A SUITABLE JOB FOR A WOMAN

A Doubleday Large Print Lost Classics Omnibus

A SUITABLE JOB FOR A WOMAN:

COVER HER FACE
A MIND TO MURDER
AN UNSUITABLE JOB FOR A WOMAN

by

P.D. James

Doubleday Large Print
Home Library Edition

GARDEN CITY, NEW YORK

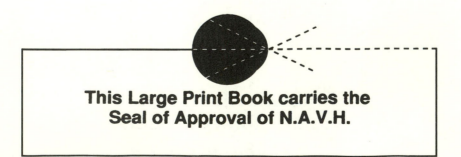

**This Large Print Book carries the
Seal of Approval of N.A.V.H.**

Contents

Cover Her Face

Chapter One

1

EXACTLY THREE MONTHS before the killing at Martingale Mrs. Maxie gave a dinner party. Years later, when the trial was a half-forgotten scandal and the headlines were yellowing on the newspaper lining of cupboard drawers, Eleanor Maxie looked back on that spring evening as the opening scene of tragedy. Memory, selective and perverse, invested what had been a perfectly ordinary dinner party with an aura of foreboding and unease. It became, in retrospect, a ritual gathering under one roof of victim and suspects, a staged preliminary to murder. In fact not all the suspects had been present. Felix Hearne, for one, was not at Martingale that week-end. Yet, in her memory, he too sat at Mrs. Maxie's table, watching with amused, sardonic eyes the opening antics of the players.

At the time, of course, the party was both ordinary and rather dull. Three of the guests, Dr. Epps, the vicar and Miss Liddell, Warden of St. Mary's Refuge for Girls, had dined together too often to expect either novelty or stimulation from each other's company. Catherine Bowers was unusually silent and Stephen Maxie and his sister, Deborah Riscoe, were obviously concealing with difficulty their irritation that Stephen's first free weekend from the hospital for over a month should have coincided with a dinner party. Mrs. Maxie had just employed one of Miss Liddell's unmarried mothers as house-parlourmaid and the girl was waiting at table for the first time. But the air of constraint which burdened the meal could hardly have been caused by the occasional presence of Sally Jupp who placed the dishes in front of Mrs. Maxie and removed the plates with a dextrous efficiency which Miss Liddell noted with complacent approval.

It is probable that at least one of the guests was wholly happy. Bernard Hinks, the vicar of Chadfleet, was a bachelor, and any change from the nourishing but unpalatable meals produced by his housekeeping sister—who was never herself tempted away from the vicarage to dine—was a relief which left small room for the niceties of social intercourse. He was a gentle, sweet-faced man who looked older than his fifty-four years and who had a reputation for vagueness and timidity except on points of doctrine. Theology was his main, almost his sole, intellectual interest and if his parishioners could not always understand his sermons they were happy enough to accept this as sure evidence of their vicar's erudition. It was, however, accepted in the village that you could get both advice and help from the vicarage and that, if the former were sometimes a little muddled, the latter could generally be relied upon.

To Dr. Charles Epps the dinner meant a first-class meal, a couple of charming women to talk to and a restful interlude from the trivialities of a country practice. He was a widower who had lived in Chadfleet for thirty years and knew most of his patients well enough to predict with accuracy whether they would live or die. He believed that there was little any doctor could do to influence the decision, that there was wisdom in knowing when to die with the least inconvenience to others and distress to oneself and that much medical progress only prolonged life for a few uncomfortable months to the greater glory of the patient's doctor. For all that, he had less stupidity and more skill than Stephen Maxie gave him credit for and few of his patients faced the inevitable before their time. He had attended Mrs. Maxie at the births of both her children and was doctor and friend to her husband in so far as Simon Maxie's bemused brain could any longer know or appreciate friendship. Now he sat at the

Maxie table and forked up chicken *soufflé* with the air of a man who has earned his dinner and has no intention of being infected by other people's moods.

"So you've taken Sally Jupp and her baby, Eleanor?" Dr. Epps was never inhibited from stating the obvious. "Nice young things both of them. Rather jolly for you to have a baby about the house again."

"Let us hope Martha agrees with you," said Mrs. Maxie dryly. "She needs help desperately, of course, but she's very conservative. She may feel the situation more than she says."

"She'll get over it. Moral scruples soon give way when it's a case of another pair of hands at the kitchen sink." Dr. Epps dismissed Martha Bultitaft's conscience with a wave of his podgy arm. "She'll be eating out of the baby's hand before long, anyway. Jimmy's an appealing child whoever his father was."

At this point Miss Liddell felt that the voice of experience should be heard.

"I don't think, Doctor, that we should talk about the problem of these children too lightly. Naturally we must show Christian charity"—here Miss Liddell gave a half bow in the direction of the vicar as if acknowledging the presence of another expert and apologizing for the intrusion into his field—"but I can't help feeling that society as a whole is getting too soft with these girls. The moral standards of the country will continue to fall if these children are to receive more consideration than those born in wedlock. And it's happening already! There's many a poor, respectable mother who doesn't get half the fussing and attention which is lavished on some of these girls."

She looked around the table, flushed and began eating again vigorously. Well, what if they did all look surprised? It had needed saying. It was her place to say it. She glanced at the vicar as if enlisting his support but Mr. Hinks, after his first puzzled glance at her, was concentrating on his dinner. Miss Liddell, baulked of an ally, thought irritably that the dear vicar really was just a little greedy over his food! Suddenly she heard Stephen Maxie speaking.

"These children are no different, surely, than any others except that we owe them more. I can't see that their mothers are so remarkable either. After all, how many people accept in practice the moral code which they despise these girls for breaking?"

"A great many, Dr. Maxie, I assure you." Miss Liddell, by nature of her job, was unaccustomed to opposition from the young. Stephen Maxie might be a rising young surgeon but that didn't make him an expert on delinquent girls. "I should be horrified if I thought that some of the behaviour I have to hear about in my work was really representative of modern youth."

"Well, as a representative of modern youth, you can take it from me that it's not so rare that we can afford to despise the ones who've been found out. This girl we have seems perfectly normal and respectable to me."

"She has a quiet and refined manner. She is quite well-educated too. A grammar-school girl! I should never have dreamed of recommending her to your mother if she weren't a most superior type of girl for St. Mary's. Actually, she's an orphan, brought up by an aunt. But I hope you won't let that play on your pity. Sally's job is to work hard and make the most of this opportunity. The past is over and is best forgotten."

"It must be difficult to forget the past when one has such a tangible memento of it," said Deborah Riscoe.

Dr. Epps, irked by a conversation which was provoking bad temper and, probably, worse digestion, hastened to contribute his placebo. Unfortunately, the result was to prolong the dissension.

"She's a good mother and a pretty girl. Probably she'll meet some chap and get married yet. Best thing too. I can't say I like this unmarried-mother-with-child relationship. They get too wrapped up in each other and sometimes end up in a mess psychologically. I sometimes think—terrible heresy I know, Miss Liddell—that the best thing would be to get these babies adopted into a good home from the start."

"The child is the mother's responsibility," pronounced Miss Liddell. "It is her duty to keep it and care for it."

"For sixteen years and without the help of the father?"

"Naturally we get an affiliation order, Dr. Maxie, whenever that is possible. Unfortunately Sally has been very obstinate and won't tell us the name of the father so we are unable to help."

"A few shillings don't go very far these days." Stephen Maxie seemed perversely determined to keep the subject alive. "And I suppose Sally doesn't even get the government children allowance."

"This is a Christian country, my dear brother, and the wages of sin are supposed to be death, not eight bob of the taxpayers' money."

Deborah had spoken under her breath but Miss Liddell had heard and felt that she had been intended to hear. Mrs. Maxie apparently felt that the time had come to intervene. At least two of her guests thought that she might well have done so earlier. It was unlike Mrs. Maxie to let anything get out of hand. "As I want to ring for Sally," she said, "perhaps it would be as well if we changed the subject. I'm going to make myself thoroughly unpopular by asking about the church fête. I know it looks as if I've got you all here on false pretences but we really ought to be thinking about the possible dates." This was a subject on which all her guests could be safely voluble. By the time Sally came in the conversation was as dull, amicable and unembarrassing as even Catherine Bowers could wish.

Miss Liddell watched Sally Jupp as she moved about the table. It was as if the conversation at dinner had stimulated her to see the girl clearly for the first time. Sally was very thin. The heavy, red-gold hair piled under her cap seemed too heavy a weight for so slender a neck. Her child-ish arms were long, the elbows jutting under the reddened skin. Her wide mouth was disciplined now, her green eyes fixed demurely on her task. Suddenly Miss Liddell was visited by an irrational spasm of affection. Sally was really doing very nicely, very nicely indeed! She looked up to catch the girl's eye and to give her a smile of approval and encouragement. Suddenly their eyes met. For a full two seconds they looked at each other. Then Miss Liddell flushed and dropped her eyes. Surely she must have been mistaken! Surely Sally would never dare to look at her like that! Confused and horrified she tried to analyse the extraordinary effect of that brief contact. Even before her own features had assumed their pro-prietal mask of commendation she had read in the girl's eyes, not the submissive gratitude which had characterized the Sally Jupp of St. Mary's Refuge, but amused contempt, a hint of conspir-acy and a dislike which was almost frightening in its intensity. Then the green eyes had dropped again and Sally the enigma became once more Sally the submissive, the subdued, Miss Liddell's favourite and most favored delinquent. But the moment left its legacy. Miss Liddell was suddenly sick with apprehension. She had recommended Sally without reserve. It was all, on the face of it, so very satisfactory. The girl was a most superior type. Too good for the job at Martingale really.

The decision had been taken. It was too late to doubt its wisdom now. The worst that could happen would be Sally's ignominious return to St. Mary's. Miss Liddell was aware for the first time that the introduction of her favourite to Martingale might produce complications. She could not be expected to foresee the magnitude of those complications nor that they would end in violent death.

Catherine Bowers, who was staying at Martingale for the weekend, had said little during dinner. Being a naturally honest person she was a little horrified to find that her sympathies were with Miss Liddell. Of course, it was very generous and gallant of Stephen to champion Sally and her kind so vigorously, but Catherine felt as irritated as she did when her non-nursing friends talked about the nobility of her profession. It was all right to have romantic ideas but they were small compensation to those who worked among the bedpans or the delinquents. She was tempted to say as much, but the presence of Deborah across the table kept her silent. The dinner, like all unsuccessful social occasions, seemed to last three times its normal length. Catherine thought that never had a family lingered so long over their coffee, never had the men been so dilatory in putting in their appearance. But it was over at last. Miss Liddell had gone back to St. Mary's, hinting that she felt happier if Miss Pollack were not left too long in sole charge. Mr. Hinks murmured about the last touches for tomorrow's

sermon and faded like a thin ghost into the spring air. The Maxies and Dr. Epps sat happily enjoying the wood fire in the drawing-room and talking about music. It was not the subject which Catherine would have chosen. Even the television would have been preferable, but the only set at Martingale was in Martha's sitting-room. If there had to be talk Catherine hoped that it would be confined to medicine. Dr. Epps might naturally say, "Of course you're a nurse, Miss Bowers, how nice for Stephen to have someone who shares his interests." Then the three of them would chat away while Deborah sat for a change in ineffectual silence and was made to realize that men do get tired of pretty, useless women, however well dressed, and that what Stephen needed was someone who understood his job, someone who could talk to his friends in a sensible and knowledgeable way. It was a pleasant dream and, like most dreams, it bore no relation to reality. Catherine sat holding her hands to the thin flames of the wood fire and tried to look at ease while the others talked about a composer called, unaccountably, Peter Warlock, of whom she had never heard except in some vague and forgotten historical sense. Certainly Deborah claimed not to understand him but she managed, as usual, to make her ignorance amusing. Her efforts to draw Catherine into the conversation by inquiring about Mrs. Bowers was evidence to Catherine of condescension, not of good manners. It was a relief when the new maid came in with a message for

Dr. Epps. One of his patients on an outlying farm had begun her labour. The doctor heaved himself reluctantly out of his chair, shook himself like a shaggy dog and made his apologies. Catherine tried for the last time. "Interesting case, Doctor?" she asked brightly. "Lord no, Miss Bowers." Dr. Epps was looking around vaguely in search of his bag. "Got three already. Pleasant little woman though, and she likes to have me there. God knows why! She could deliver herself without turning a hair. Well, good-bye, Eleanor, and thank you for an excellent dinner. I meant to go up to Simon before I left but I'll be in tomorrow if I may. You'll be needing a new prescription for the Sommeil I expect. I'll bring it with me." He nodded amiably to the company and shuffled out with Mrs. Maxie into the hall. Soon they could hear his car roaring away down the drive. He was an enthusiastic driver and loved small fast cars from which he could only extricate himself with difficulty, and in which he looked like a wicked old bear out on a spree.

"Well," said Deborah, when the sound of the exhaust had died away, "that's that. Now what about going down to the stables to see Bocock about the horses. That is, if Catherine would like a walk." Catherine was very anxious for a walk but not with Deborah. Really, she thought, it was extraordinary how Deborah couldn't or wouldn't see that she and Stephen wanted to be alone together. But if Stephen didn't make it plain she could hardly do so. The sooner he was married and away from all his female relations the better it would be for him. "They suck his blood" thought Catherine, who had met that type in her excursions into modern fiction. Deborah, happily unconscious of these vampire tendencies, led the way through the open window and across the lawn.

The stables which had once been Maxie stables and were now the property of Mr. Samuel Bocock were only two hundred yards from the house and the other side of the home meadow. Old Bocock was there, polishing harness by the light of a hurricane lamp and whistling through his teeth. He was a small brown man with a gnome-like face, slanting of eye and wide of mouth, whose pleasure at seeing Stephen was apparent. They all went to have a look at the three horses with which Bocock was attempting to establish his little business. "Really," thought Catherine, "it was ridiculous the fuss that Deborah made of them, nuzzling up to their faces with soft endearments as if they were human. Frustrated maternal instinct," she thought disagreeably. "Do her good to expend some of that energy on the children's ward. Not that she would be much use." She herself wished that they could go back to the house. The stable was scrupulously clean but there is no disguising the strong smell of horses after exercise and, for some reason, Catherine found it disturbing. At one time, Stephen's lean brown hand lay close to hers on the animal's neck. The urge to touch that hand, to stroke it, even to raise it to her lips was momentarily so strong that she had to close her eyes. And then, in the darkness, came other remembered pictures, shamefully pleasant, of that same hand half-circled around her breast, even browner against her whiteness, and moving slowly and lovingly, the harbinger of delight. She half-staggered out into the spring twilight and heard behind her the slow, hesitant speech of Bocock and the eager Maxie voices replying together. In that moment she knew again one of those devastating moments of panic which had descended upon her at intervals since she had loved Stephen. They came unheralded and all her common sense and will power were helpless against them. They were moments when everything seemed unreal and she could almost physically feel the sand shifting beneath her hopes. All her misery and uncertainty focused itself on Deborah. It was Deborah who was the enemy. Deborah who had been married, who had at least had her chance of happiness. Deborah who was pretty and selfish and useless. Listening to the voices behind her in the growing darkness Catherine felt sick with hate.

By the time they had returned to Martingale she had pulled herself together again and the black pall had lifted. She was restored to her normal condition of confidence and assurance. She went early to bed and, in the conviction of her present mood, she could almost believe that he might come to her. She told herself that it would be impossible in his father's house, an act of folly on his part, an intolerable abuse of hospitality on hers. But she waited in the darkness. After a while she heard footsteps on the stairs—his footsteps and Deborah's. Brother and sister were laughing softly together. They did not even pause as they passed her door.

2

Upstairs in the low white-painted bedroom which had been his since childhood Stephen stretched himself on his bed.

"I'm tired," he said.

"Me too." Deborah yawned and sat down on the bed beside him. "It was rather a grim dinner-party. I wish Mummy wouldn't do it."

"They're all such hypocrites."

"They can't help it. They were brought up that way. Besides, I don't think that Eppy and Mr. Hinks have much wrong with them."

"I suppose I made rather a fool of myself," said Stephen.

"Well, you were rather vehement. Rather like Sir Galahad plunging to the defence of the wronged maiden, except that she was probably more sinning than sinned against."

"You don't like her, do you?" asked Stephen.

"My sweet, I haven't thought about it. She just works here. I know that sounds very reactionary to your enlightened notions but it isn't meant to be. It's just that I'm not interested in her one way or the other, nor she, I imagine, in me."

"I'm sorry for her." There was a trace of truculence in Stephen's voice.

"That was pretty obvious at dinner," said Deborah dryly.

"It was their blasted complacency that got me down. And that Liddell woman. It's ridiculous to put a spinster in charge of a Home like St. Mary's."

"I don't see why. She may be a little limited but she's kind and conscientious. Besides, I should have thought St. Mary's already suffered from a surfeit of sexual experience."

"Oh, for heaven's sake don't be facetious, Deborah!"

"Well, what do you expect me to be? We only see each other once a fortnight. It's a bit hard to be faced with one of Mummy's duty dinner-parties and have to watch Catherine and Miss Liddell sniggering together because they thought you'd lost your head over a pretty maid. That's the kind of vulgarity Liddell would particularly relish. The whole conversation will be over the village by tomorrow."

"If they thought that they must be mad. I've hardly seen the girl. I don't think I've spoken to her yet. The idea is ridiculous!"

"That's what I meant. For heaven's sake, darling, keep your crusading instincts under control while you're at home. I should have thought that

you could have sublimated your social conscience at the hospital without bringing it home.
It's uncomfortable to live with, especially for those
of us who haven't got one."

"I'm a bit on edge today," said Stephen. "I'm
not sure I know what to do."

It was typical of Deborah to know at once what
he meant.

"She is rather dreary, isn't she? Why don't you
close the whole affair gracefully? I'm assuming
that there is an affair to close."

"You know damn well that there is—or was.
But how?"

"I've never found it particularly difficult. The art
lies in making the other person believe that he
has done the chucking. After a few weeks I practically believe it myself."

"And if they won't play?"

"'Men have died and worms have eaten them,
but not for love.'"

Stephen would have liked to have asked when
and if Felix Hearne would be persuaded that he
had done the chucking. He reflected that in this,
as in other matters, Deborah had a ruthlessness
that he lacked.

"I suppose I'm a coward about these things,"
he said. "I never find it easy to shake people off,
even party bores."

"No," replied his sister. "That's your trouble.
Too weak and too susceptible. You ought to get
married. Mummy would like it really. Someone

with money if you can find her. Not stinking, of course, just beautifully rich."

"No doubt. But who?"

"Who indeed."

Suddenly Deborah seemed to lose interest in the subject. She swung herself up from the bed and went to lean against the window-ledge. Stephen watched her profile, so like his own yet so mysteriously different, outlined against the blackness of the night. The veins and arteries of the dying day were stretched across the horizon. From the garden below he could smell the whole rich infinitely sweet distillation of an English spring night. Lying there in the cool darkness he shut his eyes and gave himself up to the peace of Martingale. At moments like this he understood perfectly why his mother and Deborah schemed and planned to preserve his inheritance. He was the first Maxie to study medicine. He had done what he wanted and the family had accepted it. He might have chosen something even less lucrative although it was difficult to imagine what. In time, if he survived the grind, the hazards, the rat race of competition, he might become a consultant. He might even become sufficiently successful to support Martingale himself. In the meantime they would struggle on as best they could, making little housekeeping economies that would never intrude on his own comfort, cutting down the donations to charity, doing more of the gardening to save old Purvis's three shillings an hour, employing untrained girls to help Martha. None of it would inconvenience him very much, and it was all to ensure that he, Stephen Maxie, succeeded his father as Simon Maxie had succeeded his. If only he could have enjoyed Martingale for its beauty and its peace without being chained to it by this band of responsibility and guilt!

There was the sound of slow careful footsteps on the stairs and then a knock on the door. It was Martha with the nightly hot drinks. Back in his childhood old Nannie had decided that a hot milk drink last thing at night would help to banish the terrifying and inexplicable nightmares from which, for a brief period, he and Deborah had suffered. The nightmares had yielded in time to the more tangible fears of adolescence, but the hot drinks had become a family habit. Martha, like her sister before her, was convinced that they were the only effective talisman against the real or imagined dangers of the night. Now she set down her small tray cautiously. There was the blue Wedgwood mug that Deborah used and the old George V coronation mug that Grandfather Maxie had bought for Stephen. "I've brought your Ovaltine too, Miss Deborah," Martha said. "I thought I should find you here." She spoke in a low voice as if they shared a conspiracy. Stephen wondered whether she guessed that they had been discussing Catherine. This was rather like the old comfortable Nannie bringing in the night drinks and ready to stay and talk. But yet not really the same. The devotion of Martha was more voluble, more self-conscious and less acceptable. It was a counterfeit of an emotion that had been as simple and necessary to him as the air he breathed. Remembering this he thought also that Martha needed her occasional sop.

"That was a lovely dinner, Martha," he said.

Deborah had turned from the window and was wrapping her thin, red-nailed hands around the steaming mug.

"It's a pity the conversation wasn't worthy of the food. We had a lecture from Miss Liddell on the social consequences of illegitimacy. What do you think of Sally, Martha?"

Stephen knew that it was an unwise question. It was unlike Deborah to ask it.

"She seems quiet enough," Martha conceded, "but, of course, it is early days yet. Miss Liddell spoke very highly of her."

"According to Miss Liddell," said Deborah, "Sally is a model of all the virtues except one, and even that was a slip on the part of nature who couldn't recognize a high-school girl in the dark."

Stephen was shocked by the sudden bitterness in his sister's voice.

"I don't know that all this education is a good thing for a maid, Miss Deborah." Martha managed to convey that she had managed perfectly well without it. "I only hope that she knows how lucky she is. Madam has even lent her our cot, the one you both slept in."

"Well, we aren't sleeping in it now." Stephen tried to keep the irritation out of his voice. Surely there had been enough talk about Sally Jupp! But Martha was not to be cautioned. It was as if she personally and not merely the family cradle had been desecrated. "We've always looked after that cot, Dr. Stephen. It was to be kept for the grandchildren."

"Damn!" said Deborah. She wiped the spilt drink from her fingers and replaced the mug on the tray. "You shouldn't count your grandchildren before they're hatched. You can count me as a non-starter and Stephen isn't even engaged—nor thinking of it. He'll probably eventually settle for a buxom and efficient nurse who'll prefer to buy a new hygienic cot of her own from Oxford Street. Thank you for the drink, Martha dear." Despite the smile, it was a dismissal.

The last "good nights" were said and the same careful footsteps descended the stairs. When they had died away Stephen said, "Poor old Martha. We do rather take her for granted and this maid-of-all-work job is getting too much for her. I suppose we ought to be thinking of pensioning her off."

"On what?" Deborah stood again at the window.

"At least there's some help for her now," Stephen temporized.

"Provided Sally isn't more trouble than she is worth. Miss Liddell made out that the baby is extraordinarily good. But any baby's considered that who doesn't bawl for two nights out of three. And then there's the washing. Sally can hardly be much help to Martha if she has to spend half the morning rinsing out nappies."

"Presumably other mothers wash nappies," said Stephen, "and still find time for other work. I like this girl and I think she can be a help to Martha if only she's given a fair chance."

"At least she had a very vigorous champion in you, Stephen. It's a pity you'll almost certainly be safely away at hospital when the trouble starts."

"What trouble, for God's sake? What's the matter with you all? Why on earth should you assume that the girl's going to make trouble?"

Deborah walked over to the door. "Because," she said, "she's making trouble already, isn't she? Good night."

Chapter Two

1

DESPITE THIS INAUSPICIOUS BEGINNING Sally Jupp's first weeks at Martingale were a success. Whether she herself shared this view was not known. No one asked for her opinion. She had been pronounced by the whole village to be a very lucky girl. If, as so often happens with the recipients of favours, she was less grateful than she ought to be, she managed to conceal her feelings behind a front of meekness, respectfulness and willingness to learn, which most people were happy enough to take at its face value. It did not deceive Martha Bultitaft and it is probable that it would not have deceived the Maxies if they had bothered to think about it. But they were too preoccupied with their individual concerns and too relieved at the sudden lightening of the domestic load to meet trouble half-way.

Martha had to admit that the baby was at first very little trouble. She put this down to Miss Liddell's excellent training since it was beyond her comprehension that bad girls could be good mothers. James was a placid child who, for his first two months at Martingale, was content to be fed at his accustomed times without advertising his hunger too loudly and who slept between his feeds in milky contentment. This could not last indefinitely. With the advent of what Sally called "mixed feeding" Martha added several substantial grievances to her list. It seemed that the kitchen was never to be free of Sally and her demands. Jimmy was fast entering that stage of childhood in which meals became less a pleasant necessity than an opportunity for the exercise of power. Carefully pillowed in his high chair he would arch his sturdy back in an orgasm of resistance, bubbling milk and cereal through his pursed lips in ecstatic rejection before suddenly capitulating into charming and submissive innocence. Sally screamed with laughter at him, caught him to her in a whirl of endearments, loved and fondled him in contemptuous disregard of Martha's muttered disapproval. Sitting there with his tight curled mop of hair, his high beaked little nose almost hidden between plump cheeks as red and hard as apples, he seemed to dominate Martha's kitchen like a throned and imperious miniature Caesar. Sally was beginning to spend more time with her child and Martha would often see her during the mornings, her bright head bent over the pram where the sudden emergence of a chubby leg or arm showed that Jimmy's long periods of sleep were a thing of the past. No doubt his demands would increase. So far Sally had managed to keep up with the work allotted to her and to reconcile the demands of her son with those of Martha. If the strain was beginning to show, only Stephen on his fortnightly visits home noticed it with any compunction. Mrs. Maxie inquired of Sally at intervals whether she was finding the work too much and was glad to be satisfied with the reply she received. Deborah did not notice, or if she did, said nothing. It was, in any case, difficult to know whether Sally was overtired. Her naturally pale face under its shock of hair and her slim brittle-looking arms gave her an air of fragility which Martha, for one, thought highly deceiving. "Tough as a nut and cunning as a wagon-load of monkeys" was Martha's opinion.

Spring ripened slowly into summer. The beech trees burst their spearheads of bright green and spread a chequered pattern of shade over the drive. The vicar celebrated Easter to his own joy and with no more than the usual recriminations and unpleasantness among his flock over the church decorations. Miss Pollack, at St. Mary's Refuge, endured a spell of sleeplessness for which Dr. Epps prescribed special tablets, and two of the Home's inmates settled for marriage with the unprepossessing but apparently repentant fathers of their babies. Miss Liddell admitted two more peccant mothers in their place. Sam Bocock advertised his stables in Chadfleet New Town and was surprised at the number of youths and girls who, in new, ill-fitting jodhpurs and bright yellow gloves, were prepared to pay 7s. 6d. an hour to amble through the village under his tutelage. Simon Maxie lay in his narrow bed and was neither better nor worse. The evenings lengthened and the roses came. The garden at Martingale was heavy with their scent. As Deborah cut them for the house she had a feeling that the garden and Martingale, itself, were waiting for something. The house was always at its most beautiful in summer, but this year she sensed an atmosphere of expectancy, almost of foreboding, which was alien to its usual cool serenity. Carrying the roses into the house, Deborah shook herself out of this morbid fancy with the wry reflection that the most ominous event now hanging over Martingale was the annual church fête. When the words "waiting for a death" came suddenly into her mind she told herself firmly that her father was no worse, might even be considered a little better, and that the house could not possibly know. She recognized that her love for Martingale was not entirely rational. Sometimes she tried to discipline that love by talking of the time "when we have to sell" as if the very sound of the words could act both as a warning and a talisman.

St. Cedd's church fête had taken place in the grounds of Martingale every July since the days of Stephen's great-grandfather. It was organized by the fête committee, which consisted of the vicar, Mrs. Maxie, Dr. Epps and Miss Liddell. Their administrative duties were never arduous since the fête, like the church it helped to support, continued virtually unchanging from year to year, a symbol of immutability in the midst of chaos. But the committee took their responsibilities seriously and met frequently at Martingale during June and early July to drink tea in the garden and to pass resolutions which they passed the year before in identical words and in the same agreeable surroundings. The only member of the committee who occasionally felt genuinely uneasy about the fête was the vicar. In his gentle way he preferred to see the best in everyone and to impute worthy motives wherever possible. He included himself in this dispensation, having discovered early in his ministry that charity is a policy as well as a virtue. But once a year Mr. Hinks faced certain unpalatable facts about his church. He worried about its exclusiveness, its negative impact on the seething fringe of Chadfleet New Town, the suspicion that it was more of a social than a spiritual force in the village life. Once he had suggested that the fête should close as well as open with a prayer and a hymn, but the only committee member to support this startling innovation was Mrs. Maxie, whose chief quarrel with the fête was that it never seemed to end.

This year Mrs. Maxie felt that she was going to be glad of Sally's willing help. There were plenty of workers for the actual fête, even if some of them were out to extract the maximum of personal enjoyment with the minimum of work, but the responsibilities did not end with the successful organization of the day. Most of the committee would expect to be asked to dinner at Martingale and Catherine Bowers had written to say that the Saturday of the fête was one of her off-duty days and would it be too much of an imposition if she invited herself for what she described as "one of your perfect week-ends away from the noise and grime of this dreadful city." This letter was not the first of its kind. Catherine was always so much more anxious to see the children than the children were to see Catherine. In some circumstances that would be just as well. It would be an unsuitable match for Stephen in every way, much as poor Katie would like to see her only child eligibly married off. She herself had married, as they said, beneath her. Christian Bowers had been an artist with more talent than money and no pretensions to anything except genius. Mrs. Maxie had met him once and had disliked him but, unlike his wife, she did believe him to be an artist. She had bought one of his early canvases for Martingale, a reclining nude which now hung in her bedroom and gave her a satisfied joy which no amount of intermittent hospitality to his daughter could adequately repay. To Mrs. Maxie it was an object-lesson in the folly of an unwise marriage. But because the pleasure it gave her was still fresh and real, and because she had once been at school with Katie Bowers and placed some importance on the obligations of old and sentimental associations, she felt that Catherine should be welcome at Martingale as her own guest, if not as her children's.

There were other things that were slightly worrying. Mrs. Maxie did not believe in taking too much notice of what other people sometimes describe as "atmosphere." She retained her serenity by coping with shattering common sense with those difficulties which were too obvious to ignore and by ignoring the others.

But things were happening at Martingale which were difficult to overlook. Some of them were to be expected, of course. Mrs. Maxie, for all her insensitivity, could not but realize that Martha and Sally were hardly compatible kitchen mates, and that Martha would be bound to find the situation difficult for a time. What she had not expected was that it should become progressively more difficult as the weeks wore on. After a succession of untrained and uneducated housemaids, who had come to Martingale because domesticity offered their only chance of employment, Sally seemed a paragon of intelligence, capability and refinement. Orders could be given in the confident assurance that they would be carried out where, before, even constant and painstaking reiteration had only resulted in the eventual realization that it was easier to do the job oneself.

An almost pre-war feeling of leisure would have returned to Martingale if it had not been for the heavier nursing which Simon Maxie now needed. Dr. Epps was already warning that they could not go on for long. Soon now it would be necessary to install a resident nurse or to move the patient to hospital. Mrs. Maxie rejected both alternatives. The former would be expensive, inconvenient and possibly indefinitely prolonged. The latter would mean that Simon Maxie would die in the hands of strangers instead of in his own house. The family could not afford a nursing home or a private ward. It would mean a bed in the local hospital for chronic cases, barrack-like, over-crowded and under-staffed. Before this final stage of his illness had fallen upon him, Simon Maxie had whispered to her, "You won't let them take me away, Eleanor?" and she had replied, "Of course I won't." He had fallen asleep then, secure in a promise which both of them knew was no light assurance. It was a pity that Martha had apparently so short a memory for the overwork which had preceded Sally's arrival. The new régime had given her time and energy to criticize what she had at first found surprisingly easy to accept. But so far she had not come into the open. There had been the veiled innuendoes but no definite complaint. Undoubtedly tension must be building up in the kitchen, thought Mrs. Maxie, and after the fête it would probably have to be coped with. But she was in no hurry; the fête was only a week away and the chief consideration was to get it successfully over.

2

On the Thursday preceding the fête Deborah spent the morning shopping in London, lunched with Felix Hearne at his club and went with him to see a Hitchcock revival at a Baker Street cinema in the afternoon. This agreeable programme was completed with afternoon tea at a Mayfair restaurant which holds unfashionable views on what constitutes an adequate afternoon meal. Replete with cucumber sandwiches and home-made chocolate éclairs Deborah reflected that the afternoon had really been very successful, even if a little low-brow for Felix's taste. But he had borne up under it well. There were advantages in not being lovers. If they had been having a love affair it would have seemed necessary to spend the afternoon together in his Greenwich house since the opportunity offered and an irregular union imposes conventions as rigid and compelling as those of marriage. And while the love-making would no doubt have been pleasant enough the easy undemanding companionship which they had enjoyed was more to her taste.

She did not want to fall in love again. Months of annihilating misery and despair had cured her of that particular folly. She had married young and Edward Riscoe had died of poliomyelitis less than a year later. But a marriage based on companionship, compatible tastes and the satisfactory exchange of sexual pleasure seemed to her a reasonable basis for life and one which could be achieved without too much disturbing emotion. Felix, she suspected, was enough in love with her to be interesting without being boring and she was only spasmodically tempted to consider seriously the expected offer of marriage. It was, nevertheless, beginning to be slightly odd that the offer was not made. It was not, she knew, that he disliked women. Certainly most of their friends considered him to be a natural bachelor, eccentric, slightly pedantic and perennially amusing. They might have been unkinder, but there was the inescapable fact of his war record to be explained away. A man cannot be either effeminate or a fool who holds both French and British decorations for his part in the Resistance Movement. He was one of those whose physical courage, that most respected and most glamorous of virtues, had been tried in the punishment cells of the Gestapo and could never again be challenged. It was less fashionable now to think of those things but they were not yet quite forgotten. What those months in France had done to Felix Hearne was anyone's guess, but he was allowed his eccentricities and presumably he enjoyed them. Deborah liked him because he was intelligent and amusing and the most diverting gossip she knew. He had a woman's interest in the small change of life and an intuitive concern for the minutiae of human relationships. Nothing was too trivial for him and he sat now listening with every appearance of amused sympathy to Deborah's report on Martingale.

"So you see, it's bliss to have some free time again, but I really can't see it lasting. Martha will have her out in time. And I don't really blame her. She doesn't like Sally and neither do I."

"Why? Is she chasing Stephen?"

"Don't be vulgar, Felix. You might give me the benefit of a more subtle reason than that. Actually, though, she does seem to have impressed him and I think it's deliberate. She asks his advice about the baby whenever he's at home, although I have tried to point out that he's supposed to be a surgeon not a paediatrician. And poor old Martha can't breathe a word of criticism without his rushing to Sally's defence. You'll see for yourself when you come on Saturday."

"Who else will be there apart from this intriguing Sally Jupp?"

"Stephen, of course. And Catherine Bowers. You met her the last time you were at Martingale."

"So I did. Rather poached-egg eyes but an agreeable figure and more intelligence than you or Stephen were willing to allow her."

"If she impressed you so much," retorted Deborah easily, "you can demonstrate your admiration this week-end and give Stephen a respite. He was rather taken with her once and now she sticks to him like a limpet and it bores him horribly."

"How incredibly ruthless pretty women are to plain ones! And by 'rather taken with her' I suppose you mean that Stephen seduced her. Well, that usually does lead to complications and he must find his own way out as better men have done before him. But I shall come. I love Martingale and I appreciate good cooking. Besides, I have a feeling that the week-end will be interesting. A house full of people all disliking each other is bound to be explosive."

"Oh, it isn't as bad as that!"

"Very nearly. Stephen dislikes me. He has never bothered to hide it. You dislike Catherine Bowers. She dislikes you and will probably extend the emotion to me. Martha and you dislike Sally Jupp and she, poor girl, probably loathes you all. And that pathetic creature, Miss Liddell, will be there, and your mother dislikes her. It will be a perfect orgy of suppressed emotion."

"You needn't come. In fact, I think it would be better if you didn't."

"But, Deborah, your mother has already asked me and I've accepted. I wrote to her last week in my nice formal way, and I shall now make a note in my little black book to settle it beyond doubt." He bent his sleek fair head over his engagement diary. His face, with the pale skin which made the hair-line almost indistinguishable, was turned away from her. She noticed how sparse were the eyebrows against that pallid forehead and the intricate folds and crinkles around his eyes. Deborah thought that he must once have had beautiful hands before the Gestapo played about with them. The nails had never fully grown again. She tried to picture those hands moving about the intricacies of a gun, curled into the cords of a parachute, clenched in defiance or endurance. But it was no good. There seemed no point of contact between that Felix who had apparently once known a cause worth suffering for and the facile, sophisticated, sardonic Felix Hearne of Hearne and Illingworth, publishers, just as there was none between the girl who had married Edward Riscoe and the woman she was today. Suddenly Deborah felt again the familiar *malaise* of nostalgia and regret. In this mood she watched Felix writing under Saturday's date in his cramped meticulous hand as if he were making a date with death.

3

After tea Deborah decided to visit Stephen, partly to avoid the rush-hour crowds but chiefly because she seldom came up to London without calling at St. Luke's Hospital. She invited Felix to accompany her but he excused himself on the grounds that the smell of disinfectant made him sick, and sent her off in a taxi with formal expressions of thanks for her company. He was punctilious about these matters. Deborah fought against the unflattering suspicion that he had tired of her conversation and was relieved to see her borne away in comfort and with speed, and concentrated on the pleasure of seeing Stephen. It was all the more disconcerting to find that he was not in the hospital. It was unusual too. Colley, the hall porter, explained that Mr. Maxie had had a telephone call and had gone out to meet someone saying that he wouldn't be long. Mr. Donwell was on duty for him. But Mr. Maxie would certainly not be long now. He had been gone nearly an hour. Perhaps Mrs. Riscoe would like to go to the resident's sitting-room? Deborah stayed for a few minutes' chat with Colley whom she liked and then took the lift to the fourth floor. Mr. Donwell, a shy and spotty young registrar, mumbled a greeting and made a speedy escape to the wards leaving Deborah in sole possession of four grubby armchairs, an untidy heap of medical periodicals and the half-cleared remnants of the residents' tea. It appeared that they had had Swiss roll again and, as usual, someone had used his saucer as an ash-tray. Deborah began to pile up the plates, but, realizing that this was a somewhat pointless activity since she did not know what to do with them, she took up one of the papers and moved to the window where she could divide her interest between waiting for Stephen and scanning the more intriguing or comprehensible of the medical articles. The window gave a view of the main hospital entrance farther along the street. In the distance she could discern the shining curve of the river and the towers of Westminster. The ceaseless rumbling of traffic was muted, an unobtrusive background to the occasional noises of the hospital, the clang of the lift gates, the ringing of telephone bells, the passing of brisk feet along the corridor. An old woman was being helped into an ambulance at the front door. From a height of four floors the figures below seemed curiously foreshortened. The ambulance door was shut without a sound and it slid away noiselessly. Suddenly she saw them. It was Stephen she noticed first, but the flaming red-gold head almost level with his shoulder was unmistakable. They paused at the corner of the building. They seemed to be talking. The black head was bent towards the gold. After a moment she saw him shake hands and then Sally turned in a flash of sunlight and walked swiftly away without a backward glance. Deborah missed nothing. Sally was wearing her grey suit. It was mass-produced and bought off the peg, but it fitted well and was a foil for the shining cascade of hair, released now from the restraint of cap and pins.

She was clever, thought Deborah. Clever to know that you had to dress simply if you wanted to wear your hair loose like that. Clever to avoid the greens for which most redheads had a predilection. Clever to have said "good-bye" outside the hospital and to have resisted the certain invitation to a hospital supper with its inevitable openings for embarrassment or regret. Afterwards Deborah was surprised that she should have noticed so keenly what Sally was wearing. It was as if she saw her for the first time through Stephen's eyes, and seeing her was afraid. It seemed a long time before she heard the drone of the lift and his quick footsteps along the corridor. Then he was by her side. She did not move away from the window so that he should know at once she had seen. She felt that she could not bear it if he did not tell her and it was easier that way. She did not know what she expected but when he spoke it was a surprise.

"Have you seen these before?" he asked.

In his outstretched palm was a rough bag made from a man's handkerchief tied together at the corners. He lifted one of the knots, gave a little jerk, and spilled out three or four of the tiny tablets. Their grey-brown colour was unmistakable.

"Aren't they some of Father's tablets?" It seemed as if he were accusing her of something. "Where did you get them?"

"Sally found them and brought them up to me. I expect you saw us from the window."

"What did she do with the baby?" The silly irrelevant question was out before she had time to think.

"The baby? Oh, Jimmy, I don't know. Sally left him with someone in the village I suppose or with Mother or Martha. She came up to bring me these and 'phoned from Liverpool Street to ask me to meet her. She found them in Father's bed."

"But how, in his bed?"

"Between the mattress cover and the mattress.

Down the side. His draw-sheet was ruckled and she was smoothing it and pulling the macintosh tight when she noticed a little bulge in the corner of the mattress underneath the fitted cover. She found this. Father must have been saving them over several weeks, perhaps months. I can guess why."

"Does he know she found them?"

"Sally doesn't think so. He was lying on his side with his face away from her as she attended to the draw-sheet. She just put the handkerchief and the tablets in her pocket and went on as if nothing had happened. Of course they may have been there for a long time—he's been on Sommeil for eighteen months or more—and he may have forgotten about them. He may have lost the power to get at them and use them. We can't tell what goes on in his mind. The trouble is that we haven't bothered even to try. Except Sally."

"But Stephen, that isn't true. We do try. We sit with him and nurse him and try to make him feel that we're there. But he just lies, not moving, not speaking, not even seeming to notice people any more. He isn't really Father. There isn't any contact between us. I have tried, I swear I have, but it isn't any use. He can't really have meant to take those tablets. I can't think how he even managed to collect them, to plan it all."

"When it's your turn to give him his tablets, do you watch him while he swallows them?"

"No, not really. You know how he used to hate

us to help him too much. Now I don't think he minds, but we still give him the tablets and then pour out the water and hold it up to his lips if he seems to want it. He must have secreted these away months ago. I can't believe he could manage it now, not without Martha knowing. She does most of the lifting and the heavier nursing."

"Well, apparently he managed to deceive Martha. But, by God, Deborah, I ought to have guessed, ought to have known. I call myself a doctor. This is the kind of thing which makes me feel like a specialized carpenter, good enough to carve patients up as long as I'm not expected to bother with them as people. At least Sally treated him as a human being."

Deborah was momentarily tempted to point out that she, her mother and Martha were at least managing to keep Simon Maxie comfortable, clean and fed at no small cost and that it was difficult to see where Sally had done more. But if Stephen wanted to indulge in remorse there was little to be gained by stopping him. He usually felt better afterwards, even if other people felt worse. She watched in silence as he rummaged about in the drawer of the desk, found a small bottle which had apparently once held aspirin, carefully counted the tablets—there were ten of them—into the bottle and labelled it with the name of the drug and the dose. They were the almost automatic actions of a man trained to keep medicines properly labelled. Deborah's mind was busy with questions she dared not ask. "Why did Sally come to you? Why not Mother? Did she really find those tablets or was it just a convenient ruse to see you alone? But she must have found them. No one could make up a story like that. Poor Father. What has Sally been saying? Why should I mind so much about this, about Sally? I hate her because she has a child and I haven't. Now I've said it, but admitting it doesn't make it any easier. That handkerchief bag. It must have taken him hours to tie it together. It looked like something made by a child. Poor Father. He was so tall when I was a child. Was I really rather afraid of him? Oh God, please help me to feel pity. I want to be sorry for him. What is Sally thinking now? What did Stephen say to her?"

He turned back from the desk and held out the bottle.

"I think you had better take this home. Put it in the medicine cupboard in his room. Don't say anything to Mother yet or to Dr. Epps. I think it would be wiser if we stopped the tablets for Father. I'll get you a prescription made up in the dispensary before you leave, the same kind of drug only in solution. Give him a tablespoonful at night in water. I should see to it yourself. Just tell Martha that I have stopped the tablets. When does Dr. Epps see him again?"

"He's coming in to see Mother with Miss Liddell after dinner. I suppose he may go up then. But I don't expect he'll ask about the tablets. They've been going on for so long now. We just say when the bottle is getting empty and he gives us a fresh prescription."

"Do you know how many tablets there are in the house now?"

"There's a new bottle with the seal unbroken. We were to start it tonight."

"Then leave it in the cupboard and give him the medicine. I shall be able to talk to Eppy about it when I see him on Saturday. I'll get down late tomorrow night. You had better come with me to the dispensary now and it would be wiser to get home straight away. I'll telephone Martha and ask her to keep you some dinner."

"Yes, Stephen." Deborah did not regret the loss of her meal. All the pleasure of the day had evaporated. It was time to be going home.

"And I would rather you said nothing to Sally about this."

"I hadn't the slightest intention of doing so. I only hope she's capable of a similar discretion. We don't want this story all over the village."

"That's an unfair thing to say, Deborah, and you don't even believe it. You couldn't have any-one safer than Sally. She was very sensible about it. And rather sweet."

"I'm sure she was."

"She was naturally worried about it. She's very devoted to Father."

"She seems to be extending her devotion to you."

"What on earth do you mean?"

"I was wondering why she didn't tell Mother about the tablets. Or me."

"You haven't done much to encourage her to confide in you, have you?"

"What on earth do you expect me to do? Hold her hand? I'm not particularly interested in her as long as she does her work efficiently. I don't like her and I don't expect her to like me."

"It's not true that you don't like her," said Stephen. "You hate her."

"Did she complain of the way she's been treated?"

"Of course she didn't. Do be sensible, Deb. This isn't like you."

"Isn't it," thought Deborah. "How do you know what's like me?" But she recognized in Stephen's last words a plea for peace and she held out her hand to him, saying, "I'm sorry. I don't know what's wrong with me lately. I'm sure Sally did what she thought best. It isn't worth quarreling about anyway. Do you want me to wait up for you tomorrow night? Felix won't be able to get down until Saturday morning, but Catherine is expected for dinner."

"Don't bother. I may have to get the last bus. But I'll ride with you before breakfast if you like to call me."

The significance of this formal offer in place of the previously happily established routine did not escape Deborah. The chasm between them had only been precariously bridged. She felt that

Stephen, too, was uneasily aware of the cracking ice beneath their feet. Never since the death of Edward Riscoe had she felt so alienated from Stephen; never since then had she been so in need of him.

4

It was nearly half past seven before Martha heard the sound she had been listening for, the squeak of pram wheels on the drive. Jimmy was whining softly and was obviously only persuaded from open bawling by the soothing motion of the pram and the soft reassurances of his mother. Soon Sally's head was seen to pass the kitchen window, the pram was wheeled into the scullery and, almost immediately, mother and child appeared through the kitchen door. There was an air of suppressed emotion about the girl. She seemed at once nervous and yet pleased with herself. Martha did not think that an afternoon wheeling Jimmy in the forest could altogether account for that look of secretive and triumphant pleasure.

"You're late," she said. "I should think the child is starving, poor mite."

"Well, he won't have to wait much longer, will you my pet? I suppose there isn't any milk boiled?"

"I'm not here to wait on you, Sally, please remember. If you want milk you must boil it yourself.

You know well enough what time the child should be fed."

They did not speak again while Sally boiled the milk and tried, rather ineffectually, to cool it quickly whilst holding Jimmy on one arm. It was not until Sally was ready to take her child upstairs that Martha spoke.

"Sally," she said, "did you take anything from the master's bed when you made it this morning? Anything belonging to him? I want the truth now!"

"It's obvious from your tone that you know I did. Do you mean that you know that he had those tablets hidden? And you said nothing about them?"

"Of course I knew. I've looked after him now for five years haven't I? Who else would know what he does, what he's feeling? I suppose you thought he'd take them. Well, that needn't worry you. What business is it of yours anyway? If you had to lie there, year after year, perhaps you might like to know that you had something, a few little tablets maybe, that would end all the pain and the tired- ness. Something that nobody else knew about, until a silly little bitch, no better than she should be, came ferreting them out. Very clever, weren't you? But he wouldn't have taken them! He's a gentleman. You wouldn't understand that either. But you can give me back those tablets. And if you mention a word of this to anyone or lay a hand on anything else belonging to the master, I'll have you out. You and that brat. I'll find a way, never fear!"

She held out her hand towards Sally. Never once had she raised her voice but her calm authority was more frightening than anger and the girl's voice was tinged with hysteria as she replied.

"I'm afraid you're unlucky. I haven't got the tablets. I took them to Stephen this afternoon. Yes, Stephen! And now I've heard your silly twaddle I'm glad I did. I'd like to see Stephen's face if I told him that you knew all the time! Dear, faithful old Martha! So devoted to the family! You don't care a damn for any of them, you old hypocrite, except for your precious master! Pity you can't see yourself! Washing him, stroking his face, cooing to him as if he were your baby. I could laugh sometimes if it weren't so pitiful. It's indecent! Lucky for him he's half gaga! Being mauled about by you would make any normal man sick!"

She swung the child on to her hip and Martha heard the door close behind her.

Martha lurched over to the sink and clutched it with shaking hands. She was seized with a physical revulsion that made her retch but her body found no relief in sickness. She put a hand to her forehead in a stock gesture of despair. Looking at her fingers she saw that they were wet with perspiration. As she fought for control the echo of that high, childish voice beat in her brain. "Being mauled about by you would make any normal man sick . . . being mauled about by you . . . mauled about." When her body stopped its shaking, nausea gave way to hate.

Her mind solaced its misery with the sweet images of revenge. She indulged in phantasies of Sally disgraced, Sally and her child banished from Martingale, Sally found out for what she was, lying, wicked and evil. And, since all things are possible, Sally dead.

Chapter Three

1

THE FICKLE SUMMER WEATHER WHICH, for the last few weeks, had provided a sample of every climatic condition known to the country with the sole exception of snow, now settled into the warm grey normality for the time of the year. There was a chance that the fête would be held in dry weather if not in sun. Deborah, pulling on her jodhpurs for her morning ride with Stephen, could see the red and white marquee from her window, and scattered around the lawn, the skeletons of a dozen half-erected stalls awaiting their final embellishment of crêpe paper and Union Jacks. Away in the home field a course had already been ringed for the children's sports and the dancing display.

An ancient car surmounted by a loudspeaker was parked under one of the elms at the end of the lawn and several lengths of wire coiled on the paths and slung between the trees bore witness to the efforts of the local wireless enthusiasts to provide a loudspeaker system for the music and the announcements. Deborah, after a good night's rest, was able to survey these preparations with stoicism. She knew from experience that a very different sight would meet her eyes by the time the fête was over. However careful people were—and many of them only began to enjoy themselves when they were surrounded by a familiar litter of cigarette packets and fruit peelings—it was at least a week's work before the garden lost its look of ravaged beauty. Already the rows of bunting stretched from side to side of the green walks gave the spinney an air of incongruous frivolity and the rooks seemed shocked into noisier than usual recriminations.

In Catherine's favourite day-dream of the Martingale fête she spent the afternoon helping Stephen with the horses, the centre of an interested, deferential and speculating group of the Chadfleet villagers. Catherine had picturesque if outdated notions of the place and importance of the Maxies in their community. This happy imagining faded in face of Mrs. Maxie's determination that both her guests should help where they were most needed. For Catherine this was plainly to be with Deborah on the white elephant stall. When the first disappointment had subsided it was surprising how pleasant the experience proved. The morning was spent in sorting, examining and pricing the miscellaneous hoard that had still to be dealt with. Deborah had an amazing knowledge, born of long experience, of the source of most of her wares, what each article was worth and who was likely to buy it. Sir Reynold Price had contributed a large shaggy coat with a detachable waterproof lining which was immediately placed on one side for the private consideration of Dr. Epps. It was just the thing he needed for winter visiting in his open car and, after all, no one noticed what you wore when you were driving. There was an old felt hat which belonged to the doctor himself and which his daily help tried to get rid of every year only to have it brought back by its irate owner. It was marked sixpence and prominently displayed. There were hand-knitted jumpers of startling style and hue, small objects in brass and china from the village mantelpieces, bundles of books and magazines and a fascinating collection of prints in heavy frames, appropriately named in spidery copper-plate. There were "The First Love Letter," "Daddy's Darling," an ornate twin pair called "The Quarrel" and "Reconciliation" and several showing soldiers either kissing their wives farewell or enjoying the chaster pleasures of reunion. Deborah prophesied that the customers would love them and declared that the frames alone were worth half a crown.

By one o'clock the preparations were complete

and the household had time for a hurried luncheon waited on by Sally. Catherine remembered that there had been some trouble that morning with Martha because the girl had overslept. Apparently she had had to rush to make up the lost time for she looked flushed and was, Catherine thought, concealing some excitement behind an outward air of docile efficiency. But the meal passed happily enough since the company was at present united in a common preoccupation and a shared activity. By two o'clock the bishop and his wife had arrived, the committee came out of the drawing-room windows to arrange themselves a little self-consciously on the circle of waiting chairs and the fête was formally opened. Although the bishop was old and retired he was not senile and his short speech was a model of simplicity and grace. As the lovely old voice came to her across the lawn, Catherine thought of the church for the first time with interest and affection. Here was the Norman font where she and Stephen would stand at the christening of their children. In these aisles were commemorated his ancestors. Here the kneeling figures of a sixteenth-century Stephen Maxie and Deborah, his wife, faced each other for ever petrified in stone, their thin hands curved in prayer. Here were the secular and ornate busts of the eighteenth-century Maxies and the plain tablets which told briefly of sons killed in Gallipoli and on the Marne. Catherine had often thought that it was as well the family obsequies had become progressively less extravagant since the Church of St. Cedd with St. Mary the Virgin, Chadfleet, was already less a public place of worship than a private repository for Maxie bones. But today, in a mood of confidence and exultation, she could think of all the family, dead and alive, without criticism and even a baroque reredos and Corinthian would have seemed no more than their due.

Deborah took her place with Catherine behind their stall and the customers began to approach and search warily for bargains. It was certainly one of the most popular attractions and business was brisk. Dr. Epps came early for his hat and was easily persuaded to buy Sir Reynold's coat for £1. The clothes and shoes were snapped up, usually by the very people Deborah had foretold would want them, and Catherine was kept busy handing out change and replenishing the stall from the large box of reinforcements which they kept under the counter. At the gate of the drive little groups of people continued to come in throughout the afternoon, the children's faces stretched into fixed unnatural smiles for the benefit of a photographer who had promised a prize for the "Happiest Looking Child" to enter the garden during the afternoon. The loudspeaker exceeded everyone's wildest hopes and poured forth a medley of Sousa marches and Strauss waltzes, announcements about teas and competitions, and occasional admonitions to use the rubbish baskets and keep the garden tidy. Miss

Liddell and Miss Pollack, helped by the plainest, oldest and most reliable of their delinquent girls, bustled from St. Mary's to the fête and back again at the call of a conscience or duty. Their stall was by far the most expensive and the hand-made underclothes display suffered from an unhappy compromise between prettiness and respectability. The vicar, his soft white hair damped by exertion, beamed happily upon his flock, who were for once at peace with the world and each other. Sir Reynold arrived late, voluble, patronizing and generous. From the tea lawn came the sound of earnest admonitions as Mrs. Cope and Mrs. Nelson, with the help of the boys' class from the Sunday school, busied themselves with bridge tables, chairs from the village hall, and assorted table-cloths which would all have to find their eventual way back to their owners. Felix Hearne seemed to be enjoying himself as a free-lance. He did appear once or twice to help Deborah or Catherine but announced that he was having a much better time with Miss Liddell and Miss Pollack. Once Stephen came to inquire after business. For someone who habitually referred to the fête as "The Curse of the Maxies," he seemed happy enough. Soon after four o'clock Deborah went into the house to see if her father needed attention and Catherine was left in charge. Deborah returned after half an hour or so and suggested that they might go in search of tea. It was being served in the larger of the two tents and late arrivals, Deborah warned, were usually faced with a weak beverage and the less attractive cakes. Felix Hearne, who had stopped at the stall to chat and pass judgment on the remaining merchandise, was commandeered to take their places and Deborah and Catherine went into the house to wash. One or two people were usually found passing through the hall either because they thought it would be a short cut or because they were strangers to the village and thought their entrance fee included a free tour of the house. Deborah seemed unconcerned. "There's Bob Gittings, our local P.C., keeping an eye on things in the drawing-room," she pointed out. "And the dining-room's locked. This always happens. No one's ever taken anything yet. We'll go in the south door now and use the small bathroom. It'll be quicker." All the same it was disconcerting for them both when a man brushed past them on the back stairs with a hasty apology. They stopped and Deborah called after him. "Were you looking for someone? This is a private house." He turned and looked back at them, a nervous, lean man with greying hair swept back from a high forehead and a thin mouth which he drew back into a propitiatory smile. "Oh, I'm sorry. I didn't realize. Please excuse me. I was looking for the toilet." It was not an attractive voice. "If you mean the lavatory," said Deborah shortly, "there's one in the garden. It seemed adequately signposted to me." He flushed and mumbled some reply and then was gone. Deborah shrugged her shoulders. "What a scared rabbit! I don't suppose he was doing any harm. But I wish they'd keep out of the house." Catherine made a mental resolve that when she was mistress of Martingale arrangements would be made to see that they did.

The tea-tent was certainly crowded and the confused clatter of crockery, the babble of voices and the hissing of the tea-urn were heard against a background of the broadcast music which muted through the canvas. The tables had been decorated by the Sunday school children as part of their competition for the best arrangements of wild flowers. Each table bore its labelled jam jar and the harvest of poppy, campion, sorrel and dog-rose, revived from the hours of clutching in hot hands, had a delicate and unselfconscious beauty, although the scent of the flowers was lost in the strong smell of trampled grass, hot canvas and food. The concentration of noise was so great that a sudden break in the clatter of voices seemed to Catherine as if a total silence had fallen. Only afterwards did she realize that not everybody had stopped talking, that not every head was turned to where Sally had come into the tent by the opposite entrance, Sally in a white dress with a low boat-shaped neckline and a skirt of swirling pleats, identical with the one Deborah was wearing, Sally with a green cummerbund which was a replica of the one round Deborah's waist, and with green ear-rings gleaming on each side of flushed cheeks. Catherine felt her own cheeks redden and could not help her quick inquiring glance at Deborah. She was not the only one. Faces were turning toward them from more and more of the tables. From the far end of the tent where some of Miss Liddell's girls were enjoying an early tea under Miss Pollack's supervision, there was a quickly suppressed giggling. Someone said softly, but not softly enough, "Good old Sal." Only Deborah appeared unconcerned. Without a second glance at Sally she walked up to the counter of trestle tables and asked equally for tea for two, a plate of bread and butter and one of cakes. Mrs. Pardy splashed tea from the urn into the cups with embarrassed haste, and Catherine followed Deborah to one of the vacant tables, clutching the plate of cakes and unhappily aware that she was the one who looked a fool.

"How dare she?" she muttered, bending her hot face over the cup. "It's a deliberate insult." Deborah gave a slight shrug of her shoulders. "Oh, I don't know. What does it matter? Presumably the poor little devil is getting a kick out of her gesture and it isn't hurting me."

"Where did she get the dress from?"

"The same place as I did, I imagine. The name's inside. It isn't a model or anything like that. Anyone could buy it who took the trouble to find it. Sally must have thought it worth the trouble."

"She couldn't have known you were going to wear it today."

"Any other occasion would have done as well, I expect. Must you go on about it?"

"I can't think why you take it so calmly. I wouldn't."

"What do you expect me to do? Go and tear it off her? There's a limit to the free entertainment the village can expect."

"I wonder what Stephen will say," said Catherine. Deborah looked surprised. "I doubt whether he will even notice, except to think how well it suits her. It's more her dress than mine. Are those cakes all right for you or would you rather forage for sandwiches?" Catherine, baulked of further discussion, went on with her tea.

2

The afternoon wore on. After the scene in the tea-tent the fun had gone out of the fête for Catherine and the rest of the jumble sale was little more than a laborious chore. They were sold out before five as Deborah had predicted, and Catherine was free to offer her help with the pony rides. She arrived in the home field to see Stephen lift Jimmy, screaming with delight, into the saddle in front of his mother. The sun, mellowing now at the ending of the day, shone through the child's hair and turned it into fire. Sally's shining hair swung forward as she leaned down to whisper to Stephen. Catherine heard his answering laugh. It was a moment of time that she was never to forget. She turned back to the lawns and tried to recapture some of the confidence and happiness with which she had started the day. But it was of no use. After wandering about in desultory search for something to occupy her mind, she decided to go up to her room and lie down before dinner. She did not see Mrs. Maxie or Martha on her way through the house. Presumably they were busy either with Simon Maxie or with preparations for the cold meal which was to end the day. Through her window she did see that Dr. Epps was still dozing beside his darts and treasure hunt, although the busiest part of the afternoon was over. The winners of the competitions would soon be announced, rewarded and acclaimed and a thin but steady stream of people was already passing out of the grounds to the bus terminus.

Apart from that moment in the home field Catherine had not seen Sally again, and when she had washed and changed and was on the way to the dining-room she met Martha on the stairs and heard from her that Sally and Jimmy were not yet in. The dining-room table had been set with cold meats, salads and bowls of fresh fruit, and all the party except Stephen were gathered there. Dr. Epps, voluble and cheerful as ever, was busying himself with the cider bottles. Felix Hearne was setting out the glasses. Miss Liddell was helping Deborah to finish laying the table. Her little squeals of dismay when she could not find what she wanted and her ineffectual jabbings at the table napkins were symptomatic of more than normal unease. Mrs. Maxie stood with her back to the others, looking into the glass above the chimney-piece. When she turned, Catherine was shocked by the lines and weariness of her face.

"Isn't Stephen with you?" she asked.

"No. I haven't seen him since he was with the horses. I've been in my room."

"He probably walked home with Bocock to help with the stabling. Or perhaps he's changing. I don't think we'll wait."

"Where's Sally?" asked Deborah.

"Not in apparently. Martha tells me that Jimmy is in his cot so she must have come in and gone out again." Mrs. Maxie spoke calmly. If this was a domestic crisis she evidently regarded it as a comparatively minor one which warranted no further comment in front of her guests. Felix Hearne glanced at her and felt a familiar tingle of anticipation and foreboding which startled him. It seemed so extravagant a reaction for so ordinary an occasion. Looking across to Catherine Bowers he had a feeling that she shared his unease. The whole party was a little jaded. Except for Miss Liddell's inconsequential and maddening chatter they had little to say. There was the sense of anticlimax which follows most long-planned social functions. The affair was over and yet too much with them to permit relaxation. The bright sun of the day had given way to heaviness. There was no breeze now and the heat was greater than ever.

When Sally appeared at the door they turned to face her as if stung by a common urgency. She leaned back against the linen-fold panelling, the white pleats of her dress fanned out against its sombre darkness like a pigeon's wing. In this strange and stormy light her hair burned against the wood. Her face was very pale but she was smiling. Stephen was at her side.

Mrs. Maxie was aware of a curious moment in which each person present seemed separately aware of Sally and in which they yet moved quietly together as if tensed to face a common challenge. In an effort to restore normality she spoke casually. "I'm glad you're in, Stephen. Sally, you had better change back into your uniform and help Martha."

The girl's self-contained little smile cracked into laughter. It took her a second to gain sufficient control to reply in a voice which was almost obsequious in its derisive respectfulness.

"Would that be appropriate, madam, for the girl your son has asked to marry him?"

3

Simon Maxie had a night which was no worse and no better than any other. It is doubtful whether anyone else beneath his roof was as fortunate. His wife kept her vigil on the day bed in his dressing-room and heard the hours strike while the luminous hand on the clock beside her bed jerked forward towards the inevitable day. She lived through the scene in the drawing-room so many times that there now seemed no second of it which was not remembered with clarity, no nuance of voice or emotion which was lost. She could recall every word of Miss Liddell's hysterical attack, the spate of vicious and half-demented abuse which had provoked Sally's retort.

"Don't talk about what you've done for me. What have you ever cared about me, you sex-starved old hypocrite? Be thankful that I know how to keep my mouth shut. There are some things I could tell the village about you."

She had gone after that and the party had been left to enjoy their dinner with as much appetite as they could muster or simulate. Miss Liddell had made little effort. Once Mrs. Maxie noticed a tear on her cheek and she was touched with the thought that Miss Liddell was genuinely suffering, had cared to the limit of her capacity for Sally and had honestly taken pleasure in her progress and happiness. Dr. Epps had champed through his meal in an unwonted silence, a sure sign that jaw and mind were together exercised. Stephen had not followed Sally from the room but had taken his seat by his sister. In reply to his mother's quiet "Is this true, Stephen?" he had replied simply, "Of course." He had made no further mention of it and brother and sister had sat through the meal together, eating little but presenting a united front to Miss Liddell's distress, and Felix Hearne's ironic glances. He, thought Mrs. Maxie, was the only member of the party who had enjoyed his dinner. She was not sure that the preliminaries had not sharpened his appetite. She knew that he had never liked Stephen and this engagement, if persisted in, was likely to afford him amusement as well as increasing his chances with Deborah. No one could suppose that Deborah would remain at Martingale once Stephen had married. Mrs. Maxie found that she could remember with uncomfortable vividness Catherine's bent face, flushed unbecomingly with grief or resentment and the calm way in which Felix Hearne had roused her to make at least a decent effort at concealment. He could be very amusing when he cared to exert himself and last night he had exerted himself to the full. Surprisingly, he had succeeded in producing laughter by the end of the meal. Was that really only seven hours ago?

The minutes ticked away sounding unnaturally loud in the quietness. It had rained heavily earlier in the night but had now stopped. At five o'clock she thought she heard her husband stirring and went to him, but he still lay in that rigid stupor which they called sleep. Stephen had changed his sleeping-drug. He had been given medicine instead of the usual tablet but the result appeared much the same. She went back to bed but not to sleep. At six o'clock she got up and put on her dressing-gown, then she filled and plugged in the electric kettle for her morning tea. The day with its problems had come at last.

It was a relief to her when there was a knock on the door and Catherine slipped in, still in her pyjamas and dressing-gown. Mrs. Maxie had a moment of acute fear that Catherine had come to talk, that the affairs of the previous evening would have to be discussed, assessed, deprecated and relived. She had spent most of the night making plans that she could not share nor would wish to share with Catherine. But she found herself unaccountably glad to see another human being. She noticed that the girl looked pale. Obviously someone else had enjoyed little sleep. Catherine confessed that the rain had kept her awake and that she had woken early with a bad headache. She did not get them very often now but, when she did, they were bad. Had Mrs. Maxie any aspirin? She preferred the soluble kind but any would do. Mrs. Maxie reflected that the headache might be an excuse for a confidential chat on the Sally-Stephen situation but a longer look at the girl's heavy eyes decided her that the pain was genuine enough. Catherine was obviously in no state for planning anything. Mrs. Maxie invited her to help herself to the aspirin from the medicine cupboard and put out an extra cup of tea on the tray. Catherine was not the companion she would have chosen, but at least the girl seemed prepared to drink her tea in silence.

They were sitting together in front of the electric fire when Martha arrived, her bearing and tone demonstrating a nice compromise between indignation and anxiety.

"It's Sally, madam," she said. "She's overslept again I suppose. She didn't answer when I called her and, when I tried the door, I found that she's bolted it. I can't get in. I'm sure I don't know what she's playing at, madam." Mrs. Maxie replaced her cup in its saucer and noticed with clinical detachment and a kind of wonder that her hand was not shaking. The imminence of evil took hold of her and she had to pause for a second before she could trust her voice. But when the words came, neither Catherine nor Martha seemed aware of any change in her.

"Have you really knocked hard?" she inquired.

Martha hesitated. Mrs. Maxie knew what that meant. Martha had not chosen to knock very hard. It was suiting her purpose better to let Sally oversleep. Mrs. Maxie, after her broken night, found this pettiness almost too much to bear.

"You had better try again," she said shortly. "Sally had a busy day yesterday as we all did. People don't oversleep without reason."

Catherine opened her mouth as if to make some comment, thought better of it, and bent her head over her tea. Within two minutes Martha was back and, this time, there was no doubt of it. Anxiety had conquered irritation and there was something very like panic in her voice.

"I can't make her hear me. The baby's awake.

He's whimpering in there. I can't make Sally hear!"

Mrs. Maxie had no memory of getting to the door of Sally's room. She was so certain, beyond any possible doubt, that the room must be open that she beat and tugged ineffectually at the door for several seconds before her mind accepted the truth. The door was bolted on the inside. The noise of the knocking had thoroughly woken Jimmy and his early morning whimpering was now rising into a crescendo of wailing fear. Mrs. Maxie could hear the rattling of his cot bars and could picture him, cocooned in his woollen sleeping-bag, pulling himself up to scream for his mother. She felt the cold sweat starting on her forehead. It was all she could do to prevent herself from beating in mad panic at the unyielding wood. Martha was moaning now and it was Catherine who laid a comforting and restraining hand on Mrs. Maxie's shoulder.

"Don't worry too much. I'll get your son." "Why doesn't she say 'Stephen'?" thought Mrs. Maxie irrelevantly. "Stephen is my son." In a moment he was with them. The knocking must have aroused him for Catherine could not have fetched him so quickly. Stephen spoke calmly.

"We'll have to get in by the window. The ladder in the outhouse will do. I'll get Hearne." He was gone and the little group of women waited in silence. The moments slowly passed.

"It's bound to take a little time," said Catherine

reassuringly. "But they won't be long. I'm sure she's all right. She's probably still asleep."

Deborah gave her a long look. "With all this noise from Jimmy? My guess is that she won't be there. She's gone."

"But why should she?" asked Catherine. "And what about the locked door?"

"Knowing Sally, I presume that she wanted to do it the spectacular way and got out through the window. She seems to have a penchant for making scenes even when she can't be present to enjoy them. Here we are shivering with apprehension while Stephen and Felix lug ladders about, and the whole of the household is disorganized. Very satisfying to her imagination."

"She wouldn't leave the baby," said Catherine suddenly. "No mother would."

"This one apparently has," replied Deborah dryly. But her mother noticed that she made no move to leave the party.

Jimmy's yells had now reached a sustained climax which drowned any sound of the men's activities with the ladder or their entrance through the window. The next sound heard from the room was the quick scraping of the lock. Felix stood in the doorway. At the sight of his face Martha gave a scream, a high-pitched animal squeal of terror. Mrs. Maxie felt rather than heard the thud of her retreating footsteps, but no one followed her. The other women pushed past Felix's restraining arm and moved silently as if under some united compulsion to where Sally lay. The window was open and the pillow of the bed was blodged with rain. Over the pillow Sally's hair was spread like a web of gold. Her eyes were closed but she was not asleep. From the clenched corner of her mouth a thin trickle of blood had dried like a black slash. On each side of her neck was a bruise where her killer's hands had choked the life from her.

Chapter Four

1

"NICE-LOOKING PLACE, SIR," said Detective-Sergeant Martin as the police car drew up in front of Martingale. "Bit of a change from our last job." He spoke with satisfaction for he was a countryman by birth and inclination and was often heard to complain of the proclivity of murderers to commit their crimes in overcrowded cities and unsalubrious tenements. He sniffed the air appreciatively and blessed whatever reasons of policy or prudence had led the local chief constable to call in the Yard. It had been rumoured that the chief constable personally knew the people concerned and, what with that and the still unsolved business on the fringe of the county, had thought it advisable to hand over this spot of trouble without delay. That suited Detective-Sergeant Martin all right. Work was work wherever you did it, but a man was entitled to his preferences.

Detective Chief-Inspector Adam Dalgleish did not reply but swung himself out of the car and stood back for a moment to look at the house. It was a typical Elizabethan manor house, simple but strongly formalized in design. The large, two-storeyed bays with their mullioned and transomed windows stood symmetrically on each side of the square central porch. Above the dripstone was a heavy carved coat of arms. The roof sloped to a small open stone balustrade also carved with symbols in relief and the six great Tudor chimneys stood up boldly against a summer sky. To the west curved the wall of a room which Dalgleish guessed had been added at a later date— probably during the last century. The french windows were of plated glass and led into the garden. For a moment he saw a face at one of them, but then it turned away. Someone was watching for his arrival. To the west a grey stone wall ran from the corner of the house in a wide sweep towards the gates and lost itself behind the shrubs and the tall beeches. The trees came very close to the house on this side. Above the wall and half-concealed behind a mosaic of leaves he could just see the top of a ladder placed against an oriel window. That presumably was the dead girl's room. Her mistress could hardly have chosen one more suitably placed for an illicit entry. Two vehicles were parked beside the porch, a police car with a uniformed man sitting impassive at the wheel, and a mortuary van. Its driver, stretched back in his seat and with his peaked cap tilted forward, took no notice of Dalgleish's arrival while his mate merely looked up perfunctorily before returning to his Sunday newspaper.

The local superintendent was waiting in the hall. They knew each other slightly as was to be expected with two men both eminent in the same job, but neither had ever wished for a closer acquaintanceship. It was not an easy moment. Manning was finding it necessary to explain exactly why his chief had thought it advisable to call in the Yard. Dalgleish replied suitably. Two reporters were sitting just inside the door with the air of dogs who have been promised a bone if they behave and who have resigned themselves to patience. The house was very quiet and smelt faintly of roses. After the torrid heat of the car the air struck so cold that Dalgleish gave an involuntary shiver.

"The family are together in the drawing-room," said Manning. "I've left a sergeant with them. Do you want to see them now?"

"No, I'll see the body first. The living will keep."

Superintendent Manning led the way up the vast square staircase talking back at them as he went.

"I got a bit of ground covered before I knew they were calling in Central Office. They've probably given you the gist. Victim is the maid here. Unmarried mother aged twenty-two. Strangled. The body was discovered at about 7.15 a.m. this morning by the family. The girl's bedroom door was bolted. Exit, and probably entrance too, was via the window. You'll find evidence of that on the stack-pipe and the wall. It looks as if he fell the last five feet or so. She was last seen alive at 10.30 p.m. last night carrying her late-night drink up to bed. She never finished it. The mug's on the bedside table. I thought it was almost certainly an outside job at first. They had a fête here yesterday and anyone cauld have got into the grounds. Into the house, too, for that matter. But there are one or two odd features."

"The drink, for example?" asked Dalgleish.

They had reached the landing now and were passing towards the west wing of the house. Manning looked at him curiously.

"Yes. The cocoa. It may have been doped. There's some stuff missing. Mr. Simon Maxie is an invalid. There's a bottle of sleeping dope missing from his medicine cupboard."

"Any evidence of doping on the body?"

"The police surgeon's with her now. I doubt it though. Looked a straightforward strangling to me. The P.M. will probably have the answer."

"She could have taken the stuff herself," said Dalgleish. "Is there any obvious motive?"

Manning paused.

"There could be. I haven't got any of the details but I've heard gossip."

"Ah. Gossip."

"A Miss Liddell came this morning to take away the girl's child. She was here to dinner last night. Quite a meal it must have been by her account. Apparently Stephen Maxie had proposed to Sally Jupp. You could call that a motive for the family, I suppose."

"In the circumstances I think I could," said Dalgleish.

The bedroom was white-walled and full of light. After the dimness of the hall and corridors bounded with oak linen-fold panelling, this room struck with the artificial brightness of a stage. The corpse was the most unreal of all, a second-rate actress trying unconvincingly to simulate death. Her eyes were almost closed, but her face held that look of faint surprise which he had often noticed on the faces of the dead. Two small and very white front teeth were clenched against the lower lip, giving a rabbit-look to a face which, in life, must, he felt, have been striking, perhaps even beautiful. An aureole of hair flamed over the pillow in incongruous defiance of death. It felt slightly damp to his hand. Almost he wondered that its brightness had not drained away with the life of her body. He stood very still looking down at her. He was never conscious of pity at moments like this and not even of anger, although that might come later and would have to be resisted. He liked to fix the sight of the murdered body firmly in his mind. This had been a habit since his first big case seven years ago when he had looked down at the battered corpse of a Soho prostitute in silent resolution and had thought, "This is it. This is my job."

The photographer had completed his work with the body before the police surgeon began his examination. He was now finishing with shots of the room and the window before packing up his equipment. The print man had likewise finished with Sally and intent on his private world of whorls and composites, was moving with unobtrusive efficiency from door-knob to lock, from cocoa-beaker to chest of drawers, from bed to window-ledge before heaving himself out on the ladder to work on the stack-pipe and on the ladder itself. Dr. Feltman, the police surgeon, balding, rotund and self-consciously cheerful, as if under a perpetual compulsion to demonstrate his professional imperturbability in the face of death, was replacing his instruments in a black case. Dalgleish had met him before and knew him for a first-class doctor who had never learned to appreciate where his job ended and the detective's began. He waited until Dalgleish had turned away from the body before speaking.

"We're ready to take her away now if that's all right by you. It looks simple enough medically speaking. Manual strangulation by a right-handed person standing in front of her. She died quickly, possibly by vagal inhibition. I'll be able to tell you more after the P.M. There's no sign of sexual interference but that doesn't mean that sex wasn't the motive. I imagine there's nothing like finding a dead body on your hands to take away the urge. When you pull him in you'll get the same old story, 'I put my hands round her neck to frighten her and she went all limp'. He got in by the window by the look of it. You might find fingerprints on that stack-pipe but I doubt whether the ground will be much help. It's a kind of courtyard underneath. No nice soft earth with a couple of handy sole marks. Anyway, it rained pretty hard last night which doesn't help matters. Well, I'll go and get the stretcher party if your man here has finished. Nasty business for a Sunday morning."

He went and Dalgleish inspected the room. It was large and sparsely furnished, but the overall impression it gave was one of sunlight and comfort. He thought that it had probably previously been the family day nursery. The old-fashioned fireplace on the north wall was surrounded by a heavy meshed fireguard behind which an electric fire had been installed. On each side of the fireplace were deep recesses fitted with bookcases and low cupboards. There were two windows. The smaller oriel window against which the ladder stood was on the west wall and looked over the courtyard to the old stables. The larger window ran almost the whole length of the south wall, giving a panoramic view of the lawns and gardens. Here the glass was old and set with occasional medallions. Only the top mullioned windows could be opened.

The cream-painted single bed was set at right-angles to the smaller window and had a chair on one side and a bedside table with a lamp on the other. The child's cot was in the opposite corner half-hidden by a screen. It was the kind of screen which Dalgleish remembered from his own child-hood, composed of dozens of coloured pictures and postcards stuck in a pattern and glazed over. There were a rug before the fireplace and a low nursing chair. Against the wall were a plain ward-robe and a chest of drawers.

There was a curious anonymity about the room. It had the intimate fecund atmosphere of almost any nursery compounded of the faint smell of talcum powder, baby-soap and warmly-aired clothes. But the girl herself had impressed little of her personality on her surroundings. There was none of the feminine clutter which he had half expected. Her few personal belongings were carefully arranged but they were uncom-municative. Primarily it was just a child's nursery with a plain bed for his mother. The few books on the shelves were popular works on baby care. The half-dozen magazines were those devoted to the interests of mothers and housewives rather than to the more romanticized and varied concerns of young working-women. He picked one from the shelf and flicked through it. From its pages dropped an envelope bearing a Venezuelan stamp. It was addressed to:

D. Pullen, Esq.,
Rose Cottage, Nessingford-road,
Little Chadfleet, Essex, England.

On the reverse were three dates scribbled in pencil—Wednesday 18th, Monday 23rd, Monday 30th.

Prowling from the bookshelf to the chest of drawers, Dalgleish pulled out each drawer and systematically turned over its contents with practised fingers. They were in perfect order. The top drawer held only baby clothes. Most of them were hand-knitted, all were well washed and cared for. The second was full of the girl's own underclothes, arranged in neat piles. It was the third and bottom drawer which held the surprise.

"What do you make of this?" he called to Martin.

The sergeant moved to his chief's side with a silent swiftness which was disconcerting in one of his build. He lifted one of the garments in his massive fist.

"Hand-made by the look of it, sir. Must have embroidered it herself, I suppose. There's almost a drawer full. It looks like a trousseau to me."

"I think that's what it is all right. And not only clothes too. Table-cloths, hand towels, cushion covers." He turned them over as he spoke. "It's rather a pathetic little dowry, Martin. Months of devoted work pressed away in lavender bags and tissue paper. Poor little devil. Do you suppose this was for the delight of Stephen Maxie? I can hardly picture these coy tray-clothes being used in Martingale."

Martin picked one up and examined it appreciatively.

"She can't have had him in mind when she did this. He only proposed yesterday according to the Super and she must have been working on this for months. My mother used to do this kind of work. You buttonhole round the pattern and then cut out the middle pits. Richelieu or something they call it. Pretty effect it gives—if you like that sort of thing," he added in deference to his Chief's obvious lack of enthusiasm. He ruminated over the embroidery in nostalgic approval before yielding it up for replacement in the drawer.

Dalgleish moved over to the oriel window. The wide window-ledge was about three feet high. It was scattered now with the bright glass fragments of a collection of miniature animals. A penguin lay wingless on its side and a brittle dachshund had snapped in two. One Siamese cat, startlingly blue of eye, was the sole survivor among the splintered holocaust.

The two largest and middle sections of the window opened outwards with a latch and the stackpipe, skirting a similar window about six feet below, ran directly to the paved terrace beneath. It would hardly be a difficult descent for anyone reasonably agile. Even the climb up would be possible. He noticed again how safe from unwanted observation such an entry or exit would be. To his right the great brick wall, half hidden by overhanging beech boughs, curved away towards the drive. Immediately facing the window and about thirty yards away were the old stables with their attractive clock turret. From their open shelter the window could be watched, but from nowhere else. To the left only a small part of the lawn was visible. Someone seemed to have been messing about with it. There was a small patch ringed with cord where the grass had been hacked or cut. Even from the window Dalgleish could see the lifted sods and the rash of brown soil beneath. Superintendent Manning had come up behind him and answered his unspoken question.

"That's Doctor Epps's treasure hunt. He's had it in the same spot for the last twenty years. They had the church fête here yesterday. Most of the bunting's down—the vicar likes to get the place cleared up before Sunday—but it takes a day or two to erase all the evidence."

Dalgleish remembered that the Super was almost a local man. "Were you here?" he asked.

"Not this year. I've been on duty almost continuously for the last week. We've still got that killing on the county border to clear up. It won't be long now, but I've been pretty tied up with it. The wife and I used to come over here once a year for the fête but that was before the war. It

was different then. I don't think we'd bother now.
They still get a fair crowd though. Someone could
have met the girl and found out from her where
she slept. It's going to mean a lot of work checking on her movements during yesterday afternoon and evening." His tone implied that he was
glad the job was not his.

Dalgleish did not theorize in advance of his
facts. But the facts he had garnered so far did
not support this comfortable thesis of an unknown casual intruder. There had been no sign
of attempted sexual assault, no evidence of theft.
He had a very open mind on the question of that
bolted door. Admittedly, the Maxie family had all
been on the right side of it at 7 a.m. that morning, but they were presumably as capable as
anyone else of climbing down stack-pipes or de-
scending ladders.

The body had been taken away, a white-
sheeted lumpy shape stiff on the stretcher, des-
tined for the pathologist's knife and the analyst's
bottle. Manning had left them to telephone his
office. Dalgleish and Martin continued their patient inspection of the house. Next to Sally's
room was an old-fashioned bathroom, the deep
bath boxed round with mahogany and the whole
of one wall covered with an immense airing-
cupboard, fitted with slatted shelves. The three
remaining walls were papered in an elegant floral design faded with age and there was an old
but still unworn fitted carpet on the floor. The
room offered no possible hiding-place. From the

landing outside a flight of drugget-covered stairs curved down to the panelled corridor which led on the one side to the kitchen quarters and on the other to the main hall. Just at the bottom of these stairs was the heavy south door. It was ajar, and Dalgleish and Martin passed out of the coolness of Martingale into the heavy heat of the day. Somewhere the bells of a church were ringing for Sunday matins. The sound came clearly and sweetly across the trees bringing to Martin a memory of boyhood's country Sundays and to Dalgleish a reminder that there was much to be done and little left of the morning.

"We'll have a look at that old stable block and the west wall beneath her window. After that I'm rather interested in the kitchen. And then we'll get on with the questioning. I've a feeling that the person we're after slept under this roof last night."

2

In the drawing-room the Maxies with their two guests and Martha Bultitaft waited to be questioned, unobtrusively watched over by a detective-sergeant who had stationed himself in a small chair by the door and who sat in apparently solid indifference, seeming far more at his ease than the owners of the house. His charges had their various reasons for wondering how long they would be kept waiting, but no one liked to reveal anxiety by asking. They had been told that Detective Chief-Inspector Dalgleish from Scotland Yard had arrived and would be with them shortly. How shortly no one was prepared to ask. Felix and Deborah were still in their riding-clothes. The others had dressed hurriedly. All had eaten little and now they sat and waited. Since it would have seemed heartless to read, shocking to play the piano, unwise to talk about the murder and unnatural to talk about anything else, they sat in almost unbroken silence. Felix Hearne and Deborah were together on the sofa but sitting a little apart and occasionally he leaned across to whisper something in her ear. Stephen Maxie had stationed himself at one of the windows and stood with his back to the room. It was a stance which, as Felix Hearne had noticed cynically, enabled him to keep his face hidden and to demonstrate an inarticulate sorrow with the back of his bent head. At least four of the watchers would have liked very much to know whether the sorrow was genuine. Eleanor Maxie sat calmly in a chair apart. She was either numbed by grief or thinking deeply. Her face was very pale but the brief panic which had caught her at Sally's door was over now. Her daughter noticed that she at least had taken trouble in her dressing and was presenting an almost normal appearance to her family and guests. Martha Bultitaft also sat a little apart, ill at ease in the edge of her chair and darting occasional furious looks at the sergeant whom she obviously held responsible for her embarrassment at having to sit with the family and in the drawing-room, too, while there was work to be done. She who had been the most upset and terrified at the morning's discovery now seemed to regard the whole thing as a personal insult, and she sat in sullen resentment. Catherine Bowers gave the greatest appearance of ease. She had taken a small notebook from her handbag and was writing in it at intervals as if refreshing her memory about the events of the morning. No one was deceived by this appearance of normality and efficiency, but they all envied her the opportunity of putting up so good a show. All of them sat in essential isolation and thought their own thoughts. Mrs. Maxie kept her eyes on the strong hands folded in her lap but her mind was on her son.

"He will get over it, the young always do. Thank God Simon will never know. It's going to be difficult to manage the nursing without Sally. One oughtn't to think about that I suppose. Poor child. There may be fingerprints on that lock. The police will have thought of that. Unless he wore gloves. We all know about gloves these days. I wonder how many people got through that window to her. I suppose I ought to have thought of it, but how could I? She had the child with her after all. What will they do with Jimmy? A mother murdered and a father he'll never know now. That was one secret she kept. One of many probably. One never knows people. What do I know about Felix? He could be dangerous. So could this chief inspector.

Martha ought to be seeing to luncheon. That is, if anyone wants luncheon. Where will the police feed? Presumably they'll only want to use our rooms today. Nurse will be here at twelve so I'll have to go to Simon then. I suppose I could go now if I asked. Deborah is on edge. We all are. If only we can keep our heads."

Deborah thought, "I ought to dislike her less now that she's dead, but I can't. She always did make trouble. She would enjoy watching us like this, sweating on the top line. Perhaps she can. I mustn't get morbid. I wish we could talk about it. We might have kept quiet about Stephen and Sally if Eppy and Miss Liddell hadn't been at dinner. And Catherine of course. There's always Catherine. She's going to enjoy this all right. Felix knows that Sally was doped. Well, if she was, it was in my drinking mug. Let them make what they like of that."

Felix Hearne thought, "They can't be much longer. The thing is not to lose my temper. These will be English policemen, extremely polite English policemen asking questions in strict compliance with judges' rules. Fear is the devil to hide. I can imagine Dalgleish's face if I decided to explain. Excuse me, Inspector, if I appear to be terrified of you. The reaction is purely automatic, a trick of the nervous system. I have a dislike of formal questioning, and even more of the carefully staged informal session. I had some experience of it in France. I have recovered completely from the effects, you understand, except for this one slight legacy. I tend to lose my temper. It is only pure bloody funk. I am sure you will understand, Herr Inspector. Your questions are so very reasonable. It is unfortunate that I mistrust reasonable questions. We mustn't get this thing out of proportion of course. This is a minor disability. A comparatively small part of one's life is spent in being questioned by the police. I got off lightly. They even left me some of my fingernails. I'm just trying to explain that I may find it difficult to give you the answers you want."

Stephen turned round.

"What about a lawyer?" he asked suddenly. "Oughtn't we to send for Jephson?"

His mother looked up from a silent contemplation of her folded hands. "Matthew Jephson is motoring somewhere on the Continent. Lionel is in London. We could get him if you feel it to be necessary."

Her voice held a note of interrogation. Deborah said impulsively, "Oh, Mummy! *Not* Lionel Jephson. He's the world's most pompous bore. Let's wait until we're arrested before we encourage him to come beetling down. Besides, he's not a criminal lawyer. He only knows about trusts and affidavits and documents. This would shock his respectable soul to the core. He couldn't help."

"What about you, Hearne?" asked Stephen.

"I'll cope unaided, thank you."

"We should apologize for mixing you up in this," said Stephen with stiff formality. "It's unpleasant for you and may be inconvenient. I don't know when you'll get back to London." Felix thought that this apology should more appropriately be made to Catherine Bowers. Stephen was apparently determined to ignore the girl. Did the arrogant young fool seriously believe that this death was merely a matter of unpleasantness and inconvenience? He looked across at Mrs. Maxie as he replied.

"I shall be very glad to stay—voluntarily or involuntarily—if I can be of use."

Catherine was adding her eager assurances to the same effect when the silent sergeant, galvanized into life, sprang to attention in a single movement. The door opened and three plainclothes policemen came in. Superintendent Manning they already knew. Briefly he introduced his companions as Detective Chief-Inspector Adam Dalgleish and Detective-Sergeant George Martin. Five pairs of eyes swung simultaneously to the taller stranger in fear, appraisal or frank curiosity.

Catherine Bowers thought, "Tall, dark and handsome. Not what I expected. Quite an interesting face really."

Stephen Maxie thought, "Supercilious-looking devil. He's taken his time coming. I suppose the idea is to soften us up. Or else he's been snooping round the house. This is the end of privacy."

Felix Hearne thought, "Well, here it comes. Adam Dalgleish, I've heard of him. Ruthless, unorthodox, working always against time. I suppose he has his own private compulsions. At least they've thought us adversaries worthy of the best."

Eleanor Maxie thought, "Where have I seen that head before? Of course. That Dürer. In Munich was it? Portrait of an Unknown Man. Why does one always expect police officers to wear bowlers and raincoats?"

Through the exchange of introductions and courtesies Deborah Riscoe stared at him as if she saw him through a web of red-gold hair.

When he spoke it was in a curiously deep voice, relaxed and unemphatic.

"I understand from Superintendent Manning that the small business room next door has been placed at my disposal. I hope it won't be necessary to monopolize either it or you for a very long time. I should like to see you separately please and in this order."

"See me in my study at nine, nine-five, nine-ten . . ." whispered Felix to Deborah. He was not sure whether he sought relief for himself or her, but there was no answering smile.

Dalgleish let his glance move briefly over the group. "Mr. Stephen Maxie, Miss Bowers, Mrs. Maxie, Mrs. Riscoe, Mr. Hearne and Mrs. Bultitaft. Will those who are waiting please stay here. If any of you need to leave this room there is a woman police officer and a constable outside in the hall who can go with you. This surveillance will be relaxed as soon as everyone has been interviewed. Would you come with me please, Mr. Maxie?"

3

Stephen Maxie took the initiative.

"I think I had better begin by letting you know that Miss Jupp and I were engaged to be married. I proposed to her yesterday evening. There's no secret about it. It can't have anything to do with her death and I might not have bothered to mention it except that she broke the news in front of the village's prize gossip, so you'd probably find out fairly soon."

Dalgleish, who had already found out and was by no means convinced that the proposal was nothing to do with the murder, thanked Mr. Maxie gravely for his frankness and expressed formal condolences on the death of his fiancée. The boy looked up at him with a sudden direct glance.

"I don't feel I've any right to accept condolences. I can't even feel bereaved. I suppose I shall when the shock of this has worn off a little. We were only engaged yesterday and now she's dead. It still isn't believable."

"Your mother was aware of this engagement?"

"Yes. All the family were except my father."

"Did Mrs. Maxie approve?"

"Hadn't you better ask her that yourself?"

"Perhaps I had. What were your relations with Miss Jupp before yesterday evening, Dr. Maxie?"

"If you are asking whether we were lovers the answer is 'no'. I was sorry for her, I admired her and I was attracted by her. I have no idea what she thought about me."

"Yet she accepted your offer of marriage?"

"Not specifically. She told my mother and her guests that I had proposed so I naturally assumed that she intended to accept me. Otherwise there would have been no point in breaking the news."

Dalgleish could think of several reasons why the girl should have broken the news, but he was not prepared to discuss them. Instead he invited his witness to give his own account of recent events from the time that the missing Sommeil tablets were first brought into the house.

"So you think she was drugged, Inspector? I told the Superintendent about the tablets when he arrived. They were certainly in my father's medicine chest early this morning. Miss Bowers noticed them when she went to the cupboard for aspirin. They aren't there now. The only Sommeil in the cupboard now is in a sealed packet. The bottle has gone."

"No doubt we shall find it, Dr. Maxie. The autopsy will discover whether or not Miss Jupp was drugged, and if so, how much of the stuff was taken. There is almost certainly something other than cocoa in that mug by the bed. She may, of course, have put the stuff in it herself."

"If she didn't, Inspector, who did? The stuff might not even have been meant for Sally. That was my sister's drinking-mug by the bed. We each have our own and they are all different. If the Sommeil was meant for Sally it must have been put in the drink after she had taken it up to her room."

"If the drinking-mugs are so distinctive it is curious that Miss Jupp should have taken the wrong one. That was an unlikely mistake surely?"

"It may not have been a mistake," said Stephen shortly.

Dalgleish did not ask him to explain but listened in silence as his witness described the visit of Sally to St. Luke's on the previous Thursday, the events of the church fête, the sudden impulse which had led him to propose marriage and the finding of his fiancée's body. The account he gave was factual, concise and almost unemotional. When he came to describe the scene in Sally's bedroom his voice was almost clinically detached. Either he had greater control than was good for him or he had anticipated this interview and had schooled himself in advance against every betrayal of fear or remorse.

"I went with Felix Hearne to get the ladder. He was dressed but I was still in my dressing-gown. I shed one of my bedroom slippers on the way to the outhouses opposite Sally's window so he reached them first and gripped the ladder. It's always kept there. Hearne had dragged it out by the time I caught up with him and was calling out to know which way to carry it. I pointed towards Sally's window. We carried the ladder between us although it's quite light. One person could manage it, although I'm not sure about a woman. We put it against the wall and Hearne went up first while I steadied it. I followed him at once. The window was open but the curtains were drawn across. As you saw, the bed is at right angles to the window with the head towards it. There's a wide window-ledge where the oriel window juts out and Sally apparently kept a collection of small glass animals there. I noticed that they had been scattered and most were broken. Hearne went over to the door and pulled back the lock. I stood looking at Sally. The bed-clothes were pulled up as far as her chin but I could see at once that she was dead. By this time the rest of the family were around the bed, and when I turned back the clothes we could see what had happened. She was lying on her back—we didn't disturb her—and she looked quite peaceful. But you know what she looked like. You saw her."

"I know what I saw," said Dalgleish. "I'm asking now what you saw."

The boy looked at him curiously and then closed his eyes for a second before replying. He spoke in a flat expressionless voice as if repeating a lesson learnt by rote. "There was a trickle of blood at the corner of her mouth. Her eyes were almost closed. There was a fairly distinct thumb impression under the right lower jaw over the cornu of the thyroid and a less clear indication of fingermarks on the left side of the neck lying along the thyroid cartilage. It was an obvious case of manual strangulation with the right hand and from the front. Considerable force must have been used, but I thought that death was possibly due to vagal inhibition and may have been very sudden. There were few of the classic signs of asphyxia. But no doubt you will get the facts from the autopsy."

"I expect them to be in line with your own views. Did you form any idea of the time of death?"

"There were some rigor mortis in the jaw and neck muscles. I don't know whether it had spread any farther. I'm describing the signs that I noticed almost subconsciously. You will hardly expect a full post-mortem account in the circumstances."

Sergeant Martin, his head bent over his notebook, detected unerringly the first note of near hysteria and thought, "Poor devil. The old man can be pretty brutal. He stood up to it all right so far, though. Too well for a man who has just discovered the body of his girl. If she was his girl."

"I shall get the full post-mortem report in due course," said Dalgleish equably. "I was interested in your assessment of the time of death."

"It was a fairly warm night despite the rain. I should say not less than five hours nor more than eight."

"Did you kill Sally Jupp, Doctor?"

"No."

"Do you know who did?"

"No."

"What were your movements from the time that you finished dinner on Saturday night until

Miss Bowers called you this morning with the news that Sally Jupp's door was bolted?"

"We had our coffee in the drawing-room. At about nine o'clock my mother suggested that we should start counting the money. It was in the safe here in the business room. I thought they might be happier without me and I was feeling restless, so I went out for a walk. I told my mother that I might be late and asked her to leave the south door open for me. I hadn't any particular idea in mind, but as soon as I'd left the house I felt I should like to see Sam Bocock. He lives alone in the cottage at the far end of the home meadow. I walked through the garden and over the meadow to his cottage and stayed there with him until pretty late. I can't exactly remember when I left, but he may be able to help. I think it was just after eleven. I walked back alone, entered the house through the south door, bolted it behind me and went to bed. That's all."

"Did you go straight home?"

The almost imperceptible hesitation was not lost on Dalgleish.

"Yes."

"That means you would have been back in the house by when?"

"It's only five minutes' walk from Bocock's cottage, but I didn't hurry. I suppose I was indoors and in bed by eleven-thirty."

"It's a pity that you can't be precise about the time, Dr. Maxie. It's also, surely, surprising in view of the fact that you have a small clock on your bedside table with a luminous dial."

"I may have. That doesn't mean that I always take a note of the times I sleep or get up."

"You spent about two hours with Mr. Bocock. What did you talk about?"

"Horses and music mainly. He has a rather fine record-player. We listened to his new record— Klemperer conducting the *Eroica* to be precise."

"Are you in the habit of visiting Mr. Bocock and spending the evening with him?"

"Habit? Bocock was groom to my grandfather. He's my friend. Don't you visit your friends when you feel like it, Inspector, or haven't you any?"

It was the first flash of temper. Dalgleish's face showed no emotion, not even satisfaction. He pushed a small square of paper across the table. On it were three minute splinters of glass.

"These were found in the outhouse opposite Miss Jupp's room, where you say that the ladder is normally kept. Do you know what they are?"

Stephen Maxie bent forward and studied this exhibit without apparent interest. "They're splinters of glass obviously. I can't tell you any more about them. They could be part of a broken watch-glass I suppose."

"Or part of one of the smashed glass animals from Miss Jupp's room."

"Presumably."

"I see you are wearing a small piece of plaster across your right knuckle. What's wrong?"

"I grazed myself slightly when I was coming home last night. I brushed my hand against the bark of a tree. At least, that's the most probable explanation. I can't remember it happening and only noticed the blood when I got to my room. I stuck this plaster on before I went to bed and I'd normally have taken it off by now. The graze wasn't really worth bothering about, but I have to look after my hands."

"May I see, please?"

Maxie came forward and placed his hand, palm down, on the desk. Dalgleish noted that it did not tremble. He picked at the corner of the plaster and ripped it off. Together they inspected the whitened knuckle underneath. Maxie still showed no sign of anxiety, but scrutinized his hand with the air of a connoisseur condescendingly inspecting an exhibit which was hardly worthy of his attention. He picked up the discarded plaster, folded it neatly and flicked it accurately into the waste-paper basket.

"That looks like a cut to me," said Dalgleish. "Or it could, of course, be a scratch from a finger-nail."

"It could, of course," agreed his suspect easily. "But if it were wouldn't you expect to find blood and skin under the nail which did the scratching? I'm sorry I can't remember how it happened." He looked at it again and added, "It certainly looks like a small cut but it's ridiculously small. In two days it won't be visible. Are you sure you don't want to photograph it?"

"No thank you," said Dalgleish. "We've had something rather more serious to photograph upstairs."

It gave him considerable satisfaction to watch the effect of his words. While he was in charge of this case none of his suspects need think that they could retreat into private worlds of detachment or cynicism from the horror of what had laid on the bed upstairs. He waited for a moment and then continued remorselessly.

"I want to be perfectly clear about this south door. It leads directly to the flight of stairs which go up to the old nursery. To that extent Miss Jupp slept in a part of the house which can be said to have its own entrance. Almost a self-contained flat in effect. Once the kitchen quarters were closed for the night she could let a visitor in through that door with little risk of discovery. If the door were left unbolted a visitor could gain entrance to her door with reasonable ease. Now you say that the south door was left unbolted for you from nine o'clock when you had finished dinner until shortly after 11 p.m. when you returned from Mr. Bocock's cottage. During that time is it true to say that anyone could have gained access to the house through the south door?"

"Yes. I suppose so."

"Surely you know definitely whether they could or not, Mr. Maxie?"

"Yes, they could. As you probably saw, the door has two heavy inside bolts and a mortice lock. We haven't used the lock for years. There are keys somewhere, I suppose. My mother might know. We normally keep the door closed during the day and bolt it at night. In the winter it is usually kept bolted all the time and is hardly used. There is another door into the kitchen quarters. We're rather slack about locking up, but we've never had any trouble here. Even if we did lock the doors carefully the house wouldn't be burglarproof. Anyone could get in through the french windows in the drawing-room. We do lock them, but the glass could easily be broken. It has never seemed worth while worrying too much about security."

"And, in addition to this ever-open door, there was a convenient ladder in the old stable block?"

Stephen Maxie gave a slight shrug.

"It has to be kept somewhere. We don't lock up the ladders just in case someone gets the idea of using them to get through the windows."

"We have no evidence yet that anyone did. I am still interested in that door. Would you be prepared to swear that it was unbolted when you returned from Mr. Bocock's cottage?"

"Of course. Otherwise I couldn't have got in."

Dalgleish said quickly, "You realize the importance of determining at what time you finally bolted that door?"

"Of course."

"I'm going to ask you once more what time you bolted it and I advise you to think very carefully before you reply."

Stephen Maxie looked at him straight in the eye and said almost casually:

"It was thirty-three minutes past twelve by my watch. I wasn't able to get to sleep and at twelve-thirty I suddenly remembered that I hadn't locked up. So I got out of bed and did so. I didn't see anyone or hear anything and I went straight back to my room. It was no doubt very careless of me, but if there's a law against forgetting to lock up I should like to hear of it."

"So that at twelve-thirty-three you bolted the south door?"

"Yes," replied Stephen Maxie easily. "At thirty-three minutes past midnight."

4

In Catherine Bowers Dalgleish had a witness after every policeman's heart, composed, painstaking and confident. She had walked in with great self-possession, showing no signs of either nervousness or grief. Dalgleish did not like her. He knew that he was prone to these personal antipathies and he had long ago learned both to conceal and evaluate them. But he was right in supposing her to be an accurate observer. She had been quick to watch people's reactions as she had been to note the sequence of events. It was from Catherine Bowers that Dalgleish learned how shocked the Maxies had been at Sally's announcement, how triumphantly the girl had laughed out her news and what an unusual effect her remarks to Miss Liddell had produced on that lady. Miss Bowers was perfectly prepared, too, to discuss her own feelings.

"Naturally it was a terrible shock when Sally gave us her news, but I can quite see how it happened. No one is kinder than Dr. Maxie. He has too much social conscience as I am always telling him and the girl just took advantage of it. I know he couldn't have loved her really. He never mentioned it to me and he would have told me before anyone. If they had really loved each other he could have relied on me to understand and release him."

"Do you mean that there was an engagement between you?"

Dalgleish had difficulty in keeping the surprise out of his voice. It needed only one more fiancée to make the case fantastic.

"Not exactly an engagement, Inspector. No ring or anything like that. But we have been close friends for so long now that it was rather taken for granted . . . I suppose you might say we had an understanding. But there were no definite plans. Dr. Maxie has a long was to go before he can think of marriage. And there is his father's illness to consider."

"So that you were not, in fact, engaged to be married to him?"

Faced with this uncompromising question Catherine admitted as much, but with a little self-satisfied smile which conveyed that it could only be a matter of time.

"When you arrived at Martingale for this week-end, did anything strike you as unusual?"

"Well, I was rather late on Friday evening. I didn't arrive until just before dinner. Dr. Maxie didn't arrive until late that night and Mr. Hearne only came on Saturday morning, so there were only Mrs. Maxie, Deborah and me at dinner. I thought they seemed worried. I don't like having to say it, but I'm afraid Sally Jupp was a scheming little girl. She waited on us and I didn't like her attitude at all." Dalgleish questioned her further but the "attitude" as far as he could judge consisted of nothing more than a slight toss of the head when Deborah had spoken to her and a neglect to call Mrs. Maxie "Madam." But he did not discount Catherine's evidence as valueless. It was likely that neither Mrs. Maxie nor her daughter had been entirely oblivious to the danger in their midst.

He changed his tack and took her carefully over the events of Sunday morning. She described how she had woken with a headache after a poor night and had gone in search of aspirin. Mrs. Maxie had invited her to help herself. It was then that she had noticed the little bottle of Sommeil. At first she had mistaken the tablets for aspirin but had quickly realized that they were too small and were the wrong colour. Apart from that, the bottle was labelled. She had not noticed how many Sommeil tablets were in the bottle but she was absolutely certain that the bottle was in the drug cupboard at seven o'clock that morning and equally certain that it was no longer there when she and Stephen Maxie had looked for it after the finding of Sally Jupp's body. The only Sommeil in the cupboard then had been an un-opened and sealed packet.

Dalgleish asked her to describe the finding of the body and was surprised at the vivid picture which she was able to give.

"When Martha came to tell Mrs. Maxie that Sally hadn't got up we thought at first that she'd just overslept again. Then Martha came back to say that her door was locked and Jimmy crying so we went to see what was wrong. There's no doubt that the door was bolted. As you know, Dr. Maxie and Mr. Hearne got in through the win-dow and I heard one of them drawing back the bolt. I think it must have been Mr. Hearne be-cause he opened the door. Stephen was stand-ing near the bed looking at Sally. Mr. Hearne said, 'I'm afraid she's dead.' Someone screamed. It was Martha, I think, but I didn't look round to see. I said, 'She can't be! She was all right last night!' We had moved over to the bed then and Stephen had drawn the sheet down from her face. Before that it had been up to her chin and folded quite neatly. I thought that it looked as if someone had tucked her up comfortably for the night. As soon as we saw the marks on her neck we knew what had happened. Mrs. Maxie closed her eyes for a moment. I thought that she was going to faint so I went over to her. But she managed to keep on her feet and stood at the bottom of the bed gripping the rail. She was shaking violently, so much that the whole bed was shaking. It is only a light single bed as you will have seen, and the shaking made the body bounce very gently up and down. Stephen said very loudly, 'Cover her face,' but Mr. Hearne reminded him that we had better not touch anything more until the police came. Mr. Hearne was the calmest of us all, I thought, but I suppose that he is used to violent death. He looked more interested than shocked. He bent over Sally and lifted one of her eyelids. Stephen said roughly, 'I shouldn't worry, Hearne. She's dead all right.' Mr. Hearne replied, 'It isn't that. I'm wondering why she didn't struggle.' Then he dipped his little finger into the mug of cocoa on the bedside table. It was just over half full and a skin had formed on the top. The skin stuck to his finger and he scraped it off against the side of the mug before putting the finger in his mouth. We were all looking at him as if he were going to demonstrate something wonderful to us. I thought that Mrs. Maxie looked—well, rather hopeful. Rather like a child at a party. Stephen said, 'Well, what is it?' Mr. Hearne shrugged his shoulders and said, 'That's for the analyst to say, I think she's been doped.' Just then Deborah gave a kind of gasp and fumbled towards the door. She was deathly white and was obviously going to be sick. I tried to get to her, but Mr. Hearne said quite sharply, 'All right. Leave her to me.' He guided her out of the room, and I think they went into the maids' bathroom next door. I wasn't surprised. I would have expected Deborah to break down like that. That left Mrs. Maxie and Stephen in the room with me. I suggested that Mrs. Maxie should find a key so that the room could be locked and she replied, 'Of course. I believe that is usual. And oughtn't we to telephone the police? The extension in the dressing-room would be best.' I suppose she meant that it would be the most private. I remember thinking, 'If we 'phone from the dressing-room the maids won't overhear,' forgetting that 'the maids' meant Sally and that Sally wouldn't be overhearing anything again."

"Do you mean that Miss Jupp was in the habit of listening to other people's conversation?" interrupted the inspector.

"I certainly always had that impression, Inspector. But I always thought she was sly. She never seemed the least grateful for all that the family had done for her. She hated Mrs. Riscoe, of course. Anyone could see that. I expect you've been told about the affair of the copied dress?"

Dalgleish expressed himself interested in this intriguing title and was rewarded with a graphic description of the incident and the reactions it had provoked.

"So you can see the type of girl she was. Mrs. Riscoe pretended to take it calmly, but I could see what she was feeling. She could have killed Sally." Catherine Bowers pulled her skirt down over her knees with complacent mock modesty. She was either a very good actress or she was unconscious of her solecism. Dalgleish continued the questioning with the feeling that he might be facing a more complex personality than he had first recognized.

"Will you tell me please what happened when Mrs. Maxie, her son and you reached the dressing-room?"

"I was just coming to that, Inspector. I had picked up Jimmy from his cot and was still holding him in my arms. It seemed terrible to me that he should have been alone in that room with his dead mother. When we all burst in he stopped crying and I don't think any of us thought about him for a time. Then suddenly I noticed him. He had pulled himself up by the bars of his cot and was balancing there with his wet nappy hanging around his ankles and such an interested look on his face. Of course, he is too young to understand, thank God, and I expect he just wondered what we were all doing round his mother's bed. He had become perfectly quiet and he came to me quite willingly. I carried him with me into the dressing-room. When we got there Dr. Maxie went straight to the medicine cupboard. He said, 'It's gone!' I asked him what he meant and he told me about the missing Sommeil. That was the first time I heard about it. I was able to tell him that the bottle had been there when I went to the cupboard for aspirin that morning. While we were talking Mrs. Maxie had gone through to her husband's room. She was only there for a minute and when she got back she said, 'He's all right. He's sleeping. Have you got the police yet?' Stephen went across to the telephone and I said that I would take Jimmy with me while I dressed and then give him his breakfast. No one replied so I went to the door. Just before I went out I turned round. Stephen had his hand on the receiver and suddenly his mother placed her hand over his and I heard her say, 'Wait. There's one thing I must know.' Stephen replied, 'You don't have to ask. I know nothing about it. I swear that.' Mrs. Maxie gave a little sigh and put her hand up to her eyes. Then Stephen picked up the receiver and I left the room."

She paused and looked up at Dalgleish as if expecting or inviting his comment. "Thank you," he said gravely. "Please go on."

"There isn't really much more to tell you, Inspector. I took Jimmy to my room, collecting a clean nappy from the small bathroom on my way. Mrs. Riscoe and Mr. Hearne were still there. She had been sick and he was helping to bathe her face. They didn't seem very pleased to see me. I said, 'When you feel better I daresay your mother would like some attention. I'm looking after Jimmy.' Neither of them replied. I found the nappies in the airing cupboard and went to my room and changed Jimmy. Then I let him play on my bed while I dressed. That only took about ten minutes. I took him to the kitchen and gave him a lightly boiled egg with bread and butter fingers and some warm milk. He was perfectly good the whole time. Martha was in the kitchen getting breakfast but we didn't speak. I was surprised to find Mr. Hearne there, too. He was making coffee. I suppose Mrs. Riscoe was with her mother. Mr. Hearne didn't seem inclined to talk either. I suppose he was annoyed with me for saying what I did to Mrs. Riscoe. She can do no wrong in his eyes as you've probably guessed. Well, as they didn't seem inclined to discuss what should be done next I decided to take matters into my own hands and I went into the hall with Jimmy and telephoned Miss Liddell. I told her what had happened and asked her to take back the baby until things had been sorted out. She came round by taxi within about fifteen minutes and, by then, Dr. Epps and the police had arrived. The rest you know."

"That has been a very clear and useful account, Miss Bowers. You have the advantage of being a trained observer, but not all trained observers can present their facts in logical sequence. I won't keep you very much longer. I just want to go back to the earlier part of the night. So far you have described very clearly for me the events of yesterday evening and this morning. What I want to establish now is the sequence of events from ten p.m. onwards. At that time I believe you were still in the business room with Mrs. Maxie, Dr. Epps and Miss Liddell. Could you please go on from there."

For the first time Dalgleish discerned a trace of hesitation in his suspect's response. Until now she had responded to his questioning with a ready fluency which had impressed him as being too spontaneous for guile. He could believe that, so far, Catherine Bowers had not found the interview unpleasant. It was difficult to reconcile such uninhibited outpourings with a guilty conscience. Now, however, he sensed the sudden withdrawal of confidence, the slight tensing to meet an unwelcome change of emphasis. She confirmed that Miss Liddell and Dr. Epps had left the business room to go home at about ten-thirty. Mrs. Maxie had seen them off and had then returned to Catherine. Together they had tidied the papers and locked the money in the safe. Mrs. Maxie had not mentioned seeing Sally. Neither of them had discussed her. After locking away the money they had gone to the kitchen. Martha had retired for the night, but had left a saucepan of milk on the top of the stove and a silver tray of beakers on the kitchen table. Catherine remembered noting that Mrs. Riscoe's Wedgwood beaker wasn't there and thought it strange that Mr. Hearne and Mrs. Riscoe could have come in from the garden without anyone knowing. It never occurred to her that Sally might have taken the beaker although, of course, one could see that it was just the sort of thing she might do. Dr. Maxie's mug had been there, together with a glass one in a holder which belonged to Mrs. Maxie and two large cups with saucers which had been put out for the guests. There were a bowl of sugar on the table and tins of two milk drinks. There was no cocoa. Mrs. Maxie and Catherine had collected their drinks and taken them up to Mr. Maxie's dressing-room where his wife was to spend the night. Catherine had helped her to make the invalid's bed and had then stopped to drink her Ovaltine before the dressing-room fire. She had offered to sit up with Mrs. Maxie for a time but the offer had not been accepted. After about an hour Catherine had left to go to her own room. She was sleeping on the opposite side of the house from Sally. She had seen no one on the way to her room. After undressing she had visited the bathroom in her dressing-gown and had been back in her room by about a quarter past eleven. As she was closing the door she thought she heard Mrs. Riscoe and Mr. Hearne coming up the stairs but she couldn't be sure. She had seen or heard nothing of Sally up to that time. Here Catherine paused and Dalgleish waited patiently, but with a quickening of interest. In the corner Sergeant Martin turned over a page of his notebook in practised silence and cast a quick sidelong glance at his chief Unless he was much mistaken the old man's thumbs were pricking now. "Yes, Miss Bowers," prompted Dalgleish inexorably. His witness went bravely on. "I'm afraid this part you may find rather strange but it all seemed perfectly natural at the time. As you can understand the scene before dinner had been a great shock to me. I couldn't believe that Stephen and this girl were engaged. It wasn't he who had broken the news after all, and I don't think for one moment that he had really proposed to her. Dinner had been a terrible meal as you can imagine and, afterwards, everyone had gone on behaving as if nothing had happened. Of course, the Maxies never do show their feelings but Mrs. Riscoe went off with Mr. Hearne and I've no doubt they had a good talk about it and what could be done. But no one said anything to me although, in a sense, I was the one who was most concerned. I thought that Mrs. Maxie might have discussed it with me after the other two guests had left, but I could see that she didn't mean to. When I got to my room I realized that if I didn't do something no one would. I couldn't bear to lie there all night without knowing the worst. I felt I just had to find out the truth. The natural thing seemed to be to ask Sally. I thought that if she and I could only have a private talk together I might be able to get it all straightened out. I knew that it was late but it seemed the only chance. I had been lying there in the dark for some time but, when I had made up my mind, I put on the bedside lamp and looked at my watch. It said three minutes to midnight. That didn't seem so very late in the mood I was in. I put on my dressing-gown and took my pocket torch with me and went to Sally's room. Her door was locked but I could see that the light was on because it was shining through the keyhole. I knocked on the door and called her softly. The door is very strong as you know, but she must have heard me because the next thing I heard was the sound of the bolt being shot home and the light from the keyhole was suddenly obscured as she stood in front of it. I knocked and called once more but it was obvious that she wasn't going to let me in, so I turned and went back to my room. On the way there I suddenly thought I had to see Stephen. I couldn't face going back to bed in the same uncertainty. I thought that he might be wanting to confide in me, but not liking to come and see me. So I turned back from my own bedroom door and went to his. The light wasn't on so I knocked gently and went in. I felt that if only I could see him everything would be all right."

"And was it?" asked Dalgleish.

This time the air of cheerful competence had gone. There could be no mistaking the sudden pain in those unattractive eyes.

"He wasn't there, Inspector. The bed was turned down ready for the night but he wasn't there." She made a sudden effort to return to her former manner and gave him a smile which was almost pathetic in its artificiality. "Of course, I know now that Stephen had been to see Bocock, but it was very disappointing at the time."

"It must have been," agreed Dalgleish gravely.

5

Mrs. Maxie seated herself quietly and composedly, offered him whatever facilities he needed and only hoped that the investigation could be carried out without disturbing her husband who was gravely ill and incapable of realizing what

had happened. Watching her across the desk
Dalgleish could see what her daughter might become in thirty years' time. Her strong, capable,
jeweled hands lay inertly in her lap. Even at that
distance he could see how alike they were to the
hands of her son. With greater interest he noticed that the nails, like the nails on the surgeon's
fingers, were cut very short. He could detect no
signs of nervousness. She seemed rather to
personify the peaceful acceptance of an inevitable trial. It was not, he felt, that she had schooled
herself to endurance. Here was a true serenity
based on some kind of central stability which
would take more than a murder investigation to
disturb. She answered his questions with a deliberate thoughtfulness. It was as if she was setting
her own value on every word. But there was
nothing new that she could tell. She corroborated
the evidence of Catherine Bowers about the discovery of the body and her account of the previous day agreed with the accounts already given.
After the departure of Miss Liddell and Dr. Epps
at about half past ten, she had locked up the
house with the exception of the drawing-room
window and the back door. Miss Bowers had
been with her. Together they had collected their
mugs of milk from the kitchen—only her son's
then remained on the tray—and together they
had gone up to bed. She had spent the night half
sleeping and half watching her husband. She
had heard and seen nothing unusual. No one
had come near her until Miss Bowers had arrived

early and had asked her for aspirin. She had known nothing of the tablets said to have been discovered in her husband's bed and found the story very difficult to believe. In her view it was impossible for him to have hidden anything in his mattress without Mrs. Bultitaft finding it. Her son had told her nothing of the incident, but had mentioned that he had substituted a medicine for the pills. She had not been surprised at this. She had thought that he was trying some new preparation from the hospital and was confident that he would have prescribed nothing without the approval of Dr. Epps.

Not until the patient probing questions of her son's engagement was her composure shaken. Even then it was irritation rather than fear which gave an edge to her voice. Dalgleish sensed that the smooth apologies with which he usually prefaced embarrassing questions would be out of place here, would be resented more than the questions themselves. He asked bluntly:

"What was your attitude, madam, to this engagement between Miss Jupp and your son?"

"It hardly lasted long enough to be dignified with that name surely. And I'm surprised that you bother to ask, Inspector. You must know that I would disapprove strongly."

"Well, that was frank enough," thought Dalgleish. "But what else could she say? We would scarcely believe that she liked it."

"Even though her affection for your son could have been genuine?"

"I am paying her the compliment of assuming that it was. What difference does that make? I would still have disapproved. They had nothing in common. He would have had to support another man's child. It would have hindered his career and they would have disliked each other within a year. These King Cophetua marriages seldom work out. How can they? No girl of spirit likes to think she's been condescended to and Sally had plenty of spirit even if she chose not to show it. Furthermore, I fail to see what they would have married on. Stephen has very little money of his own. Of course I disapproved of this so-called engagement. Would you wish for such a marriage for your son?"

For one unbelievable second Dalgleish thought that she knew. It was a commonplace, almost banal argument which any mother faced with her circumstances might casually have used. She could not possibly have realized its force. He wondered what she would say if he replied, "I have no son. My own child and his mother died three hours after he was born. I have no son to marry anyone—suitable or unsuitable." He could imagine her frown of well-bred distaste that he should embarrass her at such a time with a private grief at once so old, so intimate, so unrelated to the matter at hand. He replied briefly:

"No. I should not wish it either. I'm sorry to have taken up so much of your time with what must seem no one's business but your own. But you must see its importance."

"Naturally. From your point of view it provides a

motive for several people, myself particularly. But one does not kill to avoid social inconvenience. I admit that I intended to do all I could to stop them marrying. I was going to have a talk with Stephen next day. I've no doubt we should have been able to do something for Sally without the necessity of welcoming her into the family. There must be a limit to what these people expect."

The sudden bitterness of her last sentence roused even Sergeant Martin from the routine automatism of his note-taking. But if Mrs. Maxie realized that she had said too much she did not aggravate her error by saying more. Watching her, Dalgleish thought how like a picture she was, an advertisement in water-colour for toilet water or soap. Even the low bowl of flowers on the desk between them emphasized her serene gentility as if placed there by the cunning hand of a commercial photographer. "Picture of an English lady at home," he thought, and wondered what the Chief Superintendent would make of her and, if it ever came to that, what a jury would make of her. Even his mind, accustomed to finding wickedness in strange as well as high places, could not easily reconcile Mrs. Maxie with murder. But her last words had been revealing.

He decided to leave the marriage question at present and concentrate on other aspects of the investigation. Again he went over the account of the preparation of the nightly hot drinks. There could be no confusion about the ownership of the different mugs. The Wedgwood blue one found at

Sally's side belonged to Deborah Riscoe. The milk for the drinks was placed on top of the stove. It was a solid-fuel stove with heavy covers to each of the hot-plates. The saucepan of milk was left on top of one of these covers where there could be no danger of its boiling over. Any of the family wanting to boil the milk would transfer the saucepan to the hot-plate and replace it afterwards on top of the cover. Only the family's mugs and cups for their guests were placed on the tray. She could not say what Sally or Mrs. Bultitaft usually drank at night but, certainly, none of the family drank cocoa. They were not fond of chocolate.

"It comes to this, doesn't it," said Dalgleish. "If, as I am now assuming, the post-mortem shows that Miss Jupp was drugged and the analysis of the cocoa shows that the drug was in her late night drink, then we are faced with two possibilities. She could have taken the drug herself, perhaps for no worse reason than to get a good sleep after the excitement of the day. Or someone else drugged her for a reason which we must discover but which is not so difficult to guess. Miss Jupp, as far as is known, was a healthy young woman. If this crime was premeditated her murderer must have considered how he—or she—could get into that room and kill the girl with the least possible disturbance. To drug her is an obvious answer. That supposes that the murderer is familiar with the evening drink routine at Martingale and knew where the drugs were kept. I suppose a member of your household or a guest is familiar with your household routine?"

"Surely then he would know that the Wedgwood beaker belonged to my daughter. Are you satisfied, Inspector, that the drug was intended for Sally?"

"Not entirely. But I am satisfied that the killer did not mistake Miss Jupp's neck for Mrs. Riscoe's. Let us assume for the present that the drug was intended for Miss Jupp. It could have been put into the saucepan of milk, the Wedgwood beaker itself either before or after the drink was made, into the tin of cocoa, or into the sugar. You and Miss Bowers made your drinks from the milk in the same saucepan and sugared them from the bowl on the table without ill effects. I don't think that the drug was put in the empty beaker. It was brownish in colour and would be easily seen against the blue china. That leaves us with two possibilities. Either it was crumbled into the dry cocoa or it was dissolved in the hot drink some time after Miss Jupp made it but before she drank it."

"I don't think the latter is possible, Inspector. Mrs. Bultitaft always puts on the hot milk at ten. At about twenty-five minutes past we saw Sally carrying her mug up to her room."

"Who do you mean by 'we,' Mrs. Maxie?"

"Dr. Epps, Miss Liddell and I myself saw her. I'd been upstairs with Miss Liddell to fetch her coat. When we came back into the hall Dr. Epps joined us from the business room. As we stood there together Sally came from the kitchen end of the house and went up the main staircase carrying the blue Wedgwood beaker on its saucer. She was wearing pyjamas and a dressing-gown. We all three saw her but no one spoke. Miss Liddell and Dr. Epps left at once."

"Was it usual for Miss Jupp to use that staircase?"

"No. The back one leads more directly from the kitchen to her room. I think she was trying to make some kind of gesture."

"Although she couldn't have known that she would meet anyone in the hall?"

"No. I don't see how she could have known that."

"You say that you noticed that Miss Jupp was carrying Mrs. Riscoe's beaker. Did you mention this to either of your guests or remonstrate to Miss Jupp about it?"

Mrs. Maxie smiled faintly. For the second time the delicate claw was unsheathed.

"What old-fashioned ideas you have, Inspector! Did you expect me to tear it from her grasp to the embarrassment of my guests and the satisfaction of Sally herself? What an exciting and exhausting world yours must be."

Dalgleish pursued his question undeterred by this gentle irony. But he was interested to know that his witness could be provoked.

"What happened after Miss Liddell and Dr. Epps left?"

"I rejoined Miss Bowers in the business room where we tidied up the papers and locked away the bags of money in the safe. We then went to the kitchen and made our drinks. I had hot milk and Miss Bowers made Ovaltine. She likes it very sweet and added sugar from the bowl set ready. We carried our drinks to the dressing-room next to my husband's bedroom where I spend the nights when I am on duty nursing him. Miss Bowers helped me to re-make my husband's bed. I suppose we spent about twenty minutes together. Then she said 'good night' and left."

"Having had her Ovaltine?"

"Yes. It was too hot to drink at once but she sat down and finished it before she left me."

"Did she go to the drug cupboard while she was with you?"

"No. Neither of us did. My son had given his father something earlier to make him sleep and he appeared to be dozing. There was nothing to do for him except make his bed as comfortable as possible. I was glad of Miss Bowers's help. She is a trained nurse and, together, we were able to tidy the bed without disturbing him."

"What were Miss Bowers's relations with Dr. Maxie?"

"As far as I know Miss Bowers is a friend of both my children. That is the kind of question which it would be better to ask them and her."

"She and your son are not engaged to be married as far as you know?"

"I know nothing about their personal affairs. I should have thought it unlikely."

"Thank you," said Dalgleish. "I will see Mrs.

Riscoe now if you will be good enough to send her in."

He rose to open the door for Mrs. Maxie but she did not move. She said, "I still believe that Sally took that drug herself. There's no reasonable alternative. But if someone else did administer it then I agree with you that it must have been put into the dry cocoa. Forgive me—but wouldn't you be able to tell that from an examination of the tin and its contents?"

"We might have been," replied Dalgleish gravely. "But the empty tin was found in the dustbin. It had been rinsed out. The inner paper lining isn't there. It was probably burnt in the kitchen stove. Someone was making assurance doubly sure."

"A very cool lady, sir," said Sergeant Martin when Mrs. Maxie had left them. He added with unaccustomed humour, "She sat there like a Liberal candidate waiting for the recount."

"Yes," agreed Dalgleish dryly. "But with every confidence in her Party organization. Well, let's hear what the rest of them have to tell us."

6

It was a very different room from last time, thought Felix, but that room, too, had been quiet and peaceful. There had been pictures and a heavy mahogany desk not unlike the one Dalgleish was sitting at now. There had been flowers, too, a small posy arranged in a bowl hardly larger than a teacup. Everything about that room had been homely and comfortable, even the man behind the desk with his plump white hands, his smiling eyes behind the thick spectacles. The room had retained that look. It was surprising how many procedures there were for the extracting of truth which did not shed blood, were calculatedly unmessy, did not require very much in the way of apparatus. He wrenched memory back and made himself look at the figure at the desk. The folded hands were leaner, the eyes dark and less kind. There was only one other person in the room and he, too, was an English policeman. This was Martingale. This was England.

So far it had not gone too badly. Deborah had been absent for half an hour. When she returned she walked to her seat without looking at him and he, just as silently, got up and followed the uniformed policeman into the business room. He was glad that he had resisted the desire to have a drink before his questioning and that he had refused Dalgleish's proffered cigarette. That was an old one! They couldn't catch him that way! He wasn't going to make them a present of his nervousness. If only he could keep his temper all would be well.

The patient man behind the desk looked at his notes.

"Thank you. That's clear so far. Now may we please go back a little? After coffee you went with Mrs. Riscoe to help wash up the dinner things. At about nine-thirty you both returned to this room where Mrs. Maxie, Miss Liddell, Miss Bowers and Dr. Epps were counting the money taken at the fête. You told them that you and Mrs. Riscoe were going out and you said 'Good night' to Miss Liddell and Dr. Epps, who would probably have left Martingale by the time you returned. Mrs. Maxie said that she would leave one of the french windows in the drawing-room open for you and asked you to lock it when you had come in. This arrangement was heard by everyone who was in the room at the time?"

"As far as I know it was. No one commented on it and, as they were busy counting money, I doubt whether they took it in."

"I find it surprising that the drawing-room window was left unlatched for you when the back door was also open. Isn't that a Stubbs on the wall behind you? This house has several very fine things which are easily portable."

Felix did not turn his head.

"The cultured cop! I thought they were peculiar to detective novels. Congratulations! But the Maxies don't advertise their possessions. There's no danger from the village. People have been wandering in and out of this house pretty freely for the last three hundred years. The locking-up here is rather haphazard except for the front door. That is ritually bolted and barred every night by Stephen Maxie or his sister almost as if it had some esoteric significance. Apart from that, they aren't thorough. In that, as in other matters, they appear to rely on our wonderful police."

"Right! You went out into the garden with Mrs. Riscoe at about nine-thirty p.m. and walked there together. What did you talk about, Mr. Hearne?"

"I asked Mrs. Riscoe to marry me. I am going out to our Canadian house in two months' time and I thought it might be pleasant to combine business with a honeymoon."

"And Mrs. Riscoe accepted?"

"It's charming of you to be interested, Inspector, but I'm afraid I must disappoint you. Inexplicable as it must seem to you, Mrs. Riscoe was not enthusiastic."

The memory flooded back in a wave of emotion. Darkness, the cloying scent of roses, the hard urgent kisses which were the expression of some compelling need in her but not, he felt, of passion. And afterwards the sick weariness in her voice. "Marriage, Felix? Hasn't there been enough talk of marriage in this family? God, how I wish she were dead!" He knew then that he had been betrayed into speaking too soon. The time and the place had both been wrong. Had the words been wrong too? What exactly was it that she wanted? Dalgleish's voice recalled him to the present.

"How long did you stay in the garden, sir?"

"It would be gallant to pretend that time ceased to exist. In the interest of your investigation, however, I will admit that we came in through the drawing-room window at ten-forty-five p.m. The chiming clock on the mantelpiece struck the three-quarters as I closed and bolted the window."

"That clock is kept five minutes fast, sir. Would you go on, please."

"Then we returned at ten-forty p.m. I did not look at my watch. Mrs. Riscoe offered me a whisky which I declined. I also declined a milk drink and she went to the kitchen to get her own. She came back in a few minutes and said that she'd changed her mind. She also said that, apparently, her brother was still out. We talked for a little time and arranged to meet to ride together at seven next morning. Then we went to bed. I had a reasonably good night. As far as I know Mrs. Riscoe had, too. I had dressed and was waiting for her in the hall when I heard Stephen Maxie calling down to me. He wanted my help with the ladder. The rest you know."

"Did you kill Sally Jupp, Mr. Hearne?"

"Not so far as I am aware."

"What do you mean by that?"

"Merely that I suppose I could have done it while in a state of amnesia, but that is hardly a practical supposition."

"I think we can dismiss that possibility. Miss Jupp was killed by someone who knew what he, or she, was doing. Have you any idea who?"

"Do you expect me to take that question seriously?"

"I expect to you take all my questions seriously. This young mother was murdered. I intend to find out who killed her without wasting too much of my own time or anyone else's and I expect you to co-operate with me."

"I have no idea who killed her and I doubt whether I should tell you if I had. I haven't your evident passion for abstract justice. However, I'm prepared to co-operate to the extent of pointing out some facts which, in your enthusiasm for lengthy interrogations of your suspects, you may possibly have overlooked. Someone had got through that girl's window. She kept glass animals on the ledge and they had been scattered. The window was open and her hair was damp. It rained last night from half-past twelve until three. I deduce that she was dead before twelve-thirty or she would have closed the window. The child did not awake until its normal time. Presumably then the visitor made little noise. It is unlikely that there was a violent quarrel. I imagine that Sally herself let in her visitor through the window. He probably used the ladder. She would know where it was kept. He probably came by appointment. Your guess is as good as mine as to why. I didn't know her but, somehow, she never struck me as being highly sexed or promiscuous. The man was probably in love with her and, when she told him about her intention to marry Stephen Maxie, he killed her in a sudden access of jealousy or anger. I can't believe that this was a premeditated crime. Sally had locked the door to secure their privacy and the man got out through the window without unlocking it. He may not have realized it was bolted. Had he done so he would probably have unbolted it and made his exit with more care. That bolted door must be a great disappointment to you, Inspector. Even you can hardly visualize any of the family pounding up and down a ladder to get in and out of their own house. I know how excited you must be about the Maxie-Jupp engagement but you don't need me to point out that, if we had to commit murder to get out of an unwelcome engagement, the mortality rate among women would be very high."

Even as he was speaking Felix knew that it was a mistake. Fear had trapped him into garrulity as well as anger. The police sergeant was looking at him with the resigned and slightly pitying look of a man who has seen too many men make fools of themselves to be surprised, but still rather wishes that they wouldn't do it. Dalgleish spoke mildly.

"I thought that you had a good night. Yet you noticed that it rained from half past twelve until three."

"It was a good night for me."

"You suffer from insomnia then? What you take for it?"

"Whisky. But seldom in other people's houses."

"You described earlier how the body was discovered and how you went into the adjoining bathroom with Mrs. Riscoe while Dr. Maxie 'phoned the police. After a time Mrs. Riscoe left you to go to her mother. What did you do after that?"

"I thought I had better see if Mrs. Bultitaft was all right. I didn't suppose that anyone would feel like breakfast, but it was obvious that we should need plenty of hot coffee, and that sandwiches would be a good idea. She seemed stunned and kept repeating that Sally must have killed herself. I pointed out as gently as I could that that was anatomically impossible and that seemed to up-set her more. She gave me one curious look as if I were a stranger and then burst into loud sob-bing. By the time I had managed to calm her Miss Bowers had arrived with the child and was being rather obviously capable with its break-fast. Martha took herself in hand and we got on with the coffee and with Mr. Maxie's breakfast. By that time the police had arrived and we were told to wait in the drawing-room."

"When Mrs. Bultitaft burst into tears, was that the first sign of grief that she had shown?"

"Grief?" The pause was almost imperceptible. "She was obviously very much shocked, as we all were."

"Thank you, sir. That has been very helpful. I will have your statement typed and later I will ask you to read it over and, if you agree with it, to sign it. If you have anything else you want to tell me there'll be plenty of opportunity. I shall be about the place. If you are going back to the drawing-room will you ask Mrs. Bultitaft if she will come in next."

It was a command not a request. As he reached the door Felix heard the quiet voice speaking again.

"You will scarcely be surprised to hear that your account of things tallies almost exactly with that of Mrs. Riscoe. With one exception. Mrs. Riscoe says that you spent almost the whole of last night in her room, not your own. She says, in fact, that you slept together."

Felix stood for a moment facing the door and then turned round and faced the man behind the desk.

"That was very sweet of Mrs. Riscoe, but it makes things difficult for me, doesn't it? I'm afraid you will have to make up your mind, Inspector, as to which of us is lying."

"Thank you," said Dalgleish. "I have already done so."

7

Dalgleish had met a number of Marthas in his time and had never supposed them to be complicated people. They were concerned with the comfort of the body, the cooking of food, the unending menial tasks which someone must carry out before the life of the maid can have any true validity. Their own undemanding emotional needs found fulfilment in service. They were loyal, hardworking and truthful and made good witnesses because they lacked both the imagination and the practice necessary for successful lying. They could be a nuisance if they decided to shield those who had gained their loyalty but this was an overt danger which could be anticipated. He expected no difficulty with Martha. It was with a sense of irritation that Dalgleish realized that someone had been talking to her. She would be correct, she would be respectful, but any information he extracted would be gained the hard way. Martha had been coached and it was not hard to guess by whom. He pressed patiently on.

"So you do the cooking and help with the nursing of Mr. Maxie. That must be a heavy load. Did you suggest to Mrs. Maxie that she should employ Miss Jupp?"

"No."

"Do you know who did?"

Martha was silent for several seconds as if wondering whether to chance an indiscretion.

"It may have been Miss Liddell. Madam may have thought of it herself. I don't know."

"But I presume that Mrs. Maxie talked it over with you before she employed the girl."

"She told me about Sally. It was for Madam to decide."

Dalgleish began to find this servility irritating but his voice did not change. He had never been known to lose his temper with a witness.

"Had Mrs. Maxie ever employed an unmarried mother before?"

"It would never have been thought of in the old days. All our girls came with excellent references."

"So that this was a new venture. Do you think it was a success? You had most to do with Miss Jupp. What sort of a girl was she?"

Martha did not reply.

"Were you satisfied with her work?"

"I was satisfied enough. At first, anyway."

"What caused you to change your mind? Was it her late rising?" The heavy-lidded, obstinate eyes slewed suddenly from side to side.

"There are worse things than lying abed."

"Such as?"

"She began to get cheeky."

"That must have been trying for you. I wonder what caused Miss Jupp to get cheeky?"

"Girls are like that. They start quietly enough and then begin to act as if they are mistress in the house."

"Suppose Sally Jupp were beginning to think that she might be mistress here one day?"

"Then she was out of her mind."

"But Dr. Maxie did propose marriage to her on Saturday evening."

"I know nothing of that. Dr. Maxie couldn't have married Sally Jupp."

"Someone seems to have made that certain, don't they? Have you any idea who?"

Martha did not reply. There was, indeed, nothing to be said. If Sally Jupp really had been killed for that reason the circle of suspects was not large. Dalgleish began to take her with tedious thoroughness over the events of Saturday afternoon and evening. There was little she could say about the fête. She had apparently taken no part in it except to walk once round the garden before giving Mr. Maxie his evening meal and making him comfortable for the night. When she returned to the kitchen Sally had evidently given Jimmy his tea and taken him up for his bath because the pram was in the scullery and the child's plate and mug were in the sink. The girl did not appear and Martha had wasted no time in looking for her. The family had waited on themselves at dinner which was a cold meal and Mrs. Maxie had not rung for her. Afterwards Mrs. Riscoe and Mr. Hearne had come into the kitchen to help wash up. They hadn't asked whether Sally was back. No one had mentioned her. They had talked mostly about the fête. Mr. Hearne had laughed and joked with Mrs. Riscoe while they washed up. He was a very amusing gentleman. They hadn't helped to get the hot drinks ready. That was done later. The cocoa tin was in a cupboard with the other dry provisions and neither Mrs. Riscoe nor Mr. Hearne had been to the cupboard. She had stayed in the kitchen all the time they were there.

After they left she turned on the television for half an hour. No, she hadn't worried about Sally. The girl would come in when she felt like it. At about five minutes to ten Martha had put a saucepan of milk to heat slowly at the side of the stove. This was done most nights at Martingale so that she could get early to bed. She had put out the mugs on a tray. There were large cups and saucers put out for any guest who liked a hot drink at night. Sally knew very well that the blue beaker belonged to Mrs. Riscoe. Everyone at Martingale knew. After seeing to the hot milk Martha had gone to bed. She was in bed before half past ten and had heard nothing unusual all night. In the morning she had gone to wake up Sally and had found the door bolted. She had gone to tell Madam. The rest he knew.

It took over forty minutes to extract this unremarkable information but Dalgleish showed no sign of impatience. Now they came to the actual finding of the body. It was important to discover how far Martha's account agreed with that of Catherine Bowers. If it agreed, then at least one of his tentative theories might prove correct. The account did agree. Patiently he went on to inquire about the missing Sommeil. But here he was less successful. Martha Bultitaft did not believe that Sally had found any tablets in her master's bed.

"Sally liked to make out that she nursed the master. Maybe she took a turn at nights if Madam was extra tired. But he never liked anyone about him but me. I do all the heavy nursing. If there was anything hidden in the bed I should have found it."

It was the longest speech she had made. Dalgleish felt that it carried conviction. Finally he questioned her about the empty cocoa tin. Here, again, she spoke quietly but with unemphatic certainty. She had found the empty tin on the kitchen table when she came down to make the early morning tea. She had burned the inside paper, rinsed the tin and put it in the dustbin. Why had she rinsed it first? Because Madam disliked sticky or greasy tins being put in the dustbin. The cocoa tin hadn't been greasy, of course, but that didn't signify. All used tins were rinsed at Martingale.

And why had she burned the inside wrapper? Well, she couldn't rinse the inside of the tin with the paper lining still there, could she? The tin was empty so she rinsed it out and threw it away. Her tone suggested that no reasonable person could have done otherwise.

For the life of him Dalgleish couldn't see how her story could be effectively countered. His heart sank at the thought of interrogating Mrs. Maxie on the usual method of disposal of the family's used tins. But, once again, he suspected that Martha had been coached. He was seeing the beginning of a pattern. The infinite patience of the last hour had been well worth while.

Chapter Five

1

ST. MARY'S REFUGE was about a mile from the main part of the village, an ugly red-brick house with a multiplicity of gables and turrets which was set back from the main road behind a discreet shield of laurel bushes. The gravel drive led to a front door whose worn knocker gleamed with much polishing. The net curtains were snowy white at each of the windows. Shallow stone steps at the side of the house led down to a square lawn where several prams were clustered together. A maid in cap and apron admitted them, probably one of the mothers Dalgleish thought, and showed them into a small room at the left of the hall. She seemed uncertain what to do and could not catch Dalgleish's name although he repeated it twice. Large eyes stared at him uncomprehendingly through the steel-frame spectacles as she hovered miserably in the doorway. "Never mind," said Dalgleish kindly, "just let Miss Liddell know that there are two policemen to see her from Martingale. She'll know all about us."

"Please, I have to take the name. I'm being trained for a house parlourmaid." She hovered in desperate persistence, torn between fear of Miss Liddell's censure and embarrassment at being in the same room as two strange men, and both of them policemen at that. Dalgleish handed her his card. "Just give her this then. That will be even more proper and correct. And don't worry. You'll make a very nice house parlourmaid. Nowadays they're prized above rubies you know."

"Not saddled with an illegitimate kid, they aren't," said Sergeant Martin as the slight figure disappeared through the door with what might have been a whispered "Thank you."

"Funny to see a plain little thing like that here, sir. A bit missing by the way she acted. Someone took advantage of her I suppose."

"She's the kind of person who gets taken advantage of from the day she's born."

"Properly scared, too, wasn't she? I suppose this Miss Liddell treats the girls all right, sir?"

"Very well, I imagine, according to her own lights. It's easy to get sentimental over her job, but she has to deal with a pretty mixed bunch. What you want here is hope, faith and charity to an unlimited degree. In other words you want a saint and we can hardly expect Miss Liddell to measure up to that standard."

"Yes, sir," said Sergeant Martin. On second thoughts he felt that "No, sir" would have been more appropriate. Unconscious of having uttered any unorthodoxy Dalgleish moved slowly about the room. It was comfortable but unostentatious and was furnished, he thought, with many of Miss Liddell's personal possessions. All the wood glowed with polishing. The spinet and the rosewood table both looked as if they would have struck warm to the touch from the vigour and energy spent on them. The one large window which overlooked the lawn was curtained with flower-patterned cretonne now drawn against the sun. The carpet, although showing signs of age, was not the kind provided by official bodies however voluntary and public spirited. The room was as much Miss Liddell's in spirit as if she had owned the house. Along the walls were photographs of babies. Babies lying naked on rugs, their heads reared towards the camera in helpless absurdity. Babies smiling toothlessly from prams and cradles. Woollen-clad babies held in their mothers' arms. There were even one or two lying lumpily in the arms of an embarrassed man. These presumably were the lucky ones, the ones who had achieved an official father at last. Above a small mahogany desk was the framed print of a woman at a spinning-wheel with a plaque attached to the base of the frame. "Presented by the Chad-fleet and District Committee for Moral Welfare to Miss Alice Liddell in commemoration of twenty years' devoted service as Warden of St. Mary's Refuge." Dalgleish and Martin looked at it together. "I don't know that I'd call this place a refuge exactly," said the Sergeant. Dalgleish looked again at the furniture, the carefully tended legacies from Miss Liddell's childhood.

"It might well be to a single woman of Miss Liddell's age. She made this place her home for over twenty years. She might do a great deal to prevent herself being driven out of it."

Sergeant Martin was prevented from replying by the entrance of the lady. Miss Liddell was always most at ease on her own ground. She shook hands composedly and apologized for keeping them waiting. Looking at her Dalgleish deduced she had spent the time in applying powder to her face and resolution to her mind. She was obviously determined to treat this as a social call as far as possible and she invited them to sit down with all the conscious charm of an inexperienced hostess. Dalgleish declined her offer of tea, carefully avoiding the reproachful eye of his sergeant. Martin was perspiring freely. His own view was that punctilio towards a possible suspect could be carried too far and that a nice cup of tea on a hot day had never yet obstructed justice.

"We shall try not to keep you too long, Miss Liddell. As I'm sure you have realized, I am investigating the death of Sally Jupp. I understand that you dined at Martingale yesterday evening. You were also at the fête during the afternoon and you did, of course, know Miss Jupp while she was with you here at St. Mary's. There are one or two matters which I am hoping you may be able to explain." Miss Liddell started at the use of his last word. As Sergeant Martin drew out his notebook with something akin to resignation, Dalgleish noted her quick moistening of her lips and the almost imperceptible tensing of her hands and knew that she was on her guard.

"Anything you care to ask, of course, Inspector. It is Inspector, isn't it? Of course I knew Sally very well and the whole thing is a dreadful shock to me. It is to us all. But I'm afraid I'm not likely to be of much help. I'm not very clever at noticing and remembering things, you know. It's rather a disadvantage sometimes, but we can't all be detectives can we?" The nervous laugh was a little too high to be natural. "We've got her scared all right," thought Sergeant Martin. "Might be something here after all."

"Perhaps we could begin with Sally Jupp herself," said Dalgleish gently. "I understand that she lived here during the last five months of her pregnancy and came back to you when she left the hospital after the birth. She stayed here until she started the job at Martingale which she did when her baby was four months old. Until that time she helped here with the household duties. You must have got to know her very well during this time. Did you like her, Miss Liddell?"

"Like her?" The woman laughed nervously. "Isn't that rather a funny question, Inspector?"

"Is it? In what way?"

She made an effort to conceal her embarrassment and to give the question the compliment of careful thought.

"I hardly know what to say. If you had asked me that question a week ago I should have had no hesitation in saying that Sally was an excellent little worker and a most deserving girl who was doing her best to atone for her mistake. But now, of course, I can't help wondering whether I was wrong about her, whether she was really genuine after all." She spoke with the sorrow of a connoisseur whose previously infallible judgment has at last been proved at fault. "I suppose now that we shall never know whether she was genuine or not."

"By genuine, I assume you mean whether she was sincere in her affection for Mr. Stephen Maxie."

Miss Liddell shook her head sadly. "The appearances were against it. I was never more shocked in my life, Inspector, never. Of course she had no right to accept him whatever she felt for him. She looked positively triumphant when she stood in that window and told us. He was horribly embarrassed of course, and went as white as a sheet. It was a dreadful moment for poor Mrs. Maxie. I'm afraid I shall always blame myself for what happened. I recommended Sally to Martingale, you know. It seemed such a wonderful chance for her in every way. And now this."

"You believe, then, that Sally Jupp's death is the direct result of her engagement to Mr. Maxie?"

"Well, it does look like that, doesn't it?"

"I agree that her death was highly convenient for anyone who had a reason to dislike the proposed marriage. The Maxie family for instance."

Miss Liddell's face flamed. "But that's ridiculous, Inspector. It's a terrible thing to say. Terrible. Of course, you don't know the family as we do, but you must take it from me that the whole suggestion is fantastic. You can't have thought I meant that! It's perfectly plain to me what happened. Sally had been playing fast and loose with some man we don't know about and when he heard of the engagement—well, he lost control of himself. He got through the window, didn't he? That's what Miss Bowers told me. Well, that proves it wasn't the family."

"The murderer probably got out of the room through the window. We have no knowledge as yet how he or she got in."

"You surely can't imagine Mrs. Maxie climbing down that wall. She couldn't do it!"

"I imagine nothing. There was a ladder in the customary place for anyone who cared to use it. It could have been put in place ready even if the murderer got in through the door."

"But Sally would have heard! Even if the ladder were placed there very gently. Or she might look out of her window and see it!"

"Perhaps. If she were awake."

"I don't understand you, Inspector. You seem determined to suspect the family. If only you knew what they've done for that girl."

"I should like to be told. And you must not misunderstand me. I suspect everyone who knew Miss Jupp and who has no alibi for the time she was killed. That is why I am here now."

"Well, you know about my movements presumably. I've no wish to make a secret of them. Dr. Epps brought me back here in his car. We left Martingale at about half past ten. I wrote in this room for a little while and then took a stroll in the garden. I went to bed at about eleven which is rather late for me. I heard about this dreadful thing while I was finishing my breakfast. Miss Bowers 'phoned and asked if I could take Jimmy back for a while until they knew what was to happen to him. Naturally I left my deputy, Miss Pollack, in charge of the girls and went round at once. I telephoned George Hopgood and told him to bring round his taxi."

"You said a little earlier that you thought the news of Miss Jupp's engagement to Mr. Maxie was the reason for her death. Was that news known outside the household? I was given to understand that Mr. Maxie only proposed on Saturday night so that no one who was not at Martingale after that time could have been told."

"Dr. Maxie may have proposed on Saturday, but no doubt the girl had made up her mind to have him before then. Something had been happening, I'm sure of it. I saw her at the fête and she was flushed with excitement all the afternoon. And were you told how she copied Mrs. Riscoe's dress?"

"You are hardly suggesting that that constituted another motive."

"It showed which way her mind was working. Make no mistake about it, Sally asked for what she got. I'm only desperately sorry that the Maxies should have been involved in all this trouble on her account."

"You have told me that you went to bed about eleven after a stroll in the gardens. Have you anyone to confirm that statement?"

"No one saw me as far as I know, Inspector. Miss Pollack and the girls are in bed by ten. I have my own key of course. It was an unusual thing for me to have gone out again like that but I was disturbed. I couldn't help thinking about Sally and Mr. Maxie and I knew I shouldn't get to sleep if I went to bed too early."

"Thank you. There are just two other questions. Where in the house do you keep your private papers? I mean documents referring to the administration of this Home. Letters from the committee for example."

Miss Liddell walked over to the rosewood desk.

"They are kept in this drawer, Inspector. Naturally I keep it locked although only the most trustworthy girls are allowed to look after this room. The key is kept in this little compartment at the top."

She lifted the desk lid as she spoke and indicated the place. Dalgleish reflected that only the dullest or least curious housemaid could have missed the hidden key if she had had sufficient nerve to look. Miss Liddell was obviously used to dealing with girls who had too fearful a respect for papers and official documents to tamper with them voluntarily. But Sally Jupp had been neither dull nor, he suspected, incurious. He suggested as much to Miss Liddell and, as expected, the image of Sally's picking fingers and amused ironic eyes roused her to even greater resentment than his earlier questions about the Maxies.

"You mean that Sally may have pried about among my things? I would never have believed that once, but you could be right. Oh, yes. I see it now. That was why she liked to work in here. All that docility, that politeness was so much pretence! And to think that I trusted her! I really thought that she cared for me, that I was helping her. She confided in me, you know. But I suppose all those stories were lies. She must have been laughing at me all the time. I suppose you think I'm a fool too. Well, I may be, but I've done nothing to be ashamed of. Nothing! They've told you about that scene in the Maxie dining-room no doubt. She couldn't frighten me. There may have been little difficulties here in the past. I'm not very clever with figures and accounts. I've never pretended to be. But I've done nothing wrong. You can ask any member of the committee. Sally Jupp could pry as much as she liked. A lot of good it's done her."

She was shaking with anger and made no attempt to hide the bitter satisfaction behind her last words. But Dalgleish was unprepared for the effect of his last question.

"One of my officers has been to see the Proctors, Sally Jupp's next-of-kin. Naturally we hoped that they might be able to give us some information about her life which might help us. Their young daughter was there and she volunteered some information. Can you tell me, Miss Liddell, why it was you telephoned Mr. Proctor early on Saturday morning—the morning of the fête? The child said she answered the telephone." The transformation from furious resentment to complete surprise was almost ludicrous. Miss Liddell gazed at him literally openmouthed.

"Me? Telephoned Mr. Proctor? I don't know what you mean! I haven't been in touch with the Proctors since Sally first went to Martingale. They never took an interest in her. What on earth would I telephone Mr. Proctor about?"

"That," said Dalgleish, "was what I had been wondering."

"But it's ridiculous! If I had telephoned Mr. Proctor I should have no objection to admitting it. But I didn't. The child must be lying."

"Someone is lying, certainly."

"Well, it isn't me," reported Miss Liddell stoutly if ungrammatically. Dalgleish, on this point at least, was disposed to believe her. As she accompanied him to the door he asked casually:

"Did you tell anyone about the events at Martingale when you got home, Miss Liddell? If your deputy were still up no doubt it would be natural to mention Sally's engagement to her."

Miss Liddell hesitated then said defensively, "Well, the news was bound to get around, wasn't it? I mean, the Maxies could hardly expect to keep it secret. Actually, I did mention it to Miss Pollack. Mrs. Pullen was here, too. She came over from Rose Cottage to return some teaspoons which we'd lent for the fête teas. She was still here chatting to Miss Pollack when I got back from Martingale. So Mrs. Pullen knew and you're surely not suggesting that telling her had anything to do with Sally's death."

Dalgleish replied non-committally. He was not so sure.

2

By dinner-time the activity of the day at Martingale seemed to be slowing down. Dalgleish and the sergeant were still working in the business room from which the sergeant occasionally emerged to speak to the man on duty at the door. The police cars still mysteriously appeared, disgorged their uniformed or macintoshed passengers and, after a short wait, bore them away again. The Maxies and their guests watched these comings and goings from the windows, but no one had been sent for since the late afternoon and it looked as if the questioning was over for the day and that the party could think about dinner with some prospect of being able to eat undisturbed. The house had suddenly become very quiet and when Martha nervously and half-heartedly sounded the gong at half past seven it boomed out like a vulgar intrusion into the silence of grief, sounding unnaturally loud to the family's heightened nerves. The meal itself passed almost in silence. The ghost of Sally moved from door to sideboard, and when Mrs. Maxie rang and the door opened to admit Martha, no one looked up. Martha's own preoccupations were shown in the poverty of the meal. No one had any hunger and there was nothing to tempt hunger. Afterwards they all moved as if by unspoken but common summons into the drawing-room. It was a relief when they saw Mr. Hinks pass the window and Stephen went out to welcome him in. Here at least was a representative of the outside world. No one could accuse the vicar of murdering Sally Jupp. Presumably he had come to offer spiritual guidance and comfort. The only kind of comfort which would have been welcome to the Maxies was the assurance that Sally was not after all dead, that they had been living through a brief nightmare from which they could now awake, a little tired and distressed by the lack of sleep but raised into joy by the glorious realization that none of it was true. But if this could not be, it was at least reassuring to talk with someone who stood outside the shadow of suspicion and who could give this dreadful day the semblance of normality. They found that they had even been speaking in whispers and Stephen's call to the vicar rang out like a shout. Soon he was with them and, as he entered with Stephen behind him, four pairs of eyes looked up inquiringly as if anxious to know the verdict on them of the world outside.

"Poor girl," he said. "Poor little girl. And she was so happy yesterday evening."

"Did you speak to her after the fête then?" Stephen could not succeed in hiding the urgency in his voice.

"No, not after the fête. I get so muddled about times. Stupid of me. Now that you mention it I didn't speak to her at all yesterday, although, of course, I did see her about the gardens. Such a pretty white dress she was wearing. No, I spoke to her on Thursday evening. We walked up the road together and I asked about Jimmy. I think it was Thursday. Yes, it must have been because I was at home all the evening on Friday. Thursday evening was the last time we spoke. She was so happy. She told me about her marriage and how Jimmy was to have a father. But you know all about that, I expect. It was a surprise to me, but, of course, I was glad for her. And now this. Have the police any news yet?"

He looked round in gentle inquiry seeming oblivious of the effect of his words. No one spoke for a moment and then Stephen said, "You may as well know, Vicar, that I had asked Sally to marry me. But she couldn't have told you about it on Thursday. She didn't know then. I never mentioned marriage to her until seven-forty p.m. on Saturday."

Catherine Bowers laughed shortly and then turned away in embarrassment as Deborah turned and looked at her. Mr. Hinks creased worried brows but his gentle old voice was firm.

"I do get times muddled I know, but it was certainly Thursday when we met. I was coming out of church after Compline and Sally was passing with Jimmy in his pushchair. But I couldn't be mistaken about the conversation. Not the exact words, but the general gist. Sally said that Jimmy was soon to have a father. She asked me not to tell anyone and I said I wouldn't, but that I was very glad for her. I asked whether I knew the bridegroom but she just laughed and said she would rather let it be a surprise. She was very excited and happy. We only walked a little way together as I left her at the vicarage and I suppose she came on here. I'm afraid I rather assumed that you knew all about it. Is it important?"

"Inspector Dalgleish will probably think so," said Deborah wearily. "I suppose you ought to go and tell him. There isn't much choice really. The man has an uncanny facility for extracting uncomfortable truths."

Mr. Hinks looked troubled, but was saved from the necessity of replying by a quick knock at the door and the appearance of Dalgleish. He held out his hand towards Stephen. Loosely wrapped in a man's white handkerchief was a small mud-caked bottle.

"Do you recognize this?" he asked.

Stephen went across and looked at it for a moment but did not try to touch it.

"Yes. It's the bottle of Sommeil from Father's drug cupboard."

"There are seven three-grain tablets left. Do you confirm that three tablets are missing since you put them in this bottle?"

"Naturally I do. I told you. There were ten three-grain tablets."

"Thank you," said Dalgleish and turned again to the door.

Deborah spoke just as his hand reached the doorknob:

"Are we permitted to ask where that bottle was found?" she asked.

Dalgleish looked at her as if the question really needed his serious consideration.

"Why not? It is probable that at least one of you would genuinely like to know. It was found by one of the men working with me, buried in that part of the lawn which was used for a treasure hunt. As you know, the turf has been cut about fairly intensively there, presumably by hopeful competitors. There are several sods still lying on the surface. The bottle had been placed in one of the holes and the turf pressed down over it. The person responsible had even been considerate enough to mark the place with one of the named wooden pegs which were lying about. Curiously enough it was yours, Mrs. Riscoe. Your mug with the drugged cocoa; your peg marking the hidden bottle."

"But why? Why?" said Deborah.

"If any of you can answer that question I shall be in the business room for an hour or two yet." He turned courteously to Mr. Hinks. "I think you must be Mr. Hinks, sir. I was hoping to see you. If it is convenient perhaps you could spare me a few minutes now."

The vicar looked around at the Maxies in puzzled pity. He paused and seemed about to speak. Then, without a word, he followed Dalgleish from the room.

3

It was not until ten o'clock that Dalgleish got round to interviewing Dr. Epps. The doctor had been out nearly all day seeing cases that might or might not have been urgent enough to warrant a Sunday visit, but which had certainly provided him with an excuse to postpone questioning. If he had anything to hide he had presumably decided on his tactics by now. He was not an obvious suspect. It was difficult, for one thing, to imagine a motive. But he was the Maxie family doctor and a close family friend. He would not willingly obstruct justice but he might have unorthodox ideas about what constituted justice and he would have the loophole of professional discretion if he wanted to avoid inconvenient questions. Dalgleish had had trouble with that kind of witness before. But he need not have worried. Dr. Epps, as if conceding some semi-medical recognition to the visit, invited him willingly enough into the red-brick surgery which had been misguidedly added to his pleasant Georgian house, and squeezed himself into a swivel-chair at his desk. Dalgleish was waved towards the patients' chair, a large Windsor of disconcerting lowness in which it was difficult to appear at ease or to take the initiative. He almost expected the doctor to begin on a string of personal and embarrassing questions. And, in fact, Dr. Epps had obviously decided to do most of the talking. This suited Dalgleish who knew very well when he might learn most by silence. The doctor lit a large and peculiarly shaped pipe.

"Won't offer you a smoke. Or a drink for that matter. Know you don't usually drink with suspects." He darted a sharp glance at Dalgleish to see his reaction but, receiving no comment, he established his pipe with a few vigorous sucks and began to talk.

"Won't waste your time saying what an appalling thing this is. Difficult to believe really. Still, someone killed her. Put his hands round her neck and throttled her. Terrible for Mrs. Maxie. For the girl, too, of course, but naturally I think of the living. Stephen called me in at about seven-thirty.

No doubt the girl was dead, of course. Had been for seven hours as far as I could judge. The police surgeon knows more about that than me. Girl wasn't pregnant. I doctored her for the odd spot of trouble and I do know that. It'll be one in the eye for the village though. They do like to hear the worst. And it would have been a motive I suppose—for someone."

"If we're thinking about motive," replied Dalgleish, "we could start with this engagement to Mr. Stephen Maxie."

The doctor shifted uncomfortably in his chair.

"Lot of rot. The boy's a fool. He hasn't a bean except what he earns and God knows that's little enough. Of course, there will be something when his father dies, but these old families, living and keeping up property on capital, well, it's a wonder they haven't had to sell. The government's doing its best to tax them out of existence. And that fellow Price surrounds himself with accountants and grows fat on untaxed expenses! Makes you wonder if we've all gone mad! Still, that's not your problem. You can take it from me, though, that Maxie isn't in a position to marry anyone at present. And where did he think Sally was going to live? Stay on at Martingale with her mother-in-law? Silly fool wants his head examined."

"All of which makes it plain," said Dalgleish, "that this projected match would have been calamitous for the Maxies. And that gives several people an interest in seeing that it didn't happen."

The doctor leaned across the desk at him challengingly.

"At the cost of killing the girl? By making that child motherless as well as fatherless? What sort of people do you think we are?"

Dalgleish did not reply. The facts were incontrovertible. Someone had killed Sally Jupp. Someone who had not even been deterred by the presence of her sleeping child. But he noted how the doctor's cry allied him with the Maxies. "What sort of people do you think we are?" There was no doubt where Dr. Epps's allegiance lay.

It was growing dark in the little room. Grunting with the slight effort, the doctor heaved himself across his desk and turned on a lamp. It was jointed and angled and he adjusted it carefully so that a pool of light fell on his hands but left his face in shadow. Dalgleish was beginning to feel weary but there was much to be done before his working day was over. He introduced the main object of his visit.

"Mr. Simon Maxie is your patient, I believe?"

"Of course. Always has been. Not much to be done for him now, of course. Just a matter of time and good nursing. Martha sees to that mostly. But, yes, he's my patient. Quite helpless. Advanced arteriosclerosis with other complications of one kind and another. If you're thinking that he crawled upstairs to do in the maid, well, you're wrong. I doubt if he knew she existed."

"I believe you've been prescribing some special sleeping tablets for him for the last year or so?"

"Wish you wouldn't keep on saying you believe this, that and the other. You know damn well I have. There's no secret about them. Can't see what they've got to do with this business though." He stiffened suddenly. "You don't mean she was doped first?"

"We haven't the post-mortem report yet, but it looks very like it."

The doctor did not pretend that he did not understand.

"That's bad."

"It does rather narrow down the field. And there are other disquieting features."

Dalgleish then told the doctor about the missing Sommeil, where Sally was alleged to have found it, what Stephen did with the ten tablets and the finding of the bottle in the treasure-hunt plot. When he had finished there was a silence for a moment. The doctor was sagging back into the chair which at first seemed too small to withstand his cheerful and comfortable rotundity. When he spoke the deep rumbling voice was suddenly an old and tired voice.

"Stephen never told me. Not much chance with the fête, of course. Might have changed his mind though. Probably thought I wouldn't be much help. I ought to have known, you see. He wouldn't overlook carelessness like that. His father . . . my patient. I've known Simon Maxie for thirty years.

Brought his children into the world. You ought to know your patients, know when they want help. I just left the prescription week after week. Didn't even go up to him very often recently. Didn't seem much point in it. Can't think what Martha was doing though. She nursed him, did everything. She must have known about those tablets. That is, if Sally was telling the truth."

"It's difficult to imagine her making the whole thing up. Besides, she had the tablets. I presume they can only be obtained by a doctor's prescription?"

"Yes. Can't just walk into a chemist's and buy them. Oh, it's true all right. Never doubted it really. I blame myself. Should have seen what was happening at Martingale. Not only to Simon Maxie. To all of them."

"So he thinks one of them did it," thought Dalgleish. "He can see clearly enough which way things are moving and he doesn't like it. Small blame to him. He knows this is a Martingale crime all right. The thing is, does he know for certain? And if so, which one?"

He asked about the Saturday evening at Martingale. Dr. Epps's account of Sally's appearance before dinner and the disclosure of Stephen's proposal was considerably less dramatic than that of Catherine Bowers or Miss Liddell, but the versions fundamentally agreed. He confirmed that neither he nor Miss Liddell had left the business room during the counting of the money and that he had seen Sally Jupp mounting the main staircase as he and his hostess were passing through the hall to the front door. He thought Sally was wearing a dressing-gown and carrying something, but he couldn't recall what. It might have been a cup and saucer or perhaps a beaker. He had not spoken to her. That was the last time he had seen her alive.

Dalgleish asked who else in the village had been prescribed Sommeil.

"I'll have to look up my records if you want accuracy. May take half an hour or so. It wasn't a common prescription. I can remember one or two patients who had it. May be others, of course. Sir Reynold Price and Miss Pollack at St. Mary's had it, I know. Mr. Maxie, of course. By the way, what's happening about his medicine now?"

"We're holding the Sommeil. I understand that Dr. Maxie has prescribed its equivalent. And now, Doctor, perhaps I might have a word with your housekeeper before I go."

It was a full minute before the doctor seemed to hear. Then he shuffled out of his chair with a muttered apology and led the way from the surgery into the house. There Dalgleish was able tactfully to confirm that the doctor had arrived home at 10.45 the evening before and had been called out to a confinement at 11.10. He hardly expected to hear otherwise. He would have to check with the patient's family, but no doubt they would provide an alibi for the doctor up to 3.30

in the morning when he had finally left Mrs. Baines of Nessingford in proud possession of her first-born son. Dr. Epps had been busy helping life into the world for most of Saturday night, not choking it out of Sally Jupp.

The doctor muttered something about a late visit and walked with Dalgleish to the gate, first protecting himself from the evening air by an opulent and voluminous coat at least a size too large for him. When they were at the gate the doctor, who had plunged his hands into his pockets, gave a little start of surprise and opened his right hand to reveal a small bottle. It was nearly full of small brown tablets. The two men looked at it in silence for a moment. Then Dr. Epps said, "Sommeil."

Dalgleish took a handkerchief, wrapped up the bottle and slipped it into his own pocket. He noted with interest the doctor's first instinctive gesture of resistance.

"That would be Sir Reynold's stuff, Inspector. Nothing to do with the family. This was Price's coat." His tone was defensive.

"When did the coat come into your possession, Doctor?" asked Dalgleish. Again there was a long pause. Then the doctor seemed to remember that there were facts which it was pointless to try to hide.

"I bought it on Saturday. At the church fête. I bought it rather as a joke between myself and . . . and the stallholder."

"And that was . . . who?" asked Dalgleish inexorably.

Dr. Epps did not meet his eyes as he answered dully, "Mrs. Riscoe."

4

Sunday had been secularized and timeless, its legacy a week so out-of-joint that Monday dawned without any colour or individuality, a mere limbo of a day. The post was heavier than usual, a tribute to the efficiency both of the ubiquitous telephone and to those subtler and less scientific methods of country communications. Presumably tomorrow's post would be heavier still when the news of the Martingale murder reached those who depended on print for their information. Deborah had ordered half a dozen papers. Her mother wondered whether this extravagance was a gesture of defiance or a sop to genuine curiosity.

The police were still using the business room, although they had notified their intention of moving to the Moonraker's Arms later in the day. Mrs. Maxie privately wished them joy of the cooking. Sally's room was kept locked. Only Dalgleish held the key and he gave no explanation of his frequent visits there nor of what he had found or hoped to find.

Lionel Jephson had arrived early in the morning, fussy, scandalized, and ineffectual. The family only hoped that he was being as big a nuisance to the police as he was to them. As Deborah predicted he was at a loss in a situation so divorced from his normal concerns and experience. His obvious anxiety and reiterated admonitions suggested that he had either grave doubts of his clients' innocence or little faith in the efficiency of the police. It was a relief to the whole household when he scurried back to town before luncheon to consult with a colleague.

At twelve o'clock the telephone rang for the twentieth time.

Sir Reynold Price's voice boomed across the wire to Mrs. Maxie.

"But it's disgraceful, my dear lady. What are the police doing?"

"I think at the moment they're trying to trace the baby's father."

"Good God! Whatever for? I should think they'd do better to concentrate on finding who killed her."

"They seem to think there could be a connection."

"Damn silly ideas they would get. They've been here, you know. Wanted to know about some pills that Epps prescribed for me. Must have been months ago. Fancy him remembering after all that time. Now why do you suppose they worried about those? Most extraordinary thing. Not going to arrest me yet, Inspector, I said. You could see he was amused." Sir Reynold's hearty laughter crackled unpleasantly in Mrs. Maxie's ear.

"How very tiresome for you," said Mrs. Maxie. "I am afraid this sad business is causing a lot of trouble to everyone. Did you send them away happy?"

"The police? My dear lady, the police are never happy. I told them plainly that it's no use expecting to find anything in this house. Maids tidy up everything that isn't actually kept under lock and key. Fancy looking for a bottle of tablets which I had months ago. Damn silly idea. The inspector seemed to think I ought to remember just how many I took and what happened to the others. Well, I ask you! I told him that I was a busy man with something better to do with my time. They were asking, too, about that spot of bother we had at St. Mary's about two years ago. The inspector seemed very interested in it. Wanted to know why you had resigned from the committee and so on."

"I wonder how they got on to that?"

"Some fool's been talking too much, I suppose. Funny how people can't keep their mouths shut, especially to the police. That chap Dalgleish said to me that it was a funny thing you weren't on the St. Mary's committee when you ran practically everything else in the village. I told him you'd resigned two years ago when we had that spot of trouble and, naturally, he wanted to know what spot of trouble. Asked why we hadn't got rid of Liddell at the time. I said to him, 'My dear chap, you can't just chuck a woman out after twenty-five years' service. It's not as if there was actual dishonesty.' I take my stand on that, you know. Always have. Always will. Carelessness and general muddle with the accounts, maybe, but that's a far cry from deliberate dishonesty. I told

the man that we'd had her before the committee—
all very hushed up and tactful of course—and
sent her a letter confirming the new financial arrangements so that there couldn't be any misun-
derstanding. Damn stiff letter, too, all things
considered. I know you thought at the time that
we should have turned over the Home to the di-
ocesan welfare committee or one of the national
associations for unmarried mothers, instead of
keeping it on as a private charitable concern,
and so I told the inspector."

"I thought it was time we handed over a difficult job to trained and experienced people, Sir
Reynold." Even as she spoke Mrs. Maxie cursed
the unwariness which had trapped her into this
recapitulation of old history.

"That's what I mean. I told Dalgleish, 'Mrs.
Maxie may well have been right. I'm not saying
she wasn't. But Lady Price was keen on the
Home—practically founded it, in fact—and naturally I wasn't keen to hand it over. Not enough of
these small individual places left now. Personal
touch is what counts. No doubt, though, that Miss
Liddell had made a nonsense of the accounts.
Too much worry for her. Figures not really woman's work.' He agreed of course. Had quite a
laugh about it."

Mrs. Maxie could well believe it. The picture was
not a pretty one. No doubt this facility for being
all things to all men was a prerequisite of success as a detective. When the hearty man-to-man

amusement had died down Mrs. Maxie had no
doubt that Dalgleish's mind was busy with a new
theory. Yet how was it possible? The mugs and
cups for those last night drinks had certainly been
placed ready by ten. After that time Miss Liddell
had never been out of her hostess's sight. Together they had stood in the hall and watched
that glowing triumphant figure carrying Deborah's
beaker up to bed. Miss Liddell might possibly
have a motive if Sally's taunt had any significance,
but there was no evidence that she had the
means, and certainly not that she had had the
opportunity. Mrs. Maxie, who had never liked Miss
Liddell, was still able to hope that the half-forgotten
humiliations of two years ago could remain hidden and that Alice Liddell, not very efficient, not
very intelligent, but fundamentally kind and
well-meaning, would be left in peace.

But Sir Reynold was still speaking.

"And by the way, I wouldn't take any notice of
these extraordinary rumours that are going round
the village. People are bound to talk you know,
but it will all die down as soon as the police get
their man. Let's hope they get a move on. Now
don't forget, let me know if there's anything I
can do. And mind you lock up carefully at night.
It might be Deborah or yourself next. And there's
another thing." Sir Reynold's voice became
hoarsely conspiratorial and Mrs. Maxie had to
strain to hear. "It's about the boy. Nice little fellow as far as I could see. Was watching him in
his pram at the fête, you know. Thought this

morning I'd like to do something there. Not much fun losing your mother. No real home. Someone ought to keep an eye on him. Where is he now? With you?"

"Jimmy's back at St. Mary's. It seemed best that way. I don't know what will be arranged for him. It's early yet, of course, and I don't know if anyone's given much thought to it."

"Time they did, dear lady. Time they did. Perhaps they'll put him up for adoption. Better get on the list, eh? Miss Liddell would be the person to ask, I suppose."

Mrs. Maxie was at a loss for an answer. She was more familiar with the laws of adoption than Sir Reynold and doubted whether he could be considered the most suitable applicant to have charge of a child. If Jimmy were to be adopted his situation would ensure that there were plenty of offers. She herself had already given thought to the child's future. She did not mention this, however, but contented herself by pointing out that Sally's relations might yet accept the boy and that nothing could be done until their views were known. It was possible, even, that the father would be traced. Sir Reynold dismissed this possibility with a hoot of derision but promised to do nothing in a hurry. With renewed warnings against homicidal maniacs he rang off. Mrs. Maxie wondered whether anyone could be as stupid as Sir Reynold appeared to be and what could have prompted his sudden concern for Jimmy.

She replaced the receiver with a sigh and turned to the day's letters. Half a dozen were from friends who, obviously in some social embarrassment, expressed their sympathy with the family and their confidence in Maxie innocence by invitations to dine. Mrs. Maxie found this demonstration of support more diverting than reassuring. The next three envelopes bore unfamiliar handwriting and she opened them reluctantly. Perhaps it would be better to destroy them unread but one never knew. Some information of value might be lost that way. Besides, it was more courageous to face unpleasantness and Eleanor Maxie had never lacked courage. But the first two letters were less objectionable than she had feared. One, indeed, was meant to be heartening. It contained three little printed texts with robins and roses in unreasonable proximity and an assurance that whosoever endured to the end would be saved. It asked for a contribution to enable this good news to be spread and suggested that the texts should be copied and distributed to those friends who were also in trouble. Most of Mrs. Maxie's friends were discreet about their troubles but, even so, she felt a tinge of guilt as she dropped the texts into the wastepaper basket. The next letter was in a mauve scented envelope from a lady who claimed psychic powers and was prepared, for a fee, to organize a séance at which Sally Jupp might be expected to appear and name her murderer. The assumption that Sally's disclosures would be completely acceptable to the Maxies did at least suggest that the writer gave them the benefit of the doubt. The last communication bore the local postmark and merely inquired, "Why weren't you content to work her to death, you dirty murderess?" Mrs. Maxie looked at the writing carefully but could not remember seeing it before. But the postmark was clear and she recognized a challenge. She decided to go down to the village and do some shopping.

The little village store was rather busier than usual and the buzz of talk which stopped as soon as she appeared left her in no doubt as to the subject of conversation. Mrs. Nelson was there, Miss Pollack, old Simon from the Weir cottage who was claimed as the oldest inhabitant and seemed to think that this absolved him from any effort at personal hygiene, and one or two of the women from the new agricultural cottages whose faces and personalities, if any, were still strange to her. There was a general murmur of "Good morning" in reply to her own greeting and Miss Pollack went so far as to say, "Lovely day again, isn't it?" before hurriedly consulting her shopping list and trying to conceal her red face behind the barricades of breakfast cereal. Mr. Wilson himself left the invoicing which was concerning him behind the scenes and came forward, quietly deferential as ever, to attend to Mrs. Maxie. He was a tall, lean, cadaverous-looking man with a face of such startling unhappiness that it was difficult to believe that he was not on the brink of bankruptcy instead of the owner of a flourishing little business. He heard more gossip than almost anyone in the village, but expressed an opinion himself so rarely that his pronouncements were listened to with great respect and commonly remembered. So far he had been uniformly silent on the subject of Sally Jupp, but it was not therefore supposed that he considered it an unsuitable subject for comment or was restrained by any reverence in the face of sudden death. Sooner or later, it was felt, Mr. Wilson would pronounce judgment, and the village would be very surprised if the judgment of the Law itself, given later and with more ceremony, were not substantially the same. He accepted Mrs. Maxie's order in silence and occupied himself with serving his most valued customer, while one by one the little group of women muttered their good-byes and crept or swept out of his shop.

When they had gone Mr. Wilson gave a conspiratorial glance around, cast his watery eyes upwards as if seeking guidance and then leaned across the counter towards Mrs. Maxie.

"Derek Pullen," he said. "That's who."

"I'm afraid I don't know what you mean, Mr. Wilson." Mrs. Maxie spoke the truth. She might have added that she had no particular desire to know.

"I'm saying nothing, mind you, madam. Let the police do their own work I say. But if they bother you at Martingale, ask them where Derek Pullen was going last Saturday night. Ask them that. He passed here at twelve or thereabouts. Saw him myself from the bedroom window."

Mr. Wilson drew himself up with the self-satisfied air of a man who has pronounced a final unanswerable argument and returned with a complete change of mood to the business of totalling Mrs. Maxie's bill. She felt that she ought to say that any evidence he possessed or thought that he possessed should be communicated to the police, but she could not bring herself to say words to this effect. She remembered Derek Pullen as she had last seen him, a small, rather spotty youth who wore overcut city suits and cheap shoes. His mother was a member of the Women's Institute and his father worked for Sir Reynold on the larger of his two farms. It was too silly and unfair. If Wilson couldn't keep his mouth shut there would be the police at the Pullens' cottage before nightfall and it was anyone's guess what they would ferret out. The boy looked timid and would probably be scared out of the few wits he looked as if he possessed. Then Mrs. Maxie remembered that someone had been in Sally's room that night. It could have been Derek Pullen. If Martingale were to be saved any further suffering she must keep her allegiance clear. "If you have information, Mr. Wilson," she said, "I think you should give it to Inspector Dalgliesh. In the meantime you might harm a great many innocent people by making accusations of that kind."

Mr. Wilson received this mild rebuke with the liveliest satisfaction as if it were the only confirmation needed of his own theories. He had obviously said all he intended to and the subject was now closed. "Four and five and ten and nine and one pound one shilling is one pound sixteen and two, if you please, madam," he intoned. Mrs. Maxie paid.

5

Meanwhile Johnnie Wilcox, a grubby and undersized twelve-year-old, was being interviewed by Dalgleish in the business room. He had presented himself at Martingale with the announcement that the vicar had sent him to see the inspector and please it was important. Dalgleish received him with grave courtesy and invited him to sit down and tell his story in comfort. He told it clearly and well and it was the most intriguing piece of evidence that Dalgleish had heard for some time.

Apparently Johnnie had been detailed with other members of his Sunday school class to help with the teas and the washing-up. There had been some feeling over this arrangement which was generally felt by the boys to be domestic, degrading and, frankly, not much fun. True, there had been promises of feasting later with the leftovers but the teas were always popular and last year several helpers had arrived to lend a belated hand and to share the meagre spoils with those who had borne the heat of the day. Johnnie Wilcox had seen no advantage in lingering longer than necessary and as soon as enough children had arrived to make his absence less noticeable he had possessed himself of two fish sandwiches, three chocolate buns and a couple of jam tarts and had borne them off to Bocock's stable loft in the confidence that Bocock was safely occupied giving pony rides.

Johnnie had been sitting peacefully in the loft munching and reading his comic for some time—it was useless to expect him to estimate for how long but only one bun remained—when he had heard footsteps and voices. He had not been alone in a desire for privacy and two other people were coming into the stable. He did not wait to see whether they were also intending to climb the loft, but took the sensible precaution of removing himself and his bun to a corner where he hid behind a large bale of straw. This action did not seem unnecessarily timid. In Johnnie's world a great deal of unpleasantness from spankings to going to bed at an early hour was avoided by the simple expedient of knowing when not to be seen. This time his caution was again justified. The footsteps did come up into the hay loft and he heard the soft thud of the trap-door being replaced. After that he was forced to sit in silence and some boredom, nibbling quietly at his bun and trying to make it last out until the visitors should depart. There were only two of them, he was certain of that—and one of them was Sally Jupp. He had caught a brief glimpse of her hair as she came through the trap-door, but had been forced to dodge back before she was in full view. But there was no doubt about it. Johnnie knew Sally well enough to be quite certain that he had both seen and heard her in the hay loft on Saturday afternoon. But he had not seen nor recognized the man with her. Once Sally had entered the loft it would have been risky to peer round the bundle of hay since even the smallest movement caused an unexpectedly loud rustling, and Johnnie had employed all his energies in keeping perfectly, and most unnaturally, still. Partly because the heavy hay bundle had muffled the voices and partly because he was used to finding the conversations of grown-up people both boring and incomprehensible, he made no effort to understand what was being said. All that Dalgleish could count on as reliable was that the two visitors had been arguing, but in low voices, that there was some mention of forty pounds, and that Sally Jupp had ended up by saying something about there being no risk if he kept his head and "watching for the light." Johnnie said that there had been a great deal of talk but most of it was spoken quietly and quickly. Only those few phrases remained in his memory. He could not say how long the three of them remained in the loft. It had seemed a dreadfully long time and he was stiff and thoroughly bored before he heard the sound of the trap-door being banged back and the girl and her companion left the loft. Sally had gone first and the man had followed. Johnnie had not felt safe in peering from his hiding-place until the sound of their footsteps was heard disappearing down the steps. Then he was in time to see a brown gloved hand replacing the trap-door. He had waited another few minutes himself then had run back to the fête where his absence had aroused very little interest. That, indeed, was the sum total of Johnnie Wilcox's Saturday afternoon adventure and it was irritating to consider how a few changes in circumstances might have added to its value. If Johnnie had been a little more adventurous he might have seen the man. If he had been a few years older or of a different sex he certainly would have considered this clandestine meeting in a more intriguing light than the mere interruption of a feast and would have certainly listened to and remembered as much of the conversation as possible. Now it was difficult to place any interpretation on the scraps he had overheard. He seemed an honest and reliable little boy, but ready enough to admit that he might have made a mistake. He thought that Sally had talked about "the light" but he might have imagined it. He hadn't really been listening and they were speaking quietly. On the other hand he had no doubt at all that it was Sally he had seen and was equally firm in his belief that it was not a friendly meeting. He couldn't be sure of the time when he left the stable. Teas began about half past three and lasted as long as people wanted them and the food held out. Johnnie thought it must have been about half past four when he first made his escape from Mrs. Cope. He couldn't remember how long he was hidden in the stable. It had seemed a very long time. With that Dalgleish had to be content. The whole thing was suspiciously like a case of blackmail and it seemed likely that another assignation had been made. But the fact that Johnnie had not recognized the man's voice seemed to prove conclusively that it could not have been either Stephen Maxie or a local man, most of whom would be well known to him. That at least supported the theory that there was another man to be considered. If Sally were blackmailing this stranger and he was actually at the church fête, then things looked brighter for the Maxies. As he thanked young Johnnie, warned him against talking to anyone else about his experience, and dismissed him to the comforting pleasure of revealing all that had passed to the vicar, Dalgleish's mind was already busy with new evidence.

Chapter Six

1

THE INQUEST WAS FIXED for three o'clock on Tuesday and the Maxies found they were almost looking forward to it as at least one known obligation which might help to speed the slow, uncomfortable hours. There was a sense of constant unease like the tension of a thundery day when the storm is inevitable and yet will not break. The tacit assumption that no one at Martingale could be a murderer precluded any realistic discussion of Sally's death. They were all afraid of saying too much or of saying it to the wrong person. Sometimes Deborah wished that the household could get together and at least decide on some solid basis of strategy. But when Stephen hesitantly voiced the same wish she drew back in sudden panic. Stephen talking about Sally was not to be borne.

Felix Hearne was different. With him it was possible to discuss almost anything. He did not fear death for himself nor was he shy of it and he apparently saw no breach of good taste in discussing Sally Jupp's death dispassionately and even lightly. At first Deborah took part in these conversations in a spirit of bravado. Later she realized that humour was only a feeble attempt to denigrate fear. Now, before Tuesday luncheon, she paced between the roses at Felix's side while he poured out his spate of blessedly foolish chatter, provoking her to an equally dispassionate and diverting flow of theories.

"Seriously, though, Deborah. If I were writing a book I should make it one of the village boys. Derek Pullen, for example."

"But he didn't. Anyway, he hasn't a motive."

"Motive is the last thing to look for. You can always find a motive. Perhaps the corpse was blackmailing him. Perhaps she was pressing him to marry her and he wouldn't. She could tell him that there was another baby on the way. It isn't true, of course, but he wasn't to know that. You see, they had been having the usual passionate *affaire*. I should make him one of the quiet, intense kind. They're capable of anything. In fiction, anyway."

"But she didn't want him to marry her. She had Stephen to marry. She wouldn't want Derek Pullen if she could have Stephen."

"You speak, if I may say so, with the blind partiality of a sister. But have it your own way. Whom do you suggest?"

"Suppose we make it Father."

"You mean the elderly gentleman, tied to his bed?"

"Yes. Except that he wasn't. It could be one of those Grand Guignol plots. The elderly gentleman didn't want his son to marry the scheming hussy so he crawled upstairs step by step and strangled her with his old school tie."

Felix considered this effort and rejected it.

"Why not make it the mysterious visitor with a name like a cinema cat. Who is he? Where does he come from? Could he be the father of her child?"

"Oh, I don't think so."

"Well, he was. He had met the corpse when she was an innocent girl at her first job. I shall draw a veil over that painful episode but you can imagine his surprise and horror when he meets her again, the girl he has wronged, in the home of his fiancée. And with his child too!"

"Has he a fiancée?"

"Of course. An extremely attractive widow whom he is determined to snare. Anyway, the poor wronged girl threatens to tell all so he has to silence her. I should make him one of those cynical, unlikeable characters so that no one would worry when he got copped."

"You don't think that would be rather sordid? What about making it the Warden of St. Mary's?

It could be one of those psychological thrillers with highbrow quotations at the beginning of the chapters and a lot of Freud."

"If it's Freud you fancy I'd put my money on the corpse's uncle. Now there would be a fine excuse for some deep psychological stuff. You see, he was a hard, narrow-minded man who had turned her out when he heard about the baby. But like all Puritans in fiction, he was just as bad himself. He had been carrying on with a simple little girl whom he met singing in the choir and she was in the same Home as the corpse having her baby. So the whole horrible truth came out and, of course, Sally was blackmailing him for thirty bob a week and nothing said. Obviously he couldn't risk exposure. He was far too respectable for that."

"What did Sally do with the thirty bob?"

"Opened a savings account in the baby's name of course. All that will come to light in due course."

"It would be nice if it did. But aren't you forgetting about the corpse's prospective sister-in-law? No difficulty about motive there."

Felix said easily, "But she wasn't a murderess."

"Oh, damn you, Felix! Must you be so blatantly tactful?"

"Since I know very well that you didn't kill Sally Jupp, do you expect me to go about registering embarrassment and suspicion just for the fun of it?"

"I did hate her, Felix. I really hated her."

"All right, my sweet. So you really hated her. That is bound to put you at a disadvantage with yourself. But don't be too anxious to confide your feelings to the police. They are worthy men, no doubt, and their manners are beautiful. They may, however, be limited in imagination. After all, their great strength is their common sense. That is the basis of all sound detective work. They have the method and the means so don't go handing them the motive. Let them do some work for the taxpayers' money."

"Do you think Dalgleish will find out who did it?" asked Deborah after a little pause.

"I think he may know now," replied Felix calmly. "Getting enough evidence to justify a charge is a different matter. We may find out this afternoon how far the police have got and how much they're prepared to tell. It may amuse Dalgleish to keep us in suspense but he's bound to show his hand sooner or later."

But the inquest was both a relief and a disappointment. The coroner sat without a jury. He was a mild-voiced man with the face of a depressed St. Bernard dog who gave the impression of having wandered into the proceedings by mistake. For all that, he knew what he wanted and he wasted no time. There were fewer villagers present than the Maxies had expected. Probably they were conserving time and energy for the better entertainment of the funeral. Certainly, those present were little wiser than they were before. The coroner made it all seem deceptively simple. Evidence of identification was given by a nervous, insignificant little woman who proved to be Sally's aunt. Stephen Maxie gave evidence and the factual details of finding the body were briefly elicited. The medical evidence showed that death was caused by vagal inhibition during manual strangulation and had been very sudden. There were about one and a half grains of barbiturate acid derivative in the stomach. The coroner asked no questions other than those necessary to establish these facts. The police asked for an adjournment and this was granted. It was all very informal, almost friendly. The witnesses crouched on the low chairs used by the Sunday school children while the coroner drooped over the proceedings from the superintendent's dais. There were jam jars of summer flowers on the window-sills and a flannelgraph on one wall showed the Christian's journey from baptism to burial in crayoned pictures. In these innocent and incongruous surroundings the law, with formality but without fuss, took note that Sarah Lillian Jupp had been feloniously done to death.

2

Now there was the funeral to face. Here, unlike the inquest, attendance was optional and the decision whether or not to appear was one which none but Mrs. Maxie found easy. She had no difficulty and made it clear that she had every intention of being present. Although she did not discuss the matter, her attitude was obvious. Sally Jupp had died in their house and in their employ. Her only relations had obviously no intentions of forgiving her for being as embarrassing and unorthodox in death as she had been in life. They would have no part in the funeral and it would take place from St. Mary's and at the expense of that institution. But, apart from the need for someone to be there, the Maxies had a responsibility. If people died in your house the least you could do was to attend the funeral. Mrs. Maxie did not express herself in these words, but her son and daughter were unmistakably given to understand that such attendance was mere courtesy and that those who extended to others the hospitality of their homes should, if it unfortunately proved necessary, extend that hospitality to seeing them safely into their graves. In all her private imaginings of what life at Martingale would be during a murder investigation Deborah had never considered the major part which comparatively minor matters of taste or etiquette would play. It was strange that the overriding anxiety for all their futures would be, temporarily at least, less urgent than the worry of whether or not the family should send a wreath to the funeral, and if so, what appropriate condolence should be written on the card. Here again the question did not worry Mrs. Maxie who merely inquired whether they wished to club together or whether Deborah would send a wreath of her own.

Stephen, it appeared, was exempt from these obsequies. The police had given him permission to return to hospital after the inquest and he would not be at Martingale again until the following Saturday night, except for fleeting visits. No one expected him to provide a chaste wreath for the delectation of the village gossips. He had every excuse for returning to London and carrying on with his job. Even Dalgleish could not expect him to hang about at Martingale indefinitely for the convenience of the police.

If Catherine had almost as valid an excuse for returning to London she did not avail herself of it. Apparently she had still seven days of her annual leave in hand and was willing and happy to stay on at Martingale. Matron had been approached and was sympathetic. There would be absolutely no difficulty if she could help Mrs. Maxie in any way. Undeniably she could. There was still the heavy nursing of Simon Maxie to be coped with, there was the continual interruption of household routine caused by Dalgleish's investigation, and there was the lack of Sally.

Once it was established that her mother intended to be at the funeral, Deborah set about subduing her natural abhorrence of the whole idea and announced abruptly that she would be there. She was not surprised when Catherine expressed a similar intention, but it was both unexpected and a relief to find that Felix meant to go with them.

"It's not in the least necessary," she told him angrily. "I can't think what all the fuss is about. Personally I find the whole idea morbid and distasteful, but if you want to come and be gaped at, well, it's a free show." She left the drawing-room quickly but returned a few minutes later to say with the disconcerting formality which he found so disarming in her, "I'm sorry I was so rude, Felix. Please do come if you will. It was sweet of you to think of it."

Felix felt suddenly angry with Stephen. It was true that the boy had every excuse for returning to work, but it was nevertheless typical and irritating that he should have so ready and simple an excuse for evading responsibility and unpleasantness. Neither Deborah nor her mother, of course, would see it that way and Catherine Bowers, poor besotted fool, was ready to forgive Stephen anything. None of the women would intrude their troubles or difficulties on Stephen. But, thought Felix, if that young man had disciplined his more quixotic impulses none of this need have happened. Felix prepared for the funeral in a mood of cold anger and fought resolutely against the suspicion that part of his resentment was frustration and part was envy.

It was another wonderful day. The crowd were dressed in summer dresses, some of the girls in clothes which would have been more suitable on a bathing-beach than in a cemetery. A large number had evidently been picnicking and had only heard of the better entertainment to be offered in the churchyard by chance. They were laden with the remains of their feasts and some were actually still engaged in finishing their sandwiches or oranges. They were perfectly well behaved once they got near to the grave. Death has an almost universally sobering effect and a few nervous giggles were soon repressed by the outraged glances of the more orthodox. It was not their behaviour that enraged Deborah, it was the fact that they should be there at all. She was filled with a cold contempt and an anger that was frightening in its intensity. Afterwards she was glad of this since it left no room for grief or for embarrassment.

The Maxies, Felix Hearne and Catherine Bowers stood together at the open graveside with Miss Liddell and a handful of girls from St. Mary's bunched behind them. Opposite them stood Dalgleish and Martin. Police and suspects faced each other across the open grave. A little way away another funeral was in progress taken by some alien clergyman from another parish. The little group of mourners were all in black and huddled so close to the grave in a tight circle that they seemed engaged in some secret and esoteric rite that was not for the eyes of others. No one took any notice of them and the voice of their priest could not be heard above the minor rustlings of Sally's crowd. Afterwards they went quietly away. They, thought Deborah, had at least buried their dead with some dignity. But now Mr. Hinks was speaking his few words. Wisely he did not mention the circumstances of the girl's death, but said gently that the ways of Providence were strange and mysterious, an assertion which few of his listeners were competent to disprove, even though the presence of the police suggested that some at least of this present mystery was the work of human agency.

Mrs. Maxie took an active interest in the whole ceremony, her audible "Amens" sounded emphatic agreement at the end of each petition, she found her way about the Book of Common Prayer with capable fingers and helped two of the St. Mary's girls to find the place when they were too overcome with grief or embarrassment to manage their books themselves. As the end of the service she stepped up to the grave and stood for a moment gazing down at the coffin. Deborah felt rather than heard her sigh. What it meant no one could have told from the composed face that turned itself again to confront the crowd. She pulled on her gloves and leaned down to read one of the mourning-cards before joining her daughter.

"What an appalling crowd. One would think people had something better to do. Still, if that poor child Sally were half the exhibitionist she seems to have been, this funeral would meet with her approval. What is that boy doing? Is this your mother? Well, surely your little boy knows that one doesn't jump about on graves. You must control him better if you want to bring him into the churchyard. This is consecrated ground, not the school playground. A funeral isn't suitable entertainment for a child anyway."

The mother and child gaped after them, two pale astounded faces with the same sharp noses, the same scrawny hair. Then the woman pulled her child away with a frightened backward glance. Already the bright splurge of colour was dispersing, the bicycles were being dragged from among the Michaelmas daisies by the churchyard wall, the photographers were packing up their cameras. One or two little groups still waited about, whispering together and watching an opportunity to snoop among the wreaths. The sexton was already picking up the legacy of orange peel and paper bags, muttering under his breath. Sally's grave was a sheet of colour. Reds, blues and gold spread over the piled turfs and wooden planks like a gaudy patchwork quilt and the scent of rich earth mixed with the scent of flowers.

3

"Isn't that Sally's aunt?" asked Deborah. A thin, nervous-looking woman with hair which might once have been red was talking to Miss Liddell. They walked away together towards the churchyard gate. "Surely it's the same woman who identified Sally at the inquest. If it is the aunt perhaps we could drive her home. The buses are dreadfully infrequent at this time of day."

"It might be worth while having a word with her," said Felix consideringly. Deborah's suggestion had originally been prompted by simple kindness, the wish to save someone a long wait in the hot sun. But now the practical advantages of her proposal asserted themselves.

"Do get Miss Liddell to introduce you, Felix. I'll bring the car round. You might find out where Sally worked before she got pregnant, and who Jimmy's father is and whether Sally's uncle really liked her."

"In two or three moments of casual conversation? I hardly think so."

"We should have all the drive to pump her. Do try, Felix."

Deborah sped after her mother and Catherine with as much speed as decency permitted, leaving Felix to his task. The woman and Miss Liddell had reached the road now and were pausing for a last few words. From a distance the two figures seemed to be executing some kind of ceremonial dance. They moved together to shake hands, then bobbed apart. Then Miss Liddell, who had turned away, swung back with some fresh remark and the figures drew together again.

As Felix moved towards them they turned to watch him and he could see Miss Liddell's lips moving. He joined them and the inescapable introductions were made. A thin hand, gloved in cheap black rayon, held his hand timidly for a

brief second and then dropped. Even in that apa-
thetic and almost imperceptible contact he
sensed that she was shaking. The anxious grey
eyes looked away from his as he spoke.

"Mrs. Riscoe and I were wondering if we might
drive you home," he said gently. "There will be a
long wait for a bus and we should be very glad of
the drive." That at least was the truth. She hesitated. Just as Miss Liddell had apparently decided that the offer, although unexpected, could
not in decency be ignored and might even be
safely accepted and had begun to urge this
course, Deborah drew up beside them in Felix's
Renault and the matter was settled. Sally's aunt
was introduced to her as Mrs. Victor Proctor and
was comfortably ensconced beside her in the
front of the car before anyone had time for argument. Felix settled himself in the back, aware of
some distaste for the enterprise but prepared to
admire Deborah in action. "Painless extractions
a specialty" he thought as the car swung away
down the hill. He wondered how far they were
going and whether Deborah had bothered to tell
her mother how long they would be away. "I think
I know roughly where you live," he heard her saying. "It's just outside Canningbury, isn't it? We go
through it on our way to London. But I shall have
to rely on you for the road. It's very sweet of you to
let us drive you home. Funerals are so awful. It really is a relief to get away for a time." The result of
this was unexpected. Suddenly Mrs. Proctor was
crying, not noisily, hardly even without moving

her face. Almost as if her tears were without any possibility of control she let them slide in a stream down her cheeks and fall on to her folded hands. When she spoke her voice was low but clear enough to be heard above the engine. And still the tears fell silently and without effort.

"I shouldn't have come really. Mr. Proctor wouldn't like it if he knew I'd come. He won't be back when I get home and Beryl is at school, so he won't know. But he wouldn't like it. She's made her own bed so let her lie on it. That's what he says and you can't blame him. Not after what he's done for her. There was never any difference made between Sally and Beryl. Never. I'll say that to the day I die. I don't know why it had to happen to us."

This perennial cry of the unfortunate struck Felix as unreasonable. He was not aware that the Proctors had accepted any responsibility for Sally since her pregnancy and they had certainly succeeded in dissociating themselves from her death. He leaned forward to hear more clearly. Deborah may have made some kind of encouraging sound, he could not be sure. But there was to be no question of pumping this witness. She had been keeping things to herself for too long. "We brought her up decently. No one can say we didn't. It hasn't always been easy. She did get the scholarship but we still had to feed her. She wasn't an easy child. I used to think it was the bombing but Mr. Proctor wouldn't have that. They were with us at the time, you know. We had a

house in Stoke Newington then. There hadn't
been many raids and somehow we felt safe with
the Anderson shelter and everything. It was one
of those VI rockets that did for Lil and George. I
don't remember anything about it nor about being dug out. They never told me about Lil for a
week afterwards. They got us all out but Lil was
dead and George died in hospital. We were the
lucky ones. At least I suppose we were. Mr. Proctor was really bad for a long time and, of course,
he's got his disability. But they said we were the
lucky ones."

"Like me," thought Felix bitterly. "One of the
lucky ones."

"And then you took Sally and brought her up,"
prompted Deborah.

"There wasn't anyone else really. Mother
couldn't have taken her. She wasn't fit for it. I
tried to think that Lil would have liked it, but those
sort of thoughts can't help you to love a child.
She wasn't loving really. Not like Beryl. But then
Sally was ten before Beryl arrived and I suppose
it was hard on her after being the only one for so
long. But we never made a difference. They always had the same, piano lessons and everything. And now this. The police came round after
she died. They weren't in uniform or anything,
but you could see who they were. Everyone knew
about it. They asked who the man was but, of
course, we couldn't say."

"The man who killed her?" Deborah sounded
incredulous.

"Oh no. The father of the baby. I suppose they thought he might have done it. But we couldn't tell them anything."

"I suppose they asked a lot of questions about where you were on the night."

For the first time Mrs. Proctor seemed aware of her tears. She fumbled in her handbag and wiped them away. Interest in her story seemed to have assuaged whatever grief she was indulging. Felix thought that it was unlikely that she wept for Sally. Was it the resurrected memory of Lil, of George and of the helpless child they had left behind which had caused those tears, or was it just weariness and a sense of failure? Almost as if she sensed his question she said, "I don't know why I'm crying. Crying can't bring back the dead. I suppose it was the service. We had that hymn for Lil. 'The King of Love my Shepherd Is.' It doesn't seem right for either of them really. You were asking about the police. I suppose you've had your share of them, too. They came to us all right. I told them I was at home with Beryl. They asked if we went to the fête at Chadfleet. I told them we didn't know anything about it. Not that we would have gone. We didn't see Sally ever and we didn't want to come nosing around where she worked. I could remember the day all right. It was funny really. Miss Liddell telephoned in the morning to talk to Mr. Proctor which she hadn't done since Sally took her new job. Beryl answered the 'phone and it made her feel quite queer. She thought something must have happened to Sally for Miss Liddell to 'phone. But it was only to say that Sally was doing all right. It was funny though. She knew we didn't want to hear."

It must have struck Deborah as strange, too, for she asked, "Had Miss Liddell telephoned before to tell you how Sally was getting on?"

"No. Not since Sally went to Martingale. She telephoned to tell us that. At least I think she did. She may have written to Mr. Proctor, but I can't be sure. I suppose she thought that we ought to know about Sally leaving the Home, Mr. Proctor being her guardian. At least he used to be, but now she's over twenty-one and on her own it's nothing to us where she goes. She never cared for us not for any of us, not even Beryl. I thought I'd better come today because it looks queer if no one from the family's there, whatever Mr. Proctor may say. But he was right really. You can't help the dead by being there and it's only upsetting. All those people, too. They ought to have something better to do."

"So Mr. Proctor hadn't seen Sally since she left your house?" pursued Deborah.

"Oh, no. There wouldn't be any point in it, would there?"

"I expect the police asked him where he was on the night she died. They always do. Of course it's only a formality."

If Deborah had been afraid of causing offence she was worrying unnecessarily.

"It's funny the way they go on. You'd have thought we knew something about it by the way they talked. Asking questions about Sally's life and whether she had any expectations and who her friends were. Anyone would think she was someone important. They had Beryl in to ask about the telephone call from Miss Liddell. They even asked Mr. Proctor what he was doing the night Sally died. Not that we were likely to forget that night. It was the one he had his cycle accident. He wasn't home till twelve and he was in a proper bad state with his lip all swollen and the cycle bent up. He lost his watch, too, which was upsetting as his father left it to him and it was real gold. Very valuable they always told us. We aren't likely to forget that night in a hurry I can tell you."

Mrs. Proctor had now recovered completely from the emotional effects of the funeral and was chatting away with the eagerness of someone who is more accustomed to listening than to getting a hearing. Deborah was making light work of the driving. Her hands lay gently on the wheel and her blue eyes gazed steadily on the road ahead, but Felix had little doubt that most of her mind was on other matters. She made sympathetic sounds in reply to Mrs. Proctor's story and replied, "What a horrid shock for you both! You must have been terribly worried when he was so late. How did it happen?"

"He came off at the bottom of a hill somewhere Finch-worthy way. I don't know exactly where. He was coming down fast and someone had left broken glass in the road. Of course it ripped the front tyre and he lost control and went into the ditch. He might have been killed as I told him, or badly injured, and if he had, goodness knows what would have happened because those roads are very lonely. You could lie there for hours and no one come by. Mr. Proctor doesn't like the busy roads for cycling and I don't wonder. There's no peace if you don't get away by yourself."

"Is he fond of cycling?" asked Deborah.

"Cycling mad. Always has been. Of course he doesn't go in for the real road work now. Not since the war and being bombed. He did a lot of it when he was young though. But he still likes to get about and we don't usually see much of him on Saturday afternoons."

Mrs. Proctor's voice held a shade of relief which was not lost on either of her listeners. A bicycle and an accident can be a useful alibi, thought Felix, but he can't be a serious suspect if he was indoors by twelve. It would take him at least an hour to get home from Martingale even if the accident were faked, and he had the use of the bicycle all the way. It was difficult, too, to imagine an adequate motive since Proctor had obviously found no reason to murder his niece before her admission to St. Mary's and had apparently had no contact with her since. Felix's mind played with the possibility of a future inheritance for Sally which, at her death, would conveniently devolve upon Beryl Proctor. But in his heart he knew that he was looking not for the murderer of Sally Jupp but for someone with sufficient motive and opportunity to divert the police investigation from more likely suspects. It seemed a forlorn hope so far as the Proctors were concerned, but Deborah had obviously made up her mind that there was something to be discovered from them. The time factor was apparently worrying her, too.

"Did you wait up for your husband, Mrs. Proctor? You must have been getting pretty desperate by midnight unless he was usually late."

"Well, he was usually a bit late and he always said not to wait up so I didn't. I go to the pictures most Saturdays with Beryl. We've got the telly, of course, and we sometimes watch that, but it makes a change to get out of the house once a week."

"So you were in bed when your husband returned?" Deborah insisted gently.

"He had his own key, of course, so there wasn't any point in waiting up. If I'd known he was going to be so late it would have been different. I usually go up to bed about ten when Mr. Proctor's out. Mind you, there's not the same rush on a Sunday morning, but I was never one for late nights. That's what I told the police. 'I was never one for late nights,' I said. They were asking about Mr. Proctor's accident, too. The inspector was very sympathetic. 'Not home until nearly twelve,' I told them. They could see it had been a worrying night without Sally getting herself murdered like that."

"I expect Mr. Proctor woke you when he arrived home. It must have been terribly worrying to see him in that condition."

"Oh, it was! I heard him in the bathroom and when I called out he came in to me. His face looked awful, a terrible green colour streaked with blood, and he was shaking all over. I don't know how he got home. I got up to make him a cup of tea while he had a bath. I remember the time because he called down to me to ask me what it was. He'd lost his watch you see after the accident, and we'd only got the little kitchen clock and the one in the front room. That said ten minutes past midnight and the kitchen one said the same. It was a shock to me I can tell you. It must have been half past twelve before we were back in bed and I never thought he'd be fit to get up the next morning. But he did, the same as usual. He always goes down first and makes the tea. He thinks no one can make tea like him and he does bring up a good cup. But I never thought he'd get up early that Sunday, not after what he looked like the night before. He's still shaken up by it even now. That's why he didn't go to the inquest. And then to have the police arriving that morning to tell us about Sally. We shan't forget that night in a hurry."

4

They had reached Canningbury now and there was a long wait at the traffic lights which regulated the surge of traffic meeting at the High

Road and the Broadway. It was obviously a popular shopping afternoon in this over-crowded
suburb of east London. The pavements were
spilling with housewives who every now and then,
as if propelled by some primeval urge, streamed
with maddening slowness across the path of the
traffic. The shops on both sides of the road had
once been a row of houses and their grandiose
windows and frontages were in incongruous contrast to the modest roofs and windows above.
The town hall, which looked as if it had been designed by a committee of morons in an excess of
alcohol and civic pride, stood in isolated splen-
dour bounded by two bombed sites where re-
building had only just begun.

Closing his eyes against the heat and the noise
Felix reminded himself sternly that Canningbury
was one of the more enlightened suburbs with
an enviable record of good public services and
that not everyone wanted to live in a quiet Georgian house in Greenwich where the mist came
up from the river in white fingers and only the
most persistent friends found their way to his
door. He was glad when the traffic lights changed
and, under Mrs. Proctor's guidance, they moved
forward in a series of gentle jerks and turned left
away from the main road. Here was the back-
wash of the shopping centre, the women walking
home with their laden baskets, the few smaller
gown shops and hairdressers with pseudo-French
names over the converted front-room windows.
After a few minutes they turned again into a quiet

street where a row of identical houses stretched as far as the eye could see. Although they were identical in structure, however, they were very different in appearance for hardly two of the small front gardens were alike. All were carefully sown and tended. A few householders had expressed their individuality with monkey-puzzle trees, coy stone gnomes fishing from basins or spurious rock gardens, but the majority had contented themselves by creating a little show of colour and fragrance which shamed the dull nonentity of the house behind. The curtains showed signs of careful if misguided choosing and of frequent washing, and were supplemented by additional half-curtains of draped lace or net which were carefully drawn against the curiosity of a vulgar world. Windermere Crescent had the respectable look of a street that is a cut above its neighbours and whose inhabitants are determined to maintain that superiority.

This then had been the home of Sally Jupp who had fallen so lamentably from its standards. The car drew in to the kerb at the gate of number 17 and Mrs. Proctor clutched her black shapeless handbag to her chest and began to fumble at the door. "Let me," said Deborah, and leaned across her to release the catch. Mrs. Proctor extricated herself and began her profuse thanks which Deborah cut short.

"Please don't. We were very glad to come. I wonder if I might bother you for a glass of water before we leave. It's silly, I know, but driving is so thirst-making in this heat. Really only water. I hardly ever drink anything else."

"Don't you, by God!" thought Felix as the two women disappeared into the house.

He wondered what Deborah was up to now and hoped that the wait wouldn't be too long. Mrs. Proctor had been offered no choice about inviting her benefactor into the house. She could hardly have brought a glass of water out to the car. Nevertheless Felix was certain that she had not welcomed the intrusion. She had glanced anxiously up the road before they went in and he guessed that the time was getting dangerously late and that she was desperately anxious that the car should be gone before her husband came home. Some of the anxiety she had shown when they first met her in the churchyard had returned. He felt a momentary spasm of irritation with Deborah. The exercise was unlikely to be useful and it was a shame to worry that pathetic little woman.

Deborah, untouched by such nice refinement of feeling, was being shown into the front room. A schoolgirl was arranging her music on the piano in evident preparation for her practice but was bundled out of the room with a hasty injunction to "Fetch a glass of water, dear" spoken in the falsely bright tone often used by parents in the presence of strangers. The child went out rather reluctantly Deborah thought and not without giving her a long and deliberate stare. She was a remarkably plain child, but the likeness to her dead cousin was unmistakable. Mrs. Proctor had not introduced her and Deborah wondered whether this was an oversight due to nervousness or a deliberate wish to keep the child in ignorance of her mother's afternoon's activities. If so, presumably some story would be concocted to explain the visit, although Mrs. Proctor had not struck her as possessing much inventive faculty.

They sat down in opposite armchairs, each with its embroidered chair-back of a crinolined and bonneted female gathering hollyhocks and its plump unsullied cushions. This was obviously the best room, used only for entertaining or for piano practice. It had the faint musty smell compounded of wax polish, new furniture and seldom-opened windows. On the piano were two photographs of young girls in ballet dresses, their graceless bodies bent into unnatural and angular poses and their faces set into determined smiles beneath the wreaths of artificial roses. One of them was the child who had just left the room. The other was Sally. It was strange how, even at that age, the same family colouring and similar bone structure should have produced in one an essential distinction and in the other a heavy plainness that held little promise for the future. Mrs. Proctor saw the direction of her glance.

"Yes," she said, "we did everything for her. Everything. There was never any difference made. She had piano lessons, too, the same as Beryl although she never had Beryl's gift. But we always treated them alike. It's a dreadful thing that it's all ended like this. That other photo is the group we had took after Beryl's christening. That's me and Mr. Proctor with the baby and Sally. She was a pretty little thing then, but it didn't last."

Deborah moved over to the photograph. The group had been stiffly posed in heavy carved chairs and against a contrived background of draped curtains which made the photograph look older than it was. Mrs. Proctor, younger and more buxom, held her child awkwardly and looked ill at ease in her new clothes.

Sally looked sulky. The husband was posed behind them, his gloved hands leaning proprietorially on the backs of the chairs. There was something unnatural in his stance, but his face gave nothing away. Deborah looked at him carefully. Somewhere she was certain that she had seen that face before, but the recognition was tenuous and unsatisfactory. It was, after all, an unremarkable face and the photograph was more than ten years old. She turned away from the photograph with a sense of disappointment. It had told her very little and she hardly knew what else she had expected to gain from it.

Beryl Proctor came back with the glass of water, one of the best glasses carried on a small papiermâché tray. No introductions were made and Deborah was conscious as she drank that both of them wished her away. Suddenly she wished nothing more herself than to be out of the house and free of them. Her coming in had been an incomprehensible impulse. It had been prompted partly by boredom, partly by hope and very largely by curiosity. Sally dead had become more interesting than Sally alive and she had wanted to see from what sort of home Sally had been rejected. That curiosity now seemed presumption and her entry into the house an intrusion which she did not want to prolong.

She said her "good-byes" and rejoined Felix. He took the wheel and they did not speak until the town was behind them and the car was shaking free of the suburban tentacles and climbing into the country.

"Well," said Felix at last, "was the exercise in detection worth while? Are you sure you want to go on with it?"

"Why not?"

"Only that you might discover facts which you would prefer not to know."

"Such as my family contains a murderer?"

"I didn't say that."

"You have been studiously careful not to say it, but I would prefer honesty to tact. That is what you think, isn't it?"

"Speaking as a murderer myself, I admit that it's a possibility."

"You're thinking of the Resistance. That wasn't murder. You didn't kill women."

"I killed two. I admit it was by shooting, not by strangulation, and it seemed at the time to be expedient."

"This killing was expedient all right—for someone," said Deborah.

"Then why not leave it to the police? Their greatest difficulty will be to get enough evidence to justify a charge. If we start interfering we may only hand them the evidence they want. The case is wide open. Stephen and I got through Sally's window. So could almost anyone else. Most people in the village must have known where that ladder was kept. The evidence of that locked door is incontrovertible. However her murderer got in he didn't go out through the door. There's only the Sommeil to connect this crime with Martingale and the two need not be related. Other people had access to the stuff even if they are."

"Aren't you relying too much on coincidence?" asked Deborah coldly.

"Coincidences happen every day. An average jury will be able to think up half a dozen instances in their own experience. The most likely interpretation of the facts so far is that someone known to Sally got in through her window and killed her. He may or may not have used the ladder. There are scratches on the walls as if he slid down by the stack pipe and lost his hold when he was nearly at the ground. The police must have noticed these, but I don't see how they can prove when the scratches were made. Sally may have been admitting callers that way on previous occasions."

"It seems a curious thing to say but somehow I can't believe that. It's not in character. I'd like to believe it for all our sakes, but I don't. I never liked Sally, but I don't believe that she was pro-

miscuous. I don't want safety at the price of black-
ening the poor little devil's reputation further now
that she isn't here to defend herself."

"I think you are right about her," said Felix. "But
I don't advise you to make the inspector a present of your opinion. Let him make his own psychological assessment of Sally. The whole case
may run into the sand if we keep our heads cool
and our mouths shut. The Sommeil is the greatest danger. The hiding of that bottle makes the
two things seem connected. Even so, the drug
was put into your drinking-mug. It could have
been put there by anyone."

"Even by me."

"Even by you. It could have been put there by
Sally. She may have taken the mug to annoy
you. I think she did. But she may have put the
drug in her cocoa for no more sinister reason
that the desire for a good night. It wasn't a lethal
dose."

"In which case, why was the bottle hidden?"

"Let us say that it was hidden either by someone who erroneously believed that the drugging
and the murder were connected and who wanted
to conceal that fact, or by someone who knew
that they weren't but who wanted to implicate the
family. As your stake marked the hiding-place we
may assume that such a person specifically
wished to implicate you. That's a pleasant thought
for you to be going on with."

They were cresting the hill above Little Chadfleet now. Below them lay the village and there

was a glimpse of the tall grey chimneys of Martingale above the trees. With the return home the oppression and fear which the drive had only partially relieved fell like a black cloud.

"If they never solve this crime," said Deborah, "can you really imagine us living on happily at Martingale? Don't you ever feel that you must know the truth? Do you honestly never convince yourself that Stephen did it, or I?"

"You? Not with those hands and finger-nails. Didn't you notice that very considerable force was used and that her neck was bruised, but not scratched? Stephen is a possibility. So are Catherine and your mother and Martha. So am I. The superfluity of suspects is our greatest protection. Let Dalgleish take his pick. As for not living on at Martingale with an unsolved crime hanging over you—I imagine that the house has seen its share of violence in the past three hundred years. Not all your ancestors lived such well-regulated lives even if their deaths were with benefit of clergy. In two hundred years the death of Sally Jupp will be one of the legends told on All-Hallows to frighten your great-grand-children. And if you really can't stand Martingale there will always be Greenwich. I won't bore you with that again, but you know what I feel."

His voice was almost expressionless. His hands lay lightly on the wheel and his eyes still looked at the road ahead with easy and unstrained concentration. He must have known what she was thinking for he said:

"Don't let it worry you. I shan't complicate things more than I can help. I just don't want any of those beefy types you run around with to misunderstand my interest."

"Would you want me, Felix, if I were running away?"

"Isn't that being melodramatic? What else have most of us been doing for the last ten years? But if you want marriage as an escape from Martingale you may yet find the sacrifice unnecessary. As we left Canningbury we passed Dalgleish and one of his minions on the way in. My guess is that they were on the same errand. Your instinct about Proctor may not have been so far wrong after all."

They garaged the car in silence and passed into the coolness of the hall. Catherine Bowers was mounting the stairs. She was carrying a linen-covered tray and the white nylon overall which she usually wore when nursing Simon Maxie looked cool, efficient and not unbecoming. It is never agreeable to see another person competently and publicly performing duties which conscience suggests are one's own and Deborah was honest enough to recognize the reason for her spasm of irritation. She tried to hide it by an unusual burst of confidence.

"Wasn't the funeral awful, Catherine? I'm terribly sorry that Felix and I ran off like that. We drove Mrs. Proctor home. I had a sudden urge to fix the murder on the wicked uncle."

Catherine was unimpressed.

"I asked the inspector about the uncle when he questioned me for the second time. He said that the police are satisfied that Mr. Proctor couldn't have killed Sally. He didn't explain why. I should leave the job to him. Goodness knows there's enough work here."

She went on her way. Looking after her, Deborah said:

"I may be uncharitable, but if anyone at Martingale killed Sally I should prefer it to have been Catherine."

"It isn't likely, though, is it?" said Felix. "I can't see her capable of murder."

"And the rest of us are? Even Mother?"

"She particularly, I think, if she felt it were necessary."

"I don't believe it," said Deborah. "But even if it were true, can you see her saying nothing while police overrun Martingale and people like Miss Liddell and Derek Pullen are suspected?"

"No," replied Felix. "No, I can't see that."

Chapter Seven

1

ROSE COTTAGE on the Nessingford Road was a late eighteenth century labourer's cottage with enough superficial charm and antiquity to tempt the passing motorist to an opinion that something could be made of it. In the Pullens' hands something had, a replica of a thousand urban council houses. A large plaster model of an Alsatian dog occupied all the window space in the front room. Behind it the lace curtains were elegantly draped and tied with blue ribbon. The front door opened straight into the living-room. Here the Pullens' enthusiasm for modern décor had outrun discretion and the result was curiously irritating and bizarre. One wall was papered with a design of pink stars against a blue background. The opposite wall was painted in matching pink. The chairs were covered with blue striped material obviously carefully chosen to tone with the paper. The hair-cord carpet was a pale pink and had suffered from the inevitable comings and goings of muddy feet. Nothing was clean, nothing made to last, nothing was simple or honest. Dalgleish found it all profoundly depressing.

Derek Pullen and his mother were at home. Mrs. Pullen showed none of the normal reactions to the arrival of police officers engaged in a murder investigation, but greeted them with a spate of welcoming miscellanea, as if she had stayed at home specially to receive them and had long awaited their arrival. The phrases tumbled against one another. Delighted to see them . . . her brother a police constable . . . perhaps they had heard of him . . . Joe Pullen over at Barkingway . . . always better to tell the truth to the police . . . not that they's anything to tell . . . poor Mrs. Maxie . . . couldn't hardly believe it when Miss Liddell told her . . . come home and told Derek and he didn't believe it neither . . . not the sort of girl a decent man would want . . . very proud the Maxies were . . . a girl like that asked for trouble. As she spoke the pale eyes wavered over Dalgleish's face but with little comprehension. In the background stood her son, braced to the inevitable.

So Pullen had known about the engagement late on Saturday night although, as the police

had already ascertained, he had spent the evening at the Theatre Royal, Stratford, with a party
from his office and had not been at the fête.

Dalgleish had difficulty in persuading the voluble Mrs. Pullen to retire to her kitchen and leave
the boy to answer for himself but he was helped
by Pullen's fretful insistence that she should leave
them alone. He had obviously been expecting a
visit. When Dalgleish and Martin were announced
he had risen from his chair and faced them with
the pathetic courage of a man whose meagre
reserves have scarcely carried him through the
waiting period. Dalgleish dealt with him gently.
He might have been speaking to a son. Martin
had seen this technique in use before. It was a
cinch with the nervous, emotional types, especially if they were burdened with guilt. Guilt,
thought Martin, was a funny thing. This boy, now,
had probably done nothing worse than meet Sally
Jupp for a bit of kiss and cuddle but he wouldn't
feel at peace until he'd spilt the beans to someone. On the other hand he might be a murderer.
If he were, then fear would keep his mouth shut
for a little longer. But in the end he'd crack. Before long he would see in Dalgleish, patient, uncensorious and omnipotent, the father confessor
whom his conscience craved. Then it would be
difficult for the shorthand writer to catch up with
the spate of self-accusation and guilt. It was a
man's own mind which betrayed him in the end
and Dalgleish knew that better than most. There
were times when Sergeant Martin, not the most

sensitive of men, felt that a detective's job was not a pretty one.

But, so far, Pullen was standing up well to the questioning. He admitted that he had walked past Martingale late on Saturday night. He was studying for an examination and liked to get some air before going to bed. He often went for a late walk. His mother could confirm that. He took the Venezuelan envelope found in Sally's room, pushed a pair of bent spectacles up on his forehead and peered short-sightedly at the scribbled dates. Quietly he admitted that the writing was his. The envelope had come from a pen friend in South America. He had used it to jot down the times when he could meet Sally Jupp. He couldn't remember when he had given it to her but the dates referred to their meetings last month.

"She used to lock her door and then come down the stack-pipe to you, didn't she?" asked Dalgleish. "You needn't be afraid of breaking her confidence. We found her palm-marks on the pipe. What did you do when you had those meetings?"

"We went for walks in the garden once or twice. Mostly we sat in the old stable block opposite her room and talked." He must have fancied that he saw incredulity in Dalgleish's face for he flushed and said defensively:

"We didn't make love if that's what you're thinking. I suppose all policemen have to cultivate dirty minds but she wasn't like that."

"What was she like?" asked Dalgleish gently. "What did you talk about?"

"Anything. Everything really. I think she was lonely for someone her own age. She wasn't happy when she was at St. Mary's but there were the other girls to have a laugh with. She was a wonderful mimic. I could almost hear Miss Liddell talking. She talked about her home too. Her parents were killed in the war. Everything would have been different for her if they had lived. Her father was a university don and she would have had a different kind of home from her aunt's. Cultured and . . . well, different."

Dalgleish thought that Sally Jupp had been a young woman who enjoyed exercising imagination and in Derek Pullen she had at least found a credulous listener. But there was more in these meetings than Pullen was choosing to say. The girl had been using him for something. But for what?

"You looked after her child for her, didn't you, when she went up to London on the Thursday before she died?"

It was a complete shot in the dark but Pullen did not even seem surprised that he knew.

"Yes, I did. I work in a local government office and I can take a day's leave now and then. Sally said that she wanted to go up to town and I didn't see why she shouldn't. I expect she wanted to see a flick or go shopping. Other mothers can."

"It seems strange that Sally didn't leave her

child at Martingale if she wanted to go up to London. Mrs. Bultitaft would probably have been willing to look after him occasionally. All this secrecy was surely rather unnecessary."

"Sally liked it that way. She liked things to be secret. I think that was half the attraction of sneaking out at night. I had a feeling sometimes that she wasn't really enjoying it. She was worried about the baby or just plain sleepy. But she had to come. It made her pleased to know next day that she had done it and got away with it."

"Didn't you point out that it would make trouble for both of you if it were discovered?"

"I don't see how it could affect me," said Pullen sulkily.

"I think you're pretending to be a great deal more simple than you are, surely. I'm ready to believe that you and Miss Jupp weren't lovers because I like to think I know when people are telling the truth and because it fits in with what I know so far of both of you. But you can't honestly believe that other people would be so accommodating. The facts bear one obvious interpretation and that is the one most people would put on them, especially in the circumstances."

"That's right. Just because the kid had an illegitimate child then she must be a nymphomaniac." The boy used this last word self-consciously as if it were one he had only recently known and had not used before.

"You know, I doubt whether they'd understand what that word means. Perhaps people have rather nasty minds, but then it's surprising how often the nastiness is justified. I don't think Sally Jupp was being very fair to you when she used these stables as a retreat from Martingale. Surely you must have thought that, too?"

"Yes, I suppose so." The boy looked away unhappily and Dalgleish waited. He felt that there was still something to be explained but that Pullen was enmeshed in his own inarticulateness and frustrated with the difficulty of explaining the girl he had known, alive, gay and foolhardy, to two officers of police who had never even met her. The difficulty was easily understood. He had no doubt how Pullen's story would look to a jury and was glad that it would never be his job to convince twelve good men and true that Sally Jupp, young, pretty and already lapsed from grace, had been sneaking out of her bedroom at night and leaving her baby alone, however briefly, for the sole pleasure of intellectual discussion with Derek Pullen.

"Did Miss Jupp ever suggest to you that she was afraid of anyone or had an enemy?" he asked.

"No. She wasn't important enough to have enemies."

"Not until Saturday night, perhaps," thought Dalgleish.

"She never confided in you about her child, who the father was, for example?"

"No." The boy had mastered some of his terror and his voice was sullen.

"Did she tell you why she wanted to go to London last Thursday afternoon?"

"No. She asked me to look after Jimmy because she was sick of carting him around the forest and wanted to get away from the village. We arranged where she was to hand him over at Liverpool Street Station. She brought the folding pram and I took him to St. James's Park. In the evening I handed him back and we travelled home separately. We weren't going to give the village tabbies anything else to gossip about."

"You never thought she might be falling in love with you?"

"I knew damn well she wasn't." He gave Dalgleish one quick direct glance and then said, as if the confidence surprised him:

"She wouldn't even let me touch her."

Dalgleish waited for a moment and then said quietly:

"Those aren't your normal spectacles, are they? What happened to the ones you usually wear?"

The boy almost snatched them from his nose and closed his hands over the lenses in a gesture which was pathetic in its futility. Then, realizing the significance of that instinctive gesture, he dug in his pocket for a handkerchief and made a show of cleaning the lenses.

His hands shook as he pushed the spectacles back on his nose where they rested lopsidedly, his voice croaked with fright:

"I lost them. That is, I broke them. I'm having them mended."

"Did you break them at the same time as you got that bruise over your eye?"

"Yes. I knocked into a tree."

"Indeed. The trees around here seem curiously hazardous. Dr. Maxie grazed his knuckle on the bark of one, I'm told. Could it have been the same tree?"

"Dr. Maxie's troubles are nothing to do with me. I don't know what you mean."

"I think you do," said Dalgleish gently. "I'm going to ask you to think over what we've said and later I shall want you to make a statement and sign it. There isn't any tremendous hurry. We know where to find you if we want you. Talk it over with your father when he comes in. If either of you want to see me let me know. And remember this: someone killed Sally. If it wasn't you, then you've got nothing to fear. Either way, I hope you'll find the courage to tell us what you know." He waited for a moment but his eyes met only the glazed stare of fear and resolution. After a minute he turned away and beckoned Martin to follow.

Half an hour later the telephone rang at Martingale. Deborah, carrying her father's tray through the hall, paused, balanced it on her hip, and lifted the receiver. A minute later she put her head round the drawing-room door.

"It's for you, Stephen. The 'phone. Derek Pullen of all people."

Stephen, home unexpectedly for a few hours only, did not look up from his book but Deborah could see the sudden arrest of movement and the slight tensing of his back.

"Oh Lord, what does he want?"

"He wants you. He sounds pretty worried."

"Tell him I'm busy, Deb."

Deborah translated this message into the semblance of civility. The voice at the end of the line rose into incoherence. Holding the receiver away from her ear Deborah made soothing noises and felt the well of hysterical laughter which nowadays was never far submerged. She went back to the drawing-room.

"You'd better come, Stephen. He really is in a bad way. What on earth have you been up to? He says the police have been with him."

"Is that all? He's not the only one. Tell him they've been with me for about six hours all told. And they haven't finished yet. Tell him to keep his mouth shut and stop flapping."

"Hadn't you better tell him yourself?" suggested Deborah sweetly. "I'm not in your confidence arid I'm certainly not in his."

Stephen swore softly and went to the telephone. Pausing in the hall to balance her tray, Deborah could hear his quick impatient expostulations.

"All right. All right. Tell them if you want to. I'm not stopping you. They're probably listening in to this conversation anyway. . . . No, as a matter of fact I didn't, but don't let that influence you . . . Quite the little gentleman, aren't you. . . . My dear man, I don't care a damn what you tell them, or when or how, only for God's sake don't be such a bore about it. Good-bye."

Moving out of earshot along the gallery, Deborah thought sadly, "Stephen and I have grown so far apart that I could ask him outright whether he killed Sally without being certain what answer I'd get."

2

Dalgleish and Martin sat in the small parlour of The Moonraker's Arms in that state of repletion without satisfaction which commonly follows a poor meal. They had been assured that Mrs. Piggott who, with her husband, kept the inn, was noted for her good plain cooking and plenty of it. The expression had struck ominously on the ears of men whose travels had inured them to most of the vagaries of good plain English fare. It is probable that Martin suffered most. His war service in France and Italy had given him a taste for continental food which he had been indulging ever since on holidays abroad. Most of his spare time and all of his spare money was spent in this way. He and his cheerful, enterprising wife were enthusiastic and unsophisticated travellers, confident of their ability to be understood, tolerated and well fed in almost any corner of Europe. So far, strangely enough, they had never been disappointed. Sitting in deep abdominal distress

Martin let his mind rumble on *cassoulet de Toulouse* and remembered with yearning the *poularde en vessu* he had first eaten in a modest hotel in the Ardèche. Dalgleish's needs were at once simpler and more exacting. He merely craved simple English food properly cooked.

Mrs. Piggott was reputed to take trouble with her soups. This was true in so far as the packaged ingredients had been sufficiently well mixed to exclude lumps. She had even experimented with flavours and today's mixture of tomato (orange) and oxtail (reddish brown), thick enough to support the spoon unaided, was as startling to the palate as to the eye. Soup had been followed by a couple of mutton chops nestling artistically against a mound of potato and flanked with tinned peas larger and shinier than any peas which had ever seen pod. They tasted of soya flour. A green dye which bore little resemblance to the colour of any known vegetable seeped from them and mingled disagreeably with the gravy. An apple and black-currant pie had followed in which neither of the fruits had met each other nor the pastry until they had been arranged on the plate by Mrs. Piggott's careful hand and liberally blanketed with synthetic custard.

Martin wrenched his mind from a contemplation of these culinary horrors and fixed it on the matter in hand.

"It's curious, sir, that Dr. Maxie should have fetched Mr. Hearne to help with the ladder. It's one that a strong man can manage on his own.

The quickest way to the old stable block would have been down the back stairs. Instead of that, Maxie goes to find Hearne. It looks as if he wanted a witness to the finding of the body."

"That's possible, of course. Even if he didn't kill the girl he may have wanted a witness to whatever was to be found in that room. Besides that, he was in pyjamas and dressing-gown. Hardly the most convenient garb for climbing up ladders and through windows."

"Sam Bocock confirmed Dr. Maxie's story to some extent. Not that it means much until the time of death is established. Still, it does prove he was telling the truth on one point."

"Sam Bocock would confirm anything the Maxies said. That man would be a gift to the defending counsel. Apart from his natural gift for saying little while creating an impression of absolute and incorruptible veracity he honestly believes that the Maxies are innocent. You heard him. 'They're good people up at the house.' A simple statement of truth. He would maintain it against the evidence of God Almighty at the Judgment Seat itself. The Old Bailey isn't likely to frighten him."

"I thought him an honest witness, sir."

"Of course you did, Martin. I would have liked him better if he hadn't looked at me with that curious expression, half amused, half pitying, which I've noticed before on the faces of old country people. You're a countryman yourself. No doubt you can explain it."

No doubt Martin could, but his was a nature in

which discretion had long taken precedence of valour.

"He seemed a very musical old gentleman. That was a fine record-player he had. It looked funny seeing a hi-fi instrument in a cottage like that."

The player, with its surrounding racks of long-play records, had indeed struck an incongruous note in the cottage sitting-room where almost every other article was a legacy from the past. Bocock evidently shared the normal countryman's respect for fresh air. The two small windows were shut; showed, indeed, no signs of ever having been opened. The wallpaper bore the entwined and faded roses of another era. Hung in erratic profusion were the trophies and mementoes of the First World War, a posse of mounted cavalrymen, a small glass frame of medals, a luridly coloured reproduction of King George V and his Queen. There were the family photographs, relations whom no casual observer could hope to identify. Was the serious bewhiskered young man with his Edwardian bride Bocock's father or grandfather? Could he really have a personal memory of a family loyalty for these sepia groups of bowler-hatted countrymen in their Sunday best with their solid sloping-bosomed wives and daughters? Above the mantelpiece were the newer photographs. Stephen Maxie, proud on his first shaggy pony with an unmistakable but younger Bocock by his side. A pigtailed Deborah Maxie bending from the saddle to receive her rosette. For all its conglomeration of old and new, the room bore evidence of an old soldier's disciplined care of his personal chattels.

Bocock had welcomed them in with an easy dignity. He had been having his tea. Although he lived alone he had the woman's habit of putting everything edible on the table at once, presumably to provide for any sudden whim of taste. There had been a loaf of crusty bread, a pot of jam supporting its spoon, an ornate glass jar of sliced beetroot and one of spring onions, and a cucumber stuck precariously in a small jug. In the middle of the table a bowl of lettuce disputed with a large and obviously home-baked cake for pride of place. Dalgleish had recalled that Bocock's daughter was married to a farmer in Nessingford and kept an eye on her father. The cake was probably a recent offering of filial duty. In addition to this bounty there was evidence by sight and smell that Bocock had just finished a meal of fried fish and chipped potatoes.

Dalgleish and Martin were ensconced in the heavy armchairs which flanked the fireplace—even on that warm July day there was a small fire burning, its faint incandescent flame hardly visible in a shaft of sunlight from the western window—and were offered cups of tea. This done, Bocock obviously felt that the obligations of hospitality had been met and that it was the duty of his guests to announce their business. He carried on with his tea, snapping off pieces of bread with lean brown hands and casting them almost absent-mindedly into his mouth where they were chewed and turned in silent concentration. He volunteered no remarks of his own, answered Dalgleish's questions with a deliberation which gave the impression of lack of interest rather than any unwillingness to co-operate and he regarded both policemen with that frank amused appraisal which Dalgleish, his thighs prickled by the horsehair and his face sweating with the heat, found a little disconcerting and more than a little irritating.

The slow catechism had produced nothing new, nothing unexpected. Stephen Maxie had been at the cottage the previous evening. He had arrived during the nine o'clock news. Bocock couldn't say when he had left. It had been latish. Mr. Stephen would know. Very late? "Aye. After eleven. Maybe later. Maybe a goodish bit later." Dalgleish remarked dryly that no doubt Mr. Bocock would remember more precisely when he had had time to think about it. Bocock admitted the force of this possibility. What had they talked about? "Listened to Beethoven mostly. Mr. Stephen wasn't much of a one for talking." Bocock spoke as if deploring his own volubility and the distressing garrulity of the world at large and of policemen in particular. Nothing else emerged. He had not noticed Sally at the fête except during the latish part of the afternoon when she gave the baby a ride in her arms on one of the horses, and about six o'clock when one of the Sunday school children's balloons had got caught in an elm and Mr. Stephen had fetched the ladder to get it down.

Sally had been with him then with her child in the pram. Bocock remembered her holding the foot of the ladder. Apart from that he hadn't noticed her about. Yes, he had seen young Johnnie Wilcox. That was at ten to four or thereabouts. Sneaking away from the tea-tent he was with as suspicious-looking a bundle as Bocock had seen. No, he hadn't stopped the boy. Young Wilcox was a good enough lad. None of the boys liked helping with the teas. Bocock hadn't much cared for it in his young days. If Wilcox said he left the tent at four-thirty he was a bit out, that's all. That lad hadn't put in more than thirty minutes' work at the most. If the old man wondered why the police should be interested in Johnnie Wilcox and his peccadilloes he gave no sign. All Dalgleish's questions were answered with equal composure and apparent candour. He knew nothing of Mr. Maxie's engagement and had heard no talk of it in the village, either before or after the murder. "Some folks'll say anything. You've no call to mind village talk. They're good people up at the house." That had been his final word. No doubt, if and when he had talked to Stephen Maxie and knew what was wanted, he would remember more clearly the time when Maxie had left him the previous night. At the moment he was wary. But his intelligence was clear. They had left him still eating, sitting in solitary and impressive state among his music and his memories.

"No," said Dalgleish. "We're not likely to get anything helpful about the Maxies out of Bocock.

If young Maxie was looking for an ally he knew where to go. We've gained something though. If Bocock is right about times, and he's certainly more likely to be accurate than Johnnie Wilcox, the meeting in the loft probably took place before four-thirty. That would fit in with what we know of Jupp's subsequent movements, including the scene in the tea-tent when she appeared in a duplicate of Mrs. Riscoe's dress. Jupp hadn't been seen in it before four-forty-five p.m. so that she must have changed after the interview in the stable loft."

"It was a funny thing to do, sir. And why wait until then?"

"She may have bought the dress with the idea of wearing it publicly on some occasion or other. Perhaps something happened at that interview which freed her from any future dependence on Martingale. She could afford to make a last gesture. On the other hand, if she knew before last Saturday that she was going to marry Maxie, she was presumably free to make her gesture whenever the fancy took her. There's a curious conflict of evidence about that proposal of marriage. If we are to believe Mr. Hinks—and why not?—Sally Jupp certainly knew that she was to marry someone when she met him on the previous Thursday. I find it difficult to believe that she had two prospective bridegrooms and there isn't a surfeit of obvious candidates. And while we're considering young Maxie's love life here's something you haven't seen."

He handed over a thin sheet of official-looking writing-paper. It bore the name of a small coastal hotel.

Dear Sir,

Although I have my reputation to think of and am not particularly anxious to be mixed up in police matters, I think it my duty to inform you that a Mr. Maxie stayed at this hotel last May 24th with a lady he signed for as his wife. I have seen a photograph in the *Evening Clarion* of Dr. Maxie who is mixed up in the Chadfleet murder case and who the papers say is a bachelor and it is the same one. I have not seen any photographs of the dead girl so could not swear to her, but I thought it my duty to bring the above to your notice. Of course it may not mean anything and I do not wish to be mixed up in anything unpleasant so I would be grateful if my name could be kept out of this. Also the name of my hotel which has always catered for a very good class of people. Mr. Maxie only stayed for one night and they were a very quiet couple, but my husband thinks it is our duty to bring this information to your notice. It is, of course, entirely without prejudice.

Yours faithfully,

LILY BURWOOD (Mrs.)

"The lady seems curiously concerned with her duty," said Dalgleish, "and it is a little difficult to see what she can mean by 'without prejudice'. I feel that her husband has a great deal to do with this letter, including the phraseology, without quite managing to bring himself to signing it. Anyway, I sent that eager young fledgeling, Robson, down to investigate and I've no doubt he enjoyed himself hugely. He managed to convince them that the night in question has nothing to do with the murder and that the best interests of the hotel will be served by forgetting the whole thing. It isn't quite as simple as that, though. Robson took some photographs down with him, one or two of those taken at the fête, and they confirmed a rather interesting little theory. Any idea who young Maxie's partner in sin was?"

"Would it be Miss Bowers, sir?"

"It would. I hoped that might surprise you."

"Well, sir, if it had to be someone from here she was the only one. There isn't any evidence that Dr. Maxie and Sally Jupp had been carrying on. And that was nearly a year ago."

"So you aren't inclined to pay much attention to it?"

"Well, the young today don't seem to make so much of it as I was taught to."

"It's not that they sin less but that they bear their sins more lightly. But we have no evidence that Miss Bowers feels the same. She may easily have been very hurt by what happened. She doesn't strike me as an unconventional person and she is very much in love and not particularly clever at concealing the fact. I think she is desperately anxious to marry Dr. Maxie and her chances have, after all, increased since Saturday night. She was present at the scene in the drawing-room. She knew what she had to lose."

"Do you think it's still going on, sir?" Sergeant Martin could never bring himself to be more explicit about these sins of the flesh. He had seen and heard enough in thirty years of police work to have shattered most men's illusions, but he was of a tough yet gentle disposition and could never believe that men were either as wicked or as weak as the evidence consistently proved them to be.

"I should think it very unlikely. That week-end was probably the only excursion into passion. Perhaps it wasn't particularly successful. Perhaps it was, as you rather unkindly suggest, a mere bagatelle. It's a complication though. Love, that kind of love, is always a complication. Catherine Bowers is the sort of woman who tells her man that she will do anything for him, and sometimes does."

"Could she have known about the tablets though, sir?"

"No one admits to having told her and I think she was telling the truth when she said she knew nothing. Sally Jupp might have told her but they weren't on particularly good terms, in fact they weren't on any terms at all as far as I can see, and it seems unlikely. But that proves nothing. Miss Bowers must have known that there were sleeping-tablets of some kind in the house and where they were likely to be kept and the same thing applies to Hearne."

"It seems strange that he's able to stay around."

"That probably means that he thinks one of the family did it and wants to be on the spot to see that we don't get the same idea. He may actually know who did it. If so, he's not likely to slip up, I'm afraid. I got Robson on to him, too. His report, stripped of a lot of psychological jargon about everyone he interviewed, is much what I expected. Here we are. All the details on Felix Georges Mortimer Hearne. He has a fine war record, of course. God knows how he did it or what it did to him. Ever since 1945 he seems to have flitted around doing a little writing and not much else. He is a partner in Hearne and Illingworth the publishers. His great-grandfather was old Mortimer Hearne who founded the firm. His father married a French woman, Mlle Annette D'Apprius, in 1919. The marriage brought more money into the family. Felix was born in 1921. Educated in the usual and expensive places. Met Deborah Riscoe through her husband who was at school with him, although considerably his junior, and as far as Robson can tell, never saw Sally Jupp until he met her in this house. He has a very pleasant little house in Greenwich, still true to type you see, and an ex-batman to look after him. Gossip says that he and Mrs. Riscoe are lovers, but there's no evidence, and Robson says you would get nothing out of the man-servant. I doubt whether there's anything to get. Mrs. Riscoe was certainly lying when she said they spent all Saturday night together. I suppose Felix Hearne might have murdered Sally Jupp to save Deborah Riscoe from embarrassment, but a jury wouldn't believe it and neither would I."

"There is no mention of his having the drug in his possession?"

"None at all. I don't think there's much doubt that the Sommeil used to drug Sally Jupp came from the bottle which was taken from Mr. Maxie's cupboard. Still, other people did have the stuff. The Martingale bottle could have been hidden in that melodramatic way as a blind. According to Dr. Epps he prescribed Sommeil for Mr. Maxie, Sir Reynold Price and Miss Pollack of St. Mary's. None of these insomniacs can account for the correct dose. I'm not surprised at that. People are very careless about medicines. Where's that report? Yes, here we are. Mr. Maxie we know all about. Sir Reynold Price. His Sommeil was prescribed in January of this year and dispensed by Goodliffes of the City on January 14th. He had twenty three-gr. tablets and says that he took about half and then forgot all the rest. Apparently his insomnia was quickly overcome. Taking the common-sense view his was the bottle of nine tablets left in his overcoat pocket and found by Dr. Epps. Sir Reynold is ready enough to claim them without being able to remember putting them in his pocket. It's not a very likely place to keep sleeping-tablets, but he spends nights away from home and says that he probably picked them up in a hurry. We know all about Sir Reynold Price, our local business man *cum* farmer, making a calculated loss on the second activity to compensate for his profits on the first. He fumes against what he calls the desecration of Chadfleet New Town from a Victorian pseudo-castle so ugly that I'm surprised someone hasn't formed a trust to preserve it. Sir Reynold is a philistine, no doubt, but not, I think, a murderer. Admittedly he has no alibi for last Saturday night and all we know from his staff is that he left home in his car at about ten p.m. and didn't return until early Sunday morning. Sir Reynold is being so guilty and embarrassed by this absence, is so patently trying to preserve a gentlemanly reticence, that I think we can take it that there's a 'little woman' in the case. When we really put on the pressure and he appreciates that there's a murder charge involved I think we shall get the lady's name. These one-night excursions are fairly regular with him and I don't think they had anything to do with Jupp. He would hardly make himself conspicuous by taking his Daimler on a surreptitious visit to Martingale.

"We know about Miss Pollack. She seems to have regarded the tablets as a cocaine addict ought to regard cocaine, but so seldom does. She wrestled long with the twin evils of temptation and insomnia and ended by trying to put the Sommeil down the w.c. Miss Liddell dissuades her and returns them to Dr. Epps. Dr. Epps, according again to Robson, thinks he may have had them back but isn't sure. There weren't enough to

be a really dangerous dose and they were labelled. Shockingly careless of someone I suppose, but then people are careless. And Sommeil,
of course, isn't on the D.D.A. Besides, it only
took three tablets to drug Sally Jupp and, taking
the common-sense view, those tablets came
from the Martingale bottle."

"Which leads us back to the Maxies and their
guests."

"Of course. And it's not such a stupid crime as
it appears on the face of it. Unless we can find
those tablets and get some evidence that one of
the Maxies administered them, there's no hope
of getting a conviction. You can see how it would
go. Sally Jupp knew about the tablets. She might
have taken them herself. They were put into Mrs.
Riscoe's mug. No evidence to show they were
meant for Sally Jupp. Anyone could have got into
the house during the fête and lain in wait for the
girl. No adequate motive. Other people had access to Sommeil. And as far as I know at present
he might be right."

"But if the murderer had used more of the tablets and killed the girl that way there might have
been no suspicion of murder."

"It couldn't be done. Those barbiturates are
notoriously slow-acting if you want to kill. The
girl might have been in a coma for days and then
recovered. Any doctor would know that. On the
other hand it would be difficult to smother a
strong and healthy girl, or even to get into her
bedroom unobserved, unless she were drugged.

The combination was risky for the murderer, but not as risky as one method on its own. Besides, I doubt whether anyone would swallow a fatal dose without suspecting something. Sommeil is supposed to be less bitter than most of these sleeping-tablets, but it's not tasteless. That is probably why Sally Jupp left most of the cocoa. She could hardly have felt sleepy with so small a dose in her, and yet she still died without a struggle. That's the curious part of it. Whoever entered that bedroom must have been either expected by Jupp or at least not feared. And if that were so, why the drugging? They may be unconnected but it's really too much of a coincidence that someone should put a dangerous dose of barbiturate in her drink on the same night as someone else chooses to throttle her. Then there is the curious distribution of fingerprints. Someone went down that stack-pipe, but the only prints are those of Jupp herself and they're possibly not recent. The cocoa tin was found empty in the dustbin with the paper lining missing. The tin bore the prints of Jupp and Bultitaft. The lock of the bedroom has a print of Jupp only, although it's badly smudged. Hearne says that he protected the lock with his handkerchief when he opened the door which, considering the circumstances, shows some presence of mind. Perhaps too much presence of mind. Hearne of all these people is the one least likely to lose his head in an emergency or to overlook any essential points."

"Something had rattled him pretty badly by the time he came to be questioned, though."

"It had indeed, Sergeant. I might have reacted more positively to his offensiveness if I hadn't known it was only pure funk. It takes some people that way. The poor devil was almost pitiable. It was a surprising exhibition coming from him. Even Proctor put up a better show and heaven knows he was scared enough."

"We know Proctor couldn't have done it."

"So presumably does Proctor. Yet he was lying about a number of things and we shall break him when the time's right. I think he was telling the truth about that telephone call, though, or at least part of the truth. It was unlucky for him that his daughter took the call. If he had answered the 'phone I doubt whether we should have been told about it. He still maintains that the call was from Miss Liddell and Beryl Proctor confirms that the caller gave that name. First of all Proctor tells his wife and us that she was merely ringing to give him news of Sally. When we question him again and tell him that Liddell denies making the call he still persists that the call was either from her or from someone impersonating her, but admits that she told him that Sally was engaged to be married to Stephen Maxie. That would certainly be a more reasonable motive for the call than a general report on his niece's progress."

"It's interesting how many people claim to have known about this engagement before it actually took place."

"Or before Maxie admits that it took place. He still insists that he proposed as a result of an impulse when they met in the garden at about seven-forty p.m. on Saturday night and that he had never previously considered asking her to marry him. That doesn't mean that she hadn't considered it. She may even have expected it. But surely it was asking for trouble to spread the glad news in advance. And what possible motive had she for telling her uncle unless it was an understandable urge to gloat over him or disconcert him? Even so, why pretend to be Miss Liddell?"

"You're satisfied that Sally Jupp made that call then, sir?"

"Well—we've been told, haven't we, what a good mimic she was? I think we can be certain that Jupp made that call and it's significant that Proctor isn't yet willing to admit as much. Another minor mystery, which we'll very likely never solve, is where Sally Jupp spent the hours between putting her child to bed on Saturday night and her final appearance on the main staircase at Martingale. No one admits to having seen her."

"Doesn't that make it likely that she stayed in her room with Jimmy and then went to get her last night drink when she knew that Martha would have gone to bed and the coast be clear?"

"It's certainly the likeliest explanation. She would hardly have been welcome either in the drawing-room or the kitchen. Perhaps she wanted to be alone. God knows, she must have had plenty to think about!"

They sat in silence for a moment. Dalgleish pondered on the curious diversity of the clues which he felt were salient in the case. There was Martha's significant reluctance to dwell on one of Sally's shortcomings. There was the bottle of Sommeil pressed hastily into the earth. There were an empty cocoa tin, a golden-haired girl laughing up at Stephen Maxie as he retrieved a child's balloon from a Martingale elm, an anonymous telephone call and a gloved hand briefly glimpsed as it closed the trap-door into Bocock's loft. And at the heart of the mystery, the clue which could make all plain, lay the complex personality of Sally Jupp.

Chapter Eight

1

THE THURSDAY MORNING list at St. Luke's had been a heavy one and it was not until he sat down for lunch that Stephen Maxie remembered Sally. Then, as always, the remembrance came down like a knife severing appetite, cutting him off from the careless and undemanding pleasure of everyday life. The talk at table sounded false; a barrage of trivialities put up to cover his colleagues' embarrassment at his presence. The newspapers were too tidily folded away in case a chance headline should draw attention to the presence among them of a suspected murderer. They included him too carefully in their conversation. Not too much in case he should think they were sorry for him. Not too little in case he should think they were avoiding him. The meat on his plate was as tasteless as cardboard. He forced down a few more mouthfuls—it would never do if the suspect went right off his food—and made a show of despising the pudding. The need for action was upon him. If the police could not bring this thing to a head perhaps he could. With a murmured apology he left the residents to their speculation. And why not? Was it so very surprising that they wanted to ask him the one crucial question. His mother, her hand over his on the telephone, her ravaged face turned to him in desperate inquiry, had wanted to ask the same. And he had replied, "You don't have to ask. I know nothing about it. I swear it."

He had a free hour and he knew what he wanted to do. The secret of Sally's death must lie in her life, and probably in her life before she came to Martingale. Stephen had the conviction that the baby's father would hold the key if only he could be found. He did not analyse his motives, whether this urge to find an unknown man had its roots in logic, curiosity or jealousy. It was enough to find relief in action, however fruitless its results.

He remembered the name of Sally's uncle but not the full address and it took some time to hunt through the Proctors in search of a Canningbury number. A woman answered in the stilted, artificial voice of one unused to the telephone. When he announced himself there was a silence so

long that he thought they must have been cut off.
He sensed her distrust like a physical impulse
along the wire and tried to propitiate it. When she
still hesitated he suggested that she might prefer
him to ring later and speak to her husband. The
proposal was not meant as a threat. He had merely
imagined that she was one of those women who
are incapable of even the simplest independent
action. But the result of his suggestion was surprising. She said quickly, "Oh, no! No! There
wasn't any need for that. Mr. Proctor didn't want
to talk about Sally. It wouldn't do to telephone Mr.
Proctor. After all it couldn't do any harm to tell Mr.
Maxie what he wanted to know. Only it would be
better if Mr. Proctor didn't know that he had
'phoned." Then she gave the address Stephen
wanted. When she became pregnant, Sally had
been working for the Select Book Club, at Fal-
coner's Yard in the City.

The Select Book Club had its offices in a courtyard near St. Paul's Cathedral. It was approached
through a narrow passage, dark and difficult to
find, but the courtyard itself was full of light and
as quiet as a provincial cathedral close. The grind-
ing crescendo of city traffic was muted to a faint
moan like the far sound of the sea. The air was
full of the river smell. There was no difficulty in
finding the right house. On the sunlit side of the
court a small bay window was dressed with the
Select Book Club choices arranged with carefully
contrived casualness against a draped back-cloth
of purple velvet. The Club had been carefully

named. Select Books catered for that class of reader which likes a good story without caring much who writes it, prefers to be spared the tedium of personal choice, and believes that a bookcase of volumes equal in size and bound in exactly the same colour gives tone to any room. Select Books preferred virtue to be rewarded and vice suitably punished. They eschewed salacity, avoided controversy and took no risks with unestablished writers. Not surprisingly they often had to look far back in the publishers' lists to produce a current choice. Stephen noticed that only a few of the selected volumes had originally borne the imprint of Hearne and Illingworth. He was surprised that there were any.

The front door steps were scrubbed white and the open door led into a small office obviously furnished for the convenience of those customers who preferred to collect their monthly book in person. As Stephen entered an elderly clergyman was suffering the prolonged and sprightly farewells of the woman in charge who was determined that he should not escape until the merits of the current choice, including details of the plot and the really astonishing surprise ending, had been explained in detail. This done, there were the members of his family to inquire for and his opinion of last month's choice to be solicited. Stephen waited in patience until this was concluded and the woman was free to turn her determinedly bright glance on him. A small framed card on the desk proclaimed her as Miss Titley.

"I'm so sorry to have kept you waiting. You're a new customer, aren't you? I don't think I've had the pleasure before? I get to know everyone in time and they all know me. That was Canon Tatlock. A very dear customer. But he won't be hurried, you know. He won't be hurried."

Stephen exerted all his charm and explained that he wanted to see whoever was in charge. The matter was personal and very important. He wasn't trying to sell anything and would honestly not take long. He was sorry that he couldn't be more explicit but it really was important. "To me, anyway," he added with a smile.

The smile was successful. It always had been. Miss Titley, flustered into normality by the unusual, retired to the back of her office and made a furtive telephone call. It was a little prolonged. She gave several glances at him during her conversation as if to reassure herself as to his respectability. Eventually she replaced the receiver and came back with the news that Miss Molpas was prepared to see him.

Miss Molpas had her office on the third floor. The drugget-covered stairs were steep and narrow and Stephen and Miss Titley had to stand aside on each of the landings while women clerks passed. There were no men to be seen. When he was finally shown into Miss Molpas's room he saw that she had chosen well. Three steep flights were a small price to pay for this view over city roofs, this glimpse of a silver ribbon threading down from Westminster. Miss Titley breathed an introduction which was as reverent as it was inarticulate and faded away. From behind her desk Miss Molpas rose stockily to her feet and waved him to a chair. She was a short, dark woman of remarkable plainness. Her face was round and large and her hair was cut in a thick straight fringe above her eyebrows. She wore horn-rimmed spectacles so large and heavy that they seemed an obvious aid to caricature. She was dressed in a short tweed skirt and man's white shirt with a yellow and green woven tie which reminded Stephen unpleasantly of a squashed cabbage caterpillar. She had one of the pleasantest speaking voices he had ever heard in a woman and the hand which she held out to him was cool and firm.

"You're Stephen Maxie, aren't you? Saw your picture in the *Echo.* People are saying that you killed Sally Jupp. Did you?"

"No," said Stephen. "And neither did any member of my family. I haven't come to argue about that. People can believe what they like. I wanted to know something more about Sally. I thought you might be able to help. It's the child I'm really worrying about. Now that he hasn't a mother it seems important to try to find his father. No one's come forward, but it did strike me that the man may not know. Sally was very independent. If he doesn't know and would like to do something about Jimmy—well, I think he should be given the chance."

Miss Molpas pushed a packet of cigarettes across the table at him.

"D'you smoke? No? Well, I will. You're meddling a bit, aren't you? Better get your own motives straight. You can't believe the man didn't know. Why shouldn't he? He must know now anyway. There's been enough publicity. The police have been here on the same tack but I don't imagine they're interested in the child's welfare. More likely looking for a motive. They're very thorough. You'd do better to leave them to it."

So the police had been there. It was stupid and irrational to suppose otherwise, but he found the news depressing. They would always be one step ahead. It was presumptuous to suppose that there was anything significant to be discovered about Sally that the police, experienced, persevering and infinitely patient, would not already have found. The disappointment must have shown in his face for Miss Molpas gave a shout of laughter.

"Cheer up! You may beat them to it yet. Not that I can help you much. I told the police all I know and they wrote it down most conscientiously, but I could see it wasn't getting them anywhere."

"Except to fix the guilt more firmly where they already believe it rests—on someone in my family."

"Well, it certainly doesn't rest on anyone here. I can't even produce a possible father for the child. We haven't a man on the premises. She certainly got herself pregnant while she was working here, but don't ask me how."

"What was she really like, Miss Molpas?" asked Stephen. He forced out the question against his own realization of its absurdity. They were all asking the same thing. It was as if, in the heart of this maze of evidence and doubt, someone would at last be found who could say, "This was Sally."

Miss Molpas looked at him curiously.

"You should know what she was like. You were in love with her."

"If I were I should be the last person to know."

"But you weren't." It was a statement not an impertinent question and Stephen met it with a frankness which surprised him.

"I admired her and I wanted to go to bed with her. I suppose you wouldn't call that love. Never having felt more than that for any woman, I wouldn't know."

Miss Molpas looked away from him and out towards the river.

"I should settle for that. I doubt whether you'll ever feel more. Your kind don't." She turned towards him again and spoke more briskly:

"But you were asking what I thought of her. So did the police. The answer's the same. Sally Jupp was pretty, intelligent, ambitious, sly and insecure."

"You seem to have known her very well," said Stephen quietly.

"Not really. She wasn't easy to know. She worked here for three years and I knew no more about her home circumstances when she left than I did the day I engaged her. Taking her on was an experiment. You've probably noticed that we haven't any youngsters here. They're difficult to get except at double the wages they're worth and they don't keep their minds on the job. I don't blame them. They've only a few years to find a husband and this isn't a promising hunting-ground. They can be cruel, too, if you put them to work with an older woman. Have you seen young hens pecking away at an injured bird? Well, we only employ old birds here. They may be a bit slow but they're methodical and reliable. The work doesn't call for much intelligence. Sally was too good for the job. I never understood why she stayed. She worked for a secretarial agency after finishing her training and came to us as a temporary relief when we were short of staff during a 'flu epidemic. She liked the job and asked to stay on. The Club was growing and the business justified another shorthand-typist. So I took her on. As I said, it was an experiment. She was the only member of the staff who was under forty-five."

"Staying in this job doesn't suggest ambition to me," said Stephen. "What made you think she was sly?"

"I watched her and listened to her. We're rather a collection of has-beens here and she must have known it. But she was clever, was our Sally. 'Yes, Miss Titley. Certainly, Miss Croome. Can I get it for you, Miss Melling?' Demure as a nun and respectful as a Victorian parlourmaid. She had the poor fools eating out of her hand of course. They said how nice it was to have a young thing about the office. They bought her birthday and Christmas presents. They talked to her about her career. She even asked for advice about her clothes! As if she cared a damn what we wore or what we thought! I should have thought her a fool if she had. It was a very pretty piece of acting. It wasn't altogether surprising that, after a few months of Sally, we had an office atmosphere. That's probably not a phenomenon which you have experienced. You can take it from me that it isn't comfortable. There are tensions, whispered confidence, barbed remarks, unexplained feuds. Old allies no longer speak to each other. Incongruous friendships spring up. It all plays havoc with the work, of course, although some people seem to thrive on it. I don't. I could see what the trouble was here. She'd got them all in a tizzy of jealousy and the poor fools couldn't see it. They were really fond of her. I think Miss Melling loved her. If Sally confided in anyone about her pregnancy it would have been Beatrice Melling."

"Could I talk to Miss Melling?" asked Stephen.

"Not unless you're clairvoyant. Beatrice died following an uncomplicated operation for appendicitis the week after Sally left. Left, incidentally, without even saying 'good-bye' to her. Do you believe in death from a broken heart, Dr. Maxie? No, of course you don't."

"What happened when Sally became pregnant?"

"Nothing. No one knew. We're hardly the most

likely community to spot that kind of trouble. And Sally! Meek, virtuous, quiet little Sally! I noticed that she looked wan and even thinner than usual for a few weeks. Then she was prettier than ever. There was a kind of radiance about her. She must have been about four months' pregnant when she left. She gave in her week's notice to me and asked me to tell no one. She gave me no reasons and I asked for none. Frankly, it was a relief. I had no tangible excuse for getting rid of her, but I had known for some time that the experiment was a failure. She went home one Friday and, on Monday, I told the rest of the staff that she had left. They drew their own conclusions, but no one as far as I know drew the right one. We had one glorious row. Miss Croome accused Miss Melling of having driven the girl away by her over-possessiveness and unnatural affection. To do Miss Croome justice I don't think she meant anything more sinister than that Jupp felt obliged to eat her luncheon sandwiches in Melling's company when she would rather have visited the nearest Lyons with Croome."

"So you have no idea who the man was or where she could have met him?"

"None at all. Except they met on Saturday mornings. I got that from the police. We work a five-day week here and the office is never open on Saturdays. Apparently Sally told her uncle and aunt that it was. She came up to town nearly every Saturday morning as if to work. It was a neat deception. They apparently took no interest in her job and, even had they tried to telephone her on a Saturday morning, the assumption would be that the line had been left unattended. She was a clever little liar was Sally."

The dislike in her voice was surely too bitter to be the result of anything but a personal hurt. Stephen wondered what else could have been told about Sally's office life.

"Were you surprised to hear of her death?" he asked.

"As surprised and shocked as one usually is when something as horrible and unreal as murder touches one's own world. When I thought about it I was less surprised. She seemed in some ways a natural murderee. What did astound me was the news that she was an unmarried mother. She struck me as too careful, too scheming for that kind of trouble. I would have said, too, that she was undersexed rather than the reverse. We had one curious incident when she had been here a few weeks. The packing was done in the basement then and we had a male packer. He was a quiet, middle-aged, undersized little man with about six children. We didn't see much of him, but Sally was sent down to the packing-room with a message. Apparently he made some kind of sexual advance to her. It can't have been serious. The man was genuinely surprised when he got the sack for it. He may only have tried to kiss her. I never did get the whole story. But from the fuss she made you'd have thought she was stripped naked and raped.

It was all very estimable of her to be so shocked, but most girls today seem to be able to cope with that kind of situation without having hysterics. And she wasn't play-acting that time. It was real, all right. You can't mistake genuine fear and disgust. I felt rather sorry for Jelks. Luckily I have a brother with a business in Glasgow, which was the man's home town, and I was able to get him fixed up there. He's doing well and, no doubt, he's learnt his lesson. But, believe me, Sally Jupp was no nymphomaniac."

That much Stephen had known for himself. There seemed nothing more to be learnt from Miss Molpas. He had already been away from the hospital for over an hour and Standen would be getting impatient. He said his "good-byes" and made his own way back to the ground-floor office. Miss Titley was still in attendance and had just finished pacifying an aggrieved subscriber whose last three books had failed to satisfy. Stephen waited for a moment while they finished their conversation. The neat rows of maroon-backed volumes had touched a chord of memory. Someone he knew subscribed to Select Books Limited. It was no one at the hospital. Methodically he let his mind range over the bookcases of his friends and acquaintances and time brought the answer.

"I'm afraid I haven't much time for reading," he said to Miss Titley. "But the books look wonderful value. I think one of my friends is a member. Do you ever see Sir Reynold Price?"

Miss Titley did indeed see Sir Reynold. Sir Reynold was a dear member. He came in himself for his monthly books and they had such interesting talks together. A charming man in every way was Sir Reynold Price.

"I wonder if he ever met Miss Sally Jupp here?" Stephen asked his question diffidently. He expected it to provoke some surprise, but Miss Titley's reaction was unexpected. She was affronted. With infinite kindness but great firmness, she explained that Miss Jupp could not have met Sir Reynold at Select Books Limited. She, Miss Titley, was in charge of the public office. She had held that job for over ten years now. All the customers knew Miss Titley and Miss Titley knew them. Dealing personally with the members was a job requiring tact and experience. Miss Molpas had every confidence in Miss Titley and would never dream of putting anyone else in the public office. Miss Jupp, concluded Miss Titley, had only been the office junior. She was just an inexperienced girl.

And with this ironic parting shot Stephen had to be content.

It was nearly four when Stephen got back to the hospital. As he passed by the porter's room Colley called to him and leaned over his counter with the wariness of a conspirator. His kind old eyes were troubled. Stephen remembered that the police had been to the hospital. It was Colley they would have spoken to. He wondered how much harm the old man might have done by a too-loyal determination to give nothing away. And there was nothing to give away. Sally had only been to the hospital once. Colley could only have confirmed what the police already knew. But the porter was speaking.

"There's been a telephone call for you, sir. It was from Martingale. Miss Bowers said would you please ring as soon as you came in. It's urgent, sir."

Stephen fought down panic and made himself scan the letter-rack as if for an expected letter before replying.

"Did Miss Bowers leave a message, Colley?"

"No, sir. No message."

He decided to telephone from the public call box in the hall. There was a greater chance of privacy there even if it did mean that he was in full view of Colley. He counted out the necessary coins deliberately before entering the box. As usual there was a slight delay in getting the Chadfleet exchange but at Martingale Catherine must have been sitting by the telephone. She answered almost before the bell had rung.

"Stephen? Thank God you're back. Look, can you come home at once. Someone's tried to kill Deborah."

2

Meanwhile in the little front room of 17 Windermere Crescent, Inspector Dalgleish faced his man and moved relentlessly towards the moment of truth. Victor Proctor's face held the look of a trapped animal which knows that the last escape hole is barred but cannot even yet bring itself to turn and face the end. His dark little eyes moved restlessly from side to side. The propitiatory voice and smile had gone. Now there was nothing left but fear. In the last few minutes the lines from nose to mouth seemed to have deepened. In his red neck, scraggy as a chicken's, the Adams apple moved convulsively.

Dalgleish pressed remorselessly on.

"So you admit that this return which you made to the 'Help Them Now Association' in which you claimed that your niece was a war orphan without means was untrue?"

"I suppose I should have mentioned about the £2,000, but that was capital not income."

"Capital which you had spent?"

"I had to bring her up. It may have been left to me in trust for her but I had to feed her, didn't I? We've never had much to come and go on. She got her scholarship but we still had her clothes. It hasn't been easy let me tell you."

"And you still say that Miss Jupp was unaware that her father had left this money?"

"She was only a baby at the time. Afterwards there didn't seem any point in telling her."

"Because, by then, the trust money had been converted to your own use?"

"I used it to help keep her, I tell you. I was entitled to use it. My wife and I were made trustees and we did our best for the girl. How long would it have lasted if she'd had it when she was twenty-one? We fed her all those years without another penny."

"Except the three grants which the 'Help Them Now Association' gave."

"Well, she was a war orphan, wasn't she? They didn't give much. It helped with her school uniform, that's all."

"And you still deny having been in the grounds of Martingale House last Saturday?"

"I've told you. Why do you keep on badgering? I didn't go to the fête. Why should I?"

"You might have wanted to congratulate your niece on her engagement. You said that Miss Liddell telephoned early on the Saturday morning to tell you about it. Miss Liddell still denies that she did any such thing."

"I can't help that. If it wasn't the Liddell woman it was someone pretending to be her. How do I know who it was?"

"Are you quite sure that it wasn't your niece?"

"It was Miss Liddell I tell you."

"Did you, as a result of that telephone conversation, go to see Miss Jupp at Martingale?"

"No. No. I keep telling you. I was out cycling all day."

Deliberately Dalgleish took two photographs from his wallet and spread them out on the table. In each a bunch of children were seen entering the vast wrought-iron gates of Martingale, their faces contorted into wide grimaces in an effort to persuade the hidden photographer that there was the "Happiest-looking child to enter the fête." At their backs a few adults made their less spectacular entrances. The furtive, macintoshed figure turning hands in pockets towards the pay table was not very clearly in focus but was still unmistakable. Proctor half reached out his left hand as if to tear the photograph in two and then sank back in his chair.

"All right," he said. "I'd better tell you. I was there."

3

It had taken a little time to arrange for his work to be covered. Not for the first time Stephen envied those whose personal problems were not always secondary to the demands of their profession. By the time the arrangements were complete and he had borrowed a car he felt something like hatred for the hospital and every one of his demanding, insatiable patients. Things would have been easier if he could have spoken frankly of what had happened, but something held him back. They probably thought that the police had sent for him, that an arrest was imminent. Well, let them. Let them all bloody well think what they liked. God, he was glad to get away from a place where the living were perpetually sacrificed to keep the half-dead alive!

Afterwards he could remember nothing of the

drive home. Catherine had said that Deborah was all right, that the attempt had failed, but Catherine was a fool. What were they all doing to have let it happen? Catherine had been perfectly calm on the telephone but the details she had given, although clear, had explained nothing. Someone had got into Deborah's room early this morning and had attempted to strangle her. She had shaken herself free and screamed for help. Martha had reached her first and Felix a second later. Deborah had recovered sufficiently by then to pretend that she had awoken from a nightmare. But she had obviously been terrified and had spent the rest of the night sitting by the fire in Martha's room, with the door and windows locked and her dressing-gown collar hugged high round her neck. She had come down to breakfast with a chiffon scarf at her throat but, apart from looking pale and tired, had been perfectly composed. It was Felix Hearne who, sitting next to Deborah at luncheon, had noticed the edge of the bruise above the scarf and who had subsequently got the truth from her. He had consulted Catherine. Deborah had implored them not to worry her mother and Felix had been willing to give in to this, but Catherine had insisted on sending for the police. Dalgleish was not in the village. One of the constables thought that he and Sergeant Martin were in Canningbury. Felix had left no message except to ask that Dalgleish should visit Martingale as soon as convenient. They had told Mrs. Maxie nothing. Mr. Maxie was too ill now to be left for long and they were hoping that the bruise on Deborah's neck would have faded before her mother became suspicious. Deborah, explained Catherine, seemed more terrified of upsetting her mother than of being attacked for a second time. They were waiting for Dalgleish now, but Catherine thought that Stephen ought to know what had happened. She hadn't consulted Felix before telephoning. Probably Felix wouldn't have approved of her sending for Stephen. But it was time someone took a firm line. Martha knew nothing. Deborah was terrified that she might refuse to stay at Martingale if the truth came out. Catherine had no sympathy with that attitude. With a murderer at large Martha had the right to protect herself. It was ridiculous of Deborah to think that the attack could be kept secret much longer. But she had threatened to deny everything if the police told Martha or her mother. So would Stephen please come at once and see what he could do. Catherine really couldn't take any more responsibility herself. Stephen was not surprised. Hearne and Catherine between them seemed to have taken too much responsibility already. Deborah must be mad to try and conceal a thing like that. Unless she had her own reasons. Unless even the fear of a second attempt was better than knowing the truth. While his feet and hands worked with automatic co-ordination at brakes and throttle, wheel and gear lever, his mind, sharpened by apprehension, posed its questions. How long had it been

after Deborah's scream before Martha arrived—
and Felix? Martha slept next door. It was natural
that she should have woken first. But Felix? Why
had he agreed to hush it up? It was madness to
think that murder and attempted murder could
be treated like one of his wartime escapades.
They all knew that Felix was a bloody hero, but
his brand of heroics wasn't wanted at Martingale. How much did they know about him anyway? Deborah had behaved strangely. It was
unlike Deborah he knew to scream for help.
Once she would have fought back with more
fury than fear. But he remembered her stricken
face when Sally's body was discovered, the sudden retching, the blind stumbling for the door.
One couldn't guess how people would behave
under stress. Catherine had behaved well, Deborah badly. But Catherine had more experience
of violent death. And a better conscience?

The heavy front door of Martingale was open.
The house was strangely quiet. He could hear
only a murmur of voices from the drawing-room.
As he entered four pairs of eyes looked up at him
and he heard Catherine's quick sigh of relief.
Deborah was sitting in one of the winged chairs
before the fireplace. Catherine and Felix stood
behind her, Felix upright and watchful, Catherine
with her arms stretched over the back of the
chair and her hands resting on Deborah's shoulders in an attitude which was half-protective, half-
comforting. Deborah did not seem to resent it.
Her head was thrown back. Her high-necked

shirt was open and a yellow chiffon scarf dangled from her hand. Even from the door Stephen could see the purpling bruise above the thin shoulder-blades. Dalgleish was sitting opposite her, re-laxed on the edge of his chair, but his eyes were watchful. He and Felix Hearne confronted each other like cats across a room. Somewhere in the background Stephen was conscious of the ubiq-uitous Sergeant Martin with his notebook. In the second before anyone spoke or moved the little gilded clock chimed the three-quarters, dropping each beautiful note into the silence like a crystal pebble. Stephen moved swiftly to his sister's side and bent his head to kiss her. The smooth cheek was icy cold against his lips. As he drew back her eyes met his with a look which was hard to interpret. Could it have been entreaty—or warn-ing? He looked at Felix.

"What happened?" he asked. "Where's my mother?"

"Upstairs with Mr. Maxie. She spends most of the day with him now. We told her that inspector Dalgleish was making a routine visit. There's no need to add to her worries. Or Martha's either. If Martha takes fright and decides to go it will mean importing another trained nurse and we can't cope with that just now. Even if we could find one who would be willing to come."

"Aren't you forgetting something," said Stephen roughly. "What about Deborah? Do we all sit back quietly and wait for another attempt?" He resented both Felix's calm assumption of responsibility for the family arrangements and the inference that someone had to cope with these matters while the son of the house put his professional responsibilities before his family. It was Dalgleish who answered:

"I am looking after Mrs. Riscoe's safety, Doctor. Would you please examine her throat and let me know what you think."

Stephen turned to him.

"I prefer not to. Dr. Epps treats my family. Why not call him?"

"I'm asking you to look at the throat, not to treat it. This isn't the time to indulge in spurious professional scruples. Do as I say, please."

Stephen bent his head again. After a moment he straightened up and said, "He grasped the neck with both hands just above and behind the shoulder-blades. There is fairly extensive bruising but no nail scratches and no thumb-marks. The grip could have been with the base of the thumbs in front and the fingers behind. The larynx is almost certainly untouched. I should expect the bruises to fade in a day or two. There's no real harm done." He added, "Physically at any rate."

"In other words," said Dalgleish, "it was rather an amateur effort?"

"If you care to put it like that."

"I do care. Doesn't it suggest to you that this assailant knew his job rather well? Knew where to apply pressure and how much to apply without causing harm? Are we expected to believe that the person who killed Miss Jupp with such expertise couldn't do better than this? What do you think, Mrs. Riscoe?"

Deborah was buttoning up her shirt. She shrugged herself free of Catherine's proprietary grasp and rewound the chiffon scarf round her neck.

"I'm sorry you're disappointed, Inspector. Perhaps next time he'll make a better job of it. He was quite expert enough for me, thank you."

"I must say you seem to be taking it very coolly," cried Catherine indignantly. "If Mrs. Riscoe hadn't managed to shake herself free and scream she wouldn't be alive now. Obviously he got the best grip he could in the dark but was scared off when she called out. And this may not have been the first attempt. Don't forget that the sleeping-drug was put into Deborah's mug."

"I haven't forgotten that, Miss Bowers. Nor that the missing bottle was found under her name stake. Where were you last night?

"Helping to nurse Mr. Maxie. Mrs. Maxie and I were together for the whole of the night; except when we went to the bathroom. We were certainly together from midnight onwards."

"And Dr. Maxie was in London. This attack has certainly happened at a convenient time for you all. Did you see this mysterious strangler, Mrs. Riscoe? Or recognize him?"

"No. I wasn't sleeping very deeply. I think I was having a nightmare. I woke up when I felt the first touch of his hands on my throat. I could feel his breath on my face but I couldn't recognize him.

When I screamed and felt for the light switch he made off through the door. I put on the light and screamed. I was terrified. It wasn't a rational fear even. Somehow my dream and the attack had merged together. I couldn't tell where one horror ended and the other began."

"And yet when Mrs. Bultitaft arrived you said nothing?"

"I didn't want to frighten her. We all know there's a strangler about but we've got to get on with our jobs. It wouldn't help her to know."

"That shows a commendable concern for her peace of mind, but less for her safety. I must congratulate you all on your insouciance in the face of this homicidal maniac. For that is obviously what he is. Surely you are not trying to tell me that Miss Jupp was killed by mistake, that she was mistaken for Mrs. Riscoe?"

Felix spoke for the first time. "We're not trying to tell you anything. It's your job to tell us. We only know what happened. I agree with Miss Bowers that Mrs. Riscoe is in danger. Presumably you're prepared to offer her the protection she's entitled to."

Dalgleish looked at him.

"What time did you reach Mrs. Riscoe's room this morning?"

"About half a minute after Mrs. Bultitaft, I suppose. I got out of bed as soon as Mrs. Riscoe called out."

"And neither you nor Mrs. Bultitaft saw the intruder?"

"No. I presume he was down the stairs before we came out of our rooms. Naturally I made no search as I wasn't told until this afternoon what had happened. I've looked since, but there's no trace of anyone."

"Have you any idea of how this person got in, Mrs. Riscoe?"

"It could have been through one of the drawing-room windows. We went into the garden last night and must have forgotten to lock it. Martha mentioned that she found it open this morning."

"By 'we' do you mean yourself and Mr. Hearne?"

"Yes."

"Were you wearing your dressing-gown by the time your maid arrived in your room?"

"Yes. I had just put it on."

"And Mrs. Bultitaft accepted your story of a nightmare and suggested that you should spend the remainder of the night by the electric fire in her room?"

"Yes. She didn't want to go back to bed herself, but I made her. First of all we had a pot of tea together by her fire."

"So it comes to this," said Dalgleish. "You and Mr. Hearne take an evening walk in the garden of a house where there has recently been a murder and leave a french window open when you come in. In the night some unspecified man comes to your room, makes an inexpert attempt at strangling you for no motive which you or anyone else can suggest and then vanishes, leaving no trace.

Your throat is so little affected that you are able to scream with enough force to attract the people sleeping in near-by rooms yet, by the time they arrive in a matter of minutes, you have recovered from your fright sufficiently to lie about what has happened, a lie made more effective by the fact that you have taken the trouble to get out of bed and put on your dressing-gown with its concealing collar. Does that strike you as rational behaviour, Mrs. Riscoe?"

"Of course it doesn't," said Felix roughly. "Nothing that has happened in this house since last Saturday has been rational. But even you can hardly suppose that Mrs. Riscoe tried to strangle herself. Those bruises can't have been self-inflicted, and if they weren't, who inflicted them? Do you really suppose that a jury wouldn't believe the two crimes to be related?"

"I don't think a jury will be asked to consider that possibility," said Dalgleish evenly. "I have nearly completed my investigation into Miss Jupp's death. What happened last night isn't likely to affect my conclusions. It has made one difference. I think it's time the matter was settled and I propose to take a short cut. If Mrs. Maxie has no objection I want to see you all together in this house at eight o'clock tonight."

"Did you want something of me, Inspector?" They turned towards the door. Eleanor Maxie had come in so quietly that only Dalgleish had noticed her. She did not wait for his reply but moved swiftly to her son.

"I'm glad you're here, Stephen. Did Deborah telephone? I meant to myself if he didn't improve. It's difficult to tell, but I think there's a change. Could you get Mr. Hinks? And Charles, of course."

It was natural, Stephen thought, for her to ask for the priest before the doctor.

"I'll come up myself first," he said. "That is, if the inspector will excuse me. I don't think there is anything more we can usefully discuss."

"Not until eight o'clock tonight, Doctor."

Stung by his tone Stephen wanted, not for the first time, to point out that surgeons were addressed as "Mister." He was saved from this pedantic pettiness by a realization of its futility and of his mother's need. For days now he had hardly thought of his father. Now there were amends which he must make. For a second Dalgleish and his investigation, the whole horror of Sally's murder faded before this new and more immediate need. In this at least he could act like a son.

But suddenly Martha was blocking the door. She stood there, white and shaking, her mouth opening and shutting soundlessly. The tall young man behind her stepped past her into the room. With one terrified glance at her mistress and a stiff little gesture of her arm which was less one of ushering the stranger in than of abandoning him to the company, Martha gave an animal-like moan and disappeared. The man looked back at her with amusement and then turned to face them. He was very tall, over six feet, and his fair hair, cut short all over the head, was bleached by the sun. He was dressed in brown corduroy trousers with a leather jacket. From its open neck the throat rose sunburnt and thick, supporting a head which was arresting in its animal health and virility. He was long-legged, long-armed. Over one shoulder was slung a ruck-sack. In his right hand he carried an airline hold-all, pristine new with its golden wings. It looked as incongruous as a woman's toy in his great brown fist. Beside him Stephen's good looks paled into a commonplace elegance and all the weariness and futility which Felix had known for fifteen years seemed at once graven on his face. When he spoke his voice, confident with happiness, held no trace of diffidence. It was a soft voice slightly American in tone, and yet there could be no doubt of his Englishness.

"It seems I've given your maid a bit of a shock. I'm sorry to butt in like this but I guess Sally never told you about me. The name's James Ritchie. She'll be expecting me all right. I'm her husband." He turned to Mrs. Maxie. "She never told me exactly what sort of a job she's got here and I don't want to cause inconvenience, but I've come to take her away."

4

In the years that followed when Eleanor Maxie sat quietly in her drawing-room she would often see again in her mind's eye that gangling and confident ghost from the past confronting her from the doorway and could sense again the shocked silence which followed his words. That silence could only have lasted for seconds yet, in retrospect, it seemed as if minutes passed while he looked round at them in confident ease and they gazed back at him in incredulous horror. Mrs. Maxie had time to think how like a tableau it was, the very personification of surprise. She felt none herself. The last few days had drained her of so much emotion that this final revelation fell like a hammer on wool. There was nothing left to discover about Sally Jupp which had power to surprise any more. It was surprising that Sally was dead, surprising that she had been engaged to Stephen, surprising to learn that so many people were implicated in her life and death. To learn now that Sally had been a wife as well as a mother was interesting but not shocking. Detached from their common emotion she did not miss the quick glance that Felix Hearne gave Deborah. He was shaken all right but that swift appraisal held something, too, of amusement and triumph. Stephen looked merely dazed. Catherine Bowers had flushed deep red and was literally open-mouthed, the stock registration of surprise. Then she turned to Stephen as if throwing on him the burden of spokesman for them all. Finally Mrs. Maxie looked at Dalgleish and for a second their eyes held. In them she read a momentary but unmistakable compassion. She was conscious of thinking irrelevantly "Sally Ritchie. Jimmie Ritchie. That's why she called the child Jimmy after his father. I could never understand why it had to be Jimmy Jupp. Why are they staring at him like that? Someone ought to say something." Someone did. Deborah, white to her lips, spoke like someone in a dream:

"Sally's dead. Didn't they tell you? She's dead and buried. They say that one of us killed her." Then she began to shake uncontrollably and Catherine, getting to her before Stephen, caught her before she fell and supported her into a chair. The tableau broke. There was a sudden spate of words. Stephen and Dalgleish moved over to Ritchie. There was a murmur of "better in the business room" and the three of them were suddenly gone. Deborah lay back in her chair, her eyes closed. Mrs. Maxie could witness her distress without feeling more than a faint irritation and a passive curiosity as to what lay behind it all. Her own preoccupations were more compelling. She spoke to Catherine.

"I must go back to my husband now. Perhaps you would come to help. Mr. Hinks will be here soon and I don't expect Martha will be much use at present. This arrival seems to have unnerved her." Catherine might have replied that Martha was not the only one to be unnerved, but she murmured an acquiescence and came at once. Her real usefulness and genuine care of the invalid did not blind Mrs. Maxie to her guest's self-imposed role of the cheerful little helpmeet competent to cope with all emergencies. This last emergency might prove one too many but Catherine had plenty of stamina and the more Deborah weakened the more Catherine grew in strength. At the door Mrs. Maxie turned to Felix Hearne.

"When Stephen has finished talking to Ritchie I think he should come to his father. He's deeply unconscious, of course, but I think Stephen should be there. Deborah should come up, too, when she has recovered. Perhaps you would tell her." Answering his unspoken comment, she added, "There's no need to tell Dalgleish. His plans for tonight can stand. It will all be over before eight." Deborah was stretched back in her chair, her eyes closed. The chiffon scarf had loosened around her neck.

"What is the matter with Deborah's throat?" Mrs. Maxie sounded only vaguely interested.

"Some rather childish horseplay, I'm afraid," replied Felix. "It was as unsuccessful as it deserved to be."

Without another glance at her daughter, Eleanor Maxie left them together.

5

Half an hour later Simon Maxie died. The long years of half-life were over at last. Emotionally and intellectually he had been dead for three years. His last breath was the technicality which finally and officially severed him from a world which he had once known and loved. It was not within his capacity now to die with courage or with dignity but he died without fuss. His wife and children were with him and his parish priest said the prescribed prayers as though they could be heard and shared by that stiffened grotesque figure on the bed. Martha was not there. Afterwards the family were to say that there seemed no point in asking her. At the time they knew that her sentimental weeping would have been more than they could bear. This death-bed was only the culmination of a slow process of dying. Although they stood white-faced about the bed and tried to evoke some pietas of remembrance and grief their thoughts were with that other death and their minds reached towards eight o'clock.

Afterwards all of them met in the drawing-room, except Mrs. Maxie, who was either without curiosity about Sally's husband, or who had decided to detach herself momentarily from the murder and all its ramifications. She merely instructed the family not to let Dalgleish know that her husband was dead, then walked with Mr. Hinks back to the vicarage.

In the drawing-room Stephen poured the drinks and told his story:

"It's simple enough really. Of course I had only time for the bare details. I wanted to get up to Father. Dalgleish stayed on with Ritchie after I left and I suppose he got all the information he wanted. They were married all right. They met while Sally was working in London and married there secretly about a month before he went to Venezuela on a building job."

"But why didn't she say?" asked Catherine. "Why all the mystery?"

"Apparently he wouldn't have got the job abroad if the firm had known. They wanted an unmarried man. The pay was good and it would have given them a chance to set up house. Sally was mad keen to get married before he went. Ritchie rather thinks she liked the idea of putting one over on her aunt and uncle. She was never happy with them. The idea was that she would have stayed with them and kept on with her job. She planned to save £50 before Ritchie came back. Then, when she found the baby was coming, she decided to stick to her side of the bargain. Heaven knows why. But that part didn't surprise Ritchie. He said that was just the kind of thing that Sally would do."

"It's a pity he didn't make sure that she wasn't pregnant before he left her," said Felix dryly.

"Perhaps he did," said Stephen shortly. "Perhaps he asked her and she lied. I didn't question him about his sexual relationship. What business is that of mine? I was faced by a husband who had returned to find his wife murdered in this house, leaving a child he never even knew existed. I don't want a half an hour like that again. It was hardly the time to suggest that he might have been more careful. So might we, by God!"

He gulped down his whisky. The hand which

held the glass was shaking. Without waiting for them to speak he went on:

"Dalgleish was wonderful with him. I could like him after tonight if he were here in any other capacity. He's taken Ritchie with him. They're calling in at St. Mary's to see the child and then they hope to get a room for Ritchie at The Moonraker's Arms. Apparently he hasn't any family to go to." He paused to refill his glass. Then he went on:

"This explains a lot, of course. Sally's conversation with the vicar on Thursday, her telling him that Jimmy was going to have a father."

"But she was engaged to you!" cried Catherine. "She accepted you."

"She never actually said she'd marry me. Sally loved a mystery all right and this one was at my expense. I don't suppose she ever told anyone that she was engaged to me. We all assumed it. She was in love with Ritchie all the time. She knew he was soon coming home. He was pathetically anxious to let me know just how much in love they were. He kept crying and trying to force some of her letters on me. I didn't want to read them. Heaven knows I was hating myself enough without that. God, it was awful! But once I'd started reading I had to go on. He kept pulling them out of that bag he had and pushing them into my hand, the tears running down his face. They were pathetic, sentimental and naïve. But they were real, the emotion was genuine."

No wonder you're upset then, thought Felix. You never felt a genuine emotion in your life.

Catherine Bowers said reasonably, "You mustn't blame yourself. None of this would have happened if Sally had told the truth about her marriage. It's asking for trouble to pretend about a thing like that. I suppose he wrote to her through an intermediary."

"Yes. He wrote through Derek Pullen. The letters were sent in an envelope enclosed in one addressed to Pullen. He handed them over to Sally at pre-arranged meetings. She never told him they were from a husband. I don't know what story she concocted, but it must have been a good one. Pullen was pledged to secrecy and, as far as I know, he never gave her away. Sally knew how to choose her dupes."

"She liked amusing herself with people," said Felix. "They can be dangerous playthings. Obviously one of her dupes thought that the joke had gone far enough. It wasn't you by chance, was it, Maxie?"

The tone was deliberately offensive and Stephen took a quick step towards him. But before he could answer they heard the clang of the front door-bell and the clock on the mantelpiece struck eight.

Chapter Nine

1

BY COMMON CONSENT they met in the business room. Someone had arranged the chairs in a half circle around the heavy table, someone had filled the water carafe and placed it at Dalgleish's right hand. Sitting alone at the table with Martin behind him, Dalgleish watched his suspects as they came in. Eleanor Maxie was the most composed. She took a chair facing the light and sat, detached and at peace, looking out at the lawns and the far trees. It was as if her ordeal were already over. Stephen Maxie strode in, threw Dalgleish a glance of mingled contempt and defiance, and sat down by his mother. Felix Hearne and Deborah Riscoe came in together but did not look at each other and sat apart. Dalgleish felt that their relationship had subtly altered since the unsuccessful play-acting of the night before. He wondered that Hearne should have lent himself to so palpable a deceit. Looking at the darkening bruise on the girl's neck, only half hidden by the knotted scarf, he wondered more at the force which Hearne had apparently found it necessary to use. Catherine Bowers came in last. She flushed as she saw their eyes on her and scurried to the only vacant chair like an anxious probationer arriving late for a lecture. As Dalgleish opened his dossier he heard the first slow notes of the church bell. The bells had been ringing when he first arrived at Martingale. They had sounded often as a background to his investigation, the mood music of murder. Now they tolled like a funeral bell and he wondered irrelevantly who in the village had died; someone for whom the bells were tolling as they had not tolled for Sally.

He looked up from his papers and began to talk in his calm deep voice.

"One of the most unusual features of this crime was the contrast between the apparent premeditation and the actual execution. All the medical evidence pointed to a crime of impulse. This was not a slow strangulation. There were few of the classical signs of asphyxiation. Considerable force had been used and there was a fracture of the superior cornu of the thyroid at its base. Nevertheless, death was due to vagal inhibition and was very sudden. It may well have taken place even if the strangler had used considerably less force. The picture on the face of it was of a single unpremeditated attack. This is borne out, too, by the use of hands. If a murderer intends to kill by strangulation, it is usually done with a cord, or with a scarf, or stocking, perhaps. This isn't invariable, but you can see the reason for it. Few people can be confident of their ability to kill with the bare hands. There is one person in this room who might feel that confidence, but I don't think he would have used this method. There are more effective ways of killing without a weapon and he would have known them."

Felix Hearne murmured under his breath, "But that was in another country and besides, the wench is dead." If Dalgleish heard the quotation or sensed the slight tensing of muscles as his audience controlled the impulse to look at Hearne he made no sign but went on quietly:

"In contrast to this apparent impulse in the deed we were faced with the evidence of the attempted and partial drugging of the victim which certainly indicated an intention to render the girl insensible. This could have been with the object of getting into her bedroom more easily and without waking her or of murdering her in her sleep. I dismissed the theory of two separate and different attempts on her life in the same night. No one in this room had any reason to like Sally and some of you may even have had reason to hate her. But it was straining incredulity too far seriously to consider that two people chose the same night to attempt murder."

"If we did hate her," said Deborah quietly, "we weren't the only ones."

"There was that Pullen boy," said Catherine. "You can't tell me that there was nothing between them." She saw Deborah's wince at the solecism and went on belligerently.

"And what about Miss Liddell? It's all over the village how Sally had found out something discreditable about her and was threatening to tell. If she could blackmail one she could blackmail another."

Stephen Maxie said wearily:

"I can hardly see poor old Liddell climbing up stack-pipes, or sneaking in at the back door, to face Sally alone. She wouldn't have the nerve. And you can't imagine her seriously setting out to kill Sally with her bare hands."

"She might," said Catherine, "if she knew that Sally was drugged."

"But she couldn't have known," Deborah pointed out. "And she couldn't have put the drug in Sally's beaker, either. She and Eppy were leaving the house as Sally took the beaker up to bed. And it was my beaker she took, remember. Before that they were both in this room with Mummy."

"She took your beaker in the same way that she copied your dress," said Catherine. "But the Sommeil must have been put in it later. No one could want to drug you."

"It couldn't have been put in later," said Deborah

shortly. "What chance would there have been? I suppose one of us tiptoed in with Father's bottles of tablets, pretended to Sally that it was just a cosy social call, and then waited until she was bending over the baby and popped a tablet or two into her cocoa. It doesn't make sense."

Dalgleish's quiet voice broke in:

"None of it makes sense if the drugging and the strangling are connected. Yet, as I said, it was too great a coincidence that someone should have decided to strangle Sally Jupp on the same night as someone else set out to poison her. But there could be another explanation. What if this drugging were not an isolated incident? Suppose someone had regularly been doping Sally's evening drink. Someone who knew that only Sally drank cocoa so that the Sommeil could safely be put into the cocoa tin. Someone who knew where the drug was kept and was experienced enough to use the right amount. Someone who wanted Sally discredited and out of the house, and could complain if she persistently overslept. Someone who had probably suffered more from Sally than the rest of the household realized and was glad of any action, however apparently ineffective, which would give her a sense of power over the girl. In a sense, you see, it was a substitute for murder."

"Martha," said Catherine involuntarily. The Maxies sat silent. If they had known or guessed, none of them gave a sign. Eleanor Maxie thought with compunction of the woman she had left weeping in the kitchen for her dead master. Martha had stood up at her entrance, her thick coarse-grained hands folded over her apron. She had made no sign when Mrs. Maxie told her. The tears were the more distressing for their silence. When she spoke her voice had been perfectly controlled, although the tears still ran down her face and dripped over the quiet hands. With no fuss and without explanation she had given in her notice. She would like to leave at the end of the week. There was a friend in Herefordshire to whom she could go for a time. Mrs. Maxie had neither argued nor persuaded. That was not her way. But, bending now a courteous and attentive gaze on Dalgleish, her honest mind explored the motives which had prompted her to exclude Martha from the death-bed and interested itself in this revelation that a loyalty which the family had all taken for granted had been more complicated, less acquiescent than any of them had suspected and had at last been strained too far.

Catherine was speaking. She was apparently without apprehension and was following Dalgleish's explanation as if he were expounding an interesting and atypical case history:

"Martha could always get Sommeil of course. The family were appallingly careless over Mr. Maxie's drugs. But why should she want to dope Sally on that particular night? After the scene at dinner Mrs. Maxie had more to worry about than Sally's late rising. It was too late to get rid of her that way. And why did Martha hide the bottle under Deborah's name-peg? I always thought she was devoted to the family."

"So did the family," said Deborah dryly.

"She drugged the cocoa again that night because she didn't know about the supposed engagement," said Dalgleish. "She wasn't in the dining-room at the time and no one told her. She went to Mr. Maxie's room and she took the Sommeil and hid it in a panic because she thought she had killed Sally with the drug. If you think back you will realize that Mrs. Bultitaft was the only member of the household who didn't actually enter Sally's room. While the rest of you stood around the bed her one thought was to hide the bottle. It wasn't a reasonable thing to do but she was beyond behaving reasonably. She ran into the garden with it and hid it in the first soft earth she found. It was meant, I think, to be a temporary hiding-place. That's why she hastily marked it with the nearest peg. It was by chance that it happened to be yours, Mrs. Riscoe. Then she went back to the kitchen, emptied the remaining cocoa powder and the lining-paper into the stove, washed out the tin and put it in the dustbin. She was the only person who had the opportunity to do these things. Then Mr. Hearne came into the kitchen to see if Mrs. Bultitaft was all right and to offer his help. This is what Mr. Hearne told me." Dalgleish turned a page of his dossier and read:

"She seemed stunned and kept repeating

that Sally must have killed herself. I pointed out that that was anatomically impossible and that seemed to upset her more. She gave me one curious look . . . and burst into loud sobbing."

Dalgleish looked up at his audience. "I think we can take it," he said, "that Mrs. Bultitaft's emotion was the reaction of relief. I suspect, too, that before Miss Bowers arrived to feed the child Mr. Hearne had coached Mrs. Bultitaft for the inevitable police questioning. Mrs. Bultitaft tells me that she didn't admit to him or to any of you that she was responsible for drugging Sally. That may be true. It doesn't mean that Mr. Hearne didn't guess. He was quite ready, as he has been throughout the case, to leave well alone if it were likely to mislead the police. Towards the end of this investigation, with the faked attack on Mrs. Riscoe, he took a more positive line in attempting to deceive."

"That was my idea," said Deborah quietly. "I asked him. I made him do it."

Hearne ignored the interruption and merely said:

"I may have guessed about Martha. But she was perfectly truthful. She didn't tell me and I didn't ask. It wasn't my affair."

"No," said Dalgleish bitterly. "It wasn't your affair." His voice had lost its controlled neutrality and they looked up at him startled by his sudden vehemence.

"That has been your attitude throughout, hasn't it? Don't let's pry into each other's affairs. Don't let's be vulgarly interested. If we must have a murder let it be handled with taste. Even your efforts to hamper the police would have been more effective if you had bothered to find out a little more from each other. Mrs. Riscoe need not have persuaded Mr. Hearne to stage an attack on her while her brother was safely in London if that brother had confided in her that he had an alibi for the time of Sally Jupp's death. Derek Pullen need not have tortured himself wondering whether he ought to shield a murderer if Mr. Stephen Maxie had bothered to explain what he was doing with a ladder in the garden on Saturday night. We finally got the truth from Pullen, but it wasn't easy."

"Pullen wasn't interested in shielding me," said Stephen indifferently. "He just couldn't bear not to behave like a little gent! You should have heard him telephoning to explain just how old-school-tie he was going to be. Your secret is safe with me, Maxie, but why not do the decent thing? Damn his insolence!"

"I suppose there's no objection to us knowing what you were doing with a ladder," inquired Deborah.

"Why should there be? I was bringing it back from outside Bocock's cottage. We used it during the afternoon to retrieve one of the balloons which got caught up in his elm. You know what Bocock is. He would have dragged it up here first thing in the morning and it's too heavy for him. I suppose I was in the mood for a little masochism so I slung it over my shoulder. I wasn't to know that I'd find Pullen lurking about in the old stables. Apparently he made a habit of it. I wasn't to know, either, that Sally would be murdered and that Pullen would use his great mind to put two and two together and assume that I'd used the ladder to climb into her room and kill her. Why climb in anyway? I could have got through the door. And I wasn't even carrying the ladder from the right direction."

"He probably thought that you were trying to cast suspicion on an outside person," suggested Deborah. "Himself, for instance."

Felix's lazy voice broke in:

"It didn't occur to you, Maxie, that the boy might be in genuine distress and indecision?"

Stephen moved uneasily in his chair.

"I didn't lose any sleep over him. He had no right on our property and I told him so. I don't know how long he'd been waiting there but he must have watched me while I put down the ladder. Then he stepped out of the shadows like an avenging fury and accused me of deceiving Sally. He seems to have curious ideas about class distinctions. Anyone would think I had been exercising *droit de seigneur.* I told him to mind his own business, only less politely, and he lunged out at me. I'd had about as much as I could stand by then so I struck out and caught him on the eye, knocking off his spectacles. It was all pretty vulgar and stupid. We were too near the house to be safe so we daren't make much noise. We stood there hissing insults at each other in whispers and grovelling around in the dust to find his glasses. He's pretty blind without them so I thought I'd better see him as far as the corner of Nessingford Road. He took it that I was escorting him off the premises, but his pride would have been hurt either way so it didn't matter much. By the time we came to say good night he had obviously persuaded himself into what he imagined was an appropriate frame of mind. He even wanted to shake hands! I didn't know whether to burst out laughing or to knock him down again. I'm sorry, Deb, but he's that sort of person."

Eleanor Maxie spoke for the first time:

"It is a pity that you didn't tell us about this earlier. That poor boy should certainly have been spared a great deal of worry."

They seemed to have forgotten the presence of Dalgleish, but now he spoke:

"Mr. Maxie had a reason for his silence. He realized that it was important for you all that the police should think that a ladder had been available within easy reach of Sally's window. He knew the approximate time of death and he wasn't anxious for the police to know that the ladder hadn't been returned to the old stable before twenty past twelve. With luck we should assume that it had been there all night. For much the same reason he was vague about the time he left Bocock's cottage and lied about the time he got to bed. If Sally was killed at midnight by someone under this roof he was anxious that there should be no lack of suspects. He realized that most crimes are solved by a process of elimination. On the other hand I think he was telling the truth about the time he locked the south door. That was at about twelve thirty-three and we know now that at twelve thirty-three Sally Jupp had been dead for over half an hour. She died before Mr. Maxie left Bocock's cottage and about the same time as Mr. Wilson of the village store got out of bed to shut a creaking window and saw Derek Pullen walking quickly past, head bent, towards Martingale. Pullen was hoping, perhaps, to see Sally and to hear her explanation. But he only reached the cover of the old stables before Mr. Maxie arrived, carrying the ladder. And by then Sally Jupp was dead."

"So it wasn't Pullen?" said Catherine.

"How could it have been," said Stephen roughly. "He certainly hadn't killed her when he spoke to me and he was in no condition to turn back and kill her after I had left him. He could hardly see his way to his own front gate."

"And if Sally was dead before Stephen got back from visiting Bocock, it couldn't have been him either," pointed out Catherine. It was, Dalgleish noticed, the first time that any of them had specifically referred to the possible guilt or innocence of a member of the family.

Stephen Maxie said:

"How do you know that she was dead then? She was alive at ten-thirty p.m. and dead by the morning. That's as much as anyone knows."

"Not really," replied Dalgleish. "Two people can put the time of death closer than that. One is the murderer, but there is someone else who can help too."

2

There was a knock on the door and Martha stood there, capped and aproned, stolid as always. Her hair was strained back beneath her curiously high old-fashioned cap, her ankles bulged above the barred black shoes. If the Maxies were seeing in their mind's eye a desperate woman, clutching to herself that incriminating bottle and homing to her familiar kitchen like a frightened animal, they gave no sign. She looked as she had always looked and if she had become a stranger she was less alien than they now were to each other. She gave no explanation of her presence except to announce "Mr. Proctor for the Inspector." Then she was gone again and the shadowy figure behind her stepped forward into the light. Proctor was too angry to be disconcerted at being shown thus summarily into a roomful of people obviously occupied with their private concerns. He seemed to notice no one but Dalgleish and advanced towards him belligerently.

"Look here, Inspector, I've got to have protection. It isn't good enough. I've been trying to get you at the station. They wouldn't tell me where you were, if you please, but I wasn't going to be fobbed off with that station sergeant. I thought I'd find you here. Something's got to be done about it."

Dalgleish considered him in silence for a minute.

"What isn't good enough, Mr. Proctor?" he inquired.

"That young fellow. Sally's husband. He's been round home threatening me. He was drunk if you ask me. It's not my fault if she got herself murdered and I told him so. I won't have him upsetting my wife. And there are the neighbours. You could hear him shouting his insults right down the avenue. My daughter was there, too. It's not nice in front of a child. I'm innocent of this murder as you very well know, and I want protection."

He looked indeed as if he could have done with protection against more than James Ritchie. He was a scrawny red-faced little man with the look of an angry hen and a trick of jerking his head as he talked. He was neatly but cheaply dressed. The grey raincoat was clean and the trilby hat, held stiffly in his gloved hands, had recently acquired a new band. Catherine said suddenly, "You were in this house on the day of the murder, weren't you? We saw you on the stairs. You must have been coming from Sally's room."

Stephen glanced at his mother and said:

"You'd better come in and join the prayer meeting, Mr. Proctor. Public confessions are said to be good for the soul. Actually you've timed your entrance rather well. You are, I assume, interested in hearing who killed your niece?"

"No!" said Hearne suddenly and violently. "Don't be a fool, Maxie. Keep him out of it."

His voice recalled Proctor to a sense of his surroundings. He focused his attention on Felix and seemed to dislike what he saw. "So I'm not to stay! Suppose I choose to stay. I've a right to know what's going on." He glared round at the watchful, unwelcoming faces. "You'd like it to be me, wouldn't you? All of you. Don't think I don't know. You'd like to pin it on me all right if you could. I'd have been in queer street if she'd been poisoned or knocked on the head. Pity one of you couldn't keep your hands off her, wasn't it? But there's one thing you can't pin on me and that's a strangling. And why? That's why!"

He gave a sudden convulsive movement, there was a click and a moment of sheer unbelievable comedy as his artificial right hand fell with a thud on the desk in front of Dalgleish. They gazed at it fascinated while it lay like some obscene relic, its rubber fingers curved in impotent supplication. Breathing heavily, Proctor hitched a chair beneath himself with a deft twist of his left hand and sat there triumphantly, while Catherine turned her pale eyes on him reproachfully as if he were a difficult patient who had behaved with more than customary petulance.

Dalgleish picked up the hand.

"We knew about this, of course, although I'm glad to say that my own attention was first brought to it less spectacularly. Mr. Proctor lost his right hand in a bombing incident. This ingenious substitute is made of moulded linen and glue. It's light and strong and has three articulated fingers with knuckle joints like a real hand. By flexing his left shoulder and slightly moving his arm away from his body, the wearer can tighten a control cord which runs from the shoulder to the thumb. This opens the thumb against the pressure of a spring. Once the tension on the shoulder is released the spring automatically closes the thumb against the firm fixed index finger. It is, as you can see, a clever contraption, and Mr. Proctor can do a great deal with it. He can get through his work, ride a bicycle and present an almost normal appearance to the world. But there's one thing he can't do, and that is to kill by manual strangulation."

"He could be left-handed."

"He could be, Miss Bowers, but he isn't, and the evidence shows that Sally was killed by a strong right-handed grip." He turned the hand over and pushed it across the cable to Proctor.

"This, of course, was the hand which a certain small boy saw opening the trap-door of Bocock's stables. There could only be one person connected with this case who would be wearing leather gloves on a hot summer day and at a garden fête. This was one clue to his identity and there were others. Miss Bowers is quite right. Mr. Proctor was in Martingale that afternoon."

"What if I was? Sally asked me to come. She was my niece, wasn't she?"

"Oh, come now, Proctor," said Felix. "You aren't

going to tell us that this was a dutiful social call, that you were just dropping in to inquire after the baby's health! How much was she asking?"

"Thirty pounds," said Proctor. "Thirty pounds she was after and much good they would do her now."

"And being in need of thirty pounds," went on Felix remorselessly, "she naturally turned to her next of kin who might be expected to help. It's a touching story."

Before Proctor could answer Dalgleish broke in:

"She was asking for thirty pounds because she wanted to have some money ready for the return of her husband. It had been arranged that she should go on working and save what she could. Sally meant to keep the bargain to the last pound, baby or no baby. She intended to get this money from her uncle by a not uncommon method. She told him that she was shortly to get married, she didn't say to whom, and that she and her husband would make his treatment of her public unless he bought her silence. She threatened to expose him to his employers and the respectable neighbours of Canningbury. She talked about being done out of her rights. On the other hand, if he chose to pay up, neither she nor her husband would ever see or worry the Proctors again."

"But that was blackmail," cried Catherine. "He should have told her to go ahead and say what she liked. No one would have believed her. She wouldn't have got a penny out of me!" Proctor sat silent. The others seemed to have forgotten his presence. Dalgleish continued.

"I think Mr. Proctor would have been very willing to take your advice, Miss Bowers, if his niece hadn't made use of one particular phrase. She talked about being done out of her rights. She probably meant no more than that a difference was made in the treatment of herself and her cousin, although Mrs. Proctor would deny that this was so. She may have known more than we realize. But for reasons which we needn't discuss here that phrase struck uncomfortably on her uncle's ear. His reaction must have been interesting and Sally was intelligent enough to take the clue. Mr. Proctor is no actor. He tried to find out how much his niece knew and the more he probed the more he gave away. By the time they parted Sally knew that those thirty pounds, and perhaps more, were well within her grasp."

Proctor's grating voice broke in:

"I said I'd want a receipt from her, mind you. I knew what she was up to. I said I was willing to help her this once as she was getting married and there was bound to be expense. But that would be the end. If she tried it on again I'd go to the police, and I'd have the receipt to prove it."

"She wouldn't have tried it on again," said Deborah quietly. The men's eyes swung round to her. "Not Sally. She was only playing with you, pulling the strings for the fun of watching you dance. If she could get thirty pounds as well as her fun so

much the better, but the real attraction was seeing you sweat. But she wouldn't have bothered
to go on with it. The entertainment palled after a
time. Sally liked to eat her victims fresh."

"Oh no, no." Eleanor Maxie opened her hands
in a little gesture of protest. "She wasn't really
like that. We never really knew her." Proctor ignored her and suddenly and surprisingly smiled
across at Deborah as if accepting an ally.

"That's true enough. You knew what she was
like. I was on a string all right. She had it all
worked out. I was to get the thirty pounds that
night and bring it to her. She made me follow her
into the house and up to her room. That was bad
enough, the sneaking in and out. That's when I
met you on the stairs. She showed me the back
door and said that she would open it for me at
midnight. I was to stay in the trees at the back of
the lawn until she switched her bedroom light on
and off. That was to be the signal."

Felix gave a shout of laughter.

"Poor Sally. What an exhibitionist! She had to
have drama if it killed her."

"In the end it did," said Dalgleish. "If she hadn't
played with people Sally would be alive today."

"She was in a funny mood that day," remembered Deborah. "There was a kind of madness
about her. I don't only mean copying my dress or
pretending to accept Stephen. She was as full of
mischief as a child. I suppose it could have been
her kind of happiness."

"She went to bed happy," said Stephen. And

suddenly they were all quiet, remembering. Somewhere a clock struck sweetly and clearly but there was no other sound except the thin rasp of paper as Dalgleish turned over a page. Outside, rising into coolness and silence, was the staircase up which Sally had carried that last bedtime drink. As they listened it was almost possible to imagine the sound of a soft footfall, the brush of wool against the stairs, the echo of a laugh. Outside in the darkness the edge of the lawn was a faint blur and the desk light reflected above it like a row of Chinese lanterns hung in the scented night. Was there the suspicion of a white dress floating between them, a swirl of hair? Somewhere above them was the nursery, empty now, white and aseptic as a morgue. Could any of them face that staircase and open that nursery door without the fear that the bed might not be empty? Deborah shivered and spoke for them all. "Please," she said. "Please tell us what happened!"

Dalgleish lifted his eyes and looked at her. Then the deep level voice went on.

3

"I think the killer went to Miss Jupp's room driven by an uncontrollable impulse to find out exactly what the girl felt, what she intended, the extent of the danger from her. Perhaps there was some idea of pleading with her—although I don't think that is very likely. It is more probable that the intention was to try to arrange some kind of a bargain. The visitor went to Sally's room and either walked in or knocked and was let in. It was a person, you see, from whom nothing was feared. Sally would be undressed and in bed. She must have been sleepy but she had only taken a little of the cocoa and was not drugged, only too tired to be bothered with finesse or rational argument. She didn't trouble to get up from her bed nor to put on her dressing-gown. You may think, in view of what we have learned about her character, that she would have done so had her visitor been a man. But that is hardly the kind of evidence which is worth very much.

"We don't know yet what happened between Sally and her visitor. We only know that, when that visitor left and closed the door, Sally was dead. If we assume that this was an unpremeditated killing we can make a guess at what happened. We know now that Sally was married, was in love with her husband, was waiting for him to come to fetch her, was even expecting him daily. We can guess from her attitude to Derek Pullen and from the careful way in which she kept her secret, that she enjoyed the feeling of power that this hidden knowledge gave her. Pullen has said, "She liked things to be secret.' A woman I interviewed for whom Sally had worked said, 'She was a secretive little thing. She was with me for three years and I knew no more about her at the end of them than when she first came.' Sally Jupp kept the news of her marriage secret under very difficult circumstances. Her behaviour wasn't reasonable. Her husband was overseas and doing well. The firm would hardly have sent him home. The firm need not even have known. If Sally had told the truth someone could have been found to help her. I think she kept her secret partly because she wanted to prove her loyalty and trustworthiness and partly because she was the kind of person to whom secrecy made its appeal. It gave her an opportunity of hurting her uncle and aunt for whom she had no affection, and it provided her with considerable entertainment. It also gave her a free home for seven months. Her husband has told me, 'Sally always did say that the unmarried mothers had the best of it.' I don't suppose anyone here agrees with that, but Sally Ritchie obviously believed that we live in a society which salves its conscience more by helping the interestingly unfortunate than the dull deserving and was in the position to put her theory to the test. I think she enjoyed herself at St. Mary's Refuge. I think she sustained herself by the knowledge that she was different from the others. I imagine that she relished in advance the look on Miss Liddell's face when she knew the truth and the fun that she would have mimicking the inmates of St. Mary's to her husband. You know the sort of thing. 'Let Sal tell you about the time she was an unmarried mother.' I think, too, that she enjoyed the feeling of power which her hidden knowledge gave her. She enjoyed watching the consternation of the Maxies at a danger which only she knew had no reality."

Deborah moved uncomfortably in her chair.

"You seem to know a great deal about her. If she knew the engagement had no reality why did she consent to it? She would have saved everyone a great deal of trouble by telling Stephen the truth."

Dalgleish looked across at her.

"She would have saved her own life. But was it in character for her to tell? There was not much longer to wait. Her husband would be flying home, perhaps in the next day or two. Dr. Maxie's proposal was merely one additional complication, adding its own stimulus of excitement and amusement to the total situation. Remember, she never overtly accepted the proposal. No, I would have expected her to act as she did. She obviously disliked Mrs. Riscoe and was becoming more audacious in showing it as the time for her husband's return drew nearer. This proposal offered new chances of private amusement. I think that, when her visitor came to her, she was lying back on her bed in sleepy, happy, amused confidence, feeling, perhaps, that she held the Maxie family, the whole situation, the world itself in the hollow of her hand. Not one of the dozens of people I have interviewed have described her as kind. I don't think she was kind to her visitor. She underestimated the force of the anger and desperation which were confronting her. Perhaps she laughed. And when she did that the strong fingers closed around her throat."

There was a silence. Felix Hearne broke in by saying roughly:

"You've mistaken your profession, Inspector. That dramatic histrionic was worthy of a larger audience."

"Don't be a fool, Hearne." Stephen Maxie lifted a face drained of colour and etched with weariness. "Can't you see that he's satisfied enough with the reactions we're providing." He turned to Dalgleish with a sudden spurt of anger. "Whose hands?" he demanded. "Why go on with this farce? Whose hands?"

Dalgleish ignored him.

"Our killer goes to the door and turns out the light. This is to be the moment of escape. And then, perhaps, there comes a doubt. It may be the need to make certain just once more that Sally Jupp is dead. It may be that the child turns in his sleep and there is the natural and human wish not to leave him crying and alone with his dead mother. It may be the more selfish concern that his cries will awaken the household before the killer can make good his escape. Whatever the reason, the light is momentarily switched on again. On and then off. Waiting at the edge of the lawn and in the shelter of the trees Sydney Proctor sees what he thinks is the awaited signal. He has no watch. He must depend on the flashing light. He makes his way along the edge of the lawn towards the back door still keeping in the shadow of the trees and the shrubs."

As Dalgleish paused his audience looked towards Proctor. He was more self-possessed now and seemed, indeed, to have lost both his earlier nervousness and his defensive truculence. He took up the story simply and calmly as if the recollection of that dreadful night and the intense and concentrated interest of his audience had released him from self-consciousness and guilt. Now that he was beyond noisy self-justification they found him easier to tolerate. Like them he had been in some sense a victim of Sally. Listening, they shared the desperation and fear which had driven him forward to her door.

"I thought I must have missed the first flash. She'd said two flashes so I waited for a bit and watched. Then I thought I'd better take a chance. There wasn't any sense in messing about. I'd come so far and I might as well go on with it. She'd see that I did, anyway. It hadn't been easy to raise the thirty quid. I'd got what I could from my Post Office account, but that was only ten. I hadn't much at home, only what I'd put by for the instalments on the telly. I took that and pawned my watch at a shop in Canningbury. The chap could see I was pretty desperate I suppose, and didn't give me what it was worth. Still, I had enough to keep her quiet. I'd written out a receipt for her to sign, too. I wasn't taking any chances with her after that scene in the stables. I thought I'd just hand over the cash, make her sign the receipt and get off home. If she tried any more funny business I could threaten to charge her with blackmail. The receipt would be useful if it came to that, but I didn't think it would. She just wanted the money and afterwards she'd leave me in peace. Well, there wouldn't be much sense in trying it on again, would there? I can't raise money to order and Sally knew that well enough. She was no fool was our Sally.

"The heavy outside door was open just as she said. I had my torch and it was easy to find the stairs and get up to her room. She'd shown me the way that afternoon. It was a piece of cake. The house was dead quiet. You'd have thought it was empty. Sally's door was shut and there was no light showing through the keyhole or under the door. That struck me as queer. I wondered whether to knock, but I wasn't keen on making a sound. The whole place was so quiet it was eerie. In the end I opened the door and called to her quietly. She didn't answer. I shone the light of the torch across the room and on to the bed. She was lying there. At first I thought she was asleep and—well, it was like a reprieve. I wondered whether I ought to leave the cash on her pillow and then I thought, 'Why the hell should I?' She had asked me to come. It was up to her to stay awake. Besides, I wanted to get out of the house. I don't know when I first realized that she wasn't asleep. I went up to the bed. It was then that I knew that she was dead. Funny how you can't mistake it. I knew that she wasn't ill or unconscious. Sally was dead. One eye was closed but the other was half open. It seemed to be looking at me, so I put out my left hand and drew down the lid. I don't know what made me touch her. Damn silly thing to do really. It was just that I had to close that staring eye. The sheet was folded down under her chin just as if someone had made her comfortable. I drew it down and then I saw the bruise on her neck. Until then I don't think the word 'murder' had come into my mind. When it did, well I suppose I lost my head. I ought to have known that it was a right-handed job and that no one could suspect me, but you don't think like that when you're frightened. I still held my torch and I was shaking so that it made little circles of light round her head. I couldn't hold it steady. I was trying to think straight, wondering what to do. Then it came over me that she was dead and I was in her room and with the money on me. You could see what people would think. I knew I'd got to get away. I don't remember reaching the door but I was too late. I could hear footsteps coming along the passage. They were only faint. I suppose I wouldn't have heard them in the ordinary way. But I was keyed up so that I could hear my own heart beating. In a second I drew the bolt across the door and leaned back against it, holding my breath. It was a woman on the other side of the door. She knocked very quietly and called out, 'Sally. Are you asleep, Sally?' She called quite softly. I don't see how she expected to be heard. Perhaps she didn't really care. I've thought about it a good deal since but, at the time, I didn't wait to see what she would do. She might have knocked louder and set the kid bawling or she might have realized that something was wrong and fetched the family. I had to get away. Luckily I kept myself fit and heights don't worry me. Not that there was much in it. I got out of the side window, the one sheltered by the trees, and the stack-pipe was handy enough. I couldn't hurt my hands and my soft cycling shoes gave me a grip. I fell the last few feet and turned my ankle, but I didn't feel it at the time. I ran into the shelter of the trees before I looked back. Sally's room was still in darkness and I began to feel safe.

"I'd hidden my cycle in the hedge at the side of the lane and I was glad to see it again, I can tell you. It wasn't until I got on that I realized about my foot. I couldn't grasp the pedal with it. Still, I got on all right. I was beginning to think out a plan, too. I had to have an alibi. When I got to Finch-worthy I staged my accident. It wasn't difficult. It's a quiet road and a high wall runs on the left of it. I drove the cycle hard against it until the front wheel buckled. Then I slashed the front tyre with my pocket-knife. I didn't need to worry about myself. I looked the part all right. My ankle was swelling by now and I felt sick. It must have started raining some time in the night because I was wet and cold, although I don't remember the rain. It took some doing to drag myself and the bike into Canningbury and it was well after one before I got home. I had to be pretty quiet so I left the bike

in the front garden and let myself in. It was important not to wake Mrs. Proctor before I had a
chance to alter the two downstairs clocks. We
haven't a clock or watch in the bedroom. I used
to wind the gold one every night and keep it by
the bed. If I could only get in without waking the
wife I reckoned I should be all right. I thought I
was going to be unlucky. She must have been
awake and listening for the door because she
came out to the top of the stairs and called out.
I'd had about as much as I could take by then, so
I shouted at her to get back to bed and I'd be up.
She did what she was told—she usually does—
but I knew she'd be down before long. Still, it
gave me my chance. By the time she'd got on
her dressing-gown and come pussy-footing down
I'd got the clocks put back to midnight. She fussed
about getting me a cup of tea. I was in a sweat to
get her back into bed before any of the town
clocks struck two. It was the sort of thing she
might notice. Anyway, I did get her back upstairs
eventually and she went off to sleep quickly
enough. It was different with me, I can tell you.
My God, I never want to live through another
night like that! You can say what you like about
us and the way we treated Sally. She didn't do so
badly out of us to my way of thinking. But if she
felt hard done by, well, the little bitch got her own
back that night."

He spat the shocking word at them and then,
in the silence, muttered something which might
have been an apology and covered his face with

that grotesque right hand. No one spoke for a moment and then Catherine said:

"You didn't come to the inquest, did you? We wondered about that at the time, but there was some talk that you were ill. Was that because you were afraid of being recognized? But you must have known by then how Sally died and that no one could possibly suspect you."

Under the stress of emotion Proctor had told his story with unselfconscious fluency. Now the need for self-justification reasserted itself and brought a return of his former truculence.

"Why should I go? I wasn't in a fit state for it anyway. I knew how she had died all right. The police told us that when they sent someone round on Sunday morning. He didn't take long before he was asking when I'd last seen her, but I had my story ready. I suppose you all think that I ought to have told them what I knew. Well, I didn't! Sally had caused enough trouble while she was alive and she wasn't going to add to it now she was dead if I could help it. I didn't see why my private affairs should have to come out in court. It isn't easy to explain these things. People might get the wrong ideas."

"Worse still, they might understand only too well," said Felix dryly.

Proctor's thin face flushed. Getting to his feet he deliberately turned his back on Felix and spoke to Eleanor Maxie.

"If you'll excuse me now I'll be on my way. I didn't mean to intrude. It was just that I had to see the inspector. I'm sure I hope this all turns out satisfactorily, but you don't want me here."

"He talks as if we're about to give birth," thought Stephen. The wish to assert an independence of Dalgleish and to show that at least one of the family still considered himself a free agent made him ask:

"Can I drive you home? The last bus went at eight."

Proctor made a gesture of refusal but did not look at him.

"No. No thank you. I have my bicycle outside. They've made a good job of it, all things considered. Please don't bother to see me out."

He stood there, his gloved hands hanging loosely, an unlikeable and pathetic figure but not without dignity.

"At least," thought Felix, "he has the grace to know when he's not wanted." Suddenly, and with a stiff little gesture, Proctor held out his left hand to Eleanor Maxie and she took it.

Stephen went with him to the door. While he was away no one spoke. Felix felt the heightening of tension and his nostrils twitched at the remembered smell of fear. They must know now. They had been told everything except the actual name. But how far were they letting themselves recognize the truth? From under lowered eyelids he watched them. Deborah was curiously tranquil as if the end of lying and deceit had brought their own peace. He did not believe that Deborah knew what was coming. Eleanor Maxie's face was grey, but the folded hands lay relaxed in her lap. He could almost believe that her thoughts were elsewhere. Catherine Bowers sat stiffly, her lips pursed as if in disapproval. Earlier Felix had thought that she was enjoying herself. Now he was not so sure. He noticed with sardonic satisfaction the clenching of her hands, the nervous twitching at the corner of her eyes.

Suddenly Stephen was back with them and Felix spoke.

"Hasn't this gone on long enough? We've heard the evidence. That back door was opened until Maxie locked it at twelve-thirty-three a.m. Some time before then someone got in and killed Sally. The police haven't found out who and they aren't likely to find out. It could have been anyone. I suggest that we none of us say anything more." He looked round at them. The warning was unmistakable. Dalgleish said mildly:

"You are suggesting that a perfect stranger entered the house, made no attempt to steal, went unerringly to Miss Jupp's room and strangled her while, with no attempt of raising the alarm, she lay back obligingly on the bed?"

"She could have invited him to come, whoever he was," said Catherine.

Dalgleish turned to her.

"But she was expecting Proctor. We can't imagine that she wanted to make a party of that little transaction. And whom would she invite? We have checked on everyone who knew her."

"For God's sake stop discussing it," cried Felix.

"Can't you see that's what he wants you to do! There's no proof!"

"Isn't there?" said Dalgleish softly. "I wonder."

"We know who didn't do it, anyway," said Catherine. "It wasn't Stephen or Derek Pullen because they've got alibis and it wasn't Mr. Proctor because of his hand. Sally couldn't have been killed by her uncle."

"No," said Dalgleish. "Nor by Martha Bultitaft who didn't know how the girl had died until Mr. Hearne told her. Nor by you, Miss Bowers, who knocked at her door and tried to speak to her after she was dead. Nor by Mrs. Riscoe, whose fingernails would inevitably have left scratches. No one can grow nails that length overnight and the murderer didn't wear gloves. Nor by Mr. Hearne, whatever he might like me to think. Mr. Hearne didn't know which room Sally slept in. He had to ask Mr. Maxie where he should carry the ladder."

"Only a fool would have shown that he knew. I could have pretended."

"Only you weren't pretending," said Stephen roughly. "You can keep your bloody patronage to yourself. You were the last person to want Sally dead. Once Sally was installed here Deborah might have married you. Believe me, you wouldn't have got her on any other terms. She'll never marry you now and you know it."

Eleanor Maxie looked up and said quietly:

"I went to her room to talk to her. It seemed that the marriage might not be so bad a thing if she were really fond of my son. I wanted to find out what she felt. I was tired and I should have waited till the morning. She was lying there on her bed and singing to herself. It would have been all right if she hadn't done two things. She laughed at me. And she told me, Stephen, that she was going to have your child. It was so very quick. One second she was alive and laughing. The next she was a dead thing in my hands."

"Then it was you!" said Catherine in a whisper. "It was you."

"Of course," said Eleanor Maxie gently. "Think it out for yourself. Who else could it have been?"

4

The Maxies thought that going to prison must be rather like going to hospital, except that it was even more involuntary. Both were abnormal and rather frightening experiences to which the victim reacted with a clinical detachment and the on-lookers with a determined cheerfulness which was intended to create confidence without giving the suspicion of callousness. Eleanor Maxie, ac-companied by a calm and tactful woman police sergeant, went to enjoy the comfort of a last bath in her own house. She had insisted on this and, as with the final preparations for hospital, no one liked to point out that bathing was the first proce-dure inflicted on admission. Or was there, per-haps, a difference between prisoners in custody and those convicted? Felix might have known but no one cared to ask. The police car driver waited in the background, watchful and unobtrusive as an ambulance attendant. There were the last instructions, the messages for friends, the telephone calls and the hurried packing. Mr. Hinks arrived from the vicarage, breathless and unsurprised, steeling himself to give advice and comfort but looking so desperately in need of them himself that Felix took him firmly by the arm and walked with him back to the vicarage. From a window Deborah watched them talking together as they passed out of sight and wondered briefly what they were saying. As she was mounting the stairs to her mother Dalgleish was telephoning from the hall. Their eyes met and held. For a second she thought he was going to speak, but his head bent again to the receiver and she passed on her way, recognizing suddenly and without surprise that, had things been different, here was the man to whom she would have instinctively turned for reassurance and advice.

Stephen, left alone, recognized his misery for what it was, an overmastering pain which had nothing in common with the dissatisfaction and ennui which he had previously thought of as unhappiness. He had taken two drinks but realized in time that drinking wasn't helping. What he needed was someone to minister to his misery and assure him of its essential unfairness. He went in search of Catherine.

He found her kneeling before a small case in his mother's room wrapping jars and bottles in tissue paper. When she looked up at him he saw that she had been crying. He was shocked and irritated. There was no room in the house for a lesser grief. Catherine had never mastered the art of crying appealingly. Perhaps that was one reason why she had learnt early to be stoical in grief as in other things. Stephen decided to ignore this intrusion on his own misery.

"Cathy," he said. "Why on earth did she confess? Hearne was perfectly right. They would never have proved it if she'd only kept quiet."

He had only called her Cathy once before and then, too, he had wanted something from her. Even in the moment of physical love it had struck her as an affectation. She looked up at him. "You don't know her very well, do you? She was only waiting for your father to die before she confessed. She didn't want to leave him and she promised him that he wouldn't be sent away. That was the only reason why she kept silent. She told Mr. Hinks about Sally when she walked back to the vicarage with him earlier tonight."

"But she sat so calmly through all the disclosures!"

"I suppose she wanted to know just what happened. None of you told her anything. I think she worried most thinking that it was you who had visited Sally and locked the door."

"I know. She tried to ask me. I thought she was asking me if I was the murderer. They'll have to reduce the charge. It wasn't premeditated after all. Why doesn't Jephson hurry up and come. We've telephoned for him."

Catherine was sorting a few books she had taken from the bedside table, considering whether to pack them. Stephen went on:

"They'll send her to prison either way. Mother in prison! Cathy, I don't think I can bear it!"

And Catherine, who had grown to like and respect Eleanor Maxie very much, was not sure that she could bear it either and lost her patience.

"You can't bear it! I like that! You don't have to bear it. She does. And it's you that put her there, remember."

Catherine, once started, found it hard to stop and her irritation found a more personal expression.

"And there's another thing, Stephen. I don't know what you feel about us . . . about me if you like. I don't want to talk about this again so I'm just saying now that it's all over. Oh, for heaven's sake get your feet out of that tissue paper! I'm trying to pack."

She was crying in earnest now like an animal or a child. The words were thickened so that he could only just hear them.

"I was in love with you, but not any more. I don't know what you expect now, but it doesn't matter. It's all off."

And Stephen, who had never for one moment intended that it should be on, looked down on the blotched face, the swollen protuberant eyes and felt, irrationally, a spasm of chagrin and regret.

5

One month after Eleanor Maxie had been found guilty on the lesser charge of manslaughter Dalgleish, on one of his rare off-duty days, drove through Chadfleet on his way back to London from the Essex estuary where he had laid up his 30-foot sailing-boat. It was not much out of his way, but he did not choose to analyse too precisely the motives which had prompted him to these three additional miles of winding, tree-shadowed roads. He passed the Pullens' cottage. There was a light in the front room and the plaster Alsatian dog stood darkly outlined against the curtains. And now came St. Mary's Refuge. The house looked empty with only a lone pram at the front door steps to hint at the life inside. The village itself was deserted, somnolent in its teatime five o'clock calm. As he was passing Wilson's General Stores the front door blinds were being drawn and the last customer was leaving. It was Deborah Riscoe. There was a heavy-looking shopping-basket on her arm and he stopped the car instinctively. There was no time for indecision or awkwardness and he had taken the basket from her and she had slid into the seat beside him before it had struck him to wonder at his boldness or her compliance. Stealing a quick glance at her calm uplifted profile, he saw that the look of strain had gone. She had lost none of her beauty but there was a serenity about her which reminded him of her mother.

As the car turned into the drive of Martingale he hesitated but she gave an almost imperceptible shake of the head and he drove on. The beeches were golden now but the twilight was draining them of colour. The first fallen leaves crackled into dust beneath the tyres. The house came into view as he had first seen it, but greyer now and slightly sinister in the fading light. In the hall Deborah slipped off her leather jacket and unwound her scarf.

"Thank you. I was glad of that. Stephen has the car in town this week and Wilson's can only deliver on Wednesdays. I'm always running out of things I've forgotten. Would you like a drink, or tea or something?" She gave him a quick mocking smile. "You aren't on duty now. Or are you?"

"No," he said. "I'm not on duty now. Just indulging myself."

She did not ask for an explanation and he followed her into the drawing-room. It was dustier than he remembered, and somehow more bare but his trained eye saw that there was no real change, only the naked look of a room from which the small personal change of living has been tidied away.

As if she guessed what he was thinking, she said:

"There's only me here most of the time. Martha has left and I've replaced her by a couple of dailies from the new town. At least, they call themselves dailies but I can never be sure they'll turn up. It adds spice to our relationship. Stephen is home most week-ends, of course, and that helps. There will be plenty of time for a good clean-up before Mummy comes home. It's mostly paper work at present, Daddy's will and death duties and lawyers fussing."

"Ought you to be here alone?" asked Dalgleish.

"Oh, I don't mind. One of the family has to stay. Sir Reynold did offer me one of his dogs but they're a little too bite-happy for me. Besides, they aren't trained to exorcise ghosts."

Dalgleish took the drink she handed him and asked after Catherine Bowers. She seemed the safest person to mention. He had little interest in Stephen Maxie and too much interest in Felix Hearne. To ask after the child was to evoke that golden-haired wraith whose shadow was already between them.

"I see Catherine sometimes. Jimmy is still at St. Mary's for the present and Catherine comes down with his father quite often to take him out. She and James Ritchie will get married, I think."

"That's rather sudden, isn't it?"

She laughed.

"Oh, I don't think Ritchie knows it yet. It will be rather a good thing really. She loves the child, really cares about him, and I think Ritchie will be lucky. I don't think there's anyone else to tell you about. Mummy's very well really and not too unhappy. Felix Hearne is in Canada. My brother is at hospital most of the time and terribly busy. Everyone's been very kind though, he says."

"They would be," thought Dalgleish. His mother was serving her sentence and his sister was coping unaided with death duties, housework and the hostility or—and she would hate this worse—the sympathy of the village. But Stephen Maxie was back at hospital with everyone being very kind. Something of what he felt must have shown in his face for she said quickly:

"I'm glad he's busy. It was worse for him than for me."

They sat together in silence for a little time. Despite their apparent easy companionship Dalgleish was morbidly sensitive to every word. He longed to say something of comfort or reassurance but rejected each of the half formulated sentences before they reached his lips. "I'm sorry I had to do it." Only he wasn't sorry and she was intelligent and honest enough to know it. He had never yet apologized for his job and wouldn't insult her by pretending to now. "I know you must dislike me for what I had to do." Mawkish, sentimental, insincere and with an arrogant presumption that she could feel about him one way or the other. They walked to the door in silence and she stood to watch him out of sight. As he turned his head and saw the lonely figure, outlined momentarily against the light from the hall, he knew with sudden and heart-lifting certainty that they would meet again. And when that happened the right words would be found.

A Mind to Murder

**For
Edward Gordon James**

Author's Note

There is only a small number of autonomous psychiatric out-patient clinics in London and it is obvious that these units, dealing as they do with the same medical specialty and organized within a unified National Health Service, must inevitably have some methods of treatment and administrative procedures in common. A number of these they share with the Steen Clinic. It is the more important to state clearly that the Steen is an imaginary clinic situated in an imaginary London square, that none of its patients or staff, medical or lay, represent living people, and that the deplorable events which took place in its basement have their origin only in that curious psychological phenomenon—the imagination of the crime novelist.

P.D.J.

Chapter One

DR. PAUL STEINER, consulting psychiatrist at the
Steen Clinic, sat in the front ground floor
consulting-room and listened to his patient's
highly rationalized explanation of the failure of
his third marriage. Mr. Burge lay in comfort on a
couch the better to expound the complications of
his psyche. Dr. Steiner sat at his head in a chair
of the carefully documented type which the Hospital Management Committee had decreed for
the use of consultants. It was functional and not
unattractive but it gave no support to the back of
the head. From time to time a sharp jerk of his
neck muscles recalled Dr. Steiner from momentary oblivion to the realities of his Friday evening
psychotherapy clinic. The October day had been
very warm. After a fortnight of sharp frosts during

which the staff of the clinic had shivered and pleaded, the official date for starting the central heating had coincided with one of those perfect autumn days when the city square outside had brimmed with yellow light and the late dahlias in the railed garden, bright as a paintbox, had shone like the gauds of high summer. It was now nearly seven o'clock. Outside, the warmth of the day had long given way, first to mist and then to chilly darkness. But here, inside the clinic, the heat of noon was trapped, the air, heavy and still, seemed spent with the breath of too much talking.

Mr. Burge enlarged on the immaturity, coldness and insensitivity of his wives in a querulous falsetto. Dr. Steiner's clinical judgment, not uninfluenced by the late effects of a large lunch and the unwise choice of a cream doughnut with his afternoon tea, told him that the time was not yet ripe to point out that the one defect shared by the three mesdames Burge had been a singular lack of judgment in their choice of husband. Mr. Burge was not yet ready to face the truth of his own inadequacy.

Dr. Steiner felt no moral indignation about his patient's behaviour. It would indeed have been most unethical had any such improper emotion clouded his judgment. There were few things in life which aroused Dr. Steiner's moral indignation and most of them affected his own comfort. Many of them were, indeed, concerned with the Steen Clinic and its administration. He disapproved strongly of the administrative officer, Miss

Bolam, whose preoccupation with the number of patients he saw in a session and the accuracy of his travelling expense form he saw as part of a systematic policy of persecution. He resented the fact that his Friday evening clinic coincided with Dr. James Baguley's electro-convulsive therapy session so that his psychotherapy patients, all of them of high intelligence and sensible of the privilege of being treated by him, had to sit in the waiting-room with the motley crowd of depressed suburban housewives and ill-educated psychotics that Baguley seemed to delight in collecting. Dr. Steiner had refused the use of one of the third-floor consulting-rooms. These had been formed by partitioning the large and elegant Georgian rooms and he despised them as badly proportioned and unpleasing cells, ill-suited either to his grade or to the importance of his work. Nor had he found it convenient to change the time of his session. Baguley, therefore, should change his. But Dr. Baguley had stood firm and in this, too, Dr. Steiner had seen the influence of Miss Bolam. His plea that the ground floor consulting-rooms should be soundproofed had been turned down by the Hospital Management Committee on the grounds of expense. There had, however, been no demur over providing Baguley with a new and highly expensive contraption for shocking his patients out of the few wits they still possessed. The matter, had, of course, been considered by the Clinic Medical Committee, but Miss Bolam had made no secret of where her sympathies lay. In his diatribes against the administrative officer, Dr. Steiner found it convenient to forget that her influence over the Medical Committee was non-existent.

It was difficult to forget the irritations of the E.C.T. session. The clinic building had been put up when men built to last, but even the sturdy oak door of the consulting-room could not muffle the comings and goings of a Friday night. The front door was closed at 6 P.M. and patients at the evening clinics were booked in and out since the time, over five years ago, when a patient had entered unobserved, secreted herself in the basement lavatory and chosen that insalubrious place in which to kill herself. Dr. Steiner's psychotherapy sessions were punctuated by the ringing of the front-door bell, the passing of feet as patients came and went, the hearty voices of relatives and escorts exhorting the patient or calling goodbyes to Sister Ambrose. Dr. Steiner wondered why relatives found it necessary to shout at the patients as if they were deaf as well as psychotic. But possibly after a session with Baguley and his diabolic machine they were. Worst of all was the clinic domestic assistant, Mrs. Shorthouse. One might imagine that Amy Shorthouse could do the cleaning early in the mornings as was surely the normal arrangement. That way there would be the minimum of disturbance to the clinic staff. But Mrs. Shorthouse maintained that she couldn't get through the work without an extra two hours in the evenings and Miss Bolam had agreed. Naturally, she would. It appeared to Dr. Steiner that very little domestic work was done on Friday evenings. Mrs. Shorthouse had a predilection for the E.C.T. patients—indeed, her own husband had once been treated by Dr. Baguley—and she was usually to be seen hanging around the hall and the ground floor general office while the session was being held. Dr. Steiner had mentioned it at the Medical Committee more than once and had been irritated by his colleagues' general uninterest in the problem. Mrs. Shorthouse should be kept out of sight and encouraged to get on with her work, not permitted to stand around gossiping with the patients. Miss Bolam, so unnecessarily strict with other members of the staff, showed no inclination to discipline Mrs. Shorthouse. Everyone knew that good domestic workers were hard to get but an administrative officer who knew her job would recruit them somehow. Weakness solved nothing. But Baguley could not be persuaded to complain about Mrs. Shorthouse and Bolam would never criticize Baguley. The poor woman was probably in love with him. It was up to Baguley to take a firm line instead of sloping around the clinic in that ridiculously long white coat which made him look like a second-rate dentist. Really, the man had no idea of the dignity with which a consultant clinic should be conducted.

Clump, clump went someone's boots along the passage. It was probably old Tippett, a chronic schizophrenic patient of Baguley's who, for the

past nine years, had regularly spent Friday evenings carving wood in the art therapy department.
The thought of Tippett increased Dr. Steiner's
petulance. The man was totally unsuitable for the
Steen. If he were well enough to be out of hospital, which Dr. Steiner doubted, he ought to attend
a Day Hospital or one of the County Council's
sheltered workshops. It was patients like Tippett
who gave the clinic a dubious reputation and obscured its real function as an analytically orientated centre of psychotherapy. Dr. Steiner felt
positively embarrassed when one of his own carefully selected patients encountered Tippett creeping about the clinic on a Friday evening. Tippett
wasn't even safe to be out. One day there would
be an incident and Baguley would find himself in
trouble.

Dr. Steiner's happy contemplation of his colleague in trouble was punctured by the ring of
the front-door bell. Really, it was impossible! This
time it was apparently a hospital car service driver
calling for a patient. Mrs. Shorthouse went to the
door to speed them away. Her eldritch screech
echoed through the hall. "Cheerio, ducks. See
you next week. If you can't be good be careful."

Dr. Steiner winced and shut his eyes. But his
patient, happily engaged in his favourite hobby of
talking about himself, seemed not to have heard.
Mr. Burge's high whine had not, in fact, faltered
for the past twenty minutes.

"I don't pretend I'm an easy person. I'm not,

I'm a complicated devil. That's something which Theda and Sylvia had never understood. The roots of it go deep of course. You remember that session we had in June? Some pretty basic stuff came out then I thought."

His therapist did not recall the session in question but was unconcerned. With Mr. Burge pretty basic stuff was invariably near the surface and could be trusted to emerge. An unaccountable peace fell. Dr. Steiner doodled on his notepad, regarded his doodle with interest, and concern, looked at it again with the pad held upside down and became for a moment more preoccupied with his own subconscious than with that of his patient. Suddenly he became aware of another sound from outside, faint at first and then becoming louder. Somewhere a woman was screaming. It was a horrible noise, high, continuous, and completely animal. Its effect on Dr. Steiner was peculiarly unpleasant. He was naturally timid and highly strung. Although his job involved him in the occasional emotional crises he was more adept at circumventing than coping with an emergency. Fear gave vent to irritation and he sprang from his chair exclaiming.

"No! Really, this is too bad! What's Miss Bolam doing? Isn't anyone supposed to be in charge here?"

"What's up?" inquired Mr. Burge, sitting up like a jack-in-the-box and dropping his voice half an octave to its more normal tone.

"Nothing. Nothing. Some woman having an attack of hysteria that's all. Stay where you are. I'll be back," commanded Dr. Steiner.

Mr. Burge collapsed again but with eye and ear cocked for the door. Dr. Steiner found himself in the hall.

Immediately a little group swung round to face him. Jennifer Priddy, the junior typist, was clinging to one of the porters, Peter Nagle, who was patting her shoulder in embarrassed pity and looking puzzled. Mrs. Shorthouse was with them. The girl's screams were subsiding into whimpers but her whole body was shaking, and she was deathly pale.

"What's the matter?" asked Dr. Steiner sharply. "What's wrong with her?"

Before anyone had a chance to reply the door of the E.C.T. room opened and Dr. Baguley came out followed by Sister Ambrose and his anaesthetist, Dr. Mary Ingram. The hall seemed suddenly full of people. "Calm down, that's a good girl," said Dr. Baguley mildly. "We're trying to run a clinic." He turned to Peter Nagle and asked in a low voice: "What's the matter anyway?"

Nagle seemed about to speak when, suddenly, Miss Priddy gained control. Breaking free of him she turned to Dr. Baguley and said with absolute clearness:

"It's Miss Bolam. She's dead. Someone's killed her. She's in the basement record room and she's murdered. I found her. Enid's been murdered!"

She clung to Nagle and began to cry again but

more quietly. The dreadful shaking had ceased.
Dr. Baguley said to the porter:

"Take her into the treatment-room. Make her lie
down. Better give her something to drink. Here's
the key. I'll be back."

He made for the basement stairs and the rest,
abandoning the girl to Nagle's ministrations, followed in a jostling bunch. The basement at the
Steen was well lit; all its rooms were used by the
clinic which, like most psychiatric units, was chron-
ically short of space. Here, below stairs, in addition
to the boiler-room, the telephone equipment-room
and the porters' quarters, was the art therapy department, a medical records storeroom and, at
the front of the building, a treatment-room for the
lysergic acid patients. As the little group reached
the bottom of the stairs the door of this room
opened and Nurse Bolam, Miss Bolam's cousin,
looked out briefly—a shadowy wraith in her white
uniform against the darkness of the room behind.
Her gentle, puzzled voice floated to them down
the corridor. "Is there anything wrong? I thought I
heard a scream a few minutes ago."

Sister Ambrose said with brusque authority:

"There's nothing wrong, Nurse. Get back to your
patient."

The white figure disappeared and the door
was shut. Turning to Mrs. Shorthouse, Sister Ambrose went on:

"And there's nothing for you to do here, Mrs.
Shorthouse. Please stay upstairs. Miss Priddy
might like a cup of tea."

Mrs. Shorthouse was heard to mutter rebelliously but beat a reluctant retreat. The three doctors, with sister in tow, pressed on.

The medical record-room was on their right, between the porters' rest-room and the art therapy department. The door was ajar and the light was on.

Dr. Steiner, who had become unnaturally aware of every small detail, noticed the key was in the lock. No one was about. The steel racks, with their tight-packed rows of manilla folders, ran ceiling high and at right angles to the door forming a series of narrow aisles, each lit by a fluorescent light. The four high windows were barred and dissected by the racks; it was an airless little room rarely visited and seldom dusted. The little group pushed its way down the first passage and turned left to where there was a small windowless space clear of shelving and furnished with a table and chair where records could be sorted for filing or information copied from the notes without the need to take the file away. Here was chaos. The chair was overturned. The floor was littered with records. Some had their covers wrenched apart and their pages torn, others lay dumped in shifting layers beneath gaps on the shelves which looked too narrow to have held such a weight of paper. And in the middle of this confusion, like a plump and incongruous Ophelia afloat on a tide of paper, was the body of Enid Bolam. On her chest rested a heavy and grotesque image carved in wood, her hands folded about its base so that she looked, horribly, like a parody of motherhood with her creature ritually laid to her breast.

There could be no doubt that she was dead. Even in the midst of his fear and repugnance Dr. Steiner could not miss that final diagnosis. Staring at the wooden figure he cried:

"Tippett! That's his fetish! That's the carving he's so proud of. Where is he? Baguley, he's your patient! You'd better handle this!"

He looked round nervously as if expecting Tippett to materialize, arm raised to strike, the very personification of violence.

Dr. Baguley was kneeling by the body. He said quietly:

"Tippett isn't here this evening."

"But he's always here on Fridays! That's his fetish! That's the weapon!" Dr. Steiner wailed against such obtuseness.

Dr. Baguley gently lifted Miss Bolam's left eyelid with his thumb. Without looking up he said:

"We had a phone call from St. Luke's this morning. Tippett's been admitted with pneumonia. Last Monday, I think. Anyway, he wasn't here this evening." Suddenly he gave a exclamation. The two women bent closer to the body. Dr. Steiner, who could not bring himself to watch the examination, heard him say:

"She's been stabbed, too. Through the heart by the look of it and with a black-handled chisel. Isn't this one of Nagle's, Sister?" There was a pause and Dr. Steiner heard Sister's voice:

"It looks very like it, Doctor. All his tools have

black handles. He keeps them in the porters' rest-room." She added defensively, "Anyone could get at them."

"It looks as if someone has." There was the sound of Dr. Baguley getting to his feet. Still keeping his eyes on the body he said: "Phone Cully on the door, will you, Sister. Don't alarm him, but tell him that no one is to be admitted or to leave the building. That includes the patients. Then get Dr. Etherege and ask him to come down. He'll be in his consulting-room I imagine."

"Oughtn't we to phone the police?" Dr. Ingram spoke nervously and her pink face, so ridiculously like that of an angora rabbit, flushed pinker. It was not only in moments of high drama that one was apt to overlook the presence of Dr. Ingram, and Dr. Baguley stared blankly at her as if he had momentarily forgotten her existence.

"We'll wait for the medical director," he said.

Sister Ambrose disappeared with a rustle of starched linen. The nearest telephone was just outside the record-room but, insulated by tiers of paper from every outside noise, Dr. Steiner strained his ears in vain to hear the lift of the receiver or the murmur of Sister's voice. He forced himself to look once more at Miss Bolam's body. In life he had thought of her as graceless and unattractive, and death had lent her no dignity. She lay on her back, her knees raised and parted so that there was an expanse of pink woollen knicker clearly visible, looking far more indecent than naked flesh. Her round, heavy face was quite peaceful. The two thick plaits which she wore wound above her broad forehead were undisturbed. But then, nothing had ever been known to disturb Miss Bolam's archaic hair style. Dr. Steiner was reminded of his private fantasy that the thick, lifeless plaits exuded their own mysterious secretion and were fixed for ever, immutably, about that placid brow. Looking at her in the defenceless indignity of death, Dr. Steiner tried to feel pity and knew that he felt fear. But he was fully conscious only of repugnance. It was impossible to feel tenderly towards something so ridiculous, so shocking, so obscene. The ugly word spun unbidden to the surface of thought. Obscene! He felt a ridiculous urge to pull down her skirt, to cover that puffy, pathetic face, to replace the spectacles which had slipped from her nose and hung, askew, from her left ear. Her eyes were half closed, her small mouth pursed as if in disapproval of so undignified and unmerited an end. Dr. Steiner was not unfamiliar with that look; he had seen it on her face in life. He thought, "She looks as if she's just confronting me with my travelling expense form."

Suddenly he was seized with an intolerable need to giggle. Laughter welled up uncontrollably. He recognized that this horrible urge was the result of nervousness and shock but understanding did not bring control. Helplessly, he turned his back on his colleagues and fought for composure, grasping the edge of a filing rack and pressing his forehead for support against the cold metal, his mouth and nostrils choked with the musty smell of old records.

He was not aware of Sister Ambrose's return but, suddenly, he heard her speaking.

"Dr. Etherege is on his way down. Cully is on the door and I've told him that no one is to leave. Your patient is making rather a fuss, Dr. Steiner."

"Perhaps I'd better go up to him." Faced with the need for decision, Dr. Steiner regained control. He felt that it was somehow important that he should stay with the others and be there when the medical director arrived; that it would be wise to ensure that nothing important was said or done out of his hearing. On the other hand he was not anxious to stay with the body. The records-room, brightly lit as an operating theatre, claustrophobic and overheated, made him feel like a trapped animal. The heavy close-packed shelves seemed to press upon him, compelling his eyes again and again to that lumpen figure on its paper bier.

"I'll stay here," he decided. "Mr. Burge must wait like everyone else."

They stood together without speaking. Dr. Steiner saw that Sister Ambrose, white-faced but otherwise apparently unmoved, stood stockily calm with her hands loosely clasped over her apron. So must she have stood time without number in nearly forty years of nursing, waiting at the bedside of a patient, quietly deferential, for the doctor's orders. Dr. Baguley pulled out his cigarettes, looked at the packet for a moment as if surprised to find it in his hand, and replaced it in his pocket. Dr. Ingram seemed to be silently crying. Once Dr. Steiner thought he heard her murmur: "Poor woman. Poor woman!"

Soon they heard footsteps and the medical director was with them followed by the senior psychologist, Frederica Saxon. Dr. Etherege knelt down beside the body. He did not touch it but put his face close to Miss Bolam's as if he were about to kiss her. Dr. Steiner's sharp little eyes did not miss the glance that Miss Saxon gave Dr. Baguley, that instinctive move towards each other and the quick withdrawal.

"What happened?" she whispered. "Is she dead?"

"Yes. Murdered apparently." Baguley's tone was flat. Miss Saxon made a sudden gesture. For one unbelievable moment Dr. Steiner thought that she was going to cross herself.

"Who did it? Not poor old Tippett? That's his fetish surely."

"Yes, but he isn't here. He's in St. Luke's with pneumonia."

"Oh, my God! Then who?" This time she moved close to Dr. Baguley and they did not draw apart. Dr. Etherege scrambled to this feet.

"You're right, of course. She's dead. Stunned first apparently and then stabbed through the heart. I'll go upstairs to phone the police and let the rest of the staff know. We'd better keep people together. Then we three had better search the building. Nothing must be touched of course."

Dr. Steiner dared not meet Dr. Baguley's eyes.

Dr. Etherege in his role of the calm, authoritative administrator had always struck him as slightly ridiculous. He suspected that Baguley felt the same.

Suddenly they heard footsteps and the senior psychiatric social worker Miss Ruth Kettle appeared from behind the filing racks, peering at them short-sightedly.

"Ah, there are you, Director," said Miss Kettle, in her fluting, breathless voice. (She was the only staff member, thought Dr. Steiner, to give Dr. Etherege that ridiculous title and God only knew why. It made the place sound like a nature-cure clinic.)

"Cully told me you were down here. Not busy, I hope? I'm so distressed, I don't want to make trouble but it really is too bad! Miss Bolam has booked me a new patient for ten on Monday. I've just seen the appointment in my diary. No consultation with me of course. She knows I always see the Worrikers then. It's quite deliberate, I'm afraid. You know, Director, someone has really got to do something about Miss Bolam."

Dr. Baguley stood aside and said grimly: "Someone has."

At the other end of the square Superintendent Adam Dalgliesh of the Criminal Investigation Department was attending the ritual autumn sherry party given by his publishers which had coincided with the third reprint of his first book of verse. He didn't overestimate his talent or the success of his book. The poems, which reflected his detached, ironic and fundamentally restless spirit, had happened to catch a public mood. He did not believe that more than half a dozen would live even in his own affections. Meanwhile he found himself awash on the shallows of an unfamiliar sea in which agents, royalties and reviews were agreeable hazards. And now there was this party. He had thought of it without enthusiasm as something to be endured, but it had proved unexpectedly enjoyable. Messrs Hearne and Illingworth were as incapable of providing poor sherry as they were of publishing poor work; Dalgliesh estimated that his publishers' share of his own book's profits had been drunk in the first ten minutes. Old Sir Hubert Illingworth had made his brief appearance in the course of it, had shaken Dalgliesh sadly by the hand, and had shuffled off muttering under his breath as if deploring that yet another writer on the firm's list was exposing himself and his publisher to the doubtful gratifications of success. To him all writers were precocious children; creatures to be tolerated and encouraged but not overexcited in case they cried before bedtime.

There were less welcome diversions than the brief appearance of Sir Hubert. Few of the guests knew that Dalgliesh was a detective and not all of them expected him to talk about his job. But there were inevitably those who thought it inappropriate that a man who caught murderers should also write verse and who said so with varying degrees of tact. Presumably they wanted murderers caught however much they might argue about what should happen to them afterwards; but they displayed a typical ambivalence towards those who did the catching. Dalgliesh was used to this attitude and found it less offensive than the common assumption that there was a particular glamour in being a member of the murder squad. But if there had been the expected quota of furtive curiosity and the inanities common to all such parties, there had also been agreeable people saying agreeable things. No writer, however apparently detached about his talent, is immune to the subtle reassurance of disinterested praise and Dalgliesh, fighting the suspicion that few of those who admired had actually read and fewer still had bought, found that he was quietly enjoying himself and was honest enough to admit why.

The first hour had been hectic but, soon after seven o'clock, he found himself standing alone glass in hand beside the ornate James Wyatt chimney-piece. A thin wood fire was burning, filling the room with a faint country smell. It was one of those inexplicable moments when one is suddenly completely alone in the middle of a crowd, when the noise is muted and the pressing bodies seem to recede and become remote and mysterious as actors on some distant stage. Dalgliesh leaned the back of his head against the mantelpiece, savouring this momentary privacy and noting appreciatively the elegant proportions of the room. Suddenly he saw Deborah

Riscoe. She must have come into the room very quietly. He wondered how long she had been there. Immediately his diffuse sense of peace and happiness gave way to a pleasure as keen and painful as that of a boy in love for the first time. She saw him at once and, glass in hand, edged her way across the room to him.

Her appearance was wholly unexpected and he did not deceive himself that she was there on his account. After their last encounter that would hardly be likely.

He said, "It's very pleasant to see you here."

"I should have come anyway," she replied. "But actually I work here. Felix Hearne got me the job after Mummy died. I'm quite useful. I'm the general dogs-body. Shorthand and typing, too. I took a course."

He smiled.

"You make it sound like a cure."

"Well, in a way it was."

He did not pretend not to understand. They were both silent. Dalgliesh knew that he was morbidly sensitive to any allusion to the case which, nearly three years ago, had led to their first meeting. That sore could not stand even the gentlest of probes. He had seen the announcement of her mother's death in the paper about six months ago, but it had seemed impossible and impertinent then to send her a message or to speak the customary words of condolence. After all, he was partly responsible for her death. It was no easier now. Instead they talked of his verse and of her job. Taking his share of this casual undemanding small talk he wondered what she would say if he asked her to have dinner with him. If she didn't turn him down flat—and she probably would—it could be for him the beginning of involvement. He didn't deceive himself that he only wanted an agreeable meal with a woman he happened to think beautiful. He had no idea what she thought of him, but ever since their last meeting, he had known himself to be on the brink of love. If she accepted—for this or for an evening—his solitary life would be threatened. He knew this with complete certainty and the knowledge frightened him. Ever since the death of his wife in childbirth he had insulated himself carefully against pain; sex little more than an exercise in skill; a love affair merely an emotional pavanne, formalized, danced according to the rules, committing one to nothing. But, of course, she wouldn't accept. He had absolutely no reason to think that she was interested in him. It was only this certainty that gave him the confidence to indulge his thoughts. But he was tempted to try his luck. As they talked he mentally rehearsed the words, wryly amused to recognize after so many years the uncertainties of adolescence.

The light tap on his shoulder took him by surprise. It was the chairman's secretary to say that he was wanted on the telephone. "It's the Yard, Mr. Dalgliesh," she said with well-controlled interest as if Hearne and Illingworth's authors were accustomed to calls from the Yard.

He smiled his excuses at Deborah Riscoe and she gave a little resigned shrug of her shoulders.

"I won't be a moment," he said. But even as he threaded his way through the crush of chatterers he knew that he wouldn't be back.

He took the call in a small office next to the boardroom, struggling to the telephone through chairs heaped with manuscripts, rolled galley proofs and dusty files. Hearne and Illingworth fostered an air of old-fashioned leisureliness and general muddle which concealed—sometimes to their author's discomfiture—a formidable efficiency and attention to detail.

The familiar voice boomed in his ear.

"That you, Adam? How's the party? Good. Sorry to break it up but I'd be grateful if you'd look in over the way. The Steen Clinic, Number 31. You know the place. Upper class neuroses catered for only. It seems that their secretary or administrative officer or what have you has got herself murdered. Bashed on the head in the basement and then stabbed expertly through the heart. The boys are on their way. I've sent you Martin, of course. He'll have your gear with him."

"Thank you, sir. When was it reported?"

"Three minutes ago. The medical director rang. He gave me a concise account of practically everyone's alibi for the supposed time of death and explained why it couldn't possibly be one of the patients. He was followed by a doctor called Steiner. He explained that we met about five years ago at a dinner party given by his late brother-in-law. Dr. Steiner explained why it couldn't have been him and favoured me with his interpretation of the psychological makeup of the killer. They've read all the best detective fiction. No one has touched the body, they're not letting anyone in or out of the building and they've all collected into one room to keep an eye on each other. You'd better hurry over, Adam, or they'll solve the crime before you arrive."

"Who is the medical director?" asked Dalgliesh.

"Dr. Henry Etherege. You must have seen him on television. He's the establishment psychiatrist, dedicated to making the profession respectable. Distinguished looking, orthodox and earnest."

"I've seen him in court," said Dalgliesh.

"Of course. Remember him in the Routledge case? He practically had me weeping into my hankie and I knew Routledge better than most. Etherege is the natural choice of any defence counsel—if he can get him. You know their bleat. Find me a psychiatrist who looks respectable, speaks English and won't shock the jury or antagonize the judge. Answer. Etherege. Ah well, good luck!"

The A.C. was optimistic in supposing that his message could break up the party. It had long reached the stage when the departure of a solitary guest disconcerted no one. Dalgliesh thanked his host, waved a casual good-bye to the few people who caught his eye and passed almost unnoticed out of the building. He did not see

Deborah Riscoe again. And made no effort to find her. His mind was already on the job ahead and he felt that he had been saved, at best from a snub and, at worst, from folly. It had been a brief, tantalizing, inconclusive and unsettling encounter but, already, it was in the past.

Walking across the square to the tall Georgian building that housed the Steen Clinic, Dalgliesh recalled some of the scant items of information about the place that had come his way. It was a well-known witticism that you had to be exceptionally sane to be accepted for treatment at the Steen. Certainly it had a reputation—Dalgliesh thought probably undeserved—for selecting its patients with more regard to their intelligence and social class than their mental condition, subjecting them to diagnostic procedures designed to deter all but the most enthusiastic, and then placing them on a waiting list for treatment long enough to ensure that the curative effect of time could exert their maximum influence before the patient actually attended for his first psychotherapy session. The Steen, Dalgliesh remembered, had a Modigliani. It was not a well-known painting, nor did it represent the artist at his best, but it was, undeniably, Modigliani. It hung in the first-floor boardroom, the gift of a former grateful patient, and it represented much that the clinic stood for in the public eye. Other National Health Service clinics brightened their walls with reproductions from the Red Cross picture library. The Steen staff made no secret that they preferred a second-rate original to a first-class reproduction any day. And they had a second-rate original to prove it.

The house itself was one of a Georgian terrace. It stood at the south corner of the square, comfortable, unpretentious and wholly pleasing. At the rear a narrow passage ran into Lincoln Square Mews. There was a railed basement; in front of the house the railings curved on each side of the broad steps which led to the door and supported two wrought-iron lamp standards. On the right of the door an unpretentious bronze plaque bore the name of the Hospital Management Committee which administered the unit and, underneath, the words, "The Steen Clinic". No other information was given. The Steen did not advertise its function to a vulgar world nor did it wish to invite an influx of the local psychotics seeking treatment or reassurance. There were four cars parked outside but no signs yet of the police. The house looked very quiet. The door was shut but a light shone from the elegant Adam fanlight above the door and between the folds of drawn curtains in the ground floor rooms.

The door was opened almost before he had taken his finger from the bell. They had been waiting for him. A stockily-built young man in porter's uniform opened the door and let him in without speaking. The hall blazed with light and struck very warm after the coolness of the autumn night. To the left of the door was a glass-panelled reception kiosk with a telephone switchboard. A second, and much older, porter sat at the board in an attitude of utter misery. He looked round and glanced briefly at Dalgliesh with rheumy eyes, then returned to his contemplation of the board as if the arrival of the superintendent was the last straw of an intolerable burden which, if ignored, might be lifted from him. In the main body of the hall the reception committee came forward, the medical director with outstretched hand as if welcoming a guest. "Superintendent Dalgliesh? We're very glad to see you. May I introduce my colleague, Dr. James Baguley, and the secretary of the Hospital Management Committee, Mr. Lauder."

"You got here very promptly, sir," said Dalgliesh to Lauder. The group secretary said:

"I didn't know about the murder until I arrived ten minutes ago. Miss Bolam telephoned me at lunchtime today and said she wanted to see me urgently. Something was going on at the clinic and she needed advice. I came as soon as I could and found that she'd been murdered. In the circumstances, I had more reasons than one for deciding to stay around. It looks as if she needed advice more than she knew."

"Whatever it was you've come too late, I'm afraid," said Dr. Etherege.

Dalgliesh saw that he was much shorter than his television appearances suggested. His large, high-domed head, with its aureole of white hair soft and fine as a baby's, looked too weighty for the slight supporting body which seemed to have aged independently giving him an oddly disintegrated appearance. It was difficult to guess his age but Dalgliesh thought that he must be nearer seventy than sixty-five, the normal retiring age for a consultant. He had the face of an indestructible gnome, the cheeks mottled with high colour so that they looked painted, the eyebrows springing above eyes of a piercing blue. Dalgliesh felt that those eyes and the soft, persuasive voice were not the least of the medical director's professional assets.

In contrast, Dr. James Baguley was six feet tall, nearly as tall as Dalgliesh, and the immediate impression he gave was of intense weariness. He was wearing a long white coat which hung loosely from his bowed shoulders. Although he was much the younger man he had none of the medical director's vitality. His hair was straight and turning iron-grey. From time to time he swept it out of his eyes with long nicotine-stained fingers. His was a handsome, bony face, but the skin and eyes were dulled as if with permanent tiredness.

The medical director said:

"You will, of course, want to see the body straight away. I'll ask Peter Nagle, our second porter, to come down with us if you've no objection. His chisel was one of the weapons used—not that he could help that, poor fellow—and no doubt you will want to ask him questions."

"I shall want to question everyone here in due course," replied Dalgliesh.

It was apparent that the medical director had taken charge. Dr. Baguley, who had not yet spoken, seemed glad to accept that position. Lauder had apparently decided to adopt a watching brief. As they moved towards the basement stairs at the back of the hall he caught Dalgliesh's eye. The momentary glance was hard to analyse, but Dalgliesh thought he detected an amused gleam and a certain wry detachment.

They stood in silence as Dalgliesh knelt by the body. He did not touch it except to part the cardigan and blouse, both of which were unbuttoned, and expose the handle of the chisel. It had been driven in up to the hilt. There was very little bruising of the tissues and no blood. The woman's vest had been rolled up above her breasts to expose the flesh for that vicious, calculated thrust. Such deliberation suggested that the killer had a confident knowledge of anatomy. There were easier ways of killing than to pierce the heart with one thrust. But for those with the knowledge and the strength there were few ways so sure.

He got to his feet and turned to Peter Nagle.

"Is that your chisel?"

"Apparently. It looks like it and mine isn't in the box." Despite the omission of the usual "sir" the voice, educated and unemphatic, held no trace of insolence or resentment. Dalgliesh asked:

"Any idea how it got here?"

"None at all. But I'd hardly be likely to say if I had, would I?"

The medical director gave Nagle a quick frown of warning or admonition and placed his hand briefly on the porter's shoulder. Without consulting Dalgliesh he said gently:

"That will be all for the present, Nagle. Just wait outside, will you?"

Dalgliesh made no demur as the porter quietly detached himself from the group and left without another word.

"Poor boy! The use of his chisel has naturally shocked him. It looks unpleasantly like an attempt to implicate him. But you will find, Superintendent, that Nagle is one of the few members of the staff with a complete alibi for the presumed time of death." Dalgliesh did not point out that this was, in itself, highly suspicious.

"Did you make any estimate of the time of death?" he asked.

Dr. Etherege replied:

"I thought that it must have been very recent. That is Dr. Baguley's view too. The clinic is very warm today—we've just started our central heating—so the body would cool very slowly. I didn't try for rigor. I am, of course, little more than a layman in such matters. Subsequently I knew that she must have died within the hour. Naturally we have been talking among ourselves while waiting for you and it appears that Sister Ambrose was the last person to see Miss Bolam alive. That was at twenty-past six. Cully, our senior porter, tells me that Miss Bolam rang him on the internal phone at about six-fifteen to say that she was going down to the basement and that Mr. Lauder should be directed to her office if he arrived. A few minutes later, as far as she can judge, Sister came out of the E.C.T. room on the ground floor and crossed the hall to the patients' waiting-room to let a husband know that his wife was ready to be taken home. Sister saw Miss Bolam going down the hall towards the basement stairs. No one saw her alive again after that."

"Except her murderer," said Dalgliesh.

Dr. Etherege looked surprised.

"Yes, that would be so, of course. I mean that none of us saw her alive again. I have asked Sister Ambrose about the time and Sister is quite sure . . ."

"I shall be seeing Sister Ambrose and the other porter."

"Of course. Naturally you will want to see everybody. We expect that. While waiting we telephoned our homes to say that we would be delayed tonight but gave no explanation. We had already searched the building and ascertained that the basement door and the ground floor rear entrance were both bolted. Nothing has been touched in here naturally. I arranged for the staff to stay together in the front consulting-room except for Sister and Nurse Bolam who are with the remaining patients in the waiting-room. No one but Mr. Lauder and you have been allowed in."

"You seem to have thought of everything, Doctor," said Dalgliesh. He got up from his knees and stood looking down at the body.

"Who found her?" he asked.

"One of our medical secretaries, Jennifer Priddy. Cully, the senior porter, has been complaining of stomach-ache most of the day and Miss Priddy went to find Miss Bolam to ask if he could go home early. Miss Priddy is very upset but she was able to tell me . . ."

"I think it would be better if I heard it from her direct. Was this door kept locked?"

His tone was perfectly courteous but he felt their surprise. The medical director's tone did not change as he replied:

"Usually it is. The key is kept on a board with other clinic keys in the porters' duty-room here in the basement. The chisel was kept there, too."

"And this fetish?"

"Taken from the basement art-therapy-room across the passage. It was carved by one of our patients."

It was still the medical director who replied. So far Dr. Baguley hadn't spoken a word. Suddenly he said:

"She was knocked out with the fetish and then stabbed through the heart by someone who was either knowledgeable or damned lucky. That much is obvious. What isn't obvious is why they had this free-for-all with the medical records. She's lying on them so it must have happened before the murder."

"The result of a struggle, perhaps," suggested Dr. Etherege.

"It doesn't look like it. They were pulled out of

the shelves and deliberately chucked about. There must have been a reason. There wasn't anything impulsive about this murder."

It was then that Peter Nagle, who had apparently been standing outside the door, came into the room.

"There's been a ring at the door, sir. Would that be the rest of the police?"

Dalgliesh noted that the records-room was almost soundproof. The front-door bell was strident but he had not heard it.

"Right," he said. "We'll go up."

As they moved together towards the stairs Dr. Etherege said:

"I wonder, Superintendent, if you could see the patients fairly soon. We have only two still with us, a male psychotherapy patient of my colleague Dr. Steiner, and a woman who has been receiving lysergic acid treatment down here in the basement front treatment-room. Dr. Baguley will be able to explain the treatment to you—she is his patient—but you can be assured that she wasn't capable of leaving her bed until twenty minutes ago and certainly wouldn't know anything about the murder. These patients become quite disorientated during treatment. Nurse Bolam was with her all the evening."

"Nurse Bolam? She is a relation to the dead woman?"

"Her cousin," said Dr. Baguley briefly.

"And your disorientated patient, Doctor. Would

she know if Nurse Bolam left her alone during treatment?"

Dr. Baguley said curtly:

"Nurse Bolam would not have left her."

They mounted the stairs together to meet the murmur of voices in the hall.

That ring at the door brought into the Steen Clinic the paraphernalia and skills of an alien world. Quietly and without fuss the experts in violent death got busy. Dalgliesh disappeared into the record-room with the police surgeon and photographer. The print man, small and plump-cheeked as a hamster, with tiny delicate hands, gave his attention to door handles, locks, the tool case and Tippett's fetish. Plain-clothes men, looking disconcertingly like television actors playing plain-clothes men, made their methodical search of every room and cupboard in the clinic verifying that there was indeed no unauthorized person on the premises and that the back doors both of the ground floor and the basement were securely locked from the inside. The clinic staff, excluded from these activities and congregated in the front ground-floor consulting-room, which had been hastily furnished with additional easy chairs from the patients' waiting-room, felt that their familiar ground had been taken over by strangers and that they were caught up in the inexorable machinery of justice and being ground forward to God knew what embarrassments and disasters.

Only the group secretary appeared unperturbed. He had stationed himself in the hall like a watchdog and sat there patient and alone until his turn came to be interviewed.

Dalgliesh took Miss Bolam's office for his use. It was a small room on the ground floor situated between the large general office at the front of the building and the E.C.T. treatment-room and recovery-room at the rear. Opposite it was a suite of two consulting-rooms and the patients' waiting-room. The office had been formed by partitioning the end of a larger room so that it was oddly proportioned and unattractively narrow for its height. It was sparsely furnished and lacked all evidence of personal taste except for a large bowl of chrysanthemums set on one of the filing cabinets. There was an old-fashioned safe against one wall and the other was lined with green metal filing cabinets. The desk was unostentatious and held nothing but a stationery office desk calendar, a jotting pad, and a small stack of manilla folders. Dalgliesh looked through them and said, "This is odd. These are staff dossiers apparently, but only of the female staff. Her own isn't here incidentally. I wonder why she got these out?"

"Checking on people's annual leave entitlement or something like that perhaps," suggested Sergeant Martin.

"Could be, I suppose. But why only the women? Oh well, it's hardly of immediate importance. Let's have a look at that jotter."

Miss Bolam was apparently one of those administrators who prefer not to trust to memory. The top leaf of the jotter, headed with the date, was well filled with notes in a sloping, rather childish handwriting.

Medical Committee—speak M.D. re proposed Adolescent Dept.

Speak Nagle—broken sash cord Miss Kallinski's room.

Mrs. Shorthouse—? leave.

These notes were at least self-explanatory but the jottings below them—written it appeared in some hurry—were less explicit.

Woman. Here eight years. To arrive 1st Monday.

Dalgliesh said: "These look like the jottings of a telephone call. It could have been a private call, of course, and nothing to do with the clinic. It could have been a doctor trying to trace a patient, or vice versa. Something, or someone, is apparently expected to arrive on the first Monday or on Monday the first. There are a dozen possible interpretations and none of them relevant to the murder. Still, someone phoned recently about a woman and Miss Bolam was obviously examining the dossiers of every woman on the staff except herself. Why? To check which of them were here eight years ago? It's all pretty farfetched. We'll leave the pleasures of conjecture for the moment and get down to seeing these people. I'd like that typist in first. The girl who found the body. Etherege said she was upset.

Let's hope she's calmed down by now or we'll be here half the night."

But Jennifer Priddy was perfectly calm. She had obviously been drinking and her grief was overlaid with a barely suppressed excitement. Her face, still swollen from crying, was blotched with high colour and her eyes were unnaturally bright. But the drink had not fuddled her and she told her story well. She had been busy in the ground-floor general office for most of the evening and had last seen Miss Bolam at about five-forty-five when she had gone into the A.O.'s office with a query about a patient's appointment. Miss Bolam had seemed the same as usual to her. She had returned to the general office and had been joined by Peter Nagle at about six-ten. He was wearing his coat and had come to collect the outgoing post. Miss Priddy had registered the last few letters in the post book and handed them to him. At about quarter- or twenty-past six Mrs. Shorthouse had joined them. Mrs. Shorthouse had mentioned that she had just come from Miss Bolam's office where she had been settling a query about her annual leave entitlement. Peter Nagle had gone out with the post and she and Mrs. Shorthouse had stayed together until his return some ten minutes later. Nagle had then gone down to the basement porters' room to hang up his coat and feed Tigger, the office cat, and she had followed him down almost immediately. She had helped him feed Tigger and they had returned to the general office together. At about seven the senior porter, Cully, complained again about his stomach-ache which had been troubling him all day. Miss Priddy, Mrs. Bostock, the other medical secretary, and Peter Nagle had all had to take Cully's place at the switchboard from time to time because of his stomach-ache, but he had refused to go home. Now he was willing to go and Miss Priddy had gone to the A.O.'s office to ask Miss Bolam if he could leave early. Miss Bolam wasn't in her office so she had looked in the nurses' duty-room on the ground floor. Sister Ambrose told her that she had seen the A.O. passing down the hall towards the basement stairs about thirty minutes or so earlier, so Miss Priddy had looked in the basement. The record-room was usually kept locked but the key was in the lock and the door just ajar, so she had looked inside. The light was on. She had found the body—here Miss Priddy's voice faltered—and had rushed upstairs at once to get help. No, she hadn't touched anything. She didn't know why the medical records were strewn around. She didn't know how she had known that Miss Bolam was dead. It was just that Miss Bolam had looked so very dead. She didn't know why she had been so sure it was murder. She thought she had seen a bruise on Miss Bolam's head. And, then, there had been Tippett's fetish laying on the body. She was afraid that Tippett was hiding among the record racks and would jump out at her. Everyone said that he wasn't dangerous—at least everyone except Dr. Steiner—but he had been in a mental hospital and, after all, you couldn't be really sure, could you? No, she hadn't known that Tippett wasn't in the clinic. Peter Nagle had taken the call from the hospital and had told Miss Bolam but he hadn't told her. She hadn't seen the chisel in Miss Bolam's chest but Dr. Etherege had told the staff about the stabbing when they weregatheredtogetherinthefrontconsulting-room waiting for the police. She thought that most of the staff knew where Peter Nagle kept his tools and also which key opened the door of the basement record-room. It hung on hook number 12 and was shinier than the other keys, but it wasn't labelled. Dalgliesh said:

"I want you to think very hard and very carefully. When you went downstairs to help Mr. Nagle feed the cat was the record-room door ajar and the light on as it was when you went down later and found Miss Bolam?"

The girl pushed back her dark blonde hair and said with sudden weariness:

"I . . . I can't remember. I didn't go past that door you see. I went straight into the porters' room at the bottom of the stairs. Peter was there clearing up Tigger's plate. He hadn't eaten all of his last meal so we scraped it off his plate and washed it at the sink. We didn't go near the record-room."

"But you could see the door as you came down the stairs. Would you be likely to notice if the door were ajar? The room isn't often used, is it?"

"No, but anyone might go there if they wanted a record. I mean, if the door were open I wouldn't go to see who was there or anything like that. I think I would notice if the door was wide open so I suppose it wasn't, but I can't remember, honestly I can't."

Dalgliesh ended by asking her about Miss Bolam. It appeared that Miss Priddy knew her outside the clinic, that the Priddy family attended the same church and that Miss Bolam had encouraged her to take the job at the clinic.

"I shouldn't have got this job if it hadn't been for Enid. Of course, I never called her that inside the clinic. She wouldn't have liked it." Miss Priddy gave the impression that she had only reluctantly brought herself to use the Christian name outside the clinic. She went on: "I don't mean she actually appointed me. I had to be interviewed by Mr. Lauder and by Dr. Etherege, but I know she spoke up for me. My shorthand and typing weren't very good then—it was nearly two years ago when I came—and I was lucky to get here. I didn't see very much of Enid at the clinic but she was always very kind and keen for me to get on. She wanted me to take the Institute of Hospital Administration Diploma so that I needn't be a shorthand typist all my life."

This ambition for Miss Priddy's future career struck Dalgliesh as a little odd. The child gave no impression of being ambitious and she would surely marry in time. It hardly needed the Institute's diploma, whatever that might be, to save her from being a shorthand typist for life. He felt a little sorry for Miss Bolam who could scarcely have picked a less promising protégée. She was pretty, honest and naïve, but not, he thought, particularly intelligent. He had to remind himself that she had given her age as twenty-two not seventeen. She had a shapely and oddly mature body, but her thin face with its frame of long, straight hair, was the face of a child.

There was little she could tell him about the administrative officer. She hadn't noticed any change recently in Miss Bolam. She didn't know that the A.O. had sent for Mr. Lauder and had no idea what could be worrying Miss Bolam at the clinic. Everything was going on very much as usual. Miss Bolam had no enemies as far as she knew, certainly no one who would wish to kill her.

"She was happy here, then, as far as you know? I was wondering whether she had asked for a move. A psychiatric clinic can't be the easiest unit to administer."

"Oh, it isn't! I don't know how Enid carried on sometimes. But I'm sure she would never ask for a move. Someone must have given you the wrong impression. She was never one to give up. If she thought people wanted her to go she'd dig her toes in. The clinic was a kind of challenge to her."

It was probably the most illuminating thing she had said about Miss Bolam. As he thanked her and asked her to wait with the rest of the staff until his preliminary interviews were over,

Dalgliesh pondered on the possible nuisance value of an administrator who regarded her job as a challenge, a battleground from which she would never willingly retreat. He asked next to see Peter Nagle.

If the junior porter was worried by the killer's choice of his chisel as a weapon he gave no sign. He answered Dalgliesh's questions calmly and politely, but so dispassionately that they might have been discussing some minor point of clinic procedure which was only doubtfully his concern. He gave his age as twenty-seven and an address in Pimlico and confirmed that he had been employed at the clinic for just over two years and was previously at a provincial art school. His voice was level and educated, his mud-brown eyes were large, almost expressionless. Dalgliesh noticed that he had unusually long arms which, held loosely from his short and powerful body, gave an impression of simian strength. His hair was black, coiling tightly over the scalp. It was an interesting face, withdrawn but intelligent. There could scarcely have been a greater contrast with poor old Cully, long since despatched home to nurse both his stomach-ache and his grievance at being kept late.

Nagle confirmed Miss Priddy's story. He again identified his chisel with no more emotion than a brief moue of distaste and said that he had last seen it at eight o'clock that morning when he arrived on duty and—for no particular reason—had made a check of his toolbox. Everything was in order then. Dalgliesh asked whether it was generally known where the box was kept. Nagle replied:

"I'd be a fool if I said no, wouldn't I?"

"You'd be a fool to say anything but the truth now or later."

"I suppose most of the staff knew. Those who didn't could find out easily enough. We don't keep the porters' room locked."

"Isn't that rather unwise? What about the patients?"

"They don't go down to the basement on their own. The lysergic acid patients are always escorted and the art therapy people usually have someone keeping an eye on them. The department hasn't been down there for long. The light's bad and it isn't really suitable. It's a temporary department."

"Where used it to be, then?"

"On the third floor. Then the clinic Medical Committee decided they wanted the large room there for the marital problems discussion groups, so Mrs. Baumgarten—she's the art therapist—lost it. She's been agitating to get it back, but the M.P.D. patients say it would be psychologically disturbing for them to meet in the basement."

"Who runs the M.P.D.?"

"Dr. Steiner and one of the psychiatric social workers, Miss Kallinski. It's a club where the divorced and the single tell the patients how to be happy though married. I don't see how it can concern the murder."

"Nor do I. I asked about it to satisfy my curiosity as to why the art therapy department was so unsuitably housed. When did you hear that Tippett wasn't attending today, by the way?"

"At about nine o'clock this morning. The old boy had been worrying St. Luke's Hospital to telephone and let us know what had happened. So they did. I told Miss Bolam and Sister."

"Anyone else?"

"I think I mentioned it to Cully when he came back on the board. He's had belly-ache for most of the day."

"So I'm told. What's wrong with him?"

"Cully? Miss Bolam made him go to hospital for an examination but nothing was found. He gets these belly-aches if anyone upsets him. They say here it's psychosomatic."

"What upset him this morning?"

"I did. He got here before me this morning and started sorting the post. That's my job. I told him to concentrate on his own work."

Dalgliesh took him patiently over the events of the evening. His story agreed with Miss Priddy's and, like her, he was unable to say whether the door of the basement record-room had been ajar when he returned from posting the letters. He admitted that he had passed the door when he went to ask Nurse Bolam if the laundry was sorted. It was usual for the door to be closed as the room was seldom visited and he thought he would have noticed had it been open. It was frustrating and maddening that this crucial point could not be cleared up, but Nagle stood firm. He hadn't noticed. He couldn't say. He hadn't noticed, either, whether the record-room key was on the board in the porters' rest-room. This was easier to understand. There were twenty-two hooks on the board and most of the keys were in use and missing. Dalgliesh said:

"You realize that Miss Bolam's body was almost certainly lying in the record-room when you and Miss Priddy were together feeding the cat? You realize how important it is to remember whether the door was open or shut?"

"It was ajar when Jenny Priddy went down later. That's what she says and she's no liar. If it was shut when I got back from the post someone must have opened it between six-twenty-five and seven. I don't see what's so impossible about that. It would be better for me if I could remember about the door, but I can't. I hung up my coat in my locker, went straight to ask Nurse Bolam about the clean laundry, and then returned to the rest-room. Jenny met me at the bottom of the stairs."

He spoke without heat, almost unemotionally. It was as if he said, "That's what happened. Like it or not, it happened that way." He was too intelligent not to see that he was in some danger. Perhaps he was also intelligent enough to know that the danger was minimal to an innocent man who kept his head and told the truth.

Dalgliesh told him to let the police know at

once if he remembered anything fresh and let him go.

Sister Ambrose was seen next. She strutted into the room, armour-plated in white linen, belligerent as a battleship. The bib of her apron, starched rigid as a board, curved against a formidable bosom on which she wore her nursing badges like medals of war. Grey hair spurted from each side of her cap which she wore low on her forehead above a face of uncompromising plainness. Her colour was high; Dalgliesh thought that she was finding it difficult to control her resentment and distrust. He dealt with her gently, but his questions were answered in an atmosphere of rigid disapproval. She confirmed briefly that she had last seen Miss Bolam walking through the hall towards the basement stairs at about twenty-past six. They had not spoken and the administrative officer had looked the same as usual. Sister Ambrose was back in the E.C.T. room before Miss Bolam was out of sight and had been there with Dr. Ingram until the body was found. In reply to Dalgliesh's question whether Dr. Baguley had also been with them for the whole of that time, Sister Ambrose suggested that he should ask the doctor direct. Dalgliesh replied mildly that this was his intention. He knew that the Sister could give him a great deal of useful information about the clinic if she chose but, apart from a few questions about Miss Bolam's personal relationships from which he gained nothing, he did not press her. He thought that she was probably more shocked by the murder, by the calculated violence of Miss Bolam's death, than anyone he had yet seen. As sometimes happens with unimaginative and inarticulate people, this shock gave vent to ill-temper. She was very cross; with Dalgliesh because his job gave him the right to ask impertinent and embarrassing questions; with herself because she could not conceal her feelings; with the victim, even, who had involved the clinic in this bizarre predicament. It was a re-action Dalgliesh had met before and no good came of trying to force co-operation on such a witness. Later on Sister Ambrose might be induced to talk more freely; at present, it was a waste of time to do more than elicit the facts which she was prepared to give. One fact at least was cru-cial. Miss Bolam was alive and making her way towards the basement stairs at about twenty-past six. At seven o'clock her body was discovered. Those forty minutes were vital and any member of the staff who could produce an alibi covering them could be eliminated from the enquiry. On the face of it the case presented little difficulty. Dalgliesh did not believe that an outsider had somehow gained access to the clinic and lain in wait for Miss Bolam. The killer was almost cer-tainly still in the building. It was now a matter for careful questioning, for the methodical checking of alibis, for the seeking out of a motive. Dalgliesh decided to talk to the one man whose alibi ap-peared unassailable and who would have the detached, outsider's view of the clinic and its varied personalities. He thanked Sister Ambrose for her valuable co-operation—a flicker of the eyes behind the steel-rimmed spectacles suggested that the irony was not lost on her—and asked the constable at the door to send in Mr. Lauder.

Chapter Two

IT WAS THE FIRST CHANCE Dalgliesh had had to observe the group secretary closely. He saw a
thick-set, chubby-featured man, mild-eyed behind the heavy square spectacles, who looked,
in his well-cut tweeds, more like a country doctor
or small-town solicitor than a bureaucrat. He was
completely at ease and bore himself like a man
confident of his powers, unwilling to be hurried,
keeping always something in reserve, including,
Dalgliesh thought, a keener intelligence than his
appearance might suggest.

He seated himself opposite Dalgliesh, drew
his chair comfortably forward and, without either
apology or excuse, took a pipe from one pocket
and sought in the other for his tobacco pouch.
Nodding towards Martin and his open note book

he said, in a slow voice with a trace of north-country accent:

"Reginald Iven Lauder. Date of birth, 21st April 1905. Address, 42 Makepeace Avenue, Chigwell, Essex. Occupation, Group Secretary, East Central Hospital Management Committee. And now, Superintendent, what do you want to know?"

"A great deal, I'm afraid," said Dalgliesh. "And firstly, have you any idea at all who could have killed Miss Bolam?" The group secretary established his pipe and, leaning his elbows on the desk, regarded its glowing head with satisfaction.

"I wish I had. I'd have been in here to tell you before now, never fear. But, no. I've no help of that kind for you."

"Miss Bolam had no enemies as far as you were aware?"

"Enemies? Well now, Superintendent, that's a strong word! She had people who didn't much like her, the same as I have. You, too, no doubt. But we don't go in fear of being murdered. No, I wouldn't have said she had enemies. Mind you, I know nothing of her private life. That's not my concern."

"Could you tell me something about the Steen and the position she held? I know something of the clinic's reputation, of course, but it would be helpful if I could have a clear picture of what goes on here."

"A clear picture of what goes on?" It might have been imagination, but Dalgliesh thought he saw the group secretary's mouth twitch.

"Well, the medical director could tell you more about that than I—on the medical side, that is. But I can give you a gist. The place was founded between the wars by the family of a Mr. Hyman Stein. The story goes that the old man suffered from impotence, got himself some psychotherapy and subsequently fathered five children. So far from impoverishing him they all did well and when papa died they put the clinic on a sound financial footing as a memorial to him. After all, they did owe the place something. The sons all changed their name to Steen—for the usual reason I suppose—and the clinic was given the anglicized name. I often wonder what old Hyman would have thought."

"Is it well endowed?"

"It was. The state got the endowments of course on the Appointed Day following the 1946 Act. A bit has come in since, but not much. People aren't so keen to will money to institutions run by the Government. But the place was quite well off before 1948 as these places go. They did themselves well in the way of equipment and facilities. The Hospital Management Committee's had quite a job providing for them in the way to which they'd become accustomed."

"Is the clinic difficult to administer? I imagine there may be personality problems."

"No more difficult than any other small unit. You get personality problems anywhere. I'd rather deal with a difficult psychiatrist than a difficult surgeon any day. They're the real *prima donnas*."

"Did you consider Miss Bolam a successful administrative officer?"

"Well . . . she was efficient. I hadn't really any complaints. She was a bit rigid, I suppose. After all, Ministry circulars haven't even the force of law, so there's no sense in treating them as if they are personally dictated by God Almighty. I doubt whether Miss Bolam would have got much further. Mind you, she was a competent, methodical and highly conscientious officer. I don't think she ever sent in an inaccurate return."

"Poor devil!" thought Dalgliesh, stung by the bleak anonymity of that official epitaph. He asked:

"Was she popular here? With the medical staff, for example?"

"Well, now, Superintendent, you'll have to ask them. I can't think of any reason why she shouldn't be."

"You were not then under any pressure from the medical committee to remove her from the clinic?"

The mild grey eyes grew suddenly blank. There was a momentary pause before the group secretary calmly replied:

"I have had no official request of that kind made to me."

"But unofficially?"

"There has been a feeling here from time to time, I believe, that a change of job might be helpful to Miss Bolam. Now that's not such a bad idea, Superintendent! Any officer in a small unit, particularly a psychiatric clinic, can benefit from a change of experience. But I don't transfer my staff at the whim of medical committees. Bless me, no! And, as I said, no official request was made. If Miss Bolam herself had asked for a transfer, that would have been a different matter. Even so, it wouldn't have been easy. She was a general administrative officer and we haven't many posts in that grade."

Dalgliesh then asked again about Miss Bolam's telephone call and Lauder confirmed that he had spoken to her about ten to one. He remembered the time because he was just about to go for lunch. Miss Bolam had asked to speak to him personally and had been put through by his secretary. She had asked whether she could see him urgently.

"Can you remember the exact conversation?"

"More or less. She said: 'Can I have an appointment to see you as soon as possible? I think there may be something going on here that you ought to know about. I should like your advice. Something that started well before my time here.' I said that I couldn't see her this afternoon as I would be in the Finance and General Purposes Committee from two-thirty onwards and had a Joint Consultative Committee immediately afterwards. I asked whether she could give me any idea what it was all about and whether it couldn't wait until Monday. She hesitated, so, before she could reply, I said I'd drop in on my way home this evening. I knew they had a late clinic on Fridays. She said that she would arrange to be alone in her office from six-thirty onwards, thanked me, and rang off. The J.C.C. lasted longer than I expected—that Committee always does—and I got here just before seven-thirty. But you know that. I was still in Committee at the time they found the body, as no doubt you'll be checking in due course."

"Did you take Miss Bolam's message seriously? Was she the sort of woman who ran to you with trifles or would a request to see you really mean that something serious was wrong?"

The group secretary thought for a moment before replying: "I took it seriously. That's why I came round tonight."

"And you have no idea at all what it might be?"

"None, I'm afraid. It must have been something that she learned about since Wednesday. I saw Miss Bolam then at the House Committee meeting in the late afternoon and she told me afterwards that things were pretty quiet here at present. That is the last time I saw her incidentally. She was looking rather well I thought. Better than for some time."

Dalgliesh asked the group secretary what, if anything, he knew of Miss Bolam's private life.

"Very little. I believe she has no near relations and lives alone in a flat in Kensington. Nurse Bolam will be able to tell you more about her. They're cousins, and Nurse Bolam is probably the nearest living relative. I've got an idea that she had private means. All the official information about her career will be on her dossier. Knowing Miss

Bolam, I expect her file will be as meticulously kept as any other staff dossier. It'll be here no doubt."

Without moving from his chair he leaned sideways, jerked open the top drawer of the filing cabinet and inserted a chubby hand between the manilla folders.

"Here we are. Bolam, Enid Constance. I see she came to us in October 1949 as a shorthand typist. She spent eighteen months in Group Headquarters, was transferred to one of our chest clinics on 19th April 1951 on Grade B and applied for the vacant post of administrative officer here on 14th May 1957. The post was then Grade D and she was lucky to get it. We hadn't a very strong field, I remember. All administrative and clerical jobs were regraded in 1958 following the Noel Hall report and, after some argument with the Regional Board, we managed to get this one graded as general administrative. It's all down here. Date of birth, 12th December 1922. Address, 37a Ballantyne Mansions, S.W.8. Then come details about her tax code, national insurance number and incremental date. She's only had one week off sick since she came here and that was in 1959 when she had 'flu. There isn't much more here. Her original application form and letters of appointment will be on her main dossier at Group Headquarters."

He handed the file to Dalgliesh who looked through it and then said:

"This states that her previous employers were

the Botley Research Establishment. Isn't that Sir Mark Etherege's show? They dabble in Aeronautical research. He's Dr. Etherege's brother, isn't he?

"I think Miss Bolam did mention to me when she was appointed to this post that she knew Dr. Etherege's brother slightly. Mind you now, it can't have been more than that. She was only a shorthand typist at Botley. It's a bit of a coincidence, I suppose, but then she had to come from somewhere. I seem to remember it was Sir Mark who gave her a reference when she applied to us. That will be on her Group dossier, of course."

"Would you mind telling me, Mr. Lauder, what arrangements you propose making here now that she's dead?"

The group secretary replaced the file in the cabinet.

"I don't see why not. I shall have to consult my Committee, of course, as the circumstances are unusual, but I shall recommend that the senior medical stenographer here, Mrs. Bostock, takes over in an acting capacity. If she can do the job— and I think she can—she'll be a strong candidate for the vacancy, but the post will be advertised in the usual way."

Dalgliesh did not comment but he was interested. Such a quick decision on Miss Bolam's successor could only mean that Lauder had earlier given some thought to it. The approaches of the medical staff may have been unofficial, but they had probably been more effective than the group secretary cared to admit. Dalgliesh returned to the telephone call which had brought Mr. Lauder to the clinic. He said:

"The words Miss Bolam used strike me as significant. She said that there may be something very serious going on here which you ought to know about and that it started before her time. That suggests, firstly that she wasn't yet certain but only suspicious, and secondly that she wasn't worried about a particular incident but about something of long standing. A systematic policy of thieving, for example, as opposed to one isolated theft."

"Well now, Superintendent, it's odd you should mention theft. We have had a theft recently, but it was an isolated incident, the first we've had here for years, and I can't see how it could be connected with murder. It was just over a week ago, last Tuesday if I remember rightly. Cully and Nagle were the last to leave the clinic as usual and Cully asked Nagle to have a drink with him at the 'Queen's Head.' You know it, I expect. It's the pub on the far corner of Beefsteak Street. There are one or two odd things about this story and one of the strangest is that Cully should invite Nagle for a drink. They've never struck me as buddies. Anyway, Nagle accepted and they were in 'Queen's Head' together from about seven. At about half-past, a pal of Cully's came in and said he was surprised to see Cully there as he had just passed the clinic and there was a faint light in one of the windows—as if someone was moving around with a torch, he said. Nagle and Cully went off to investigate and found one of the back basement windows broken, or rather, cut out. Quite a clever job it was. Cully didn't feel inclined to investigate further without reinforcements and I'm not sure that I blame him. He's sixty-five, remember, and not strong. After some whispering together, Nagle said that he'd go in and Cully had better telephone the police from the kiosk on the corner. Your people came pretty smartly but they didn't get the intruder. He gave Nagle the slip inside the building, and when Cully got back from telephoning he was just in time to see the man slip out of the mews."

"I'll check how far our people have got with the investigation," said Dalgliesh. "But I agree that a connection between the crimes seems unlikely on the face of it. Was much taken?"

"Fifteen pounds from a drawer in the psychiatric social worker's office. The door was locked but he wrenched it open. The money was in an envelope addressed in green ink to the administrative secretary of the clinic and had been received a week earlier. There was no letter with it, only a note to say that the money was from a grateful patient. The other contents of the drawer were torn and scattered but nothing else was stolen. Some attempt had been made to force open the cabinets of records in the general office and Miss Bolam's desk drawers had been forced but nothing taken."

Dalgliesh asked whether the fifteen pounds should have been placed in the wall safe.

"Well now, Superintendent, you're right, of course. It should have been. But there was a little difficulty about using the money. Miss Bolam phoned me about its arrival and said that she thought it should be paid immediately into the clinic's free money account to be used in due course on the authority of the House Committee. That was a very proper course of action, and so I told her. Shortly afterwards the medical director phoned me to ask if he could have authority to spend the money on some new flower vases for the patients' waiting-room. The vases were certainly needed and it seemed a correct use for non-Exchequer funds, so I rang the chairman of the House Committee and got his approval. Apparently Dr. Etherege wanted Miss Kettle to choose the vases and asked Miss Bolam to hand over the cash. I had already notified Miss Bolam of the decision so she did so, expecting that the vases would be bought at once. Something happened to change Miss Kettle's plans and, instead of returning the cash to the A.O. for safe custody, she locked it in her drawer."

"Do you know how many of the staff knew that it was there?"

"That's what the police asked. I suppose most people knew that the vases hadn't been bought or Miss Kettle would have shown them around. They probably guessed that, having been handed the cash, she wouldn't be likely to return it even temporarily. I don't know. The arrival of that fifteen pounds was mysterious. It caused nothing but trouble and its disappearance was equally mysterious. Anyway, Superintendent, no one here stole it. Cully only saw the thief for a second but he was certain that he didn't know the man. He did say, though, that he thought the chap looked like a gentleman. Don't ask me how he knew or what his criteria are. But that's what he said."

Dalgliesh thought that the whole incident was odd and would bear further investigation but he could see no apparent connection between the two crimes. It was not even certain that Miss Bolam's call to the group secretary for advice was related to her death, but here the presumption was much stronger. It was very important to discover, if possible, what she had suspected. He asked Mr. Lauder once more whether he could help.

"I told you, Superintendent, I haven't an idea what she meant. If I suspected that anything was wrong I shouldn't wait for Miss Bolam to phone me. We're not quite so remote from the units at group offices as some people think and I usually get to know anything I ought to know. If the murder is connected with that phone message something pretty serious must be happening here. After all, you don't kill just to prevent the group secretary knowing that you've fiddled your travelling claim or overspent your annual leave. Not that anyone has as far as I know."

"Exactly," said Dalgliesh. He watched the group secretary's face very closely and said, without emphasis:

"It suggests something that might ruin a man professionally. A sexual relationship with a patient perhaps—something as serious as that." Mr. Lauder's face did not change.

"I imagine every doctor knows the seriousness of that, particularly psychiatrists. They must have to be pretty careful with some of the neurotic women they treat. Frankly, I don't believe it. All the doctors here are eminent men, some of them with world-wide reputations. You don't get that sort of reputation if you're a fool and men of that eminence don't commit murder."

"And what about the rest of the staff? They may not be eminent, but presumably you consider them honest?"

Unruffled, the group secretary replied:

"Sister Ambrose has been here for nearly twenty years and Nurse Bolam for five. I would trust them both absolutely. All the clerical staff came with good references and so did the two porters, Cully and Nagle." He added wryly: "Admittedly I didn't check that they hadn't committed murder but none of them strike me as homicidal maniacs. Cully drinks a bit and is a pathetic old fool with only another four months' service to complete. I doubt whether he could kill a mouse without making a hash of it. Nagle is a cut above the usual hospital porter. I understand he's an art student and works here for pocket money. He's only been with us a couple of years so he wasn't here before Miss Bolam's time. Even if he's been seducing all the female staff, which seems unlikely, the worst that could happen to him would be the sack and that wouldn't worry him as things are today. Admittedly she was killed with his chisel but anyone could have got their hands on that."

"I'm afraid this was an inside job, you know," said Dalgliesh gently. "The murderer knew where Tippett's fetish and Nagle's chisel were kept, knew which key opened the old record-room, knew where that key was hung on the board in the porters' duty-room, probably wore one of the rubber aprons from the art therapy room as a protection, certainly had medical knowledge. Above all, of course, the murderer couldn't have left the clinic after the crime. The basement door was bolted and so was the ground floor back door. Cully was watching the front door."

"Cully had a belly-ache. He could have missed someone."

"Do you really believe that's possible?" asked Dalgliesh. And the group secretary did not reply.

At first sight Marion Bolam could be thought beautiful. She had the fair, classical good looks which, enhanced by her nurse's uniform, gave an immediate impression of serene loveliness. Her blonde hair, parted above a broad forehead and twisted into a high roll at the back of her head, was bound by the simple white cap. It was only at second glance that the illusion faded and beauty gave way to prettiness. The features, individually analysed, were unremarkable, the nose a little too long, the lips a little too thin. In ordinary clothes, hurrying home perhaps at the end of the day, she would be undistinguished. It was the combination of the starched formal linen with that fair skin and yellow hair which dazzled the eye. Only in the broad forehead and the sharpness of the nose could Dalgliesh detect any likeness to her dead cousin. But there was nothing ordinary about the large grey eyes which met his fully for a brief second before she lowered her glance and gazed fixedly at the clasped hands in her lap.

"I understand that you are Miss Bolam's next of kin. This must be a terrible shock for you."

"Yes. Oh, yes, it is! Enid was my cousin."

"You have the same name. Your fathers were brothers?"

"Yes, they were. Our mothers were sisters, too. Two brothers married two sisters so that we were doubly related."

"Had she no other relations living?"

"Only Mummy and me."

"I shall have to see Miss Bolam's solicitor, I expect," said Dalgliesh, "but it would be helpful if you would tell me as much as you know about her affairs. I'm afraid I have to ask these personal questions. Usually they have no bearing on the crime, but one must know as much as possible about everyone concerned. Had your cousin any income apart from her salary?"

"Oh, yes. Enid was quite well off. Uncle Sydney left her mother about £25,000 and it all came to Enid. I don't know how much was left, but I think she had about £1,000 a year coming in apart from her salary here. She kept on auntie's flat in Ballantyne Mansions and she . . . she was always very good to us."

"In what way, Miss Bolam? Did she make you an allowance?"

"Oh, no! Enid wouldn't want to do that. She gave us presents. Thirty pounds at Christmas and fifty in July for our summer holiday. Mummy has disseminated sclerosis and we couldn't go away to an ordinary hotel."

"And what happens to Miss Bolam's money now?"

The grey eyes lifted to meet his with no trace of embarrassment. She answered simply:

"It will come to Mummy and me. There wasn't anyone else to leave it to, was there? Enid always said it would come to us if she died first. But, of course, it wasn't likely that she would die first; not while Mummy was alive anyway."

It was indeed unlikely, in the ordinary course of events, that Mrs. Bolam would ever have benefited from that £25,000 or what was left of it, thought Dalgliesh. Here was the obvious motive, so understandable, so universal, so dear to any prosecuting counsel. Every juryman understood the lure of money. Could Nurse Bolam really be unaware of the significance of the information which she was handing him with such unembarrassed candour? Could innocence be so naïve or guilt so confident? He said suddenly:

"Was your cousin popular, Miss Bolam?"

"She hadn't many friends. I don't think she would have called herself popular. She wouldn't want that. She had her church activities and the Guides. She was a very quiet person really."

"But you know of no enemies?"

"Oh, no! None at all. Enid was very much respected."

The formal, old-fashioned epithet was almost inaudible.

Dalgliesh said:

"Then it looks as if this is a motiveless, unpremeditated crime. Normally that would suggest one of the patients. But it hardly seems possible and you are all insistent that it isn't likely."

"Oh, no! It couldn't be a patient! I'm quite sure none of our patients would do a thing like that. They aren't violent."

"Not even Mr. Tippett?"

"But it couldn't have been Tippett. He's in hospital."

"So I'm told. How many people here knew that Mr. Tippett wouldn't be coming to the clinic this Friday?"

"I don't know. Nagle knew because he took the message and he told Enid and Sister. Sister told me. You see, I usually try to keep an eye on

Tippett when I'm specialling the LSD patients on Fridays. I can't leave my patient for more than a second, of course, but I do pop out occasionally to see if Tippett is all right. Tonight it wasn't necessary. Poor Tippett, he does love his art therapy! Mrs. Baumgarden has been away ill for six months now, but we couldn't stop Tippett from coming. He wouldn't hurt a fly. It's wicked to suggest that Tippett could have anything to do with it. Wicked!"

She spoke with sudden vehemence. Dalgliesh said mildly:

"But no one is suggesting anything of the sort. If Tippett is in hospital—and I haven't the least doubt we shall find that he is—then he couldn't have been here."

"But someone put his fetish on the body, didn't they? If Tippett had been here you would have suspected him straight away and he would have been so upset and confused. It was a wicked thing to do. Really wicked!"

Her voice broke and she was very near to tears. Dalgliesh watched the thin fingers twisting in her lap. He said gently:

"I don't think we need worry about Mr. Tippett. Now I want you to think carefully and tell me everything that you know happened in the clinic from the time you came on duty this evening. Never mind about other people, I just want to know what you did."

Nurse Bolam remembered very clearly what she had done and, after a second's hesitation, she gave a careful and logical account. It was her job on Friday evenings to "special" any patient undergoing treatment with lysergic acid. She explained that this was a method of releasing deep-seated inhibitions so that the patient was able to recall and recount the incidents which were being repressed in his subconscious and were responsible for his illness. As she spoke about the treatment Nurse Bolam lost her nervousness and seemed to forget that she was talking to a layman. But Dalgliesh did not interrupt.

"It's a remarkable drug and Dr. Baguley uses it quite a lot. Its name is lysergic acid diethylamide and I think it was discovered by a German in 1942. We administer it orally, and the usual dose is 0.25 mg. It's produced in ampoules of 1 mg. and mixed with from 15 to 30 c.c.'s of distilled water. The patients are told not to have any breakfast. The first effects are noticed after about half an hour and the more disturbing subjective experiences occur from one to one and a half hours after administration. That's when Dr. Baguley comes down to be with the patient. The effects can last for as long as four hours and the patient is flushed and restless and quite withdrawn from reality. They're never left alone, of course, and we use the basement room because it's secluded and quiet and other patients aren't distressed by the noise. We usually give LSD treatments on Friday afternoon and evening, and I always 'special' the patient."

"I suppose that, if any noise, such as a cry, were heard on Fridays in the basement most of the staff would assume that it was the LSD patient?"

Nurse Bolam looked doubtful.

"I suppose they might. Certainly these patients can be very noisy. My patient today was more disturbed than usual which was why I stayed close to her. Usually I spend a little time in the linen-room which adjoins the treatment-room sorting the clean laundry as soon as the patient is over the worst. I keep the door open between the rooms, of course, so that I can watch the patient from time to time."

Dalgliesh asked what exactly had happened during the evening.

"Well, the treatment began just after three-thirty and Dr. Baguley looked in shortly after four to see if all was well. I stayed with the patient until four-thirty when Mrs. Shorthouse came to tell me that tea was made. Sister came down while I went upstairs to the nurses' duty-room and drank tea. I came down again at quarter to five and rang for Dr. Baguley at five. He was with the patient for about three-quarters of an hour. Then he left to return to his E.C.T. clinic. I stayed with the patient, and as she was so restless I decided to leave the laundry until later in the evening. At about twenty to seven Peter Nagle knocked on the door and asked for the laundry. I told him that it wasn't sorted and he looked a bit surprised but didn't say anything. A little time after that I thought I heard a scream. I didn't take any notice at first as it didn't seem very close and I thought it was children playing in the square. Then I thought I ought to make sure and I went to the door. I saw Dr. Baguley and Dr. Steiner coming into the basement with Sister and Dr. Ingram. Sister told me that nothing was wrong and to go back to my patient, so I did."

"Did you leave the treatment-room at all after Dr. Baguley left you at about quarter to six?"

"Oh, no! There wasn't any need. If I'd wanted to go to the cloakroom or anything like that"— Nurse Bolam blushed faintly—"I would have phoned for Sister to come and take my place."

"Did you make any telephone calls from the treatment-room at all during the evening?"

"Only the one to the E.C.T. room at five to call Dr. Baguley."

"Are you quite sure you didn't telephone Miss Bolam?"

"Enid? Oh, no! There wouldn't be any reason to call Enid. She . . . that is, we didn't see very much of each other in the clinic. I am responsible to Sister Ambrose, you see, and Enid wasn't concerned with the nursing staff."

"But you saw quite a lot of her outside the clinic?"

"Oh, no! I didn't mean that. I went to her flat once or twice, to collect the cheque at Christmas and in the summer, but it isn't easy for me to leave Mummy. Besides, Enid had her own life to live. And then she's quite a lot older than me. I didn't really know her very well."

Her voice broke and Dalgliesh saw that she was crying. Fumbling under her apron for the pocket in her nurse's dress, she sobbed:

"It's so dreadful! Poor Enid! Putting that fetish on her body as if he was making fun of her, making it look as if she was nursing a baby!"

Dalgliesh hadn't realized that she had seen the body and said so.

"Oh, I didn't! Dr. Etherege and Sister wouldn't let me go in to her. But we were all told what had happened."

Miss Bolam had indeed looked as if she were nursing a baby. But he was surprised that someone who hadn't seen the body should say so. The medical director must have given a graphic description of the scene.

Suddenly Nurse Bolam found her handkerchief and drew it out of her pocket. With it came a pair of thin, surgical gloves. They fell at Dalgliesh's feet. Picking them up he asked:

"I didn't realize that you used surgical gloves here."

Nurse Bolam seemed unsurprised by his interest. Checking her sobs with surprising control she replied:

"We don't use them very often but we keep a few pairs. The whole Group's gone over to disposable gloves now, but there are a few of the old kind about. That's one of them. We use them for odd cleaning jobs."

"Thank you," said Dalgliesh. "I'll keep this pair

if I may. And I don't think I need worry you any more at present."

With a murmured word which could have been "thank you", Nurse Bolam almost backed out of the room.

The minutes dragged heavily to the clinic staff waiting in the front consulting-room to be interviewed. Fredrica Saxon had fetched some papers from her room on the third floor and was scoring an intelligence test. There had been some discussion about whether she ought to go upstairs alone, but Miss Saxon had stated firmly that she didn't intend to sit there wasting time and biting her nails until the police chose to see her, that she hadn't the murderer hidden upstairs, nor was she proposing to destroy incriminating evidence and that she had no objection to any member of the staff accompanying her to satisfy themselves on this point. This distressing frankness had provoked a murmur of protests and reassurance, but Mrs. Bostock had announced abruptly that she would like to fetch a book from the medical library and the two women had left the room and returned together. Cully had been seen early, having established his right to be classed as a patient, and had been released to cosset his stomach-ache at home. The only remaining patient, Mrs. King, had been interviewed and allowed to depart with her husband in attendance. Mr. Burge had also left, protesting loudly at the interruption of his session and the trauma of the whole experience.

"Mind you, he's enjoying himself, you can see that," confided Mrs. Shorthouse to the assembled staff. "The Superintendent had a job getting rid of him, I can tell you."

There was a great deal which Mrs. Shorthouse seemed able to tell them. She had been given permission to make coffee and prepare sandwiches in her small ground-floor kitchen at the rear of the building, and this gave her an excuse for frequent trips up and down the hall. The sandwiches were brought in almost singly. Cups were taken individually to be washed. This coming and going gave her an opportunity of reporting the latest situation to the rest of the staff who awaited each instalment with an anxiety and eagerness which they could only imperfectly conceal. Mrs. Shorthouse was not the emissary they would have chosen but any news, however obtained and by whomever delivered, helped to lighten the weight of suspense and she was certainly unexpectedly knowledgeable about police procedure.

"There's several of them searching the building now and they've got their own chap on the door. They haven't found anyone, of course. Well, it stands to reason! We know he couldn't have got out of the building. Or in for that matter. I said to the sergeant: 'This clinic has had all the cleaning from me that it's getting today, so tell your chaps to mind where they plant their boots. . . .'

"The police surgeon's seen the body. The fingerprint man is still downstairs and they're taking everyone's prints. I've seen the photographer. He went through the hall with a tripod and a big case, white on top and black at the bottom. . . .

"Here's a funny thing now. They're looking for prints in the basement lift. Measuring it up, too."

Fredrica Saxon lifted her head, seemed about to say something, then went on with her work. The basement lift, which was about four feet square and operated by a rope pulley, had been used to transport food from the basement kitchen to the first-floor dining-room when the clinic was a private house. It had never been taken out. Occasionally medical records from the basement record-room were hoisted in it to the first- and second-floor consulting-rooms, but it was otherwise little used. No one commented on a possible reason why the police should test it for prints.

Mrs. Shorthouse departed with two cups to be washed. She was back within five minutes.

"Mr. Lauder's in the general office phoning the chairman. Telling him about the murder, I suppose. This'll give the H.M.C. something to natter about and no mistake. Sister is going through the linen inventory with one of the police. Seems there's a rubber apron from the art therapy-room missing. Oh, and another thing. They're letting the boiler out. Want to rake it through, I suppose. Nice for us, I must say. This place'll be bloody cold on Monday. . . .

"The mortuary van's arrived. That's what they call it. The mortuary van. They don't use an ambulance, you see. Not when the victim's dead. You probably heard it arrive. I dare say if you draw the curtains back a bit you'll see her being took in."

But no one cared to draw back the curtains and, as the soft, careful feet of the stretcher-bearers shuffled past the door, no one spoke. Fredrica Saxon laid down her pencil and bowed her head as if she were praying. When the front door closed their relief was heard in the soft hiss of breath released. There was a brief silence and then the van drove off. Mrs. Shorthouse was the only one to speak.

"Poor little blighter! Mind you I only gave her another six months here what with one thing and another, but I never thought she'd leave feet first."

Jennifer Priddy sat apart from the rest of the staff on the edge of the treatment couch. Her interview with the superintendent had been unexpectedly easy. She didn't know quite what she had expected but certainly it wasn't this quiet, gentle, deep-voiced man. He hadn't bothered to commiserate with her on the shock of finding the body. He hadn't smiled at her. He hadn't been paternal or understanding. He gave the impression that he was interested only in finding out the truth as quickly as possible and that he expected everyone else to feel the same. She thought that it would be difficult to tell him a lie and she hadn't tried. It had all been quite easy to remember, quite straightforward. The superintendent had questioned her closely about the ten minutes or so she had spent in the basement with Peter. That was only to be expected. Naturally he was wondering whether Peter could have killed Miss Bolam after he returned from the post and before she joined him. Well, it wasn't possible. She had followed him downstairs almost immediately and Mrs. Shorthouse could confirm it. Probably it hadn't taken long to kill Enid—she tried not to think about that sudden, savage, calculated violence—but however quickly it was done, Peter hadn't time.

She thought about Peter. Thinking about him occupied most of her few solitary hours. Tonight, however, the familiar warm imaginings were needled with anxiety. Was he going to be cross about the way she had behaved? She remembered with shame her delayed scream of terror after finding the body, the way she had thrown herself into his arms. He had been very kind and considerate, of course, but then he always was considerate when he wasn't working and remembered she was there. She knew that he hated fuss and that any demonstration of affection irked him. She had learned to accept that their love, and she dared no longer doubt that it was love, must be taken on his terms. Since their brief time together in the nurses' duty-room after the finding of Miss Bolam she had scarcely spoken to him. She couldn't guess what he felt. She was only sure of one thing. She couldn't possibly pose for him tonight. It hadn't anything to do with shame or guilt; he had long since cut her free of those twin encumbrances. He would expect her to arrive at the studio as planned. After all, her alibi was fixed and her parents would accept that she was at her evening class. He would see no reasonable grounds for altering their arrangements and Peter was a great one for reason. But she couldn't do it! Not tonight. It wasn't so much the posing as what would follow. She wouldn't be able to refuse him. She wouldn't want to refuse him. And tonight, with Enid dead, she felt that she couldn't bear to be touched.

When she returned from her talk with the superintendent, Dr. Steiner had come to sit beside her and had been very kind. But then Dr. Steiner was kind. It was easy enough to criticize his indolence or laugh at his odd patients. But he did care about people, whereas Dr. Baguley, who worked so hard and wore himself out with his heavy clinics, didn't really like people at all, but only wished that he did. Jenny wasn't sure how she knew this so clearly. She hadn't really thought about it before. Tonight, however, now that the first shock of finding the body had passed, her mind was unnaturally clear. And not only her mind. All her perceptions were sharpened. The tangible objects about her, the chintz covering on the couch, the red blanket folded at its foot, the bright varied greens and golds of the chrysanthemums on the desk, were clearer, brighter, more real to her than ever before. She saw the line of Miss Saxon's arm as it rested on the desk curved around the book she was reading and the way in which the small hairs on her forearm were tipped with light from the desk lamp. She wondered whether Peter always saw the life around him with this wonder and clarity as if one were born into an unfamiliar world with all the first bright hues of creation fresh upon it. Perhaps this was what it felt like to be a painter.

"I suppose it's the brandy," she thought, and giggled a little. She remembered hearing the muttered grumblings of Sister Ambrose half an hour earlier.

"What's Nagle been feeding to Priddy? That child's half drunk." But she wasn't drunk and she didn't really believe it was the brandy.

Dr. Steiner had drawn his chair close to her and had laid his hand briefly on her shoulder. Without thinking, Miss Priddy had said:

"She was kind to me and I didn't like her."

She no longer felt sad or guilty about it. It was a statement of fact.

"You mustn't worry about it," he said gently, and patted her knee. She didn't resent the pat. Peter would have said: "Lecherous old goat! Tell him to keep his paws to himself." But Peter would have been wrong. Jenny knew that it was a gesture of kindliness. For a moment she was tempted to put her hand over his to show that she understood. He had small and very white hands for a man, so different from Peter's long, bony, paint-stained fingers. She saw how the hairs curled beneath his shirt cuffs, the stubble of black along the knuckles. On his little finger he wore a gold signet ring, heavy as a weapon.

"It's natural to feel as you do," he said. "When people die we always wish that we had been kinder to them, had liked them better. There is nothing to be done about it. We shouldn't pretend about our feelings. If we understand them we learn in time to accept them and to live with them."

But Jenny was no longer listening. For the door had opened quietly and Peter Nagle had come in.

Bored with sitting in the reception desk and exchanging commonplace remarks with the uncommunicative policeman on duty there, Nagle sought diversion in the front consulting-room. Although his formal interview was over he wasn't yet free to leave the clinic. The group secretary obviously expected him to stay until the building could be locked for the night and it would be his job to open it again on Monday morning. The way things were going it looked as if he would be stuck in the place for another couple of hours at least. That morning he had planned to get home early and work on the picture, but it was no use thinking of that now. It might well be after eleven o'clock before this business was settled and he was free to go home. But even if they could go to the Pimlico flat together Jenny wouldn't pose for him tonight. One glance at her face told him that. She did not come across to him as he entered the room and he was grateful for that amount of restraint at least. But she gave him her shy, elliptical glance, half conspiratorial and half pleading. It was her way of asking him to understand, of saying sorry. Well, he was sorry, too. He had hoped to put in a good three hours tonight and time was getting short. But if she was only trying to convey that she wasn't in the mood for making love, well, that suited him all right. It suited him most nights if she only knew. He wished that he could take her—since she was so tiresomely insistent on being taken—as simply and quickly as he took a meal, a means of satisfying an appetite that was nothing to be ashamed of but nothing to fuss about either. But that wasn't Jenny. He hadn't been as clever as he thought and Jenny was in love. She was hopelessly, passionately and insecurely in love, demanding a constant reassurance, facile tenderness and time-consuming technique which left him exhausted and barely satisfied. She was terrified of becoming pregnant so that the preliminaries to love-making were irritatingly clinical, the aftermath, more often than not, her wild sobbing in his arms. As a painter he was obsessed by her body. He couldn't think of changing his model now and he couldn't afford to change. But the price of Jenny was getting too high.

He was almost untouched by Miss Bolam's death. He suspected that she had always known just how little work he did for his money. The rest of the staff, deluded by comparing him with that poor fool, Cully, thought they had a paragon of industry and intelligence. But Bolam had been no fool. It was not that he was lazy. One could have an easy life at the Steen—and most people, including some psychiatrists, did—without risking that imputation. Everything required of him was well within his capabilities and he gave no more than was required. Enid Bolam knew that all right, but it worried neither of them. If he went she could only hope to replace him by a porter who did less and did it less efficiently. And he was educated, personable and polite. That had meant a great deal to Miss Bolam. He smiled as he remembered how much it had meant. No, Bolam had never bothered him. But he was less confident about her successor.

He glanced across the room to where Mrs. Bostock sat alone gracefully relaxed in one of the more comfortable patients' chairs that he had brought in from the waiting-room. Her head was studiously bent over a book, but Nagle had little doubt that her mind was otherwise occupied. Probably working out her incremental date as A.O., he thought. This murder was a break for her all right. You couldn't miss compulsive ambition in a woman. They burnt with it. You could almost smell it sizzling their flesh. Underneath that air of calm unflappability she was as restless and nervous as a cat on heat. He sauntered across the room to her and lounged against the wall beside her chair, his arm just brushing her shoulder.

"Nicely timed for you, isn't it?" he said.

She kept her eyes on the page but he knew that she would have to answer. She could never resist defending herself even when defence only made her more vulnerable. She's like the rest of them, he thought. She can't keep her bloody mouth shut.

"I don't know what you mean, Nagle."

"Come off it. I've been admiring your performance for the last six months. Yes, Doctor. No, Doctor. Just as you like, Doctor. Of course, I'd like to help, Doctor, but there are certain complications here. . . . You bet there were! She wasn't giving up without a struggle. And now she's dead. Very nice for you. They won't have to look far for their new A.O."

"Don't be impertinent and ridiculous. And why aren't you helping Mrs. Shorthouse with the coffee?"

"Because I don't choose to. You're not the A.O. yet, remember."

"I've no doubt the police will be interested in knowing where you were this evening. After all, it was your chisel."

"I was out with the post and fetching my evening paper. Disappointing, isn't it? And I wonder where you were at six-twenty-two."

"How do you know she died at six-twenty-two?"

"I don't. But Sister saw her going down to the basement at six-twenty and there wasn't anything in the basement to keep her as far as I know. Not unless your dear Dr. Etherege was there, of course. But surely he wouldn't demean himself cuddling Miss Bolam. Not quite his type I'd have said. But you know his tastes in that direction better than I do, of course."

Suddenly she was out of her chair and, swinging her right arm, she slapped his cheek with a force that momentarily rocked him. The sharp crack of the blow echoed in the room. Everyone looked at them. Nagle heard Jennifer Priddy's gasp, saw Dr. Steiner's worried frown as he looked from one to the other in puzzled inquiry, saw Fredrica Saxon's contemptuous glance at them before her eyes fell again to her book. Mrs. Shorthouse, who was piling plates on to a tray at a side table, looked round a second too late. Her sharp little eyes darted from one to the other, frustrated at having missed something worth seeing. Mrs. Bostock, her colour heightened, sank back in her chair and picked up her book. Nagle, holding his hand to his cheek, gave a shout of laughter.

"Is anything the matter?" asked Dr. Steiner. "What happened?"

It was then that the door opened and a uniformed policeman put his head in and said:

"The superintendent would like to see Mrs. Shorthouse now, please."

Mrs. Amy Shorthouse had seen no reason why she should stay in her working clothes while waiting to be interviewed so that, when called in to Dalgliesh, she was dressed ready to go home.

The metamorphosis was striking. Comfortable working slippers had been replaced by a modish pair of high-heeled court shoes, white overall by a fur coat, and head scarf by the latest idiocy in hats. The total effect was curiously old-fashioned. Mrs. Shorthouse looked like a relic of the gay twenties, an effect which was heightened by the shortness of her skirt and the careful curls of peroxided hair which lay cunningly arranged on forehead and cheeks. But there was nothing false about her voice and little, Dalgliesh suspected, about her personality. The little grey eyes were shrewd and amused. She was neither frightened nor distressed. He suspected that Amy Shorthouse craved more excitement than her life customarily afforded and was enjoying herself. She would not wish anyone violently dead but, since it had happened, one might as well make the most of it.

When the preliminaries were over and they got down to the events of the evening, Mrs. Shorthouse came out with her prize piece of information.

"No good saying I can tell you who did it because I can't. Not that I haven't got my own ideas. But there's one thing I can tell you. I was the last person to talk to her, no doubt about that. No, scrub that out! I was the last person to talk to her, face to face. Excepting the murderer, of course."

"You mean that she subsequently spoke on

the telephone? Hadn't you better tell me about it plainly? I've got enough mystery here for one evening."

"Smart, aren't you?" said Mrs. Shorthouse without rancour. "Well, it was in this room. I came in at about ten-past six to ask how much leave I'd got left on account of wanting a day off next week. Miss Bolam got out my dossier—leastwise it was already out come to think of it—and we fixed that up and had a bit of a chat about the work. I was on my way out really, just standing at the door for a few last words as you might say, when the phone rang."

"I want you to think very carefully, Mrs. Shorthouse," said Dalgliesh. "That call may be important. I wonder if you can remember what Miss Bolam said?"

"Think someone was enticing her down to her death, do you?" said Mrs. Shorthouse with alliterative relish. "Well, could be, come to think of it."

Dalgliesh thought that his witness was far from being a fool. He watched while she screwed up her face in a simulated agony of effort. He had no doubt that she remembered very well what had been said.

After a nicely judged pause for suspense, Mrs. Shorthouse said:

"Well, the phone rang like I said. That would be about six-fifteen, I suppose. Miss Bolam picked up the receiver and said, "Administrative officer speaking." She always answered like that. Very keen on her position she was. Peter Nagle used to say, 'Who the hell does she think we're expecting to hear? Khrushchev?' Not that he said it to her. No fear! Anyway, that's what she said. Then there was a little pause and she looked up at me and said: 'Yes, I am.' Meaning, I suppose, that she was alone, not counting me. Then there was a longer pause while the chap at the other end spoke. Then she said: 'All right, stay where you are. I'll be down.' Then she asked me to show Mr. Lauder into her office if I was about when he arrived, and I said I would and pushed off."

"You're quite sure about her conversation on the telephone?"

"Sure as I'm sitting here. That's what she said all right."

"You talked about the chap at the other end. How could you tell it was a man?"

"Never said I could. Just assumed it was a chap, I suppose. Mind you, if I'd been closer I might have known. You can sometimes get an idea who's speaking from the crackly noise the phone makes. But I was standing against the door."

"And you couldn't hear the other voice at all?"

"That's right. Suggests he was talking low."

"What happened then, Mrs. Shorthouse?"

"I said cheerio and toddled off to do a bit in the general office. Peter Nagle was there taking young Priddy's mind off her work as usual, and Cully was in the reception kiosk, so it wasn't them. Peter went out with the post as soon as I arrived. He always does at about a quarter-past six."

"Did you see Miss Bolam leaving her office?"

"No, I didn't. I told you. I was in with Nagle and Miss Priddy. Sister saw her, though. You ask her. Sister saw her going down the hall."

"So I understand. I have seen Sister Ambrose. I wondered whether Miss Bolam followed you out of the room."

"No, she didn't. Not at once anyway. Perhaps she thought it would do the chap good to be kept waiting."

"Perhaps," said Dalgliesh. "But she would have gone down promptly I expect if a doctor had phoned for her."

Mrs. Shorthouse gave a shriek of laughter.

"Maybe. Maybe not. You didn't know Miss Bolam."

"What was she like, Mrs. Shorthouse?"

"All right. We got on. She liked a good worker and I'm a good worker. Well—you can see how the place is kept."

"I can indeed."

"Her yea was yea and her nay, nay, I'll say that for her. Nothing unpleasant behind your back. Mind you, quite a bit of unpleasantness in front of your face sometimes if you didn't watch out. Still, I'd rather have it that way. She and me understood each other."

"Had she any enemies—anyone who bore her a grudge?"

"Must have had, mustn't she? That wasn't no playful tap on the head. Carrying a grudge a bit far, if you ask me." She planted her feet apart and leaned towards Dalgliesh confidentially.

"Look, ducks," she said. "Miss B put people's backs up. Some people do. You know how it is. They can't make no allowances. Right was right and wrong was wrong and nothing in between. Rigid. That's what she was. Rigid." Mrs. Shorthouse's tone and tightened mouth expressed the ultimate in virtuous inflexibility. "Take the little matter of the attendance book now. All the consultants are supposed to sign it so that Miss Bolam could make her monthly return to the Board. All very right and proper. Well, the book used to be kept on a table in the doctors' cloakroom and no trouble to anyone. Then Miss B gets to noticing that Dr. Steiner and Dr. McBain are coming in late, so she moves the book to her office and they all have to go in there to sign. Mind you, as often as not Dr. Steiner won't do it. 'She knows I'm here,' he says. 'And I'm a consultant not a factory hand. If she wants her stupid book signed she can put it back in the medical cloakroom.' The doctors have been trying to get rid of her for a year or more, I do know that."

"How do you know, Mrs. Shorthouse?"

"Let's just say that I know. Dr. Steiner couldn't stand her. He goes in for psychotherapy. Intensive psychotherapy. Ever heard of it?"

Dalgliesh admitted that he had. Mrs. Shorthouse gave him a look in which disbelief fought with suspicion. Then she leaned forward conspiratorially as if about to divulge one of Dr. Steiner's less reputable idiosyncrasies.

"He's analytically orientated, that's what he is. Analytically orientated. Know what that means?"

"I've some idea."

"Then you know that he doesn't see many patients. Two a session, three if you're lucky, and a new patient once every eight weeks. That doesn't push up the figures."

"The figures?"

"The attendance figures. They go to the Hospital Management Committee and the Regional Board every quarter. Miss Bolam was a great one for pushing up the figures."

"Then she must have approved thoroughly of Dr. Baguley. I understand that his E.C.T. sessions are usually very busy."

"She approved all right. Not about his divorce, though."

"How could that affect the figures?" asked Dalgliesh, innocently obtuse. Mrs. Shorthouse looked at him pityingly.

"Who said anything about the figures? We were talking about the Baguleys. Getting a divorce, they were, on account of Dr. Baguley having an affair with Miss Saxon. It was in all the papers, too. Psychiatrist's wife cites psychologist. Then suddenly Mrs. Baguley withdrew the case. Never said why. No one said why. Didn't make any difference here, though. Dr. B and Miss

Saxon went on working together easy as you please. Still do."

"And Dr. Baguley and his wife were reconciled?"

"Who said anything about reconciled? They stayed married. That's all I know. Miss Bolam couldn't say a good word for Miss Saxon after that. Not that she ever talked about it; she wasn't one for gossip I'll give her that. But she let Miss Saxon see what she felt. She was against that sort of thing Miss Bolam was. No carrying on with her, I can tell you!"

Dalgliesh inquired whether anyone had tried. It was a question he usually put with the maximum of tact, but he felt that subtlety would be lost on Mrs. Shorthouse. She gave a scream of laughter.

"What do you think? She wasn't one for the men. Not as far as I know, anyway. Mind you, some of the cases they have here would put you off sex for life. Miss Bolam went to the medical director once to complain about some of the reports Miss Priddy was given to type. Said they weren't decent. Of course, she was always a bit odd about Priddy. Tried to fuss round the kid too much if you ask me. Priddy used to be in Miss Bolam's Guide Company or something when she was young, and I suppose Bolam wanted to keep an eye on her in case she forgot what captain had taught her. You could see the kid was embarrassed by it. There wasn't anything wrong, though. Don't you go believing it if they hint that there was. Some of them here have dirty minds and there's no denying it."

Dalgliesh asked whether Miss Bolam had approved of Miss Priddy's friendship with Nagle.

"Oh, you're on to that, are you? Nothing to approve of, if you ask me. Nagle's a cold fish and as mean as hell. Just try getting his tea money out of him! He and Priddy play around a bit and I dare say Tigger could tell a thing or two if cats could speak. I don't think Bolam noticed though. She kept pretty much to her own office. Anyway, Nagle isn't encouraged in the general office and the medical stenogs are kept pretty busy, so there isn't much time for hanky-panky. Nagle took good care to keep in Miss B's good books. Quite the little blue-eyed boy he was. Never absent, never late, that's our Peter. Leastways, he got stuck in the Underground on Monday and wasn't he in a state about it! Spoilt his record, you see. He even came in on May first when he had the 'flu because we had a visit from the Duke and, naturally, Peter Nagle had to be here to see everything was done proper. Temperature of 103 he had. Sister took it. Miss Bolam sent him home pretty soon, I can tell you. Dr. Steiner took him in his car."

"Is it generally known that Mr. Nagle keeps his tools in the porters' duty-room?"

"Of course it is! Stands to reason. People are always wanting him to mend this or that and where else would he keep his tools? A proper old woman he is about them, too. Talk about fussy. Cully isn't allowed to touch them. Mind you they aren't clinic tools. They belong to Nagle. There wasn't half a row about six weeks ago when Dr. Steiner borrowed a screwdriver to do something to his car. Being Dr. Steiner he mucked up the job and bent the screwdriver. Talk about trouble! Nagle thought it was Cully and they had one hell of a row which brought on Cully's belly-ache again, poor old blighter. Then Nagle found out that someone had seen Dr. Steiner coming out of the porters' duty-room with the tool so he complained to Miss Bolam and she spoke to Dr. Steiner and made him buy another screwdriver. We do see life here, I can tell you. Never a dull moment. Never had a murder before, though. That's something new. Nice goings-on, I don't think."

"As you say. If you've any idea who did it, Mrs. Shorthouse, now's the time to say so."

Mrs. Shorthouse adjusted one of the curls on her forehead with a licked finger, wriggled more comfortably into her coat and got to her feet, thus indicating that, in her opinion, the interview was over.

"No fear! Catching murderers is your job, mate, and you're welcome to it. I'll say this much, though. It wasn't one of the doctors. They haven't the guts. These psychiatrists are a timid lot. Say what you like about this killer, the chap has nerve."

Dalgliesh decided to question the doctors next. He was surprised and interested by their patience, by their ready acceptance of his role. He had kept them waiting because he judged it more important to his inquiry to see other people first, even such an apparently less important witness as the domestic assistant. It looked as if they appreciated that he wasn't trying to irritate them or keep them unnecessarily in suspense. He wouldn't have hesitated to do either if it would have served his purpose, but it was his experience that useful information could most often be obtained when a witness hadn't been given time to think and could be betrayed by shock or fear into garrulity and indiscretion. The doctors had not kept themselves apart. They had waited in the front consulting-room with the others, quietly and without protest. They gave him the credit of knowing his job and let him get on with it. He wondered whether consultant surgeons or physicians would have been so accommodating and felt with the group secretary that there were worse people to deal with than psychiatrists.

Dr. Mary Ingram was seen first by request of the medical director. She had three young children at home and it was important that she get back to them as soon as possible. She had been crying spasmodically while waiting, to the embarrassment of her colleagues who had difficulty in comforting a grief which seemed to them unreasonable and ill-timed. Nurse Bolam was bearing up well, after all, and she was a relative. Dr. Ingram's tears added to the tension and provoked an irrational guilt in those whose emotions were less uncomplicated. There was a general feeling that she should be allowed to go home to her children without delay. There was little she could tell Dalgliesh. She attended the clinic only twice weekly to help with the E.C.T. sessions and had hardly known Miss Bolam. She had been in the E.C.T. room with Sister Ambrose for the whole of the crucial time from six-twenty until seven. In reply to Dalgliesh's question she admitted that Dr. Baguley may have left them for a short time after six-fifteen, but she couldn't remember when exactly or for how long. At the end of the interview she looked at Dalgliesh from reddened eyes and said:

"You will find out who did it, won't you? That poor, poor girl."

"We shall find out," replied Dalgliesh.

Dr. Etherege was interviewed next. He gave the necessary personal details without waiting to be asked and went on:

"As regards my own movements this evening, I'm afraid I can't be very helpful. I arrived at the clinic just before five and went into Miss Bolam's office to speak to her before going upstairs. We had a little general conversation. She seemed perfectly all right to me and didn't tell me that she had asked to see the group secretary. I rang the general office for Mrs. Bostock at about five-fifteen and she was with me taking dictation until about ten to six when she went downstairs with the post. She came back after ten minutes or so and we continued with the dictation, until some time before half past six, when she went next door to type material directly from a tape machine. Some of my treatment sessions are recorded and the material subsequently played back and a typescript made either for research purposes or for the medical record. I worked alone in my consulting-room except for one brief visit to the medical library—I can't remember when, but it was very shortly after Mrs. Bostock left me—until she returned to consult me on a point. That must have been just before seven because we were together when Sister rang to tell me about Miss Bolam. Miss Saxon came down from her room on the third floor to go home and caught us up on the stairs, so she and I went to the basement. You know what we found and the subsequent steps I took to ensure that no one left the clinic."

"You seem to have acted with great presence of mind, Doctor," said Dalgliesh. "As a result the field of inquiry can be considerably narrowed. It looks, doesn't it, as if the murderer is still in this building?"

"Certainly Cully has assured me that no one got past him after 5 P.M. without being entered in his register. That is our system here. The implication of that locked back door is disturbing, but I'm sure you are too experienced an officer to jump to conclusions. No building is impregnable. The . . . the person responsible could have got in at any time, even early this morning, and lain hidden in the basement."

"Can you suggest where such a person lay concealed or how he got out of the clinic?"

The medical director did not reply.

"Have you any idea who that person might be?"

Dr. Etherege slowly traced the line of his right eyebrow with his middle finger. Dalgliesh had seen him do this on television and reflected, now as then, that it served to draw attention to a fine hand and a well-shaped eyebrow even if as an indication of serious thought the gesture seemed slightly spurious.

"I have no idea at all. The whole tragedy is incomprehensible. I'm not going to claim that Miss Bolam was an altogether easy person to get on with. She sometimes aroused resentment." He smiled deprecatingly. "We're not always very easy to get on with ourselves and the most successful administrator of a psychiatric unit is probably someone far more tolerant than Miss Bolam, less obsessional perhaps. But this is murder! I can't think of anyone, patient or staff, who would want to kill her. It's very horrible to me as medical director to think that there might be someone as disturbed as that working at the Steen and I never knew."

"As disturbed or as wicked," said Dalgliesh, unable to resist the temptation. Dr. Etherege smiled again, patiently explaining a difficult point to an obtuse member of the television panel. "Wicked? I'm not competent to discuss this in theological terms."

"Nor am I, Doctor," replied Dalgliesh. "But this crime doesn't look like the work of a madman. There's an intelligence behind it."

"Some psychopaths are highly intelligent, Superintendent. Not that I am knowledgeable about psychopathy. It's a most interesting field but not mine. We have never claimed at the Steen to be able to treat the condition."

Then the Steen was in good company, thought Dalgliesh. The Mental Health Act, 1959, may have defined psychopathy as a disorder requiring or susceptible to medical treatment, but there appeared little enthusiasm on the part of doctors to treat it. The word seemed little more than a psychiatrist's term of abuse and he said as much. Dr. Etherege smiled, indulgent, unprovoked.

"I have never accepted a clinical entity because it is defined in an Act of Parliament. However, psychopathy exists. I'm not convinced at present that it is susceptible to medical treatment. What I am sure is that it is not susceptible to a prison sentence. But we have no certainty that we're looking for a psychopath."

Dalgliesh asked Dr. Etherege whether he knew where Nagle kept his tools and which key opened the door of the record-room.

"I knew about the key. If I'm working late and alone I sometimes need one of the old files and I fetch it myself. I do a certain amount of research and, of course, lecturing and writing, and it's important to have access to the medical records. I last fetched a file about ten days ago. I don't think

I've ever seen the box of tools in the porters' room, but I knew that Nagle had his own set and was particular about them. I suppose if I'd wanted a chisel I should have looked in the porters' room. The tools would hardly be kept anywhere else. Obviously, too, I should expect Tippett's fetish to be in the art therapy department. It was a most curious choice of weapons! What I find interesting is the apparent care taken by the murderer to fix suspicion on the clinic staff."

"Suspicion can hardly rest elsewhere in the face of those locked doors."

"That's what I meant, Superintendent. If a member of the staff present this evening did kill Miss Bolam surely he would want to divert suspicion from the relatively few people known to be in the building at the time. The easiest way to do that would be to unlock one of the doors. He'd need to wear gloves, of course, but then, I gather that he did wear them."

"There are no prints on either of the weapons, certainly. They were wiped, but it is probable that he did wear gloves."

"And yet, those doors were kept locked, the strongest evidence that the murderer was still in the building. Why? It would be risky to unlock the back door on the ground floor. That, as you know, is between the E.C.T. room and the medical staffroom and it leads into a well-lit road. It would be difficult to unlock it without the risk of being seen and a murderer would hardly make his exit that way. But there are two fire-escape doors on the second and third floors and the door in the base-ment. Why not unlock one of those? It can only be, surely, because the murderer hadn't the op-portunity between the time of the crime and the finding of the body, or that he deliberately wished to throw suspicion on the clinic staff even at the inevitable cost of increasing his own danger."

"You talk about 'he,' Doctor. Do you think, as a psychiatrist, that we should be looking for a man?"

"Oh, yes! I would expect this to be the work of a man."

"Although it didn't require great strength?" asked Dalgliesh.

"I wasn't thinking primarily of the strength re-quired but of the method and the choice of weapon. I can only give my opinion, of course, and I'm not a criminologist. I would expect it to be a man's crime. But, of course, a woman could have done it. Psychologically, it's unlikely. Physically, it's per-fectly possible."

It was indeed, thought Dalgliesh. It required merely knowledge and nerve. He pictured for a moment an intent, pretty face bent over Miss Bo-lam's body; a thin, girlish hand slipping open the sweater buttons and rolling up the fine cashmere jumper. And then, that clinical selection of exactly the right place to pierce, and the grunt of effort as the blade went home. And, last of all the sweater drawn lightly back to conceal the chisel handle, the ugly fetish placed in position on the still twitching body in an ultimate gesture of derision and defiance. He told the medical director about Mrs. Shorthouse's evidence of the phone call.

"No one has admitted to making that call. It looks very much as if she were tricked down to the basement."

"That is mere supposition, Superintendent."

Dalgliesh pointed out mildly that it was also common sense, the basis of all sound police work. The medical director said:

"There is a card hung beside the telephone outside the record-room. Anyone, even a stranger to the clinic, could discover Miss Bolam's number."

"But what would be her reaction to an internal call from a stranger? She went downstairs without question. She must have recognized the voice."

"Then it was someone she had no reason to fear, Superintendent. That doesn't tie up with the suggestion that she was in possession of some dangerous knowledge and was killed to prevent her passing it on to Lauder. She went down to her death without fear or suspicion. I can only hope that she died quickly and without pain."

Dalgliesh said that he would know more when he got the autopsy report but that death was almost certainly instantaneous. He added:

"There must have been one dreadful moment when she looked up and saw her murderer with the fetish raised, but it happened very quickly.

She would feel nothing after she was stunned. I doubt whether she even had time to cry out. If she did the sound would be muffled by the tiers of paper and I'm told that Mrs. King was being rather noisy during her treatment." He paused for a moment, then said quietly: "What made you describe to the staff just how Miss Bolam died? You did tell them?"

"Of course. I called them together in the front consulting-room—the patients were in the waiting-room—and made a brief statement. Are you suggesting that the news could have been kept from them?"

"I am suggesting that they need not have been told the details. It would have been useful to me if you hadn't mentioned the stabbing. The murderer might have given himself away by showing more knowledge than an innocent person could have possessed."

The medical director smiled.

"I'm a psychiatrist not a detective. Strange as it may seem to you, my reaction to this crime was to assume that the rest of the staff would share my horror and distress, not to lay traps for them. I wanted to break the news to them myself, gently and honestly. They have always had my confidence and I saw no reason for withholding that confidence now."

That was all very well, thought Dalgliesh, but an intelligent man must surely have seen the importance of saying as little as possible. And the medical director was a very intelligent man. As he thanked his witness and drew the interview to its close, his mind busied itself with the problem. How carefully had Dr. Etherege considered the position before he spoke to the staff? Had his disclosure of the stabbing been as thoughtless as it appeared? It would, after all, have been impossible to deceive most of the staff. Dr. Steiner, Dr. Baguley, Nagle, Dr. Ingram and Sister Ambrose had all seen the body. Miss Priddy had seen it but had apparently fled without a second look. That left Nurse Bolam, Mrs. Bostock, Mrs. Shorthouse, Miss Saxon, Miss Kettle and Cully. Possibly Dr. Etherege was satisfied that none of these was the murderer. Cully and Mrs. Shorthouse both had an alibi. Had the medical director been reluctant to lay a trap for Nurse Bolam, Mrs. Bostock or Miss Saxon? Or was he so certain in his own mind that the murderer must be a man that any subterfuge to mislead the women seemed a waste of time, likely to result only in embarrassment and resentment? The medical director had certainly been almost blatant in his hints that anyone working on the second or third floor could be eliminated since they would have had the opportunity of opening one of the fire-escape doors. But then, he himself had been in his consulting-room on the second floor. In any case, the obvious door for the killer to unlock was the one in the basement and it was hard to believe that he had lacked the opportunity. It would be a second's work only to draw back that lock and provide evidence that the murderer could have left the clinic that way. Yet the basement door had been fast bolted. Why?

Dr. Steiner came in next, short, dapper, outwardly self-composed. In the light from Miss Bolam's desk lamp his pale smooth skin looked slightly luminous. Despite his calmness he had been sweating heavily. The heavy smell hung about his clothes, about the well cut, conventional black coat of a consultant. Dalgliesh was surprised when he gave his age as forty-two. He looked older. The smooth skin, the sharp black eyes, the bouncy walk gave a superficial impression of youth but he was already thickening and his dark hair, cunningly sleeked back, could not quite conceal the tonsure-like patch on the crown of the head.

Dr. Steiner had apparently decided to treat his encounter with a policeman as a social occasion. Extending a plump, well-kept hand, he smiled a benign "how d'you do" and inquired whether he was speaking to the writer, Adam Dalgliesh.

"I have read your verse," he announced complacently. "I congratulate you. Such a deceptive simplicity. I started at the first poem and read straight through. That is my way of experiencing verse. At the tenth page I began to think that we might have a new poet."

Dalgliesh admitted to himself that Dr. Steiner had not only read the book but showed some critical insight. It was at the tenth page that he, too, sometimes felt they might have a new poet. Dr. Steiner inquired whether he had met Ernie

Bales the new young playwright from Notting-ham. He looked so hopeful that Dalgliesh felt positively unkind as he disclaimed acquaintance with Mr. Bales and steered the conversation from literary criticism back to the purpose of the inter-view. Dr. Steiner at once assumed an air of shocked gravity.

"The whole affair is dreadful, quite dreadful. I was one of the first people to see the body as you may know and it has distressed me greatly. I have always had a horror of violence. It is an ap-palling business. Dr. Etherege, our medical di-rector, is due to retire at the end of the year. This is a most unfortunate thing to happen in his last months here."

He shook his head sadly, but Dalgliesh fancied that the little black eyes held something very like satisfaction.

Tippett's fetish had yielded its secrets to the fingerprint expert and Dalgliesh had stood it on the desk before him. Dr. Steiner put out his hand to touch it then drew back and said:

"I had better not handle it, I suppose, because of fingerprints." He darted a quick look at Dal-gliesh and getting no response went on: "It's an interesting carving, isn't it? Quite remarkable. Have you ever noticed, Superintendent, what excellent art the mentally ill can produce, even patients without previous training or experience? It raises interesting questions on the nature of artistic achievement. As they recover their work deteriorates. The power and originality go. By

the time they are well again the stuff they produce is valueless. We've got several interesting
examples of patients' work in the art therapy department, but this fetish is outstanding. Tippett
was very ill when he carved it and went to hospital shortly afterwards. He's a schizophrenic. The
fetish has the typical facies of the chronic disease,
the frog-like eyes and spreading nostrils. Tippett
looked very like that himself at one time."

"Everyone knew where this thing was kept, I
suppose?" said Dalgliesh.

"Oh, yes! It was kept on the shelf in the art
therapy department. Tippett was very proud of it
and Dr. Baguley often showed it to House Committee members when they made visits of inspection. Mrs. Baumgarden, the art therapist, likes to
keep some of the best work on show. That's why
she had the shelves put up. She's on sick leave
at the present but you've been shown the department, I expect?"

Dalgliesh said that he had.

"Some of my colleagues feel that the art therapy is a waste of money," confided Dr. Steiner.
"Certainly I never use Mrs. Baumgarden. But one
must be tolerant. Dr. Baguley refers patients now
and again, and it probably does them less harm
to dabble about down there than to be subjected
to E.C.T. But to pretend that the patients' artistic
efforts can help towards a diagnosis seems very
far fetched to me. Of course that claim is all part
of the effort to get Mrs. Baumgarden graded as a

lay psychotherapist, quite unwarrantably, I'm afraid. She has no analytical training."

"And the chisel? Did you know where that was kept, Doctor?"

"Well, not really, Superintendent. I mean, I knew that Nagle had some tools and presumably kept them in the porters' duty-room, but I didn't know exactly where."

"The toolbox is large and clearly labelled and is kept on the small table in the duty-room. It would be difficult to miss."

"Oh, I'm sure it would! But then, I have no reason to go into the porters' duty-room. That is true of all the doctors. We must get a key for that box now and see that it's kept somewhere safe. Miss Bolam was very wrong to allow Nagle to keep it unlocked. After all, we do occasionally have disturbed patients and some tools can be lethal."

"So it appears."

"This clinic wasn't intended to treat grossly psychotic patients, of course. It was founded to provide a centre for analytically orientated psychotherapy, particularly for middle class and highly intelligent patients. We treat people who would never dream of entering a mental hospital—and who would be just as out of place in the ordinary psychiatric outpatient department. In addition, of course, there is a large research element in our work."

"What were you doing between six o'clock and seven this evening, Doctor?" inquired Dalgliesh.

Dr. Steiner looked pained at this sudden intrusion of sordid curiosity into an interesting discussion but answered, meekly enough, that he had been conducting his Friday night psychotherapy session.

"I arrived at the clinic at five-thirty when my first patient was booked. Unfortunately he defaulted. His treatment has arrived at a stage when poor attendance is to be expected. Mr. Burge was booked for six-fifteen and he is usually very prompt. I waited for him in the second consulting-room on the ground floor and joined him in my own room at about ten-past six. Mr. Burge dislikes waiting with Dr. Baguley's patients in the general waiting-room and I really don't blame him. You've heard of Burge, I expect. He wrote that interesting novel *The Souls of the Righteous*, a quite brilliant exposure of the sexual conflicts concealed beneath the conventionality of a respectable English suburb. But I'm forgetting. Naturally you have interviewed Mr. Burge."

Dalgliesh had indeed. The experience had been tedious and not unenlightening. He had also heard of Mr. Burge's book, an opus of some two hundred thousand words in which the scabrous episodes are inserted with such meticulous deliberation that it only requires an exercise in simple arithmetic to calculate on what page the next will occur. Dalgliesh did not suspect Burge of any part in the murder. A writer who could produce such a hotchpotch of sex and sadism was probably impotent and certainly timid.

But he was not necessarily a liar. Dalgliesh said:

"Are you quite sure of your times, Doctor? Mr. Burge says that he arrived at six-fifteen and Cully has booked him in at that time. Burge says he went straight into your own consulting-room, having checked with Cully that you weren't seeing a patient, and that it was a full ten minutes before you joined him. He was getting impatient and was thinking of going to inquire where you were."

Dr. Steiner did not appear either frightened or angry at his patient's perfidy. He did, however, look embarrassed.

"It's interesting Mr. Burge should say that. I'm afraid he may be right. I thought he seemed a little put out when he began the session. If he says that I joined him at six-twenty-five I have no doubt he's telling the truth. The poor man has had a very short and interrupted session this evening. It's very unfortunate at this particular stage in his treatment."

"So, if you weren't in the front consulting-room when your patient arrived, where were you?" persisted Dalgliesh gently.

An astonishing change came over Dr. Steiner's face. Suddenly he looked as shamefaced as a small boy who has been caught in the middle of mischief. He didn't look frightened but he did look extremely guilty. The metamorphosis from consultant psychiatrist to embarrassed delinquent was almost comical.

"But I told you, Superintendent! I was in number

two consulting-room, the one between the front one and the patients' waiting-room."

"Doing what, Doctor?"

Really, it was almost laughable! What could Steiner have been up to to produce this degree of embarrassment? Dalgliesh's mind toyed with bizarre possibilities. Reading pornography? Smoking hemp? Seducing Mrs. Shorthouse? It surely couldn't be anything so conventional as planning murder. But the doctor had obviously decided that the truth must be told. He said with a burst of shamefaced candour:

"It sounds silly, I know, but . . . well . . . it was rather warm and I'd had a busy day and the couch was there." He gave a little giggle. "In fact, Superintendent, at the time Miss Bolam is thought to have died, I was, in the vulgar parlance, having a kip!"

Once this embarrassing confession was off his chest Dr. Steiner became happily voluble and it was difficult to get rid of him. But at last he was persuaded that he could help no more for the present and his place was taken by Dr. Baguley.

Dr. Baguley, like his colleagues, made no complaint of his long wait, but it had taken its toll. He was still wearing his white coat and he hugged it around himself as he drew the chair under him. He seemed to have difficulty in settling comfortably, twitching his lean shoulders and crossing and recrossing his legs. The clefts from nose to mouth looked deeper, his hair was dank, his eyes black pools in the light of the desk lamp. He lit a cigarette and, fumbling in his coat pocket, produced a slip of paper and passed it to Martin.

"I've written down my personal details. It'll save time."

"Thank you, sir," said Martin stolidly.

"I may as well say now that I haven't an alibi for the twenty minutes or so after six-fifteen. I expect you've heard that I left the E.C.T. clinic a few minutes before Sister saw Miss Bolam for the last time. I went into the medical staff cloakroom at the end of the hall and had a cigarette. The place was empty and no one came in. I didn't hurry back to the clinic so I suppose it was about twenty to seven before I rejoined Dr. Ingram and Sister. They were together for the whole of that time, of course."

"So Sister tells me."

"It's ridiculous even to consider that either of them would be involved but I'm glad they happened to stick together. The more people you can eliminate the better from your point of view, I suppose. I'm sorry not to be able to produce an alibi. I can't help in any other way either, I'm afraid. I heard and saw nothing."

Dalgliesh asked the doctor how he had spent the evening.

"It was the usual pattern, until seven o'clock that is. I arrived just before four and went into Miss Bolam's office to sign the medical attendance book. It used to be kept in the medical staff cloakroom until recently when she moved it into her office. We talked for a short time—she had some queries about the servicing arrangements for my new E.C.T. machine—and then I went to start my clinic. We were pretty busy until just after six and I also had my lysergic acid patient to visit periodically. She was being specialled by Nurse Bolam in the basement treatment-room. But I'm forgetting. You've seen Mrs. King."

Mrs. King and her husband had been sitting in the patients' waiting-room on Dalgliesh's arrival and he had taken very little time to satisfy himself that they could have had nothing to do with the murder. The woman was still weak and a little disorientated and sat holding tightly to her husband's hand. He had not arrived at the clinic to escort her home until a few minutes after Sergeant Martin and his party. Dalgliesh had questioned the woman briefly and gently and had let her go. He had not needed the assurances of the medical director to be satisfied that this patient could not have left her bed to murder anyone. But he was equally sure that she was in no state to give an alibi to anyone else. He asked Dr. Baguley when he had last visited his patient.

"I looked in on her shortly after I arrived, before I started the shock treatments actually. The drug had been given at 3.30 and the patient was beginning to react. I ought to say that LSD is given in an effort to make the patient more accessible to psychotherapy by releasing some of the more deep-seated inhibitions. It's only given under close supervision and the patient is never left. I was called down again by Nurse Bolam at five and stayed for about forty minutes. I went back upstairs and gave my last shock treatment at about twenty to six. The last E.C.T. patient actually left the clinic a few minutes after Miss Bolam was last seen. From about six-thirty I was clearing up and writing my notes."

"Was the door of the medical record-room open when you passed it at five o'clock?"

Dr. Baguley thought for a moment or two and then said:

"I think it was shut. It's difficult to be absolutely certain, but I'm pretty sure I should have noticed if it had been open or ajar."

"And at twenty to six when you left your patient?"

"The same."

Dalgliesh asked again the usual, the inevitable, the obvious questions. Had Miss Bolam any enemies? Did the doctor know of any reason why someone might wish her dead? Had she seemed worried lately? Had he any idea why she might have sent for the group secretary? Could he decipher the notes on her jotting pad? But Dr. Baguley could not help. He said:

"She was a curious woman in some ways, shy, a little aggressive, not really happy with us. But she was perfectly harmless, the last person I'd have said to invite violence. One can't go on saying how shocking it is. Words seem to lose their meaning with repetition. But I suppose we all feel the same. The whole thing is fantastic! Unbelievable!"

"You said she wasn't happy here. Is this a difficult clinic to administer? From what I've heard, Miss Bolam wasn't particularly skilled at dealing with difficult personalities."

Dr. Baguley said easily:

"Oh, you don't want to believe all you hear. We're individualists, but we get along with each other pretty well on the whole. Steiner and I scrap a bit but it's all quite amiable. He wants the place to become a psychotherapy training unit with registrars and lay professional staff running around like mice and a bit of research on the side. One of those places where time and money are spent lavishly on anything but actually treating patients—especially psychotics. There's no danger he'll get his way. The Regional Board wouldn't wear it for one thing."

"And what were Miss Bolam's views, Doctor?"

"Strictly speaking she was hardly competent to hold any, but that didn't inhibit her. She was anti-Freudian and pro-eclectic. Anti-Steiner and pro-me if you like. But that didn't mean anything. Neither Dr. Steiner nor I were likely to knock her on the head because of our doctrinal differences. As you see we haven't even taken a knife to each other yet. All this is utterly irrelevant."

"I'm inclined to agree with you," said Dalgliesh. "Miss Bolam was killed with great deliberation and considerable expertise. I think the motive was a great deal more positive and important than a mere difference of opinion or clash of personality. Did you know, by the way, which key opens the record-room?"

"Of course. If I want one of the old records I usually fetch it myself. I also know, if it's any help to you, that Nagle keeps his box of tools in the porters' rest room. Furthermore, when I arrived this afternoon, Miss Bolam told me about Tippett. But that's hardly relevant, is it? You can't seriously believe that the murderer hoped to implicate Tippett."

"Perhaps not. Tell me, Doctor. From your knowledge of Miss Bolam what would be her reaction to finding those medical records strewn about the floor?"

Dr. Baguley looked surprised for a second then gave a curt laugh.

"Bolam? That's an easy one! She was obsessionally neat. Obviously she'd start to pick them up!"

"She wouldn't be more likely to ring for a porter to do the work or to leave the records where they were as evidence until the culprit was discovered?"

Dr. Baguley thought for a moment and seemed to repent of his first categorical opinion.

"One can't possibly know for certain what she'd do. It's all conjecture. Probably you're right and she'd ring for Nagle. She wasn't afraid of work but she was very conscious of her position as A.O. I'm sure of one thing, though. She wouldn't have left the place in a mess like that. She couldn't pass a rug or a picture without straightening it."

"And her cousin? Are they alike? I understand that Nurse Bolam works for you more than for any other consultant."

Dalgliesh noticed the quick frown of distaste that this question provoked. Dr. Baguley, however co-operative and frank about his own motives, was not disposed to comment on those of any-one else. Or was it that Nurse Bolam's gentle defencelessness had aroused his protective in-stincts? Dalgliesh waited for a reply. After a min-ute the doctor said curtly:

"I shouldn't have said the cousins were alike. You will have formed your own impression of Nurse Bolam. I can only say that I have complete trust in her, both as a nurse and a person."

"She is her cousin's heir. Or perhaps you knew that?"

The inference was too plain to be missed and Dr. Baguley too tired to resist the provocation.

"No, I didn't. But I hope for her sake that it's a bloody great sum and that she and her mother will be allowed to enjoy it in peace. And I hope, too, that you won't waste time suspecting inno-cent people. The sooner this murder is cleared up the better. It's a pretty intolerable position for all of us."

So Dr. Baguley knew about Nurse Bolam's mother. But, then, it was likely that most of the clinic staff knew. He asked his last question:

"You said, Doctor, that you were alone in the

medical staff cloakroom from about six-fifteen until twenty to seven. What were you doing?

"Going to the lavatory. Washing my hands. Smoking a cigarette. Thinking."

"And that was absolutely all you did during the twenty-five minutes?"

"Yes—that was all, Superintendent."

Dr. Baguley was a poor liar. The hesitation was only momentary; his face did not change colour; the fingers holding his cigarette were quite steady. But his voice was a little too nonchalant, the disinterest a little too carefully controlled. And it was with a palpable effort that he made himself meet Dalgliesh's eyes. He was too intelligent to add to his statement but his eyes held those of the detective as if willing Dalgliesh to repeat his question, and bracing himself to meet it.

"Thank you, Doctor," said Dalgliesh calmly. "That will be all for the present."

Chapter Three

AND SO IT WENT ON; the patient questioning; the meticulous taking of notes, the close watch of suspects' eyes and hands for the revealing flicker of fear, the tensed reaction to an unwelcome change of emphasis. Fredrica Saxon followed Dr. Baguley. As they passed each other in the doorway Dalgliesh saw that they were careful not to meet each other's eyes. She was a dark, vital, casually-dressed woman of twenty-nine who would do no more than give brief but straightforward answers to his questions and who seemed to take a perverse pleasure in pointing out that she had been alone scoring a psychological test in her own room from six until seven and could neither claim an alibi for herself nor give one to anyone else. He got little help or information from

Fredrica Saxon but did not, on that account, assume that she had none to give.

She was followed by a very different witness. Miss Ruth Kettle had apparently decided that the murder was none of her affair and, although she was willing to answer Dalgliesh's questions, it was with a vague lack of interest which suggested that her thoughts were on higher things. There is only a limited number of words to express horror and surprise and the clinic staff had used most of them during the evening. Miss Kettle's reaction was less orthodox. She gave her opinion that the murder was peculiar . . . really very odd indeed, and sat blinking at Dalgliesh through her thick spectacles in gentle bewilderment as if she did indeed find it odd, but hardly sufficiently odd to be worth discussing at length. But at least two pieces of information which she was able to give were interesting. Dalgliesh could only hope that they were reliable.

She had been vague about her own movements during the evening, but Dalgliesh's persistence elicited that she had been interviewing the wife of one of the E.C.T. patients until about twenty to six when Sister had telephoned to say that the patient was ready to be taken home. Miss Kettle had walked downstairs with her client, said "good night" in the hall, and had then gone straight down to the record-room to fetch a file. She had found the room in perfect order and had locked it after her. Despite her gentle incertitude about most of the evening's activities she was positive about the time. In any case, thought Dalgliesh, it could probably be verified by Sister Ambrose. The second clue was more nebulous and Miss Kettle mentioned it with apparent indifference to its importance. Some half-hour after returning to her room on the second floor she had heard the unmistakable sound of the service lift thumping to a stop.

Dalgliesh was tired now. Despite the central heating he felt spasms of cold and recognized the familiar malaise that preceded an attack of neuralgia. The right side of his face already felt stiff and heavy, and the needling pain was beginning to stab spasmodically behind his eyeball. But his last witness was here.

Mrs. Bostock, the senior medical stenographer, had none of the doctors' tolerant acceptance of a long wait. She was angry and her anger came into the room with her like a chill wind. She seated herself without speaking, crossed a pair of long and remarkably shapely legs, and looked at Dalgliesh with frank dislike in her pale eyes. She had a striking and unusual head. Her long hair, golden as a guinea, was coiled in intricate folds above a pale, arrogant, sharp-nosed face. With her long neck, poised, colourful head and slightly protuberant eyes, she looked like some exotic bird. Dalgliesh had difficulty in concealing his shock when he saw her hands. They were as huge, red and raw-boned as the hands of a butcher and looked as if they had been incongruously grafted on to the slim wrists by some malignant fate. It was almost a deformity. She made no attempt to conceal them, but her nails were short and she wore no polish. She had a beautiful figure and was well and expensively dressed, an object lesson in the art of minimizing one's defects and emphasizing one's advantages. She probably lived her life, thought Dalgliesh, on much the same principle.

She gave details of her movements since six o'clock that evening briefly and with no apparent reluctance. She had last seen Miss Bolam at six o'clock when, as was usual, she had taken in the post for the administrative officer to sign. There were only five letters. Most of the post consisted of medical reports and letters to general practitioners from the psychiatrists and Miss Bolam was not, of course, concerned with these. All the outgoing mail was registered in the post book either by Mrs. Bostock or Miss Priddy, and was then taken across the road by Nagle to catch the six-thirty from the pillar-box. Miss Bolam had seemed her usual self at six o'clock. She had signed her own letters and Mrs. Bostock had returned to the general office, handed them with the doctors' post to Miss Priddy, and had then gone upstairs to take dictation from Dr. Etherege for the last hour of the day. It was an understood thing that she helped Dr. Etherege on Friday evenings for one hour with his research project. She and the medical director had been together except for a few short periods. Sister rang at about seven o'clock with the news of Miss Bolam's death.

As she and Dr. Etherege left the consulting-room they met Miss Saxon who was just leaving. She went down to the basement with the medical directors. Mrs. Bostock, at Dr. Etherege's request, had gone to join Cully at the front door to ensure that the instructions were followed about no one leaving the building. She had stayed with Cully until the party from the basement appeared and they had then all collected in the waiting-room to await the arrival of the police, except for the two porters who remained on duty in the hall.

"You said that you were with Dr. Etherege from just after six onwards except for short periods. What were you both doing?"

"We were both working, naturally." Mrs. Bostock managed to suggest that the question had been both stupid and a little vulgar: "Dr. Etherege is writing a paper on the treatment of twin schizophrenic women by psycho-analysis. As I said, it has been agreed that I shall assist him for one hour on Friday evenings. That is quite inadequate for his needs, but Miss Bolam took the view that the work wasn't strictly a clinic concern and that Dr. Etherege should do it in his own consulting-room with the help of his private secretary. Naturally that's impossible. All the material, including some on tape, is here. My part of the job is varied. For some of the time I take dictation. Sometimes I work in the little office typing directly from the tape. Sometimes I look up references in the staff library."

"And what did you do this evening?"

"I took dictation for about thirty minutes. Then I went into the adjoining office and worked from the tape. Dr. Etherege rang for me to come in at about ten to seven. We were working together when the phone rang."

"That would mean that you were with Dr. Etherege taking dictation until about six-thirty-five."

"Presumably."

"And for the whole of that time you were together?"

"I think Dr. Etherege went out for a minute or so to verify a reference."

"Why should you be uncertain, Mrs. Bostock? Either he did or he didn't."

"Naturally, Inspector. As you say, either he did or he didn't. But there is no reason why I should particularly remember. This evening was in no way remarkable. My impression is that he did go out for a short time but I really couldn't recall exactly when. I expect he may be able to help you."

Suddenly Dalgliesh changed the course of questioning. He paused for a full half-minute and then asked quietly:

"Did you like Miss Bolam, Mrs. Bostock?"

It was not a welcome question. Under the patina of makeup he saw a flush of anger or embarrassment die along her neck.

"She wasn't an easy person to like. I tried to be loyal to her."

"By loyal you mean, no doubt, that you tried to smooth down rather than exacerbate her difficulties with the medical staff and refrained from any overt criticism of her as an administrator?"

The tinge of sarcasm in his voice awoke, as was intended, all her latent hostility. Behind the mask of hauteur and detachment he glimpsed the insecure schoolgirl. He knew that she would have to justify herself even against an implied criticism. She did not like him but she could not bear to be underrated or ignored.

"Miss Bolam wasn't really a suitable administrator for a psychiatric unit. She hadn't any sympathy with what we're trying to do here."

"In what way was she unsympathetic?"

"Well, for one thing, she didn't like neurotics."

"Neither do I, God help me," thought Dalgliesh. "Neither do I." But he said nothing and Mrs. Bostock went on:

"She was difficult, for example, about paying out some of the patients' travelling expenses. They only get them if they're on National Assistance, but we help other cases from the Samaritan Fund. We have one girl, a most intelligent person, who comes here twice a week from Surrey to work in the art therapy department. Miss Bolam thought she ought to get treatment nearer home—or go without. Actually she made it pretty plain that, in her view, the patient ought to be discharged to do a job of work, as she put it."

"She didn't say this sort of thing to the patient."

"Oh, no! She was careful enough what she actually said. But I could see that the sensitive ones weren't at ease with her. Then she was very critical of intensive psychotherapy. It's a time-consuming procedure. It has to be. Miss Bolam tended to judge a psychiatrist's worth by the number of patients he saw in a session. But that was less important than her attitude to the patients. There was a reason for it, of course. Her mother was mentally ill and in analysis for years before she died. I understand that she killed herself. Miss Bolam can't have had an easy time. Naturally she couldn't allow herself to hate her mother, so she projected her resentment on to the patients here. She was subconsciously afraid of her own neurosis too. That was pretty obvious."

Dalgliesh did not feel qualified to comment on these theories. He was prepared to believe that there was truth in them but not that Mrs. Bostock had thought them out for herself. Miss Bolam may have irritated the psychiatrists by her lack of sympathy, but here at least, they had a believer.

"Do you know who treated Mrs. Bolam?" he asked.

Mrs. Bostock uncrossed her elegant legs and settled herself more comfortably in the chair before deigning to reply.

"I do, as a matter of fact. But I hardly see its relevance to this inquiry."

"Shall we leave that to me to decide? I can find out quite easily. If you don't know or aren't sure it would save time if you said so."

"It was Dr. Etherege."

"And who do you think will be appointed to succeed Miss Bolam?"

"As administrative officer? Really," said Mrs. Bostock coolly, "I've no idea."

At last the main work of the evening was over for Dalgliesh and Martin. The body had been taken away and the record-room sealed. All the clinic staff had been questioned and most of them had left for their homes. Dr. Etherege had been the last doctor to leave and had hung around uneasily for some time after Dalgliesh had said he might go. Mr. Lauder and Peter Nagle were still in the clinic and were waiting together in the hall where two uniformed policemen were on duty. The group secretary had said with quiet determination that he preferred to be on the premises while the police were still there, and Nagle could not leave until the front door had been locked and the key handed over since it was his job to open the clinic at eight o'clock on Monday morning.

Dalgliesh and Martin made their last round of the premises together. Watching them at work a casual observer might have been misled into the facile assumption that Martin was merely a foil for the younger, more successful man. Those at the Yard who knew them both judged differently. In appearance they were certainly unalike. Martin was a big man, nearly six feet and broad-shouldered and looking, with his open ruddy face, more like a successful farmer than a detective. Dalgliesh was even taller, dark, lean and easy moving. Beside him Martin seemed ponderous. No one watching Dalgliesh at work could fail to recognize his intelligence. With Martin one was less sure. He was ten years older than his chief and it was unlikely now that he would gain further promotion. But he had qualities that made him an admirable detective. He was never tormented by doubt of his own motives. Right and wrong stood for him as immutable as the two poles. He had never wandered in that twilight country where the nuances of evil and good cast their perplexing shadows. He had great determination and infinite patience. He was kind without being sentimental and meticulous for detail without losing sight of the whole. Looking at his career, no one could have called him brilliant. But if he was incapable of high intelligence he was equally incapable of stupidity. Most police work consists of the boring, repetitive and meticulous checking of detail. Most murders are sordid little crimes bred out of ignorance and despair. It was Martin's job to help solve them and, patiently and uncensoriously, that is what he did. Faced with the murder at the Steen Clinic with its frightening undertones of a trained intelligence at work, he remained unimpressed. Methodical attention to detail had solved other murders and would solve this one. And murderers, intelligent or subnormal, devious or impulsive had to be caught. He walked, as was usual, a pace or two behind Dalgliesh and said little. But when he spoke it was usually to the point.

They went through the building for the last time that evening, starting on the third floor. Here the eighteenth-century rooms had been divided to provide accommodation for psychiatric social workers, psychologists and lay therapists, together with two larger treatment-rooms for the use of psychiatrists. There was one pleasant and unconverted room at the front of the building furnished comfortably with easy chairs and a number of small tables. This, apparently, was the rendezvous of the marital problem group who could enjoy an agreeable view over the square in the intervals of analysing their domestic and sexual incompatibilities. Dalgliesh could understand the chagrin of the absent Mrs. Baumgarden. The room was admirably suited for the art therapy department.

The more important rooms were on the floor below and here there had been little alteration or adaptation so that ceilings, doors and windows could contribute their own graciousness to the atmosphere of elegance and calm. The Modigliani was out of place in the boardroom but not aggressively so. The smaller medical library next door with its antique bookcases, each bearing the name of the donor, could have been an eighteenth-century gentleman's library until one looked at the titles on the books. There were low bowls of flowers set on the bookcases and a number of armchairs which looked right together although they had obviously come originally from half a dozen different houses.

On this floor, too, the medical director had his consulting-room and it was one of the most elegant in the clinic. The treatment couch, which stood against the far wall, was the same pattern as that in each of the other psychiatrists' rooms, a low single divan, covered in chintz and with a red blanket folded at its foot and one pillow. But no H.M.C. had provided the rest of the furniture. The eighteenth-century desk was uncluttered by cardboard calendars or stationery office diaries and held merely a leather-bound blotter, a silver inkstand and a tray for papers. There were two leather armchairs and a mahogany corner cupboard. It appeared that the medical director collected old prints and was particularly interested in mezzotints and eighteenth-century engravings. Dalgliesh inspected a collection of works by James McArdell and Valentine Green, arranged on each side of the chimney-piece, and noted that Dr. Etherege's patients unburdened their subconscious beneath a couple of fine lithographs by Hullmandel. He reflected that the unknown clinic thief might have been a gentleman if Cully's opinion was to be trusted, but he was certainly no connoisseur. It was more typical of the small-time professional to neglect two Hullmandels for fifteen pounds in cash. It was certainly a pleasant room, proclaiming its owner as a man with taste and the money to indulge it, the room of a man

who sees no reason why his working life should
be spent in less agreeable surroundings than his
leisure. And yet it was not wholly successful.
Somewhere there was a lack. The elegance was
a little too contrived, the good taste a little too
orthodox. Dalgliesh felt that a patient might well
be happier in the warm, untidy, oddly-shaped cell
upstairs where Fredrica Saxon worked in a litter
of papers, pot-plants and the paraphernalia of
tea-brewing. Despite the engravings the room
lacked the nuances of personality. In that it was
somehow typical of its owner. Dalgliesh was reminded of a recent conference which he had attended on mental illness and the law at which Dr.
Etherege had been one of the speakers. At the
time his paper had seemed a model of felicitous
wisdom; afterwards Dalgliesh was unable accurately to recall a single word.

They went down to the ground floor where the
group secretary and Nagle, chatting quietly to
the police constables, turned to watch but made
no move to join them. The four waiting figures
were standing together in a sad group like mourners after a funeral, uncertain and disorganized in
the hiatus that follows grief. When they talked together their voices sounded muted in the silence
of the hall.

The ground-floor plan was simple. Immediately
inside the front door and to the left as one entered was the glass-panelled reception kiosk.
Dalgliesh noted again that it commanded a good
view of the whole hall, including the great curved

staircase at the end. Yet Cully's observations during the evening had been curiously selective. He was positive that everyone entering or leaving the clinic after 5 p.m. had been seen by him and entered in his book, but many of the comings and goings in the hall had passed unnoticed. He had seen Mrs. Shorthouse come out of Miss Bolam's office and into the front general office but had not seen the administrative officer passing down the hall to the basement stairs. He had seen Dr. Baguley coming out of the medical staff cloakroom but not entering it. Most of the movements of patients and their relations had not escaped him and he was able to confirm the comings and goings of Mrs. Bostock. He was certain that Dr. Etherege, Miss Saxon and Miss Kettle had not passed through the hall after 6 p.m. If they had he hadn't noticed. Dalgliesh would have felt more confidence in Cully's evidence if it were not apparent that the pathetic little man was terrified. When they arrived at the clinic he had been merely depressed and a little surly. By the time he was allowed to go home he was in a state of terror. At some stage of the investigation, thought Dalgliesh, he would have to find out why.

Behind the reception kiosk and with windows facing the square was the general office, part of which had been partitioned to form a small filing-room for the current medical records. Next to the general office was Miss Bolam's room and, beyond that, the E.C.T. suite with its treatment-room, nurses' duty-room and male and female recovery bays. This suite was separated by a hallway from the medical staff cloakroom, clerical staff lavatories and the domestic assistant's pantry. At the end of the hallway was the locked side door, seldom used except by members of the staff who had been working late and who did not want to give Nagle the trouble of undoing the more complicated locks, bolts and chains on the front door.

At the opposite side of the main hall were two consulting-rooms and the patients' waiting-room, and lavatories. The front room had been divided to form two fairly large psychotherapy-rooms which were separated from the waiting-room by a passage. Dr. Steiner could, therefore, move from one to the other without coming within Cully's view. But he could hardly move down the hall to the basement stairs without risk of being seen. Had he been seen? What was Cully keeping back and why?

Together, Dalgliesh and Martin examined the basement rooms for the last time that night. At the rear was the door which led to the area steps. Dr. Etherege had said that this door was bolted when he and Dr. Steiner had examined it after finding the body. It was still bolted. It had been tested for fingerprints, but the only decipherable ones had been Peter Nagle's. Nagle had said that he was probably the last person to touch the lock since it was his habit to check that the door was securely bolted before he locked up at night. It was rare for him or for any member of the staff to use the basement exit and the door was usually only opened when the coal or other heavy supplies were delivered. Dalgliesh shot back the bolt. There was a short flight of iron steps leading to the rear railings. Here, again, the wrought-iron door was bolted and fitted with a lock and chain. But an intruder would have no difficulty in getting into the basement area, particularly as the mews at the back were ill lit and unoccupied. The clinic itself would be less easy of access. All the basement windows, except the small lavatory window, were barred. It was through that window the clinic thief had cut his way.

Dalgliesh bolted the door again and they went back into the porters' rest-room which occupied most of the back of the building. Nothing was changed since they had first examined it. Two clothes lockers stood against one wall. The centre of the floor was occupied by a heavy square table. There was a small old-fashioned gas cooker in one corner and, beside it, a cupboard containing cups and saucers and tins of tea, sugar and biscuits. Two shabby leather chairs were drawn up one on each side of the gas fire. To the left of the door was a keyboard with the hooks numbered but not named. On this board had hung, among others, the key to the basement record-room. That key was now in possession of the police.

A large striped cat was curled in a basket before the unlit gas fire. When the light was switched on it stirred and, lifting its heavy barred head, gave the intruders a stare, blank and expression-less, from immense yellow eyes. Dalgliesh knelt beside the basket and stroked the top of its head. The cat shivered then sat immobile under his touch. Suddenly it rolled on its back, and stretched out its legs, rigid as poles, to display a ridge of soft belly hair for Dalgliesh's ministrations. The superintendent stroked and talked while Martin, whose preference was for dogs, looked on in tolerant patience. He said: "I've heard about him from Mrs. Shorthouse. It's Tigger, Miss Bolam's cat."

"We deduce that Miss Bolam read A.A. Milne as a child. Cats are nocturnal. Why isn't he let out at night?"

"I heard about that, too. Miss Bolam thought he'd keep the mice down if he were shut in. Nagle goes out at lunch time for a beer and a sandwich, but Cully eats his grub here and Miss B was always on to him about crumbs. The cat is shut in here every night and let out during the day. He's got his food and his scratch tin."

"So I see. Furnished with cinders from the boiler."

"Pity he can't talk, sir. He was in here for most of the evening waiting to be fed. He was probably here when the murderer came in for the record-room key."

"And for the chisel. Oh, yes, Tigger saw it all right. But what makes you think he'd tell you the truth?"

Sergeant Martin didn't reply. People who went

for cats in a big way were like that, of course. Childish you might call it. Unusually talkative, he said:

"Miss B had him doctored at her own expense. Mrs. Shorthouse told P.C. Holliday that Dr. Steiner was very upset about it. He likes cats seemingly. They had words over it. Dr. Steiner told Mrs. Bostock that Miss Bolam would like everything male at the clinic doctored if she had her way. He put it rather crudely, I gather. Of course, it wasn't meant to get back to Miss Bolam but Mrs. Bostock saw that it did."

"Yes," said Dalgliesh shortly. "She would."

They continued their inspection.

It was not an uncomfortable room. It smelled of food and leather and, just perceptibly, of gas. There were a number of pictures which looked as if they had found a home with the porters when their previous owners had seen enough of them. One was of the founder of the Steen surrounded, appropriately enough, by his five sons. It was a faded sepia photograph in a gilt frame more indicative, Dalgliesh thought, of old Hyman's character than the more orthodox commemorative oil which hung upstairs in the hall.

On a smaller table against the rear wall lay Nagle's box of tools. Dalgliesh lifted the lid. The tools, meticulously cared for, lay each in its correct place. There was only one missing and that was unlikely ever again to find its place in Nagle's toolbox.

"He could have come in through that rear door

if he left it unlocked," said Martin, voicing Dalgliesh's thought.

"Of course. I admit to a perverse disposition to suspect the one person who was apparently not even in the building when the murder was committed. There's little doubt, though, that Nagle was with Miss Priddy in the general office when Mrs. Shorthouse left Miss Bolam. Cully confirms that. And Miss Priddy states that she never left the general office except momentarily to fetch a file from the next room. What did you think of Shorthouse by the way?"

"I thought she was telling the truth, sir. I wouldn't put her above a bit of lying when it suited her. She's the sort who likes things to happen and isn't averse to giving them a bit of a shove in the right direction. But she had plenty to tell us without adding any frills."

"She had, indeed," agreed Dalgliesh. "There isn't any reasonable doubt that Miss Bolam came down to the basement as a result of that call which fixes the approximate time of death for us very satisfactorily. It ties up with the police surgeon's view, too, but we shall know more about that when we get the result of the P.M. The call could have been genuine, of course. It's possible that someone phoned from the basement, spoke to Miss Bolam somewhere down here, then left her to go back to his or her own room and is now too afraid to admit making the call. As I say, it's possible, but I don't think it's likely."

"If the call was genuine it could have been someone calling her down to look at the mess in the record-room. Those files were certainly chucked about before the murder. Some of them were under the body. It looked to me as if she was struck as she crouched to pick them up."

"That's how it looked to me," said Dalgliesh. "Well, let's press on."

They passed the service lift door without comment and went next into the basement treatment-room at the front of the building. Here Nurse Bolam had sat with her patient through the early hours of the evening. Dalgliesh switched on the lights. The heavy curtains had been drawn back but the windows were hung with thin net, presumably to give privacy during the day. The room was simply furnished. There was a low stretcher bed in one corner with a hospital screen at its foot and a small armchair at its head. Against the front wall was a small table and chair, apparently for the use of the nurse in attendance. The table held a rack of nursing report forms and blank medical record sheets. The left-hand wall was lined with cupboards where the clinic's clean linen was stored. Some attempt had been made to sound-proof the fourth wall. It had been lined with acoustic panels and the door, strong and well built, was hung with a heavy curtain.

Dalgliesh aid:

"If her patient were noisy I doubt whether Nurse Bolam would hear much that went on outside.

Walk down the passage will you, Martin, and make a call on the telephone, the one just outside the medical record-room."

Martin closed the door behind him and Dalgliesh was alone with the heavy silence. His hearing was acute and Martin's heavy tread was just audible. He doubted whether he would have heard it against the noise of a distressed patient. He could not hear the faint ring as Martin took off the receiver nor the swing of the dial. In a few seconds he heard the footsteps again and Martin was back. He said:

"There's a card giving the internal numbers so I rang 004. That's Miss Bolam's room. Funny how eerie a telephone bell sounds when there's no one to answer. Then someone did. It gave me quite a shock when the ringing stopped. It was Mr. Lauder, of course. He sounded a bit surprised, too. I told him we wouldn't be long now."

"Nor shall we. I couldn't hear you, by the way. And yet Nurse Bolam did hear the Priddy child scream. Or so she says."

"She took her time doing anything about it, didn't she, sir? What's more she apparently heard the doctors and Sister when they came down."

"That's reasonable enough. There were four of them clattering about. She's the obvious suspect, of course. She could have telephoned her cousin from this room, saying perhaps that someone had been creating chaos in the record-room. Her patient would be far too disorientated to hear or understand. I saw her with Dr. Baguley and it was obvious that she wasn't capable of giving anyone an alibi. Nurse Bolam could have left the treatment-room and waited for her cousin in the record-room with a fair degree of safety. She had the best opportunity to kill, she has the necessary medical knowledge, she has an obvious motive. If she is the murderer the crime probably had nothing to do with the phone call to Lauder. We shall have to find out what Bolam did think was going on here, but it needn't necessarily have anything to do with her death. If Nurse Bolam knew that the group secretary was coming she might have decided to kill now with the idea of obscuring the real motive."

"She doesn't strike me as clever enough for that kind of planning, sir."

"She doesn't strike me as a murderer, Martin, but we've known less likely ones. If she is innocent then her being down here alone was very convenient for the murderer. Then there are those rubber gloves. Of course, she had an explanation for them. There are plenty of pairs about and it's perfectly reasonable for a member of the nursing staff to have a used pair in her apron pocket. But the fact remains that we haven't found any dabs on either of the weapons nor on the door key, not even old prints. Someone wiped them first and handled them with gloves. And what more suitable than thin surgical gloves. Driving that chisel in was practically a surgical operation."

"If she had the sense to use the gloves, then

she'd have the sense to destroy them afterwards. The boiler was alight. What about that missing rubber apron from the art department? If the killer used that as possible protection and disposed of it in the boiler, it would be daft to hang on to the gloves."

"So daft that we're probably meant to think that no sane person would do it. I'm not sure about that apron, anyway. Apparently there's one missing and it's possible that the killer wore it. But this was a clean death and it was planned that way. Anyway, we'll know tomorrow when the boiler's cold and can be raked out. Those aprons have metal studs on the shoulder straps and, with luck, we might find them."

They closed the treatment door behind them and went upstairs. Dalgliesh began to be conscious of his tiredness and the stabbing pain behind his eye was now almost continuous. It had not been an easy week and the sherry party, which promised an agreeably relaxing finish to a busy day, had proved an unsettling preliminary to an even busier night. He wondered briefly where Deborah Riscoe had dined, and with whom. Their meeting now seemed part of a different world. Perhaps because he was tired he felt none of the confidence with which he usually began a case. He did not seriously believe that the crime would defeat him. Professionally he had never yet known the taste of failure. It was all the more irritating, therefore, to be visited by this vague sensation of inadequacy and unrest. For the first time he felt unsure of his own mastery, as if he were opposed by an intelligence actively working against him and equal to his own. And he did not think that Nurse Bolam had that intelligence.

The group secretary and Nagle were still waiting in the hall. Dalgliesh handed over the clinic keys and was promised that an additional set, now held at group headquarters, would be delivered to the police next day. Martin and he, with the two constables, waited while Nagle checked that all lights were out. Soon the whole clinic was in darkness and the six men stepped into the foggy chill of the October night and went their separate ways.

Chapter Four

DR. BAGULEY KNEW that he couldn't in decency neglect to offer Miss Kettle a lift home. She lived in Richmond and her house was directly on the route to his Surrey village. Usually he managed to avoid her and her attendance at the clinic was so erratic that they seldom left at the same time and he could usually drive alone without compunction. He enjoyed driving. Even the frustrations of getting through the city in the rush hour were a small price to pay for those few miles of straight road before he reached home when he could feel the power of the car like a physical thrust in his back and the tensions of the day were ripped from him in the singing air. Just before he reached Stalling it was his custom to stop at a quiet pub for a pint of beer. He never drank more nor less. This nightly ritual, the formal division of day from night, had become necessary to him since he had lost Fredrica. The night brought no relief from the strain of coping with neurosis. He was accustoming himself to a life in which the greatest demands on his patience and professional skill were made in his own home. But it was good to sit alone and in peace, savouring the brief interlude between two different but essentially similar worlds.

He drove slowly at first since Miss Kettle was known to dislike speed. She sat beside him, close-wrapped in a heavy tweed coat, her grey cropped head incongruously crowned with a knitted red cap. Like many professional social workers she had little instinctive understanding of people, a lack which had gained her an undeserved reputation for insensitivity. It was, of course, different if they were her clients—and how Baguley hated that word! Once they were securely caged behind the bars of a professional relationship she gave them a dedicated and meticulous attention which left few of their privacies intact. They were understood whether they liked it or not, their weaknesses exposed and condoned, their efforts applauded and encouraged, their sins forgiven. Apart from her clients the rest of the Steen Clinic hardly existed for Miss Kettle. Baguley did not dislike her. He had long come to the melancholy conclusion that psychiatric social work held a strong attraction for those least suited to it, and Miss Kettle was better than most. The reports

she provided for him were over-long and spattered with the peculiar jargon of the job, but at
least she provided them. The Steen Clinic had its
share of those P.S.W.s who, driven by their irresistible urge to treat patients, were restless until
they had trained as lay psychotherapists and left
behind such lesser excitements as the writing of
social reports and the arranging of recuperative
holidays. No, he did not dislike Ruth Kettle, but
tonight, of all nights, he would have been happier
to drive alone.

She did not speak until they had reached
Knightsbridge, then her high breathy voice fluted
in his ear.

"Such a very complicated murder, wasn't it?
And so oddly timed. What did you think of the
superintendent?"

"He's efficient, I suppose," replied Dr. Baguley.
"My attitude to him is a little ambivalent, probably
because I haven't an alibi. I was alone in the medical staff cloakroom when Miss Bolam is thought
to have died."

He knew that he was hoping for reassurance,
expecting to hear her eager protestations that,
naturally, no one could think of suspecting him.
Despising himself he added quickly:

"It's a nuisance, of course, but not important. I
expect he'll clear the matter up pretty quickly."

"Oh, do you think so? I wonder. I thought he
seemed rather puzzled by the whole thing. I was
alone in my room most of the evening so I prob-

ably haven't an alibi either. But then I don't know when she's supposed to have died."

"Probably at about six-twenty," said Baguley briefly.

"Is that so? Then I most certainly haven't an alibi." Miss Kettle spoke with the liveliest satisfaction. After a moment she said: "I shall be able to arrange a country holiday from Free Money for the Worrikers now. Miss Bolam was always so difficult about spending Free Money on patients. Dr. Steiner and I feel that if the Worrikers can have a quiet fortnight together in some pleasant country hotel they may be able to sort things out. It may save the marriage."

Dr. Baguley was tempted to say that the Worriker marriage had been in jeopardy for so many years that its salvation or otherwise was hardly likely to be settled in a fortnight, however pleasant the hotel. Being precariously married was the Worrikers' main emotional preoccupation and one they were unlikely to relinquish without a struggle. He asked:

"Isn't Mr. Worriker in work then?"

"Oh, yes! He's in work," replied Miss Kettle, as if that fact could have no relevance to his ability to pay for a holiday. "But his wife is a poor manager, I'm afraid, although she does her best. They can't really afford to go away unless the clinic pays. Miss Bolam wasn't very sympathetic, I'm sorry to say. There was another matter, too. She would make appointments for me to see patients without telling me. It happened today. When I looked at my diary just before I left there was a new patient booked for ten on Monday. Mrs. Bostock had written it in, of course, but she added 'on Miss Bolam's instructions.' Mrs. Bostock would never do a thing like that herself. She's a very pleasant and efficient secretary."

Dr. Baguley thought that Mrs. Bostock was an ambitious trouble-maker, but saw no point in saying so. Instead, he asked how Miss Kettle had got on during her interview with Dalgliesh.

"I wasn't able to help him very much, I'm afraid, but he was interested to hear about the lift."

"What about the lift, Miss Kettle?"

"Someone was using it this evening. You know how it creaks when someone's using it and then bangs when it reaches the second floor? Well, I heard it bang. I don't know exactly when, of course, as it didn't seem important at the time. It wasn't very early in the evening. I suppose it could have been about six-thirty."

"Surely Dalgliesh isn't seriously thinking that someone used the lift to get down to the basement. It's large enough, of course, but it would need two people."

"Yes, it would, wouldn't it? No one could hoist himself up in it. It would need an accomplice." She spoke the word conspiratorially as if it were part of some criminal patois, a naughty expression which she was daring to use. She went on: "I can't imagine dear Dr. Etherege squatting in the lift like a plump little buddha while Mrs. Bostock heaved on the ropes with her strong red hands, can you?"

"No," said Dr. Baguley curtly. The description had been unexpectedly vivid. To change the image he said:

"It would be interesting to know who was last in the medical record-room. Before the murder, I mean. I can't remember when I last used the place."

"Oh, can't you! How strange! It's such a dusty claustrophobic room that I can always remember when I have to go down there. I was there at a quarter to six this evening."

Dr. Baguley nearly stopped the car in his surprise.

"At five-forty-five this evening? But that was only thirty-five minutes before the time of death!"

"Yes, it must have been, mustn't it, if she died at about six-twenty? The superintendent didn't tell me that. But he was interested to hear that I'd been in the basement. I fetched one of the old Worriker records. It must have been about five-forty-five when I went down and I didn't stay; I knew just where the record was."

"And the room was as usual? The records weren't chucked on the floor?"

"Oh, no, everything was perfectly tidy. The room was locked, of course, so I got the key from the porters' rest-room and locked the room again when I'd finished. I put the key back on the board."

"And you didn't see anyone?"

"No, I don't think so. I could hear your LSD patient, though. She seemed very noisy, I thought. Almost as if she were alone."

"She wasn't alone. She never is. As a matter of fact I was with her myself up to about five-forty. If you'd been a few minutes earlier we should have seen each other."

"Only if we'd happened to pass on the basement stairs or if you'd come into the record-room. But I don't think I saw anyone. The superintendent kept asking me. I wonder if he's a capable man. He seemed very puzzled by the whole thing, I thought."

They did not speak again about the murder although, to Dr. Baguley, the air of the car was heavy with unspoken questions. Twenty minutes later he drew up outside Miss Kettle's flat off Richmond Green and leaned over to open the car door for her with a sense of relief. As soon as she had disappeared from view he got out of the car and, in defiance of the chilly dampness, opened the roof. The next few miles fled in a gold thread of winking cats'-eyes marking the crown of the road, a rush of cold autumnal air. Outside Stalling he turned from the main road to where the dark, uninviting little pub was set well back among its surrounding elms. The bright boys of Stalling Coombe had never discovered it or had rejected it in favour of the smart pubs edging the green belt; their Jaguars were never seen parked against its black brick walls. The saloon bar was empty as usual, but there was a murmur of voices across the wooden partition which separated it from the public bar. He took his seat by the fire which burned summer and winter, evidently stoked with malodorous chunks of the publican's old furniture. It was not a welcoming room. The chimney smoked in an east wind, the stone floor was bare and the wooden benches lining the walls were too hard and narrow for comfort. But the beer was cold and good, the glasses clean, and there was a kind of peace about the place bred out of its bareness and the solitude.

George brought over his pint.

"You're late this evening, Doctor."

George had called him that since his second visit. Dr. Baguley neither knew nor cared how George had discovered what his job was.

"Yes," he replied. "I was kept late at the clinic."

He said no more and the man went back to his bar. Then he wondered whether he had been wise. It would be in all the papers tomorrow. They would probably be talking about it in the public bar. It would be natural for George to say:

"The doctor was in as usual on Friday. He didn't say anything about the murder. . . . Looked upset, though."

Was it suspicious to say nothing? Wasn't it more natural for an innocent man to want to talk about a murder case in which he was involved? Suddenly the little room became unbearably stuffy, the peace dissolved in an uprush of anxiety and pain. He had got to tell Helen somehow, and the sooner she knew the better.

But although he drove fast it was well after ten before he reached home and saw through the tall beech hedge the light in Helen's bedroom. So she had gone up without waiting for him; that was always a bad sign. Garaging the car he braced himself for whatever lay ahead. Stalling Coombe was very quiet. It was a small private estate of architect-designed houses, built in the traditional manner, and set each in a spacious garden. It had little contact with the neighbouring village of Stalling and was, indeed, an oasis of prosperous suburbia whose inhabitants, bound by ties of common prejudices and snobberies, lived like exiles determinedly preserving the decencies of civilization in the midst of an alien culture. Baguley had bought his house fifteen years ago, soon after his marriage. He had disliked the place then and the past years had taught him of the folly of disregarding first impressions. But Helen had liked it; and Helen had been pregnant then so that there was an additional reason for trying to make her happy. To Helen the house, spacious mock Tudor, had promised much. There was the huge oak in the front lawn ("just the place for the pram on hot days"), the wide entrance hall ("the children will love it for parties later on"), the quiet of the estate ("so peaceful for you, darling, after London and all those dreadful patients").

But the pregnancy had ended in a miscarriage and there had never again been the hope of children. Would it have made any difference if there had? Would the house have been any less an expensive repository of lost hopes? Sitting quietly in the car and watching that ominous square of lighted window, Dr. Baguley reflected that all unhappy marriages were fundamentally alike. He and Helen were no different from the Worrikers. They stayed together because they expected to be less miserable together than apart. If the strain and miseries of marriage became greater than the expense, the inconvenience and the trauma of a legal separation, then they would part. No sane person continued to endure the intolerable. For him there had been only one valid and overriding need for a divorce, his hope of marrying Fredrica Saxon. Now that the hope was over for ever he might as well continue to endure a marriage which, for all its strain, at least gave him the comfortable illusion of being needed. He despised his private image, the stock predicament of the psychiatrist unable to manage his own personal relationships. But at least something remained from the marriage; a fugitive surge of tenderness and pity which for most of the time enabled him to be kind.

He locked the garage gates and crossed the wide lawn to the front door. The garden was looking unkempt. It was expensive to maintain and Helen took little interest in it. It would be better in every way if they sold and bought a smaller place. But Helen wouldn't talk of selling. She was as happy at Stalling Coombe as she could hope to be anywhere. Its narrow and undemanding social life gave her at least a semblance of security. This cocktail-and-*canapé* existence, the bright chatter of its smart, lean, acquisitive women, the gossip over the iniquities of foreign maids and *au pair* girls, the lamentations over school fees and school reports and the boorish ingratitude of the young, were preoccupations which she could sympathize with or share. Baguley had long known with pain that it was in her relationship with him that she was least at home.

He wondered how he could best break the news of Miss Bolam's murder. Helen had only met her once, that Wednesday at the clinic, and he had never learned what they had said to each other. But that brief, catalytic encounter had established some kind of intimacy between them. Or was it perhaps an offensive alliance directed against himself? But not on Bolam's part, surely? Her attitude to him had never altered. He could even believe that she approved of him more than of most psychiatrists. He had always found her co-operative, helpful and correct. It was without malice, without vindictiveness, without even disliking him particularly that she had called Helen into her office that Wednesday afternoon and, in half an hour's conversation, destroyed the greatest happiness he had ever known. It was then that Helen appeared at the top of the stairs.

"Is that you, James?" she called.

For fifteen years he had been greeted every night with that unnecessary question.

"Yes. I'm sorry I'm late. I'm sorry, too, that I

couldn't tell you more on the phone. But something pretty dreadful has happened at the Steen and Etherege thought it better to say as little as possible. Enid Bolam has been killed."

But her mind had seized on the medical director's name.

"Henry Etherege! He would, of course. He lives in Harley Street with an adequate staff and about twice our income. He might consider me a little before keeping you at the clinic until this hour. His wife isn't stuck in the country alone until he chooses to come home."

"It wasn't Henry's fault that I was kept. I told you. Enid Bolam's been killed. We've had the police at the clinic most of the evening."

This time she heard. He sensed her sharp intake of breath, saw her eyes narrow as she came down the stairs to him, clutching her dressing-gown around her.

"Miss Bolam killed?"

"Yes, murdered."

She stood motionless, seeming to consider, then asked calmly:

"How?"

As he told her she still didn't speak. Afterwards they stood facing each other. He wondered uneasily whether he ought to go to her, to make some gesture of comfort or sympathy. But why sympathy? What, after all, had Helen lost? When she spoke her voice was as cold as metal.

"You none of you liked her, did you? Not one of you!"

"That's ridiculous, Helen! Most of us hardly came into touch with her except briefly and in her capacity as A.O."

"It looks like an inside job, doesn't it?"

He winced at the crude, police-court jargon, but said curtly:

"On the face of it, yes. I don't know what the police think."

She laughed bitterly.

"Oh, I can guess what the police think!"

Again she stood silent, then suddenly asked: "Where were you?"

"I told you. In the medical staff cloakroom."

"And Fredrica Saxon?"

It was hopeless now to wait for that spring of pity or tenderness. It was useless, even, to try to keep control. He said with a deadly calm:

"She was in her room, scoring a Rorschach. If it's any satisfaction to you, neither of us had an alibi. But if you're hoping to pin this murder on Fredrica or me you'll need more intelligence than I give you credit for. The superintendent's hardly likely to listen to a neurotic woman, acting out of spite. He's seen too many of that type. But make an effort! You might be lucky! Why not come and examine my clothes for blood?"

He threw out his hands towards her, his whole body shaking with anger. Terrified, she gave him one glance, then turned and stumbled up the stairs, tripping over her dressing-gown and crying like a child. He gazed after her, his body cold from tiredness, hunger and self-disgust. He must go to her. Somehow it must be put right. But not now, not at once. First he must find a drink. He leaned for a moment against the banister and said with infinite tiredness:

"Oh, Fredrica. Darling Fredrica. Why did you do it? Why? Why?"

Sister Ambrose lived with an elderly nurse friend who had trained with her thirty-five years ago and who had recently retired. Together they had bought a house in Gidea Park where they had lived together for the last twenty years on their joint income in comfort and happy accord. Neither of them had married and neither of them regretted it. In the past they had sometimes wished for children, but observation of the family life of their relations had convinced them that marriage, despite a common belief to the contrary, was designed to benefit men at the expense of women, and that even motherhood was not an unmixed blessing. Admittedly this conviction had never been put to the test since neither of them had ever received a proposal. Like any professional worker in a psychiatric clinic, Sister Ambrose was aware of the dangers of sexual repression, but it had never once occurred to her that these might apply to herself and, indeed, it would be difficult to imagine anyone less repressed. It is possible that she would have dismissed most of the psychiatrists' theories as dangerous nonsense if she had ever considered them critically. But Sister Ambrose had been trained to think of consultants as only one degree lower than God. Like God they moved in mysterious ways their wonders to perform but, like God, they were not subject to open criticism. Some, admittedly, were more mysterious in their ways than others, but it was still the privilege of a nurse to minister to these lesser deities, to encourage the patients to have confidence in their treatment, especially when its success appeared most doubtful, and to practise the cardinal professional virtue of complete loyalty.

"I've always been loyal to the doctors," was a remark frequently heard at Acacia Road, Gidea Park. Sister Ambrose often noted that the young nurses who occasionally worked at the Steen as holiday reliefs were trained in a less accommodating tradition, but she had a poor opinion of most young nurses, and an even poorer opinion of modern training.

As usual she took the Central Line to Liverpool Street, changed to an electric train on the eastern suburban line, and twenty minutes later was letting herself into the neat semidetached house which she shared with Miss Beatrice Sharpe. Tonight, however, she fitted her key in the lock without her customary inspection of the front garden, without running a critical eye over the paintwork on the door, and even without reflecting as was her custom on the generally satisfactory appearance of the property and on the gratifying capital investment that its purchase had proved to be.

"Is that you, Dot?" called Miss Sharpe from the kitchen. "You're late."

"It's a wonder I'm not later. We've had a murder at the clinic and the police have been with us for most of the evening. As far as I know they're still there. I've had my fingerprints taken and so have the rest of the staff."

Sister Ambrose deliberately kept her voice level but the effect of the news was gratifying. She had expected no less. It is not every day one has such excitement to relate and she had spent some time in the train rehearsing how most effectively to break the news. The selected sentence expressed concisely the salient details. Supper was temporarily forgotten. Murmuring that a casserole could always wait, Miss Sharpe poured her friend and herself a glass of sherry, specific against shock, and settled down with it in the sitting-room to hear the full story. Sister Ambrose, who had a reputation at the clinic for discretion and taciturnity, was a great deal more forthcoming at home, and it wasn't long before Miss Sharpe knew as much about the murder as her friend was able to tell.

"But who do you think did it, Dot?" Miss Sharpe refilled their glasses—an unprecedented extravagance—and applied her mind to analysis.

"As I see it the murder must have been done between six-twenty when you saw Miss Bolam going towards the basement stairs and seven o'clock when the body was discovered."

"Well, that's obvious! That's why the superintendent kept asking me whether I was sure about the time. I was the last person to see her alive, there's no doubt about that. Mrs. Belling had finished treatment and was ready to go home at about six-fifteen and I went across to the waiting-room to let her husband know. He's always fussed about time because he's on night duty and has to be fed and at work by eight. So I looked at my watch and saw that it was just six-twenty. As I came out of the E.C.T. room door Miss Bolam passed me and went towards the basement stairs. The superintendent asked me what she looked like and whether we spoke. Well, we didn't and, as far as I could see, she looked the same as usual."

"What's he like?" asked Miss Sharpe, visions of Maigret and Inspector Barlow crowding her mind.

"The superintendent? Perfectly polite, I must say. One of those lean, bony faces. Very dark. I didn't say a great deal. You could see he's used to smarming things out of people. Mrs. Shorthouse was with him for hours and I bet he got plenty out of her. Well, I wasn't playing that game. I've always been loyal to the clinic."

"All the same, Dot, it is murder."

"That's all very fine, Bea, but you know what the Steen is. There's enough gossip without adding to it. None of the doctors liked her and nor did anyone else as far as I know. But that's no reason for killing her. Anyway, I kept my mouth shut and if the others have any sense they'll do the same."

"Well, you're all right, anyway. You've got an alibi if you and Dr. Ingram were together in the E.T.C. room all the time."

"Oh, we're all right. So are Shorthouse and Cully and Nagle and Miss Priddy. Nagle was out with the post after six-fifteen and the others were together. I'm not sure about the doctors, though, and it's a pity that Dr. Baguley left the E.C.T. room after the Belling treatment. Mind you, no one in their senses could suspect him but it's unfortunate all the same. While we were waiting for the police, Dr. Ingram came over to suggest that we ought not to say anything about it. A nice mess we'd get Dr. Baguley into with that kind of hanky-panky! I pretended not to understand. I just gave her one of my looks and said: 'I'm sure that if we all tell the truth, Doctor, the innocent will have nothing to fear.' That shut her up all right. And that's what I did. I told the truth. But I wasn't going any further. If the police want gossip they can go to Mrs. Shorthouse."

"What about Nurse Bolam?" inquired Miss Sharpe.

"It's Bolam I'm worried about. She was on the spot all right and you can't say an LSD patient is an alibi for anyone. The superintendent was on to her quick enough. He tried to pump me. Were she and her cousin friendly? No doubt they worked at the Steen to be together? You can tell that to the Marines, I thought, but I kept my mouth shut. He didn't get much change out of me. But you could see which way his mind was working.

You can't wonder, really. We all know Miss Bolam had money and if she hasn't willed it to a cats' home it will go to her cousin. There's no one else to leave it to after all."

"I can't see her leaving it to a cats' home," said Miss Sharpe, who had a literal mind.

"I didn't mean that exactly. As a matter of fact she never took much notice of Tigger although he's supposed to be her cat. I always thought that was typical of Miss Bolam. She found Tigger practically starving in the square and took him into the clinic. Ever since then she's bought three tins of cat meat for him every week. But she never petted him or fed him or let him into any of the upstairs rooms. On the other hand, that fool Priddy is always down in the porters' room with Nagle making a fuss of Tigger, but I've never seen either of them bringing in food for him. I think Miss Bolam just bought the food out of a sense of duty. She didn't really care for animals. But she might leave her money to that church she's so keen on, or to the Guides, for that matter."

"You'd think she'd leave it to her own flesh and blood," said Miss Sharpe. She herself had a poor opinion of her own flesh and blood, and found much to criticize in the conduct of her nephews and nieces, but her small and slowly accumulated capital had been carefully willed between them. It was beyond her understanding that money should be left out of the family.

They sipped their sherry in silence. The two

bars of the electric fire glowed and the synthetic coals shone and flickered as the little light behind them revolved. Sister Ambrose looked around at the sitting-room and found it good. The standard lamp threw a soft light on the fitted carpet and the comfortable sofa and chairs. In the corner a television set stood, its small twin aerials disguised as two flowers on their stems. The telephone nestled beneath the crinolined skirt of a plastic doll. On the opposite wall, above the piano, hung a cane basket from which an indoor plant, cascading streamers of green, almost concealed the wedding group of Miss Sharpe's eldest niece which had pride of place on the piano. Sister Ambrose took comfort from the unchanged homeliness of these familiar things. They at least were the same. Now that the excitement of telling her news was over she felt very tired. Planting her stout legs apart she bent to loosen the laces of her regulation black shoes, grunting a little with the effort. Usually she changed out of uniform as soon as she got home. Tonight she couldn't be bothered. Suddenly she said:

"It isn't easy to know what to do for the best. The superintendent said that anything, however small, might be important. That's all very well. But suppose it's important in the wrong way? Suppose it gives the police the wrong ideas?"

Miss Sharpe was not imaginative nor sensitive, but she had not lived in the same house as her friend for twenty years without recognizing a plea for help.

"You'd better tell me what you have in mind, Dot."

"Well, it happened on Wednesday. You know what the ladies' cloakroom is like at the Steen? There's the large outside room with the wash-basin and the lockers and two lavatories. The clinic was rather later than usual. I suppose it was well after seven when I went to wash. Well, I was in the lavatory when Miss Bolam came into the outer room. Nurse Bolam was with her. I thought they'd both gone home, but I suppose Miss Bolam must have wanted something from her locker and Nurse just followed her in. They must have been in the A.O.'s office together because they'd obviously been talking and were just carrying on with the argument. I couldn't help hearing. You know how it is. I could have coughed or flushed the pan, I suppose, to show I was there but, by the time I thought of it, it was too late."

"What were they arguing about?" inquired her friend. "Money?"

In her experience this was the most frequent cause of family dissension.

"Well, that's what it sounded like. They weren't talking loudly and I certainly didn't try to hear. I think they must have been having words about Nurse Bolam's mother—she's a D.S., you know, and more or less confined to bed now—because Miss Bolam said she was sorry, but she was doing as much as she could and that it would be wiser if Marion accepted the situation and placed her mother's name on a waiting list for a hospital bed."

"That's reasonable enough. You can't nurse these cases at home indefinitely. Not without giving up outside work and saying at home all the time."

"I don't suppose Marion Bolam could afford that. Anyway, she started arguing and saying that her mother would only end up in a geriatric ward with a lot of senile old women and Enid had a duty to help them because that's what her mother would have wanted. Then she said something about the money coming to her if Enid died and how much better to have some now when it would make such a difference to them."

"What did Miss Bolam reply to that?"

"That's what's worrying me," said Sister Ambrose. "I can't remember the actual words, but what it amounted to was that Marion shouldn't rely on getting any of the money because she was going to change her will. She said that she meant to tell her cousin quite openly as soon as she had really made up her mind. She talked about what a great responsibility the money was and how she had been praying for guidance to do the right thing."

Miss Sharpe sniffed. She found it impossible to believe that the Almighty would ever counsel leaving cash away from the family. Miss Bolam was either an ineffectual petitioner or had wilfully misinterpreted the divine instructions. Miss Sharpe was not even sure that she approved of the praying. There are some things, surely, which one ought to be able to decide on one's own. But she saw her friend's difficulty.

"It would look bad if it came out," she admitted. "No doubt about that."

"I think I know Bolam pretty well, Bea, and that child wouldn't lay hands on a fly. The idea of her murdering anyone is ridiculous. You know what I think about young nurses generally. Well, I wouldn't mind Bolam taking over when I retire next year and that's saying something. I'd trust her completely."

"Maybe, but the police wouldn't. Why should they? She's probably their first suspect already. She was on the spot; she hasn't an alibi; she has medical knowledge and would know where the skull is most vulnerable; and where to put that chisel in. She was told that Tippett wouldn't be in the clinic. And now this!"

"And it's not as if it's a small sum." Sister Ambrose leaned forward and dropped her voice. "I thought I heard Miss Bolam mention thirty thousand pounds. Thirty thousand, Bea! It would be like winning the pools!"

Miss Sharpe was impressed despite herself, but remarked merely that people who went on working when they had thirty thousand wanted their brains examined.

"What would you do, Bea? Do you think I ought to say anything?"

Sister Ambrose, sturdily independent and used

to settling her own affairs, recognized that this decision was beyond her and threw half the burden on her friend. Both of them knew that the moment was unique. Never had two friends made fewer demands on each other. Miss Sharpe sat in silence for a moment or two, then said:

"No. Not yet, anyway. After all she is your colleague and you trust her. It wasn't your fault that you overheard the conversation, but it was only overhearing. It was only chance that you happened to be in the loo. I should try to forget it. The police will find out how Bolam has left her money anyway and whether the will has been changed. Either way Nurse Bolam will be suspected. And if it should come to a trial—I'm only saying 'if,' remember—well, you don't want to get involved unnecessarily. Remember those nurses in the Eastbourne case, the hours they spent in the box. You wouldn't want that kind of publicity."

Indeed she wouldn't, thought Sister Ambrose. Her imagination set the scene only too vividly. Sir Somebody or Other would be prosecuting, tall, beak-nosed, bending his terrifying gaze on her, thumbs hooked in the bands of his gown.

"And now, Sister Ambrose, perhaps you will tell his Lordship and the jury what you were doing when you overheard this conversation between the accused and her cousin."

Titters in court. The judge, terrifying in scarlet and white wig, leans down from his seat.

"If there is any more of this laughter I shall clear the court."

Silence. Sir Somebody on the ball again.

"Well, Sister Ambrose . . . ?"

No, she certainly wouldn't want that kind of publicity.

"I think you're right, Bea," she said. "After all, it's not as if the superintendent actually asked me whether I'd over overheard them quarrelling." Certainly he hadn't and, with luck, he never would.

Miss Sharpe felt that it was time to change the subject.

"How did Dr. Steiner take it?" she asked. "You always said that he was working to get Bolam moved to another unit."

"That's another extraordinary thing! He was terribly upset. You know I told you that he was with us when we first saw the body? D'you know he could hardly control himself? He had to turn his back on us and I could see his shoulders shaking. He was actually crying, I think. I've never seen him so upset. Aren't people extraordinary, Bea?"

It was a vehement cry of resentment and protest. People were extraordinary! You thought you knew them. You worked with them, sometimes for years. You spent more time with them than you would with family or close friends. You knew every line of their faces. And all the time they were private. As private as Dr. Steiner who cried over the dead body of a woman he had never liked. As private as Dr. Baguley who had been having a love affair with Fredrica Saxon for years with no one knowing until Miss Bolam found out and told his wife. As private as Miss Bolam who had taken God knows what secrets to the grave. Miss Bolam, dull, ordinary, unremarkable Enid Bolam, who had inspired so much hate in someone that she had ended with a chisel in her heart. As private as that unknown member of the staff who would be at the clinic on Monday morning, dressed as usual, looking the same as usual, speaking and smiling as usual and who was a murderer.

"Damned smiling villain!" said Sister Ambrose suddenly. She thought that the phrase was a quotation from some play or other. Shakespeare probably. Most quotations were. But its terse malevolence suited her mood.

"What you need is food," said Miss Sharpe positively. "Something light and nourishing. Suppose we leave the casserole until tomorrow night and just have boiled eggs on a tray?"

She was waiting for him at the entrance to St. James's Park just as he had expected her to be. As he crossed the Mall and saw the slight figure drooping a little disconsolately by the war memorial Nagle could almost feel sorry for her. It was the hell of a raw night to be standing about. But her first words killed any impulse to pity.

"We should have met somewhere else. This is all right for you, of course. You're on the way home."

She sounded as peevish as a neglected wife.

"Come back to the flat, then," he taunted her softly. "We can get a bus down."

"No. Not the flat. Not tonight."

He smiled into the darkness and they moved together into the black shadow of the trees. They walked a little way apart and she made no move towards him. He glanced down at the calm, up-lifted profile cleansed now of all traces of crying. She looked desperately tired. Suddenly she said:

"That superintendent is very good-looking, isn't he? Do you think he suspects us?"

So here it was, the grasping at reassurance, the childish need to be protected. And yet she had sounded almost uncaring. He said roughly:

"For God's sake why should he? I was out of the clinic when she died. You know that as well as I do."

"But I wasn't. I was there."

"No one's going to suspect you for long. The doctors will see to that. We've had all this out before. Nothing can go wrong if you keep your head and listen to me. Now this is what I want you to do."

She listened as meekly as a child but watching that tired, expressionless face he felt that he was in the company of a stranger. He wondered idly whether they would ever get free of each other again. And suddenly he felt that it was not she who was the victim.

As they came to the lake she stopped and gazed out over the water. Out of the darkness came the subdued cry and shuffle of ducks. He could smell the evening breeze, salt as a sea wind, and shivered. Turning to study her face, ravaged now with fatigue, he saw, in his mind's eye, another picture; a broad brow under a white nurse's cap, a swathe of yellow hair, immense grey eyes which gave nothing away. Tentatively he pondered a new idea. It might come to nothing, of course. It might easily come to nothing. But the picture would soon be finished and he could get rid of Jenny. In a month he would be in Paris, but Paris was only an hour's flight away and he would be coming back often. And with Jenny out of the way a new life in his grasp it would be worth trying. There were worse fates than marrying the heiress to thirty thousand pounds.

Nurse Bolam let herself into the narrow terraced house at 17 Rettinger Street, N.W.1, and was met by the familiar ground-floor smell compounded of frying fat, furniture polish and stale urine. The twins' pram stood behind the door with its stained under-blanket thrown across the handle. The smell of cooking was less strong than usual. She was very late tonight and the ground-floor tenants must long have finished their evening meal. The wail of one of the babies sounded faintly from the back of the house, almost drowned by the noise of the television. She could hear the National Anthem. The B.B.C. service was closing for the day.

She mounted to the first floor. Here the smell of food was fainter and was masked by the tang of a household disinfectant. The first-floor tenant was addicted to cleanliness as the basement tenant was to drink. There was the usual note on the landing window ledge. Tonight it read: "Do not stand your dirty milk bottles here. This ledge is private. This means you." From behind the brown polished door, even at this late hour, came the roar of a vacuum cleaner in full throttle.

Up now to the third floor, to their own flat. She paused on the bottom step of the last flight and saw, as if with a stranger's eyes, the pathetic attempt she had made to improve the look of the place. The walls here were painted with white emulsion paint. The stairs were covered with a grey drugget. The door was painted a bright citrus yellow and sported a brass knocker in the shape of a frog's head. On the wall, carefully disposed one above the other, were the three flower prints she had picked up in Berwick Street market. Until tonight she had been pleased with the result of her work. It really had given the entrance quite an air. There had been times when she had felt that a visitor, Mrs. Bostock from the clinic, perhaps, or even Sister Ambrose, might safely be invited home for coffee without the need to apologize or explain. But tonight, freed, gloriously freed for ever, from the self-deceit of poverty, she could see the flat for what it was, sordid, dark, airless, smelly and pathetic. Tonight, for the first time, she could safely recognize how much she hated every brick of 17 Rettinger Street.

She trod very softly, still not ready to go in. There was so little time in which to think, in which to plan. She knew exactly what she would see when she opened the door of her mother's room. The bed stood against the window. In summer evenings Mrs. Bolam could lie and watch the sun setting behind a castellation of sloping roofs and twisting chimneys with, in the distance, the turrets of St. Pancras Station darkening against a flaming sky. Tonight the curtains would be drawn. The district nurse would have put her mother to bed, would have left the telephone and portable wireless on the bedside table, together with the handbell which could, if necessary, summon aid from the tenant of the flat below. Her mother's bedside lamp would be lit, a small pool of light in the surrounding gloom. At the other end of the room one bar of the electric fire would be burning, one bar only, the nicely calculated allocation of comfort for an October evening. As soon as she opened the door her mother's eyes would meet her, brightened by pleasure and anticipation. There would be the same intolerably bright greeting, the same minute inquiries about the doings of the day.

"Did you have a good day at the clinic, darling? Why were you late? Did anything happen?"

And how did one answer that?

"Nothing of any importance, Mummy, except that someone has stabbed Cousin Enid through the heart and we're going to be rich after all."

And what did that mean? Dear God, what didn't it mean? No more smell of polish and napkins. No more need to propitiate the second-floor harpy in case she were needed to answer that bell. No more watching the electricity meter and wondering whether it were really cold enough for that extra bar of the fire. No more thanking Cousin Enid for her generous cheque twice a year, the one in December that made such a difference to Christmas, the one late in July that paid for the hired car, the expensive hotel which catered for invalids who could afford to pay for being a nuisance. No longer any need to count the days, to watch the calendar, to wonder whether Enid were going to oblige this year. No need to take the cheque with becoming gratitude to conceal behind lowered eyes the hate and resentment that longed to tear it up and throw it in that smug, plain, condescending face. No need to climb these stairs any more. They could have the house in a suburb which her mother talked about. One of the better-class suburbs, of course, near enough to London for easy travelling to the clinic—it wouldn't be wise to give up the job before she really had to—far enough out for a small garden, perhaps, even for a country view. They might even afford a little car. She could learn to drive. And then, when it was no longer possible for her mother to be left, they could be together. It meant the end of this nagging anxiety about the future. There was no reason now to picture her mother in a chronic sick ward, cared for by overworked

strangers, surrounded by the senile and inconti-
nent, waiting hopelessly for the end. And money
could buy less vital but not unimportant pleasures. She would get some clothes. It would no
longer be necessary to wait for the biennial sales
if she wanted a suit with some evidence of quality. It would be possible to dress well, really well,
on half the amount Enid had spent on those unattractive skirts and suits. There must be ward-
robes full of them in the Kensington flat. Someone
would have the job of sorting them out. And
who would want them? Who would want anything that had belonged to Cousin Enid? Except
her money. Except her money. Except her money.
And suppose she had already written to her solicitor about changing the will. Surely that wasn't
possible! Nurse Bolam fought down panic and
forced herself once again to consider the possibility rationally. She had thought it out so many
times before. Suppose Enid had written on
Wednesday night. All right, suppose she had. It
would be too late to catch the post that evening so the letter would have been received
only this morning. Everyone knew how long solicitors took to do anything. Even if Enid had
stressed the urgency, had caught the Wednesday post, the new will couldn't possibly be ready
for signature yet. And if it were ready, if it were
waiting to be posted in its solid official-looking
envelope, what did it matter? Cousin Enid
wouldn't sign it now with that round, upright, un-
adult hand which had always seemed so typical

of her. Cousin Enid would never sign anything again.

She thought again about the money. Not about her own share. That was hardly likely to bring her happiness now. But, even if they arrested her for murder they couldn't stop Mummy inheriting her share. No one could stop that. But somehow she must get hold of some cash urgently. Everyone knew that a will took months to prove. Would it look very suspicious or heartless if she went to Enid's solicitor to explain how poor they were and to ask what could be arranged? Or would it be wiser to approach the bank? Perhaps the solicitor would send for her. Yes, of course he would. She and her mother were the next of kin. And as soon as the will was read she could tactfully raise the question of an advance. Surely that would be natural enough? An advance of one hundred pounds wouldn't be much to ask by someone who was going to inherit a share of thirty thousand.

Suddenly she could bear it no longer. The long tension broke. She wasn't conscious of covering those last few stairs, of putting her key in the lock. At once she was in the flat and through to her mother's room. Howling with fear and misery, crying as she had not cried since childhood, she hurled herself on her mother's breast and felt around her the comfort and the unexpected strength of those brittle, shaking arms. The arms rocked her like a baby. The beloved voice cooed its reassurance. Under the cheap nightdress she smelt the soft familiar flesh.

"Hush, my darling. My baby. Hush. What is it? What's happened. Tell me, darling."

And Nurse Bolam told her.

Since his divorce two years earlier Dr. Steiner had shared a house in Hampstead with his widowed sister. He had his own sitting-room and kitchen, an arrangement which enabled Rosa and him to see little of each other, thus fostering the illusion that they got on well together. Rosa was a culture snob. Her house was the centre for a collection of resting actors, one-volume poets, aesthetes posing on the fringe of the ballet world, and writers more anxious to talk about their craft in an atmosphere of sympathetic understanding than to practise it. Dr. Steiner did not resent them. He merely ensured that they ate and drank at Rosa's expense, not his. He was aware that his profession had a certain cachet for his sister and that to introduce "my brother Paul—the famous psycho-analyst" was in some measure a compensation for the low rent which he spasmodically paid and the minor irritations of propinquity. He would hardly have been housed so economically and comfortably had he been a bank manager.

Tonight Rosa was out. It was exasperating and inconsiderate of her to be missing on the one evening when he needed her company, but that was typical of Rosa. The German maid was out, too, presumably illicitly, since Friday was not her half-day. There was soup and salad put ready for him in his kitchen, but even the effort of heating the soup seemed beyond him. The sandwiches he had eaten without relish at the clinic had taken away his appetite but left him hungry for protein, preferably hot and properly cooked. But he did not want to eat alone. Pouring himself a glass of sherry he recognized his need to talk to someone—anyone, about the murder. The need was imperative. He thought of Valda.

His marriage to Valda had been doomed from the start, as any marriage must be when husband and wife have a basic ignorance of each other's needs coupled with the illusion that they understand each other perfectly. Dr. Steiner had not been desolated by his divorce, but he had been inconvenienced and distressed, and had been harried afterwards by an irrational sense of failure and guilt. Valda, on the other hand, apparently throve on freedom. When they met he was always struck with her glow of physical well-being. They did not avoid each other, since meeting her ex-husband and discarded lovers with the greatest appearance of friendliness and good humour was what Valda meant when she talked about civilized behaviour. Dr. Steiner did not like or admire her. He liked the company of women who were well-informed, well-educated, intelligent and fundamentally serious. But these were not the kind of women he liked to go to bed with. He knew all about this inconvenient dichotomy. Its causes had occupied many expensive hours with his analyst. Unfortunately, knowing is one thing and changing is another, as some of his patients could have told him. And there had been times with Valda (christened Millicent) when he hadn't really wanted to be different.

The telephone rang for about a minute before she answered and he told her about Miss Bolam against a background noise of music and clinking glasses. The flat was apparently full of people. He wasn't even sure she had heard him.

"What is it?" he asked irritably. "Are you having a party?"

"Just a few chums. Wait while I turn down the gramophone. Now, what did you say?"

Dr. Steiner said it again. This time Valda's reaction was entirely satisfactory.

"Murdered! No! Darling, how too frightful for you! Miss Bolam. Isn't she that dreary old A.O. you hated so much? The one who kept trying to do you down over your travelling claims?"

"I didn't hate her, Valda. In some ways I respected her. She had considerable integrity. Of course, she was rather obsessional, frightened of her own subconscious aggressions, possibly sexually frigid. . . ."

"That's what I said, darling. I knew you couldn't bear her. Oh, Paulie, they won't think you did it, will they?"

"Of course not," said Dr. Steiner, beginning to regret his impulse to confide.

"But you always did say that someone should get rid of her."

The conversation was beginning to have a nightmare quality. The gramophone thudded its insistent bass to the treble cacophony of Valda's party and the pulse in Dr. Steiner's temple beat in unison. He was going to start one of his headaches.

"I meant that she should be transferred to another clinic, not bashed on the head with a blunt instrument."

The hackneyed phrase sharpened her curiosity. Violence had always fascinated her. He knew that she saw in imagination a spatter of blood and brains.

"Darling, I must hear all about it. Why not come over?"

"Well, I was thinking of it," said Dr. Steiner. He added cunningly: "There are one or two details I can't give you over the phone. But if you've got a party it's rather difficult. Frankly, Valda, I'm not capable of being sociable just now. I've got one of my heads starting. This has all been a terrible shock. After all, I did more or less discover the body."

"You poor sweet. Look, give me half an hour and I'll get rid of the chums."

The chums sounded to Dr. Steiner as if they were well entrenched and he said so.

"Not really. We were all going on to Toni's. They can manage without me. I'll give them a shove and you set off in about half an hour. All right?"

It was certainly all right. Replacing the receiver, Dr. Steiner decided that he would just have time to bathe and change in comfort. He pondered on a choice of tie. The headache unaccountably seemed to have gone. Just before he left the house the telephone rang. He felt a spasm of apprehension. Perhaps Valda had changed her mind about seeing off the chums and having some time alone together. That, after all, had been a recurring pattern in his marriage. He was irritated to find that the hand reaching for the receiver was not quite steady. But the caller was only Dr. Etherege to say that he was calling an emergency meeting of the clinic Medical Committee for 8 p.m. the following evening. In his relief Dr. Steiner, momentarily forgetting Miss Bolam, just saved himself in time from the folly of asking why.

If Ralfe and Sonia Bostock had lived in Clapham their flat would have been called a basement. Since, however, it was in Hampstead, half a mile in fact from Dr. Steiner's house, a small wooden notice, lettered with impeccable taste, directed one to the garden flat. Here they paid nearly twelve pounds a week for a socially acceptable address and the privilege of seeing a green sloping lawn from the sitting-room window. They had planted this lawn with crocuses and daffodils and in spring those plants which managed to bloom in the almost complete lack of sun, at least fostered the illusion that the flat had access to a garden. In autumn, however, the view was less agreeable and dampness from the sloping soil seeped into the room. The flat was noisy. There was a nursery school two houses away and a young family in the ground-floor flat. Ralfe Bostock, dispensing drinks to their carefully selected friends and raising his voice against the wail of bath-time tantrums, would say:

"Sorry for the row. I'm afraid the intelligentsia have taken to breeding but not—also—to controlling their brats." He was given to malicious remarks, some of which were clever, but he overworked them. His wife lived in constant apprehension that he would make the same witticism twice to the same people. There were few things more fatal to a man's chances than the reputation for repeating his jokes.

Tonight he was out at a political meeting. She approved of the meeting which might be an important one for him and she did not mind being alone. She wanted time to think. She went into the bedroom and took off her suit, shaking it carefully and hanging it in the wardrobe, then put on a housecoat of brown velvet. Next she sat at her dressing-table. Binding a *crèpe* bandage about her brow she began to cream the make-up from her face. She was more tired than she had realized and needed a drink, but nothing would deter her from her evening ritual. There was much to think about; much to plan. The grey-green eyes, ringed with cream, gazed calmly back at her from the glass. Leaning forward she inspected the delicate folds of skin beneath each eye, watching for the first lines of age. She was only twenty-eight after all. There was no need to worry yet. But Ralfe was thirty this year. Time was passing. If they were to achieve anything there was no time to lose.

She considered tactics. The situation would need careful handling and there was no room for mistakes. She had made one already. The temptation to slap Nagle's face had proved irresistible, but it was still a mistake and possibly a bad one, too like vulgar exhibitionism to be safe. Aspiring administrative officers did not slap a porter's face, even when under strain, particularly if they wanted to create an impression of calm, authoritative competence. She remembered the look on Miss Saxon's face. Well, Fredrica Saxon was in no position to be censorious. It was a pity that Dr. Steiner was there, but it had all happened so quickly that she couldn't be sure that he had really seen. The Priddy child was of no importance.

Nagle would have to go, of course, once she was appointed. Here, too, she would have to be careful. He was an insolent devil, but the clinic could do much worse and the consultants knew it. An efficient porter made quite a difference to their comfort, especially when he was willing and able to carry out the many small repair jobs that were needed. It wouldn't be a popular move if they had to wait for someone to come from the group engineer's department every time a sash cord broke or a fuse needed replacing. Nagle would have to go, but she would put out feelers for a good replacement before taking any action.

The main concern at present must be to get the consultants' support for her appointment. She could be sure of Dr. Etherege and his was the most powerful voice. But it wasn't the only one. He would be retiring in six months' time and his influence would be on the wane. If she were offered an acting appointment, and all went well, the Hospital Management Committee might not be in too much of a hurry to advertise the post. Almost certainly they would wait until the murder was either solved or the police shelved the case. It was up to her to consolidate her position in the intervening months. It wouldn't do to take anything for granted. When there had been trouble at a unit, Committees tended to make an outside appointment. There was safety in bringing in a stranger uncontaminated by the previous upset. The group secretary would be an influence there. It had been a wise move to see him last month and ask his advice about working for the diploma of the Institute of Hospital Administrators. He liked his staff to qualify and, being a man, he was flattered to be asked for advice. But he wasn't a fool. He didn't have to be. She was as suitable a candidate as the H.M.C. were likely to find, and he knew it.

She lay back, relaxed, on her single bed, her feet raised on a pillow, her mind busy with the images of success. "My wife is administrative officer of the Steen Clinic." So much more satisfactory than, "Actually, my wife is working as a secretary at present. The Steen Clinic, as a matter of fact."

And less than two miles away, in a mortuary in north London, Miss Bolam's body, tight-packed as a herring in an ice box, stiffened slowly through the autumn night.

Chapter Five

IF THERE HAD TO BE a murder at the Steen, Friday was the most convenient day for it. The clinic did not open on Saturday so that the police were able to work in the building without the complications presented by the presence of patients and staff. The staff, presumably, were glad of two days' grace in which to recover from the shock, determine at leisure what their official reaction should be and seek the comfort and reassurance of their friends.

Dalgliesh's day began early. He had asked for a report from the local C.I.D. about the Steen burglary and this, together with typescripts of the previous day's interviews, was waiting on his desk. The burglary had puzzled the local men. There could be no doubt that someone had broken into the clinic and that the £15 was missing. It was not so certain that these two facts were related. The local sergeant thought it odd that a casual thief had picked the one drawer which held cash while neglecting the safe and leaving untouched the silver inkstand in the medical director's office. On the other hand, Cully had undoubtedly seen a man leaving the clinic and both he and Nagle had alibis for the time of entry. The local C.I.D. were inclined to suspect Nagle of having helped himself to the cash while he was alone in the building, but it had not been found on him and there was no real evidence. Besides, the porter had plenty of opportunities for dishonesty at the Steen if he were so inclined, and nothing was known against him. The whole affair was puzzling. They were still working on it but weren't very hopeful. Dalgliesh asked that any progress should be reported to him at once and set off with Sergeant Martin to examine Miss Bolam's flat.

Miss Bolam had lived on the fifth floor of a solid, red-brick block near Kensington High Street. There was no difficulty over the key. The resident caretaker handed it over with formal and perfunctory expressions of regret at Miss Bolam's death. She seemed to feel that some reference to the murder was necessary, but managed to give the impression that the company's tenants usually had the good taste to quit this life in more orthodox fashion.

"There will be no undesirable publicity, I hope,"

she murmured, as she escorted Dalgliesh and Sergeant Martin to the lift. "These flats are very select and the company are most particular about their tenants. We have never had trouble of this kind before."

Dalgliesh resisted the temptation to say that Miss Bolam's murderer had obviously not recognized one of the company's tenants.

"The publicity is hardly likely to affect the flats," he pointed out. "It's not as if the murder took place here." The caretaker was heard to murmur that she hoped not indeed!

They ascended to the fifth floor together in the slow, old-fashioned panelled lift. The atmosphere was heavy with disapproval.

"Did you know Miss Bolam at all?" Dalgliesh inquired. "I believe she had lived here for some years."

"I knew her to say good morning to, nothing more. She was a very quiet tenant. But then all our tenants are. She has been in residence for fifteen years, I believe. Her mother was the tenant previously and they lived here together. When Mrs. Bolam died her daughter took over the tenancy. That was before my time."

"Did her mother die here?"

The caretaker closed her lips repressively.

"Mrs. Bolam died in a nursing home in the country. There was some unpleasantness, I believe."

"You mean that she killed herself?"

"I was told so. As I said, it happened before I

took this job. Naturally I never alluded to the fact
either to Miss Bolam or to any of the other tenants. It is not the kind of thing one would wish to
talk about. They really do seem a most unfortunate family."

"What rent did Miss Bolam pay?"

The caretaker paused before replying. This
was obviously high on her list of questions that
should not properly be asked. Then, as if reluctantly admitting the authority of the police, she
replied:

"Our fourth and fifth floor two-bedroom flats
are from £490 excluding rates."

That was about half Miss Bolam's salary,
thought Dalgliesh. It was too high a proportion
for anyone without private means. He had yet to
see the dead woman's solicitor, but it looked as if
Nurse Bolam's assessment of her cousin's income was not far wrong.

He dismissed the caretaker at the door of the
flat and he and Martin went in together.

This prying among the personal residue of a
finished life was a part of his job that Dalgliesh
had always found a little distasteful. It was too
much like putting the dead at a disadvantage.
During his career he had examined with interest
and with pity so many petty leavings. The soiled
underclothes pushed hurriedly into drawers, personal letters which prudence would have destroyed, half-eaten meals, unpaid bills, old
photographs, pictures and books which the dead
would not have chosen to represent their taste to

a curious or vulgar world, family secrets, stale make-up in greasy jars, the muddle of ill-disciplined or unhappy lives. It was no longer the fashion to dread an unshriven end but most people, if they thought at all, hoped for time to clear away their debris. He remembered from childhood the voice of an old aunt exhorting him to change his vest. "Suppose you got run over, Adam. What would people think?" The question was less absurd than it had seemed to a ten-year-old. Time had taught him that it expressed one of the major preoccupations of mankind, the dread of losing face.

But Enid Bolam might have lived each day as if expecting sudden death. He had never examined a flat so neat, so obsessively tidy. Even her few cosmetics, the brush and comb on her dressing-table were arranged with patterned precision. The heavy double bed was made. Friday was obviously her day for changing the linen. The used sheets and pillow-cases were folded into a laundry box which lay open on a chair. The bed-side table held nothing but a small travelling clock, a carafe of water and a Bible with a booklet beside it appointing the passage to be read each day and expounding the moral. There was nothing in the table drawer but a bottle of aspirin and a folded handkerchief. A hotel room would have held as much individuality.

All the furniture was old and heavy. The ornate mahogany door of the wardrobe swung open soundlessly to reveal a row of tightly packed clothes. They were expensive but unexciting.

Miss Bolam had bought from that store which still caters mainly for country-house dowagers. There were well-cut skirts of indeterminate colour, heavy coats tailored to last through a dozen English winters, woollen dresses which could offend no one. Once the wardrobe was closed it was impossible accurately to recall a single garment. At the back of them all, closeted from the light, were bowls of fibre, planted no doubt with bulbs whose Christmas flowering Miss Bolam would never see.

Dalgliesh and Martin had worked together for too many years to find much talking necessary and they moved about the flat almost in silence. Everywhere was the same heavy, old-fashioned furniture, the same ordered neatness. It was hard to believe that these rooms had been recently lived in, that anyone had cooked a meal in this impersonal kitchen. It was very quiet. At this height and muffled by the solid Victorian walls the clamour of traffic in Kensington High Street was a faint, distant throbbing. Only the insistent ticking of a grandfather clock in the hall stabbed the still silence. The air was cold and almost odourless except for the smell of the flowers. They were everywhere. There was a bowl of chrysanthemums on the hall table and another in the sitting-room. The bedroom mantelpiece held a small jug of anemones. On the kitchen dresser was a taller brass jug of autumn foliage, the gatherings perhaps of some recent country walk. Dalgliesh did not like autumn flowers, the chrysanthemums which obstinately refuse to die, flaunting their shaggy heads even on a rotting stem, scentless dahlias fit only to be planted in neat rows in municipal parks. His wife had died in October and he had long recognized the minor bereavements which follow the death of the heart. Autumn was no longer a good time of the year. For him the flowers in Miss Bolam's flat emphasized the general air of gloom, like wreaths at a funeral.

The sitting-room was the largest room in the flat and here was Miss Bolam's desk. Martin fingered it appreciatively.

"It's all good solid stuff, sir, isn't it? We've got a piece rather like this. The wife's mother left it to us. Mind you, they don't make furniture like it today. You get nothing for it, of course. Too big for modern rooms, I suppose. But it's got quality."

"You can certainly lean against it without collapsing," said Dalgliesh.

"That's what I mean, sir. Good solid stuff. No wonder she hung on to it. A sensible young woman on the whole, I'd say, and one who knew how to make herself comfortable." He drew a second chair up to the desk where Dalgliesh was already seated, planted his heavy thighs in it, and did indeed look comfortable and at home.

The desk was unlocked. The top rolled back without difficulty. Inside was a portable typewriter and a metal box containing files of paper, each file neatly labelled. The drawers and compartments of the desk held writing paper, envelopes, and correspondence. As they expected, everything was in perfect order. They went through the files together. Miss Bolam paid her bills as soon as they were due and kept a running account of all her household expenditure.

There was much to be gone through. Details of her investments were filed under the appropriate heading. At her mother's death the trustee securities had been redeemed and the capital reinvested in equities. The portfolio was skilfully balanced and there could be little doubt that Miss Bolam had been well advised and had increased her assets considerably during the past five years. Dalgliesh noted the name of her stockbroker and solicitor. Both would have to be seen before the investigation was complete.

The dead woman kept few of her personal letters; perhaps there had been few worth keeping. But there was one, filed under P, which was interesting. It was written in a careful hand on cheap lined paper from a Balham address, and read:

Dear Miss Bolam,

These are just a few lines to thank you for all you done for Jenny. It hasn't turned out as we wished and prayed for but we shall know in His good time what His purpose is. I still feel we did right to let them marry. It wasn't only to stop talk as I think you know. He has gone for good, he writes. Her Dad and me didn't know that things had got that bad between them. She doesn't talk much to us but we shall wait patiently and maybe, one day, she will be our girl again. She seems very quiet and won't talk about it so we don't know whether she grieves. I try not to feel bitterness against him. Dad and I think it would be a good idea if you could get Jenny a post in the health service. It is really good of you to offer and be interested after all that's happened. You know what we think about divorce so she must look to her job now for happiness. Dad and I pray every night that she'll find it.

Thanking you again for all your interest and help. If you do manage to get Jenny the post I'm sure she won't let you down. She's learnt her lesson and it's been a bitter one for us all. But His will be done.

Yours respectfully,
Emily Priddy (Mrs.)

It was extraordinary, thought Dalgliesh, that people still lived who could write a letter like that, with its archaic mixture of subservience and self-respect, its unashamed yet curiously poignant emotionalism. The story it told was ordinary enough, but he felt detached from its reality. The letter could have been written fifty years ago; almost he expected to see the paper curling with age and smell the tentative scent of potpourri. It had no relevance, surely, to that pretty, ineffectual child at the Steen.

"It's unlikely to have any importance," he said to Martin. "But I'd like you to go over to Clapham and have a word with these people. We'd better know who the husband is. But, somehow, I don't think he'll prove to be Dr. Etherege's mysterious marauder. The man—or woman—who killed Miss Bolam was still in the building when we arrived. And we've talked to him."

It was then that the telephone rang, sounding ominously strident in the silence of the flat as if it were calling for the dead. Dalgliesh said:

"I'll take it. It will be Dr. Keating with the P.M. report. I asked him to ring me here if he got through with it."

He was back with Martin within two minutes. The report had been brief. Dalgliesh said:

"Nothing surprising. She was a healthy woman. Killed by a stab through the heart after being stunned, which we could see for ourselves, and *virgo intacta* which we had no reason to doubt. What have you got there?"

"It's her photograph album, sir. Pictures of Guide camps mostly. It looks as if she went away with the girls every year."

Probably making her annual holiday, thought Dalgliesh. He had a respect bordering on simple wonder for those who voluntarily gave up their leisure to other people's children. He was not a man who liked children and he found the company of most of them insupportable after a very brief time. He took the album from Sergeant Martin. The photographs were small and technically unremarkable, taken apparently with a small box camera. But they were carefully disposed on the page, each labelled in neat white printing. There were Guides hiking, Guides cooking on primus stoves, erecting tents, blanket-swathed around the camp-fire, lining up for kit inspection. And in many of the photographs there was the figure of their captain, plump, motherly, smiling. It was difficult to connect this buxom, happy extrovert with that pathetic corpse on the record-room floor—or with the obsessional, authoritative administrator described by the staff of the Steen. The comments under some of the photographs were pathetic in their evocation of happiness remembered:

"The Swallows dish up. Shirley keeps an eye on the spotted dick."

"Valerie 'flies up' from the Brownies."

"The Kingfishers tackle the washing-up. Snap taken by Susan."

"Captain helps the tide in! Taken by Jean."

This last showed Miss Bolam's plump shoulders rising from the surf, surrounded by some half-dozen of her girls. Her hair was down and hanging in flat swaths, wet and dank as seaweed, on either side of her laughing face. Together the two detectives looked at the photograph in silence. Then Dalgliesh said:

"There haven't been many tears shed for her yet, have there? Only her cousin's and they were more shock than grief. I wonder whether the Swallows and the Kingfishers will weep for her."

They closed the album and went back to their search. It disclosed only one further item of interest, but that was very interesting indeed. It was the carbon copy of a letter from Miss Bolam to her solicitor, dated the day before her death, and making an appointment to see him "in connection with the proposed changes to my will which we discussed briefly on the telephone yesterday night."

After the visit to Ballantyne Mansions there followed a hiatus in the investigation, one of those inevitable delays which Dalgliesh had never found it easy to accept. He had always worked at speed. His reputation rested on the pace as well as the success of his cases. He did not ponder too deeply the implications of this compulsive need to get on with the job. It was enough to know that delay irritated him more than it did most men.

   This hold up was, perhaps, to be expected. It was hardly likely that a London solicitor would be in his office after midday on Saturday. It was more dispiriting to learn by telephone that Mr. Babcock of Babcock and Honeywell had flown with his wife to Geneva on Friday afternoon to attend the funeral of a friend and would not be back in his City office until the following Tuesday. There was now no Mr. Honeywell in the firm, but Mr. Babcock's chief clerk would be in the office on Monday morning if he could help the superintendent. It was the caretaker speaking. Dalgliesh was not sure how far the chief clerk could help him. He much preferred to see Mr. Babcock. The solicitor was likely to be able to give a great deal of useful information about Miss Bolam's family as well as her financial affairs, but much of it would probably be given with at least a token show of resistance and obained only by the exercise of tact. It would be folly to jeopardize success by a prior approach to the clerk.

Until the details of the will were available there was little point in seeing Nurse Bolam again. Frustrated in his immediate plans Dalgliesh drove without his sergeant to call on Peter Nagle. He had no clear aim in view but that didn't worry him. The time would be well spent. Some of his most useful work was done in these unplanned, almost casual encounters when he talked, listened, watched, studied a suspect in his own home, or gleaned the thin stalks of unwittingly dropped information about the one personality which is central to any murder investigation—that of the victim.

Nagle lived in Pimlico on the fourth floor of a large, white, stuccoed Victorian house near Eccleston Square. Dalgliesh had last visited this street three years previously when it had seemed irretrievably sunk into shabby decay. But the tide had changed. The wave of fashion and popularity which flows so inexplicably in London, sometimes missing one district while sweeping through its near neighbour, had washed the broad street bringing order and prosperity in its wake. Judging by the number of house agents' boards, the property speculators, first as always to sniff the returning tide, were reaping the usual profits. The house on the corner looked newly painted. The heavy front door stood open. Inside, a board gave the names of the tenants, but there were no bells. Dalgliesh deduced that the flats were self-contained and that, somewhere, there was a resident caretaker who would answer the front-door bell when the house was locked for the night. He could see no lift so set himself to climb the four flights to Nagle's flat.

It was a light, airy house and very quiet. There was no sign of life until the third floor where someone was playing the piano and playing well; perhaps a professional musician, practising. The treble cascade of sound fell over Dalgliesh and receded as he reached the fourth floor. Here there was a plain wooden door with a heavy brass knocker and a card pinned above it on which was lettered the one word—Nagle. He rapped and heard Nagle shout an immediate "come in."

The flat was surprising. He hardly knew what he had expected, but it was certainly not this immense, airy, impressive studio. It ran the whole length of the back of the house, the great north window, uncurtained, giving a panoramic view of twisted chimney-pots and irregular sloping roofs. Nagle was not alone. He was sitting, knees apart, on a narrow bed which stood on a raised platform at the east side of the room. Curled against him, clad only in a dressing-gown, was Jennifer Priddy. They were drinking tea from two blue mugs; a tray holding the teapot and a bottle of milk was on a small table beside them. The painting on which Nagle had recently been working stood on an easel in the middle of the room.

The girl showed no embarrassment at seeing Dalgliesh but swung her legs from the bed and gave him a smile which was frankly happy, almost welcoming, certainly without coquetry.

"Would you like some tea?" she asked.

Nagle said:

"The police never drink on duty and that includes tea. Better get your clothes on, kid. We don't want to shock the superintendent."

The girl smiled again, gathered up her clothes with one arm and the tea tray with the other and disappeared through a door at the far end of the studio. It was difficult to recognize in this confident sensual figure the tear-stained, diffident child Dalgliesh had first seen at the Steen. He watched her as she passed. She was obviously naked except for the dressing-gown of Nagle's; her hard nipples pointed the thin wool. It came to Dalgliesh that they had been making love. As she passed from view he turned to Nagle and saw in his eyes the transitory gleam of amused speculation. But neither of them spoke.

Dalgliesh moved about the studio, watched by Nagle from the bed. The room was without clutter. In its almost obsessional neatness it reminded him of Enid Bolam's flat with which it had otherwise nothing in common. The dais with its plain wooden bed, chair and small table obviously served as a bedroom. The rest of the studio was taken up with the paraphernalia of a painter, but there was none of that undisciplined muddle which the uninitiated associate with an artist's life. About a dozen large oils were stacked against the south wall and Dalgliesh was surprised by their power. Here was no amateur indulging his little talent. Miss Priddy was apparently Nagle's only model. Her heavy-busted, adolescent body gleamed at him from a diversity of poses, here foreshortened, there curiously elongated as if the painter gloried in his technical competence. The most recent picture was on the easel. It showed the girl sitting astride a stool with the childish hands hanging relaxed between her thighs, the breasts bunched forward. There was something in this flaunting of technical expertise, in the audacious use of greens and mauve and in the careful tonal relationships, which caught at Dalgliesh's memory.

"Who teaches you?" he asked. "Sugg?"

"That's right." Nagle did not seem surprised. "Know his work?"

"I have one of his early oils. A nude."

"You made a good investment. Hang on to it."

"I've every intention of doing so," said Dalgliesh mildly. "I happen to like it. Have you been with him long?"

"Two years. Part time, of course. In another three years I'll be teaching him. If he's capable of learning, that is. He's getting an old dog now and too fond of his own tricks."

"You appear to have imitated some of them," said Dalgliesh.

"You think so? That's interesting." Nagle did not seem affronted. "That's why it will be good to get away. I'm off to Paris by the end of the month at the latest. I applied for the Bollinger scholarship. The old man put in a word for me and last week I had a letter to say that it's mine."

Try as he would he could not entirely keep the note of triumph from his voice. Underneath the assumption of nonchalance there was a spring of joy. And he had reason to be pleased with himself. The Bollinger was no ordinary prize. It meant, as Dalgliesh knew, two years in any European city with a generous allowance and freedom for the student to live and work as he chose. The Bollinger trust had been set up by a manufacturer of patent medicines who had died wealthy and successful, but unsatisfied. His money had come from stomach powders but his heart was in painting. His own talent was small and, to judge by the collection of paintings which he bequeathed to the embarrassed trustees of his local gallery, his taste had been on a par with his performance. But the Bollinger scholarship had ensured that artists should remember him with gratitude. Bollinger did not believe that art flourished in poverty or that artists were stimulated to their best efforts by cold garrets and empty bellies. He had been poor in his youth and had not enjoyed it. He had travelled widely in his old age and been happy abroad. The Bollinger scholarship enabled young artists of promise to enjoy the second without enduring the first and it was well worth winning. If Nagle had been awarded the Bollinger he was hardly likely to be much concerned now with the troubles of the Steen Clinic.

"When are you due to go?" Dalgliesh asked.

"When I like. By the end of the month, anyway. But I may go earlier and without notice. No sense in upsetting anyone." He jerked his head towards the far door as he spoke and added: "That's why this murder is such a nuisance. I was afraid it might hold things up. After all, it was my chisel. And that wasn't the only attempt made to implicate me. While I was in the general office waiting for the post someone phoned to ask me to go down for the laundry. It sounded like a woman. I'd got my coat on and was more or less on my way out, so I said I'd collect it when I got back."

"So that's why you went to see Nurse Bolam on your return from the post and asked her whether the laundry was ready?"

"That's right."

"Why didn't you tell her about the phone call at the time?"

"I don't know. There didn't seem any point. I wasn't anxious to hang about the LSD room. Those patients give me the creeps with their moaning and muttering. When Bolam said the stuff wasn't ready I thought it was Miss Bolam who had phoned and it wouldn't have done to have said so. She was a bit too apt to interfere with the nursing responsibilities, or so they thought. Anyway, I didn't say anything about the call. I might have done but I didn't."

"And you didn't tell me either when you were first interviewed."

"Right again. The truth is that the whole thing struck me as a bit odd and I wanted time to think about it. Well, I've thought, and you're welcome to the story. You can believe it or not, as you like. It's all the same to me."

"You seem to be taking it pretty calmly if you really believe that someone was trying to involve you in the murder."

"I'm not worrying. They didn't succeed for one thing, and for another, I happen to believe that the chance of an innocent man getting convicted of murder in this country is practically nil. You ought to find that flattering. On the other hand— given the jury system—the chances of the guilty getting off are high. That's why I don't think you're going to solve this murder. Too many suspects. Too many possibilities."

"We shall see. Tell me more about this call. When exactly did you receive it?"

"I can't remember. About five minutes before Shorthouse came into the general office, I think. It could have been earlier. Jenny may remember."

"I'll ask her when she gets back. What exactly did the voice say?"

"Just, 'The laundry's ready if you'd fetch it now, please.' I took it that Nurse Bolam was phoning. I replied that I was just going out with the post and would see to it when I got back. Then I put down the receiver before she had a chance to argue."

"You were sure it was Nurse Bolam speaking?"

"I'm not sure at all. I naturally thought it was at the time because Nurse Bolam usually does phone about the laundry. As a matter of fact the woman spoke softly and it could have been anyone."

"But it was a woman's voice?"

"Oh, yes. It was a woman all right."

"At any rate it was a false message because we know that, in fact, the laundry wasn't sorted."

"Yes. But what was the point of it? It doesn't add up. If the idea was to lure me down to the basement to frame me, the killer stood the risk that I'd arrive at the wrong moment. Nurse Bolam, for example, wouldn't want me on the spot inquiring for the laundry if she were planning to be in the record-room slugging her cousin. Even if Miss Bolam were dead before the call was made it still doesn't make sense. Suppose I'd nosed around and found the body? The killer couldn't have wanted it discovered that soon! Anyway, I didn't go down until I got back from the post. Lucky for me I was out with it. The box is only just across the road, but I usually go down to Beefsteak Street to buy a *Standard.* The man there probably remembers me."

Jennifer Priddy had returned during the last few words. She had changed into a plain woollen dress. Clasping a belt around her waist, she said:

"It was the row over your paper that finished poor old Cully. You might have let him have it, darling, when he asked. He only wanted to check on his horses."

Nagle said without rancour:

"Mean old devil. He'd do anything to save himself threepence. Why can't he pay for it occasionally? I'm no sooner in the door before he puts out his hand for it."

"Still, you were rather unkind to him, darling. It isn't as if you wanted it yourself. We only glanced at it downstairs then used it to wrap up Tigger's food. You know what Cully is. The least upset goes to his stomach."

Nagle expressed his opinion of Cully's stomach with force and originality. Miss Priddy glanced at Dalgliesh as if inviting his shocked admiration of the vagaries of genius and murmured:

"Peter! Really, darling, you are awful!"

She spoke with coy indulgence, the little woman administering a mild rebuke. Dalgliesh looked at Nagle to see how he bore it, but the painter seemed not to have heard. He still sat, immobile, on the bed and looked down at them. Clad now in brown linen trousers, thick blue jersey and sandals, he yet looked as formal and neat as he had in his porter's uniform, his mild eyes unworried, his long, strong arms relaxed.

Under his gaze the girl moved restlessly about the studio, touching with happy possessiveness the frame of a painting, running her fingers along the window ledge, moving a jug of dahlias from one window to the next. It was as if she sought to impose the soft nuances of femininity on this disciplined masculine workshop, to demonstrate that this was her home, her natural place. She was entirely unembarrassed by the pictures of her naked body. It was possible that she gained satisfaction from this vicarious exhibitionism. Suddenly Dalgliesh asked:

"Do you remember, Miss Priddy, whether anyone telephoned Mr. Nagle while he was in the office with you?"

The girl looked surprised but said unconcernedly to Nagle:

"Nurse Bolam phoned about the laundry, didn't she? I came in from the record-room—I'd only been gone a second—and heard you say that you were just on your way out and would go down when you came back." She laughed. "After you put the receiver down you said something much less polite about the way the nurses expect you to be at their beck and call. Remember?"

"Yes," said Nagle shortly. He turned to Dalgliesh. "Any more questions, Superintendent? Jenny'll have to be getting home soon and I usually go part of the way. Her parents don't know she sees me."

"Only one or two. Have either of you any idea why Miss Bolam would send for the group secretary?"

Miss Priddy shook her head. Nagle said:

"It was nothing to do with us, anyway. She

didn't know that Jenny poses for me. Even if she found out she wouldn't send for Lauder. She wasn't a fool. She knew he wouldn't concern himself with anything the staff did in their own time. After all, she found out about Dr. Baguley's affair with Miss Saxon, but she wasn't daft enough to tell Lauder."

Dalgliesh did not ask whom Miss Bolam had told. He said:

"It was obviously something concerned with the administration of the clinic. Had anything unusual happened lately?"

"Nothing but our famous burglary and the missing fifteen quid. But you know about that."

"That's nothing to do with Peter," said the girl with quick defensiveness. "He wasn't even at the clinic when the fifteen pounds arrived." She turned to Nagle. "You remember, darling? That was the morning you got stuck in the Underground. You didn't even know about the money!"

She had said something wrong. The flash of irritation in those large mud-brown eyes was momentary, but Dalgliesh did not miss it. There was a pause before Nagle spoke, but his voice was perfectly controlled.

"I knew soon enough. We all did. What with the fuss over who sent it and the row over who was to spend it, the whole damn group must have known." He looked at Dalgliesh.

"Is that all?"

"No. Do you know who killed Miss Bolam?"

"I'm glad to say I don't. I shouldn't think it was

one of the psychiatrists. Those boys are the strongest reason I know for staying sane. But I can't see any of them actually killing. They haven't the nerve."

Someone very different had said much the same thing.

As he reached the door, Dalgliesh paused and looked back at Nagle. He and the girl were sitting together on the bed as he had first seen them, neither of them made any move to see him out, but Jenny gave him her happy valedictory smile.

Dalgliesh asked his last question:

"Why did you go for a drink with Cully on the night of the burglary?"

"Cully asked me."

"Wasn't that unusual?"

"So unusual that I went with him out of curiosity to see what was up."

"And what was?"

"Nothing really. Cully asked me to lend him a quid which I refused, and while the clinic was left empty someone broke in. I don't see how Cully could have foreseen that. Or maybe he did. Anyway, I can't see what it's got to do with the murder."

Nor, on the face of it, could Dalgliesh. As he passed down the stairs he was vexed by the thought of time passing, time wasted, the drag of hours before Monday morning when the clinic would reopen and his suspects reassemble in the place where they were likely to be most vulnerable. But the last forty minutes had been well spent. He was beginning to trace the dominant thread in this tangled skein. As he passed by the third-floor flat the pianist was playing Bach. Dalgliesh paused for a moment to listen. Contrapuntal music was the only kind he truly enjoyed. But the pianist stopped suddenly with a crash of discordant keys. And then nothing. Dalgliesh passed down the stairs in silence and left the quiet house unseen.

When Dr. Baguley arrived at the clinic for the Medical Committee meeting, the parking space reserved for doctors' cars was already occupied. Dr. Etherege's Bentley was there parked next to Steiner's Rolls. On the other side of it was the battered Vauxhall which proclaimed that Dr. Albertine Maddox had decided to attend.

Upstairs in the first-floor boardroom the curtains were drawn against the blue-black October sky. In the middle of the heavy mahogany table was a bowl of roses. Baguley remembered that Miss Bolam had always supplied flowers for the meetings of the Medical Committee. Someone had decided to continue the practice. The roses were the slim, hothouse buds of autumn, rigid and scentless on their thornless stems. In a couple of days they would open for their brief and barren flowering. In less than a week they would be dead. Baguley thought that so extravagant and evocative a flower was inappropriate to the mood of the meeting. But the empty bowl would have been unbearably poignant and embarrassing.

"Who supplied the roses?" he asked.

"Mrs. Bostock, I think," said Dr. Ingram. "She was up here getting the room ready when I arrived."

"Remarkable," said Dr. Etherege. He put out a finger and stroked one of the buds so gently that the stem did not even tremble. Baguley wondered whether the comment referred to the quality of the roses or to Mrs. Bostock's perspicacity in supplying them.

"Miss Bolam was very fond of flowers, very fond," said the medical director. He looked round as if challenging his colleagues to disagree.

"Well," he said. "Shall we get started?"

Dr. Baguley, as honorary secretary, seated himself on the right of Dr. Etherege. Dr. Steiner took the chair next to him. Dr. Maddox sat on Steiner's right. No other consultant was there. Dr. McBain and Dr. Mason-Giles were in the States attending a conference. The rest of the medical staff, torn between curiosity and a disinclination to interrupt their weekend break, had apparently decided to wait in patience for Monday. Dr. Etherege had thought it proper to telephone them all and let them know of the meeting. He gave their apologies formally and they were as gravely received.

Albertine Maddox had been a surgeon and a highly successful one before she qualified as a psychiatrist. It was perhaps typical of her colleagues' ambivalence towards their specialty that Dr. Maddox's double qualification enhanced her standing their eyes. She represented the clinic on the Group Medical Advisory Committee, where she defended the Steen against the occasional snipings of physicians and surgeons with a wit and vigour which made her respected and feared. At the clinic she took no part in the Freudian versus eclectic controversy being, as Baguley observed, equally beastly to both sides. Her patients loved her, but this did not impress her colleagues. They were used to being loved by their patients and merely observed that Albertine was particularly skilful in handling a strong transference situation. Physically she was a plump, grey-haired, unremarkable woman who looked what she was, the comfortable mother of a family. She had five children, the sons intelligent and prosperous, the girls well-married. Her insignificant-looking husband and the children treated her with a tolerant, faintly amused solicitude which never failed to astonish her colleagues at the Steen to whom she was a formidable personality. She sat now with Hector, her old Pekinese, squatting malevolently on her lap looking as comfortably anticipatory as a suburban housewife at a matinée. Dr. Steiner said testily:

"Really, Albertine, need you have brought Hector? I don't want to be unkind but that animal is beginning to smell. You should have him put down."

"Thank you, Paul," replied Dr. Maddox in her deep, beautifully modulated voice. "Hector will be put down, as you so euphemistically describe it, when he ceases to find life pleasant. I judge that he has not yet reached that state. It is not my habit to kill off living creatures simply because I find certain of their physical characteristics displeasing; nor, I may say, because they have become somewhat of a nuisance."

Dr. Etherege said quickly:

"It was good of you to find time to come tonight, Albertine. I'm sorry that the notice was so short."

He spoke without irony, although he was as well aware as were his colleagues that Dr. Maddox only attended one committee meeting in four on the grounds, which she made no effort to conceal, that her contract with the Regional Board contained no clause compelling her to a monthly session of boredom laced with claptrap, and that the company of more than one psychiatrist at a time made Hector sick. The truth of this last assertion had been demonstrated too often to be safely challenged.

"I am a member of this committee, Henry," replied Dr. Maddox graciously. "Is there any reason why I should not make the effort to attend?"

Her glance at Dr. Ingram implied that not everyone present had an equal right. Mary Ingram was the wife of a suburban general practitioner and attended the Steen twice a week to give the anaesthetic at E.C.T. sessions. Not being either a psychiatrist or a consultant she was not normally present at meetings of the Medical Committee. Dr. Etherege interpreted the glance correctly and said firmly:

"Dr. Ingram has been good enough to come along tonight at my request. The main business of the meeting is naturally concerned with Miss Bolam's murder, and Dr. Ingram was in the clinic on Friday evening."

"But is not a suspect, so I understand," replied Dr. Maddox. "I congratulate her. It is gratifying that there is one member of the medical staff who has been able to produce a satisfactory alibi."

She looked at Dr. Ingram severely, her tone implying that an alibi was, in itself, suspicious and hardly becoming to the most junior member of the staff since three senior consultants had been unable to produce one. No one asked how Dr. Maddox knew about the alibi. Presumably she had been speaking to Sister Ambrose. Dr. Steiner said pettishly:

"It's ridiculous to talk about alibis as if the police could seriously suspect one of us! It's perfectly obvious to me what happened. The murderer was lying in wait for her in the basement. We know that. He may have been hidden down there for hours, perhaps even since the previous day. He could have slipped past Cully with one of the patients or have pretended to be a relative or a hospital-car attendant. He could even have broken in during the night. That has been known, after all. Once in the basement there would be plenty of time to discover which key opened the record-room door and plenty of time to select a weapon. Neither the fetish nor the chisel were hidden."

"And how do you suggest this unknown murderer left the building?" asked Dr. Baguley. "We searched the place pretty thoroughly before the police arrived and they went over it again. The basement and first-floor doors were both bolted on the inside, remember."

"Climbed up the lift shaft by the pulley ropes and out through one of the doors leading to the fire-escape," replied Dr. Steiner, playing his trump card with a certain panache. "I've examined the lift and it's just possible. A small man—or a woman, of course—could squeeze over the top of the box and get into the shaft. The ropes are quite thick enough to support a considerable weight and the climb wouldn't be too difficult for anyone reasonably agile. They'd need to be slim, of course." He glanced at his own rounding paunch with complacency.

"It's a pleasant theory," said Baguley. "Unfortunately all the doors opening on the fire-escape were also bolted on the inside."

"There is no building in existence which a desperate and experienced man cannot break into or get out of," proclaimed Dr. Steiner, as if from a plenitude of experience. "He could have got out of a first-floor window and edged along the sill until he could get a foothold on the fire-escape.

All I'm saying is that the murderer isn't necessarily one of the staff who happened to be on duty yesterday evening."

"It couldn't be I, for example," said Dr. Maddox.

Dr. Steiner was undaunted.

"That, of course, is nonsense, Albertine. I make no accusations. I merely point out that the circle of suspects is less restricted than the police seem to think. They should direct their inquiries to Miss Bolam's private life. Obviously she has an enemy."

But Dr. Maddox was not to be diverted.

"Fortunately for me," she proclaimed, "I was at the Bach recital at the Royal Festival Hall last night with my husband and dined there before the concert. And while Alasdair's testimony on my behalf might be suspect, I was also with my brother-in-law who happens to be a bishop. A High Church bishop," she added complacently, as if incense and chasuble set a seal on episcopal virtue and veracity.

Dr. Etherege smiled gently and said:

"I should be relieved if I could produce even an evangelical curate to vouch for me between six-fifteen and seven o'clock yesterday evening. But isn't all this theorizing a waste of time? The crime is in the hands of the police and there we must leave it. Our main concern is to discuss its implications for the work of the clinic and, in particular, the suggestion of the chairman and the group secretary that Mrs. Bostock should carry on for the present as acting administrative officer. But we'd better proceed in order. Is it your pleasure that I sign the minutes of the last meeting?"

There was the unenthusiastic but acquiescent mumble which this question usually provokes and the medical director drew the minute book towards him and signed. Dr. Maddox said suddenly:

"What is he like? This superintendent, I mean."

Dr. Ingram, who hadn't so far spoken, surprisingly replied:

"He's about forty, I should think. Tall and dark. I liked his voice and he has nice hands." Then she blushed furiously, remembering that, to a psychiatrist, the most innocent remark could be embarrassingly revealing. That comment about nice hands was, perhaps, a mistake. Dr. Steiner, ignoring Dalgliesh's physical characteristics, launched into a psychological assessment of the superintendent to which his fellow psychiatrists gave the polite attention of experts interested in a colleague's theories. Dalgliesh, had he been present, would have been surprised and intrigued by the accuracy and percipience of Dr. Steiner's diagnosis. The medical director said:

"I agree that he's obsessional and also that he's intelligent. That means that his mistakes will be the mistakes of an intelligent man—always the most dangerous. We must hope for all our sakes he makes none. The murder, and the inevitable publicity, are bound to have an effect on the patients and on the work of the clinic. And that brings us to this suggestion about Mrs. Bostock."

"I have always preferred Bolam to Bostock," said Dr. Maddox. "It would be a pity if we lost one unsuitable A.O.—however regrettably and fortuitously—only to be saddled with another."

"I agree," said Dr. Baguley. "Of the two I personally always preferred Bolam. But this would only be a temporary arrangement presumably. The job will have to be advertised. In the meantime someone's got to take over and Mrs. Bostock does at least know the work."

Dr. Etherege said:

"Lauder made it plain that the H.M.C. wouldn't favour putting in an outsider until the police have finished their investigation, even if they could find anyone willing to come. We don't want any additional upheaval. There will be enough disturbance to cope with. And that brings me to the problem of the press. Lauder suggested, and I have agreed, that all inquiries are referred to group headquarters and that no one here makes any statements. It seems much the best plan. It's important in the interests of the patients that we don't have reporters running all over the clinic. Therapy is likely to suffer enough without that. Have I this Committee's formal confirmation of the decision?"

He had. No one evinced any enthusiasm for coping with the press. Dr. Steiner did not contribute to the general murmur of consent. His thoughts

were still with the problem of Miss Bolam's successor. He said querulously:

"I can't understand why Dr. Maddox and Dr.
Baguley have this animus against Mrs. Bostock.
I've noticed it before. It's ridiculous to compare
her adversely with Miss Bolam. There's no doubt
which of them is—was—is—the more suitable
administrator. Mrs. Bostock is a highly intelligent
woman, psychologically stable, efficient and with
a real appreciation of the importance of the work
we do here. No one could have said as much
of Miss Bolam. Her attitude to the patients was
sometimes most unfortunate."

"I didn't know that she came into contact much
with the patients," said Dr. Baguley. "Anyway,
none of mine complained."

"She made appointments occasionally and
paid out travelling expenses. I can quite believe
that your patients didn't remark on her attitude.
But mine are a rather different class. They're also
more sensitive to these things. Mr. Burge, for example, mentioned the matter to me."

Dr. Maddox laughed unkindly.

"Oh, Burge! Is he still coming? I see that his
new opus is promised for December. It will be
interesting to see, Paul, whether your efforts have
improved his prose. If so, it's probably public
money well spent."

Dr. Steiner burst into pained expostulation.
He treated a fair number of writers and artists,
some of them protégés of Rosa in search of a

little free psychotherapy. Although he was sensitive to the arts his usually keen critical insight failed completely where his patients were concerned. He could not bear to hear them criticized, lived in perpetual hope that their great talents would at last be recognized, and was roused to quick defensive anger on their behalf. Dr. Baguley thought that it was one of Steiner's more endearing qualities; in many ways he was touchingly naïve. He launched now into a muddled defence both of his patient's character and his prose style, ending:

"Mr. Burge is a most talented and sensitive man, very distressed by his inability to sustain a satisfactory sexual relationship, particularly with his wives."

This unfortunate solecism seemed likely to provoke Dr. Maddox to further unkindness. It was certainly, thought Baguley, her night to be proeclectic.

Dr. Etherege said mildly:

"Could we forget our professional differences for a moment and concentrate on the matter in hand? Dr. Steiner, have you any objection to accepting Mrs. Bostock as a temporary administrative officer?

Dr. Steiner said grumpily:

"The question is purely academic. If the group secretary wishes her to be appointed she will be appointed. This farce of appearing to consult us is ridiculous. We have no authority either to approve or disapprove. That was made perfectly clear to me by Lauder when I approached him last month about getting Bolam transferred."

"I didn't know you had approached him," said Dr. Etherege.

"I spoke to him after the September meeting of the House Committee. It was merely a tentative suggestion."

"And was met with a pretty positive brush off, no doubt," said Baguley. "You would have been wiser to keep your mouth shut."

"Or to have brought the matter before this Committee," said Etherege.

"And with what result?" cried Steiner. "What happened last time I complained about Bolam? Nothing! You all admitted that she was a unsuitable person to hold the post of administrative officer. You all agreed—well, most of you agreed—that Bostock—or even an outsider—would be preferable. But when it came to action not one of you was prepared to put your signature to a letter to the Hospital Management Committee. And you know very well why! You were all terrified of that woman. Yes, terrified!"

Amid a murmur of outraged denial, Dr. Maddox said:

"There was something intimidating about her. It may have been that formidable and self-conscious rectitude. You were as affected by it as anyone, Paul."

"Possibly. But I did try to do something about her. I spoke to Lauder."

"I spoke to him, too," said Etherege quietly,

"and possibly with more effect. I made it clear that this Committee realized that we had no control over the administrative staff, but I said that Miss Bolam appeared to me, speaking as a psychiatrist and as chairman of the Medical Committee, to be temperamentally unsuitable for her job. I suggested that a transfer would be in her own interests. There could be no criticism of her efficiency and I made none. Lauder was noncommittal, of course, but he knew perfectly well that I was entitled to make the point. And I think he took it."

Dr. Maddox said:

"Allowing for his natural caution, his suspicion of psychiatrists and the usual speed of his administrative decisions, I suppose we should have been rid of Miss Bolam within the next two years. Someone has certainly speeded things up."

Suddenly Dr. Ingram spoke. Her pink, rather stupid face flushed unbecomingly. She sat stiffly upright and her hands, clasped on the table in front of her, were shaking.

"I don't think you ought to say things like that. It . . . it isn't right. Miss Bolam is dead, brutally murdered. You sit here, all of you, and talk as if you didn't care! I know she wasn't very easy to get on with but she's dead, and I don't think this is the time to be unkind about her."

Dr. Maddox looked at Dr. Ingram with interest and a kind of wonder as if she were faced by an exceptionally dull child who had somehow succeeded in making an intelligent remark. She said:

"I see that you subscribe to the superstition that one should never tell the truth about the dead. The origins of that atavistic belief have always interested me. We must have a talk about it sometime. I should like to hear your views."

Dr. Ingram, scarlet with embarrassment and close to tears, looked as if the proposed talk were a privilege she would be happy to forgo. Dr. Etherege said:

"Unkind about her? I should be sorry to think that anyone here was being unkind. There are some things, surely, which don't need saying. There can't be a member of this Committee who isn't horrified at the senseless brutality of Miss Bolam's death and who wouldn't wish her back with us no matter what her defects as an administrator."

The bathos was too blatant to be missed. As if conscious of their surprise and discomfiture, he looked up and said challengingly:

"Well, is there? Is there?"

"Of course not," said Dr. Steiner. He spoke soothingly, but the sharp little eyes slewed sideways to meet Baguley's glance. There was embarrassment in that look, but Baguley recognized also the smirk of malicious amusement. The medical director wasn't playing this too cleverly. He had allowed Albertine Maddox to get out of hand and his control over the Committee was less sure than formerly. The pathetic thing about it, thought Baguley, was that Etherege was sincere. He meant every word. He had—and so had they all, come to that—a genuine horror of violence. He was a compassionate man shocked and saddened by the thought of a defenceless woman brutally done to death. But his words sounded false. He was taking refuge in formality, deliberately trying to lower the emotional tone of the meeting to one of platitudinous convention. And he only succeeded in sounding insincere.

After Dr. Ingram's outburst the meeting seemed to lose heart. Dr. Etherege made only spasmodic attempts to control it and the conversation ranged in a tired, desultory way, from one subject to another but, always and inevitably, returned to the murder. There was a feeling that the Medical Committee should express some common view. Groping from theory to theory the meeting eventually came to accept Dr. Steiner's proposition. The killer had obviously entered the clinic earlier in the day when the system of booking people in and out was not in force. He had secreted himself in the basement, selected his weapons at leisure, and called Miss Bolam down by noting the number of her extension from the card hung beside the telephone. He had made his way to the upper floors without being observed and left by one of the windows, managing to close it behind him before edging his way on to the fire-escape. That this procedure argued considerable luck, coupled with unusual and remarkable agility, was not over-emphasized. Under Dr. Steiner's leadership the theory was elaborated. Miss Bolam's telephone call to the group secretary was dismissed as irrelevant. She had undoubtedly wished to complain about some trifling misdemeanour, real or imagined, and which was quite unconnected with her subsequent death. The suggestion that the killer had swarmed up the pulley in the lift shaft was generally discounted as somewhat fanciful although, as Dr. Maddox pointed out, a man who could shut a heavy window while balancing on the outside sill, then swing himself some five feet through space to reach the fire-escape, would hardly find the lift shaft an insuperable problem.

Dr. Baguley, wearying of his part in the fabrication of this mythical killer, half-closed his eyes and gazed from under lowered lids, at the bowl of roses. Their petals had been opening gently and almost visibly in the warmth of the room. Now the red, green and pink swam together in an amorphous pattern of colour which, as his gaze shifted, was reflected in the shining table. Suddenly he opened his eyes fully and saw Dr. Etherege looking fixedly at him. There was concern in that sharp, analytic regard; Dr. Baguley thought that there was also pity. The medical director said:

"Some of our members have had enough. So, I think, have I. If no one has any urgent business to bring forward I declare the meeting closed."

Dr. Baguley thought that it was not altogether by chance that he and the medical director found themselves alone in the room, the last to leave. As he tested the windows to check that they were locked, Dr. Etherege said:

"Well, James, have you come to a decision yet about succeeding me as medical director?"

"It's more a question of deciding whether or not to apply for the job when it's advertised, surely?" said Baguley. He asked: "What about Mason-Giles or McBain?"

"M.G. isn't interested. It's maximum sessions, of course, and he doesn't want to give up his teaching hospital connection. McBain is tied up with the new regional unit for adolescents."

It was typical of the medical director's occasional insensitivity that he didn't try to soften the fact that he had tried others first. He's scraping the bottom of the barrel, thought Baguley.

"And Steiner?" he asked. "He'll be applying, I imagine?"

The medical director smiled.

"Oh, I don't think the Regional Board will appoint Dr. Steiner. This is a multi-discipline clinic. We must have someone who can hold the place together. And there may be very great changes. You know my views. If there is to be a closer integration of psychiatry with general medicine a place like this may have to die for the greater good. We ought to have access to beds. The Steen may find its natural home in a general hospital out-patient department. I don't say it's probable. But it's possible."

So that was the way the Board was thinking? Dr. Etherege had his ear well to the ground. A small out-patient unit with no registrars, no training function and no link with a general hospital might well become anachronistic in the eyes of the planners. Dr. Baguley said:

"I don't mind where I see my patients as long as I get peace and quiet, a certain tolerance, and not too much of the hierarchical claptrap and starched linen. These proposed psychiatric units in general hospitals are all very well so long as the hospital appreciates what we're going to need in staff and space. I'm too tired to do battle."

He looked at the medical director.

"Actually, I had more or less decided not to apply. I telephoned your room yesterday evening from the medical staff-room to ask if we could chat about it after the clinic."

"Indeed? At what time?"

"At about six-twenty or six-twenty-five. There was no reply. Later, of course, we had other things to think about."

The medical director said:

"I must have been in the library. I'm very glad I was if it means that you've had time to reconsider your decision. And I hope that you will reconsider it, James."

He turned out the lights and they went downstairs together. Pausing at the foot, the medical director turned to Dr. Baguley and said:

"It was at about six-twenty that you telephoned? I find that very interesting, very interesting indeed."

"Well, about then, I suppose."

Dr. Baguley realized with irritation and surprise, that it was he, not the medical director, who sounded guilty and embarrassed. He was seized by an intense desire to get out of the clinic, to escape from the blue, speculative gaze which was so adept at putting him at a disadvantage. But there was something else which must be said. At the door he forced himself to pause and face Dr. Etherege. But despite his attempt at nonchalance his voice sounded forced, even belligerent:

"I'm wondering whether we ought to do something about Nurse Bolam."

"In what way?" asked the medical director gently. Receiving no reply, he went on: "All the staff know that they can ask to see me at any time. But I'm not inviting confidences. This is a murder investigation, James, and it's out of my hands. Out of my hands completely. I think you would be wise to take the same attitude. Good night."

Chapter Six

EARLY MONDAY MORNING, the anniversary of his wife's death, Dalgliesh called in at a small Catholic church behind the Strand to light a candle. His wife had been a Catholic. He had not shared her religion and she had died before he could begin to understand what it meant to her or what importance this fundamental difference between them might have for their marriage. He had lit the first candle on the day she died out of the need to formalize an intolerable grief and, perhaps, with a childish hope of somehow comforting her spirit. This was the fourteenth candle. He thought of this most private action in his detached and secretive life, not as superstition or piety, but as a habit which he could not now break even if he wished. He dreamed of his wife only seldom, but then with absolute clarity; waking he could no longer accurately recall her face. He pushed his coin through the slot and held his candle's wick to the dying flame of a moist stump. It caught immediately and the flame grew bright and clear. It had always been important to him that the wick should catch at once. He gazed through the flame for a moment feeling nothing, not even anger. Then he turned away.

The church was nearly empty, but it held for him an atmosphere of intense and silent activity which he sensed but could not share. As he walked to the door he recognized a woman, red-coated and with a dark green scarf over her head, who was pausing to dip her fingers in the water stoup. It was Fredrica Saxon, senior psychologist of the Steen Clinic. They reached the outer door together and he forced it open for her against the sudden swirl of an autumn wind. She smiled at him, friendly and unembarrassed.

"Hullo. I haven't seen you here before."

"I only come once a year," Dalgliesh replied. He gave no explanation and she asked no questions. Instead she said:

"I wanted to see you. There's something I think you ought to know. Are you off duty? If you aren't could you be unorthodox and talk to a suspect in a coffee bar? I'd rather not come to your office and it isn't easy to ask for an interview at the clinic. I need some coffee anyway. I'm cold."

"There used to be a place round the corner,"

said Dalgliesh. "The coffee is tolerable and it's pretty quiet."

The coffee bar had changed in a year. Dalgliesh remembered it as a clean but dull café with a row of deal tables covered with plastic cloths and a long service counter embellished with a tea urn and layers of substantial sandwiches under glass domes. It had risen in the world. The walls had been panelled with imitation old oak against which hung a formidable assortment of rapiers, ancient pistols and cutlasses of uncertain authenticity. The waitresses looked like *avantegarde* débutantes earning their pin money and the lighting was so discreet as to be positively sinister. She led the way to a table in the far corner.

"Just coffee?" asked Dalgliesh.

"Just coffee, please."

She waited until the order had been given and then said:

"It's about Dr. Baguley."

"I thought it might be."

"You were bound to hear something, I suppose. I'd rather tell you about it now than wait to be asked and I'd rather you heard it from me than from Amy Shorthouse."

She spoke without rancour or embarrassment. Dalgliesh replied:

"I haven't asked about it because it doesn't seem relevant, but if you like to tell me it may be helpful."

"I don't want you to get a wrong idea about it that's all. It would be so easy for you to imagine that we had a grudge against Miss Bolam. We didn't, you know. At one time we even felt grateful to her."

Dalgliesh had no need to ask who she meant by that "we."

The waitress, uninterested, came with their coffee, pale foam served in small transparent cups. Miss Saxon slipped her coat from her shoulders and unknotted her head scarf. Both of them wrapped their fingers round the hot cups. She heaped the sugar into her coffee then pushed the plastic bowl across the table to Dalgliesh. There was no tension about her, no awkwardness. She had the directness of a schoolchild drinking coffee with a friend. He found her curiously peaceful to be with, perhaps because he did not find her physically attractive. But he liked her. It was difficult to believe that this was only their second meeting and that the matter that had brought them together was murder. She skimmed the froth from her coffee and said, without looking up:

"James Baguley and I fell in love nearly three years ago. There wasn't any great moral struggle about it. We didn't invite love but we certainly didn't fight against it. After all, you don't voluntarily give up happiness unless you're a masochist or a saint, and we aren't either. I knew that James had a neurotic wife in the way one does get to know these things, but he didn't talk much about her. We both accepted that she needed him and that a divorce was out of the question. We convinced ourselves that we weren't doing her any harm and that she need never know. James used to say that loving me made his marriage happier for both of them. Of course, it is easier to be kind and patient when one is happy, so he may have been right. I don't know. It's a rationalization that thousands of lovers must use.

"We couldn't see each other very often, but I had my flat and we usually managed to have two evenings a week together. Once Helen—that's his wife—went to stay with her sister and we had a whole night together. We had to be careful at the clinic, of course, but we don't really see very much of each other there."

"How did Miss Bolam find out about it?" asked Dalgliesh.

"It was silly, really. We were at the theatre seeing Anouilh and she was sitting alone in the row behind. Who would suppose that Bolam would want to see Anouilh, anyway? I suppose she was sent a free ticket. It was our second anniversary and we held hands all through the play. We may have been a little drunk. Afterwards we left the theatre still hand in hand. Anyone from the clinic, anyone we knew, could have seen us. We were getting careless and someone was bound to see us sooner or later. It was just chance that it happened to be Bolam. Other people would probably have minded their own business."

"Whereas she told Mrs. Baguley? That seems an unusually officious and cruel thing to have done."

"It wasn't, really. Bolam wouldn't see it that way. She was one of those rare and fortunate people who never for one moment doubt that they know the difference between right and wrong. She wasn't imaginative so she couldn't enter into other people's feelings. If she were a wife whose husband was unfaithful I'm sure that she would want to be told about it. Nothing would be worse than not knowing. She had the kind of strength that relishes a struggle. I expect she thought it was her duty to tell. Anyway, Helen came to the Steen to see her husband unexpectedly one Wednesday afternoon and Miss Bolam invited her into the A.O.'s office and told her. I often wonder what exactly she said. I imagine that she said we were 'carrying on.' She could make practically anything sound vulgar."

"She was taking a risk, wasn't she?" said Dalgliesh. "She had very little evidence, certainly no proof."

Miss Saxon laughed.

"You're talking like a policeman. She had proof enough. Even Bolam could recognize love when she saw it. Besides, we were enjoying ourselves together without a licence and that was infidelity enough."

The words were bitter but she did not sound resentful or sarcastic. She was sipping her coffee with evident satisfaction. Dalgliesh thought that she might have been talking about one of the clinic patients, discussing with detached and mild professional interest the vagaries of human nature. Yet he did not believe that she loved easily or that her emotions were superficial. He asked what Mrs. Baguley's reaction had been.

"That's the extraordinary thing, or at least it seemed so at the time. She took it wonderfully well. Looking back I wonder whether we weren't all three mad, living in some kind of imaginary world that two minutes' rational thought would have shown us couldn't exist. Helen lives her life in a series of attitudes and the one she decided to adopt was the pose of the brave, understanding wife. She insisted on a divorce. It was going to be one of those friendly divorces. That kind is only possible, I imagine, when people have ceased to care for each other, perhaps never have cared or been capable of caring. But that was the kind we were going to have. There was a great deal of discussion. Everyone's happiness was to be safeguarded. Helen was going to open a dress shop—it's a thing she's talked about for years. We all three got interested in it and looked for suitable premises. It was pathetic really. We actually fooled ourselves that it was all going to come right. That's why I said that James and I felt grateful to Enid Bolam. People at the clinic got to know that there was to be a divorce and that Helen would name me—it was all part of the policy of frankness and honesty—but very little was said to us. Bolam never mentioned the divorce to anyone. She wasn't a gossip and she wasn't malicious, either. Somehow her part in it got about in the way these things do. I think Helen may have told someone, but Miss Bolam and I never talked about it ever.

"Then the inevitable happened. Helen began to crack. James had left her with the Surrey house and was living with me in the flat. He had to see her fairly often. He didn't say very much at first, but I knew what was happening. She was ill, of course, and we both knew it. She had played out the role of the patient, uncomplaining wife and, according to the novels and the films, her husband should, by now, have been returning to her. And James wasn't. He kept most of it from me, but I had some idea what it was doing to him, the scenes, the tears, the entreaties, the threats of suicide. One minute she was going through with the divorce, the next she would never give him his freedom. She couldn't, of course. I see that now. It wasn't hers to give. It's degrading to talk about a husband as if he's a dog chained up in the back yard. All the time that this was happening I was realizing more and more that I couldn't go on. Something that had been a slow process over years came to a head. There's no point in talking about it or trying to explain. It isn't relevant to your inquiry, is it? Nine months ago I started to receive instruction with the hope of being received into the Catholic Church. When that happened Helen withdrew her petition and James went back to her. I think he no longer cared what happened to him or where he went. But you can see, can't you, that he had no reason to hate Bolam. I was the enemy."

Dalgliesh thought that there could have been very little struggle. Her rosy, healthy face with the broad and slightly tip-tilted nose, the wide cheerful mouth, was ill-suited to tragedy. He recalled how Dr. Baguley had looked, seen in the light of Miss Bolam's desk lamp. It was stupid and presumptuous to try to assess suffering by the lines on a face or the look in the eyes. Miss Saxon's mind was probably as tough and resilient as her body. It did not mean that she felt less because she could withstand more. But he felt profoundly sorry for Baguley, rejected by his mistress at the moment of greatest trial in favour of a private happiness which he could neither share nor understand. Probably no one could fully know the magnitude of that betrayal. Dalgliesh did not pretend to understand Miss Saxon. It wasn't hard to imagine what some people at the clinic would make of it. The facile explanations came easily to mind. But he could not believe that Fredrica Saxon had taken refuge in religion from her own sexuality or had ever refused to face reality.

He thought of some of the things she had said about Enid Bolam.

"Who would suppose that Bolam would want to see Anouilh. I suppose she was sent a free ticket. . . . Even Bolam could recognize love when she saw it. . . . She could make practically anything sound vulgar." People did not automatically become kind because they had become religious. Yet there had been no real malice in her words. She spoke what she thought and would be equally detached about her own motives. She was probably the best judge of character in the clinic. Suddenly, and in defiance of orthodoxy, Dalgliesh asked:

"Who do you think killed her, Miss Saxon?"

"Judging by character and the nature of the crime and taking no account of mysterious telephone calls from the basement, creaking lifts, and apparent alibis?"

"Judging by character and the nature of the crime."

She said without hesitation and with no apparent reluctance:

"I'd have said it was Peter Nagle."

Dalgliesh felt a stab of disappointment. It was irrational to have thought that she might actually know.

"Why Nagle?" he asked.

"Partly because I think this was a masculine crime. The stabbing is significant. I can't see a woman killing in just that way. Faced with an unconscious victim I think a woman would strangle. Then there's the chisel. To use it with such expertise suggests an identification of the weapon with the killer. Why use it otherwise? He could have struck her again and again with the fetish."

"Messy, noisy and less sure," said Dalgliesh.

"But the chisel was only sure in the hands of a man who had confidence in his ability to use it, someone who is literally 'good with his hands.' I can't see Dr. Steiner killing in that way, for instance. He couldn't even knock in a nail without breaking the hammer."

Dalgliesh was inclined to agree that Dr. Steiner was innocent. His clumsiness with tools had been mentioned by more than one member of the clinic staff. Admittedly he had lied in denying that he knew where the chisel was kept, but Dalgliesh judged that he had acted from fear rather than guilt. And his shame-faced confession of falling asleep while awaiting Mr. Burge had the ring of truth.

Dalgliesh said:

"The identification of the chisel with Nagle is so certain that I think we were meant to suspect him. And you do?"

"Oh, no! I know he couldn't have done it. I only answered the question as you posed it. I was judging by character and the nature of the crime."

They had finished their coffee now and Dalgliesh thought that she would want to go. But she seemed in no hurry. After a moment's pause, she said:

"I have one confession to make; on another person's behalf actually. It's Cully. Nothing important but something you ought to know and I promised I'd tell you about it. Poor old Cully is scared out of his wits and they aren't plentiful at the best of times."

"I knew he was lying about something," said Dalgliesh. "He saw someone passing down the hall, I suppose."

"Oh, no! Nothing as useful as that. It's about the missing rubber apron from the art therapy department. I gather you thought that the murderer might have worn it. Well, Cully borrowed it from the department last Monday to wear while he emulsion-painted his kitchen. You know what a mess paint makes. He didn't ask Miss Bolam if he could take it because he knew what the answer would be and he couldn't ask Mrs. Baumgarden because she's away sick. He meant to bring it back on Friday but when Sister was checking the inventory with your sergeant and they asked him if he'd seen it he lost his head and said 'no.' He's not very bright and he was terrified that you'd suspect him of the murder if he owned up."

Dalgliesh asked when Cully had told her of this.

"I knew he had the apron because it just happened that I saw him take it. I guessed that he'd be in a state about it so I went round to see him yesterday morning. His stomach gets upset when he worries and I thought someone had better keep an eye on him."

"Where is the apron now?" asked Dalgliesh.

Miss Saxon laughed.

"Disposed about London in half a dozen litter baskets if they haven't been emptied. Poor old Cully daren't put it in his own dustbin in case it was searched by the police and couldn't burn it because he lives in a council flat with electric heating and no stove. So he waited until his wife was in bed, then sat up until eleven cutting it into pieces with the kitchen scissors. He put the pieces into a number of paper bags, shoved the bags into a hold-all, and took a 36 bus up the Harrow Road until he was well away from his home ground. Then he slipped one of the bags into each litter bin he came across and dropped the metal buttons down the gutter grating. It was a formidable undertaking and the poor fellow could hardly creep home what with fear, tiredness— he'd lost the last bus—and the belly-ache. He wasn't in too good a shape when I called next morning, but I did manage to convince him that it wasn't a matter of life and death—particularly death. I told him I'd let you know about it."

"Thank you," said Dalgliesh gravely. "You haven't any other confessions to pass on, I suppose? Or have you a conscientious objection to handing over an unfortunate psychopath to justice."

She laughed, pulling on her coat and tying the scarf over her dark, springing hair.

"Oh, no! If I knew who did it I'd tell you. I don't like murder and I'm quite law-abiding, really. But I didn't know we were talking about justice. That's your word. Like Portia, I feel that in the course of justice none of us would see salvation. Please, I would much rather pay for my own coffee."

She doesn't want to feel that I bought information from her, thought Dalgliesh, not even a shilling's worth. He resisted the temptation to say that the coffee could come from expenses, wondering a little at this impulse to sarcasm which she aroused in him. He liked her, but there was something about her certainty, her self-sufficiency, which he found irritating. Perhaps what he felt was envy.

As they left the café he asked her whether she was on her way to the Steen.

"Not today. I don't have a session on Monday mornings. But I shall be there tomorrow."

She thanked him formally for the coffee and they parted. He turned eastwards towards the Steen and she disappeared in the direction of the Strand. As he watched her slim, dark figure swinging out of sight he pictured Cully creeping through the night with his pathetic bundle, half petrified with fright. He was not surprised that the old porter had confided so fully in Fredrica Saxon; in Cully's place, he would probably have done the same. She had, thought Dalgliesh, given him a great deal of interesting information. But what she hadn't been able to give him was an alibi for Dr. Baguley or for herself.

Mrs. Bostock, shorthand-notebook at the ready, sat beside Dr. Etherege's chair, her elegant legs crossed at the knees and her flamingo head lifted to receive, with becoming gravity, the medical director's instructions.

"Superintendent Dalgliesh has telephoned to say that he will be here shortly. He wants to see certain members of the staff again and has asked for an interview with me before lunch."

"I don't see how you can fit him in before lunch, Doctor," said Mrs. Bostock repressively. "There's the Professional Staff Committee at two-thirty and you haven't had time to look at the agenda. Dr. Talmage from the States is booked for twelve-thirty and I was hoping for an hour's dictation from 11 a.m."

"That will have to wait. The superintendent will be taking up a great deal of your own time, I'm afraid. He has some questions about the working of the clinic."

"I'm afraid I don't quite understand, Doctor. Do you mean he's interested in the general administrative arrangements?" Mrs. Bostock's tone was a nice blend of surprise and disapproval.

"Apparently so," replied Dr. Etherege. "He mentioned the appointments diary, the diagnostic index, the arrangements for registering incoming and outgoing post, and the medical record system. You had better deal with him personally. If I want to dictate I'll send for Miss Priddy."

"I'll do what I can to help, naturally," said Mrs. Bostock. "It's unfortunate that he should have picked one of our busiest mornings. It would be simpler to arrange a programme for him if I knew what he had in mind."

"We should all like to know that, I imagine," replied the medical director. "I should just answer his questions as fully as you can. And please get Cully to ring me as soon as he wants to come up."

"Yes, Doctor," said Mrs. Bostock, recognizing defeat. And took her leave.

Downstairs, in the E.C.T. room, Dr. Baguley

twitched himself into his white coat, helped by Nurse Bolam.

"Mrs. King will be here for her LSD treatment on Wednesday as usual. I think it will be best if we give it in one of the P.S.W. rooms on the third floor. Miss Kettle isn't in on Wednesday evenings, is she? Have a word with her. Alternatively we could use Mrs. Kallinski's room or one of the small interviewing rooms at the back."

Nurse Bolam said:

"It won't be so convenient for you, Doctor. It means coming up two flights when I phone."

"That isn't going to kill me. I may look in my dotage but I still have the use of my legs."

"There's the question of a bed, Doctor. I suppose we could put up one of the recovery stretchers from the E.C.T. clinic."

"Get Nagle to see to it. I don't want you alone in that basement."

"I'm not in the least frightened, really, Dr. Baguley."

Dr. Baguley lost his temper.

"For God's sake, use your brain, Nurse. Of course you're frightened! There's a murderer loose somewhere in this clinic and no one— except one person—is going to be happy about staying alone for any length of time in the basement. If you really aren't frightened then have the good sense to conceal the fact, especially from the police. Where's Sister? In the general office?"

He picked up the receiver and dialled jerkily.

"Sister? Baguley here. I've just told Nurse Bolam that I don't feel happy about using the basement room for LSD this week."

Sister Ambrose's voice came back clearly:

"Just as you like, Doctor, of course. But if the basement is more convenient and we could get a relief nurse from one of the general hospitals in the group for the E.C.T. clinic, I should be quite happy to stay downstairs with Nurse Bolam. We could special Mrs. King together."

Dr. Baguley said shortly:

"I want you in the E.C.T. clinic as usual, Sister, and the LSD patient will go upstairs. I hope that's finally understood."

In the medical director's room two hours later, Dalgliesh placed three black metal boxes on Dr. Etherege's desk. The boxes, which had small round holes punched in each of the shorter sides, were packed with buff-colored cards. It was the clinic diagnostic index. Dalgliesh said:

"Mrs. Bostock has explained this to me. If I've understood her correctly, each of these cards represents a patient. The information on the case record is coded and the patient's code punched on the card. The cards are punched with even rows of small holes and the space between each hole is numbered. By punching any number with the hand machine I cut out the card between the two adjacent holes to form an oblong slit. If this metal rod is then inserted through, say, hole number 20 on the outside of the box, and pushed right through the cards, and the box is rotated, any card which has been punched through that number will stand out. It is, in fact, one of the simplest of the many punch-card systems on the market."

"Yes. We use it principally as a diagnostic index and for research." If the medical director was surprised at Dalgliesh's interest he made no sign. The superintendent went on:

"Mrs. Bostock tells me that you don't code from the case record until the patient has completed treatment and that the system was started in 1952. That means that patients at present attending won't yet have a card—unless, of course, they were treated here earlier—and that patients who completed treatment before 1952 aren't included."

"Yes. We should like to include the earlier cases, but it's a question of staff time. The coding and punching are time-consuming and it's the kind of job that gets put on one side. At present we're coding the February 1962 discharges, so we're quite a bit behind."

"But once the patient's card is punched you can select any diagnosis or category of patient at will?"

"Yes, indeed." The medical director gave his slow sweet smile.

"I won't say that we can pick out immediately all the indigenous depressives with blue-eyed grandmothers who were born in wedlock because we haven't coded information about grandparents. But anything coded can be extracted without trouble."

Dalgliesh laid a slim manilla file on the desk.

"Mrs. Bostock has lent me the coding instructions. I see that you code sex, age, marital status, address by local authority area, diagnosis, consultant who treated the patient, dates of first and subsequent attendances and a considerable amount of detail about symptoms, treatment and progress. You also code social class. I find that interesting."

"It's unusual, certainly," replied Dr. Etherege. "Chiefly, I suppose, because it can be a purely subjective assessment. But we wanted it because it's sometimes useful in research. As you see we use the Registrar-General's classes. They're accurate enough for our purposes."

Dalgliesh ran the thin metal rod through his fingers.

"So I could select, for example, the cards of patients in class one who were treated eight to ten years ago, were married with a family, and were suffering from, say, sexual aberration, kleptomania, or any other socially unacceptable personality disorder."

"You could," admitted the medical director quietly. "But I can't see why you should want to."

"Blackmail, Doctor. It occurs to me that we have here a neatly contrived apparatus for the preselection of a victim. You push through the rod and out pops your card. The card bears a number on the top right-hand corner. And down in the basement record-room the medical record is filed and waiting."

The medical director said:

"This is nothing but guesswork. There isn't a shred of evidence."

"There's no proof, certainly, but it's a reasonable possibility. Consider the facts. On Wednesday afternoon Miss Bolam saw the group secretary after the House Committee meeting and told him that all was well at the clinic. At twelve-fifteen on Friday morning she telephoned to ask for an urgent visit because 'something is going on here that he ought to know about.' It was something serious and continuing and something that started before her time here, that is more than three years ago."

"Whatever it was we've no evidence that it was the reason for her death."

"No."

"In fact, if the murderer wanted to prevent Miss Bolam seeing Lauder he left it rather late. There was nothing to stop the group secretary turning up here any time after one o'clock."

Dalgliesh said:

"She was told over the telephone that he couldn't arrive until after the J.C.C. meeting that evening. That leads us to ask who could have overheard the telephone call. Cully was officially on the board, but he was unwell most of the day and, from time to time, other members of the staff took over, sometimes only for a few minutes. Nagle, Mrs. Bostock, Miss Priddy and even

Mrs. Shorthouse, all say that they helped on the board. Nagle thinks he took over for a short time at midday before he went out for his lunchtime beer, but says that he can't be sure. Nor can Cully. No one admits to having put through this particular call."

"They might not know if they had," replied Dr. Etherege. "We're insistent that the operator doesn't listen in to calls. That, after all, is important in our work. Miss Bolam may have merely asked for group offices. She must put through calls fairly often to the finance and supplies departments as well as the group secretary. The operator couldn't know there was anything special about this call. She might even have asked for an outside line and put through the call herself. That is possible, of course, with the P.A.B.X. system."

"But it could still be overheard by the person on the board."

"If he plugged in I suppose it could."

Dalgliesh said: "Miss Bolam told Cully late in the afternoon that she was expecting Mr. Lauder and she may have mentioned the visit to other people. We don't know. No one will admit to having been told except Cully. In the circumstances, that isn't perhaps surprising. We're not going to get much further with it at present. What I must do now is to find out what Miss Bolam wanted to tell Mr. Lauder. One of the first possibilities to be considered in a place like this must be blackmail. God knows that's continuing and it's serious enough."

The medical director did not speak for a moment. Dalgliesh wondered whether he was contemplating a further remonstrance, selecting appropriate words to express concern or disbelief. Then he said quietly:

"Of course it's serious. There's no point in wasting time discussing just how serious. Obviously, having thought up this theory, you have to carry through your investigation. Any other course of action would be most unfair to the members of my staff. What do you want me to do?"

"To help me select a victim. Later, perhaps, to make some telephone calls."

"You appreciate, Superintendent, that the case records are confidential?"

"I'm not asking to see a single case record. But if I did I don't think either you or the patient need worry. Shall we get started? We can take out our class 1 patients. Perhaps you would call out the codes for me."

A considerable number of the Steen patients were in class 1. "Upper-class neuroses catered for only", thought Dalgliesh. He surveyed the field for a moment and then said:

"If I were the blackmailer would I choose a man or a woman? It would depend on my own sex probably. A woman might pick on a woman. But, if it's a question of a regular income a man is probably a better bet. Let's take out the males next. I imagine our victim will live out of London. It would be risky to select an ex-patient who could too easily succumb to the temptation to pop into the clinic and let you know what was going on. I think I'd select my victim from a small town or village."

The medical director said:

"We only coded the county if it were an out-London address. London patients are coded by borough. Our best plan will be to take out all the London addresses and see what's left."

This was done. The number of cards still in the survey was now only a few dozen. Most of the Steen patients, as might be expected, came from the county of London. Dalgliesh said:

"Married or single? It's difficult to decide whether one or the other would be most vulnerable. Let's leave it open and start on the diagnosis. This is where I need your help particularly, Doctor. I realize this is highly confidential information. I suggest that you call out the codes for the diagnoses or symptoms which might interest a blackmailer. I don't want details."

Again the medical director paused. Dalgliesh waited patiently, metal rod in hand, while the doctor sat in silence, the code book opened before him. He seemed not to be seeing it. After a minute he roused himself and focused his eyes on the page. He said quietly:

"Try codes 23, 68, 69 and 71."

There were now only eleven cards remaining. Each of them bore a case record number on the top right-hand margin. Dalgliesh made a note of the numbers, and said:

"This is as far as we can go with the diagnostic index. We must now do what I think our blackmailer did, have a look at the case records, and learn more of our prospective victims. Shall we go down to the basement?"

The medical director got up without a word. As they went down the stairs they passed Miss Kettle on her way up. She nodded to the medical director and gave Dalgliesh a brief, puzzled glance as if wondering whether he were someone she had met and ought to recognize. In the hall Dr. Baguley was talking with Sister Ambrose. They broke off and turned to watch with grave, unsmiling faces as Dr. Etherege and Dalgliesh made their way to the basement stairs. At the other end of the hall the grey outline of Cully's head could be seen through the glass of the reception kiosk. The head did not turn and Dalgliesh guessed that Cully, absorbed in his contemplation of the front door, had not heard them.

The records-room was locked, but no longer sealed. In the porters' restroom Nagle was putting on his coat, evidently on his way out to an early lunch. He made no sign as the medical director took the record-room key from its hook, but the flash of interest in his mild, mud-brown eyes was not lost on Dalgliesh. They had been well observed. By early afternoon everyone in the clinic would know that he had examined the diagnostic index with the medical director and then visited the record-room. To one person that information would be of crucial interest. What

Dalgliesh hoped was that the murderer would become frightened and desperate; what he feared was that he would become more dangerous.

Dr. Etherege switched on the light in the record-room and the fluorescent tubes flickered, yellowed and blazed into whiteness. The room stood revealed. Dalgliesh smelt again its characteristic smell, compounded of mustiness, old paper and the tang of hot metal. He watched without betraying any emotion while the medical director locked the door on the inside and slipped the key in his pocket.

There was no sign now that the room had been the scene of murder. The torn records had been repaired and replaced on the shelves, the chair and table placed upright in their usual position.

The records were tied together with string in bundles of ten. Some of the files had been stored for so long that they seemed to adhere to each other. The string bit into the bulging manilla covers; across their tops was a thin patina of dust. Dalgliesh said:

"It should be possible to tell which of these bundles have been untied since the records were weeded out and brought down for storage. Some of them look as if they haven't been touched for years. I realize that a bundle may have been untied to extract a record for a perfectly innocent purpose, but we may as well make a start with files from those bundles which have obviously been untied within the last year or so. The first two numbers are in the eight thousand range. These seem to be on the top shelf. Have we a ladder?"

The medical director disappeared behind the first row of shelves and reappeared with a small step-ladder which he manœuvred with difficulty into the narrow aisle. Looking up at Dalgliesh as the detective mounted, he said:

"Tell me, Superintendent. Does this touching confidence mean that you have eliminated me from your list of suspects? If it does I should be interested to know by what process of deduction you came to that conclusion. I can't flatter myself that you believe me incapable of murder. No detective would accept that, surely, of any man."

"And no psychiatrist possibly," said Dalgliesh. "I don't ask myself whether a man is capable of murder, but whether he is capable of this particular murder. I don't think you're a petty blackmailer. I can't see how you could have known about Lauder's proposed visit. I doubt whether you've either the strength or skill to kill in that way. Lastly, I think you're probably the one person here whom Miss Bolam wouldn't have kept waiting. Even if I'm wrong you can hardly refuse to cooperate, can you?"

He was deliberately curt. The bright blue eyes were still gazing into his, inviting a confidence which he did not want to give but found it difficult to resist. The medical director went on:

"I have only met three murderers. Two of them are buried in quicklime. One of the two hardly knew what he was doing and the other couldn't have stopped himself. Are you satisfied, Superintendent, with that solution?"

Dalgliesh replied:

"No man in his senses would be. But I don't see how that affects what I'm trying to do now; catch this murderer before he—or she—kills again."

The medical director said no more. Together they found the eleven case records they sought and took them up to Dr. Etherege's room. If Dalgliesh had expected the medical director to make difficulties over the next stage of the investigation he was agreeably surprised. The hint that this killer might not stop at one victim had struck home. When Dalgliesh explained what he wanted the medical director did not protest. Dalgliesh said:

"I'm not asking for the names of these patients. I'm not interested in what was wrong with them. All I want you to do is to telephone each of them and ask tactfully whether they rang the clinic recently, probably on Friday morning. You could explain that someone made a call which it's important to trace. If one of these patients did ring I want the name and address. Not the diagnosis. Just the name and address."

"I must ask the patient's consent before I give that information."

"If you must," said Dalgliesh. "I leave that to you. All I ask is to get that information."

The medical director's stipulation was a formality and both of them knew it. The eleven case records were on the desk and nothing but force could keep the addresses from Dalgliesh if he wanted them. He sat at some distance from Dr. Etherege in one of the large, leather-covered chairs, and prepared to watch, with professional interest, his unusual collaborator at work. The medical director picked up his receiver and asked for an outside line. The patients' telephone numbers had been noted on the case records and the first two tries at once reduced the eleven possibles to nine. In each case the patient had changed his address since his attendance. Dr. Etherege apologized for disturbing the new subscribers to the numbers concerned and dialled for the third time. The third number answered and the medical director asked if he might speak to Mr. Caldecote. There was a prolonged crackling from the other end and Dr. Etherege made the appropriate response.

"No, he hadn't heard. How very sad. Really? No, it was nothing important. Just an old acquaintance who would be driving through Wiltshire and hoped to meet Mr. Caldecote again. No, he wouldn't speak to Mrs. Caldecote. He didn't want to distress her."

"Dead?" asked Dalgliesh, as the receiver was replaced.

"Yes. Three years ago, apparently. Cancer, poor fellow. I must note that on his record."

He did so while Dalgliesh waited.

The next number was difficult to get and there was much talk with the exchange. When at last the number was rung there was no reply.

"We seem to be having no success, Superintendent. It was a clever theory of yours, but it appears, more ingenious than true."

"There are still seven more patients to try," said Dalgliesh quietly. The medical director murmured something about a Dr. Talmage whom he was expecting, but referred to the next file and dialled again. This time the patient was at home and, apparently, not in the least surprised to hear from the medical director of the Steen. He poured out a lengthy account of his present pychological condition to which Dr. Etherege listened with patient sympathy and made appropriate replies. Dalgliesh was interested and a little amused at the skill with which the call was conducted. But the patient had not recently telephoned the clinic. The medical director put down the receiver and spent some time noting what the patient had told him on the case record.

"One of our successes, apparently. He wasn't at all surprised that I telephoned. It's rather touching the way patients take it for granted that their doctors are immensely concerned for their welfare and are thinking of them personally at all times of the day and night. But he didn't phone. He wasn't lying, I assure you. This is very time-consuming, Superintendent, but I suppose we must go on."

"Yes, please. I'm sorry, but we must go on."

But the next call brought success. At first it sounded like another failure. From the conversation Dalgliesh gathered that the patient had recently been taken to hospital and that it was his wife who had answered. Then he saw the medical director's face change, and heard him say:

"You did? We knew that someone had telephoned and were trying to trace the call. I expect you've heard about the very dreadful tragedy that we've had here recently. Yes, it is in connection with that." He waited while the voice spoke at some length from the other end. Then he put down the receiver and wrote briefly on his desk jotting pad. Dalgliesh did not speak. The medical director looked up at him with an expression half puzzled, half surprised.

"That was the wife of a Colonel Fenton of Sprigg's Green in Kent. She telephoned Miss Bolam about a very serious matter at about midday last Friday. She didn't want to talk to you on the phone about it and I thought it better not to press her. But she'd like to see you as soon as possible. I've written down the address."

"Thank you, Doctor," said Dalgliesh, and took the proffered paper. He showed neither surprise nor relief, but his heart was singing. The medical director shook his head as if the whole thing were beyond his understanding. He said:

"She sounds rather a formidable old lady and very formal. She said that she would be very glad if you would take afternoon tea with her."

Just after four o'clock Dalgliesh drove slowly into Sprigg's Green. It revealed itself as an undistinguished village lying between the Maidstone and Canterbury roads. He could not remember having passed through it before. There were few people about. The village, thought Dalgliesh, was too far from London to tempt the commuter and had no period charm to attract retired couples or artists and writers in search of country peace with a country cost of living. Most of the cottages were obviously lived in by farm workers, their front gardens clumped with cabbages and brussels sprouts, straggly and stem-scarred from recent pickings, their windows shut close against the treachery of an English autumn. Dalgliesh passed the church, its short flint-and-stone tower and clear glass windows only half visible behind the surrounding chestnut trees. The churchyard was untidy but not offensively so. The grass had been mown between the graves and some attempt made to weed the gravel paths. Separated from the churchyard by a tall laurel hedge stood the vicarage, a sombre Victorian house built to accommodate a Victorian-size family and its appendages. Next came the green itself, a small square of grass bounded by a row of weather-boarded cottages and faced by a more than usually hideous modern pub and petrol station. Outside the "King's Head" was a concrete bus shelter where a group of women waited dispiritedly. They gave Dalgliesh a brief and uninterested glance as he passed. In spring, no doubt, the surrounding cherry orchards would lend their charm even to Sprigg's Green. Now, however, there was a chill dampness in the air, the fields looked perpetually sodden, a slow mournful procession of cows being driven to the evening milking churned the road verges to mud. Dalgliesh slowed to a walking pace to pass them, keeping his watch for Sprigg's Acre. He did not want to ask the way.

He was not long in finding it. The house lay a little back from the road and was sheltered from it by a six-foot beech hedge which shone golden in the fading light. There appeared to be no drive and Dalgliesh edged his Cooper Bristol carefully on to the grass verge before letting himself in through the white gates of the garden. The house lay before him, rambling, low built and thatched, with an air of comfort and simplicity. As he turned from latching the gate behind him a woman turned the corner of the house and came down the path to meet him. She was very small. Somehow this surprised Dalgliesh. He had formed a mental picture of a stout, well-corseted colonel's wife condescending to see him, but at her own time and place. The reality was less intimidating and more interesting. There was something gallant and a little pathetic in the way she came down the path towards him. She was wearing a thick skirt and a tweed jacket and was hatless, her thick white hair lifting with the evening breeze. She wore gardening gloves, incongruously large with vast gauntlets which made the trowel she carried look like a child's toy. As they met she pulled off the right glove and held out her hand to him,

looking up at him with anxious eyes which light-
ened, almost imperceptibly, with relief. But when
she spoke her voice was unexpectedly firm.

"Good afternoon. You must be Superintendent
Dalgliesh. My name is Louise Fenton. Did you
come by car? I thought I heard one."

Dalgliesh explained where he had left it and
said that he hoped that it would not be in anyone's way.

"Oh, no! Not at all. Such an unpleasant way to
travel. You could have come by train quite easily
to Marden and I would have sent the trap for you.
We haven't a car. We both dislike them very
much. I'm sorry you had to sit in one all the way
from London."

"It was the fastest way," said Dalgliesh, wondering if he should apologize for living in the
twentieth century. "And I wanted to see you as
soon as possible."

He was careful to keep the urgency from his
voice, but he could see the sudden tensing of her
shoulders.

"Yes. Yes, of course. Would you like to see the
garden before we go in? The light is fading but
we might just have time."

An interest in the garden was apparently expected and Dalgliesh acquiesced. A light east
wind, rising as the day died, whipped uncomfortably around his neck and ankles. But he never
hurried an interview. This one promised to be difficult for Mrs. Fenton and she was entitled to take
her time. He wondered at his own impatience

even as he concealed it. For the last two days he had been irked by a foreboding of tragedy and failure which was the more disturbing because it was irrational. The case was young yet. His intelligence told him that he was making progress. Even at this moment he was within grasp of motive, and motive, he knew, was crucial to this case. He hadn't failed yet in his career at the Yard and this case, with its limited number of suspects and careful contriving, was an unlikely candidate for a first failure. Yet he remained worried, vexed by this unreasonable fear that time was running out. Perhaps it was the autumn. Perhaps he was tired. He turned up his coat collar and prepared himself to look interested and appreciative.

They passed together through a wrought-iron gate at the side of the house and entered the main garden. Mrs. Fenton was saying:

"I love the garden dearly, but I'm not much good at it. Things don't grow for me. My husband has the green fingers. He's in Maidstone Hospital at present having an operation for hernia. It's all been very successful I'm happy to say. Do you garden, Superintendent?"

Dalgliesh explained that he lived in a flat high above the Thames in the City and had recently sold his Essex cottage.

"I really know very little about gardening," he said.

"Then you will enjoy looking at ours," replied Mrs. Fenton, with gentle if illogical persistence.

There was, indeed, plenty to see even in the fading light of an autumn day. The colonel had given his imagination full play, compensating perhaps for the enforced regimentation of much of his life by indulgence in a picturesque and undisciplined profusion. There was a small lawn surrounding a fish pond and edged with crazy paving. There was a succession of trellis archways leading from one carefully tended plot to another. There was a rose garden with a sundial where a few last roses still gleamed white on their leafless stems. There were hedges of beech, yew and hawthorn as gold and green backcloths to the banked chrysanthemums. At the bottom of the garden ran a small stream, crossed every ten yards by wooden bridges which were a monument to the colonel's industry, if not to his taste. The appetite had grown by what it fed on. The colonel, having once successfully bridged his brook, had been unable to resist further efforts. Together they stood for a moment on one of the bridges. Dalgliesh could see the colonel's initials cut into the wood of the handrail. Beneath their feet the little stream, already half choked with the first fallen leaves, made its own sad music. Suddenly, Mrs. Fenton said:

"So somebody killed her. I know I ought to feel pity for her whatever she did. But I can't. Not yet. I should have realized that Matthew wouldn't be the only victim. These people never stop at one victim, do they? I suppose someone couldn't stand it any more and took that way out. It's a very terrible thing, but I can understand it. I read about it in the papers, you know, before the medical director telephoned. Do you know, Superintendent, for a moment I was glad. That's a terrible thing to say, but it's true. I was glad she was dead. I thought that now Matthew needn't worry any more."

Dalgliesh said gently:

"We don't think that Miss Bolam was blackmailing your husband. It's possible that she was, but not likely. We think she was killed because she had found out what was happening and meant to stop it. That's why it's so important that I talk to you."

Mrs. Fenton's knuckles whitened. The hands grasping the bridge began to shake. She said:

"I'm afraid I've been very stupid. I mustn't waste any more of your time. It's getting cold, isn't it? Shall we go indoors?"

They turned towards the house, neither of them speaking. Dalgliesh shortened his stride to the slow pace of the thin, upright figure at his side. He glanced at her anxiously. She was very pale and he thought he saw her lips moving soundlessly. But she walked firmly. She was going to be all right. He told himself that he mustn't hurry things. In half an hour, perhaps less, he would have the motive securely in his hands like a bomb that would blow the whole case wide open. But he must be patient. Once again he was touched by an indefinable unrest as if, even at this moment of imminent triumph, his heart held the sure knowledge of failure. The dusk closed in around them. Somewhere a bonfire smouldered, filling his nostrils with acrid smoke. The lawn was a wet sponge under his feet.

The house welcomed them, blessedly warm and smelling faintly of home-baked bread. Mrs. Fenton left him to put her head into a room at the far end of the hall. He guessed that tea was being ordered. Then she led him into the drawing-room to the comfort of a wood fire which threw immense shadow over the chintz-covered chairs and sofa and the faded carpet. She switched on a huge standard lamp at the side of the fireplace and tugged the curtains across the windows, shutting out desolation and decay. Tea arrived, the tray set on a low table by a stolid and aproned maid almost as old as her mistress who carefully avoided looking at Dalgliesh. It was a good tea. Dalgliesh saw with an emotion which was too like compassion to be comfortable, that trouble had been taken on his behalf. There were fresh-baked scones, two kinds of sandwiches, home-made cakes and an iced sponge. There was too much of everything, a schoolboy's tea. It was as if the two women, faced with their unknown and most unwelcome visitor, had sought relief from uncertainty in the provision of this embarrassingly liberal feast. Mrs. Fenton herself seemed surprised at the variety which faced her. She manœuvred cups on the tray like an anxious,

inexperienced hostess. It was only when Dalgliesh was provided with his tea and sandwich
that she spoke again about the murder.

"My husband attended the Steen Clinic for
about four months, nearly ten years ago, soon
after he left the army. He was living in London at
the time and I was in Nairobi staying with my
daughter-in-law who was expecting her first baby.
I never knew about my husband's treatment until
he told me a week ago."

She paused and Dalgliesh said:

"I ought to say now that we aren't, of course,
interested in what was wrong with Colonel Fenton. That is a confidential medical matter and it
isn't the concern of the police. I didn't ask Dr.
Etherege for any information and he wouldn't
have given it to me if I had. The fact that your
husband was being blackmailed may have to
come out—I don't think that can be avoided—but
his reason for going to the clinic and the details
of his treatment are no one's business but his
and yours."

Mrs. Fenton replaced her cup on the tray with
infinite care. She looked into the fire and said:

"I don't think it is my business, really. I wasn't
upset because he didn't tell me. It's so easy to
say now that I would have understood and would
have tried to help, but I wonder. I think he was wise
not to speak about it. People make such a fuss
about absolute honesty in marriage, but it isn't
very sensible to confess hurtful things unless
you really mean to hurt. I wish Matthew had told

me about the blackmail, though. Then he really needed help. Together I'm sure we could have thought of something."

Dalgliesh asked how it had started.

"Just two years ago, Matthew says. He had a telephone call. The voice reminded him about his treatment at the Steen and actually quoted some of the very intimate details Matthew had told the psychiatrist. Then the voice suggested that he would like to help other patients who were trying to overcome similar difficulties. There was a lot of talk about the dreadful social consequences of not getting cured. It was all very subtle and clever, but there wasn't the least doubt what the voice was after. Matthew asked what he was expected to do and was told to send fifteen pounds in notes to arrive by the first post on the first day of every month. If the first was a Saturday or Sunday, the letter was to arrive on Monday. He was to address the envelope in green ink to the administrative secretary and enclose with the money a note to say that it was a donation from a grateful patient. The voice said that he could be sure that the cash would go where it could do most good."

"It was a clever enough plan," said Dalgliesh. "Blackmail would be difficult to prove and the amount was nicely calculated. I imagine that your husband would have been forced to take a different line if the demand had been too exorbitant."

"Oh, he would! Matthew would never let us be ruined. But you see, it was such a small amount really. I don't mean that we could afford to lose fifteen pounds a month, but it was a sum which Matthew could just find by personal economies without making me suspicious. And the demand never rose. That was the extraordinary thing about it. Matthew said that he always understood a blackmailer was never satisfied but kept increasing the demand until the victim couldn't pay another penny. It wasn't like that at all. Matthew sent the money to arrive on the first day of the next month and he had another call. The voice thanked him for his kind donation and made it quite clear that no more than fifteen pounds was expected. And no more ever was. The voice said something about sharing the sacrifice equally. Matthew said he could almost persuade himself that the thing was genuine. About six months ago he decided to miss a month and see what happened. It wasn't very pleasant. There was another call and the menace was unmistakable. The voice talked about the need to save patients from social ostracism and said how distressed the people of Sprigg's Green would be to hear about his lack of generosity. My husband decided to go on. If the village really got to know, it would mean leaving this house. My family have lived here for two hundred years and we both love it. Matthew would be heartbroken to leave the garden. And then there's the village. Of course, you haven't seen it at its best, but we love it. My husband is a churchwarden. Our small son, who was killed in a road accident, is buried here. It isn't easy to pull up your roots at seventy."

No, it wouldn't be easy. Dalgliesh didn't question her assumption that discovery would mean that they must leave. A younger, tougher, more sophisticated couple would no doubt ride the publicity, ignore the innuendoes and accept the embarrassed sympathy of their friends in the sure knowledge that nothing lasts for ever and that few things in village life are as dead as last year's scandal. Pity was less easy to accept. It was probably the fear of pity that would drive most victims to retreat. He asked what had brought the matter to a head. Mrs. Fenton replied:

"Two things, really. The first is that we needed more money. My husband's younger brother died unexpectedly a month ago and left his widow rather badly off. She is an invalid and not likely to live more than a year or two, but she is very happily settled in a nursing-home near Norwich and would like to stay there. It was a question of helping with the fees. She needed about another five pounds a week and I couldn't understand why Matthew seemed so worried about it. It would mean careful planning, but I thought we ought to be able to manage it. But he knew, of course, that we couldn't if he had to go on sending the fifteen pounds to the Steen. Then there was his operation. It wasn't a very serious one I know, but any operation is a risk at seventy and he was afraid that he might die and the whole story come out without his being able to explain. So he told me. I was very glad he did. He went into hospital perfectly happy as a result and the operation went very well. Really very well indeed. Could I give you some more tea, Superintendent?" Dalgliesh passed her his cup and asked what action she had decided to take. They were now coming to the crux of the story, but he was careful neither to hurry her nor to appear over-anxious. His comments and questions might have been those of any afternoon guest, dutifully taking a polite share in his hostess's conversation. She was an old lady who had been through a severe strain and was faced with one even greater. He guessed a little of what this revelation to a stranger must be costing her. Any formal expression of sympathy would have been a presumption, but at least he could help, with patience and understanding.

"What did I decide to do? Well, that was the problem, of course. I was determined that the blackmailing should be stopped, but I wanted to spare us both if I could. I'm not a very intelligent woman—it's no use shaking your head, if I were this murder wouldn't have happened—but I thought it out very carefully. It seemed to me that the best thing was to visit the Steen Clinic and see someone in authority. I could explain what was happening, perhaps even without mentioning my name, and ask them to make their own investigation and put a stop to the blackmail. After all, they would know about my husband, so I wouldn't be confiding his secret to anyone new and they would be just as anxious to avoid publicity as I was. It wouldn't do the clinic any good if this came out, would it? They could probably find out who was responsible without a great deal of difficulty. Psychiatrists are supposed to understand people's characters after all, and it must be someone who was at the clinic when my husband attended. And then, being a woman, would narrow the field."

"Do you mean the blackmailer was a woman?" asked Dalgliesh, surprised.

"Oh, yes! At least, the voice on the telephone was a woman's voice, my husband says."

"Is he quite sure of that?"

"He didn't express any doubt to me. It wasn't only the voice, you see. It was some of the things she said. Things like it not being only members of my husband's sex who had these illnesses, and had he ever thought what unhappiness they could cause to women, and so on. There were definite references to her being a woman. My husband remembers the telephone conversations very clearly and he will be able to tell you what the remarks were. I expect you will want to see him as soon as possible, won't you?"

Touched by the obvious anxiety in her voice, he replied:

"If his doctor thinks Colonel Fenton is well enough to have a brief talk to me I should like to see him on my way back to London tonight. There are one or two points—this matter of the blackmailer's sex is one—that only he can help with. I shan't bother him more than necessary."

"I'm sure he will be able to see you. He has a little room of his own—an amenity bed they call them—and he's doing very well. I told him that you were coming today so he won't be surprised to see you. I don't think I'll come too, if you don't mind. I think he would rather see you alone. I shall write a note for you to take."

Dalgliesh thanked her and said:

"It's interesting that your husband should say it was a woman. He could be right, of course, but it would be a clever deception on the blackmailer's part and difficult to disprove. Some men are able to mimic a woman's voice very convincingly and the casual references to establish sex would be even more effective than a disguised voice. If the colonel had decided to prosecute and the matter had come to court, it would have been very difficult to convict a man of this particular crime unless the evidence was very strong. And as far as I can see the evidence would be almost non-existent. I think we keep a very open mind on the question of the blackmailer's sex. But I'm sorry. I interrupted."

"It was rather an important point to establish, wasn't it? I hope that my husband will be able to help with it. Well, as I was saying, I decided that the best move was to visit the clinic. I went up to London last Friday morning on an early train. I had to see my chiropodist and there were one or two things Matthew needed in hospital. I decided to shop first. I should have gone direct to the clinic, of course. That was another mistake. It was cowardice, really. I wasn't looking forward to it and I tried to behave as if it were nothing so

very special, just a casual visit I could fit in between the shopping and the chiropodist. In the
end I didn't go at all. I telephoned instead. You
see, I told you I wasn't very intelligent."

Dalgliesh asked what had led to the change of
plan.

"It was Oxford Street. I know that sounds silly,
but it happened that way. I hadn't been up to
London alone for a very long time and I had forgotten how dreadful it is now. I used to love it
when I was a girl. It seemed a gracious city then.
Now the skyline has changed and the streets
seem full of freaks and foreigners. One shouldn't
resent them, I know—the foreigners, I mean. It's
just that I felt so alien. And then there were the
cars. I tried to cross Oxford Street and was
stranded among them on one of the islands. Of
course, they weren't killing anyone or knocking
anyone down. They couldn't. They couldn't even
move. But they smelt so horrible that I had to
hold my handkerchief to my nose and I felt so
faint and ill. When I reached the pavement I went
into one of the stores to find the women's rest
room. It was on the fifth floor and it took me a long
time to get to the right lift. The crowds were dreadful and we were all squashed in together. When I
got to the rest room all the chairs were taken. I
was standing against the wall wondering whether
I could summon enough energy to queue for my
lunch when I saw the row of telephone boxes.
Suddenly I realized that I could telephone the
clinic and save myself the journey and the ordeal

of telling my story face to face. It was stupid of me, I see that now, but at the time it seemed a very good idea. It would be easier to conceal my identity on the telephone and I felt that I should be able to explain more fully. I also gained a great deal of comfort from the thought that, if the conversation became too difficult, I could always ring off. You see, I was being very cowardly and my only excuse is that I was very tired, far more tired than I imagined possible. I expect you will say that I ought to have gone straight to the police, to Scotland Yard. But Scotland Yard is a place I associate with detective stories and murders. It hardly seems possible that it actually exists and you can call there and tell your story. Besides, I was still very anxious to avoid publicity. I didn't think the police would welcome someone who wanted help, but wasn't prepared to co-operate by telling the whole story or being willing to prosecute. All I wanted, you see, was to stop the blackmailer. It wasn't very public-spirited of me, was it?"

"It was very understandable," replied Dalgliesh. "I thought it very possible that Miss Bolam got the warning by telephone. Can you remember what you said to her?"

"Not very clearly, I'm afraid. When I had found the four pennies for the call and looked up the number in the directory I spent a few minutes deciding what I would say. A man's voice answered and I asked to speak to the administrative secretary. Then there was a woman's voice which said, 'Administrative officer speaking.' I hadn't expected to hear a woman and I suddenly got it into my mind that I was speaking to the black-mailer. After all, why not? So I said that someone from the clinic, and probably she, had been black-mailing my husband and that I was telephoning to say that she wouldn't get another penny from now on and that if we received any more tele-phone calls we should go straight to the police. It all came out in a rush. I was shaking rather badly and had to lean against the wall of the telephone box for support. I must have sounded a little hys-terical. When she could get a word in she asked me whether I was a patient and who was treating me and said something about asking one of the doctors to have a word with me. I suppose she thought I was out of my mind. I replied that I had never attended the clinic and that, if ever I needed treatment, which God forbid, I should know better than to go to a place where a patient's in-discretions and unhappiness were made an op-portunity for blackmail. I think I ended up by saying that there was a woman involved, that she must have been at the clinic for nearly ten years, and that, if the administrative officer wasn't the person concerned, I hoped that she would make it her duty to discover who was. She tried to get me to leave my name or to come to see her, but I rang off."

"Did you give her any details about how the blackmail was organized?"

"I told her that my husband had sent fifteen pounds a month in an envelope addressed in green ink. That's when she became suddenly very anxious that I should visit the clinic or at least leave my name. It was rude of me to ring off without ending the conversation, but I suddenly became frightened. I don't know why. And I had said all that I meant to say. One of the chairs in the restroom was vacant by then, so I sat down for half an hour until I felt better. Then I went straight to Charing Cross and had some coffee and sandwiches in the buffet there and waited for my train home. I read about the murder in the paper on Saturday and I'm afraid I took it for granted that one of the other victims—for there must have been others, surely—had taken that way out. I didn't connect the crime with my telephone call, at least, not at first. Then I began to wonder whether it might not be my duty to let the police know what had been going on at that dreadful place. Yesterday I talked to my husband about it and we decided to do nothing in a hurry. We thought it might be best to wait and see whether we received any further calls from the blackmailer. I wasn't very happy about our silence. There haven't been many details of the murder in the papers, so I don't know what exactly happened. But I did realize that the blackmail might be in some way connected with the crime and that the police would wish to know about it. While I was still worrying about what to do, Dr. Etherege telephoned. You know the rest. I'm still wondering how you managed to trace me."

"We found you in the same way as the black-mailer picked out Colonel Fenton, from the clinic diagnostic index and the medical record. You mustn't think that they don't look after their confidential papers at the Steen. They do. Dr. Etherege is very distressed indeed about the blackmail. But no system is completely proof against clever and deliberate wickedness."

"You will find him, won't you?" she asked. "You will find him?"

"Thanks to you, I think we shall," Dalgliesh replied. As he held out his hand to say good-bye, she suddenly asked:

"What was she like, Superintendent? I mean the woman who was murdered. Tell me about Miss Bolam."

Dalgliesh said:

"She was forty-one years old. Not married. I never saw her alive, but she had light brown hair and blue-grey eyes. She was rather stout, wide browed, thin mouthed. She was an only child and both her parents were dead. She lived rather a lonely life, but her church meant a great deal to her and she was a Guide captain. She liked children and flowers. She was conscientious and efficient, but not very good at understanding people. She was kind when they were in trouble but they thought her rigid, humourless and censorious. I think they were probably right. She had a great sense of duty."

"I am responsible for her death. I have to accept that."

Dalgliesh said gently:

"That's nonsense, you know. Only one person is responsible and, thanks to you, we shall get him."

She shook her head.

"If I had come to you in the first place or even had the courage to turn up at the clinic instead of telephoning she would be alive today."

Dalgliesh thought that Louise Fenton deserved better than to be pacified with easy lies. And they would have brought no comfort. Instead he replied:

"I suppose that could be true. There are so many 'ifs.' She would be alive today if her group secretary had cancelled a meeting and hurried to the clinic, if she herself had gone at once to see him, if an old porter hadn't had stomachache. You did what you thought right and no one can do more."

"So did she, poor woman," replied Mrs. Fenton. "And look where it led her."

She patted Dalgliesh briefly on the shoulder, as if it were he who needed the comfort and reassurance.

"I didn't mean to bore you. Please forgive me. You've been very patient and kind. Might I ask one more question? You said that, thanks to me, you would get this murderer. Do you know now who it is?"

"Yes," said Dalgliesh. "I think I now know who it is."

Chapter Seven

BACK IN HIS OFFICE at the Yard just over two hours later, Dalgliesh talked over the case with Sergeant Martin. The file lay open on the desk before him.

"You got corroboration of Mrs. Fenton's story all right, sir?"

"Oh, yes. The colonel was quite forthcoming. Now that he's recovered from the twin ordeals of his operation and the confession to his wife, he's inclined to take both experiences rather lightly. He even suggested that the request for money could have been genuine and that it was reasonable to assume that it was. I had to point out that a woman has been murdered before he faced the realities of the situation. Then he gave me the full story. It agreed with what Mrs. Fenton had told me except for one interesting addition. I give you three guesses."

"Would it be about that burglary? It was Fenton I suppose?"

"Damn you Martin, you might make an effort sometimes to look surprised. Yes, it was our colonel. But he didn't take the fifteen pounds. I wouldn't have blamed him if he had. The money was his after all. He admits himself that he would have taken it back if he'd seen it, but, of course, he didn't. He was there for quite another purpose, to get hold of that medical record. He was a bit out of his depth in most things but he did realize that the medical record was the only real evidence of what happened when he was a patient at the Steen. He mucked up his burglary attempt of course despite having practised glass-cutting in his greenhouse, and made an undignified exit when he heard Nagle and Cully arriving. He got nowhere near the record he wanted. He assumed it was in one of the files in the general office and managed to prise those open. When he saw that the records were filed numerically he knew he couldn't succeed. He had long forgotten his clinic number. I expect he put it firmly out of his mind when he felt he was cured."

"Well, the clinic did that for him, anyway."

"He doesn't admit it I can tell you. I believe that's not uncommon with psychiatric patients. It must be rather disheartening for psychiatrists. After all, you don't get surgical patients claiming that they could have performed their own operation given half a chance. No, the colonel isn't feeling particularly grateful to the Steen, nor inclined to give the clinic much credit for keeping him out of trouble. I suppose he could be right. I don't imagine that Dr. Etherege would claim that you can do a great deal for a psychiatric patient in four months which was the length of time Fenton attended. His cure—if you can call it that— probably had something to do with leaving the army. It's difficult to judge whether he welcomed that or dreaded it. Anyway, we'd better resist the temptation to be amateur psychologists."

"What sort of a man is the colonel, sir?"

"Small. Probably looks smaller because of his illness. Sandy hair; bushy eyebrows. Rather like a small fierce animal glaring out from its hole. A much weaker personality than his wife, I'd say, despite Mrs. Fenton's apparent frailty. Admittedly it's difficult to be at one's best lying in a hospital bed wearing a striped bedjacket and with a formidable Sister warning one to be a good boy and not talk too long. He wasn't very helpful about the telephone voice. He says that it sounded like a woman and it never occurred to him that it mightn't be. On the other hand he wasn't surprised when I suggested that the voice could have been disguised. But he's honest, and, obviously, he can't go further than that. He just doesn't know. Still, we've got the motive. This is one of those rare cases in which knowing why is knowing who."

"Are you applying for a warrant?"

"Not yet. We're not ready. If we don't go carefully now the whole case could come apart in our hands."

Again he was visited by the chilling presentiment of disaster. He found himself analysing the case as if he had already failed. Where had it gone wrong? He had shown his hand to the murderer when he had taken the clinic diagnostic index so openly into the medical director's room. That fact would be round the clinic quickly enough. He had meant it to be. There came a time when it was useful to frighten your man. But was this killer the kind who could be frightened into betraying himself? Had it been an error of judgment to move so openly? Suddenly Martin's plain, honest face looked irritatingly bovine as he stood there unhelpfully waiting for instructions. Dalgliesh said:

"You went to the Priddys' place, I suppose. Well, let's have the dirt about that. The girl is married, I suppose?"

"There's no doubt about that, sir. I was there earlier this evening and I had a chat with the parents. Luckily Miss Priddy was out, fetching fish and chips for supper. They're in quite poor circumstances."

"That's a *non sequitur.* However, go on."

"There isn't much to report. They live in one of those terrace houses leading down to the southern railway line in Clapham. Everything's very comfortable and neat but there's no television or anything like that. I suppose their religion's against it. Both the Priddys are over sixty I reckon. Jennifer's the only child and her mother must have been more than forty when she was born. It's the usual story about the marriage. I was surprised they told me but they did. The husband's a warehouseman; used to work with the girl at her last job. Then there was a baby on the way so they had to get married."

"It's almost pitiably common. You'd think that her generation, who think they know all the answers about sex, would make themselves familiar with a few basic facts. However, we're told these little mishaps don't worry anyone these days."

Dalgliesh was shocked by the bitterness in his own voice. Was it really necessary, he wondered, to protest quite so vehemently about so common a little tragedy. What was happening to him? Martin said stolidly:

"They worry people like the Priddys. These kids get themselves into trouble but it's usually the despised older generation who have to cope. The Priddys did their best. They made the kids marry of course. There isn't much room in the house but they gave up the first floor and made it into a small flat for the young couple. Very nicely done it was too. They showed me."

Dalgliesh thought how much he disliked the expression "young couple" with its cosy undertones of dewy-eyed domesticity, its echo of disillusion.

"You seem to have made a hit in your brief visit," he said.

"I liked them, sir. They're good people. The marriage didn't last of course, and I think that they wonder now whether they did the right thing in forcing it. The chap left Clapham over two years ago and they don't know where he is now. They told me his name and I saw his photograph. He's got nothing to do with the Steen Clinic, sir."

"I didn't think he had. We hardly expected to discover that Jennifer Priddy was Mrs. Henry Etherege. Neither her parents nor her husband have anything to do with this crime."

Nor had they, except that their lives, like flying tangents, had made brief contact with the circle of death. Every murder case produced such people. Dalgliesh had sat more times than he could remember in sitting-rooms, bedrooms, pubs and police stations talking to people who had come, however briefly, in touch with murder. Violent death was a great releaser of inhibitions, the convulsive kick which spun open the top of so many ant hills. His job, in which he could deceive himself that non-involvement was a duty, had given him glimpses into the secret lives of men and women whom he might never see again except as half-recognized faces in a London crowd. Sometimes he despised his private image, the patient, uninvolved, uncensorious inquisitor of other people's misery and guilt. How long could you stay detached, he wondered, before you lost your own soul.

"What happened to the child?" he asked suddenly.

"She had a miscarriage, sir," answered Martin.

"Of course," thought Dalgliesh. "She would." Nothing could go right for such as the Priddys. Tonight he felt that he, too, was tainted with their ill luck. He asked what Martin had learned about Miss Bolam.

"Not much that we didn't know already. They went to the same church and Jennifer Priddy used to be a girl guide in Bolam's company. The old people spoke of her with a great deal of respect. She was helpful to them when the baby was on the way—I got the impression that she paid to have the house converted—and when the marriage failed she suggested that the Priddy child should work at the Steen. I think the old people were glad to think that someone was keeping an eye on Jenny. They couldn't tell me much about Miss Bolam's private life, at least, nothing that we don't know. There was one odd thing though. It happened when the girl got back with the supper. Mrs. Priddy asked me to stay and have a meal with them but I said I'd better be getting back. You know what it is with fish and chips. You just buy the right number of pieces and it isn't easy to fit in an extra. Anyway, they called the girl in to say 'good-bye' and she came in from the kitchen looking like death. She only stayed a second or two and the old people didn't seem to notice anything. But I did. Something had scared the kid properly."

"Finding you there, perhaps. She may have

thought that you'd mentioned her friendship with Nagle."

"I don't think it was that, sir. She looked into the sitting-room when she first got back from the shop and said 'good evening' without turning a hair. I explained that I was just having a chat with her parents because they were friends of Miss Bolam and might be able to tell us something useful about her private life. It didn't seem to worry her. It was about five minutes later that she came back looking so odd."

"No one arrived at the house or telephoned during that time?"

"No. I heard no one anyway. They aren't on the phone. I suppose it was something that occurred to her while she was alone in the kitchen. I couldn't very well ask her. I was on my way out and there wasn't anything you could put tongue to. I just told them all that if they thought of anything that might help they should let us know at once."

"We've got to see her again, of course, and the sooner the better. That alibi's got to be broken and she's the only one who can do it. I don't think the girl was consciously lying, or even deliberately withholding evidence. The truth simply never occurred to her."

"Nor to me, sir, until we got the motive. What do you want to do now? Let him sweat a bit?"

"I daren't, Martin. It's too dangerous. We've got to press on. I think we'll go now and have a little chat with Nagle."

But when they reached the Pimlico house twenty minutes later they found the flat locked and a folded scrap of paper wedged under the knocker. Dalgliesh smoothed it out and read aloud. "Darling. Sorry I missed you. I must speak to you. If I don't see you tonight I'll be at the clinic early. Love, Jenny."

"Any point in waiting for him, sir?"

"I doubt it. I think I can guess where he is. Cully was on the board when we did our phoning this morning but I made sure that Nagle, and probably everyone else at the Steen, knew that I was interesting myself in the medical records. I asked Dr. Etherege to put them back after I left. Nagle goes into the Steen on one or two evenings in the week to see to the boiler and turn off the art therapy department kiln. I imagine that he's there tonight, taking the opportunity of seeing which records have been moved. We'll look in anyway."

As the car moved northwards towards the river, Martin said:

"It's easy to see that he needed the cash. You couldn't rent a flat like that on a porter's pay. And then there would be his painting gear."

"Yes. The studio is pretty impressive. I should like you to have seen it. And there were the lessons from Sugg. Nagle may have got those on the cheap but Sugg doesn't teach for nothing. I don't think the blackmailing was particularly lucrative. That's where he was clever. There was probably more than one victim and the amounts were nicely calculated. But even if he only made fifteen to thirty pounds a month, tax free, it would be enough to carry him over until he won the Bollinger or made his name."

"Is he any good?" asked Sergeant Martin. There were subjects on which he never expressed an opinion but took it for granted that his Super was an expert.

"The trustees of the Bollinger Trust think so apparently."

"There's not much doubt is there, sir?" And Martin was not referring to Nagle's talent for painting. Dalgliesh said irritably:

"Of course there's doubt. There always is at this stage of an investigation. But consider what we know. The blackmailer instructed that the cash should be sent in a distinctively addressed envelope, presumably so that he could pick it out before the post was opened. Nagle gets to the clinic first and is responsible for sorting and distributing the post. Colonel Fenton was asked to send the money so that it arrived on the first of each month. Nagle came to the clinic on 1st May although he was ill and had to be taken home later. I don't think it was anxiety about the Duke's visit that brought him in. The only time he didn't manage to get first to work was the day he got stuck in the tube and that was the day Miss Bolam received fifteen pounds from an unknown grateful patient.

"And now we come to the murder and theory replaces fact. Nagle was helping on the switchboard that morning because of Cully's belly-ache. He listens to Mrs. Fenton's call. He knows what Miss Bolam's reaction will be and, sure enough, he is asked to put through a call to the group offices. He listens again and learns that Mr. Lauder will be at the Steen after the J.C.C. meeting. Sometime before then Miss Bolam has got to die. But how? He can't hope to entice her away from the Steen. What excuse could he use and how could he provide himself with an alibi? No, it must be done in the clinic. And perhaps that isn't such a bad plan after all. The A.O. isn't popular. With luck there will be plenty of suspects to keep the police occupied, some of them with pretty good reasons for wishing Miss Bolam dead.

"So he makes his plans. It was obvious, of course, that the phone call to Miss Bolam wasn't necessarily made from the basement. Nearly all the rooms have telephones. But if the murderer wasn't in the record-room waiting for her how could he ensure that she would stay there until he could get down? That's why Nagle chucked the records about. He knew Miss Bolam well enough to be fairly sure that she couldn't bear not to pick them up. Dr. Baguley thought that her first reaction might be to phone for Nagle to help. She didn't, of course, because she was expecting him to appear any minute. Instead she made a start on the job herself, giving him the two or three minutes that he needed.

"This is what I think happened. At about ten past six he goes down to the porters' rest-room to put on his outdoor coat. It's then that he unlocks the record-room door and throws the files on the floor. He leaves the light on and shuts the door but doesn't bolt it. Then he unlocks the back door. Next he goes into the general office to collect the outgoing post. Miss Priddy is there but periodically visits the adjoining filing-room. He only needs half a minute to telephone Miss Bolam and to ask her to come down to the record-room as he has something serious to show her. We know how she reacted to that message. Before Nagle has a chance to replace the receiver Jennifer Priddy is back. He keeps his head, depresses the receiver rest, and pretends to be speaking to Nurse Bolam about the laundry. Then, without wasting any more time, he leaves with the post. He has only to take it to the box across the road. Then he darts down the mews, enters the basement by the unlocked back door, slips the chisel in his pocket, collects Tippett's fetish and enters the record-room. Miss Bolam is there as he expects, kneeling to pick up the torn and scattered files. She looks up at him, ready no doubt to ask where he's been. But, before she has time to speak, he strikes. Once she's unconscious he can take his time over the stabbing. There mustn't be any mistake, and there isn't. Nagle paints from the nude and his knowledge of anatomy is probably as good as that of most psychiatrists. And he was handy with that chisel. For this most important job he chose a tool he had confidence in and knew how to use." Martin said:

"He couldn't have got down to the basement in time if he'd walked to the corner of Beefsteak Street for his *Standard.* But the newsboy there couldn't swear that he'd seen him. He was carrying a paper when he returned to the Steen but he could have got that in his lunch hour and kept it in his pocket."

"I think he did," said Dalgliesh. "That's why he wouldn't let Cully see it to check the racing results. Cully would have seen at once that it was the midday edition. Instead Nagle takes it downstairs and later uses it to wrap up the cat's food before burning it in the boiler. He wasn't in the basement alone for long, of course. Jenny Priddy was hard on his heels. But he had time to bolt the back door again and visit Nurse Bolam to ask if the clean laundry was ready to be carried upstairs. If Priddy hadn't come down Nagle would have joined her in the general office. He would take care not to be alone in the basement for more than a minute. The killing had to be fixed for the time when he was out with the post." Martin said:

"I wondered why he didn't unbolt the basement door after the killing but like as not he couldn't bring himself to draw attention to it. After all, if an outsider could have gained access that way it wouldn't take long for people to start thinking 'and so could Nagle.' He took that fifteen quid no doubt after Colonel Fenton's break-in. The local boys always did think it odd that the thief knew where to find it. Nagle thought he had a right to it I suppose."

"More likely he wanted to obscure the reason for the break-in, to make it look like a common burglary. It wouldn't do for the police to start wondering why an unknown intruder should want to get his hands on the medical records. Pinching that fifteen pounds—which only Nagle had the chance to do—confused the issue. So did that business with the lift, of course. That was a nice touch. It would only take a minute to wind it up to the second floor before he slipped out of the basement door and there was a reasonable chance that someone would hear it and remember."

Sergeant Martin thought that it all hung together very well but that it was going to be the devil to prove and said so.

"That's why I showed my hand at the clinic yesterday. We've got to get him rattled. That's why it's worth looking in at the Steen tonight. If he's there we'll put on the pressure a bit. At least we know now where we're going."

Half an hour before Dalgliesh and Martin called at the Pimlico flat, Peter Nagle let himself into the Steen by the front door and locked it behind him. He did not put on the lights but made his way to the basement with the aid of his heavy torch. There wasn't much to be done; just the kiln to be turned off, the boiler inspected. Then there was a little matter of his own to be attended to. It would mean entering the record-room but that warm, echoing place of death had no terror for him. The dead were dead, finished, powerless, silenced for ever. In a world of increasing uncertainty that much was certain. A man with the nerve to kill had much that he might reasonably fear. But he had nothing to fear from the dead.

It was then that he heard the front-door bell. It was a hesitant, tentative ring but it sounded unnaturally loud in the silence of the clinic. When he opened the door the figure of Jenny slid through so quickly that she seemed to pass by him like a wraith, a slim ghost born of the darkness and mist of the night. She said breathlessly:

"I'm sorry darling, I had to see you. When you weren't at the studio I thought you might be here."

"Did anyone see you at the studio?" he asked. He felt that the question was important without knowing why.

She looked up at him surprised.

"No. The house seemed empty. I didn't meet anyone. Why?"

"Nothing. It doesn't matter. Come on downstairs. I'll light the gas stove. You're shivering."

They went down to the basement together, their footsteps echoing in the eerie, presageful calm of a house which, with tomorrow, will awaken to voices, movement and the ceaseless hum of purposeful activity. She began walking on tiptoe and when she spoke it was in whispers. At the top of the stairs she reached for his hand and he could feel hers trembling. Halfway down there was a sudden faint noise and she started.

"What is it? What's that noise?"

"Nothing. Tigger in his scratch tin I imagine."

When they were in the rest-room and the fire was lit he threw himself into one of the armchairs and smiled up at her. It was the devil of a nuisance that she should turn up now but somehow he must hide his irritation. With any luck he could get rid of her fairly quickly. She would be out of the clinic well before ten.

"Well?" he asked.

Suddenly she was on the rug at his feet and clasping his thighs. Her pale eyes searched his in passionate entreaty.

"Darling I've got to know! I don't mind what you've done as long as I know. I love you and I want to help. Darling, you must tell me if you're in any trouble."

It was worse than he feared. Somehow she had got hold of something. But how, and what? Keeping his voice light he asked:

"What sort of trouble for God's sake? You'll be saying next that I killed her."

"Oh, Peter, please don't joke! I've been so worried. There is something wrong, I know there is. It's the money isn't it? You took that fifteen pounds."

He could have laughed aloud with relief. In a surge of emotion he put his arms round her and drew her down upon him, his voice muffled in her hair.

"You silly kid. I could have helped myself to the petty cash any time if I wanted to steal. What the hell started you off on this nonsense?"

"That's what I've been telling myself. Why should you take it? Oh, darling, don't be angry with me. I've been so worried. You see, it was the paper."

"What paper, for God's sake." It was all he could do not to shake her into coherence. He was glad that she could not see his face. So long as he need not meet her eyes he could fight his anger and the fatal, insidious panic. What in God's name was she trying to say?

"The *Standard.* That sergeant came to see us this evening. I'd been to fetch the fish and chips. When I was unwrapping them in the kitchen I looked at the paper they were wrapped in. It was Friday's *Standard* and it had a large picture of that air crash, all over the front page. Then I remembered that we had used your *Standard* to wrap up Tigger's food and the front page was different. I hadn't seen that picture before."

He tightened his hold on her and said very quietly:

"Did you say anything about this to the police?"

"Darling, of course I didn't! Suppose it made them suspect you! I didn't say anything to anyone; but I needed to see you. I don't care about the fifteen pounds. I don't care if you did meet her in the basement. I know you didn't kill her. All I want is for you to trust me. I love you and I want to help. I can't bear it if you keep things from me."

That's what they all said but there wasn't one in a million who really wanted to know the truth about a man. For a second he was tempted to tell her, spit the whole brutal story into her silly pleading face and watch the sudden draining away of pity and love. She could probably bear to know about Bolam. What she couldn't bear would be the knowledge that he hadn't blackmailed for her sake, that he hadn't acted to preserve their love, that there wasn't any love to preserve and never had been. He would have to marry her, of course. He had always known that it might be necessary. Only she could effectively witness against him and there was one sure way to stop her tongue. But time was short. He planned to be in Paris by the end of the week. Now it looked as if he wouldn't be travelling alone. He thought quickly. Shifting her weight to the arm of the chair but still keeping his arms around her, his face resting against her cheek he said softly:

"Listen darling. There's something you've got to know. I didn't tell you before because I didn't want to worry you. I did take the fifteen quid. It was a bloody stupid thing to do but there's no sense in worrying about that now. I suppose Miss Bolam might have guessed. I don't know. She didn't say anything to me and it wasn't I who phoned her. But I was in the basement after she was killed. I left the back door open and came back that way. I get sick of that old fool Cully booking me in and out as if I were as nutty as a patient and asking for the paper as soon as I appear. Why can't he buy his own, the mean old devil. I thought I'd fool him for once. When I came in at the basement door I saw that there was a light in the record-room and the door was ajar, so I went to look. I found her body. I knew that I daren't be found there, particularly if they ever discovered about the fifteen quid, so I said nothing and left again by the back door and came in as usual by the front. I've kept quiet ever since. I must darling. I've got to take up the Bollinger by the end of this week and the police wouldn't let me go if they started suspecting me. If I don't get away now I'll never have the chance again as long as I live."

That at least was true. He had to get away now. It had become an obsession. It wasn't only the money, the freedom, the sun and the colours. It was the final vindication of the lean, pallid years of struggle and humiliation. He had to take up the Bollinger. Other painters could fail here and still succeed in the end. But not him.

And, even now, he might fail. It was a thin story. He was struck, as he spoke, by the inconsistencies, the improbabilities. But it hung together—just. He couldn't see how she could prove it false. And she wouldn't want to try. But he was surprised by her reaction.

"By the end of this week! You mean, you're going to Paris almost at once. What about the clinic . . . your job?"

"For God's sake, Jenny, what the hell does that matter? I shall leave without notice and they'll find someone else. They'll have to do without me."

"And me?"

"You're coming with me of course. I always meant that you should. Surely you knew that?"

"No," she said, and it seemed to him that her voice held a great sadness. "No, I never knew that."

He tried to assume a tone of confidence tinged with slight reproach.

"I never discussed it because I thought there were some things we didn't need to say. I know the time's short but it'll be easier if you don't have to stick around too long at home waiting. They'd only get suspicious. You've got a passport, haven't you? Didn't you go to France with the guides that Easter? What I suggest is that we marry by special licence as soon as possible— after all we've got the money now—and write to your parents when we get to Paris. You do want to come, don't you, Jenny?"

Suddenly she was shaking in his arms and he felt the warm wetness of her tears stinging his face.

"I thought you meant to go without me. The days went by and you never said anything. Of course, I want to come. I don't care what happens as long as we're together. But we can't get married. I never told you because I was afraid you'd be angry and you've never asked me anything about myself. I can't get married because I'm married already."

The car had turned in to Vauxhall Bridge Road but traffic was heavy and they were making poor time. Dalgliesh sat back in his seat as if all day were before him, but inwardly he was fidgeting with anxiety. He could discover no rational cause for this impatience. The call at the Steen was merely speculative. The chances were that Nagle, if indeed he had called at the clinic, would have left before they arrived. Probably he was even now putting down his evening pint in some Pimlico pub. At the next corner the traffic lights were against them and the car slowed to a halt for the third time in a hundred yards. Suddenly Martin said:

"He couldn't have got away with it for long, even by killing Bolam. Sooner or later Mrs. Fenton— or another victim maybe—would have turned up at the Steen."

Dalgliesh replied:

"But he might well have got away with it for long enough to take up the Bollinger. And even if the blackmailing came to light before he got away—what could we prove? What can we prove now, come to that? With Bolam dead what jury could be sure beyond reasonable doubt that she wasn't the blackmailer? Nagle's only got to say that he remembers seeing the odd envelope addressed in green ink and that he placed it with the A.O.'s post. Fenton will confirm that he thought the telephone calls came from a woman. And blackmailers do occasionally come to a violent end. Nagle wouldn't go on with it after Mrs. Fenton's call. Even that would help his case. Bolam dies and the blackmailing stops. Oh, I know all the arguments against it! But what can anyone prove?"

Martin said stolidly:

"He'll try to be too clever. They always do. The girl's under his thumb of course, poor little devil. If she sticks to her story that he wasn't alone long enough to make that call. . . ."

"She'll stick all right, Sergeant."

"I'm pretty sure he doesn't know about the husband. If she looks dangerous he probably thinks that he can stop her tongue by marrying her."

Dalgliesh said quietly:

"What we've got to do is to pull him in before he finds out that he can't."

In the porters' room at the Steen, Nagle was writing a letter. He wrote easily. The glib and lying phrases flowed with unexpected ease. He would have died rather than send such a letter. It would have been unbearable to think that any eyes could see this spate of emotional clap-trap and recognize it as his. But the letter never would be read except by Jenny. Within thirty minutes it would be thrust into the boiler, its purpose served and the oily phrases only an uncomfortable memory. In the meantime he might as well make it convincing. It was easy enough to guess what Jenny would want him to say. He turned over the paper and wrote:

"By the time you read this we shall be in France together. I know that this will cause you very great unhappiness, but please believe me when I say that we can't live without each other. I know that one day we shall be free to marry. Until then Jenny will be safe with me and I shall spend my life trying to make her happy. Please try to understand and to forgive."

It was a good ending, he thought. It would appeal to Jenny, anyway, and no one else was going to see it. He called to her and pushed the paper across the table.

"Will this do?"

She read it in silence.

"I suppose so."

"Damn it all kid, what's wrong with it?" He felt a surge of anger that his careful effort should be found inadequate. He had expected, and had braced himself to meet, her astonished gratitude. She said quietly:

"Nothing's wrong with it."

"You'd better write your bit then. Not on the end. Take a fresh sheet."

He slid the paper across the table at her, not meeting her eyes. This was taking time, and he could not be sure how much time there was.

"Better make it short," he said.

She took up the pen but made no effort to write.

"I don't know what to say."

"There isn't much you need say. I've said it all."

"Yes," she said with great sadness. "You've said it all."

He kept the rising irritation from his voice and told her:

"Just write that you're sorry to cause them unhappiness, but you can't help yourself. Something like that. Damn it all, you're not going to the end of the world. It's up to them. If they want to see you I shan't stop them. Don't pile the agony on too much. I'm going upstairs to mend that lock in Miss Saxon's room. When I come down we're going to celebrate. There's only beer, but tonight you'll drink beer my darling and like it."

He took a screwdriver from the tool box and went out quickly before she had time to protest. His last glimpse was of her frightened face staring after him. But she didn't call him back.

Upstairs it was a moment's work only to slip on a pair of rubber gloves and prise open the door of the dangerous-drugs cupboard. It gave with a terrifyingly loud crack so that he stood rooted for a moment half expecting to hear her call. But there was no sound. He remembered clearly that scene from six months ago when one of Dr. Baguley's patients had become violent and disorientated. Nagle had helped to control him while Baguley had called to Sister for paraldehyde. Nagle recalled the words:

"We'll give it in beer. It's pretty filthy stuff but they can hardly taste it in beer. Odd that. Two drams, Sister, to 2 cc."

And Jenny, who disliked beer, would taste it even less.

Quickly he put the screwdriver and the small

blue bottle of paraldehyde in his jacket pocket and slipped out, lighting his way with the torch. All the clinic curtains were drawn, but it was important to show as little light as possible. He needed at least another undisturbed half-hour.

She looked up in surprise at his quick reappearance. He went over to her and kissed the back of her neck.

"I'm sorry sweetie, I shouldn't have left you. I'd forgotten that you might be nervous. The lock can wait, anyway. How's the letter going?"

She pushed it over to him. He turned his back on her to read the few carefully penned lines deliberately, taking his time. But his luck had held. It was as neat and convincing a suicide note as was ever read in a Coroner's court. He couldn't have dictated anything better. He felt a surge of confidence and excitement as he did when a painting was going well. Nothing could spoil it now. Jenny had written:

"I can't say I'm sorry for what I've done. I haven't any choice. I feel so happy and it would all be perfect if I didn't know that I'm making you miserable. But it's the only and best thing for me. Please try to understand. I love you very much. Jenny."

He put the letter back on the table and went to pour out the beer, his actions hidden by the open door of the cupboard. God, the stuff did stink! Quickly he added the foaming light ale and called to her.

"Are you happy?"

"You know I am."

"Then let's drink to it. To us, darling."

"To us."

She grimaced as the liquid met her lips. He laughed.

"You look as if you're drinking poison. Knock it back, girl. Like this!"

He opened his throat and drained his own glass. Laughing, she shuddered slightly and gulped down her ale. He took the empty glass from her and folded her in his arms. She clung to him, her hands like a cold compress on the back of his neck. Releasing himself he drew her down beside him on to the armchair. Then, clasped together they slid to the floor and lay together on the rug in front of the gas fire. He had turned off the light and her face shone in the fierce red glow of the fire as if she lay in the full sun. The hiss of the gas was the only sound in the silence.

He pulled a cushion from one of the armchairs and pushed it under her head. Only one cushion; he had a use for the other. It could rest on the bottom of the gas stove. She would be less likely to wake if he made her comfortable on that last brief slide from unconsciousness to death. He put his left arm around her and they lay tight clasped without speaking. Suddenly she turned her face to his and he felt her tongue, wet and slippery as a fish, infiltrating between his teeth. Her eyes, their pupils black in the gaslight, were heavy with desire. "Darling," she whispered. "Darling." Christ, he thought, not that. He couldn't make love to her now. It would keep her quiet but it wasn't possible. There wasn't time. And surely the police pathologist could tell how recently that had happened to a woman. He thought for the first time with relief of her obsession with safety and whispered, "We can't darling. I haven't got anything with me. We can't risk it now."

She gave a little murmur of acquiescence and nuzzled against him, moving her left leg over his thighs. It lay there, heavy and inert, but he dare not move nor speak in case he broke that insidious drop into unconsciousness. She was breathing more deeply now, hotly and irritatingly into his left ear. God, how much longer was it going to take! Holding his own breath he listened. Suddenly she gave a little snort like a contented animal. Under his arm he sensed a change in the rhythm of her breathing. There was an almost physical release of tension as her body relaxed. She was asleep.

Better give her a few minutes, he thought. There wasn't much time to spare, but he dare not hurry. It was important that there were no bruises on her body and he knew he couldn't face a struggle. But there could be no turning back now. If she woke and resisted it would still have to be done.

So he waited, lying so still that they might both have been dead bodies stiffening together into a final stylized embrace. After a little time he raised himself cautiously on his right elbow and looked at her. Her face was flushed, her mouth with its short upper lip curved against the white childish

teeth was half open. He could smell the paraldehyde on her breath. He watched her for a moment, noting the length of the pale lashes against
her cheeks, the upward slant of the eyebrows
and the shadows under the broad cheek bones.
Strange that he had never got round to drawing
her face. But it was too late to think of that now.

He murmured to her as he lifted her gently
across the room to the black mouth of the gas
oven.

"It's all right, Jenny darling. It's only me. I'm
making you comfortable. It's all right, darling."

But it was himself that he was reassuring.

There was plenty of room in the large, old-
fashioned oven, even with the cushion. The bottom of the oven was only a few inches from
the ground. Feeling for her shoulder blades he
edged her gently forward. As the cushion took
the weight of her head he looked to make sure
that the gas jets were still unimpeded. Her head
rolled gently sideways so that the half-open
mouth, moist and vulnerable as a baby's, hung
just above them, poised and ready to suck up
death. As he slid his hands from under her body
she gave a little sigh as if she were comfortable
at last.

He gave one last look at her, satisfied with his
handiwork.

And now it was time to hurry. Feeling in his
pocket for the rubber gloves, he moved with fantastic speed, treading lightly, his breath coming
in shallow gasps as if he could no longer bear

the sound of his own breathing. The suicide note was on the table. He took the chisel and wrapped her right hand gently round it, pressing the palm around the shining handle, the right finger-tip against the base of the blade. Was that how she would have held it? Near enough. He placed the chisel on top of the suicide note.

Next he washed up his own glass and put it back in the cupboard, holding the dish-cloth in front of the gas fire for a second until the damp stain had evaporated. He turned off the fire. No need to worry about prints here. There was nothing to show when last it had been lit. He wondered briefly about the paraldehyde bottle and Jenny's glass, but decided to leave them on the table with the note and the chisel. The natural thing would surely be for her to drink sitting at the table and then to move to the stove when she felt the first signs of drowsiness. He wiped his own prints from the bottle and clasped her left hand around it, her right-hand index finger and thumb on the stopper. He was almost afraid to touch her, but she was now deeply asleep. Her hand was very warm to his touch and so relaxed that it felt boneless. He was repelled by its limp flaccidity, by this touch which was without communication, without desire. He was glad when he had dealt similarly with the drinking glass and the bottle of beer. It would only be necessary now to touch her once again.

Last of all he took his own letter to the Priddys and the pair of gloves and threw them into the boiler. There was only the gas tap to turn on. It was on the right of the stove and within easy reach of her limp right arm. He lifted the arm, pressed her index finger and thumb against the tap, and turned it on. There was the soft hiss of escaping gas. How long, he wondered, was it likely to take. Not long surely? Perhaps only a matter of minutes. He put out the light and backed out, closing the door behind him.

It was then that he remembered the front-door keys. They must be found on her. His heart struck cold as he realized how fatal that one mistake could have been. He edged into the room again by the light of his torch. Taking the keys from his pocket and holding his breath against the gas, he placed them in her left hand. He had reached the door before he heard Tigger's mew. The cat must have been sleeping under the cupboard. It was moving slowly round the body now, putting out a tentative paw towards the girl's right foot. Nagle found that he could not bear to go near her again.

"Come here Tigger," he whispered. "Come here boy."

The cat turned its great amber eyes on him and seemed to be considering, but without emotion and without haste. Then it came slowly across to the door. Nagle hooked his left foot under the soft belly and lifted the cat through the door in one swift movement.

"Come out of it, you bloody fool. D'you want to lose all nine lives at one go? That stuff's lethal."

He closed the door, and the cat, suddenly active, shot away into the dark.

Nagle made his way without lights to the back door, felt for the bolts, and let himself out. He paused for a moment, back against the door, to check that the mews was empty. Now that it was over he had time to note the signs of strain. His forehead and hands were wet with sweat and he had difficulty with his breathing. He drew in deep gasps of the damp and blessedly cool night air. The fog wasn't thick, hardly more than a heavy mist, through which the street lamp which marked the end of the mews gleamed like a yellow smudge in the darkness. That gleam, only forty yards away, represented safety. Yet all at once it seemed unattainable. Like an animal in its lair he gazed in horrified fascination at the dangerous beacon and willed his legs to move. But their power had gone. Crouching in the darkness and shelter of the doorway, his back pressed against the wood, he fought off panic. After all, there was no great hurry. In a moment he would leave this spurious sanctuary and put the mews behind him. Then it was only a matter of re-entering the square from the other side and waiting until there was a casual passer-by to witness his vain hammering at the front door. Even the words he would speak were ready. "It's my girl. I think she's in there, but she won't open up. She was with me earlier this evening and when she'd gone I found the keys were missing. She *was* in a queer state. Better get a copper. I'm going to smash this window."

Then the crash of broken glass, the dash to the basement and the chance to lock the back door again before the hurrying footsteps were at his heels. The worst was over. From now on it was all so easy. By ten o'clock the body would have been removed, the clinic empty. In a moment he would move on to the final act. But not yet. Not quite yet.

Along the Embankment the traffic was almost stationary. There seemed to be some kind of function on at the Savoy. Suddenly Dalgliesh said:

"There's no guard at the clinic now, of course?"

"No, sir. You remember I asked you this morning if we need keep a man there and you said no."

"I remember."

"After all, sir, it hardly seemed necessary. We'd examined the place thoroughly and there aren't all those men to spare."

"I know, Martin," replied Dalgliesh testily. "Surprisingly enough those were the reasons for my decision." The car came to a stop once more. Dalgliesh put his head out of the window. "What the hell does he think he's doing?"

"I think he's doing his best, sir."

"That's what I find so depressing. Come on, Sergeant. Get out! We'll do the rest on foot. I'm probably being a bloody fool, but when we get to the clinic, we'll cover both exits. You go round to the back."

If Martin felt surprise it was not his nature to

show it. Something seemed to have got into the old man. As like as not Nagle was back in his flat and the clinic locked and deserted. A couple of fools they'd look creeping up on an empty building. Still, they'd know soon enough. He bent his energies to keeping up with the superintendent.

Nagle never knew how long he waited in the doorway, bent almost double and panting like an animal. But after a time, calmness returned and with it the use of his legs. He moved stealthily forward, hoisted himself over the rear railings and set off down the mews. He walked like an automaton, hands stiffly by his sides, his eyes closed. Suddenly he heard the footfall. Opening his eyes, he saw, silhouetted against the street lamp, a familiar bulky figure. Slowly, inexorably, it moved towards him through the mist. His heart leapt in his chest then settled into a regular tumultuous throbbing that shook his whole body. His legs felt heavy and cold as death, checking that first fatal impulse to flight. But at least his mind worked. While he could think there was hope. He was cleverer than they. With luck they wouldn't even think of entering the clinic. Why should they? And surely she would be dead by now! With Jenny dead they could suspect what they liked. They'd never prove a thing.

The torch shone full on his face. The slow unemphatic voice spoke:

"Good evening, lad. We were hoping to meet you. Going in or coming out?"

Nagle did not reply. He stretched his mouth into the semblance of a smile. He could only guess how he looked in that fierce light; a death's head, the mouth agape with fright, the eyes staring.

It was then that he felt the tentative rub against his legs. The policeman bent and scooped up the cat, holding it between them. Immediately it began to purr, throbbing its contentment at the warmth of that huge hand.

"So here's Tigger. You let him out, did you? You and the cat came out together."

Then, instantaneously, they were both aware of it and their eyes met. From the warmth of the cat's fur there rose between them, faint but unmistakable, the smell of gas.

The next half-hour passed for Nagle in a confused whirl of noise and blinding lights out of which a few vivid tableaux sprang into focus with unnatural clarity and stayed fixed in his mind for the rest of his life. He had no memory of the sergeant dragging him back over the iron railings, only of the grip, firm as a tourniquet, numbing his arm and the hot rasp of Martin's breath in his ear. There was a smash and the sad, delayed tinkle of broken glass as someone kicked out the windows of the porters' room, the shrill screech of a whistle, a confusion of running feet on the clinic stairs, a blaze of lights hurting his eyes. In one of the tableaux Dalgliesh was crouched over the girl's body, his mouth wide-stretched as a gargoyle's, clamped over her mouth as he forced his breath into her lungs. The two bodies seemed to be fighting, locked in an obscene embrace like the rape of the dead. Nagle didn't speak. He was almost beyond thought, but instinct warned him that he must say nothing. Pinned against the wall by strong arms and watching fascinated the feverish heave of Dalgliesh's shoulders, he felt tears start in his eyes. Enid Bolam was dead, and Jenny was dead, and he was tired now, desperately tired. He hadn't wanted to kill her. It was Bolam who had forced him into all the trouble and danger of murder. She and Jenny between them had left him no choice. And he had lost Jenny. Jenny was dead. Faced with the enormity, the unfairness of what they had made him do, he felt without surprise the tears of self-pity flow in a warm stream down his face.

The room was suddenly full. There were more uniformed men, one of them burly as a Holbein, pig-eyed, slow-moving. There was the hiss of oxygen, a murmur of consulting voices. Then they were edging something on to a stretcher with gentle, experienced hands, a red-blanketed shape which rolled sideways as the poles were lifted. Why were they carrying it so carefully? It couldn't feel jolting any more.

Dalgliesh didn't speak until Jenny had been taken away. Then, without looking at Nagle, he said:

"Right, Sergeant. Get him down to the station. We can hear his story there."

Nagle moved his mouth. His lips were so dry that he heard them crack. But it was some seconds before the words would come and then there was no stopping them. The carefully rehearsed story tumbled out in a spate, bald and unconvincing:

"There's nothing to tell. She came to see me at my flat and we spent the evening together. I had to tell her that I was going away without her. She took it pretty badly, and after she'd left I found that the clinic keys were missing. I knew she was in a bit of a state so I thought I'd better come along. There's a note on the table. She's left a note. I could see she was dead and I couldn't help, so I came away. I didn't want to be mixed up in it. I've got the Bollinger to think of. It wouldn't look good getting mixed up with a suicide."

Dalgliesh said:

"You'd better not say anything else for the present. But you'll have to do better than that. You see, it isn't quite what she has told us. That note on the table isn't the only one she left."

With slow deliberation he took from his breast pocket a small folded sheet of paper and held it an inch from Nagle's fascinated, fear-glazed eyes:

"If you were together this evening in your flat, how do you explain this note which we found under your door knocker?"

It was then that Nagle realized with sick despair that the dead, so impotent and so despised, could bear witness against him after all. Instinctively he put out his hand for the note, then dropped his arm. Dalgliesh replaced the note in his pocket. Watching Nagle closely, he said:

"So you rushed here tonight because you were concerned for her safety? Very touching! In that case let me put your mind at rest. She's going to live."

"She's dead," said Nagle dully. "She killed herself."

"She was breathing when we'd finished with her. Tomorrow, if all goes well, she'll be able to tell us what happened. And not only what happened here tonight. We shall have some questions about Miss Bolam's murder."

Nagle gave a shout of harsh laughter:

"Bolam's murder! You'll never get me for that! And I'll tell you why, you poor boobs. Because I didn't kill her! If you want to make fools of yourselves, go ahead. Don't let me stop you. But I warn you. If I'm arrested for Bolam's murder I'll make your names stink in every newspaper in the country."

He held out his wrists to Dalgliesh.

"Come on, Superintendent! Go ahead and charge me. What's stopping you? You've worked it all out very cleverly, haven't you? You've been too clever by half, you bloody supercilious copper!"

"I'm not charging you," said Dalgliesh. "I'm inviting you to come to headquarters to answer some questions and to make a statement. If you want a solicitor present you're entitled to have one."

"I'll have one all right. But not just at the moment. I'm in no hurry, Superintendent. You see, I'm expecting a visitor. We arranged to meet here at ten and it's nearly that now. I must say we'd planned to have the place to ourselves and I don't think my visitor will be particularly pleased to see you. But if you want to meet Miss Bolam's killer you'd better stick around. It won't be long. The person I'm expecting has been trained to be on time."

Suddenly all his fear seemed to have left him. The large brown eyes were expressionless again, muddy pools in which only the black iris burned with life. Martin, still clasping Nagle's arms, could feel the muscles bracing, could sense the physical return of confidence. But before anyone had time to speak their ears caught simultaneously the sound of footsteps. Someone had come in by the basement door and was moving quietly down the passage.

Dalgliesh moved to the door in one silent stride and braced himself against it. The footsteps, timid, hesitant, stopped outside. Three pairs of eyes watched as the door-knob turned, first right, then left. A voice called softly:

"Nagle! Are you there, Nagle! Open the door."

With a single movement Dalgliesh stepped to one side and crashed open the door. The slight figure moved forward involuntarily under the blaze of the fluorescent lights. The immense grey eyes widened and slewed from face to face, the eyes of an uncomprehending child. Whimpering, she clutched a handbag to her breast in a sudden protective gesture as if she were shielding a baby. Wrenching himself from Martin's grip Nagle snatched it from her and tossed it to Dalgliesh. It fell plumply into the detective's hands, the cheap plastic sticking warmly to his fingers. Nagle tried to keep his voice level, but it cracked with excitement and triumph.

"Take a look inside, Superintendent. It's all there. I'll tell you what you'll find. A signed confession of Enid Bolam's murder and one hundred pounds in notes, a first payment on account to keep my mouth shut."

He turned to his visitor.

"Sorry, kid. I didn't plan it this way. I was willing enough to keep quiet about what I'd seen, but things have changed since Friday night. I've got troubles of my own to worry about now and no one's going to pin a murder charge on me. Our little arrangement's off."

But Marion Bolam had fainted.

Two months later a Magistrate's court committed Marion Grace Bolam for trial on a charge of her cousin's murder. A capricious autumn had hardened into winter and Dalgliesh walked back alone to headquarters under a grey blanket of sky which sagged with its weight of snow. The first moist flakes were already falling, melting gently against his face. In his chief's office the lights were lit and the curtains drawn, shutting out the glittering river, the necklace of light along

the Embankment and all the cold inertia of a winter afternoon. Dalgliesh made his report briefly.
The A.C. listened in silence, then said:

"They'll try for diminished responsibility, I suppose. How did the girl seem?"

"Perfectly calm, like a child who knows she's
been naughty and is on her best behaviour in
the hope that the grown-ups will overlook it. She
feels no particular guilt, I suspect, except the
usual female guilt at being found out."

"It was a perfectly straightforward case," said
the A.C. "The obvious suspect, the obvious motive."

"Too obvious for me, apparently," said Dalgliesh
bitterly. "If this case doesn't cure me of conceit,
nothing will. If I'd paid more attention to the obvious I might have questioned why she didn't get
back to Rettinger Street until after eleven when
the television service was closing down. She'd
been with Nagle, of course, arranging the blackmail payments. They met in St. James's Park, apparently. He saw his chance all right when he
went into that record-room and found her bending over her cousin's body. He must have been
on her before she heard a sound. He took over
from there with his usual efficiency. It was he who
put the fetish so carefully on the body, of course.
Even that detail misled me. Somehow I couldn't
see Marion Bolam making that final contemptuous gesture. But it was an obvious crime, all right.
She hardly made an attempt at concealment. The
rubber gloves she wore were stuffed back in her

uniform pocket. The weapons she chose were the ones nearest to hand. She wasn't trying to incriminate anyone else. She wasn't even trying to be clever. At about six-twelve she telephoned the general office and asked Nagle not to come down yet for the laundry; he couldn't resist lying about that call, incidentally which gave me another opportunity for being over-subtle. Then she rang for her cousin. She couldn't be absolutely sure that Enid would come alone and the excuse had to be valid so she threw the medical records on the floor. Then she waited in the record-room for her victim, fetish in hand and chisel in her uniform pocket. It was unfortunate for her that Nagle returned secretly to the clinic when he was out with the post. He'd overheard Miss Bolam's call to the group secretary and wanted to get his hands on the Fenton record. It seemed safer to chuck it in the basement furnace. Coming upon the murder forced him to change his plan and he didn't get another chance once the body was discovered and the record-room sealed. Nurse Bolam, of course, had no choice of time. She discovered on Wednesday night that Enid intended to alter her will. Friday was the earliest evening when there was a lysergic acid session and she would have the basement to herself. She couldn't act earlier: she daren't act later."

"The murder was highly convenient for Nagle," said his chief. "You can't blame yourself for concentrating on him. But if you insist on indulging in self-pity don't let me spoil your fun."

"Convenient, perhaps, but not necessary," Dalgliesh replied. "And why should he have killed Bolam? His one aim, apart from making easy money, was to take up the Bollinger and get away to Europe without fuss. He must have known that it would be difficult to pin the Fenton blackmail on him even if the group secretary decided to call in the police. And, in fact, we still haven't enough evidence to charge him. But murder is different. Anyone connected with murder is likely to have his private plans disorganized. Even the innocent can't so easily shake off that contaminating dust. To kill Bolam only increased his danger. But to kill Priddy was a different matter. At one stroke he could safeguard his alibi, get rid of an encumbrance and give himself the hope of marrying the heiress of nearly thirty thousand. He knew he'd have little chance with Marion Bolam if she learned that Priddy had been his mistress. She wasn't Enid Bolam's cousin for nothing."

The A.C. said:

"At least we've got him as an accessory after the fact and that should put him away for quite a time. I'm not sorry that the Fentons will be spared the ordeal of giving evidence. But I doubt whether the charge of attempted murder will stick—not unless Priddy changes her mind. If she persists in supporting his story we'll get nowhere."

"She won't change her mind, sir," said Dalgliesh bitterly. "Nagle doesn't want to see her, of course, but nothing makes any difference. All she thinks about is planning their life together when he comes out. And God help her when he does."

The A.C. shifted his immense bulk irritably in his chair, closed the file and pushed it across the table to Dalgliesh. He said:

"There's nothing that you or anyone else can do about that. She's the kind of woman who pursues her own destruction. I've had that artist, Sugg, on to me by the way. Extraordinary ideas about judicial procedure these people have! I told him that it's out of our hands now and referred him to the proper quarter. He wants to pay for Nagle's defence, if you please! Said that if we've made a mistake the world will lose a remarkable talent."

"It will be lost, anyway," replied Dalgliesh. Thinking aloud, he added: "I wonder just how good an artist would have to be before one let him get away with a crime like Nagle's. Michelangelo? Velazquez? Rembrandt?"

"Oh, well," said the A.C. easily. "If we had to ask ourselves that question we wouldn't be policemen."

Back in Dalgliesh's office Sergeant Martin was putting away papers. He took one look at his super's face, pronounced a stolid "Good night, sir," and left. There were some situations which his uncomplicated nature found it prudent to avoid. The door had hardly closed behind him when the telephone rang. It was Mrs. Shorthouse.

"Hullo!" she yelled. "Is that you? I had the devil of a job getting through to you. Saw you in court today. Don't suppose you noticed me, though. How are you?"

"Well, thank you, Mrs. Shorthouse."

"Don't suppose we'll be meeting again, so I thought I'd give you a ring to say cheerio and tell you the news. Things have been happening at the clinic, I can tell you. Miss Saxon's leaving for one thing. She's going to work in a home for sub-normal kids up north. Run by the R.C.s it is. Fancy going off to work in a convent! No one at the Steen ever did that before."

Dalgliesh said he could well believe it.

"Miss Priddy's been transferred to one of the group's chest clinics. Mr. Lauder thought the change would do her good. She's had a terrible row with her people and she's living alone now in a bed-sitter in Kilburn. But you know all about that, no doubt. Mrs. Bolam's gone to an expensive nursing-home near Worthing. All on her share of Cousin Enid's money, of course. Poor sod. I'm surprised she could bring herself to touch a penny of it."

Dalgliesh wasn't surprised, but did not say so. Mrs. Shorthouse went on:

"And then there's Dr. Steiner. He's getting married to his wife."

"What did you say, Mrs. Shorthouse?"

"Well, re-married. Fixed it up very sudden they did. They got divorced and now they're getting married again. What d'you think of that?"

Dalgliesh said that it was a question of what Dr. Steiner thought of it.

"Oh, he's as pleased as a dog with a new collar. And a collar is just about what he's getting, if you ask me. There's a rumour that the Regional Board may close the clinic and move everyone to a hospital out-patient department. Well, you can't wonder! First a stabbing and then a gassing, and now a murder trial. Not nice really. Dr. Etherege says it's upsetting for the patients, but I haven't noticed it to speak of. The numbers haven't half gone up since last October. That would have pleased Miss Bolam. Always worrying about the numbers she was. Mind you there are those who say we wouldn't have had that trouble with Nagle and Priddy if you'd picked up the right one first go. It was a near thing all right. But what I say is, you did you best and there's no harm done to speak of."

No harm to speak of! So these, thought Dalgliesh bitterly, as he replaced the receiver, were the concomitants of failure. It was enough to taste this sour, corroding self-pity without enduring the A.C.'s moralizing. Martin's tact, Emily Shorthouse's condolences. If he were to break free from this pervasive gloom he needed a respite from crime and death, needed to walk for one brief evening out of the shadow of blackmail and murder. It came to him that what he wanted was to dine with Deborah Riscoe. At least, he told himself wryly, it would be a change of trouble. He put his hand on the receiver and then

paused, checked by the old caution, the old uncertainties. He was not even sure that she would
wish to take a call at the office, what exactly her
place was at Hearne and Illingworth. Then he
remembered how she had looked when last they
met and he lifted the receiver. He could surely
dine with an attractive woman without this prepa-
ratory morbid self-analysis. The invitation would
commit him to nothing more crucial than seeing
that she had a pleasant evening and paying the
bill. And a man was surely entitled to call his own
publishers.

An Unsuitable Job
for a Woman

**For Jane and Peter
who kindly allowed two of my characters
to live at 57 Norwich Street.**

Author's Note

A crime novelist, by virtue of his unpleasant craft, has the duty to create at least one highly reprehensible character in each book and it is perhaps inevitable that from time to time their sanguinary misdeeds should impinge upon the dwellings of the just. A writer whose characters have chosen to act out their tragicomedy in an ancient university city is in particular difficulty. He can, of course, call it Oxbridge, invent colleges named after improbable saints and send his characters boating on the Camsis, but this timid compromise merely confuses characters, readers and the author alike, with the result that no one knows precisely where he is and two communities are offered opportunities for offence instead of one.

The greater part of this story is unrepentantly set in Cambridge, a city in which, undeniably, there live and work policemen, coroners, doctors, students, college servants, flower sellers, Dons, scientists, and even, no doubt, retired Majors. None of them, to my knowledge, bears the slightest resemblance to his counterpart in this book. All the characters, even the most unpleasant, are imaginary; the city, happily for us all, is not.

P. D. J.

Chapter One

ON THE MORNING of Bernie Pryde's death—or it may have been the morning after, since Bernie died at his own convenience, nor did he think the estimated time of his departure worth recording— Cordelia was caught in a breakdown of the Bakerloo Line outside Lambeth North and was half an hour late at the office. She came up from Oxford Circus underground into the bright June sunshine, sped past the early morning shoppers scanning the windows of Dickins and Jones and plunged into the cacophony of Kingly Street threading her way between the blocked pavement and the shining mass of cars and vans which packed the narrow street. The hurry she knew was irrational, a symptom of her obsession with order and punctuality. There were no

appointments booked; no clients to be interviewed; no case outstanding; not even a final
report to be written. She and Miss Sparshott,
the temporary typist, at Cordelia's suggestion
were circulating, information about the Agency
to all the London solicitors in the hope of attract-
ing custom; Miss Sparshott would probably be
busy with it now, eyes straying to her watch, tap-
ping out her staccato irritation at every minute of
Cordelia's lateness. She was an unprepossessing woman with lips permanently taut as if to
prevent the protruding teeth from springing from
her mouth, a receding chin with one coarse hair
which grew as quickly as it was plucked, and fair
hair set in stiff corrugated waves. That chin and
mouth seemed to Cordelia the living refutation
that all men are born equal and she tried from
time to time to like and sympathize with Miss
Sparshott, with a life lived in bedsitting rooms,
measured in the five-penny pieces fed to the
gas stove and circumscribed by fell seams and
hand hemming. For Miss Sparshott was a skilled
dressmaker, an assiduous attender at the G.L.C.
evening classes. Her clothes were beautifully
made but so dateless that they were never actually in fashion; straight skirts in grey or black
which were exercises in how to sew a pleat or
insert a zip fastener; blouses with mannish collars and cuffs in insipid pastel shades on which
she distributed without discretion her collection
of costume jewellery; intricately cut dresses with

hems at the precise length to emphasize her shapeless legs and thick ankles.

Cordelia had no premonition of tragedy as she pushed open the street door which was kept perpetually on the latch for the convenience of the secretive and mysterious tenants and their equally mysterious visitors. The new bronze plaque to the left of the door gleamed brightly in the sun in incongruous contrast to the faded and dirt-encrusted paint. Cordelia gave it a short glance of approval:

PRYDE'S DETECTIVE AGENCY
(*Props:* Bernard G. Pryde   Cordelia Gray)

It had taken Cordelia some weeks of patient and tactful persuasion to convince Bernie that it would be inappropriate to append the words "ex-C.I.D. Metropolitan Police" to his name or prefix "Miss" to hers. There had been no other problem over the plaque since Cordelia had brought no qualifications or relevant past experience to the partnership and indeed no capital, except her slight but tough twenty-two-year-old body, a considerable intelligence which Bernie, she suspected, had occasionally found more disconcerting than admirable, and a half exasperated, half pitying affection for Bernie himself. It was obvious very early to Cordelia that in some undramatic but positive way life had turned against him. She recognized the signs. Bernie never got the enviable front left hand seat in the bus; he couldn't admire the view from the train window without another train promptly obscuring it; the bread he dropped invariably fell buttered side downwards; the Mini, reliable enough when she drove it, stalled for Bernie at the busiest and most inconvenient intersections. She sometimes wondered whether, in accepting his offer of a partnership in a fit of depression or of perverse masochism, she was voluntarily embracing his ill-luck. She certainly never saw herself as powerful enough to change it.

The staircase smelt as always of stale sweat, furniture polish and disinfectant. The walls were dark green and were invariably damp whatever the season as if they secreted a miasma of desperate respectability and defeat. The stairs, with their ornate wrought-iron balustrade, were covered with split and stained linoleum patched by the landlord in various and contrasting colours only when a tenant complained. The Agency was on the third floor. There was no clatter of typewriter keys as Cordelia entered and she saw that Miss Sparshott was engaged in cleaning her machine, an ancient Imperial which was a constant cause of justified complaint. She looked up, her face blotched with resentment, her back as rigid as the space bar.

"I've been wondering when you would turn up, Miss Gray. I'm concerned about Mr. Pryde. I think he must be in the inner office but he's quiet, very quiet, and the door's locked."

Cordelia, chill at heart, wrenched at the door handle:

"Why didn't you do something?"

"Do what, Miss Gray? I knocked at the door and called out to him. It wasn't my place to do that, I'm only the temporary typist, I've no authority here. I should have been placed in a very embarrassing position if he had answered. After all, he's entitled to use his own office I suppose. Besides, I'm not even sure if he's there."

"He must be. The door's locked and his hat is here."

Bernie's trilby, the stained brim turned up all round, a comedian's hat, was hanging on the convoluted hat-stand, a symbol of forlorn decrepitude. Cordelia was fumbling in her shoulder bag for her own key. As usual, the object most required had fallen to the bottom of the bag. Miss Sparshott began to clatter on the keys as if to disassociate herself from impending trauma. Above the noise she said defensively:

"There's a note on your desk."

Cordelia tore it open. It was short and explicit. Bernie had always been able to express himself succinctly when he had something to say:

"I'm sorry, partner, they've told me it's cancer and I'm taking the easy way out. I've seen what the treatment does to people and I'm not having any. I've made my will and it's with my solicitor. You'll find his name in the desk. I've left the business to you. Everything, including *all* the equipment. Good luck and thank you." Underneath with the inconsiderateness of the doomed he had scribbled a final unfair plea:

"If you find me alive, for God's sake wait before calling help. I rely on you for this, partner. Bernie."

She unlocked the door of the inner office and went inside, closing the door carefully behind her.

It was a relief to see that there was no need to wait. Bernie was dead. He lay slumped over the desk as if in an extremity of exhaustion. His right hand was half-clenched and an open cut-throat razor had slithered over the desk top leaving a thin trail of blood like a snail's track and had come to rest precariously poised on the extreme edge of the desk. His left wrist, scored with two parallel cuts, lay palm upwards in the enamel bowl which Cordelia used for the washing-up. Bernie had filled it with water but it was now brimfull with a pale pinky liquid smelling sickly sweet, through which the fingers, curved as if in supplication and looking as white and delicate as those of a child, gleamed as smooth as wax. The blood and water had overflowed on to the desk and floor soaking the oblong of garish rug which Bernie had recently bought in the hope of impressing visitors with his status but which Cordelia privately thought had only drawn attention to the shabbiness of the rest of the office. One of the cuts was tentative and superficial but the other had gone deep as the bone and the severed edges of the wound, drained of blood, gaped cleanly like an illustration in an anatomy text book. Cordelia remembered how Bernie had

once described the finding of a prospective suicide when he was first on the beat as a young
constable. It was an old man huddled into a warehouse doorway who had slashed his wrist with a
broken bottle—but who had later been dragged
back to reluctant half-life because an immense
clot of blood had blocked the severed veins. Bernie, remembering, had taken precautions to ensure that his blood would not clot. He had, she
noticed, taken another precaution; there was an
empty tea cup, the one in which she served his
afternoon tea, on the right of the desk with a
grain or two of powder, aspirin perhaps or a barbiturate, staining the rim and side. A dried trickle
of mucus, similarly stained, hung from the corner
of his mouth. His lips were pursed and half open
like those of a sleeping child, petulant and vulnerable. She put her head round the office door
and said quietly:

"Mr. Pryde is dead; don't come in. I'll ring the
police from here."

The telephone message was taken calmly,
someone would come round. Sitting beside the
body to wait and feeling that she needed to make
some gesture of pity and comfort Cordelia laid
her hand gently on Bernie's hair. Death had as
yet no power to diminish these cold and nerveless cells and the hair felt roughly and unpleasantly alive like that of an animal. Quickly she took
her hand away and tentatively touched the side of
his forehead. The skin was clammy and very cold.
This was death; this was how Daddy had felt. As

with him, the gesture of pity was meaningless and irrelevant. There was no more communication in death than there had been in life.

She wondered when exactly Bernie had died. No one now would ever know. Perhaps Bernie himself had not known. There must, she supposed, have been one measurable second in time in which he had ceased to be Bernie and had become this unimportant but embarrassingly unwieldy weight of flesh and bone. How odd that a moment of time so important to him should pass without his knowledge. Her second foster mother, Mrs. Wilkes, would have said that Bernie did know, that there was a moment of indescribable glory, shining towers, limitless singing, skies of triumph. Poor Mrs. Wilkes! Widowed, her only son dead in the war, her small house perpetually noisy with the foster children who were her livelihood, she had needed her dreams. She had lived her life by comfortable maxims stored like nuggets of coal against the winter. Cordelia thought of her now for the first time in years and heard again her tired, determinedly cheerful voice, "If the Lord doesn't call on his way out, He'll call on his way back." Well, going or coming, He hadn't called on Bernie.

It was odd but somehow typical of Bernie that he should have retained a dogged and invincible optimism about the business even when they had nothing in the cash box but a few coins for the gas meter and yet had given up hope of life without even a struggle. Was it perhaps that he had subconsciously recognized that neither he nor the Agency had any real future and had decided that this way he could yield up both life and livelihood with some honour? He had done it effectively but messily, surprisingly so for an ex-policeman versed in the ways of death. And then she realized why he had chosen the razor and the drugs. The gun. He hadn't really taken the easy way out. He could have used the gun, but he had wanted her to have it; he had bequeathed it to her together with the rickety filing cabinets, the antique typewriter, the scene-of-crime kit, the Mini, his shock-proof and waterproof wrist watch, the blood-soaked rug, the embarrassingly large stock of writing paper with the ornate heading *Pryde's Detective Agency—We take a Pride in our Work.* All the equipment; he had underlined all. He must have meant to remind her about the gun.

She unlocked the small drawer at the base of Bernie's desk to which only she and he had a key and drew it out. It was still in the suede draw-string bag which she had made for it, with three rounds of ammunition packed separately. It was a pistol, a .38 semi-automatic; she had never known how Bernie had come by it but she was certain that he had no licence. She had never seen it as a lethal weapon, perhaps because Bernie's boyishly naive obsession with it had reduced it to the impotence of a child's toy. He had taught her to become—at any rate in theory—a creditable shot. They had driven for practice into the depths of Epping Forest and her memories of the gun were linked with dappled shade and the rich smell of decaying leaves. He had fixed a target to a convenient tree; the gun was loaded with blanks. She could still hear the excited staccato orders. "Bend your knees slightly. Feet apart. Arm full length. Now place the left hand against the barrel, cradling it. Keep your eyes on the target. Arm straight, partner, arm straight! Good! Not bad; not bad; not bad at all." "But, Bernie," she had said, "we can never fire it! We haven't a licence." He had smiled, the sly self-satisfied smile of superior knowledge. "If we ever fire in anger it will be to save our lives. In such an eventuality the question of a licence is irrelevant." He had been pleased with this rotund sentence and had repeated it, lifting his heavy face to the sun like a dog. What, she wondered, had he seen in imagination? The two of them crouching behind a boulder on some desolate moor, bullets pinging against the granite, the gun passed smoking from hand to hand?

He had said: "We'll have to go carefully with the ammunition. Not that I can't get it of course . . ." The smile had become grim, as if at the memory of those mysterious contacts, those ubiquitous and obliging acquaintances whom he had only to summon from their shadow world.

So he had left her the gun. It had been his most prized possession. She slipped it, still shrouded, into the depths of her shoulder bag. It was surely unlikely that the police would examine the drawers of the desk in a case of obvious suicide but it was as well to take no risk. Bernie had meant her to have the gun and she wasn't going to give it up easily. With her bag at her feet she sat down again by the body. She said a brief convent-taught prayer to the God she wasn't sure existed for the soul which Bernie had never believed he possessed and waited quietly for the police.

The first policeman to arrive was efficient but young, not yet experienced enough to hide his shock and distaste at the sight of violent death nor his disapproval that Cordelia should be so calm. He didn't spend long in the inner office. When he came out he meditated upon Bernie's note as if a careful scrutiny could extract some inner meaning from the bald sentence of death. Then he folded it away.

"I'll have to keep this note for the present, Miss. What did he get up to here?"

"He didn't get up to anything. This was his office. He was a private detective."

"And you worked for this Mr. Pryde? You were his secretary?"

"I was his partner. It says so in the note. I'm twenty-two. Bernie was the senior partner; he started the business. He used to work for the Metropolitan Police in the C.I.D. with Superintendent Dalgliesh."

As soon as the words were spoken, she regretted them. They were too propitiatory, too naive a defence of poor Bernie. And the name Dalgliesh, she saw meant nothing to him. Why should it? He was just one of the local uniformed branch. He couldn't be expected to know how often she had listened with politely concealed impatience to Bernie's nostalgic reminiscences of his time in the C.I.D. before he was invalided out, or to his eulogies on the virtues and wisdom of Adam Dalgliesh. "The Super—well, he was just an Inspector then—always taught us . . . The Super once described a case . . . If there was one thing the Super couldn't stand . . ."

Sometimes she had wondered whether this paragon had actually existed or whether he had sprung impeccable and omnipotent from Bernie's brain, a necessary hero and mentor. It was with a shock of surprise that she had later seen a newspaper picture of Chief Superintendent Dalgliesh, a dark, sardonic face which, on her closer scrutiny, disintegrated into an ambiguity of patterned micro dots, giving nothing away. Not all the wisdom Bernie so glibly recalled was the received gospel. Much, she suspected, was his own philosophy. She in turn had devised a private litany of disdain: supercilious, superior, sarcastic Super; what wisdom, she wondered, would he have to comfort Bernie now.

The policeman had made discreet telephone calls. He now prowled around the outer office, hardly bothering to hide his puzzled contempt at the shabby second-hand furniture, the battered filing cabinet with one drawer half-open to reveal teapot and mugs, the worn linoleum. Miss Sparshott, rigid at an ancient typewriter, gazed at him with fascinated distaste. At last he said:

"Well, suppose you make yourselves a nice cup of tea while I wait for the police surgeon. There is somewhere to make tea?"

"There's a small pantry down the corridor which we share with the other tenants on this floor. But surely you don't need a surgeon? Bernie's dead!"

"He's not officially dead until a qualified medical practitioner says so." He paused: "It's just a precaution."

Against what, Cordelia wondered—judgement, damnation, decay? The policeman went back into the inner office. She followed him and asked softly:

"Couldn't you let Miss Sparshott go? She's from a secretarial agency and we have to pay for her by the hour. She hasn't done any work since I arrived and I doubt whether she will now."

He was, she saw, a little shocked by the apparent callousness of concerning herself with so mercenary a detail while standing within touching distance of Bernie's body, but he said willingly enough:

"I'll just have a word with her, then she can go. It isn't a nice place for a woman."

His tone implied that it never had been.

Afterwards, waiting in the outer office, Cordelia answered the inevitable questions.

"No, I don't know whether he was married. I've

a feeling that he was divorced; he never talked
about a wife. He lived at 15, Cremona Road, S.E.2.
He let me have a bed-sitting room there but we
didn't see much of each other."

"I know Cremona Road; my aunt used to live
there when I was a kid—one of those streets
near the Imperial War Museum."

The fact that he knew the road seemed to reassure and humanize him. He ruminated happily
for a moment.

"When did you last see Mr. Pryde alive?"

"Yesterday at about five o'clock when I left
work early to do some shopping."

"Didn't he come home last night?"

"I heard him moving around but I didn't see
him. I have a gas ring in my room and I usually
cook there unless I know he's out. I didn't hear
him this morning which is unusual, but I thought
he might be lying in. He does that occasionally
when it's his hospital morning."

"Was it his hospital morning to-day?"

"No, he had an appointment last Wednesday
but I thought that they might have asked him to
come back. He must have left the house very
late last night or before I woke early this morning.
I didn't hear him."

It was impossible to describe the almost obsessional delicacy with which they avoided each
other, trying not to intrude, preserving the other's
privacy, listening for the sound of flushing cis-
terns, tip-toeing to ascertain whether the kitchen
or bathroom was empty. They had taken infinite

trouble not to be a nuisance to each other. Living in the same small terraced house they had hardly seen each other outside the office. She wondered whether Bernie had decided to kill himself in his office so that the little house would be un-contaminated and undisturbed.

At last the office was empty and she was alone. The police surgeon had closed his bag and departed; Bernie's body had been manoeuvred down the narrow staircase watched by eyes from the half-opened doors of other offices; the last policeman had left. Miss Sparshott had gone for good, violent death being a worse insult than a typewriter which a trained typist ought not to be expected to use or lavatory accommodation which was not at all what she had been accustomed to. Alone in the emptiness and silence Cordelia felt the need of physical action. She began vigorously to clean the inner office, scrubbing the blood stains from desk and chair, mopping the soaked rug.

At one o'clock she walked briskly to their usual pub. It occurred to her that there was no longer any reason to patronize the Golden Pheasant but she walked on unable to bring herself to so early a disloyalty. She had never liked the pub or the landlady and had often wished that Bernie would find a nearer house, preferably one with a large bosomy barmaid with a heart of gold. It was, she suspected, a type commoner in fiction than in real life. The familiar lunch-time crowd was clustered around the bar and, as usual, Mavis presided behind it wearing her slightly minatory smile, her air of extreme respectability. Mavis changed her dress three times a day, her hair style once every year, her smile never. The two women had never liked each other although Bernie had galumphed between them like an affectionate old dog, finding it convenient to believe that they were great mates and unaware of or ignoring the almost physical crackle of antagonism. Mavis reminded Cordelia of a librarian known to her in childhood who had secreted the new books under the counter in case they should be taken out and soiled. Perhaps Mavis's barely suppressed chagrin was because she was forced to display her wares so prominently, compelled to measure out her bounty before watchful eyes. Pushing a half pint of shandy and a Scotch egg across the counter in response to Cordelia's order, she said:

"I hear you've had the police round."

Watching their avid faces, Cordelia thought, they know about it, of course; they want to hear the details; they may as well hear them. She said:

"Bernie cut his wrists twice. The first time he didn't get to the vein; the second time he did. He put his arm in water to help the bleeding. He had been told that he had cancer and couldn't face the treatment."

That, she saw, was different. The little group around Mavis glanced at each other, then quickly averted their eyes. Glasses were momentarily checked upon their upward way. Cutting one's wrist was something which other people did but the sinister little crab had his claws of fear into all their minds. Even Mavis looked as if she saw his bright claws lurking among her bottles. She said:

"You'll be looking for a new job, I suppose? After all, you can hardly keep the Agency going on your own. It isn't a suitable job for a woman."

"No different from working behind a bar; you meet all kinds of people."

The two women looked at each other and a snatch of unspoken dialogue passed between them clearly heard and understood by both.

"And don't think, now he's dead, that people can go on leaving messages for the Agency here."

"I wasn't going to ask."

Mavis began vigorously polishing a glass, her eyes still on Cordelia's face.

"I shouldn't think your mother would approve of you staying on alone."

"I only had a mother for the first hour of my life, so I don't have to worry about that."

Cordelia saw at once that the remark had deeply shocked them and wondered again at the capacity of older people to be outraged by simple facts when they seemed capable of accepting any amount of perverse or shocking opinion. But their silence, heavy with censure, at least left her in peace. She carried her shandy and the Scotch egg to a seat against the wall and thought without sentimentality about her mother. Gradually out of a childhood of deprivation she had evolved a philosophy of compensation. In her imagination she had enjoyed a lifetime of love in one hour with no disappointments and no regrets. Her father had never talked about her mother's death and Cordelia had avoided questioning him, fearful of learning that her mother had never held her in her arms, never regained consciousness, never perhaps even known that she had a daughter. This belief in her mother's love was the one fantasy which she could still not entirely risk losing although its indulgence had become less necessary and less real with each passing year. Now, in imagination, she consulted her mother. It was just as she expected: her mother thought it an entirely suitable job for a woman.

The little group at the bar had turned back to their drinks. Between their shoulders she could see her own reflection in the mirror above the bar. Today's face looked no different from yesterday's face; thick, light brown hair framing features which looked as if a giant had placed a hand on her head and the other under her chin and gently squeezed the face together; large eyes, browny-green under a deep fringe of hair; wide cheek bones; a gentle, childish mouth. A cat's face she thought, but calmly decorative among the reflection of coloured bottles and all the bright glitter of Mavis's bar. Despite its look of deceptive youth it could be a secret, uncommunicative face. Cordelia had early learnt stoicism. All her foster parents, kindly and well-meaning in their different ways, had demanded one thing of her—that she should be happy. She had quickly learned that to show unhappiness was to risk the loss of love. Compared with this early discipline of conceal-ment, all subsequent deceits had been easy.

The Snout was edging his way towards her. He settled himself down on the bench, his thick rump in its appalling tweed pressed close to hers. She disliked the Snout although he had been Bernie's only friend. Bernie had explained that the Snout was a police informer and did rather well. And there were other sources of income. Sometimes his friends stole famous pictures or valuable jewellery. Then the Snout, suitably in-structed, would hint to the police where the loot could be found. There was a reward for the Snout to be subsequently shared, of course, among the thieves, and a payoff, too, for the detective, who after all, had done most of the work. As Bernie had pointed out, the insurance company got off lightly, the owners got their property back intact, the thieves were in no danger from the police and the Snout and the detective got their payoff. It was the system. Cordelia, shocked, had not liked to protest too much. She suspected that Bernie too had done some snouting in his time, although never with such expertise or with such lucrative results.

The Snout's eyes were rheumy, his hand around the glass of whisky was shaking.

"Poor old Bernie, I could see he had it coming to him. He'd been losing weight for the last year and he had that grey look to him, the cancer complexion, my dad used to call it."

At least the Snout had noticed; she hadn't. Bernie had always seemed to her grey and sick-looking. A thick, hot thigh edged closer.

"Never had any luck, poor sod. They chucked him out of the C.I.D. Did he tell you? That was Superintendent Dalgliesh, Inspector at the time. Christ, he could be a proper bastard; no second chance from him, I can tell you."

"Yes, Bernie told me," Cordelia lied. She added: "He didn't seem particularly bitter about it."

"No use, is there, in being bitter? Take what comes, that's my motto. I suppose you'll be looking for another job?"

He said it wistfully as if her defection would leave the Agency open for his exploitation.

"Not just yet," said Cordelia. "I shan't look for a new job just yet."

She had made two resolutions: she would keep on Bernie's business until there was nothing left with which to pay the rent, and she would never come into the Golden Pheasant again as long as she lived.

This resolution to keep the business going survived the next four days—survived discovery of the rent book and agreement which revealed that Bernie hadn't, after all, owned the little house in Cremona Road and that her tenancy of the bedsitting room was illegal and certainly limited; survived learning from the Bank Manager that

Bernie's credit balance would barely pay for his funeral and from the garage that the Mini was shortly due for an overhaul; survived the clearing up of the Cremona Road house. Everywhere was the sad detritus of a solitary and mismanaged life.

The tins of Irish stew and baked beans—had he never eaten anything else?—stacked in a carefully arranged pyramid as if in a grocer's window; large tins of floor and metal polish, half-used, with their contents dried or congealed; a drawer of old rags used as dusters but stiff with an amalgam of polish and dirt; a laundry basket unemptied; thick woollen combinations felted with machine washing and stained brown about the crotch—how could he have borne to leave those for discovery?

She went daily to the office, cleaning, tidying, rearranging the filing. There were no calls and no clients and yet she seemed always busy. There was the inquest to attend, depressing in its detached almost boring formality, in its inevitable verdict. There was a visit to Bernie's solicitor. He was a dispirited, elderly man with an office inconveniently situated near Mile End Station who took the news of his client's death with lugubrious resignation as if it were a personal affront, and after a brief search found Bernie's will and pored over it with puzzled suspicion, as if it were not the document he himself had recently drawn up. He succeeded in giving Cordelia the impression that he realized that she had been Bernie's mistress—why else should he have left her the business—but that he was a man of the world and didn't hold the knowledge against her. He took no part in arranging the funeral except to supply Cordelia with the name of a firm of under-takers; she suspected that they probably gave him a commission. She was relieved after a week of depressing solemnity to find that the funeral director was both cheerful and competent. Once he discovered that Cordelia wasn't going to break down in tears or indulge in the more histrionic antics of the bereaved, he was happy to discuss the relative price and the merits of burial and cre-mation with conspiratorial candour.

"Cremation every time. There's no private in-surance, you tell me? Then get it all over as quickly, easily and cheaply as possible. Take my word, that's what the deceased would want nine times out of ten. A grave's an expensive luxury these days—no use to him—no use to you. Dust to dust, ashes to ashes; but what about the pro-cess in between? Not nice to think about, is it? So why not get it over as quickly as possible by the most reliable modern methods? Mind you, Miss, I'm advising you against my own best in-terests."

Cordelia said:

"It's very kind of you. Do you think we ought to have a wreath?"

"Why not, it'll give it a bit of tone. Leave it to me."

So there had been a cremation and one wreath.

The wreath had been a vulgarly inappropriate cushion of lilies and carnations, the flowers already dying and smelling of decay. The cremation service had been spoken by the priest with carefully controlled speed and with a suggestion of apology in his tone as if to assure his hearers that, although he enjoyed a special dispensation, he didn't expect them to believe the unbelievable. Bernie had passed to his burning to the sound of synthetic music and only just on time, to judge by the impatient rustlings of the cortège already waiting to enter the chapel.

Afterwards Cordelia was left standing in the bright sunlight, feeling the heat of the gravel through the soles of her shoes. The air was rich and heavy with the scent of flowers. Swept suddenly with desolation and a defensive anger on Bernie's behalf, she sought a scapegoat and found it in a certain Superintendent of the Yard. He had kicked Bernie out of the only job he had ever wanted to do; hadn't troubled to find out what happened to him later; and most irrational indictment of all, he hadn't even bothered to come to the funeral. Bernie had needed to be a detective as other men needed to paint, write, drink or fornicate. Surely the C.I.D. was large enough to accommodate one man's enthusiasm and inefficiency? For the first time Cordelia wept for Bernie; hot tears blurred and multiplied the long line of waiting hearses with their bright coronets so that they seemed to stretch in an infinity of gleaming chrome and trembling flowers. Untying the

black chiffon scarf from her head, her only concession to mourning, Cordelia set off to walk to
the tube station.

She was thirsty when she got to Oxford Circus and decided to have tea in the restaurant at
Dickins and Jones. This was unusual and an extravagance but it had been an unusual and extravagant day. She lingered long enough to get
full value for her bill and it was after a quarter
past four when she returned to the office.

She had a visitor. There was a woman waiting,
shoulders against the door—a woman who
looked cool and incongruous against the dirty
paintwork and the greasy walls. Cordelia caught
her breath in surprise, her upward rush checked.
Her light shoes had made no sound on the stairway and for a few seconds she saw her visitor
unobserved. She gained an impression, immediate and vivid, of competence and authority and
an intimidating rightness of dress. The woman
was wearing a grey suit with a small stand-away
collar which showed a narrow band of white cotton at the throat. Her black patent shoes were
obviously expensive; a large black bag with patch
pockets was slung from her left shoulder. She
was tall and her hair, prematurely white, was cut
short and moulded to her head like a cap. Her
face was pale and long. She was reading *The
Times,* the paper folded so that she could hold it
in her right hand. After a couple of seconds, she
became aware of Cordelia and their eyes met.
The woman looked at her wrist watch.

"If you are Cordelia Gray, then you're eighteen minutes late. This notice says that you would return at four o'clock."

"I know, I'm sorry." Cordelia hurried up the last few steps and fitted the Yale key into the lock. She opened the door.

"Won't you come in?"

The woman preceded her into the outer office and turned to face her without giving the room even a glance.

"I was hoping to see Mr. Pryde. Will he be long?"

"I'm sorry; I've just come back from his cremation. I mean . . . Bernie's dead."

"Obviously. Our information was that he was alive ten days ago. He must have died with remarkable speed and discretion."

"Not with discretion. Bernie killed himself."

"How extraordinary!" The visitor seemed to be struck by its extraordinariness. She pressed her hands together and for a few seconds walked restlessly about the room in a curious pantomime of distress.

"How extraordinary!" she said again. She gave a little snort of laughter. Cordelia didn't speak, but the two women regarded each other gravely. Then the visitor said:

"Well, I seem to have had a wasted journey."

Cordelia breathed an almost inaudible "Oh no!" and resisted an absurd impulse to fling her body against the door.

"Please don't go before talking to me. I was

Mr. Pryde's partner and I own the business now. I'm sure I could help. Won't you please sit down?"

The visitor took no notice of the offered chair.

"No one can help, no one in the world. However, that is beside the point. There is something which my employer particularly wants to know—some information he requires—and he had decided that Mr. Pryde was the person to get it for him. I don't know if he would consider you an effective substitute. Is there a private telephone here?"

"In here, please."

The woman walked into the inner office, again with no sign that its shabbiness had made any impression on her. She turned to Cordelia.

"I'm sorry, I should have introduced myself. My name is Elizabeth Leaming and my employer is Sir Ronald Callender."

"The conservationist?"

"I shouldn't let him hear you call him that. He prefers to be called a micro-biologist, which is what he is. Please excuse me."

She shut the door firmly. Cordelia, feeling suddenly weak, sat down at the typewriter. The keys, oddly unfamiliar symbols encircled in black medallions, shifted their pattern before her tired eyes, then at a blink clicked back to normality. She grasped the sides of the machine, cold and clammy to the touch, and talked herself back to calmness. Her heart was thudding.

"I must be calm, must show her that I am tough. This silliness is only the strain of Bernie's funeral and too much standing in the hot sun."

But hope was traumatic; she was angry with herself for caring so much.

The telephone call took only a couple of minutes. The door of the inner office opened; Miss Leaming was drawing on her gloves.

"Sir Ronald has asked to see you. Can you come now?"

Come where, thought Cordelia, but she didn't ask.

"Yes, shall I need my gear?"

The gear was Bernie's carefully designed and fitted out scene-of-crime case with its tweezers, scissors, finger printing equipment, jars to collect specimens; Cordelia had never yet had occasion to use it.

"It depends upon what you mean by your gear, but I shouldn't think so. Sir Ronald wants to see you before deciding whether to offer you the job. It means a train journey to Cambridge but you should get back tonight. Is there anyone you ought to tell?"

"No, there's only me."

"Perhaps I ought to identify myself." She opened her handbag. "Here is an addressed envelope. I'm not a white slaver if they exist and in case you're frightened."

"I'm frightened of quite a number of things but not of white slavers and if I were, an addressed envelope would hardly reassure me. I'd insist on telephoning Sir Ronald Callender to check."

"Perhaps you would like to do so?" suggested Miss Leaming without rancour.

"No."

"Then shall we go?" Miss Leaming led the way to the door. As they went out to the landing and Cordelia turned to lock the office behind her, her visitor indicated the notepad and pencil hanging together from a nail on the wall.

"Hadn't you better change the notice?"

Cordelia tore off her previous message and after a moment's thought wrote:

I am called away to an urgent case. Any messages pushed through the door will receive my immediate and personal attention on return.

"That," pronounced Miss Leaming, "should reassure your clients." Cordelia wondered if the remark was sarcastic; it was impossible to tell from the detached tone. But she didn't feel that Miss Leaming was laughing at her and was surprised at her own lack of resentment at the way in which her visitor had taken charge of events. Meekly, she followed Miss Leaming down the stairs and into Kingly Street.

They travelled by the Central Line to Liverpool Street and caught the 17.36 train to Cambridge with plenty of time. Miss Leaming bought Cordelia's ticket, collected a portable typewriter and a briefcase of papers from the left luggage department and led the way to a first-class carriage. She said:

"I shall have to work in the train; have you anything to read?"

"That's all right. I don't like talking when I'm

travelling either. I've got Hardy's *Trumpet Major*—
I always have a paperback in my bag."

After Bishops Stortford they had the compartment to themselves but only once did Miss Leaming look up from her work to question Cordelia.

"How did you come to be working for Mr.
Pryde?"

"After I left school I went to live with my father
on the continent. We travelled around a good
deal. He died in Rome last May after a heart attack and I came home. I had taught myself some
shorthand and typing so I took a job with a secretarial agency. They sent me to Bernie and after
a few weeks he let me help him with one or two of
the cases. He'd decided to train me and I agreed
to stay on permanently. Two months ago he made
me his partner."

All that had meant was that Cordelia gave up
a regular wage in return for the uncertain rewards
of success in the form of an equal share of the
profits together with a rent-free bedsitting room
in Bernie's house. He hadn't meant to cheat. The
offer of the partnership had been made in the
genuine belief that she would recognize it for
what it was; not a good conduct prize but an ac-
colade of trust.

"What was your father?"

"He was an itinerant Marxist poet and an amateur revolutionary."

"You must have had an interesting childhood."

Remembering the succession of foster mothers, the unexplained incomprehensible moves

from house to house, the changes of school, the concerned faces of Local Authority Welfare Officers and school teachers desperately wondering what to do with her in the holidays, Cordelia replied as she always did to this assertion, gravely and without irony.

"Yes, it was very interesting."

"And what was this training you received from Mr. Pryde?"

"Bernie taught me some of the things he learnt in the C.I.D.: how to search the scene of a crime properly, how to collect exhibits, some elementary self-defence, how to detect and lift finger prints—that kind of thing."

"Those are skills which I hardly feel you will find appropriate to this case."

Miss Leaming bent her head over her papers and did not speak again until the train reached Cambridge.

Outside the station Miss Leaming briefly surveyed the car park and led the way towards a small black van. Standing beside it rigidly as a uniformed chauffeur, was a stockily built young man dressed in an open-necked white shirt, dark breeches and tall boots who Miss Leaming introduced casually and without explanation as "Lunn." He nodded briefly in acknowledgement of the introduction but did not smile. Cordelia held out her hand. His grip was momentary but remarkably strong, crushing her fingers; suppressing a grimace of pain she saw a flicker in the large mud-brown eyes and wondered if he had hurt her deliberately. The eyes were certainly memorable and beautiful, moist calves' eyes heavily lashed and with the same look of troubled pain at the unpredictability of the world's terrors. But their beauty emphasized rather than redeemed the unattractiveness of the rest of him. He was, she thought, a sinister study in black and white with his thick, short neck and powerful shoulders straining the seams of his shirt. He had a helmet of strong black hair, a pudgy slightly pox-marked face and a moist petulant mouth; the face of a ribald cherub. He was a man who sweated profusely; the underarms of his shirt were stained and the cotton stuck to the flesh emphasizing the strong curve of the back and the obtrusive biceps.

Cordelia saw that the three of them were to sit squashed together in the front of the van. Lunn held open the door without apology except to state:

"The Rover's still in dock."

Miss Leaming hung back so that Cordelia was compelled to get in first and to sit beside him. She thought: "They don't like each other and he resents me."

She wondered about his position in Sir Ronald Callender's household. Miss Leaming's place she had already guessed; no ordinary secretary however long in service, however indispensable, had quite that air of authority or talked of "my employer" in that tone of possessive irony. But she wondered about Lunn. He didn't behave like a subordinate but nor did he strike her as a scientist. True, scientists were alien creatures to her. Sister Mary Magdalen was the only one she had known. Sister had taught what the syllabus dignified as general science, a hotch-potch of elementary physics, chemistry and biology unceremoniously lumped together. Science subjects were in general little regarded at the Convent of the Immaculate Conception, although the arts were well taught. Sister Mary Magdalen had been an elderly and timid nun, eyes puzzled behind her steel-rimmed spectacles, her clumsy fingers permanently stained with chemicals, who had apparently been as surprised as her pupils at the extraordinary explosions and fumes which her activities with test tube and flask had occasionally produced. She had been more concerned to demonstrate the incomprehensibility of the universe and the inscrutability of God's laws than to reveal scientific principles and in this she had certainly succeeded. Cordelia felt that Sister Mary Magdalen would be no help to her in dealing with Sir Ronald Callender; Sir Ronald who had campaigned in the cause of conservation long before his interest became a popular obsession, who had represented his country at International Conferences on Ecology and been knighted for his services to conservation. All this Cordelia, like the rest of the country, knew from his television appearances and the Sunday Colour Supplements. He was the establishment scientist, carefully uncommitted politically, who personified to everyone's reassurance the poor boy who had made good and stayed good. How, Cordelia wondered, had he come to think of employing Bernie Pryde?

Uncertain how far Lunn was in his employer's or Miss Leaming's confidence, she asked carefully:

"How did Sir Ronald hear about Bernie?"

"John Bellinger told him."

So the Bellinger bonus had arrived at last! Bernie had always expected it. The Bellinger case had been his most lucrative, perhaps his only, success. John Bellinger was the director of a small family firm which manufactured specialized scientific instruments. The previous year his office had been plagued by an outbreak of obscene letters and, unwilling to call in the police, he had telephoned Bernie. Bernie, taken on the staff at his own suggestion as a messenger, had quickly solved a not very difficult problem. The writer had been Bellinger's middle-aged and highly regarded personal secretary. Bellinger had been grateful. Bernie, after anxious thought and consultation with Cordelia, had sent in a bill the size of which had astounded them both and the bill had been promptly paid. It had kept the Agency going for a month. Bernie had said: "We'll get a bonus from the Bellinger case, see if we don't. Anything can happen in this job. He only chose us by picking our name from the telephone directory but now he'll recommend us to his friends.

This case could be the beginning of something big."

And now, thought Cordelia, on the day of Bernie's funeral, the Bellinger bonus had arrived.

She asked no more questions and the drive, which took less than thirty minutes, passed in silence. The three of them sat thigh to thigh, but distanced. She saw nothing of the city. At the end of Station Road by the War Memorial the car turned to the left and soon they were in the country. There were wide fields of young corn, the occasional stretch of tree-lined dappled shade, straggling villages of thatched cottages and squat red villas strung along the road, low uplands from which Cordelia could see the towers and spires of the city, shining with deceptive nearness in the evening sun. Finally, there was another village, a thin belt of elms fringing the road, a long curving wall of red brick and the van turned in through open wrought iron gates. They had arrived.

The house was obviously Georgian, not perhaps the best Georgian but solidly built, agreeably proportioned and with the look of all good domestic architecture of having grown naturally out of its site. The mellow brick, festooned with wisteria, gleamed richly in the evening sun so that the green of the creeper glowed and the whole house looked suddenly as artificial and unsubstantial as a film set. It was essentially a family house, a welcoming house. But now a heavy

silence lay over it and the rows of elegantly proportioned windows were empty eyes.

Lunn, who had driven fast but skilfully, braked
in front of the porch. He stayed in his seat while
the two women got out then drove the van round
the side of the house. As she slid down from the
high seat Cordelia could glimpse a range of low
buildings, topped with small ornamental turrets,
which she took to be stables or garages. Through
the wide-arched gateway she could see that the
grounds dropped slowly away to give a far vista
of the flat Cambridgeshire countryside, patterned
with the gentle greens and fawns of early summer. Miss Leaming said:

"The stable block has been converted into lab-
oratories. Most of the east side is now glass. It
was a skilful job by a Swedish architect, functional but attractive."

For the first time since they had met her voice
sounded interested, almost enthusiastic.

The front door was open. Cordelia came into a
wide, panelled hall with a staircase curving to the
left, a carved stone fireplace to the right. She
was aware of a smell of roses and lavender, of
carpets gleaming richly against polished wood,
of the subdued ticking of a clock.

Miss Leaming led the way to a door immediately across the hall. It led to a study, a room
booklined and elegant, one with a view of wide
lawns and a shield of trees. In front of the french
windows was a Georgian desk and behind the
desk sat a man.

Cordelia had seen his photographs in the press and knew what to expect. But he was at once smaller and more impressive than she had imagined. She knew that she was facing a man of authority and high intelligence; his strength came over like a physical force. But as he rose from his seat and waved her to a chair, she saw that he was slighter than his photographs suggested, the heavy shoulders and impressive head making the body look top-heavy. He had a lined, sensitive face with a high-bridged nose, deep-set eyes on which the lids weighed heavily with a mobile, sculptured mouth. His black hair, as yet unflecked with grey, lay heavily across his brow. His face was shadowed with weariness and, as Cordelia came closer, she could detect the twitch of a nerve in his left temple and the almost imperceptible staining of the veins in the irises of the deep-set eyes. But his compact body, taut with energy and latent vigour, made no concession to tiredness. The arrogant head was held high, the eyes were keen and wary under the heavy lids. Above all he looked successful. Cordelia had seen that look before, had recognized it from the back of crowds as, inscrutable, they had watched the famous and notorious pass on their way—that almost physical glow, akin to sexuality and undimmed by weariness or ill-health, of men who knew and enjoyed the realities of power.

Miss Leaming said:

"This is all that remains of Pryde's Detective Agency—Miss Cordelia Gray."

The keen eyes looked into Cordelia's.

"We take a Pride in our Work. Do you?"

Cordelia, tired after her journey at the end of a momentous day, was in no mood for jokes about poor Bernie's pathetic pun. She said:

"Sir Ronald, I have come here because your secretary said that you might want to employ me. If she's wrong, I would be glad to know so that I can get back to London."

"She isn't my secretary and she isn't wrong. You must forgive my discourtesy; it's a little disconcerting to expect a burly ex-policeman and to get you. I'm not complaining, Miss Gray; you might do very well. What are your fees?"

The question might have sounded offensive but it wasn't; he was completely matter-of-fact. Cordelia told him, a little too quickly, a little too eagerly.

"Five pounds a day and expenses, but we try to keep those as low as possible. For that, of course, you get my sole services. I mean I don't work for any other client until your case is finished."

"And is there another client?"

"Well, not just at present but there very well could be." She went on quickly:

"We have a fair-play clause. If I decide at any stage of the investigation that I'd rather not go on with it, you are entitled to any information I have gained up to that point. If I decide to withhold it from you, then I make no charge for the work already done."

That had been one of Bernie's principles. He had been a great man for principles. Even when there hadn't been a case for a week, he could happily discuss the extent to which they would be justified in telling a client less than the full truth, the point at which the police ought to be brought into an enquiry, the ethics of deception or lying in the service of truth. "But no bugging," Bernie would say, "I set my face firmly against bugging. And we don't touch industrial sabotage."

The temptation to either wasn't great. They had no bugging equipment and wouldn't have known how to use it if they had, and at no time had Bernie been invited to touch industrial sabotage.

Sir Ronald said:

"That sounds reasonable but I don't think this case will present you with any crisis of conscience. It is comparatively simple. Eighteen days ago my son hanged himself. I want you to find out why. Can you do that?"

"I should like to try, Sir Ronald."

"I realize that you need certain basic information about Mark. Miss Leaming will type it out for you, then you can read it through and let us know what else you require."

Cordelia said:

"I should like you to tell me yourself, please."

"Is that necessary?"

"It would be helpful to me."

He settled again into his chair and picked up a stub of pencil, twisting it in his hands. After a minute he slipped it absentmindedly into his pocket. Without looking at her, he began to speak.

"My son Mark was twenty-one on the 25th April this year. He was at Cambridge reading history at my old college and was in his final year. Five weeks ago and without warning, he left the university and took a job as gardener with a Major Markland, who lives in a house called Summertrees outside Duxford. Mark gave me no explanation of this action either then or later. He lived alone in a cottage in Major Markland's grounds. Eighteen days later he was found by his employer's sister hanging by the neck from a strap knotted to a hook in the sitting-room ceiling. The verdict at the inquest was that he took his life while the balance of his mind was disturbed. I know little of my son's mind but I reject that comfortable euphemism. He was a rational person. He had a reason for his action. I want to know what it was."

Miss Leaming, who had been looking out of the french windows to the garden, turned and said with sudden vehemence:

"This lust always to know! It's only prying. If he'd wanted us to know, he'd have told us."

Sir Ronald said:

"I'm not prepared to go on in this uncertainty. My son is dead. *My* son. If I am in some way responsible, I prefer to know. If anyone else is responsible I want to know that too."

Cordelia looked from one to the other. She asked:

"Did he leave a note?"

"He left a note but not an explanation. It was found in his typewriter."

Quietly Miss Leaming began to speak:

"Down the winding cavern we groped our tedious way, till a void boundless as the nether sky appeared beneath us, and we held by the roots of trees and hung over this immensity; but I said: if you please we will commit ourselves to this void, and see whether providence is here also."

The husky, curiously deep voice came to an end. They were silent. Then Sir Ronald said:

"You claim to be a detective, Miss Gray. What do you deduce from that?"

"That your son read William Blake. Isn't it a passage from *The Marriage of Heaven and Hell*?"

Sir Ronald and Miss Leaming glanced at each other. Sir Ronald said:

"So I am told."

Cordelia thought that Blake's gently unemphatic exhortation, devoid of violence or despair, was more appropriate to suicide by drowning or by poison—a ceremonious floating or sinking into oblivion—than to the trauma of hanging. And yet there was the analogy of falling, of launching oneself into the void. But this speculation was indulgent fantasy. He had chosen Blake: he had chosen hanging. Perhaps other and more gentle means were not to hand; perhaps he had acted upon impulse. What was it that the Super always said? "Never theorize in advance of your facts." She would have to look at the cottage.

Sir Ronald said, with a touch of impatience:

"Well, don't you want the job?"

Cordelia looked at Miss Leaming but the woman did not meet her eyes.

"I want it very much. I was wondering whether you really want me to take it."

"I'm offering it to you. Worry about your own responsibilities, Miss Gray, and I'll look after mine."

Cordelia said:

"Is there anything else that you can tell me? The ordinary things. Was your son in good health? Did he seem worried about his work or his love affairs? About money?"

"Mark would have inherited a considerable fortune from his maternal grandfather had he reached the age of twenty-five. In the meantime, he received an adequate allowance from me, but from the date of leaving college he transferred the balance back to my own account and instructed his Bank Manager to deal similarly with any future payments. Presumably he lived on his earnings for the last two weeks of his life. The postmortem revealed no illnesses and his tutor testified that his academic work was satisfactory. I, of course, know nothing of his subject. He didn't confide in me about his love affairs—what young man does to his father? If he had any, I would expect them to be heterosexual."

Miss Leaming turned from her contemplation at the garden. She held out her hands in a gesture which could have been resignation or despair:

"We knew nothing about him, nothing! So why wait until he's dead and then start finding out?"

"And his friends?" asked Cordelia quietly.

"They rarely visited here but there were two I recognized at the inquest and the funeral: Hugo Tilling from his own college and his sister who is a post-graduate student at New Hall, studying philology. Do you remember her name, Eliza?"

"Sophie. Sophie Tilling. Mark brought her here to dinner once or twice."

"Could you tell me something about your son's early life? Where was he educated?"

"He went to a pre-prep school when he was five and to a prep school subsequently. I couldn't have a child here running unsupervised in and out of the laboratory. Later, at his mother's wish—she died when Mark was nine months old—he went on to a Woodard Foundation. My wife was what I believe is called a High Anglican and wanted the boy educated in that tradition. As far as I know, it had no deleterious effect on him."

"Was he happy at prep school?"

"I expect he was as happy as most eight-year-olds are, which means that he was miserable most of the time, interposed with periods of animal spirits. Is all this relevant?"

"Anything could be. I have to try to get to know him, you see."

What was it that the supercilious, sapient, superhuman Super had taught? "Get to know the dead person. Nothing about him is too trivial, too unimportant. Dead men can talk. They can lead you directly to their murderer." Only this time, of course, there wasn't a murderer. She said:

"It would be helpful if Miss Leaming could type out the information you have given to me and add the name of college and his tutor. And please may I have a note signed by you to authorize me to make enquiries."

He reached down to a left-hand drawer in the desk, took out a sheet of writing paper and wrote on it; then he passed it to Cordelia. The printed heading read: From Sir Ronald Callender, F.R.S., Garfort House, Cambridgeshire. Underneath he had written:

The bearer, Miss Cordelia Gray, is authorized to make enquiries on my behalf into the death on 26th May of my son Mark Callender. He had signed and dated it. He asked:

"Is there anything else?"

Cordelia said:

"You talked about the possibility of someone else being responsible for your son's death. Do you quarrel with the verdict?"

"The verdict was in accordance with the evidence which is all one can expect of a verdict. A court of law is not constituted to establish the truth. I'm employing you to make an attempt at that. Have you everything you need? I don't think we can help you with any more information."

"I should like a photograph." They looked at each other nonplussed. He said to Miss Leaming:

"A photograph. Have we a photograph, Eliza?"

"There is his passport somewhere but I'm not sure where. I have that photograph I took of him in the garden last summer. It shows him fairly clearly, I think. I'll get it." She went out of the room. Cordelia said:

"And I should like to see his room, if I may. I assume that he stayed here during his vacations?"

"Only occasionally, but of course he had a room here. I'll show it to you."

The room was on the second floor and at the back. Once inside, Sir Ronald ignored Cordelia. He walked over to the window and gazed out over the lawns as if neither she nor the room held any interest for him. It told Cordelia nothing about the adult Mark. It was simply furnished, a school boy's sanctum, and looked as if little had been changed in the last ten years. There was a low white cupboard against one wall with the usual row of discarded childhood toys; a teddy bear, his fur scuffed with much cuddling and one beady eye hanging loose; painted wooden trains and trucks; a Noah's Ark, its deck a-tumble with stiff-legged animals topped by a round-faced Noah and his wife; a boat with limp dejected sail; a miniature darts board. Above the toys were two rows of books. Cordelia went over to examine them. Here was the orthodox library of the middle-class child, the approved classics handed down from generation to generation, the traditional lore of Nanny and mother. Cordelia had come to them late as an adult; they had found no place in her Saturday comic and television-dominated childhood. She said:

"What about his present books?"

"They're in boxes in the cellar. He sent them here for storage when he left college and we haven't had time to unpack them yet. There hardly seems any point in it."

There was a small round table beside the bed and on it a lamp and a bright round stone intricately holed by the sea, a treasure picked up, perhaps, from some holiday beach. Sir Ronald touched it gently with long tentative fingers then began rolling it under his palm over the surface of the table. Then, apparently without thinking, he dropped it into his pocket. "Well," he said. "Shall we go down now?"

They were met at the foot of the stairs by Miss Leaming. She looked up at them as slowly they came down side by side. There was such controlled intensity in her regard that Cordelia waited almost with apprehension for her to speak. But she turned away, her shoulders drooping as if with sudden fatigue, and all she said was:

"I've found the photograph. I should like it back when you've finished with it, please. I've put it in the envelope with the note. There isn't a fast train back to London until nine thirty-seven, so perhaps you would care to stay for dinner?"

The dinner party which followed was an interesting but rather odd experience, the meal itself a blend of the formal and casual which Cordelia felt was the result of conscious effort rather than chance. Some effect, she felt, had been aimed at but whether of a dedicated band of co-workers meeting together at the end of a day for a corporate meal, or the ritual imposition of order and ceremony on a diverse company, she wasn't sure. The party numbered ten: Sir Ronald Callender, Miss Leaming, Chris Lunn, a visiting American Professor, whose unpronounceable name she forgot as soon as Sir Ronald introduced her, and five of the young scientists. All the men, including Lunn, were in dinner jackets, and Miss Leaming wore a long skirt of patchwork satin below a plain sleeveless top. The rich blues, greens and reds gleamed and changed in the candlelight as she moved, and emphasized the pale silver of her hair and the almost colourless skin. Cordelia had been rather nonplussed when her hostess left her in the drawing room and went upstairs to change. She wished that she had something more competitive than the fawn skirt and green top, being at an age to value elegance more highly than youth.

She had been shown to Miss Leaming's bedroom to wash and had been intrigued by the elegance and simplicity of the furniture and the contrasting opulence of the adjacent bathroom. Studying her tired face in the mirror and wielding her lipstick, she had wished she had some eye shadow with her. On impulse, and with a sense of guilt, she had pulled open a dressing-table drawer. It was filled with a variety of make-up; old lipsticks in colours long out-of-date; half used bottles of foundation cream; eye pencils; moisturizing creams; half-used bottles of scent. She had rummaged, and eventually found, a stick of eye shadow which, in view of the wasteful muddle of discarded items in the drawer, she had had little compunction in using. The effect had been bizarre but striking. She could not compete with Miss Leaming but at least she looked five years older. The disorder in the drawer had surprised her and she had had to resist the temptation to see if the wardrobe and the other drawers were in a similar state of disarray. How inconsistent and how interesting human beings were! She thought it astonishing that such a fastidious and competent woman should be content to live with such a mess.

The dining room was at the front of the house. Miss Leaming placed Cordelia between herself and Lunn, a seating which held little prospect of pleasurable conversation. The rest of the party sat where they wished. The contrast between simplicity and elegance showed in the table arrangements. There was no artificial light and three silver branched candlesticks were placed at regular intervals down the table. Between them were set four wine carafes made of thick green glass with curved lips, such as Cordelia had often seen in cheap Italian restaurants. The place mats were of plain cork, but the forks and spoons were antique silver. The flowers were set in low bowls, not skilfully arranged but looking as if they were casualties of a garden storm, blooms which had snapped off in the wind and which someone had thought it kind to place in water.

The young men looked incongruous in their dinner jackets, not ill at ease since they enjoyed the essential self-esteem of the clever and successful, but as if they had picked up the suits second-hand or at a fancy dress costumier and were participating in a charade. Cordelia was surprised at their youth; she guessed that only one was over thirty. Three were untidy, fast talking, restless young men with loud emphatic voices who took no notice of Cordelia after the first introduction. The other two were quieter and one, a tall black-haired boy with strong irregular features, smiled at her across the table and looked as if he would like to have sat within speaking distance.

The meal was brought in by an Italian manservant and his wife who left the cooked dishes on hot plates on a side table. The food was plentiful and the smell almost intolerably appetizing to Cordelia, who hadn't realized until then just how hungry she was. There was a dish heaped high with glistening rice, a large casserole of veal in a rich mushroom sauce, a bowl of spinach. Beside it on the cold table was a large ham, a sirloin of beef and an interesting assortment of salads and fruit. The company served themselves, carrying their plates back to the table with whatever combination of food, hot or cold, they fancied. The young scientists piled their plates high and Cordelia followed their example.

She took little interest in the conversation except to notice that it was predominantly about science and that Lunn, although he spoke less than the others, spoke as their equal. He should, she thought, have looked ridiculous in his rather tight dinner jacket but, surprisingly, he looked the most at ease, the second most powerful personality in the room. Cordelia tried to analyse why this was so, but was defeated. He ate slowly, with finicky attention to the arrangement of the food on his plate, and from time to time, smiled secretly into his wine.

At the other end of the table Sir Ronald was peeling an apple and talking to his guest, his head inclined. The green rind slid thinly over his long fingers and curved down towards his plate. Cordelia glanced at Miss Leaming. She was staring at Sir Ronald with such unwavering and speculative concern, that Cordelia uncomfortably felt that every eye present must be irresistibly drawn to that pale disdainful mask. Then, Miss Leaming seemed to become aware of her glance. She relaxed and turned to Cordelia:

"When we were travelling here together you were reading Hardy. Do you enjoy him?"

"Very much. But I enjoy Jane Austen more."

"Then you must try to find an opportunity of visiting the Fitzwilliam Museum in Cambridge. They have a letter written by Jane Austen. I think you'd find it interesting."

She spoke with the controlled, artificial brightness of a hostess trying to find a subject to interest a difficult guest. Cordelia, her mouth full of veal and mushrooms, wondered how she would manage to get through the rest of the meal. Luckily, however, the American professor had caught the word "Fitzwilliam" and now called down the table to enquire about the Museum's collection of majolica in which, apparently, he was interested. The conversation became general.

It was Miss Leaming who drove Cordelia to the station, Audley End this time instead of Cambridge; a change for which no reason was given. They didn't speak about the case during the drive. Cordelia was exhausted with tiredness, food and wine and allowed herself to be firmly taken in hand and placed in the train without attempting to gain any further information. She didn't really think she would have got it. As the train drew out, her tired fingers fumbled with the flap of the strong white envelope which Miss Leaming had handed to her and she drew out and read the enclosed note. It was expertly typed and set out, but told her little more than she had already learnt. With it was the photograph. She saw the picture of a laughing boy, his head half-turned towards the camera, one hand shielding his eyes from the sun. He was wearing jeans and a vest and was half lying on the lawn, a pile of books on the grass beside him. Perhaps he had been working there under the trees when she had come out of the french windows with her camera and called imperiously to him to smile. The photograph told Cordelia nothing except, that for one recorded second at least, he had known how to be happy. She placed it back in the envelope; her hands closed protectively over it. Cordelia slept.

Chapter Two

NEXT MORNING Cordelia left Cremona Road before seven o'clock. Despite her tiredness the night before, she had made her major preparations before she went to bed. They hadn't taken long. As Bernie had taught her, she checked systematically the scene-of-crime kit, an unnecessary routine since nothing had been touched since, in celebration of their partnership, he had first set it up for her. She put ready the Polaroid camera; sorted into order the road maps from the jumble pushed into the back of his desk; shook out the sleeping bag and rolled it ready; filled a carrier bag with iron rations from Bernie's store of tinned soup and baked beans; considered, and finally decided to take, their copy of Professor Simpson's book on forensic medicine and her own

Hacker portable radio; checked the first-aid kit. Finally, she found herself a fresh notebook, headed it *Case of Mark Callender* and ruled up the last few pages ready for her expense account. These preliminaries had always been the most satisfying part of a case, before boredom or distaste set in, before anticipation crumbled into disenchantment and failure. Bernie's planning had always been meticulous and successful; it was reality which had let him down.

Finally, she considered her clothes. If this hot weather continued her Jaeger suit, bought from her savings after much careful thought to see her through almost any interview, would be uncomfortably hot, but she might have to interview the head of a college and the dignified professionalism best exemplified by a suit would be the effect to aim at. She decided to travel in her fawn suede skirt with a short-sleeved jumper and pack jeans and warmer jumpers for any field work. Cordelia enjoyed clothes, enjoyed planning and buying them, a pleasure circumscribed less by poverty than by her obsessive need to be able to pack the whole of her wardrobe into one medium sized suitcase like a refugee perpetually ready for flight.

Once she had shaken free from the tentacles of north London, Cordelia enjoyed the drive. The Mini purred along and Cordelia thought that it had never run so sweetly. She liked the flat East Anglian countryside, the broad streets of the market towns, the way in which the fields grew unhedged to the edge of the road, the openness and freedom of the far horizons and wide skies. The country matched her mood. She had grieved for Bernie and would grieve for him again, missing his comradeship and his undemanding affection, but this, in a sense, was her first case and she was glad to be tackling it alone. It was one that she thought she could solve. It neither appalled nor disgusted her. Driving in happy anticipation through the sunbathed countryside, the boot of the car carefully packed with her gear, she was filled with the euphoria of hope.

When she finally reached Duxford village she had difficulty at first in finding Summertrees. Major Markland was apparently a man who thought that his importance warranted omitting the name of the road from his address. But the second person she stopped to ask was a villager who was able to point the way, taking infinite trouble over the simple directions as if fearing that a perfunctory answer might have seemed discourteous. Cordelia had to find a suitable place to turn and then drive back a couple of miles, for she had already passed Summertrees.

And this, at last, must be the house. It was a large Victorian edifice of red brick, set well back, with a wide turfed verge between the open wooden gate leading to the drive and the road. Cordelia wondered why anyone should have wanted to build such an intimidatingly ugly house, or having decided to do so, should have set down a suburban monstrosity in the middle of the countryside. Perhaps it had replaced an earlier more agreeable house. She drove the Mini onto the grass but at some distance from the gate and made her way up the drive. The garden suited the house; it was formal to the point of artificiality and too well kept. Even the rock plants burgeoned like morbid excrescences at carefully planned intervals between the terrace paving stones. There were two rectangular beds in the lawn, each planted with red rose trees and edged with alternate bands of lobelia and alyssum. They looked like a patriotic display in a public park. Cordelia felt the lack of a flag pole.

The front door was open, giving a view of a dark, brown-painted hall. Before Cordelia could ring, an elderly woman came round the corner of the house trundling a wheelbarrow full of plants. Despite the heat, she was wearing Wellington boots, a jumper and long tweed skirt and had a scarf tied round her head. When she saw Cordelia she dropped the handle of the wheelbarrow and said:

"Oh, good morning. You've come from the church about the jumble, I expect?"

Cordelia said:

"No, not the jumble. I'm from Sir Ronald Callender. It's about his son."

"Then I expect you've called for his things? We wondered when Sir Ronald was going to send for them. They're all still at the cottage. We haven't

been down there since Mark died. We called him
Mark, you know. Well, he never told us who he
was which was rather naughty of him."

"It isn't about Mark's things. I want to talk about
Mark himself. Sir Ronald has engaged me to try
to find out why his son killed himself. My name is
Cordelia Gray."

This news seemed to puzzle rather than disconcert Mrs. Markland. She blinked at Cordelia
rapidly through troubled, rather stupid, eyes and
clutched at the wheelbarrow handle as if for support.

"Cordelia Gray? Then we haven't met before,
have we? I don't think I know a Cordelia Gray.
Perhaps it would be better if you came into the
drawing room and talked to my husband and
sister-in-law."

She abandoned the barrow where it stood in
the middle of the path and led the way into the
house, pulling off her head scarf and making ineffective pats at her hair. Cordelia followed her
through the sparsely furnished hall, smelling of
floor polish, with its clutter of walking sticks, um-
brellas and mackintoshes draping the heavy oak
hat stand, and into a room at the back of the
house.

It was a horrible room, ill-proportioned, book-
less, furnished not in poor taste but in no taste at
all. A huge sofa of repellent design and two armchairs surrounded the fireplace and a heavy mahogany table, ornately carved and lurching on its
pedestal, occupied the centre of the room. There

was little other furniture. The only pictures were framed groups, pale oblong faces too small to identify posed in straight innominate lines in front of the camera. One was a regimental photograph; the other had a pair of crossed oars above two rows of burly adolescents, all of whom were wearing low peaked caps and striped blazers. Cordelia supposed it to be a school boating club.

Despite the warmth of the day, the room was sunless and cold. The doors of the french windows were open. On the lawn outside were grouped a large swinging sofa with a fringed canopy, three cane chairs sumptuously cushioned in a garish blue cretonne, each with its footrest, and a wooden slatted table. They looked part of a setting for a play in which the designer had somehow failed to catch the mood. All the garden furniture looked new and unused. Cordelia wondered why the family should bother to sit indoors on a summer morning while the lawn was so much more comfortably furnished.

Mrs. Markland introduced Cordelia by sweeping her arm in a wide gesture of abandonment and saying feebly to the company in general:

"Miss Cordelia Gray. It isn't about the Church jumble."

Cordelia was struck by the resemblance that husband and wife and Miss Markland bore to each other. All three reminded her of horses. They had long, bony faces, narrow mouths above strong, square chins, eyes set unattractively close, and grey, coarse-looking hair which the two women wore in thick fringes almost to the eyes. Major Markland was drinking coffee from an immense white cup, much stained about the rim and sides, which had been set on a round tin tray. He held *The Times* in his hands. Miss Markland was knitting, an occupation which Cordelia vaguely felt was inappropriate to a hot summer morning.

The two faces, unwelcoming, only partly curious, regarded her with faint distaste. Miss Markland could knit without looking at the needles, an accomplishment which enabled her to fix Cordelia with sharp, inquisitive eyes. Invited by Major Markland to sit, Cordelia perched on the edge of the sofa, half expecting the smooth cushion to let out a rude noise as it subsided beneath her. She found it, however, unexpectedly hard. She composed her face into the appropriate expression— seriousness combined with efficiency and a touch of propitiatory humility seemed about right, but she wasn't sure that she managed to bring it off. As she sat there, knees demurely together, her shoulder bag at her feet, she was unhappily aware that she probably looked more like an eager seventeen-year-old facing her first interview than a mature business woman, sole proprietor of Pryde's Detective Agency.

She handed over Sir Ronald's note of authority and said:

"Sir Ronald was very distressed on your account, I mean it was awful for you that it should happen on your property when you'd been so kind in finding Mark a job he liked. His father hopes you won't mind talking about it; it's just that he wants to know what made his son kill himself."

"And he sent you?" Miss Markland's voice was a compound of disbelief, amusement and contempt. Cordelia didn't resent the rudeness. She felt Miss Markland had a point. She gave what she hoped was a credible explanation. It was probably true.

"Sir Ronald thinks that it must have been something to do with Mark's life at university. He left college suddenly, as you may know, and his father was never told why. Sir Ronald thought that I might be more successful in talking to Mark's friends than the more usual type of private detective. He didn't feel that he could trouble the police; after all, this sort of enquiry isn't really their kind of job."

Miss Markland said grimly:

"I should have thought it was precisely their job; that is, if Sir Ronald thinks there's something odd about his son's death . . ."

Cordelia broke in:

"Oh no, I don't think there's any suggestion of that! He's quite satisfied with the verdict. It's just that he badly wants to know what made him do it."

Miss Markland said with sudden fierceness:

"He was a drop-out. He dropped out of university, apparently he dropped out of his family obligations, finally he dropped out of life. Literally."

Her sister-in-law gave a little bleat of protest.

"Oh, Eleanor, is that quite fair? He worked really well here. I liked the boy. I don't think—"

"I don't deny that he earned his money. That doesn't alter the fact that he was neither bred nor educated to be a jobbing gardener. He was, therefore, a drop-out. I don't know the reason and I have no interest in discovering it."

"How did you come to employ him?" asked Cordelia.

It was Major Markland who answered.

"He saw my advertisement in the *Cambridge Evening News* for a gardener and turned up here one evening on his bicycle. I suppose he cycled all the way from Cambridge. It must have been about five weeks ago, a Tuesday I think."

Again Miss Markland broke in:

"It was Tuesday, May 9th."

The Major frowned at her as if irritated that he couldn't fault the information.

"Yes, well, Tuesday the 9th. He said that he had decided to leave university and take a job and that he'd seen my advertisement. He admitted that he didn't know much about gardening but said that he was strong and was willing to learn. His inexperience didn't worry me; we wanted him mostly for the lawns and for the vegetables. He never touched the flower garden; my wife and I see to that ourselves. Anyway, I quite liked the look of the boy and I thought I'd give him a chance."

Miss Markland said:

"You took him because he was the only applicant who was prepared to work for the miserable pittance you were offering." The Major, so far from showing offence at this frankness, smiled complacently.

"I paid him what he was worth. If more employers were prepared to do that, the country wouldn't be plagued with this inflation." He spoke as one to whom economics were an open book.

"Didn't you think it was odd, his turning up like that?" asked Cordelia.

"Of course I did, damned odd! I thought he had probably been sent down; drinks, drugs, revolution, you know the sort of things they get up to at Cambridge now. But I asked him for the name of his tutor as a referee and rang him, a fellow called Horsfall. He wasn't particularly forthcoming but he did assure me that the boy had left voluntarily and to use his own words, his conduct while in college had been almost boringly irreproachable. I need not fear that the shades of Summertrees would be polluted."

Miss Markland turned her knitting and broke into her sister-in-law's little cry of "What can he have meant by that?" with the dry comment:

"A little more boredom of that kind would be welcome from the city of the plains."

"Did Mr. Horsfall tell you why Mark had left college?" asked Cordelia.

"I didn't enquire. That wasn't my business. I asked a plain question and I got a more or less plain answer, as plain as you can expect from those academic types. We certainly had no complaint about the lad while he was here. I speak as I find."

"When did he move into the cottage?" asked Cordelia.

"Immediately. That wasn't our idea, of course. We never advertised the job as residential. However, he'd obviously seen the cottage and taken a fancy to the place and he asked if we'd mind if he camped out there. It wasn't practicable for him to cycle in from Cambridge each day, we could quite see that, and as far as we knew there was no one in the village who could put him up. I can't say I was keen on the idea; the cottage needs a lot doing to it. Actually we have it in mind to apply for a conversion grant and then get rid of the place. It wouldn't do for a family in its present state but the lad seemed keen on roughing it there, so we agreed."

Cordelia said:

"So he must have inspected the cottage before he came for the job?"

"Inspected? Oh, I don't know. He probably snooped around to see what the property was like before he actually came to the door. I don't know that I blame him, I'd have done the same myself."

Mrs. Markland broke in:

"He was very keen on the cottage, very keen. I pointed out that there was no gas or electricity but he said that that wouldn't worry him; he'd buy a primus stove and manage with lamps. There's water laid on, of course, and the main part of the roof is really quite sound. At least I think it is. We don't go there you know. He seemed to settle in very happily. We never actually visited him, there was no need, but as far as I could see he was looking after himself perfectly well. Of course as my husband said, he was very inexperienced; there were one or two things we had to teach him, like coming up to the kitchen early every morning for the orders. But I liked the boy; he was always working hard when I was in the garden."

Cordelia said:

"I wonder if I might have a look at the cottage?"

The request disconcerted them. Major Markland looked at his wife. There was an embarrassed silence and for a moment Cordelia feared that the answer would be no. Then Miss Markland stabbed her needles into the ball of wool and got to her feet:

"I'll come with you now," she said.

The grounds of Summertrees were spacious. First there was the formal rose garden, the bushes closely planted and grouped according to variety and colour like a market garden, the name tags fixed at precisely the same height from the earth. Next was the kitchen garden cut in two by a gravel path with evidence of Mark Callender's work in the weeded rows of lettuce and cabbages, the patches of dug earth. Finally they passed through a gate into a small orchard of old and unpruned apple trees. The scythed grass, smelling richly of hay, lay in thick swathes round the gnarled trunks.

At the furthest end of the orchard was a thick hedge, so overgrown that the wicket gate into the rear garden of the cottage was at first difficult to see. But the grass around it had been trimmed and the gate opened easily to Miss Markland's hand. On the other side was a thick bramble hedge, dark and impenetrable and obviously allowed to grow wild for a generation. Someone had hacked a way through, but Miss Markland and Cordelia had to bend low to avoid catching their hair on its tangled tentacles of thorn.

Once free of this barrier, Cordelia lifted her head and blinked in the bright sunshine. She gave a little exclamation of pleasure. In the short time in which he had lived here Mark Callender had created a little oasis of order and beauty out of chaos and neglect. Old flower beds had been discovered and the surviving plants tended; the stone path had been scraped free of grass and moss; a minute square of lawn to the right of the cottage door had been cut and weeded. On the other side of the path a patch about twelve feet square had been partly dug. The fork was still in the earth, driven deep about two feet from the end of the row.

The cottage was a low, brick building under a slate roof. Bathed in the afternoon sunshine, and despite its bare, rain-scoured door, its rotted window frames and the glimpse of exposed beams in the roof, it had the gentle melancholy charm of

age which hadn't yet degenerated into decay.
Just outside the cottage door, dropped casually
side by side, was a pair of heavy gardening shoes
encrusted with earth.

"His?" asked Cordelia.

"Who else's?"

They stood together for a moment contemplating the dug earth. Neither spoke. Then they
moved to the back door. Miss Markland fitted the
key into the lock. It turned easily as if the lock
had been recently oiled. Cordelia followed her
into the sitting-room of the cottage.

The air was cool after the heat of the garden
but unfresh, with a taint of contagion. Cordelia
saw that the plan of the cottage was simple.
There were three doors; one straight ahead obviously led to the front garden but was locked and
barred, the joints hung with cobwebs as if it hadn't
been opened for generations. One to the right
led, as Cordelia guessed, to the kitchen. The third
door was ajar and she could glimpse through it
an uncarpeted wooden stairway leading to the
first floor. In the middle of the room was a wooden-
topped table, the surface scarred with much
scrubbing, and with two kitchen chairs, one at
each end. In the middle of the table a blue ribbed
mug held a posy of dead flowers, black brittle
stems bearing sad tatters of unidentifiable plants,
their pollen staining the surface of the table like
golden dust. Shafts of sunlight cut across the still
air; in their beams a myriad of motes, specks of
dust and infinitesimal life danced grotesquely.

To the right was a fireplace, an old-fashioned iron range with ovens each side of the open fire. Mark had been burning wood and papers; there was a mound of white ash in the grate and a pile of kindling wood and small logs placed ready for the next cool evening. On one side of the fire was a low wooden slatted chair with a faded cushion and on the other a wheel-backed chair with the legs sawn off, perhaps to make it low enough for nursing a child. Cordelia thought that it must have been a beautiful chair before its mutilation.

Two immense beams, blackened with age, ran across the ceiling. In the middle of one was fixed a steel hook, probably once used for hanging bacon. Cordelia and Miss Markland looked at it without speaking; there was no need for question and answer. After a moment they moved, as if by common consent, to the two fireside chairs and sat down. Miss Markland said:

"I was the one who found him. He didn't come up to the kitchen for the day's orders so after breakfast I walked down here to see if he had overslept. It was nine twenty-three exactly. The door was unlocked. I knocked, but there was no reply so I pushed it open. He was hanging from that hook with a leather belt round his neck. He was wearing his blue cotton trousers, the ones he usually worked in, and his feet were bare. That chair was lying on its side on the floor. I touched his chest. He was quite cold."

"Did you cut him down?"

"No. He was obviously dead and I thought it better to leave the body until the police arrived. But I did pick up the chair and place it so that it supported his feet. That was an irrational action, I know, but I couldn't bear to see him hanging there without releasing the pressure on his throat. It was, as I've said, irrational."

"I think it was very natural. Did you notice anything else about him, about the room?"

"There was a half-empty mug of what looked like coffee on the table and a great deal of ash in the grate. It looked as if he had been burning papers. His portable typewriter was where you see it now, on that side table; the suicide note was still in the machine. I read it, then I went back to the house, told my brother and sister-in-law what had happened and rang the police. After the police arrived I brought them to this cottage, and confirmed what I had seen. I never came in here again until this moment."

"Did you, or Major and Mrs. Markland, see Mark on the night he died?"

"None of us saw him after he stopped work at about six-thirty. He was a little later that evening because he wanted to finish mowing the front lawn. We all saw him putting the mower away, then walking across the garden towards the orchard. We never saw him alive again. No one was at home at Summertrees that night. We had a dinner party at Trumpington—an old army colleague of my brother. We didn't get home until after midnight. By then, according to the medical evidence, Mark must have been dead about four hours."

Cordelia said:

"Please tell me about him."

"What is there to tell? His official hours were eight-thirty to six o'clock, with an hour for lunch and half an hour for tea. In the evenings he would work in the garden here or round the cottage. Sometimes in his lunch hour he would cycle to the village store. I used to meet him there from time to time. He didn't buy much—a loaf of wholemeal bread, butter, the cheapest cut of bacon, tea, coffee—the usual things. I heard him ask about free-range eggs and Mrs. Morgan told him that Wilcox at Grange Farm would always sell him half a dozen. We didn't speak when we met, but he would smile. In the evenings once the light had faded, he used to read or type at that table. I could see his head against the lamplight."

"I thought Major Markland said that you didn't visit the cottage?"

"They don't; it holds certain embarrassing memories for them. I do." She paused and looked into the dead fire.

"My fiancé and I used to spend a great deal of time here before the war when he was at Cambridge. He was killed in 1937, fighting in Spain for the Republican cause."

"I'm sorry," said Cordelia. She felt the inadequacy, the insincerity of her response and yet, what else was there to say? It had all happened nearly forty years ago. She hadn't heard of him before. The spasm of grief, so brief that it was hardly felt, was no more than a transitory inconvenience, a sentimental regret for all lovers who died young, for the inevitability of human loss.

Miss Markland spoke with sudden passion as if the words were being forced out of her:

"I don't like your generation, Miss Gray. I don't like your arrogance, your selfishness, your violence, the curious selectivity of your compassion. You pay for nothing with your own coin, not even for your ideals. You denigrate and destroy and never build. You invite punishment like rebellious children, then scream when you are punished. The men I knew, the men I was brought up with, were not like that."

Cordelia said gently:

"I don't think Mark Callender was like that either."

"Perhaps not. At least the violence he practiced was on himself." She looked up at Cordelia searchingly.

"No doubt you'll say I'm jealous of youth. It's a common enough syndrome of my generation."

"It ought not to be. I can never see why people should be jealous. After all, youth isn't a matter of privilege, we all get the same share of it. Some people may be born at an easier time or be richer or more privileged than others, but that hasn't anything to do with being young. And being young is terrible sometimes. Don't you remember how terrible it could be?"

"Yes, I remember. But I remember other things too."

Cordelia sat in silence, thinking that the conversation was strange but somehow inevitable and that, for some reason, she didn't resent it. Miss Markland looked up.

"His girl friend visited him once. At least, I suppose she was his girl friend or why should she have come? It was about three days after he started work."

"What was she like?"

"Beautiful. Very fair, with a face like a Botticelli angel—smooth, oval, unintelligent. She was foreign, French, I think. She was also rich."

"How could you tell that, Miss Markland?" Cordelia was intrigued.

"Because she spoke with a foreign accent; because she arrived driving a white Renault which I took to be her own car; because her clothes, although odd and unsuitable for the country, weren't cheap; because she walked up to the front door and announced that she wanted to see him with the confident arrogance that one associates with the rich."

"And did he see her?"

"He was working in the orchard at the time, scything the grass. I took her down to him. He greeted her calmly and without embarrassment and took her to sit in the cottage garden until it was time for him to stop work. He seemed pleased enough to see her but not, I thought, either delighted or surprised. He didn't introduce her. I left them together and returned to the house before he had the chance to. I didn't see her again."

Before Cordelia could speak she said suddenly:

"You're thinking of living here for a time, aren't you?"

"Will they mind? I didn't like to ask in case they said no."

"They won't know, and if they did, they wouldn't care."

"But do you mind?"

"No. I shan't worry you and I don't mind." They were talking in whispers as if in church. Then Miss Markland got up and moved to the door. She turned.

"You've taken on this job for the money, of course. Why not? But if I were you I'd keep it that way. It's unwise to become too personally involved with another human being. When that human being is dead, it can be dangerous as well as unwise."

Miss Markland stumped off down the garden path and disappeared through the wicket gate. Cordelia was glad to see her go. She was fidgeting with impatience to examine the cottage. This was where it had happened; this was where her job really began.

What was it that the Super had said? "When you're examining a building look at it as you would a country church. Walk round it first. Look at the whole scene inside and out; then make your deductions. Ask yourself what you saw, not what you expected to see or what you hoped to see, but what you saw."

He must be a man then who liked country churches and that at least was a point in his favour; for this, surely, was genuine Dalgliesh dogma. Bernie's reaction to churches, whether country or town, had been one of half-superstitious wariness. Cordelia decided to follow the advice.

She made her way first to the east side of the cottage. Here, discreetly set back and almost smothered by the hedge, was a wooden privy with its latched stable-like door. Cordelia peeped inside. The privy was very clean and looked as if it had been recently repainted. When she pulled the chain, to her relief, the bowl flushed. There was a roll of lavatory paper hanging by a string from the door and nailed beside it a small plastic bag containing a crumpled collection of orange papers and other soft wrappings. He had been an economical young man. Next to the privy was a large dilapidated shed containing a man's bicycle, old but well cared for, a large tin of white emulsion paint with the lid rammed down hard and a clean brush upended in a jam jar beside it, a tin bath, a few clean sacks, and a collection of gardening tools. All were shining clean and were neatly disposed against the wall or supported on nails.

She moved to the front of the cottage. This was in marked contrast to the southern aspect. Here Mark Callender had made no attempt to tackle the waist-high wilderness of nettles and grass which stifled the small front garden and almost obliterated the path. A thick climbing shrub sprinkled with small white flowers had thrust its black and thorned boughs to bar the two ground floor windows. The gate leading to the lane had stuck and would open only wide enough for a visitor to squeeze through. On each side a holly tree stood sentinel, its leaves grey with dust. The front hedge of privet was head-high. Cordelia could see that on either side of the path there had once been twin flower beds edged with large round stones which had been painted white. Now most of the stones had sunk out of sight among the encroaching weeds and nothing remained of the beds but a tangle of wild and straggling roses.

As she took a last look at the front garden, her eye caught a flash of colour half trodden among the weeds at the side of the path. It was a crumpled page of an illustrated magazine. She smoothed it open and saw that it was a colour photograph of a female nude. The woman had her back to the camera and was bending forward, gross buttocks splayed above booted thighs. She was smiling saucily over her shoulder in a blatant invitation made more grotesque by the long androgynous face which even tactful lighting couldn't make other than repellent. Cordelia noted the date at the top of the page; it was the May edition. So the magazine, or at least the picture, could have been brought to the cottage while he was there.

She stood with it in her hand trying to analyse the nature of her disgust which seemed to her excessive. The picture was vulgar and salacious but no more offensive or indecent than dozens on view in the side streets of London. But as she folded it away in her bag—for it was evidence of a kind—she felt contaminated and depressed. Had Miss Markland been more percipient than she knew? Was she, Cordelia, in danger of becoming sentimentally obsessed with the dead boy? The picture probably had nothing to do with Mark; it could easily have been dropped by some visitor to the cottage. But she wished that she hadn't seen it.

She passed round to the west of the cottage and made one more discovery. Hidden behind a clump of elder bushes was a small well about four feet in diameter. It had no superstructure but was closely fitted with a domed lid made of strong slatted wood and fitted at the top with an iron hoop. Cordelia saw that the cover was padlocked to the wooden rim of the well and the lock, although rusty with age, held firm at her tug. Someone had taken the trouble to see that there was no danger here to exploring children or visiting tramps.

And now it was time to explore the interior of the cottage. First the kitchen. It was a small room with a window over the sink looking east. It had obviously been recently painted and the large table which took up most of the room had been covered with a red plastic cloth. There was a poky larder containing half a dozen tins of beer, a jar of marmalade, a crock of butter and the mouldy heel of a loaf. It was here in the kitchen that Cordelia found the explanation of the disagreeable smell which had struck her on entering the cottage. On the table was an open bottle of milk about half full, the silver top crumpled beside it. The milk was solid and furred with putrefaction; a bloated fly was sucking at the rim of the bottle and still stuck to its feast as, instinctively, she tried to flick it away. On the other side of the table was a twin-burner paraffin stove with a heavy pot on one burner. Cordelia tugged at the close-fitting lid and it came off suddenly, letting out a rich repulsive smell. She opened the table drawer and stirred the mess with a spoon. It looked like beef stew. Chunks of greenish meat, soapy looking potatoes and unidentifiable vegetables floated up through the scum like drowned and putrefying flesh. Beside the sink was an orange box placed on one side and used as a vegetable store. The potatoes were green, the onions had shrunk and sprouted, the carrots were wrinkled and limp. So nothing had been cleaned up, nothing had been removed. The police had taken away the body and any evidence they required but no one; neither the Marklands nor the boy's family or friends, had bothered to come back to clean up the pathetic leavings of his young life.

Cordelia went upstairs. A cramped landing led to two bedrooms, one obviously unused for years. Here the window frame had rotted, the ceiling plaster had crumbled and a faded paper patterned with roses was peeling away with the damp. The second and larger room was the one in which he had slept. There was a single iron bed with a hair mattress and on it a sleeping bag and a bolster folded in two to make a high pillow. Beside the bed was an old table with two candles, stuck with their own wax to a cracked plate, and a box of matches. His clothes were hung in the single cupboard; a pair of bright-green corduroy trousers, one or two shirts, pullovers and one formal suit. A few underclothes, clean but not ironed, were folded on the ledge above. Cordelia fingered the pullovers. They were hand knitted in thick wool and intricate patterns and there were four of them. Someone, then, had cared enough about him to take some trouble on his behalf. She wondered who.

She ran her hands over his meagre wardrobe, feeling for pockets. She found nothing except a slim, brown leather wallet in the bottom left-hand pocket of his suit. Excitedly she carried it over to the window hoping that it might contain a clue—a letter, perhaps, a list of names and addresses, a personal note. But the wallet was empty except for a couple of pound notes, his driving licence and a blood donor's card issued by the Cambridge blood transfusion service, which showed his group as B rhesus negative.

The uncurtained window gave a view of the garden. His books were arranged on the window shelf. There were only a few of them: several volumes of the *Cambridge Modern History;* some Trollope and Hardy; a complete William Blake; school text book volumes of Wordsworth, Browning and Donne; two paperbacks on gardening. At the end of the row was a white leather-bound book which Cordelia saw was the Book of Common Prayer. It was fitted with a finely wrought brass clasp and looked much used. She was disappointed in the books; they told her little beyond his superficial tastes. If he had come to this solitary life to study, to write or to philosophize he had come singularly ill-equipped.

The most interesting thing in the room was above the bed. It was a small oil painting about nine inches square. Cordelia studied it. It was certainly Italian and probably, she thought, late fifteenth century. It showed a very young tonsured monk reading at a table, his sensitive fingers enleafed between the pages of his book. The long, controlled face was taut with concentration, the heavy lidded eyes were fixed on the page. Behind him, a view from the open window was a miniature of delight. Cordelia thought that one would never tire of looking at it. It was a Tuscan scene showing a walled city with towers enclosed by cypresses, a river winding like a silver stream, a gaudily clad procession preceded by banners, yoked oxen working in the fields. She saw the picture as a contrast between the worlds of intellect and action and tried to remember where she had seen similar paintings. The comrades—as Cordelia always thought of that ubiquitous band of fellow-revolutionaries who attached themselves to her father—had been very fond of exchanging messages in art galleries and Cordelia had spent hours walking slowly from picture to picture, waiting for the casual visitor to pause beside her and whisper his few words of warning or information. The device had always struck her as a childish and unnecessarily histrionic way of communicating, but at least the galleries were warm and she had enjoyed looking at the pictures. She enjoyed this picture; he had obviously liked it too. Had he also liked that vulgar illustration which she had found in the front garden? Were they both an essential part of his nature?

The tour of inspection over, she made herself coffee using a packet from his store cupboard and boiling the water on the stove. She took a chair from the sitting-room and sat outside the back door with the mug of coffee in her lap, her head stretched back to feel the sun. She was filled with a gentle happiness as she sat there, contented and relaxed, listening to the silence, her half-closed lids impressed with the visage of the sun. But now it was the time to think. She had examined the cottage in accordance with the Super's instructions. What did she now know about the dead boy? What had she seen? What could she deduce?

He had been almost obsessively neat and tidy. His garden tools were wiped after use and carefully put away, his kitchen had been painted and was clean and ordered. Yet he had abandoned his digging less than two feet from the end of a row; had left the uncleaned fork in the earth; had dropped his gardening shoes casually at the back door. He had apparently burnt all his papers before killing himself, yet had left his coffee mug unwashed. He had made himself a stew for his supper which he hadn't touched. The preparation of the vegetables must have been done earlier in the same day, or perhaps the day before, but the stew was clearly intended for supper that night. The pot was still on the stove and was full to the brim. This wasn't a heated-up meal, one left from the evening before. This surely meant that he had only made the decision to kill himself after the stew had been prepared and had been put on the stove to cook. Why should he trouble to prepare a meal that he knew he wouldn't be alive to eat?

But was it likely, she wondered, that a healthy young man coming in from an hour or two of hard digging and with a hot meal waiting should be in that mood of boredom, accidie, anguish or despair which could lead to suicide? Cordelia could remember times of intense unhappiness, but she couldn't recall that they had followed purposeful outdoor exercise in the sun with a meal in prospect. And why the mug of coffee, the one which the police had taken away to analyse? There were tins of beer in the larder; if he had come in thirsty from his digging, why not open one of those? Beer would have been the quickest, the obvious way of quenching thirst. Surely no one, however thirsty, would brew and drink coffee just before a meal. Coffee came after the food.

But suppose someone had visited him that evening. It wasn't likely to have been someone calling with a casual message as he passed by; it was important enough for Mark to break off his digging even within two feet of the end of a row and invite the visitor into the cottage. It was probably a visitor who didn't like or drink beer—could that mean a woman? It was a visitor who wasn't expected to stay for supper but yet was at the cottage long enough to be offered some refreshment. Perhaps it was someone on his way to his own evening meal. Obviously, the visitor hadn't been invited to supper earlier or why would the two of them have begun the meal by drinking coffee and why would Mark have worked so late in the garden instead of coming in to change? So it was an unexpected visitor. But why was there only one mug of coffee? Surely Mark would have shared it with his guest or, if he preferred not to drink coffee, would have opened a tin of beer for himself. But there was no empty beer can in the kitchen and no second mug. Had it perhaps been washed and put away? But why should Mark wash one mug and not the other? Was it to conceal the fact that he'd had a visitor that evening?

The jug of coffee on the kitchen table was almost empty and the bottle of milk only half full. Surely more than one person had taken milk and coffee. But perhaps that was a dangerous and unwarranted deduction; the visitor might well have had his mug refilled.

But suppose it wasn't Mark who had wished to conceal the fact that a visitor had called that night; suppose it wasn't Mark who had washed and put away the second mug; suppose it was the visitor who had wished to conceal the fact of his presence. But why should he bother to do that since he couldn't know that Mark was going to kill himself? Cordelia shook herself impatiently. This, of course, was nonsense. Obviously the visitor wouldn't have washed up the mug if Mark were still there and alive. He would only have obliterated the evidence of his visit if Mark were already dead. And if Mark had been dead, had been strung up on that hook before his visitor left the cottage, then could this really be suicide? A word dancing at the back of Cordelia's mind, an amorphous half-formed jangle of letters, came suddenly into focus and, for the first time, spelt out clearly the blood-stained word. Murder.

Cordelia sat on in the sun for another five minutes finishing her coffee, then she washed up the mug and hung it back on a hook in the larder. She walked down the lane to the road to where the Mini was still parked on the grass verge outside Summertrees, glad of the instinct that had led her to leave it out of sight of the house. Letting in the clutch gently, she drove it slowly down the lane looking carefully from side to side for a possible parking place; to leave it outside the cottage would only advertise her presence. It was a pity that Cambridge wasn't closer; she could then have used Mark's bicycle. The Mini was necessary to her task but would be inconveniently conspicuous wherever she left it.

But she was lucky. About fifty yards down the lane was the entrance to a field, a wide grass verge with a small copse at one side. The copse looked damp and sinister. It was impossible to believe that flowers could spring from this tainted earth or bloom among these scarred and misshapen trees. The ground was scattered with old pots and pans, the upended skeleton of a pram, a battered and rusty gas stove. Beside a stunted oak a matted heap of blankets were disintegrating into the earth. But there was space for her to drive the Mini off the road and under cover of a kind. If she locked it carefully it would be better here than outside the cottage and at night, she thought, it would be unobserved.

But now, she drove it back to the cottage and began to unpack. She moved Mark's few underclothes to one side of the shelf and set her own beside them. She laid her sleeping bag on the bed over his, thinking that she would be glad of the extra comfort. There was a red toothbrush and half-used tube of toothpaste in a jamjar on the kitchen window ledge; she placed her yellow brush and her own tube beside them. She hung her towel next to his across the cord which he had fixed between two nails under the kitchen sink. Then she made an inventory of the contents of the larder and a list of the things she would need. It would be better to buy them in Cambridge; she would only draw attention to her presence if she shopped locally. The saucepan of stew and the half bottle of milk were a worry. She couldn't leave them in the kitchen to sour the cottage with the stench of decay but she was reluctant to throw the contents away. She considered whether to photograph them but decided against it; tangible objects were better evidence. In the end she carried them out to the shed and shrouded them thickly with a piece of old sacking.

Last of all, she thought about the gun. It was a heavy object to carry with her all the time but she felt unhappy about parting with it, even temporarily. Although the back door of the cottage could be locked and Miss Markland had left her the key, an intruder would have no difficulty in breaking-in through a window. She decided that the best plan would be to secrete the ammunition among her underclothes in the bedroom cupboard but to hide the pistol itself separately in or near the cottage. The exact place cost her a little thought, but then she remembered the thick and twisting limbs of the elder bush by the well; by reaching high, she was able to feel for a convenient hollow near the fork of a branch and could slip the gun, still shrouded in its draw-string bag, among the concealing leaves.

At last she was ready to leave for Cambridge. She looked at her watch; it was half-past ten; she could be in Cambridge by eleven and there would still be two hours of the morning to go. She decided that her best plan would be to visit the newspaper office first and read the account of the inquest, then to see the police; after that she would go in search of Hugo and Sophie Tilling.

She drove away from the cottage with a feeling very like regret, as if she were leaving home. It was, she thought, a curious place, heavy with atmosphere and showing two distinct faces to the world like facets of a human personality; the north, with its dead thorn-barred windows, its encroaching weeds, and its forbidding hedge of privet, was a numinous stage for horror and tragedy. Yet the rear, where he had lived and worked, had cleared and dug the garden and tied up the few flowers, had weeded the path, and opened the windows to the sun, was as peaceful as a sanctuary. Sitting there at the door she had felt that nothing horrible could ever touch her; she was able to contemplate the night there alone without fear. Was it this atmosphere of healing tranquillity, she wondered, that had attracted Mark Callender? Had he sensed it before he took the job, or was it in some mysterious way the result of his transitory and doomed sojourn there? Major Markland had been right; obviously Mark had looked at the cottage before he went up to the house. Had it been the cottage he wanted or the job? Why were the Marklands so reluctant to come to the place, so reluctant that they obviously hadn't visited it even to clean up after his death? And why had Miss Markland spied on him, for surely such close observation was very close to spying? Had she only confided that story about her dead lover to justify her interest in the cottage, her obsessional preoccupation with what the new gardener was doing? And was the story even true? That ageing body heavy with latent strength, that equine expression of perpetual discontent, could she really once have been young, have lain perhaps with her lover on Mark's bed through the long, warm evenings of long-dead summers? How remote, how impossible and grotesque it all seemed.

Cordelia drove down Hills Road, past the vigorous memorial statue of a young 1914 soldier striding to death, past the Roman Catholic church and into the centre of the city. Again she wished that she could have abandoned the car in favour of Mark's bicycle. Everyone else seemed to be riding one and the air tinkled with bells like a festival. In these narrow and crowded streets even the compact Mini was a liability. She decided to park it as soon as she could find a place and set out on foot in search of a telephone. She had decided to vary her programme and see the police first.

But it didn't surprise her when at last she rang the police station to hear that Sergeant Maskell, who had dealt with the Callender case, was tied up all the morning. It was only in fiction that the people one wanted to interview were sitting ready at or in their office, with time, energy and interest to spare. In real life, they were about their own business and one waited on their convenience, even if, untypically, they welcomed the attention of Pryde's Detective Agency. Usually they didn't. She hardly expected Sergeant Maskell to welcome it. She mentioned Sir Ronald's note of authority to impress her hearer with the authenticity of her business. The name was not without influence. He went away to enquire. After less than a minute he came back to say that Sergeant Maskell could see Miss Gray at two-thirty that afternoon.

So the newspaper office came first after all. Old files were at least accessible and could not object to being consulted. She quickly found what she wanted. The account of the inquest was brief, couched in the usual formal language of a court report. It told her little that was new, but she made a careful note of the main evidence. Sir Ronald Callender testified that he hadn't spoken to his son for over a fortnight before his death, when Mark had telephoned to tell his father of his decision to leave college and take a job at Summertrees. He hadn't consulted Sir Ronald before making this decision nor had he explained his reasons. Sir Ronald had subsequently spoken to the Master, and the College authorities were prepared to take his son back for the next academic year if he changed his mind. His son had never spoken to him of suicide and had no health or money worries as far as he was aware. Sir Ronald's testimony was followed

by a brief reference to other evidence. Miss Markland described how she had found the body; a
forensic pathologist testified that the cause of
death was asphyxia due to strangulation; Sergeant Maskell recounted the measures he had
thought it proper to take and a report from the
forensic science laboratory was submitted which
stated that a mug of coffee found on the table
had been analysed and found harmless. The verdict was that the deceased died by his own hand
while the balance of his mind was disturbed.
Closing the heavy file, Cordelia felt depressed. It
looked as if the police work had been thorough.
Was it really possible that these experienced professionals had overlooked the significance of the
unfinished digging, the gardening shoes dropped
casually at the back door, the untouched supper?

And now, at mid-day, she was free until
half-past two. She could explore Cambridge. She
bought the cheapest guide book she could find
from Bowes and Bowes, resisting the temptation
to browse among the books, since time was short
and pleasure must be rationed. She stuffed her
shoulder bag with a pork pie and fruit bought
from a market stall and entered St. Mary's church
to sit quietly and work out her itinerary. Then for
an hour and a half she walked about the city and
its colleges in a trance of happiness.

She was seeing Cambridge at its loveliest. The
sky was an infinity of blue from whose pellucid
depths the sun shone in unclouded but gentle radiance. The trees in the college gardens and the

avenues leading to the Backs, as yet untouched by the heaviness of high summer, lifted their green tracery against stone and river and sky. Punts shot and curtsied under the bridges, scattering the gaudy water fowl, and by the rise of the new Garret Hostel bridge the willows trailed their pale, laden boughs in the darker green of the Cam.

She included all the special sights in her itinerary. She walked gravely down the length of Trinity Library, visited the Old Schools, sat quietly at the back of King's College Chapel marvelling at the upward surge of John Wastell's great vault spreading into curved fans of delicate white stone. The sunlight poured through the great windows staining the still air, blue, crimson and green. The finely carved Tudor roses, the heraldic beasts supporting the crown, stood out in arrogant pride from the panels. Despite what Milton and Wordsworth had written, surely this chapel had been built to the glory of an earthly sovereign, not to the service of God? But that didn't invalidate its purpose nor blemish its beauty. It was still a supremely religious building. Could a non-believer have planned and executed this superb interior? Was there an essential unity between motive and creation? This was the question which Carl alone among the comrades would have been interested to explore and she thought of him in his Greek prison, trying to shut her mind to what they might be doing to him and wishing his stocky figure at her side.

During her tour she indulged in small particular pleasures. She bought a linen tea cloth printed with a picture of the chapel from the stall near the west door; she lay on her face on the shorn grass above the river by Kings Bridge and let the cold green water eddy round her arms; she wandered among the book stalls in the market place and after careful reckoning bought a small edition of Keats printed on India paper and a cotton kaftan patterned in greens, blues and brown. If this hot weather continued it would be cooler than a shirt or jeans for wear in the evenings.

Finally, she returned to King's College. There was a seat set against the great stone wall which ran from the chapel down to the river bank and she sat there in the sun to eat her lunch. A privileged sparrow hopped across the immaculate lawn and cocked a bright insouciant eye. She threw him scraps from the crust of her pork pie and smiled at his agitated peckings. From the river floated the sound of voices calling across the water, the occasional scrunch of wood on wood, the harsh call of a duckling. Everything about her—the pebbles bright as jewels in the gravel path, the silver shafts of grass at the verge of the lawn, the sparrow's brittle legs— was seen with an extraordinary and individual intensity as if happiness had cleared her eyes.

Then memory recalled the voices. First her father's:

"Our little fascist was educated by the papists. It accounts for a lot. How on earth did it happen, Delia?"

"You remember, Daddy. They muddled me up with another C. Gray who was a Roman Catholic. We both passed the eleven plus exam the same year. When they discovered the mistake they wrote to you to ask if you minded my staying on at the Convent because I'd settled there."

He hadn't in fact replied. Reverend Mother had tried tactfully to conceal that he hadn't bothered to answer and Cordelia had stayed on at the Convent for the six most settled and happy years of her life, insulated by order and ceremony from the mess and muddle of life outside, incorrigibly Protestant, uncoerced, gently pitied as one in invincible ignorance. For the first time she learned that she needn't conceal her intelligence, that cleverness which a succession of foster mothers had somehow seen as a threat. Sister Perpetua had said:

"There shouldn't be any difficulty over your 'A' Levels if you go on as you are at present. That means that we can plan for university entrance in two years' time from this October. Cambridge, I think. We might as well try for Cambridge, and I really don't see why you shouldn't stand a chance of a scholarship."

Sister Perpetua had herself been at Cambridge before she entered the Convent and she still spoke of the academic life, not with longing or regret, but as if it had been a sacrifice worthy of her vocation. Even the fifteen-year-old Cordelia had recognized that Sister Perpetua was a real scholar and had thought it rather unfair of God to bestow a vocation on one who was so happy and useful as she was. But for Cordelia herself, the future had, for the first time, seemed settled and full of promise. She would go to Cambridge and Sister would visit her there. She had a romantic vision of wide lawns under the sun and the two of them walking in Donne's paradise: "Rivers of knowledge are there, arts and sciences flow from thence; gardens that are walled in; bottomless depths of unsearchable councils are there." By the aid of her own brain and Sister's prayers she would win her scholarship. The prayers occasionally worried her. She had absolutely no doubt of their efficacy since God must necessarily listen to one who at such personal cost had listened to Him. And if Sister's influence gave her an unfair advantage over the other candidates—well, that couldn't be helped. In a matter of such importance neither Cordelia nor Sister Perpetua had been disposed to fret over theological niceties.

But this time Daddy had replied to the letter. He had discovered a need for his daughter. There were no "A" Levels and no scholarship and at sixteen Cordelia finished her formal education and began her wandering life as cook, nurse, messenger and general camp follower to Daddy and the comrades.

But now by what devious routes and for what a strange purpose she had come at last to Cambridge. The city didn't disappoint her. In her wanderings she had seen lovelier places, but none in which she had been happier or more at peace. How indeed, she thought, could the heart be indifferent to such a city where stone and stained glass, water and green lawns, trees and flowers were arranged in such ordered beauty for the service of learning. But as regretfully she rose at last to go, brushing the few crumbs from her skirt, a quotation, untraced and unsought, came into her mind. She heard it with such clarity that the words might have been spoken by a human voice—a young masculine voice, unrecognized and yet mysteriously familiar: "Then saw I that there was a way to hell even from the gates of heaven."

The police headquarters building was modern and functional. It represented authority tempered with discretion; the public were to be impressed but not intimidated. Sergeant Maskell's office and the Sergeant himself conformed to this philosophy. He was surprisingly young and elegantly dressed, with a square, tough face wary with experience and a long but skilfully cut hair style which, Cordelia thought, could only just have satisfied the Force requirements, even for a plain clothes detective. He was punctiliously polite without being gallant and this reassured her. It wasn't going to be an easy interview, but she had no wish to be treated with the indulgence shown to a pretty but importunate child. Sometimes it helped to play the part of a vulnerable and naive young girl eager for information—this was a role in which Bernie had frequently sought to cast her—but she sensed that Sergeant Maskell would respond better to an unflirtatious competence. She wanted to appear efficient, but not too efficient. And her secrets must remain her own; she was here to get information, not to give it.

She stated her business concisely and showed him her note of authority from Sir Ronald. He handed it back to her, remarking without rancour:

"Sir Ronald said nothing to me to suggest that he was not satisfied with the verdict."

"I don't think that's in question. He doesn't suspect foul play. If he did, he would have come to you. I think he has a scientist's curiosity to know what made his son kill himself and he couldn't very well indulge that at public expense. I mean, Mark's private miseries aren't really your problem, are they?"

"They could be if the reasons for his death disclosed a criminal offence—blackmail, intimidation—but there was never any suggestion of that."

"Are you personally satisfied that he killed himself?"

The Sergeant looked at her with the sudden keen intelligence of a hunting dog on the scent.

"Why should you ask that, Miss Gray?"

"I suppose because of the trouble you took. I've interviewed Miss Markland and read the newspaper report of the inquest. You called in a forensic pathologist; you had the body photographed before it was cut down; you analysed the coffee left in his drinking mug."

"I treated the case as a suspicious death. That's my usual practice. This time the precautions proved unnecessary, but they might not have been."

Cordelia said:

"But something worried you, something didn't seem right?"

He said, as if reminiscing:

"Oh, it was straightforward enough to all appearances. Almost the usual story. We get more than our share of suicides. Here is a young man who gave up his university course for no apparent reason and went to live on his own in some discomfort. You get the picture of an introspective, rather solitary student, one who doesn't confide in his family or friends. Within three weeks after leaving college he's found dead. There's no sign of a struggle; no disturbance in the cottage; he leaves a suicide note conveniently in the typewriter, much the kind of suicide note you would expect. Admittedly, he took the trouble to destroy all the papers in the cottage and yet left the garden fork uncleaned and his work half-completed, and bothered to cook himself a supper which he didn't eat. But all that proves nothing. People do behave irrationally, particularly suicides. No, it wasn't any of those things which gave me a bit of worry; it was the knot."

Suddenly he bent down and rummaged in the left-hand drawer of his desk.

"Here," he said. "How would you use this to hang yourself, Miss Gray?"

The strap was about five feet long. It was a little over an inch wide and was made of strong but supple brown leather, darkened in places with age. One end was tapered and pierced with a row of metal-bound eye holes, the other was fitted with a strong brass buckle. Cordelia took it in her hands; Sergeant Maskell said:

"That was what he used. Obviously it's meant as a strap, but Miss Leaming testified that he used to wear it wound two or three times round his waist as a belt. Well, Miss Gray, how would you hang yourself?"

Cordelia ran the strap through her hands.

"First of all, of course, I'd slip the tapered end through the buckle to make a noose. Then, with the noose round my neck, I'd stand on a chair underneath the hook in the ceiling and draw the other end of the strap over the hook. I'd pull it up fairly tight and then make two half-hitches to hold it firm. I'd pull hard on the strap to make sure that the knot didn't slip and that the hook would hold. Then I'd kick away the chair."

The Sergeant opened the file in front of him and pushed it across the desk.

"Look at that," he said. "That's a picture of the knot."

The police photograph, stark in black and white, showed the knot with admirable clarity. It was a bowline on the end of a low loop and it hung about a foot from the hook.

Sergeant Maskell said:

"I doubt whether he would be able to tie that

knot with his hands above his head, no one could. So he must have made the noose first just as you did and then tied the bowline. But that can't be right either. There were only a few inches of strap between the buckle and the knot. If he'd done it that way, he wouldn't have had sufficient play on the strap to get his neck through the noose. There's only one way he could have done it. He made the noose first, pulled it until the strap fitted his neck like a collar and then tied the bowline. Then he got on the chair, placed the loop over the nail and kicked the chair away. Look, this will show you what I mean."

He turned over a new page of the file and suddenly thrust it towards her.

The photograph, uncompromising, unambiguous, a brutal surrealism in black and white, would have looked as artificial as a sick joke if the body were not so obviously dead. Cordelia felt her heart hammering against her chest. Beside this horror Bernie's death had been gentle. She bent her head low over the file so that her hair swung forward to shield her face and made herself study the pitiable thing in front of her.

The neck was elongated so that the bare feet, their toes pointed like a dancer's, hung less than a foot from the floor. The stomach muscles were taut. Above them the high rib cage looked as brittle as a bird's. The head lolled grotesquely on the right shoulder like a horrible caricature of a disjointed puppet. The eyes had rolled upwards under half-open lids. The swollen tongue had forced itself between the lips.

Cordelia said calmly:

"I see what you mean. There are barely four inches of strap between the neck and the knot. Where is the buckle?"

"At the back of the neck under the left ear. There's a photograph of the indentation it made in the flesh later in the file."

Cordelia did not look. Why, she wondered, had he shown her the photograph? It wasn't necessary to prove his argument. Had he hoped to shock her into a realization of what she was meddling in; to punish her for trespassing on his patch; to contrast the brutal reality of his professionalism with her amateurish meddling; to warn her perhaps? But against what? The police had no real suspicion of foul play; the case was closed. Had it, perhaps, been the casual malice, the incipient sadism of a man who couldn't resist the impulse to hurt or shock? Was he even aware of his own motives?

She said:

"I agree he could only have done it in the way you described, if he did it. But suppose someone else pulled the noose tight about his neck, then strung him up. He'd be heavy, a dead weight. Wouldn't it have been easier to make the knot first and then hoist him on to the chair?"

"Having first asked him to hand over his belt?"

"Why use a belt? The murderer could have

strangled him with a cord or a tie. Or that would have left a deeper and identifiable mark under the impression of the strap?"

"The pathologist looked for just such a mark. It wasn't there."

"There are other ways, though; a plastic bag, the thin kind they pack clothes in, dropped over his head and held tight against his face; a thin scarf; a woman's stocking."

"I can see you would be a resourceful murderess, Miss Gray. It's possible, but it would need a strong man and there would have to be an element of surprise. We found no sign of a struggle."

"But it could have been done that way?"

"Of course, but there was absolutely no evidence that it was."

"But if he were first drugged?"

"That possibility did occur to me; that's why I had the coffee analysed. But he wasn't drugged, the P.M. confirmed it."

"How much coffee had he drunk?"

"Only about half a mug, according to the P.M. report and he died immediately afterwards. Sometime between seven and nine p.m. was as close as the pathologist could estimate."

"Wasn't it odd that he drank coffee before his meal?"

"There's no law against it. We don't know when he intended to eat his supper. Anyway, you can't build a murder case on the order in which a man chooses to take his food and drink."

"What about the note he left? I suppose it isn't possible to raise prints from typewriter keys?"

"Not easily on that type of key. We tried but there was nothing identifiable."

"So in the end you accept that it was suicide?"

"In the end I accepted that there was no possibility of proving otherwise."

"But you had a hunch? My partner's old colleague—he's a Superintendent of the C.I.D.—always backed his hunches."

"Ah, well, that's the Met, they can afford to indulge themselves. If I backed all my hunches I'd get no work done; it isn't what you suspect, it's what you can prove that counts."

"May I take the suicide note and the strap?"

"Why not, if you sign for them? No one else seems to want them."

"Could I see the note now, please?"

He extracted it from the file and handed it to her. Cordelia began to read to herself the first half-remembered words:

a void, boundless as the nether sky
appeared beneath us . . .

She was struck, not for the first time, by the importance of the written word, the magic of ordered symbols. Would poetry hold its theurgy if the lines were printed as prose, or prose be so compelling without the pattern and stress of punctuation? Miss Leaming had spoken Blake's passage as if she recognized its beauty yet here, spaced on the page, it exerted an even stronger power.

It was then that two things about the quotation caught at her breath. The first was not something which she intended to share with Sergeant Maskell but there was no reason why she should not comment on the second.

She said:

"Mark Callender must have been an experienced typist. This was done by an expert."

"I didn't think so. If you look carefully you'll see that one or two of the letters are fainter than the rest. That's always the sign of an amateur."

"But the faint letters aren't always the same ones. It's usually the keys on the edges of the keyboard which the inexperienced typist hits more lightly. And the spacing here is good until nearly the end of the passage. It looks as if the typist suddenly realized that he ought to disguise his competence but hadn't time to retype the whole passage. And it's strange that the punctuation is so accurate."

"It was probably copied direct from the printed page. There was a copy of Blake in the boy's bedroom. The quotation is from Blake, you know, the Tyger Tyger burning bright poet."

"I know. But if he typed it from the book, why bother to return the Blake to his bedroom?"

"He was a tidy lad."

"But not tidy enough to wash up his coffee mug or clean his garden fork."

"That proves nothing. As I said, people do behave oddly when they're planning to kill themselves. We know that the typewriter was his and
that he'd had it for a year. But we couldn't compare the typing with his work. All his papers had
been burnt."

He glanced at his watch and got to his feet.
Cordelia saw that the interview was over. She
signed a chit for the suicide note and the leather
belt, then shook hands and thanked him formally
for his help. As he opened the door for her he
said, as if on impulse:

"There's one intriguing detail you may care to
know. It looks as if he was with a woman some
time during the day on which he died. The pathologist found the merest trace—a thin line
only—of purple-red lipstick on his upper lip."

Chapter Three

NEW HALL, with its Byzantine air, its sunken court and its shining domed hall like a peeled orange, reminded Cordelia of a harem; admittedly one owned by a sultan with liberal views and an odd predilection for clever girls, but a harem nonetheless. The college was surely too distractingly pretty to be conducive to serious study. She wasn't sure, either, whether she approved of the obtrusive femininity of its white brick, the mannered prettiness of the shallow pools where the goldfish slipped like blood-red shadows between the water lilies, its artfully planted saplings. She concentrated on her criticism of the building; it helped to prevent her being intimidated.

She hadn't called at the Lodge to ask for Miss Tilling, afraid that she might be asked her business or refused admission; it seemed prudent just to walk in and chance to luck. Luck was with her. After two fruitless enquiries for Sophie Tilling's room, a hurrying student called back at her:

"She doesn't live in college but she's sitting on the grass over there with her brother."

Cordelia walked out of the shadow of the court into bright sunlight and over turf as soft as moss towards the little group. There were four of them, stretched out on the warm-smelling grass. The two Tillings were unmistakably brother and sister. Cordelia's first thought was that they reminded her of a couple of pre-Raphaelite portraits with their strong dark heads held high on unusually long necks, and their straight noses above curved, foreshortened upper lips. Beside their bony distinction, the second girl was all softness. If this were the girl who had visited Mark at the cottage, Miss Markland was right to call her beautiful. She had an oval face with a neat slender nose, a small but beautifully formed mouth, and slanted eyes of a strikingly deep blue which gave her whole face an oriental appearance intriguingly at variance with the fairness of her skin and her long blonde hair. She was wearing an ankle-length dress of fine mauve patterned cotton, buttoned high at the waist but with no other fastening. The gathered bodice cupped her full breasts and the skirt fell open to reveal a pair of tight fitting shorts in the same material. As far as Cordelia could see, she wore nothing else. Her feet were bare and her long, shapely legs were untanned by the sun. Cordelia reflected that those white voluptuous thighs must be more erotic than a whole city of sunburnt limbs and that the girl knew it. Sophie Tilling's dark good looks were only a foil to this gentler, more entrancing beauty.

At first sight the fourth member of the party was more ordinary. He was a stocky, bearded young man with russet curly hair and a spade-shaped face. And was lying on the grass by the side of Sophie Tilling.

All of them, except the blonde girl, were wearing old jeans and open-necked cotton shirts.

Cordelia had come up to the group and had stood over them for a few seconds before they took any notice of her. She said:

"I'm looking for Hugo and Sophie Tilling. My name is Cordelia Gray." Hugo Tilling looked up:

"What shall Cordelia do, love and be silent."

Cordelia said:

"People who feel the need to joke about my name usually enquire after my sisters. It gets very boring."

"It must do. I'm sorry. I'm Hugo Tilling, this is my sister, this is Isabelle de Lasterie and this is Davie Stevens."

Davie Stevens sat up like a jack-in-the-box and said an amiable "Hi."

He looked at Cordelia with a quizzical intentness. She wondered about Davie. Her first impression of the little group, influenced perhaps by the college architecture, had been of a young sultan taking his ease with two of his favourites and attended by the captain of the guard. But, meeting Davie Stevens's steady intelligent gaze, that impression faded. She suspected that, in this seraglio, it was the captain of the guard who was the dominant personality.

Sophie Tilling nodded and said "Hullo."

Isabelle did not speak but a smile beautiful and meaningless spread over her face. Hugo said:

"Won't you sit down, Cordelia Gray, and explain the nature of your necessities?"

Cordelia knelt gingerly, wary of grass stains on the soft suede of her skirt. It was an odd way to interview suspects—only, of course, these people weren't suspects—kneeling like a suppliant in front of them. She said:

"I'm a private detective. Sir Ronald Callender has employed me to find out why his son died."

The effect of her words was astonishing. The little group, which had been lolling at ease like exhausted warriors, stiffened with instantaneous shock into a rigid tableau as if struck to marble. Then, almost imperceptibly, they relaxed. Cordelia could hear the slow release of held breath. She watched their faces. Davie Stevens was the least concerned. He wore a half-rueful smile, interested but unworried, and gave a quick look at Sophie as if in complicity. The look was not returned; she and Hugo were staring rigidly ahead. Cordelia felt that the two Tillings were carefully avoiding each other's eyes. But it was

Isabelle who was the most shaken. She gave a gasp and her hand flew to her face like a second-rate actress simulating shock. Her eyes widened into fathomless depths of violet blue and she turned them on Hugo in desperate appeal. She looked so pale that Cordelia half expected her to faint. She thought:

"If I'm in the middle of a conspiracy, then I know who is its weakest member."

Hugo Tilling said:

"You're telling us that Ronald Callender has employed you to find out why Mark died?"

"Is that so extraordinary?"

"I find it incredible. He took no particular interest in his son when he was alive, why begin now he's dead?"

"How do you know he took no particular interest?"

"It's just an idea I had."

Cordelia said:

"Well, he's interested now even if it's only the scientist's urge to discover truth."

"Then he'd better stick to his microbiology, discovering how to make plastic soluble in salt water, or whatever. Human beings aren't susceptible to his kind of experiment."

Davie Stevens said with casual unconcern:

"I wonder that you can stomach that arrogant fascist."

The gibe plucked at too many chords of memory. Wilfully obtuse, Cordelia said:

"I didn't enquire what political party Sir Ronald favours."

Hugo laughed.

"Davie doesn't mean that. By fascist Davie means that Ronald Callender holds certain untenable opinions. For example, that all men may not be created equal, that universal suffrage may not necessarily add to the general happiness of mankind, that the tyrannies of the left aren't noticeably more liberal or supportable than the tyrannies of the right, that black men killing black men is small improvement on white men killing black men in so far as the victims are concerned and that capitalism may not be responsible for all the ills that flesh is heir to from drug addiction to poor syntax. I don't suggest that Ronald Callender holds all or indeed any of these reprehensible opinions. But Davie thinks that he does."

Davie threw a book at Hugo and said without rancour:

"Shut up! You talk like the *Daily Telegraph*. And you're boring our visitor."

Sophie Tilling asked suddenly:

"Was it Sir Ronald who suggested that you should question us?"

"He said that you were Mark's friends; he saw you at the inquest and funeral."

Hugo laughed:

"For God's sake, is that his idea of friendship?"

Cordelia said:

"But you were there?"

"We went to the inquest—all of us except Isa-belle, who, we thought, would have been decora-tive but unreliable. It was rather dull. There was a great deal of irrelevant medical evidence about the excellent state of Mark's heart, lungs and digestive system. As far as I can see, he would have gone on living for ever if he hadn't put a belt round his neck."

"And the funeral—were you there too?"

"We were, at the Cambridge Crematorium. A very subdued affair. There were only six of us present in addition to the undertaker's men; we three, Ronald Callender, that secretary/house-keeper of his and an old nanny type dressed in black. She cast rather a gloom over the proceed-ings, I thought. Actually she looked so exactly like an old family retainer that I suspect she was a policewoman in disguise."

"Why should she be? Did she look like one?"

"No, but then you don't look like a private eye."

"You've no idea who she was?"

"No, we weren't introduced; it wasn't a chummy kind of funeral. Now I recall it, not one of us spoke a single word to any of the others. Sir Ronald wore a mask of public grief, the King mourning the Crown Prince."

"And Miss Leaming?"

"The Queen Consort; she should have had a black veil over her face."

"I thought that her suffering was real enough," said Sophie.

"You can't tell. No one can. Define suffering. Define real."

Suddenly Davie Stevens spoke, rolling over onto his stomach like a playful dog.

"Miss Leaming looked pretty sick to me. Incidentally, the old lady was called Pilbeam; anyway, that was the name on the wreath."

Sophie laughed:

"That awful cross of roses with the black-edged card? I might have guessed it came from her; but how do you know?"

"I looked, honey. The undertaker's men took the wreath off the coffin and propped it against the wall so I took a quick butchers. The card read 'With sincere sympathy from Nanny Pilbeam'."

Sophie said:

"So you did, I remember now. How beautifully feudal! Poor old nanny, it must have cost her a packet."

"Did Mark ever talk about a Nanny Pilbeam?" Cordelia asked.

They glanced at each other quickly. Isabelle shook her head. Sophie said "not to me."

Hugo Tilling replied:

"He never talked about her, but I think I did see her once before the funeral. She called at college about six weeks ago—on Mark's twenty-first birthday actually, and asked to see him. I was in the Porter's Lodge at the time and Robbins asked me if Mark was in college. She went up to his room and they were there together for about an hour. I saw her leaving, but he never mentioned her to me either then or later."

And soon afterwards, thought Cordelia, he gave up university. Could there be a connection? It was only a tenuous lead, but she would have to follow it. She asked out of a curiosity that seemed both perverse and irrelevant:

"Were there any other flowers?"

It was Sophie who replied:

"A simple bunch of unwired garden flowers on the coffin. No card. Miss Leaming, I suppose. It was hardly Sir Ronald's style."

Cordelia said:

"You were his friends. Please tell me about him."

They looked at each other as if deciding who should speak. Their embarrassment was almost palpable. Sophie Tilling was picking at small blades of grass and rolling them in her hands. Without looking up, she said:

"Mark was a very private person. I'm not sure how far any of us knew him. He was quiet, gentle, self-contained, unambitious. He was intelligent without being clever. He was very kind; he cared about people, but without inflicting them with his concern. He had little self-esteem but it never seemed to worry him. I don't think there is anything else we can say about him."

Suddenly Isabelle spoke in a voice so low that Cordelia could hardly catch it. She said:

"He was sweet."

Hugo said with a sudden angry impatience:

"He was sweet and he is dead. There you have it. We can't tell you any more about Mark Callender than that. We none of us saw him after he chucked college. He didn't consult us before he left, and he didn't consult us before he killed himself. He was, as my sister has told you, a very private person. I suggest that you leave him his privacy."

"Look," said Cordelia, "you went to the inquest, you went to the funeral. If you had stopped seeing him, if you were so unconcerned about him, why did you bother?"

"Sophie went out of affection. Davie went because Sophie did. I went out of curiosity and respect; you mustn't be seduced by my air of casual flippancy into thinking that I haven't a heart."

Cordelia said obstinately:

"Someone visited him at the cottage on the evening he died. Someone had coffee with him. I intend to find out who that person was."

Was it her fancy that this news surprised them? Sophie Tilling looked as if she were about to ask a question when her brother quickly broke in:

"It wasn't any of us. On the night Mark died we were all in the second row of the dress circle of the Arts Theatre watching Pinter. I don't know that I can prove it. I doubt whether the booking clerk has kept the chart for that particular night, but I booked the seats and she may remember me. If you insist on being tediously meticulous, I can probably introduce you to a friend who knew of my intention to take a party to the play; to another who saw some at least of us in the bar in the interval; and to another with whom I subsequently discussed the performance. None of this will prove anything; my friends are an accommodating bunch. It would be simpler for you to accept that I am telling the truth. Why should I lie? We were all four at the Arts Theatre on the night of 26th May."

Davie Stevens said gently:

"Why not tell that arrogant bastard Pa Callender to go to hell and leave his son in peace, then find yourself a nice simple case of larceny?"

"Or murder," said Hugo Tilling.

"Find yourself a nice simple case of murder."

As if in obedience to some secret code, they began getting up, piling their books together, brushing the grass cuttings from their clothes. Cordelia followed them through the courts and out of college. Still in a silent group they made their way to a white Renault parked in the forecourt.

Cordelia came up to them and spoke directly to Isabelle.

"Did you enjoy the Pinter? Weren't you frightened by that dreadful last scene when Wyatt Gillman is gunned down by the natives?"

It was so easy that Cordelia almost despised herself. The immense violet eyes grew puzzled.

"Oh, no! I did not care about it, I was not frightened. I was with Hugo and the others, you see."

Cordelia turned to Hugo Tilling.

"Your friend doesn't seem to know the difference between Pinter and Osborne."

Hugo was settling himself into the driving seat of the car. He twisted round to open the back door for Sophie and Davie. He said calmly:

"My friend, as you choose to call her, is living in Cambridge, inadequately chaperoned I'm happy to say, for the purpose of learning English. So far her progress has been erratic and in some respects disappointing. One can never be certain how much my friend has understood."

The engine purred into life. The car began to move. It was then that Sophie Tilling thrust her head out of the window and said impulsively:

"I don't mind talking about Mark if you think it will help. It won't, but you can come round to my house this afternoon if you like—57 Norwich Street. Don't be late; Davie and I are going on the river. You can come too if you feel like it."

The car accelerated. Cordelia watched it out of sight. Hugo raised his hand in ironic farewell but not one of them turned a head.

Cordelia muttered the address to herself until it was safely written down: 57, Norwich Street. Was that the address where Sophie lodged, a hostel perhaps, or did her family live in Cambridge? Well, she would find out soon enough. When ought she to arrive? Too early would look over eager; too late and they might have set out for the river. Whatever motive had prompted Sophie

Tilling to issue that belated invitation, she mustn't lose touch with them now.

They had some guilty knowledge; that had been obvious. Why else had they reacted so strongly to her arrival? They wanted the facts of Mark Callender's death to be left undisturbed. They would try to persuade, cajole, even to shame her into abandoning the case. Would they, she wondered, also threaten? But why? The most likely theory was that they were shielding someone. But again, why? Murder wasn't a matter of climbing late into college, a venial infringement of rules which a friend would automatically condone and conceal. Mark Callender had been their friend; to two of them he might have been more than a friend. Someone whom he knew and trusted had pulled a strap tight round his neck, had watched and listened to his agonized choking, had strung his body on a hook like the carcass of an animal. How could one reconcile that appalling knowledge with Davie Stevens' slightly amused and rueful glance at Sophie, with Hugo's cynical calm, with Sophie's friendly and interested eyes? If they were conspirators, then they were monsters. And Isabelle? If they were shielding anyone, it was most likely to be her. But Isabelle de Lasterie couldn't have murdered Mark. Cordelia remembered those frail sloping shoulders, those ineffective hands almost transparent in the sun, the long nails painted like elegant pink talons. If Isabelle were guilty, she hadn't acted alone. Only a tall and very strong woman could have heaved that inert body onto the chair and up to the hook.

Norwich Street was a one-way thoroughfare and, initially, Cordelia approached it from the wrong direction. It took her some time to find her way back to Hills Road, past the Roman Catholic church and down the fourth turning to the right. The street was terraced with small brick houses, obviously early Victorian. Equally obviously, the road was on its way up. Most of the houses looked well cared for; the paint on the identical front doors was fresh and bright; lined curtains had replaced the draped lace at the single ground-floor windows and the bases of the walls were scarred where a damp course had been installed. Number fifty-seven had a black front door with the house number painted in white behind the glass panel above. Cordelia was relieved to see that there was space to park the Mini. There was no sign of the Renault among the almost continuous row of old cars and battered bicycles which lined the edge of the pavement.

The front door was wide open. Cordelia pressed the bell and stepped tentatively into a narrow white hall. The interior of the house was immediately familiar to her. From her sixth birthday she had lived for two years in just such a Victorian terraced cottage with Mrs. Gibson on the outskirts of Romford. She recognized the steep and narrow staircase immediately ahead, the door on the right leading to the front parlour, the second door set aslant which led to the back parlour and through it to the kitchen and yard. She knew that there would be cupboards and a curved alcove on each side of the fireplace; she knew where to find the door under the stairs. Memory was so sharp that it imposed on this clean, sun-scented interior the strong odour of unwashed napkins, cabbage and grease which had permeated the Romford house. She could almost hear the children's voices calling her outlandish names across the rookery of the primary school playground across the road, stamping the asphalt with the ubiquitous Wellington boots which they wore in all seasons, flailing their thin jersied arms: "Cor, Cor, Cor!"

The furthest door was ajar and she could glimpse a room painted bright yellow and spilling over with sunlight. Sophie's head appeared.

"Oh, it's you! Come in. Davie has gone to collect some books from college and to buy food for the picnic. Would you like tea now or shall we wait? I'm just finishing the ironing."

"I'd rather wait, thank you."

Cordelia sat down and watched while Sophie wound the flex around the iron and folded the cloth. She glanced around the room. It was welcoming and attractive, furnished in no particular style or period, a cosy hotch-potch of the cheap and the valuable, unpretentious and pleasing. There was a sturdy oak table against the wall; four rather ugly dining chairs; a Windsor chair with a plump yellow cushion, an elegant Victorian sofa covered with brown velvet and set under the window; three good Staffordshire figures on the mantel shelf above the hooded wrought-iron grate. One of the walls was almost covered with a notice board in dark cork which displayed posters, cards, *aides-mémoire,* and pictures cut from magazines. Two, Cordelia saw, were beautifully photographed and attractive nudes.

Outside the yellow-curtained window the small walled garden was a riot of greenery. An immense and multi-flowered hollyhock burgeoned against a tatty looking trellis; there were roses planted in Ali Baba jars and a row of pots of bright-red geraniums lined the top of the wall.

Cordelia said:

"I like this house. Is it yours?"

"Yes, I own it. Our grandfather died two years ago and left Hugo and me a small legacy. I used mine for the down payment on this house and got a local authority grant towards the cost of conversion. Hugo spent all of his laying down wine. He was ensuring a happy middle age; I was ensuring a happy present. I suppose that's the difference between us."

She folded the ironing cloth on the end of the table and stowed it away in one of the cupboards. Sitting opposite to Cordelia, she asked abruptly:

"Do you like my brother?"

"Not very much. I thought he was rather rude to me."

"He didn't mean to be."

"I think that's rather worse. Rudeness should always be intentional, otherwise, it's insensitivity."

"Hugo isn't at his most agreeable when he's with Isabelle. She has that effect on him."

"Was she in love with Mark Callender?"

"You'll have to ask her, Cordelia, but I shouldn't think so. They hardly knew each other. Mark was my lover, not hers. I thought I'd better get you here to tell you myself since someone's bound to sooner or later if you go around Cambridge ferreting out facts about him. He didn't live here with me, of course. He had rooms in college. But we were lovers for almost the whole of last year. It ended just after Christmas when I met Davie."

"Were you in love?"

"I'm not sure. All sex is a kind of exploitation, isn't it? If you mean, did we explore our own identities through the personality of the other, then I suppose we were in love or thought that we were. Mark needed to believe himself in love. I'm not sure I know what the word means."

Cordelia felt a surge of sympathy. She wasn't sure either. She thought of her own two lovers; Georges whom she had slept with because he was gentle and unhappy and called her Cordelia, a real name, her name, not Delia, Daddy's little fascist; and Carl who was young and angry and whom she had liked so much that it seemed churlish not to show it in the only way which seemed to him important. She had never thought of virginity as other than a temporary and inconvenient state, part of the general insecurity and vulnerability of being young. Before Georges and Carl she had been lonely and inexperienced. Afterwards she had been lonely and a little less inexperienced. Neither affair had given her the longed-for assurance in dealing with Daddy or the landladies, neither had inconveniently touched her heart. But for Carl she had felt tenderness. It was just as well that he had left Rome before his lovemaking had become too pleasurable and he too important to her. It was intolerable to think that those strange gymnastics might one day become necessary. Lovemaking, she had decided, was overrated, not painful but surprising. The alienation between thought and action was so complete. She said:

"I suppose I only meant were you fond of each other, and did you like going to bed together?"

"Both of those things."

"Why did it end? Did you quarrel?"

"Nothing so natural or uncivilized. One didn't quarrel with Mark. That was one of the troubles about him. I told him that I didn't want to go on with the affair and he accepted my decision as calmly as if I were just breaking a date for a play at the Arts. He didn't try to argue or dissuade me. And if you're wondering whether the break had anything to do with his death, well you're wrong. I wouldn't rank that high with anyone, particularly not Mark. I was probably fonder of him than he was of me."

"So why did it end?"

"I felt that I was under moral scrutiny. It wasn't

true; Mark wasn't a prig. But that's how I felt, or pretended to myself that I felt. I couldn't live up to him and I didn't even want to. There was Gary Webber, for example. I'd better tell you about him; it explains a lot about Mark. He's an autistic child, one of the uncontrollable, violent ones. Mark met him with his parents and their other two children on Jesus Green about a year ago; the children were playing on the swings there. Mark spoke to Gary and the boy responded to him. Children always did. He took to visiting the family and looking after Gary one evening a week so that the Webbers could get out to the pictures. During his last two vacs he stayed in the house and looked after Gary completely while the whole family went off for a holiday. The Webbers couldn't bear the boy to go to hospital; they'd tried it once and he didn't settle. But they were perfectly happy to leave him with Mark. I used to call in some evenings and see them together. Mark would hold the boy on his lap and rock him backwards and forwards for hours at a time. It was the one way to quieten him. We disagreed about Gary. I thought he would be better dead and I said so. I still think it would be better if he died, better for his parents, better for the rest of the family, better for him. Mark didn't agree. I remember saying:

"'Oh well, if you think it reasonable that children should suffer so that you can enjoy the emotional kick of relieving them—' After that the conversation became boringly metaphysical. Mark said:

"'Neither you nor I could be willing to kill Gary.

He exists. His family exists. They need help which we can give. It doesn't matter what we feel. Actions are important, feelings aren't.'"

Cordelia said:

"But actions arise out of feelings."

"Oh, Cordelia, don't you start! I've had this particular conversation too many times before. Of course they do!"

They were silent for a moment. Then Cordelia, reluctant to shatter the tenuous confidence and friendship which she sensed was growing between them, made herself ask:

"Why did he kill himself—if he did kill himself?" Sophie's reply was as emphatic as a slammed door.

"He left a note."

"A note perhaps. But, as his father pointed out, not an explanation. It's a lovely passage of prose—at least I think so—but as a justification for suicide it just isn't convincing."

"It convinced the jury."

"It doesn't convince me. Think, Sophie! Surely there are only two reasons for killing oneself. One is either escaping from something or to something. The first is rational. If one is in intolerable pain, despair or mental anguish and there is no reasonable chance of a cure, then it's probably sensible to prefer oblivion. But it isn't sensible to kill oneself in the hope of gaining some better existence or to extend one's sensibilities to include the experience of death. It isn't possible to experience death. I'm not even sure it's possible to experience dying. One can only experience the preparations for death, and even that seems pointless since one can't make use of the experience afterwards. If there's any sort of existence after death we shall all know soon enough. If there isn't, we shan't exist to complain that we've been cheated. People who believe in an after life are perfectly reasonable. They're the only ones who are safe from ultimate disillusionment."

"You've thought it all out, haven't you. I'm not sure that suicides do. The act is probably both impulsive and irrational."

"Was Mark impulsive and irrational?"

"I didn't know Mark."

"But you were lovers! You slept with him!"

Sophie looked at her and cried out in angry pain.

"I didn't know him! I thought I did, but I didn't know the first thing about him!"

They sat without speaking for almost two minutes. Then Cordelia asked:

"You went to dinner at Garforth House, didn't you? What was it like?"

"The food and the wine were surprisingly good, but I don't suppose that's what you had in mind. The dinner party wasn't otherwise memorable. Sir Ronald was amiable enough when he noticed I was there. Miss Leaming, when she could tear her obsessive attention from the presiding genius, looked me over like a prospective mother-in-law. Mark was rather silent. I think he'd taken me there to prove something to me, or perhaps to himself; I'm not sure what. He never talked about the evening or asked me what I thought. A month later Hugo and I both went to dinner. It was then I met Davie. He was the guest of one of the research biologists and Ronald Callender was angling to get him. Davie did a vac job there in his final year. If you want the inside dope on Garforth House, you should ask him."

Five minutes later Hugo, Isabelle and Davie arrived. Cordelia had gone upstairs to the bathroom and heard the car stop and the jabber of voices in the hall. Footsteps passed beneath her towards the back parlour. She turned on the hot water. The gas boiler in the kitchen immediately gave forth a roar as if the little house were powered by a dynamo. Cordelia let the tap run, then stepped out of the bathroom, closing the door gently behind her. She stole to the top of the stairs. It was hard luck on Sophie to waste her hot water, she thought guiltily; but worse was the sense of treachery and shabby opportunism as she crept down the first three stairs and listened. The front door had been closed but the door to the back parlour was open. She heard Isabelle's high unemphatic voice:

"But if this man Sir Ronald is paying her to find out about Mark, why cannot I pay her to stop finding out?"

Then Hugo's voice, amused, a little contemptuous:

"Darling Isabelle, when will you learn that not everyone can be bought?"

"She can't, anyway. I like her."

It was Sophie speaking. Her brother replied:

"We all like her. The question is, how do we get rid of her?"

Then for a few minutes there was a murmur of voices, the words indistinguishable, broken by Isabelle.

"It is not, I think, a suitable job for a woman."

There was the sound of a chair scraping against the floor, a shuffle of feet. Cordelia darted guiltily back into the bathroom and turned off the tap. She recalled Bernie's complacent admonition when she had asked whether they needed accept a divorce case.

"You can't do our job, partner, and be a gentleman." She stood watching at the half-open door. Hugo and Isabelle were leaving. She waited until she heard the front door close and the car drive away. Then she went down to the parlour. Sophie and Davie were together, unpacking a large carrier bag of groceries. Sophie smiled and said:

"Isabelle has a party tonight. She has a house quite close to here in Panton Street. Mark's tutor, Edward Horsfall, will probably be there and we thought it might be useful for you to talk to him about Mark. The party's at eight o'clock but you can call for us here. Just now we're packing a picnic; we thought we'd take a punt on the river for an hour or so. Do come if you'd like to. It's re-

ally much the pleasantest way of seeing Cambridge."

Afterwards, Cordelia remembered the river picnic as a series of brief but intensely clear pictures, moments in which sight and sense fused
and time seemed momentarily arrested while the
sunlit image was impressed on her mind. Sunlight sparkling on the river and gilding the hairs of
Davie's chest and forearms; the flesh of his strong
upper arms speckled like an egg; Sophie lifting
her arm to wipe the sweat from her brow as she
rested between thrusts of the punt pole; green-
black weeds dragged by the pole from mysterious
depths to writhe sinuously below the surface; a
bright duck cocking its white tail before disappearing in a flurry of green water. When they had
rocked under Silver Street Bridge a friend of Sophie's swam alongside, sleek and snout-nosed
like an otter, his black hair lying like blades across
his cheeks. He rested his hands on the punt and
opened his mouth to be fed chunks of sandwiches by a protesting Sophie. The punts and
canoes scraped and jostled each other in the
turbulence of white water racing under the bridge.
The air rang with laughing voices and the green
banks were peopled with half-naked bodies lying
supine with their faces to the sun.

Davie punted until they reached the higher
level of the river and Cordelia and Sophie
stretched out on the cushions at opposite ends
of the punt. Thus distanced it was impossible to

carry on a private conversation; Cordelia guessed that this was precisely what Sophie had planned. From time to time, she would call out snatches of information as if to emphasize that the outing was strictly educational.

"That wedding cake is John's—we're just passing under Clare bridge, one of the prettiest, I think. Thomas Grumbald built it in 1639. They say he was only paid three shillings for the design. You know that view, of course; it's a good view of Queen's, though."

Cordelia's courage failed her at the thought of interrupting this desultory tourist's chat with the brutal demand:

"Did you and your brother kill your lover?"

Here, rocking gently on the sunlit river, the question seemed both indecent and absurd. She was in danger of being lulled into a gentle acceptance of defeat; viewing all her suspicions as a neurotic hankering after drama and notoriety, a need to justify her fee to Sir Ronald. She believed Mark Callender had been murdered because she wanted to believe it. She had identified with him, with his solitariness, his self-sufficiency, his alienation from his father, his lonely childhood. She had even—most dangerous presumption of all— come to see herself as his avenger. When Sophie took over the pole, just past the Garden House Hotel, and Davie edged his way along the gently rocking punt and stretched himself out beside her, she knew that she wouldn't be able to mention Mark's name. It was out of no more than a vague, unintrusive curiosity that she found herself asking:

"Is Sir Ronald Callender a good scientist?" Davie took up a short paddle and began lazily to stir the shining water.

"His science is perfectly respectable, as my dear colleagues would say. Rather more than respectable, in fact. At present the lab is working on ways of expanding the use of biological monitors to assess pollution of the sea and estuaries; that means routine surveys of plants and animals which might serve as indicators. And they did some very useful preliminary work last year on the degradation of plastics. R.C. isn't so hot himself, but then you can't expect much original science from the over fifties. But he's a great spotter of talent and he certainly knows how to run a team if you fancy that dedicated, one for all, band of brothers approach. I don't. They even publish their papers as the Callender Research Laboratory, not under individual names. That wouldn't do for me. When I publish, it's strictly for the glory of David Forbes Stevens and, incidentally, for the gratification of Sophie. The Tillings like success."

"Was that why you didn't want to stay on when he offered you a job?"

"That among other reasons. He pays too generously and he asks too much. I don't like being bought and I've a strong objection to dressing up every night in a dinner jacket like a performing monkey in a zoo. I'm a molecular biologist. I'm not looking for the holy grail. Dad and Mum brought me up as a Methodist and I don't see why I should chuck a perfectly good religion which served me very well for twelve years just to put the great scientific principle or Ronald Callender in its place. I distrust these sacerdotal scientists. It's a bloody wonder that little lot at Garforth House aren't genuflecting three times a day in the direction of the Cavendish."

"And what about Lunn? How does he fit in?"

"Oh, that boy's a bloody wonder! Ronald Callender found him in a children's home when he was fifteen—don't ask me how—and trained him to be a lab assistant. You couldn't find a better. There isn't an instrument made which Chris Lunn can't learn to understand and care for. He's developed one or two himself and Callender has had them patented. If anyone in that lab is indispensable it's probably Lunn. Certainly Ronald Callender cares a damn sight more for him than he did for his son. And Lunn, as you might guess, regards R.C. as God almighty, which is very gratifying for them both. It's extraordinary really, all that violence which used to be expressed in street fights and coshing old ladies, harnessed to the service of science. You've got to hand it to Callender. He certainly knows how to pick his slaves."

"And is Miss Leaming a slave?"

"Well, I wouldn't know just what Eliza Leaming is. She's responsible for the business management and, like Lunn, she's probably indispensable. Lunn and she seem to have a love-hate relationship, or, perhaps, a hate-hate relationship. I'm not very clever at detecting these psychological nuances."

"But how on earth does Sir Ronald pay for it all?"

"Well, that's the thousand-dollar question, isn't it? It's rumoured that most of the money came from his wife and that he and Elizabeth Leaming between them invested it rather cleverly. They certainly needed to. And then he gets a certain amount from contract work. Even so, it's an expensive hobby. While I was there they were saying that the Wolvington Trust were getting interested. If they come up with something big—and I gather it's below their dignity to come up with anything small—then most of Ronald Callender's troubles should be over. Mark's death must have hit him. Mark was due to come into a pretty substantial fortune in four years' time and he told Sophie that he intended to hand most of it over to Dad."

"Why on earth should he do that?"

"God knows. Conscience money, perhaps. Anyway, he obviously thought it was something that Sophie ought to know."

Conscience money for what, Cordelia wondered sleepily. For not loving his father enough? For rejecting his enthusiasms? For being less than the son he had hoped for? And what would happen to Mark's fortune now? Who stood to gain by Mark's death? She supposed that she ought to consult his grandfather's will and find out. But that would mean a trip to London. Was it really worth it?

She stretched back her face to the sun and trailed one hand in the river. A splash of water from the punt pole stung her eyes. She opened them and saw that the punt was gliding close to the bank and under the shade of overhanging trees. Immediately in front of her a torn branch, cleft at the end and thick as a man's body, hung by a thread of bark and turned gently as the punt passed beneath it. She was aware of Davie's voice; he must have been talking for a long time. How odd that she couldn't remember what he'd been saying!

"You don't need reasons for killing yourself; you need reasons for not killing yourself. It was suicide, Cordelia. I should let it go at that."

Cordelia thought that she must have briefly slept, since he seemed to be answering a question she couldn't remember having asked. But now there were other voices, louder and more insistent. Sir Ronald Callender's: "My son is dead. *My* son. If I am in some way responsible, I'd prefer to know. If anyone else is responsible, I want to know that too." Sergeant Maskell's: "How would you use this to hang yourself, Miss Gray?" The feel of the belt, smooth and sinuous, slipping like a live thing through her fingers.

She sat bolt upright, hands clasped around her knees, with such suddenness that the punt rocked violently and Sophie had to clutch at an overhanging branch to keep her balance. Her dark face, intriguingly fore-shortened and patterned with the shadow of leaves, looked down at Cordelia from what seemed an immense height. Their eyes met. In that moment Cordelia knew how close she had come to giving up the case. She had been suborned by the beauty of the day, by sunshine, indolence, the promise of comradeship, even friendship, into forgetting why she was here. The realization horrified her. Davie had said that Sir Ronald was a good picker. Well, he had picked her. This was her first case and nothing and no one was going to hinder her from solving it.

She said formally:

"It was good of you to let me join you, but I don't want to miss the party tonight. I ought to talk to Mark's tutor and there may be other people there who could tell me something. Isn't it time that we thought about turning back?"

Sophie turned her glance on Davie. He gave an almost imperceptible shrug. Without speaking, Sophie drove the pole hard against the bank. The punt began slowly to turn.

Isabelle's party was due to begin at eight o'clock but it was nearly nine when Sophie, Davie and Cordelia arrived. They walked to the house which was only five minutes from Norwich Street; Cordelia never discovered the exact address. She liked the look of the house and wondered how much it was costing Isabelle's father in rent. It was a long, white, two-story villa with tall curved windows and green shutters, set well back from the street, with a semi-basement and a flight of steps to the front door. A similar flight led down from the sitting-room to the long garden.

The sitting-room was already fairly full. Looking at her fellow guests, Cordelia was glad that she had bought the kaftan. Most people seemed to have changed although not necessarily, she thought, into something more attractive. What was aimed at was originality; it was preferable to look spectacular, even bizarre, than to appear nondescript.

The sitting-room was elegantly but unsubstantially furnished and Isabelle had impressed on it her own untidy, impractical and iconoclastic femininity. Cordelia doubted whether the owners had provided the ornate crystal chandelier, far too heavy and large for the room, which hung like a sunburst from the middle of the ceiling, or the many silken cushions and curtains which gave the room's austere proportions something of the ostentatious opulence of a courtesan's boudoir. The pictures, too, must surely be Isabelle's. No house owner letting his property would leave pictures of this quality on the walls. One, hanging above the fireplace, was of a young girl hugging a puppy. Cordelia gazed at it in excited pleasure. Surely she couldn't mistake that individual blue of the girl's dress, that marvellous painting of the cheeks and plump young arms, skin which simultaneously absorbed and reflected light—lovely, tangible flesh. She cried out involuntarily so that people turned to look at her:

"But that's a Renoir!"

Hugo was at her elbow. He laughed.

"Yes; but don't sound so shocked, Cordelia. It's only a small Renoir! Isabelle asked Papa for a picture for her sitting-room. You didn't expect him to provide a print of the Haywain or one of those cheap reproductions of Van Gogh's boring old chair."

"Would Isabelle have known the difference?"

"Oh, yes. Isabelle knows an expensive object when she sees one."

Cordelia wondered whether the bitterness, the hard edge of contempt in his voice, was for Isabelle or for himself. They looked across the room to where she stood, smiling at them. Hugo moved towards her like a man in a dream and took her hand. Cordelia watched. Isabelle had dressed her hair in a high cluster of curls, Grecian style. She was wearing an ankle-length dress of cream matt silk, with a very low square neckline and small intricately tucked sleeves. It was obviously a model and should, Cordelia felt, have looked out of place at an informal party. But it didn't. It merely made every other woman's dress look like an improvisation and reduced her own, whose colours had seemed muted and subtle when she bought it, to the status of a gaudy rag.

Cordelia was determined to get Isabelle alone some time during the evening but could see that it wasn't going to be easy. Hugo stuck tenaciously to her side, steering her among her guests with one proprietorial hand on her waist. He seemed to be drinking steadily and Isabelle's glass was always filled. Perhaps as the evening wore on they would get careless and there would be a chance to separate them. In the meantime, Cordelia decided to explore the house, and a more practical matter, to find out before she needed it where the lavatory was. It was the kind of party where guests were left to find out these things for themselves.

She went up to the first floor and making her way down the passage pushed gently open the door of the far room. The smell of whisky met her immediately; it was overpowering and Cordelia instinctively slipped into the room and closed the door behind her, afraid that it might permeate the house. The room, which was in an indescribable state of disarray, wasn't empty. On the bed and half covered by the counterpane a woman was lying; a woman with bright ginger hair splayed over the pillow and wearing a pink silk dressing-gown. Cordelia walked up to the bed and looked down at her. She was insensible with drink. She lay there emitting puffs of foul, whisky-laden breath which rose like invisible balls of smoke from the half-open mouth. Her lower lip and jaw were tense and creased, giving the face a look of stern censoriousness as if she disapproved strongly of her own condition. Her thin lips were thickly painted, the strong purple stain had seeped into the cracks around the mouth so that the body looked parched in an extremity of cold. Her hands, the gnarled fingers brown with nicotine and laden with rings, lay quietly on the counterpane. Two of the talon-like nails were broken and the brick-red varnish on the others was cracked or peeled away.

The window was obstructed by a heavy dressing-table. Averting her eyes from the mess of crumpled tissues, open bottles of face cream, spilt powder and half drunk cups of what looked like black coffee, Cordelia squeezed behind it and pushed open the window. She gulped in lungfulls of fresh, cleansing air. Below her in the garden pale shapes moved silently over the grass and between the trees like the ghosts of long dead revellers. She left the window open and went back to the bed. There was nothing here that she could do but she placed the cold hands under the counterpane and, taking a second and warmer gown from the hook on the door, tucked it around the woman's body. That, at least, would compensate for the fresh air blowing across the bed.

That done, Cordelia slipped back into the passage, just in time to see Isabelle coming out of the room next door. She shot out an arm and half dragged the girl back into the bedroom. Isabelle gave a little cry, but Cordelia planted her back firmly against the door and said in a low, urgent whisper:

"Tell me what you know about Mark Callender."

The violet eyes slewed from door to window as if desperate for escape.

"I wasn't there when he did it."

"When who did what?"

Isabelle retreated towards the bed as if the inert figure, who was now groaning stertorously, could offer support. Suddenly the woman turned on her side and gave a long snort like an animal in pain. Both girls glanced at her in startled alarm. Cordelia reiterated:

"When who did what?"

"When Mark killed himself; I wasn't there."

The woman on the bed gave a little sigh. Cordelia lowered her voice:

"But you were there some days earlier, weren't you? You called at the house and enquired for him. Miss Markland saw you. Afterwards you sat in the garden and waited until he'd finished work."

Was it Cordelia's imagination that the girl suddenly seemed more relaxed, that she was relieved at the innocuousness of the question?

"I just called to see Mark. They gave me his address at the college Lodge. I went to visit him."

"Why?" The harsh question seemed to puzzle her. She replied simply:

"I wanted to be with him. He was my friend."

"Was he your lover too?" asked Cordelia. This brutal frankness was surely better than asking whether they had slept together, or gone to bed together—stupid euphemisms which Isabelle might not even understand: it was hard to tell from those beautiful but frightened eyes just how much she did understand.

"No, Mark was never my lover. He was working in the garden and I had to wait for him at the cottage. He gave me a chair in the sun and a book until he was free."

"What book?"

"I don't remember, it was very dull. I was dull too until Mark came. Then we had tea with funny mugs that had a blue band, and after tea we went for a walk and then we had supper. Mark made a salad."

"And then?"

"I drove home."

She was perfectly calm now. Cordelia pressed on, aware of the sound of footsteps passing up and down the stairs, of the ring of voices.

"And the time before that? When did you see him before that tea party?"

"It was a few days before Mark left college. We went for a picnic in my car to the seaside. But first we stopped at a town—St. Edmunds town, is it?—and Mark saw a doctor."

"Why? Was he ill?"

"Oh no, he was not ill, and he did not stay long enough for what you call it—an examination. He was in the house a few minutes only. It was a very poor house. I waited for him in the car, but not just outside the house you understand."

"Did he say why he went there?"

"No, but I do not think he got what he wanted. Afterwards he was sad for a little time, but then we went to the sea and he was happy again."

She, too, seemed happy now. She smiled at Cordelia, her sweet, unmeaning smile. Cordelia thought: it's just the cottage that terrifies her. She doesn't mind talking about the living Mark, it's his death she can't bear to think about. And yet, this repugnance wasn't born of personal grief. He had been her friend; he was sweet; she liked him. But she was getting on very well without him.

There was a knock at the door. Cordelia stood aside and Hugo came in. He lifted an eyebrow at Isabelle and, ignoring Cordelia, said:

"It's your party, ducky; coming down?"

"Cordelia wanted to talk to me about Mark."

"No doubt. You told her, I hope, that you spent one day with him motoring to the sea and one afternoon and evening at Summertrees and that you haven't seen him since."

"She told me," said Cordelia. "She was practically word perfect. I think she's safe to be let out on her own now."

He said easily:

"You shouldn't be sarcastic, Cordelia, it doesn't suit you. Sarcasm is all right for some women, but not for women who are beautiful in the way that you are beautiful."

They were passing down the stairs together to meet the hubbub in the hall. The compliment irritated Cordelia. She said:

"I suppose that woman on the bed is Isabelle's chaperone. Is she often drunk?"

"Mademoiselle de Congé? Not often as drunk as that, but I admit that she is seldom absolutely sober."

"Then oughtn't you to do something about it?"

"What should I do? Hand her over to the twentieth-century Inquisition—a psychiatrist like my father? What has she done to us to deserve that? Besides, she is tediously conscientious on the few occasions when she's sober. It happens that her compulsions and my interest coincide."

Cordelia said severely:

"That may be expedient but I don't think it's very responsible and it isn't kind."

He stopped in his tracks and turned towards her, smiling directly into her eyes.

"Oh, Cordelia, you talk like the child of progressive parents who has been reared by a nonconformist nanny and educated at a convent school. I do like you!"

He was still smiling as Cordelia slipped away from them and infiltrated into the party. She reflected that his diagnosis hadn't been so very wrong.

She helped herself to a glass of wine, then moved slowly round the room listening unashamedly to scraps of conversation, hoping to hear Mark's name mentioned. She heard it only once. Two girls and a very fair, rather insipid young man were standing behind her. One of the girls said:

"Sophie Tilling seems to have recovered remarkably quickly from Mark Callender's suicide. She and Davie went to the cremation, did you know? Typical of Sophie to take her current lover to see the previous one incinerated. I suppose it gave her some kind of a kick."

Her companion laughed.

"And little brother takes over Mark's girl. If you can't get beauty, money and brains, settle for the first two. Poor Hugo! He suffers from a sense of inferiority. Not quite handsome enough; not quite clever enough—Sophie's First must have shaken him—not quite rich enough. No wonder he has to rely on sex to give him confidence."

"And, even there, not quite . . ."

"Darling, you should know."

They laughed and moved away. Cordelia felt her face burning. Her hand shook almost spilling her wine. She was surprised to find how much she cared, how much she had come to like Sophie. But that, of course, was part of the plan, that was Tilling strategy. If you can't shame her into giving up the case, suborn her; take her on the river; be nice to her; get her on our side. And it was true, she was on their side, at least against malicious detractors. She comforted herself with the censorious reflection that they were as bitchy as guests at a suburban cocktail party. She had never in her life attended one of those innocuous if boring gatherings for the routine consumption of gossip, gin and canapés but, like her father who had never attended one either, she found no difficulty in believing that they were hot beds of snobbery, spite and sexual innuendo.

A warm body was pressing against her. She turned and saw Davie. He was carrying three bottles of wine. He had obviously heard at least part of the conversation, as the girls had no doubt intended, but he grinned amiably.

"Funny how Hugo's discarded women always hate him so much. It's quite different with Sophie. Her ex-lovers clutter up Norwich Street with their beastly bicycles and broken-down cars. I'm always finding them in the sitting-room drinking my beer and confiding to her the awful trouble they're having with their present girls."

"Do you mind?"

"Not if they don't get any further than the sitting-room. Are you enjoying yourself?"

"Not very much."

"Come and meet a friend of mine. He's been asking who you are."

"No thank you, Davie. I must keep myself free for Mr. Horsfall. I don't want to miss him."

He smiled at her, rather pityingly she thought, and seemed about to speak. But he changed his mind and moved away, clutching his bottles to his chest and shouting a cheerful warning as he edged himself through the throng.

Cordelia worked her way around the room, watching and listening. She was intrigued by the overt sexuality; she had thought that intellectuals breathed too rarified air to be much interested in the flesh. Obviously this was a misapprehension.

Come to think of it, the comrades, who might have been supposed to live in randy promiscuity, had been remarkably staid. She had sometimes felt that their sexual activities were prompted more by duty than instinct, more a weapon of revolution or a gesture against the bourgeois mores they despised than a response to human need. Their basic energies were all devoted to politics. It was not difficult to see where most of the energies of those present were directed.

She needn't have worried about the success of the kaftan. A number of men showed themselves willing or even eager to detach themselves from their partners for the pleasure of talking to her. With one particularly, a decorative and ironically amusing young historian, Cordelia felt that she could have spent an entertaining evening. To enjoy the sole attention of one agreeable man and no attention at all from anyone else was all she ever hoped from a party. She wasn't naturally gregarious and, alienated by the last six years from her own generation, found herself intimidated by the noise, the underlying ruthlessness and the half-understood conventions of these tribal matings. And she told herself firmly that she wasn't here to enjoy herself at Sir Ronald's expense. None of her prospective partners knew Mark Callender or showed any interest in him, dead or alive. She mustn't get herself tied for the evening to people who had no information to give. When this seemed a danger and the talk became too beguiling, she would murmur her excuses and slip away to the bathroom or into the shadows of the garden where little groups were sitting on the grass smoking pot. Cordelia couldn't be mistaken in that evocative smell. They showed no disposition to chat and here, at least, she could stroll in privacy gaining courage for the next foray, for the next artfully casual question, the next inevitable response.

"Mark Callender? Sorry—we never met. Didn't he go off to sample the simple life and end by hanging himself or something?"

Once she took refuge in Mademoiselle de Congé's room, but she saw that the inert figure had been unceremoniously dumped on a cushion of pillows on the carpet and that the bed was being occupied for quite another purpose.

She wondered when Edward Horsfall would arrive or whether he would arrive at all. And if he did, would Hugo remember or bother to introduce her? She couldn't see either of the Tillings in the hot crush of gesticulating bodies which by now had crammed the sitting-room and spilled into the hall and halfway up the stairs. She was beginning to feel that this would be a wasted evening when Hugo's hand fell on her arm. He said:

"Come and meet Edward Horsfall. Edward, this is Cordelia Gray; she wants to talk about Mark Callender."

Edward Horsfall was another surprise. Cordelia had subconsciously conjured up the picture of an elderly don, a little distrait with the weight of his learning, a benevolent if detached mentor of the young. Horsfall could not have been much over thirty. He was very tall, his hair falling long over one eye, his lean body curved as a melon rind, a comparison reinforced by the pleated yellow shirt front under a jutting bow tie.

Any half acknowledged, half shameful hope which Cordelia may have nourished that he would immediately take to her and be happily ungrudging of his time so long as they were together was quickly dispersed. His eyes were restless, flicking obsessively back to the door. She suspected that he was alone by choice, deliberately keeping himself free from encumbrances until the hoped-for companion arrived. He was so fidgety that it was difficult not to be fretted by his anxiety. She said:

"You don't have to stay with me all evening you know, I only want some information."

Her voice recalled him to an awareness of her and to some attempt at civility.

"That wouldn't exactly be a penance. I'm sorry. What do you want to know?"

"Anything you can tell me about Mark. You taught him history didn't you? Was he good at it?"

It wasn't a particularly relevant question but one which she felt all teachers might respond to as a start.

"He was more rewarding to teach than some students I'm afflicted with. I don't know why he chose history. He could very well have read one of the sciences. He had a lively curiosity about physical phenomena. But he decided to read history."

"Do you think that was to disoblige his father?"

"To disoblige Sir Ronald?" He turned and stretched out an arm for a bottle. "What are you drinking? There's one thing about Isabelle de Lasterie's parties, the drink is excellent, presumably because Hugo orders it. There's an admirable absence of beer."

"Doesn't Hugo drink beer then?" asked Cordelia.

"He claims not to. What were we talking about? Oh, yes, disobliging Sir Ronald. Mark said that he chose history because we have no chance of understanding the present without understanding the past. That's the sort of irritating cliché people come out with at interviews, but he may have believed it. Actually, of course, the reverse is true; we interpret the past through our knowledge of the present."

"Was he any good?" asked Cordelia. "I mean, would he have got a First?"

A First, she naively believed, was the ultimate in scholastic achievement, the certificate of pronounced intelligence that the recipient carried unchallenged through life. She wanted to hear that Mark was safe for a First.

"Those are two separate and distinct questions. You seem to be confusing merit with achievement. Impossible to predict his class, hardly a

First. Mark was capable of extraordinarily good and original work but he limited his material to the number of his original ideas. The result tended to be rather thin. Examiners like originality but you've got to spew up the accepted facts and orthodox opinions first if only to show that you've learnt them. An exceptional memory and fast legible handwriting; that's the secret of a First. Where are you, incidentally?" He noticed Cordelia's brief look of incomprehension.

"At what college?"

"None; I work. I'm a private detective."

He took this information in his stride.

"My uncle employed one of those once to find out if my aunt was being screwed by their dentist. She was, but he could have found out more easily by the simple expedient of asking them. His way, he lost the services of a wife and of a dentist simultaneously and paid through the nose for information he could have got for nothing. It made quite a stir in the family at the time. I should have thought that the job was——"

Cordelia finished the sentence for him.

"An unsuitable job for a woman?"

"Not at all. Entirely suitable I should have thought, requiring, I imagine, infinite curiosity, infinite pains and a penchant for interfering with other people." His attention was wandering again. A group near to them were talking and snatches of the conversation came to them.

"——typical of the worst kind of academic writing. Contempt for logic; a generous sprinkling of vogue names; spurious profundity and bloody awful grammar."

The tutor gave the speakers a second's attention, dismissed their academic chat as beneath his notice and condescended to transfer his attention but not his regard back to Cordelia.

"Why are you so interested in Mark Callender?"

"His father has employed me to find out why he died. I was hoping that you might be able to help. I mean, did he ever give you a hint that he might be unhappy, unhappy enough to kill himself? Did he explain why he gave up college?"

"Not to me. I never felt that I got near him. He made a formal goodbye, thanked me for what he chose to describe as my help, and left. I made the usual noises of regret. We shook hands. I was embarrassed, but not Mark. He wasn't, I think, a young man susceptible to embarrassment."

There was a small commotion at the door and a group of new arrivals pushed themselves noisily into the throng. Among them was a tall, dark girl in a flame-coloured frock, open almost to the waist. Cordelia felt the tutor stiffen, saw his eyes fixed on the new arrival with an intense, half anxious, half supplicating look, which she had seen before. Her heart sank. She would be lucky now to get any more information. Desperately trying to recapture his attention, she said:

"I'm not sure that Mark did kill himself. I think it could have been murder."

He spoke inattentively, his eyes on the new-comers.

"Unlikely, surely. By whom? For what reason? He was a negligible personality. He didn't even provoke a vague dislike except possibly from his father. But Ronald Callender couldn't have done it if that's what you're hoping. He was dining in Hall at High Table on the night Mark died. It was a College Feast night. I sat next to him. His son telephoned him."

Cordelia said eagerly, almost tugging at his sleeve:

"At what time?"

"Soon after the meal started, I suppose. Benskin, he's one of the College servants, came in and gave him the message. It must have been between eight and eight-fifteen. Callender disappeared for about ten minutes then returned and got on with his soup. The rest of us still hadn't reached the second course."

"Did he say what Mark wanted? Did he seem disturbed?"

"Neither. We hardly spoke through the meal. Sir Ronald doesn't waste his conversational gifts on non-scientists. Excuse me, will you?"

He was gone, threading his way through the throng towards his prey. Cordelia put down her glass and went in search of Hugo.

"Look," she said, "I want to talk to Benskin, a servant at your college. Would he be there to-night?"

Hugo put down the bottle he was holding.

"He may be. He's one of the few who live in college. But I doubt whether you would winkle him out of his lair on your own. If it's all that urgent, I'd better come with you."

The college porter ascertained without curiosity that Benskin was in the college and Benskin was summoned. He arrived after a wait of five minutes during which Hugo chatted to the porter and Cordelia walked outside the Lodge to amuse herself reading the college notices. Benskin arrived, unhurrying, imperturbable. He was a silver-haired, formally dressed old man, his face creased and thick skinned as an anaemic blood orange, and would, Cordelia thought, have looked like an advertisement for the ideal butler, were it not for an expression of lugubrious and sly disdain.

Cordelia gave him sight of Sir Ronald's note of authority and plunged straight into her questions. There was nothing to be gained by subtlety and since she had enlisted Hugo's help, she had little hope of shaking him off. She said:

"Sir Ronald has asked me to enquire into the circumstances of his son's death."

"So I see, Miss."

"I am told that Mr. Mark Callender telephoned his father while Sir Ronald was dining at High Table on the night his son died and that you passed the message to Sir Ronald shortly after dinner began?"

"I was under the impression at the time that it

was Mr. Callender who was ringing, Miss, but I was mistaken."

"How can you be sure of that, Mr. Benskin?"

"Sir Ronald himself told me, Miss, when I saw him in college some few days after his son's death. I've known Sir Ronald since he was an undergraduate and I made bold to express my condolences. During our brief conversation I made reference to the telephone call of 26th May and Sir Ronald told me that I was mistaken, that it was not Mr. Callender who had called."

"Did he say who it was?"

"Sir Ronald informed me that it was his laboratory assistant, Mr. Chris Lunn."

"Did that surprise you—that you were wrong, I mean?"

"I confess that I was somewhat surprised, Miss, but the mistake was perhaps excusable. My subsequent reference to the incident was fortuitous and in the circumstances regrettable."

"But do you really believe that you mis-heard the name?"

The obstinate old face did not relax.

"Sir Ronald could have been in no doubt about the person who telephoned him."

"Was it usual for Mr. Callender to ring his father while he was dining in College?"

"I had never previously taken a call from him, but then answering the telephone is not part of my normal duties. It is possible that some of the other college servants may be able to help but I hardly think that an enquiry would be productive or that the news that college servants had been questioned would be gratifying to Sir Ronald."

"Any enquiry which can help ascertain the truth is likely to be gratifying to Sir Ronald," said Cordelia. Really, she thought, Benskin's prose style is becoming infectious. She added more naturally:

"Sir Ronald is very anxious to find out everything possible about his son's death. Is there anything that you can tell me, any help that you can give me, Mr. Benskin?"

This was perilously close to an appeal but it met with no response.

"Nothing, Miss. Mr. Callender was a quiet and pleasant young gentleman who seemed, as far as I was able to observe him, to be in good health and spirits up to the time he left us. His death has been very much felt in the college. Is there anything else, Miss?"

He stood patiently waiting to be dismissed and Cordelia let him go. As she and Hugo left college together and walked back into Trumpington Street she said bitterly:

"He doesn't care, does he?"

"Why should he? Benskin's an old phoney but he's been at college for seventy years and he's seen it all before. A thousand ages in his sight are but an evening gone. I've only known Benskin distressed once over the suicide of an undergraduate and that was a Duke's son. Benskin thought that there were some things that the college shouldn't permit to happen."

"But he wasn't mistaken about Mark's call.

You could tell that from his whole manner, at least I could. He knows what he heard. He isn't going to admit it, of course, but he knows in his heart he wasn't mistaken."

Hugo said lightly:

"He was being the old college servant, very correct, very proper; that's Benskin all over. 'The young gentlemen aren't what they were when I first came to college.' I should bloody well hope not! They wore side whiskers then and noblemen sported fancy gowns to distinguish them from the plebs. Benskin would bring all that back if he could. He's an anachronism, pottering through the court hand in hand with a statelier past."

"But he isn't deaf. I deliberately spoke in a soft voice and he heard me perfectly. Do you really believe that he was mistaken?"

"Chris Lunn and his son are very similar sounds."

"But Lunn doesn't announce himself that way. All the time I was with Sir Ronald and Miss Learning they just called him Lunn."

"Look, Cordelia, you can't possibly suspect Ronald Callender of having a hand in his son's death! Be logical. You accept, I suppose, that a rational murderer hopes not to be found out. You admit, no doubt, that Ronald Callender, although a disagreeable bastard, is a rational being. Mark is dead and his body cremated. No one except you has mentioned murder. Then Sir Ronald employs you to stir things up. Why should he if he's got something to hide? He doesn't even need to divert suspicion; there has been no suspicion; there has been no suspicion, there is no suspicion."

"Of course I don't suspect him of killing his son. He doesn't know how Mark died and he desperately needs to know. That's why he's taken me on. I could tell that at our interview; I couldn't be wrong about that. But I don't understand why he should have lied about the telephone call."

"If he is lying there could be half a dozen innocent explanations. If Mark did ring the college it must have been something pretty urgent, perhaps something which his father didn't particularly want to make public, something which gives a clue to his son's suicide."

"Then why employ me to find out why he killed himself?"

"True, wise Cordelia; I'll try again. Mark asked him for help, perhaps an urgent visit which Dad refused. You can imagine his reaction. 'Don't be ridiculous, Mark, I'm dining at High Table with the Master. Obviously I can't leave the cutlets and claret just because you telephone in this hysterical way and demand to see me. Pull yourself together.' That sort of thing wouldn't sound so good in open court; coroners are notoriously censorious." Hugo's voice took on a deep magisterial tone. "'It is not for me to add to Sir Ronald's distress, but it is, perhaps, unfortunate that he chose to ignore what was obviously a cry for help. Had he left his meal immediately and gone to his son's side this brilliant young student might have been saved.' Cambridge suicides, so I've noticed, are always brilliant; I'm still waiting to read the report of an inquest where the college authorities testify that the student only just killed himself in time before they kicked him out."

"But Mark died between seven and nine p.m. That telephone call is Sir Ronald's alibi!"

"He wouldn't see it like that. He doesn't need an alibi. If you know you're not involved and the question of foul play never arises, you don't think in terms of alibis. It's only the guilty who do that."

"But how did Mark know where to find his father? In his evidence Sir Ronald said that he hadn't spoken to his son for over three weeks."

"I can see you have a point there. Ask Miss Leaming. Better still, ask Lunn if it was, in fact, he who rang the college. If you're looking for a villain Lunn should suit it admirably. I find him absolutely sinister."

"I didn't know that you knew him."

"Oh, he's pretty well known in Cambridge. He drives that horrid little closed van around with ferocious dedication as if he were transporting recalcitrant students to the gas chambers. Everyone knows Lunn. Seldom he smiles and smiles in such a way as if he mocked himself and scorned his spirit that could be moved to smile at anything. I should concentrate on Lunn."

They walked on in silence through the warm scented night while the waters sang in the runnels of Trumpington Street. Lights were shining now in college doorways and in porters' lodges and the far gardens and inter-connecting courts, glimpsed as they passed, looked remote and ethereal as in a dream. Cordelia was suddenly oppressed with loneliness and melancholy. If Bernie were alive they would be discussing the case, cosily ensconced in the furthest corner of some Cambridge pub, insulated by noise and smoke and anonymity from the curiosity of their neighbours; talking low voiced in their own particular jargon. They would be speculating on the personality of a young man who slept under that gentle, and intellectual, painting, yet who had bought a vulgar magazine of salacious nudes. Or had he? And if not, how had it come to be in the cottage garden? They would be discussing a father who lied about his son's last telephone call; speculating in happy complicity about an uncleaned spade, a row of earth half dug, an unwashed coffee mug, a quotation from Blake meticulously typed. They would be talking about Isabelle who was terrified and Sophie who was surely honest and Hugo who certainly knew something about Mark's death and who was clever but not as clever as he needed to be. For the first time since the case began Cordelia doubted her ability to solve it alone. If only there were someone reliable in whom she could confide, someone who would reinforce her confidence. She thought again of Sophie, but Sophie had been Mark's mistress and was Hugo's sister. They were both involved. She was on her own and that, when she came to think about it, was no different from how essentially it had always been. Ironically, the realization brought her comfort and a return of hope.

At the corner of Panton Street they paused and he said:

"You're coming back to the party?"

"No, thank you, Hugo; I've got work to do."

"Are you staying in Cambridge?"

Cordelia wondered whether the question was prompted by more than polite interest. Suddenly cautious, she said:

"Only for the next day or two. I've found a very dull but cheap bed and breakfast place near the station."

He accepted the lie without comment and they said goodnight. She made her way back to Norwich Street. The little car was still outside number fifty-seven, but the house was dark and quiet as if to emphasize her exclusion and the three windows were as blank as dead rejecting eyes.

She was tired by the time she got back to the cottage and had parked the Mini on the edge of the copse. The garden gate creaked at her hand. The night was dark and she felt in her bag for her torch and followed its bright pool round the side of the cottage and to the back door. By its light she fitted the key into the lock. She turned it and, dazed with tiredness, stepped into the sitting-room. The torch, still switched on, hung loosely from her hand, making erratic patterns of light on the tiled floor. Then in one involuntary movement it jerked upwards and shone full on the thing that hung from the centre hook of the ceiling. Cordelia gave a cry and clutched at the table. It was the bolster from her bed, the bolster with a cord drawn tight about one end making a grotesque and bulbous head, and the other end stuffed into a pair of Mark's trousers. The legs hung pathetically flat and empty, one lower than the other. As she stared at it in fascinated horror, her heart hammering, a slight breeze wafted in from the open door and it swung slowly round as if twisted by a living hand.

She must have stood there rooted with fear and staring wild-eyed at the bolster for seconds only, yet it seemed minutes before she found the strength to pull out a chair from the table and take the thing down. Even in the moment of repulsion and terror she remembered to look closely at the knot. The cord was attached to the hook by a simple loop and two half-hitches. So, either her secret visitor had chosen not to repeat his former tactics, or he hadn't known how the first knot had been tied. She laid the bolster on the chair and went outside for the gun. In her tiredness she had forgotten it, but now she longed for the reassurance of the hard cold metal in her hand. She stood at the back door and listened. The garden seemed suddenly full of noises, mysterious rustlings, leaves moving in the slight breeze like human sighs, furtive scurryings in the undergrowth, the bat-like squeak of an animal disconcertingly close at hand. The night seemed to be holding its breath as she crept out towards the elder bush. She waited, listening to her own heart, before she found courage to turn her back and stretch up her hand to feel for the gun. It was still there. She sighed audibly with relief and immediately felt better. The gun wasn't loaded but that hardly seemed to matter. She hurried back to the cottage, her terror assuaged.

It was nearly an hour before she finally went to bed. She lit the lamp and, gun in hand, made a search of the whole cottage. Next she examined the window. It was obvious enough how he had got in. The window had no catch and was easy to push open from outside. Cordelia fetched a roll of Scotch tape from her scene-of-crime kit and, as Bernie had shown her, cut two very narrow strips and pasted them across the base of the pane and the wooden frame. She doubted whether the front windows could be opened but she took no chances and sealed them in the same way. It wouldn't stop an intruder but at least she would know next morning that he had gained access. Finally, having washed in the kitchen, she went upstairs to bed. There was no lock on her door but she wedged it slightly open and balanced a saucepan lid on the top of the frame. If anyone did succeed in getting in, he wouldn't take her by surprise. She loaded the gun and placed it on her bedside table, remembering that she was dealing with a killer. She examined the cord. It was a four-foot length of ordinary strong string, obviously not new and frayed at one end. Her heart sank at the hopelessness of trying to identify it. But she labelled it carefully, as Bernie had taught her, and packed it in her scene-of-crime kit. She did the same with the curled strap and the typed passage of Blake, transferring them from the bottom of her shoulder bag to plastic exhibit envelopes. She was so weary that even this routine chore cost her an effort of will. Then she placed the bolster back on the bed, resisting an impulse to sling it on the floor and sleep without it. But, by then, nothing— neither fear nor discomfort—could have kept her awake. She lay for only a few minutes listening to the ticking of her watch before tiredness overcame her and bore her unresisting down the dark tide of sleep.

Chapter Four

CORDELIA WAS AWAKENED early next morning by the discordant chattering of the birds and the strong clear light of another fine day. She lay for several minutes stretching herself within her sleeping-bag, savouring the smell of a country morning, that subtle and evocative fusion of earth, sweet wet grass and stronger farmyard smell. She washed in the kitchen as Mark had obviously done, standing in the tin bath from the shed and gasping as she poured saucepans of cold tap water over her naked body. There was something about the simple life which disposed one to these austerities. Cordelia thought it unlikely that, in any circumstances, she would willingly have bathed in cold water in London or so much relished the smell of the paraffin stove superimposed on the appetizing sizzle of frying bacon, or the flavour of her first strong mug of tea.

The cottage was filled with sunlight, a warm friendly sanctum from which she could safely venture out to whatever the day held. In the calm peace of a summer morning the little sitting-room seemed untouched by the tragedy of Mark Callender's death. The hook in the ceiling looked as innocuous as if it had never served its dreadful purpose. The horror of that moment when her torch had first picked out the dark swollen shadow of the bolster moving in the night breeze now had the unreality of a dream. Even the memory of the precautions of the night before were embarrassing viewed in the unambiguous light of day. She felt rather foolish as she unloaded the gun, secreted the ammunition among her underclothes, and hid the pistol in the elder bush, watching carefully to see that she wasn't observed. When the washing-up was done and the one teacloth washed through and hung out to dry, she picked a small posy of pansies, cowslips and meadow-sweet from the far end of the garden and set them on the table in one of the ribbed mugs.

She had decided that her first task must be to try to trace Nanny Pilbeam. Even if the woman had nothing to tell her about Mark's death or his reason for leaving college, she would be able to speak about his childhood and boyhood; she, probably better than anyone, would know what his essential nature had been. She had cared enough about him to attend the funeral and to send an expensive wreath. She had called on him in college on his 21st birthday. He had probably kept in touch with her, might even have confided in her. He had no mother and Nanny Pilbeam could have been, in some sense, a substitute.

As she drove into Cambridge Cordelia considered tactics. The probability was that Miss Pilbeam lived somewhere in the district. It was unlikely that she actually lived in the city since Hugo Tilling had only seen her once. From his brief account of her, it sounded as if she were old and probably poor. It was unlikely, therefore, that she would travel far to attend the funeral. It was apparent that she hadn't been one of the official mourners from Garforth House, hadn't been invited by Sir Ronald. According to Hugo, none of the party had even spoken to each other. This hardly suggested that Miss Pilbeam was the elderly and valued retainer of tradition, almost one of the family. Sir Ronald's neglect of her on such an occasion intrigued Cordelia. She wondered just what Miss Pilbeam's position in the family had been.

If the old lady lived near Cambridge, she had probably ordered the wreath at one of the city florists. Villages were very unlikely to provide this kind of service. It had been an ostentatious wreath, which suggested that Miss Pilbeam had been prepared to spend lavishly and had probably gone to one of the larger florists. The likelihood was that she had ordered it personally. Elderly ladies, apart from the fact that they were seldom on the telephone, like to attend to these matters direct, having, Cordelia suspected, a well-founded suspicion that only face-to-face confrontation and the meticulous recital of one's precise requirements extracted the best service. If Miss Pilbeam had come in from her village by train or by bus, she had probably selected a shop somewhere near the centre of the city. Cordelia decided to begin her search by enquiring of passers-by if they could recommend the name of a good florist.

She had already learned that Cambridge was not a city for the cruising motorist. She drew up and consulted the folding map at the back of her guide book and decided to leave the Mini on the car park next to Parker's Piece. Her search might take some time and would be best done on foot. She daren't risk a parking fine nor the impounding of the car. She checked her watch. It was still only a few minutes after nine o'clock. She had made a good start to the day.

The first hour was disappointing. The people of whom she enquired were anxious to be helpful but their ideas of what constituted a reliable florist somewhere near the centre of the city were peculiar. Cordelia was directed to small greengrocers selling a few bunches of cut flowers as a side line, to the supplier of gardening equipment who dealt in plants but not in wreaths, and once to a funeral director. The two florists' shops which at first sight seemed possible had never heard of

Miss Pilbeam and had provided no wreaths for
the Mark Callender funeral. A little weary with
much walking and beginning to feel despondent,
Cordelia decided that the whole quest had been
unreasonably sanguine. Probably Miss Pilbeam
had come in from Bury St. Edmunds or Newmarket and had bought the wreath in her own town.

But the visit to the undertakers was not wasted.
In reply to her enquiry, they recommended the
name of a firm which provided "a very nice class
of wreath, Miss, really very nice indeed." The
shop was further from the centre of the city than
Cordelia had expected. Even from the pavement
it smelt of weddings or funerals, as one's mood
dictated, and as she pushed open the door Cordelia was welcomed by a gush of sweet warm air
which caught at the throat. There were flowers
everywhere. Large green buckets lined the walls
holding clumps of lilies, irises and lupins; smaller
containers were packed tight with wall flowers
and marigolds and stocks; there were frigid bundles of tight budded roses on thornless stems,
each flower identical in size and colour and looking as if it had been cultivated in a test tube. Pots
of indoor plants, decorated with variegated ribbon, lined the path to the counter like a floral
guard of honour.

There was a room at the back of the shop where
two assistants were working. Through the open
door Cordelia watched them. The younger, a lan-
guid blonde with a spotted skin, was assistant ex-
ecutioner, laying out roses and freesias, predestined

victims, graded according to type and colour. Her senior, whose status was denoted by a better fitting overall and an air of authority, was twisting off the flower heads, piercing each mutilated bloom with wire and threading them closely on to a huge bed of moss in the shape of a heart. Cordelia averted her eyes from this horror.

A buxom lady in a pink smock appeared behind the counter apparently from nowhere. She was as pungently scented as the shop, but had obviously decided that no ordinary floral perfume could compete and that she had better rely on the exotic. She smelt of curry powder and pine so strongly that the effect was practically anaesthetizing.

Cordelia said her prepared speech:

"I'm from Sir Ronald Callender of Garforth House. I wonder whether you can help us? His son was cremated on 3rd of June and their old nurse very kindly sent a wreath, a cross of red roses. Sir Ronald has lost her address and very much wants to write to thank her. The name is Pilbeam."

"Oh, I don't think we executed any orders of that type for 3rd June."

"If you would be kind enough to just look in the book—"

Suddenly the young blonde looked up from her work and called out:

"It's Goddard."

"I beg your pardon, Shirley?" said the buxom lady repressively.

"The name's Goddard. The card on the wreath said Nanny Pilbeam, but the customer was a Mrs. Goddard. Another lady came to enquire from Sir Ronald Callender and that was the name she gave. I looked it up for her. Mrs. Goddard, Lavender Cottage, Ickleton. One cross, four foot long in red roses. Six pounds. It's there in the book."

"Thank you very much," said Cordelia fervently. She smiled her thanks impartially at the three of them and left quickly in case she got embroiled in an argument about the other enquirer from Garforth House. It must have looked odd, she knew, but the three of them would no doubt enjoy themselves discussing it after she had left. Lavender Cottage, Ickleton. She kept repeating the address to herself until she was at a safe distance from the shop and could pause to write it down.

Her tiredness seemed miraculously to have left her as she sped back to the car park. She consulted her map. Ickleton was a village near the Essex border about ten miles from Cambridge. It wasn't far from Duxford so that she would be retracing her steps. She could be there in less than half an hour.

But it took longer than she had expected to thread her way through the Cambridge traffic and it wasn't until thirty-five minutes later, that she came to Ickleton's fine flint and pebble church with its broach spire, and drove the Mini close to the church gate. It was a temptation to take a brief look inside, but she resisted it. Mrs. Goddard might even now be preparing to catch the Cambridge bus. She went in search of Lavender Cottage.

It wasn't, in fact, a cottage at all but a small semi-detached house of hideous red brick at the end of the High Street. There was only a narrow strip of grass between the front door and the road and neither smell nor sight of lavender. The iron knocker, in the form of a lion's head, fell heavily, shaking the door. The response came, not from Lavender Cottage, but from the next house. An elderly woman appeared, thin, almost toothless and swathed in an immense apron patterned with roses. She had carpet slippers on her feet, a woollen cap decorated with a bobble on her head and an air of lively interest in the world in general.

"You'll be wanting Mrs. Goddard, I daresay?"

"Yes. Could you tell me where I could find her?"

"She'll be over at the graveyard, I don't doubt. She usually is this time of a fine morning."

"I've just come from the church. I didn't see anyone."

"Bless you, Miss, she's not at the church! They haven't been burying us there for many a year now. Her old man is where they'll be putting her in time, in the cemetery on Hinxton Road. You can't miss it. Just keep straight on."

"I'll have to go back to the church for my car," said Cordelia. It was obvious that she was going to be watched out of sight and it seemed necessary to explain why she was departing in the opposite direction to the one indicated. The old woman smiled and nodded and came out to lean on her gate for a better view of Cordelia's progress down the High Street, nodding her head like a marionette so that the bright bobble danced in the sun.

The cemetery was easily found. Cordelia parked the Mini on a convenient patch of grass where a signpost pointed the footpath to Duxford and walked the few yards back to the iron gates. There was a small flint chapel of rest with an apse at the east end and beside it an ancient wooden seat green with lichen and spattered with bird lime which gave a view of the whole burial ground. A wide swathe of turf ran straight down the middle and on each side were the graves, variously marked with white marble crosses, grey headstones, small rusted circles of iron heeling over towards the smooth turf and bright splashes of flowers patchworked over the newly dug earth. It was very peaceful. The burial ground was surrounded by trees, their leaves scarcely stirring in the calm, hot air. There was little sound except the chirruping of crickets in the grass and from time to time the nearby ringing of a railway level-crossing bell and the swooping horn of a diesel train.

There was only one other person in the graveyard, an elderly woman bending over one of the far graves. Cordelia sat quietly on the seat, arms folded in her lap, before making her way silently down the grass path towards her. She knew with certainty that this interview was going to be crucial yet paradoxically she was in no hurry to begin. She came up to the woman and stood, still unnoticed, at the foot of the grave.

She was a small woman dressed in black whose old-fashioned straw hat, its brim wreathed with faded net, was screwed to her hair with an immense black bobbed hat pin. She knelt with her back to Cordelia showing the soles of a pair of mis-shapen shoes from which her thin legs stuck out like sticks. She was weeding the grave; her fingers, darting like a reptile's tongue over the grass, plucked at small, almost undetectable weeds. At her side was a punnet holding a folded newspaper and a gardening trowel. From time to time, she dropped into the punnet her little mush of weeds.

After a couple of minutes, during which Cordelia watched her in silence, she paused satisfied and began smoothing the surface of the grass as if comforting the bones beneath. Cordelia read the inscription carved deep on the headstone. "Sacred to the memory of Charles Albert Goddard beloved husband of Annie who departed this life 27th August 1962, aged 70 years. At rest." At rest; the commonest epitaph of a generation to whom rest must have seemed the ultimate luxury, the supreme benediction.

The woman rested back for a second on her heels and contemplated the grave with satisfaction. It was then that she became aware of

Cordelia. She turned a bright much wrinkled face towards her and said without curiosity or resentment at her presence:

"It's a nice stone, isn't it?"

"Yes, it is. I was admiring the lettering."

"Cut deep that is. It cost a mint of money but it was worth it. That'll last, you see. Half the lettering here won't, it's that shallow. It takes the pleasure out of a cemetery. I like to read the gravestones, like to know who people were and when they died and how long the women lived after they buried their men. It sets you wondering how they managed and whether they were lonely. There's no use in a stone if you can't read the lettering. Of course, this stone looks a bit top-heavy at present. That's because I asked them to leave space for me: 'Also to Annie his wife, departed this life, . . .' and then the date: That'll even it up nicely. I've left the money to pay for it."

"What text were you thinking of having?" enquired Cordelia.

"Oh, no text! At rest will be good enough for the both of us. We shan't be asking more of the good Lord than that."

Cordelia said:

"That cross of roses you sent to Mark Callender's funeral was beautiful."

"Oh, did you see it? You weren't at the funeral were you? Yes, I was pleased with it. They made a nice job of it, I thought. Poor boy, he hadn't much else, had he?"

She looked at Cordelia with benign interest:

"So you knew Mr. Mark? Would you be his young lady perhaps?"

"No, not that, but I care about him. It's odd that he never talked about you, his old nurse."

"But I wasn't his nurse, my dear, or at least, only for a month or two. He was a baby then, it meant nothing to him. No, I was nurse to his dear mother."

"But you visited Mark on his twenty-first birthday?"

"So he told you that, did he? I was glad to see him again after all those years, but I wouldn't have pushed myself on him. It wouldn't have been right, his father feeling as he did. No, I went to give him something from his mother, to do something she had asked me to do when she was dying. Do you know, I hadn't seen Mr. Mark for over twenty years—odd, really, considering that we didn't live that far apart—but I knew him at once. He had a great look of his mother about him, poor boy."

"Could you tell me about it? It's not just curiosity; it's important for me to know."

Leaning for support on the handle of her basket, Mrs. Goddard got laboriously to her feet. She picked at a few short blades of grass adhering to her skirt, felt in her pocket for a pair of grey cotton gloves and put them on. Together they made their way slowly down the path.

"Important, is it? I don't know why it should be. It's all in the past now. She's dead, poor lady, and so is he. All that hope and promise come to nothing. I haven't spoken to anyone else about it, but then who would care to know?"

"Perhaps we could sit on this bench and talk together for a time?"

"I don't see why we shouldn't. There's nothing to hurry home for now. Do you know, my dear, I didn't marry my husband until I was fifty-three and yet I miss him as if we had been childhood sweethearts. People said I was a fool to take on a man at that age but you see I had known his wife for thirty years, we were at school together, and I knew him. If a man's good to one woman, he'll be good to another. That's what I reckoned and I was right."

They sat side by side on the bench gazing over the green swathe towards the grave. Cordelia said:

"Tell me about Mark's mother."

"She was a Miss Bottley, Evelyn Bottley. I went to her mother as under-nursemaid before she was born. There was only little Harry then. He was killed in the war on his first raid over Germany. His Dad took it very hard; there was never anyone to match Harry, the sun shone out of his eyes. The master never really cared for Miss Evie, it was all the boy with him. Mrs. Bottley died when Evie was born and that may have made a difference. People say that it does, but I've never believed it. I've known fathers who loved a baby even more—poor innocent things, how can they be blamed? If you ask me, it was just an excuse for not taking to the child, that she killed her mother."

"Yes, I know a father who made it an excuse too. But it isn't their fault. We can't make ourselves love someone just because we want to."

"More's the pity, my dear, or the world would be an easier place. But his own child, that's not natural!"

"Did she love him?"

"How could she? You won't get love from a child if you don't give love. But she never had the trick of pleasing him, of humouring him—he was a big man, fierce, loud talking, frightening to a child. He would have done better with a pretty, pert little thing, who wouldn't have been afraid of him."

"What happened to her? How did she meet Sir Ronald Callender?"

"He wasn't Sir Ronald then, my dear. Oh, dear no! He was Ronny Callender the gardener's son. They lived at Harrogate you see. Oh, such a lovely house they had! When I first went into service there they had three gardeners. That was before the war, of course. Mr. Bottley worked in Bradford; he was in the wool trade. Well, you were asking about Ronny Callender. I remember him well, a pugnacious, good-looking lad but one who kept his thoughts to himself. He was clever that one, oh he was clever! He got a scholarship to the grammar school and did very well."

"And Evelyn Bottley fell in love?"

"She may have done, my dear. What there was between them when they were young, who can tell. But then the war came and he went away. She was wild to do something useful and they took her on as a V.A.D., though how she passed the medical I'll never know. And then they met again in London as people did in the war and the next thing we knew they were married."

"And came to live here outside Cambridge?"

"Not until after the war. At first she kept on with her nursing and he was sent overseas. He had what the men call a good war; we'd call it a bad war I daresay, a lot of killing and fighting, imprisonment and escaping. It ought to have made Mr. Bottley proud of him and reconciled to the marriage but it didn't. I think he thought that Ronny had his eye on the money, because there was money to come, no doubt about that. He may have been right, but who's to blame the boy? My mother used to say, 'Don't marry for money, but marry where money is!' There's no harm in looking for money as long as there's kindness as well."

"And do you think there was kindness?"

"There was never unkindness that I could see, and she was mad about him. After the war he went up to Cambridge. He'd always wanted to be a scientist and he got a grant because he was ex-service. She had some money from her father and they bought the house he lives in now so that he could live at home when he was studying. It didn't look the same then, of course. He's done a lot to it since. They were quite poor then and Miss Evie managed with practically no one to help, only me. Mr. Bottley used to come and stay from time to time. She used to dread his visits, poor darling. He was looking for a grandchild, you see, and one didn't come. And then Mr. Callender finished at the university and got a job teaching. He wanted to stay on at college to be a don or something like that, but they wouldn't have him. He used to say it was because he hadn't influence, but I think he may not have been quite clever enough. In Harrogate we thought he was the cleverest boy in the grammar school. But then, Cambridge is full of clever men."

"And then Mark was born?"

"Yes, on the 25th April 1951, nine years after they were married. He was born in Italy. Mr. Bottley was that pleased when she became pregnant that he increased the allowance and they used to spend a lot of holidays in Tuscany. My lady loved Italy, always had, and I think she wanted the child to be born there. Otherwise she wouldn't have gone on holiday in the last month of her pregnancy. I went to visit her about a month after she came home with the baby and I've never seen a woman so happy. Oh, he was a lovely little boy!"

"But why did you visit her; weren't you living and working there?"

"No, my dear. Not for some months. She wasn't well in the early days of her pregnancy. I could see that she was strained and unhappy and then one day Mr. Callender sent for me and told me that she had taken against me and that I'd have to leave. I wouldn't have believed it, but when I went to her she just put out her hand and said: 'I'm sorry, Nanny, I think it would be better if you went.'

"Pregnant women have strange fancies, I know, and the baby was so important to them both. I thought she might have asked me to come back afterwards and so she did, but not living in. I took a bedsitting room in the village with the post-mistress and used to give four mornings a week to my lady and the rest to other ladies in the village. It worked very well, really, but I missed the baby when I wasn't with him. I hadn't seen her often during her pregnancy but once we met in Cambridge. She must have been near the end of her time. She was very heavy, poor dear, dragging herself along. At first she pretended that she hadn't noticed me and then she thought better of it and came across the road. 'We're off to Italy next week, Nanny,' she said. 'Isn't it lovely?' I said: 'If you're not careful, my dear, that baby will be a little Italian,' and she laughed. It seemed as though she couldn't wait to get back to the sun."

"And what happened after she came home?"

"She died after nine months, my dear. She was never strong, as I said, and she caught influenza. I helped look after her and I'd have done more but Mr. Callender took over the nursing himself. He couldn't bear anyone to be near her. We only had a few minutes together just before she died and it was then that she asked me to give her prayer book to Mark on his twenty-first birthday. I can hear her now: 'Give it to Mark when he's twenty-one, Nanny. Wrap it up carefully and take it to him when he comes of age. You won't forget will you?' I said: 'I'll not forget, my darling, you know that.' Then she said a strange thing. 'If you do, or if you die before then, or if he doesn't understand, it won't really matter. It will mean that God wants it that way.'"

"What do you think she meant?"

"Who's to say, my dear? She was very religious was Miss Evie, too religious for her own good, I sometimes thought. I believe we should accept our own responsibilities, solve our own problems, not leave it all to God as if He hadn't enough to be thinking about with the world in the state it is. But that's what she said not three hours before she died and that's what I promised. So when Mr. Mark was twenty-one, I found out what college he was at and went to see him."

"What happened?"

"Oh, we had a very happy time together. Do you know, his father had never spoken about his mother. That sometimes happens when a wife dies but I think a son ought to know about his mother. He was full of questions, things that I thought his father would have told him.

"He was glad to get the prayer book. It was a few days later that he came to see me. He asked the name of the doctor who had treated his mother. I told him that it was old Dr. Gladwin. Mr. Callender and she had never had any other doctor. I used to think it a pity sometimes, Miss Evie being so frail. Dr. Gladwin must have been seventy then, and although there were people who wouldn't say a word against him, I never thought much of him myself. Drink, you know, my dear; he was never really reliable. But I expect he's gone to his rest long since, poor man. Anyway, I told Mr. Mark the name and he wrote it down. Then we had tea and a little chat and he left. I never saw him again."

"And no one else knows about the prayer book?"

"No one in the world, my dear. Miss Leaming saw the florist's name on my card and asked them for my address. She came here the day after the funeral to thank me for attending but I could see it was only curiosity. If she and Sir Ronald were so pleased to see me, what was to stop them from coming over and shaking hands? She as good as suggested that I was there without an invitation. An invitation to a funeral! Who ever heard of such a thing?"

"So you told her nothing?" asked Cordelia.

"I've told no one but you, my dear, and I'm not sure why I've told you. But no, I didn't tell her. I never liked her, to tell you the truth. I'm not saying there was anything between her and Sir Ronald, not while Miss Evie was alive anyway. There was never any gossip and she lived in a flat in

Cambridge and kept herself to herself, I'll give her that. Mr. Callender met her when he was teaching science at one of the village schools. She was the English mistress. It wasn't until after Miss Evie died that he set up his own laboratory."

"Do you mean that Miss Leaming has a degree in English?"

"Oh, yes, my dear! She wasn't trained as a secretary. Of course she gave up the teaching when she started working for Mr. Callender."

"So you left Garforth House after Mrs. Callender died? You didn't stay on to care for the baby?"

"I wasn't wanted. Mr. Callender employed one of those new college-trained girls and then, when Mark was still only a baby, he was sent away to school. His father made it plain that he didn't like me to see the child and after all, a father has his rights. I wouldn't have gone on seeing Mr. Mark knowing that his father didn't approve. It would have only put the boy in a false position. But now he's dead and we've all lost him. The coroner said that he killed himself, and he may have been right."

Cordelia said:

"I don't think he killed himself."

"Don't you, my dear? That's kind of you. But he's dead, isn't he, so what does it matter now? I think it's time for me to go home. If you don't mind, I won't ask you to tea, my dear, I'm a little tired today. But you know where to find me, and if ever you want to see me again, you'll always be welcome."

They made their way out of the burial ground together. At the gates, they parted. Mrs. Goddard patted Cordelia on the shoulder with the clumsy affection she might have shown to an animal, then walked off slowly towards the village.

As Cordelia drove round the curve of the road, the levelcrossing came into sight. A train had just passed and the barriers were being raised. Three vehicles had been caught at the crossing and the last in line was quickest away, accelerating past the first two cars as they bumped slowly over the rails. Cordelia saw that it was a small black van.

Later Cordelia remembered little of the journey back to the cottage. She drove fast, concentrating on the road ahead, trying to control her rising excitement by meticulous attention to gears and brakes. She drove the Mini hard against the front hedge, careless of whether it were seen. The cottage looked and smelt just as she had left it. She had almost expected to find it ransacked and the prayer book gone. Sighing with relief, she saw that the white spine was still there among the taller and darker covers. Cordelia opened it. She hardly knew what she expected to find; an inscription perhaps, or a message, cryptic or plain, a letter folded between the leaves. But the only inscription could have no possible relevance to the case. It was written in a shaky, old-fashioned hand; the steel nib had crawled spider-like over the page. "To Evelyn Mary on the occasion of her confirmation, with love from her Godmother, 5th August 1934."

Cordelia shook the book. No slip of paper fluttered out. She skimmed through the pages. Nothing.

She sat on the bed drooping with disappointment. Had it been unreasonable to imagine that there was something significant in the bequest of the prayer book; had she fabricated a promising edifice of conjecture and mystery on an old woman's confused recollections of a perfectly ordinary and understandable action—a devout and dying mother leaving a prayer book to her son? And even if she hadn't been wrong, why should the message still be there? If Mark had found a note from his mother, placed between the leaves, he might well have destroyed it after reading. And if he hadn't destroyed it, someone else might have done so. The note, if it ever existed, was now probably part of the shifting heap of white ash and charred debris in the cottage grate.

She shook herself out of her despondency. There was still a line of enquiry to pursue; she would try to trace Dr. Gladwin. After a second's thought she put the prayer book in her bag. Looking at her watch, she saw that it was nearly one o'clock. She decided to have a picnic lunch of cheese and fruit in the garden and then set off again for Cambridge to visit the central library and consult a medical directory.

Less than an hour later she found the information she wanted. There was only one Dr. Gladwin still on the register who could have attended Mrs. Callender as an old man of over seventy, twenty years ago. He was Emlyn Thomas Gladwin who had qualified at St. Thomas's Hospital in 1904. She wrote down the address in her note book; 4 Pratts Way, Ixworth Road, Bury St. Edmunds. Edmunds town! The town which Isabelle had said that she and Mark had visited on their way to the sea.

So the day hadn't been wasted after all—she was following in Mark Callender's footsteps. Impatient to consult a map she went over to the atlas section of the library. It was now two-fifteen. If she took the A45 road direct through Newmarket she could be in Bury St. Edmunds in about an hour. Allow an hour for the visit to the doctor and another for the return journey. She could be home at the cottage before half past five.

She was driving through the gentle unemphatic countryside just outside Newmarket when she noticed the black van following her. It was too far away to see who was driving but she thought it was Lunn and that he was alone. She accelerated, trying to keep the distance between them, but the van drew a little nearer. There was no reason, of course, why Lunn shouldn't be driving to Newmarket on Sir Ronald Callender's business, but the sight of the squat little van perpetually in her driving mirror was disconcerting. Cordelia decided to throw him off. There were few side turns on the road she was travelling and the country was unfamiliar to her. She decided to wait until she reached Newmarket and seize what opportunity offered.

The main through street of the town was a tangle of traffic and every turn seemed to be blocked. It was only at the second set of traffic lights that Cordelia saw her chance. The black van was caught at the intersection about fifty yards behind. As the light turned green, she accelerated quickly and swung round to the left. There was another turn to the left and she took it, then one to the right. She drove on through unfamiliar streets, then after about five minutes, stopped at an intersection and waited. The black van did not appear. It looked as if she had succeeded in shaking him off. She waited for another five minutes, then made her way slowly back to the main road and joined in the flow of eastward traffic. Half an hour later she had passed through Bury St. Edmunds and was driving very slowly down the Ixworth Road, watching for Pratts Way. Fifty yards farther on she came to it, a row of six small stucco houses standing back from a lay-by. She stopped the car outside number four remembering Isabelle, biddable and docile, who had obviously been told to drive further on and wait in the car. Was that because Mark thought the white Renault too conspicuous? Even the arrival of the Mini had provoked interest. There were faces at upper windows and a small group of children had mysteriously appeared, clustered around a neighbouring gate and watching her with wide and expressionless eyes.

Number four was a depressing house; the front garden was unweeded and the fence had gaps where the planks had rotted or had been wrenched apart. The external paint had flaked away to the bare wood and the brown front door had peeled and blistered in the sun. But Cordelia saw that the bottom windows were shining and that the white net curtains were clean. Mrs. Gladwin was probably a careful housewife, struggling to keep up her standards but too old for the heavy work and too poor to afford help. Cordelia felt benevolently towards her. But the woman who, after some minutes, finally opened to her knock—the bell was out of order—was a disconcerting antidote to her sentimental pity. Compassion died before those hard distrustful eyes, that mouth tight as a trap, the thin arms clasped in a bony barrier across her chest as if to repel human contact. It was difficult to guess her age. Her hair, screwed back into a small tight bun, was still black but her face was deeply lined and the sinews and veins stood out in the thin neck like cords. She was wearing carpet slippers and a gaudy cotton overall. Cordelia said:

"My name is Cordelia Gray. I wondered if I could talk to Dr. Gladwin, if he's in. It's about an old patient."

"He's in, where else would he be? He's in the garden. You'd better go through."

The house smelt horrible, an amalgam of extreme old age, the sour taint of excreta and stale food, with an overlay of strong disinfectant. Cordelia went through to the garden, carefully avoiding looking at the hall or kitchen since curiosity might seem impertinent.

Dr. Gladwin was sitting in a high Windsor chair placed in the sun. Cordelia had never seen a man so old. He seemed to be wearing a woollen track suit, his swollen legs were encased in immense felt slippers and there was a knitted patchwork shawl across his knees. His two hands hung over the arms of the chair as if too heavy for the frail wrists, hands stained and brittle as autumn leaves which trembled with a gentle insistence. The high-domed skull, spiked with a few grey bristles, looked as small and vulnerable as a child's. The eyes were pale yolks swimming in their glutinous blue-veined whites.

Cordelia went to him and called him gently by his name. There was no response. She knelt on the grass at his feet and looked up into his face.

"Dr. Gladwin, I wanted to talk to you about a patient. It was a long time ago. Mrs. Callender. Do you remember Mrs. Callender of Garforth House?"

There was no reply. Cordelia knew that there wouldn't be. Even to ask again seemed an outrage. Mrs. Gladwin was standing beside him as if displaying him to a wondering world.

"Go on, ask him! It's all in his head you know.

That's what he used to tell me. 'I'm not one for records and notes. It's all in my head.'"

Cordelia said:

"What happened to his medical records when he gave up practice? Did any one take them over?"

"That's what I've just told you. There never were any records. And it's no use asking me. I told the boy that too. The doctor was glad enough to marry me when he wanted a nurse, but he didn't discuss his patients. Oh, dear no! He was drinking all the practice profits away, but he could still talk about medical ethics."

The bitterness in her voice was horrible. Cordelia could not meet her eyes. Just then she thought she saw the old man's lips move. She bent down her head and caught the one word. "Cold."

"I think he's trying to say that he's cold. Is there another shawl perhaps that he could have round his shoulders?"

"Cold! In this sun! He's always cold."

"But perhaps another blanket would help. Shall I fetch it for you?"

"You let him be, Miss. If you want to look after him, then look after him. See how you enjoy keeping him clean like a baby, washing his nappies, changing the bed every morning. I'll get him another shawl, but in two minutes he'll be pushing it off. He doesn't know what he wants."

"I'm sorry," said Cordelia helplessly. She wondered whether Mrs. Gladwin was getting all the help available, whether the District Nurse called, whether she had asked her doctor to try to find a hospital bed. But these were useless questions. Even she could recognize the hopeless rejection of help, the despair which no longer had energy even to look for relief. She said:

"I'm sorry; I won't trouble either of you any further."

They walked back together through the house. But there was one question Cordelia had to ask. When they reached the front gate she said:

"You talked about a boy who visited. Was his name Mark?"

"Mark Callender. He was asking about his mother. And then about ten days later we get the other one calling."

"What other one?"

"He was a gentleman all right. Walked in as if he owned the place. He wouldn't give a name but I've seen his face somewhere. He asked to see Dr. Gladwin and I showed him in. We were sitting in the back parlour that day as there was a breeze. He went up to the doctor and said 'Good afternoon, Gladwin' loudly as if talking to a servant. Then he bent down and looked at him. Eye to eye they were. Then he straightened up, wished me good day and left. Oh, we're getting popular, we are! Any more of you and I'll have to charge for the show."

They stood together at the gate. Cordelia wondered whether to hold out her hand but sensed that Mrs. Gladwin was willing her not to go. Suddenly the woman spoke in a loud and gruff voice, looking straight ahead.

"That friend of yours, the boy who came here. He left his address. He said he wouldn't mind sitting with the doctor on a Sunday if I wanted a break; he said he could get them both a bit of dinner. I have a fancy to see my sister over at Haverhill this Sunday. Tell him he can come if he wants to."

The capitulation was ungracious, the invitation grudging, but Cordelia could guess what it had cost her to give it. She said impulsively:

"I could come on Sunday instead. I've got a car, I could get here sooner."

It would be a day lost to Sir Ronald Callender, but she wouldn't charge him. And even a private eye was surely entitled to a day off on Sundays.

"He won't want a slip of a girl. There's things to do for him that need a man. He took to that boy. I could see that. Tell him he can come."

Cordelia turned to her.

"He would have come, I know he would. But he can't. He's dead."

Mrs. Gladwin did not speak. Cordelia put out a tentative hand and touched her sleeve. There was no response. She whispered:

"I'm sorry. I'll go now." She nearly added: "If there's nothing I can do for you," but stopped herself in time. There was nothing she or anyone else could do.

She looked back once as the road bent towards Bury and saw the rigid figure still at the gate.

Cordelia wasn't sure what made her decide to stop at Bury and walk for ten minutes in the Abbey gardens. But she felt she couldn't face the drive back to Cambridge without calming her spirits and the glimpse of grass and flowers through the great Norman doorway was irresistible. She parked the Mini on Angel Hill, then walked through the gardens to the river bank. There she sat for five minutes in the sun. She remembered that there was money spent on petrol to be recorded in her notebook and felt for it in her bag. Her hand brought out the white prayer book. She sat quietly thinking. Suppose she had been Mrs. Callender and had wanted to leave a message, a message which Mark would find and other searchers might miss. Where would she place it? The answer now seemed childishly simple. Surely somewhere on the page with the collect, gospel and epistle for St. Mark's Day. He had been born on April 25th. He had been named after the Saint. Quickly she found the place. In the bright sunlight reflected from the water she saw what a quick rustle through the pages had missed. There against Cranmer's gentle petition for grace to withstand the blasts of false doctrine was a small pattern of hieroglyphics so faint that the mark on the paper was little more than a smudge. She saw that it was a group of letters and figures.

E M C

A   A

14.1.52

The first three letters, of course, were his mother's initials. The date must be that on which she wrote the message. Hadn't Mrs. Goddard said that Mrs. Callender had died when her son was about nine months old? But the double A? Cordelia's mind chased after motoring associations before she remembered the card in Mark's wallet. Surely these two letters under an initial could only show one thing, the blood group. Mark had been B. His mother was AA. There was only one reason why she should have wanted him to have that information. The next step was to discover Sir Ronald Callender's group.

She almost cried out with triumph as she ran through the gardens and turned the Mini again towards Cambridge. She hadn't thought out the implications of this discovery, or even whether her arguments were valid. But at least she had something to do, at least she had a lead. She drove fast, desperate to get to the city before the post office closed. There, she seemed to remember, it was possible to get a copy of the Executive Council's list of local doctors. It was handed over. And now for a telephone. She knew only one house in Cambridge where there was a chance of being left in peace to telephone for up to an hour. She drove to 57, Norwich Street.

Sophie and Davie were at home playing chess in the sitting-room, fair head and dark almost touching over the board. They showed no surprise at Cordelia's plea to use the telephone for a series of calls.

"I'll pay, of course. I'll make a note of how many."

"You'll want the room to yourself, I expect?" said Sophie. "We'll finish the game in the garden, Davie."

Blessedly incurious they carried the chess board with care through the kitchen and set it up on the garden table. Cordelia drew a chair to the kitchen table and settled down with her list. It was formidably long. There was no clue about where to begin but perhaps those doctors with group practices and addresses near the centre of the city would be the best bet. She would start with them, ticking off their names after each call. She remembered another reported pearl of the Superintendent's wisdom: "Detection requires a patient persistence which amounts to obstinacy." She thought of him as she dialled the first number. What an intolerably demanding and irritating boss he must have been! But he was almost certainly old now—forty-five at least. He had probably eased up a bit by now.

But an hour's obstinacy was unfruitful. Her calls were invariably answered; one advantage of ringing a doctor's surgery was that the telephone was at least manned. But the replies, given politely, curtly or in tones of harassed haste by a variety of respondents from the doctors themselves to obliging daily women prepared to convey a message, were the same. Sir Ronald Callender was not a patient of this practice. Cordelia repeated her formula. "I'm so sorry to have troubled you. I must have misheard the name."

But after nearly seventy minutes of patient dialling she struck lucky. The doctor's wife answered.

"I'm afraid you've got the wrong practice. Dr. Venables looks after Sir Ronald Callender's household."

This was luck indeed! Dr. Venables wasn't on her preliminary list and she wouldn't have reached the V's for at least another hour. She ran her finger quickly down the names and dialled for the last time.

It was Dr. Venables' nurse who answered. Cordelia spoke her prepared piece:

"I'm ringing for Miss Leaming from Garforth House. I'm sorry to trouble you but could you please remind us of Sir Ronald Callender's blood group? He wants to know it before the Helsinki Conference next month."

"Just a minute, please." There was a brief wait; the sound of footsteps returning.

"Sir Ronald is Group A. I should make a careful note of it if I were you. His son had to ring a month or so ago with the same enquiry."

"Thank you! Thank you! I'll be careful to make a note." Cordelia decided to take a risk.

"I'm new here, assisting Miss Leaming, and she did tell me to note it down last time but stupidly I forgot. If she should happen to call, please don't tell her that I had to trouble you again."

The voice laughed, indulgent to the inefficiency of the young. After all, it wasn't likely to inconvenience her much.

"Don't worry—, I shan't tell her. I'm glad she's got herself some help at last. Everyone's well, I hope?"

"Oh, yes! Everyone's fine."

Cordelia put down the receiver. She looked out of the window and saw that Sophie and Davie were just finishing their game and were putting the pieces back in the box. She had just finished in time. She knew the answer to her query but she still had to verify it. The information was too important to leave to her own vague recollection of the Mendelian rules of inheritance gleaned from the chapter on blood and identity in Bernie's book on forensic medicine. Davie would know, of course. The quickest way would be to ask him now. But she couldn't ask Davie. It would mean going back to the public library, and she would have to hurry if she were to be there before it closed.

But she got there just in time. The librarian, who by now had got used to seeing her, was as helpful as ever. The necessary reference book was quickly produced. Cordelia verified what she had already known. A man and wife both of whose bloods were A could not produce a B group child.

Cordelia was very tired by the time she got back to the cottage. So much had happened during one day; so much had been discovered. It seemed impossible that less than twelve hours previously she had started out on her search for Nanny Pilbeam with only a vague hope that the woman, if she could be found, might provide a clue to Mark Callender's personality, might tell her something about his formative years. She was exhilarated by the success of the day, restless with excitement, but too mentally exhausted to tease out the tangle of conjecture which lay knotted at the back of her mind. At present the facts were disordered; there was no clear pattern, no theory which would at once explain the mystery of Mark's birth, Isabelle's terror, Hugo and Sophie's secret knowledge, Miss Markland's obsessive interest in the cottage, Sergeant Maskell's almost reluctant suspicions, the oddities and unexplained inconsistencies which surrounded Mark's death.

She busied herself about the cottage with the energy of mental overtiredness. She washed the kitchen floor, laid a fire on top of the heap of ash in case the next evening should be chilly, weeded the back flower patch, then made herself a mushroom omelette and ate it sitting, as he must have done, at the simple table. Last of all, she fetched the gun from its hiding place and set it on the table beside the bed. She locked the back door carefully and drew the curtains across the window, checking once more that the seals were intact. But she didn't balance a saucepan on the top of her door. Tonight that particular precaution seemed childish and unnecessary. She lit her bedside candle then went to the window to choose a book. The night was balmy and windless; the flame of the candle burned steadily in the still air. Outside, darkness had not yet fallen but the garden was very quiet, the peace broken only by the distant crescendo of a car on the main road or the cry of a night bird. And then, seen dimly through the gloaming, she glimpsed a figure at the gate. It was Miss Markland. The woman hesitated, hand on the latch, as if wondering whether to enter the garden. Cordelia slipped to one side, back pressed against the wall. The shadowy figure was so still that it seemed as if she sensed a watching presence and had frozen like an animal surprised. Then, after two minutes, she moved away and was lost among the trees of the orchard. Cordelia relaxed, took a copy of *The Warden* from Mark's row of books, and wriggled into her sleeping-bag. Half an hour later, she blew out the candle and stretched her body comfortably for the slow acquiescent descent into sleep.

She stirred in the early hours and was instantly awake, eyes wide open in the half darkness. Time lay suspended; the still air was expectant as if the day had been taken by surprise. She could hear the ticking of her wrist watch on the bedside table and could see beside it the crooked, comforting outline of the pistol, the black cylinder of her torch. She lay and listened to the night. One lived so seldom in these still hours, the time most often slept or dreamt away, that one came to them tentative and unpractised like a creature newly born. She wasn't aware of fear, only of an all-embracing peace, a gentle lassitude. Her breathing filled the quiet room, and the still, uncontaminated air seemed to be breathing in unity with her.

Suddenly, she realized what had woken her. Visitors were coming to the cottage. She must subconsciously in some brief phase of uneasy sleep have recognized the sound of a car. Now there was the whine of the gate, the rustle of feet, furtive as an animal in undergrowth, a faint, broken murmur of voices. She wriggled out of her sleeping-bag and stole to the window. Mark hadn't attempted to clean the glass of the front windows; perhaps he hadn't had time, perhaps he welcomed their occluding dirt. Cordelia rubbed her fingers with desperate haste against the gritty accretion of years. But, at last, she felt the cold smooth glass. It squeaked with the friction of her fingers, high and thin like an animal's squeal so that she thought the noise must betray her. She peered through the narrow strip of clear pane into the garden below.

The Renault was almost hidden by the high hedge but she could see the front of the bonnet gleaming by the gate and the two pools of light from the side lamps shining like twin moons on the lane. Isabelle was wearing something long and clinging; her pale figure trembled like a wave against the dark of the hedge. Hugo was only a black shadow at her side. But then he turned and Cordelia saw the flash of a white shirt-front. They were both in evening dress. They came together quietly up the path and conferred briefly at the front door, then moved towards the corner of the cottage.

Snatching up her torch, Cordelia rushed on silent, naked feet down the stairs and threw herself across the sitting-room to unlock the back door. The key turned easily and silently. Hardly daring to breathe she retreated back into the shadows at the foot of the stairs. She was just in time. The door opened, letting in a shaft of paler light. She heard Hugo's voice:

"Just a minute, I'll strike a match."

The match flared, illuminating in a gentle, momentary light the two grave anticipatory faces, Isabelle's immense and terrified eyes. Then it went out. She heard Hugo's muttered curse followed by the scratch of the second match striking against the box. This time he held it high. It shone on the table, on the mute accusing hook; on the silent watcher at the foot of the stairs. Hugo gasped; his hand jerked and the match went out. Immediately, Isabelle began to scream.

Hugo's voice was sharp.

"What the hell—"

Cordelia switched on her torch and came forward.

"It's only me; Cordelia."

But Isabelle was beyond hearing. The screams rang out with such piercing intensity that Cordelia half feared that the Marklands must hear. The sound was inhuman, the shriek of animal terror. It was cut short by the swing of Hugo's arm; the sound of a slap; a gasp. It was succeeded by a second of absolute silence, then Isabelle collapsed against Hugo sobbing quietly.

He turned harshly on Cordelia:

"What the hell did you do that for?"

"Do what?"

"You terrified her, lurking there. What are you doing here anyway?"

"I could ask you that."

"We came to collect the Antonello which Isabelle lent to Mark when she came to supper with him, and to cure her of a certain morbid obsession with his place. We've been to the Pitt Club Ball. It seemed a good idea to call here on our way home. Obviously, it was a bloody stupid idea. Is there any drink in the cottage?"

"Only beer."

"Oh God, Cordelia, there would be! She needs something stronger."

"There isn't anything stronger, but I'll make coffee. You set a light to the fire. It's laid."

She stood the torch upright on the table and lit

the table lamp, turning the wick low, then helped Isabelle into one of the fireside chairs.

The girl was trembling. Cordelia fetched one of Mark's heavy sweaters and placed it round her shoulders. The kindling began to flame under Hugo's careful hands. Cordelia went into the kitchen to make coffee, laying her torch on its side at the edge of the window sill so that it shone on the oil stove. She lit the stronger of the two burners and took from the shelf a brown earthenware jug, the two blue-rimmed mugs and a cup for herself. A second and chipped cup held the sugar. It took only a couple of minutes to boil half a kettle of water and to pour it over the coffee grains. She could hear Hugo's voice from the sitting-room, low, urgent, consolatory, interposed with Isabelle's monosyllabic replies. Without waiting for the coffee to brew she placed it on the only tray, a bent tin one patterned with a chipped picture of Edinburgh castle, and carried it into the sitting-room, setting it down in the hearth. The faggots spluttered and blazed, shooting out a falling shower of bright sparks which patterned Isabelle's dress with stars. Then a stouter brand caught flame and the fire glowed with a stronger, more mellow, heart.

As she bent forward to stir the coffee Cordelia saw a small beetle scurrying in desperate haste along the ridges of one of the small logs. She picked up a twig from the kindling still in the hearth and held it out as a way of escape. But it confused the beetle still more. It turned in panic and raced back towards the flame, then doubled in its tracks and fell finally into a split in the wood. Cordelia pictured its fall into black burning darkness and wondered whether it briefly comprehended its dreadful end. Putting a match to a fire was such a trivial act to cause such agony, such terror.

She handed Isabelle and Hugo their mugs and took her own. The comforting smell of fresh coffee mingled with the resinous tang of the burning wood. The fire threw long shadows over the tiled floor and the oil lamp cast its gentle glow over their faces. Surely, thought Cordelia, no murder suspects could have been interrogated in a cosier setting. Even Isabelle had lost her fears. Whether it was the reassurance of Hugo's arm across her shoulders, the stimulus of the coffee or the homely warmth and crackle of the fire, she seemed almost at ease.

Cordelia said to Hugo:

"You said that Isabelle was morbidly obsessed by this place. Why should she be?"

"Isabelle's very sensitive; she isn't tough like you."

Cordelia privately thought that all beautiful women were tough—how else could they survive?—and that Isabelle's fibres could compare well for resilience with her own. But nothing would be gained by challenging Hugo's illusions. Beauty was fragile, transitory, vulnerable. Isabelle's sensitivities must be protected. The toughies could look after themselves. She said:

"According to you, she's only been here once

before. I know that Mark Callender died in this room, but you hardly expect me to believe that she's grieving over Mark. There's something that both of you know and it would be better if you told me now. If you don't I shall have to report to Sir Ronald Callender that Isabelle, your sister and you are somehow concerned in his son's death and it will be up to him to decide whether to call in the police. I can't see Isabelle standing up to even the mildest police questioning, can you?"

Even to Cordelia it sounded a stilted, sentenious little speech, an unsubstantiated accusation backed up by an empty threat. She half expected Hugo to counter it with amused contempt. But he looked at her for a minute as if assessing more than the reality of the danger. Then he said quietly:

"Can't you accept my word that Mark died by his own hand and that if you do call in the police it will cause unhappiness and distress to his father, to his friends and be absolutely no help to anyone?"

"No, Hugo, I can't."

"Then if we do tell you what we know, you will promise that it won't go any further?"

"How can I, any more than I can promise to believe you?"

Suddenly Isabelle cried:

"Oh, tell her, Hugo! What does it matter?"

Cordelia said:

"I think that you must. I don't think you've any choice."

"So it seems. All right." He put his coffee mug down in the hearth and looked into the fire.

"I told you that we went—Sophie, Isabelle, Davie and I—to the Arts Theatre on the night Mark died but that, as you've probably guessed, was only three-quarters true. They had only three seats left when I booked so we allocated them to the three people mostly likely to enjoy the play. Isabelle goes to the theatre to be seen rather than to see and is bored by any show with a cast of less than fifty, so she was the one left out. Thus neglected by her current lover, she very reasonably decided to seek consolation with the next."

Isabelle said with a secret, anticipatory smile:

"Mark was not my lover, Hugo."

She spoke without rancour or resentment. It was a matter of putting the record straight.

"I know. Mark was a romantic. He never took a girl to bed—or anywhere else that I could see—until he judged that there was an adequate depth of interpersonal communication, or whatever jargon he used, between them. Actually, that's unfair. It's my father who uses bloody awful meaningless phrases like that. But Mark agreed with the general idea. I doubt whether he could enjoy sex until he'd convinced himself that he and the girl were in love. It was a necessary preliminary—like undressing. I gather that with Isabelle the relationship hadn't reached the necessary depths, hadn't achieved the essential emotional rapport. It was only a matter of time, of course. Where Isabelle was concerned, Mark was as capable of self-deception as the rest of us."

The high, slightly hesitant voice was edged with jealousy.

Isabelle said, slowly and patiently, like a mother explaining to a wilfully obtuse child:

"Mark never made love to me, Hugo."

"That's what I'm saying. Poor Mark! He exchanged the substance for the shadow and now he has neither."

"But what happened that night?"

Cordelia spoke to Isabelle, but it was Hugo who replied.

"Isabelle drove here and arrived shortly after half past seven. The curtains were drawn across the back window, the front one is inpenetrable anyway, but the door was open. She came in. Mark was already dead. His body was hanging by the strap from that hook. But he didn't look as he did when Miss Markland found him next morning."

He turned to Isabelle:

"You tell her." She hesitated. Hugo bent forward and kissed her lightly on the lips.

"Go on, tell. There are some unpleasantnesses which all Papa's money can't entirely shield from you and this, darling, is one."

Isabelle turned her head and looked intently into the four corners of the room as if satisfying herself that the three of them were really alone. The irises of her remarkable eyes were purple in the firelight. She leaned towards Cordelia with something of the confiding relish of a village gossip about to relate the latest scandal. Cordelia saw that her panic had left her. Isabelle's agonies were elemental, violent but short lived, easily comforted. She would have kept her secret while Hugo instructed her to keep it, but she was glad of his order of release. Probably her instinct told her that the story, once told, would lose the sting of terror. She said:

"I thought I would call to see Mark and, perhaps, that we would have supper together. Mademoiselle de Congé was not well and Hugo and Sophie were at the theatre and I was bored. I came to the back door because Mark had told me that the front door would not open. I thought that I might see him in the garden, but he was not there, only the garden fork in the ground and his shoes at the door. So I pushed open the door. I did not knock because I thought I would be a surprise for Mark."

She hesitated and looked down into the mug of coffee, twisting it between her hands.

"And then?" prompted Cordelia.

"And then I saw him. He was hanging there by the belt from that hook in the ceiling and I knew he was dead. Cordelia, it was horrible! He was dressed like a woman in a black bra and black lace panties. Nothing else. And his face! He had painted his lips, all over his lips Cordelia, like a clown! It was terrible but it was funny too. I wanted to laugh and scream at the same time.

He didn't look like Mark. He didn't look like a human being at all. And on the table there were three pictures. Not nice pictures Cordelia. Pictures of naked women."

Her wide eyes stared into Cordelia's, dismayed, uncomprehending. Hugo said:

"Don't look like that, Cordelia. It was horrible for Isabelle at the time and disagreeable to think about now. But it isn't so very uncommon. It does happen. It's probably one of the more innocuous of sexual deviations. He wasn't involving anyone but himself. And he didn't mean to kill himself; that was just bad luck. I imagine that the buckle of the belt slipped and he never had a chance."
Cordelia said:

"I don't believe it."

"I thought you might not. But it's true, Cordelia. Why not come with us now and ring Sophie? She'll confirm it."

"I don't need confirmation of Isabelle's story. I already have that. I mean I still don't believe that Mark killed himself."

As soon as she spoke she knew that it had been a mistake. She shouldn't have revealed her suspicions. But it was too late now and there were questions she had to ask. She saw Hugo's face, his quick impatient frown at her obtuseness, her obstinacy. And then she detected a subtle change of mood; was it irritation, fear, disappointment? She spoke directly to Isabelle.

"You said that the door was open. Did you notice the key?"

"It was in this side of the door. I saw it when I went out."

"What about the curtains?"

"They were like now, across the window."

"And where was the lipstick?"

"What lipstick, Cordelia?"

"The one used to paint Mark's lips. It wasn't in the pockets of his jeans or the police would have found it, so where was it? Did you see it on the table?"

"There was nothing on the table except the pictures."

"What colour was the lipstick?"

"Purple. An old lady's colour. No one would choose such a colour I think."

"And the underclothes, could you describe them?"

"Oh, yes! They were from M & S. I recognized them."

"You mean that you recognized those particular ones, that they were yours?"

"Oh, no Cordelia! They were not mine. I never wear black underclothes. I only like white next to my skin. But they were the kind I usually buy. I always get my underclothes from M & S."

Cordelia reflected that Isabelle was hardly one of the store's best customers, but that no other witness would have been as reliable when it came to details, particularly of clothes. Even in that moment of absolute terror and revulsion, Isabelle had noticed the type of underclothes. And if she said that she hadn't seen the lipstick, then it was because the lipstick hadn't been there to see.

Cordelia went on inexorably:

"Did you touch anything, Mark's body perhaps, to see if he was dead?"

Isabelle was shocked. The facts of life she could take in her stride, but not the facts of death.

"I couldn't touch Mark! I touched nothing. And I knew that he was dead."

Hugo said: "A respectable, sensible, law-abiding citizen would have found the nearest telephone and rung the police. Luckily Isabelle is none of these things. Her instinct was to come to me. She waited until the play ended, and then met us outside the theatre. When we came out she was pacing up and down the pavement on the other side of the road. Davie, Sophie and I came back here with her in the Renault. We only stopped briefly at Norwich Street to collect Davie's camera and flash."

"Why?"

"That was my idea. Obviously, we had no intention of letting the fuzz and Ronald Callender know how Mark had died. Our idea was to fake a suicide. We planned to dress him in his own clothes, clean his face and then leave him for someone else to find. We hadn't it in mind to fake a suicide note; that was a refinement somewhat outside our powers. We collected the camera so that we could photograph him as he was. We didn't know what particular law we were breaking in faking a suicide, but there must have been one. You can't do the simplest service for your friends these days without it being liable to misconstruction by the fuzz. If there were trouble we wanted some evidence of the truth. We were all fond of Mark in our different ways, but not fond enough to risk a murder charge. However, our good intentions were frustrated. Someone else had got here first."

"Tell me about it."

"There's nothing to tell. We told the two girls to wait in the car, Isabelle because she had already seen enough and Sophie because Isabelle was too frightened to be left alone. Besides, it seemed only fair to Mark to keep Sophie out of it, to prevent her from seeing him. Don't you find it odd, Cordelia, this concern one has for the susceptibilities of the dead?"

Thinking of her father and Bernie, Cordelia said:

"Perhaps it's only when people are dead that we can safely show how much we cared about them. We know that it's too late then for them to do anything about it."

"Cynical but true. Anyway, there was nothing for us to do here. We found Mark's body and this room as Miss Markland described them at the inquest. The door was open, the curtains drawn across. Mark was naked except for his blue jeans. There were no magazine pictures on the table and no lipstick on his face. But there was a suicide note in the typewriter and a mound of ash in the grate. It looked as if the visitor had made a thorough job of it. We didn't linger. Someone else—perhaps someone from the house—might have turned up at any minute. Admittedly, it was very late by then but it seemed an evening for people to pop in. Mark must have had more visitors that night than during his whole time at the cottage; first Isabelle; then the unknown samaritan; then us."

Cordelia thought that there had been someone before Isabelle. Mark's murderer had been there first. She asked suddenly:

"Someone played a stupid trick on me last night. When I got back here from the party there was a bolster slung from that hook. Did you do that?"

If his surprise were not genuine, then Hugo was a better actor than Cordelia thought possible.

"Of course I didn't! I thought you were living in Cambridge not here. And why on earth should I?"

"To warn me off."

"But that would be crazy! It wouldn't warn you off, would it? It might scare some women, but not you. We wanted to convince you that there was nothing to investigate about Mark's death. That sort of trick would only convince you that there was. Someone else was trying to scare you. The most likely person is the one who came here after us."

"I know. Someone took a risk for Mark. He—or she—won't want me ferreting around. But he would have got rid of me more sensibly by telling me the truth."

"How could he know whether to trust you? What will you do now, Cordelia? Go back to town?"

He was trying to keep his voice casual but she thought she detected the underlying anxiety. She replied:

"I expect so. I'll have to see Sir Ronald first."

"What will you tell him?"

"I'll think of something. Don't worry."

Dawn was staining the eastern sky and the first chorus of birds was noisily contradicting the new day before Hugo and Isabelle left. They took the Antonello with them. Cordelia saw it taken down with a pang of regret as if something of Mark were leaving the cottage. Isabelle examined the picture closely with a grave professional eye before tucking it under her arm. Cordelia thought that she was probably generous enough with her possessions, both people and pictures, provided they were on loan only, to be returned promptly on demand and in the same condition as when she parted with them. Cordelia watched from the front gate as the Renault, with Hugo driving, moved out of the shadow of the hedge. She lifted her hand in a formal gesture of farewell like a weary hostess speeding her final guests, then turned back to the cottage.

The sitting room seemed empty and cold without them. The fire was dying and she hastily

pushed in the few remaining sticks from the
hearth and blew on them to kindle the flame. She
moved restlessly about the little room. She was
too lively to go back to bed, but her short and
disturbed night had left her edgy with tiredness.
But her mind was tormented by something more
fundamental than lack of sleep. For the first time
she knew that she was afraid. Evil existed—it
hadn't needed a convent education to convince
her of that reality—and it had been present in
this room. Something here had been stronger
than wickedness, ruthlessness, cruelty or expe-
dience. Evil. She had no doubt that Mark had
been murdered, but with what diabolical cleverness it had been done! If Isabelle told her story,
who now would ever believe that he hadn't died
accidentally, but by his own hand? Cordelia had
no need to refer to her book on forensic medicine
to know how it would appear to the police. As
Hugo had said, these cases weren't so very uncommon. He, as a psychiatrist's son, would have
heard or read of them. Who else would know?
Probably any reasonably sophisticated person.
But it couldn't have been Hugo. Hugo had an alibi. Her mind revolted at the thought that Davie or
Sophie could have participated in such a horror.
But how typical that they should have collected
the camera. Even their compassion had been
overlaid with self concern. Would Hugo and Davie have stood here, under Mark's grotesque
body, calmly discussing distance and exposure

before taking the photograph which would, if necessary, exonerate them at his expense?

She went into the kitchen to make tea, glad to be free of the malignant fascination of that hook in the ceiling. Previously it had hardly worried her, now it was as obtrusive as a fetish. It seemed to have grown since the previous night, to be growing still as it drew her eyes compulsively upwards. And the sitting room itself had surely shrunk; no longer a sanctum but a claustrophobic cell, tawdry and shameful as an execution shed. Even the bright morning air was redolent with evil.

Waiting for the kettle to boil she made herself contemplate the day's activities. It was still too early to theorize; her mind was too preoccupied with horror to deal rationally with its new knowledge. Isabelle's story had complicated, not illumined the case. But there were still relevant facts to be discovered. She would go on with the programme she had already planned. Today she would go to London to examine Mark's grandfather's will.

But there were still two hours to get through before it was time to start out. She had decided to travel to London by train and to leave the car at Cambridge station since this would be both quicker and easier. It was irritating to have to spend a day in town when the heart of the mystery so obviously lay in Cambridgeshire, but for once she wasn't sorry at the prospect of leaving the cottage. Shocked and restless, she wandered aimlessly from room to room and prowled around the garden, fretting to be away. Finally in desperation she took hold of the garden fork and completed the digging of Mark's unfinished row. She wasn't sure this was wise; Mark's interrupted work was part of the evidence for his murder. But other people, including Sergeant Maskell, had seen it and could testify if necessary, and the sight of the partly-completed job, of the fork still askew in the soil, was unbearably irritating. When the row was completed she felt calmer and she dug on without pausing for another hour before carefully cleaning the fork and placing it with the other tools in the garden shed.

At last it was time to go. The seven o'clock weather forecast had prophesied thundery storms in the southeast so she put on her suit, the heaviest protection she had brought with her. She hadn't worn it since Bernie's death and she discovered that the waist band was uncomfortably loose. She had lost some weight. After a moment's thought, she took Mark's belt from the scene-of-crime kit and wound it twice round her waist. She felt no repugnance as the leather tightened against her. It was impossible to believe that anything he had ever touched or owned could frighten or distress her. The strength and heaviness of the leather so close to her skin was even obscurely comforting and reassuring, as if the belt were a talisman.

Chapter Five

THE STORM BROKE just as Cordelia alighted from the number 11 bus outside Somerset House. There was a jagged flash of lightning and, almost instantaneously, the thunder crashed like a barrage round her ears and she raced across the inner courtyard between the ranks of parked cars through a wall of water while the rain spouted around her ankles as if the paving stones were being raked with bullets. She pushed open the door and stood draining pools of water on the mat and laughing aloud with relief. One or two of the people present glanced up from their perusal of wills and smiled at her, while a motherly looking woman behind the counter tut-tutted her concern. Cordelia shook her jacket over the mat then hung it on the back of one of the chairs and tried ineffectually to dry her hair with her handkerchief before approaching the counter.

The motherly woman was helpful. Consulted by Cordelia on the correct procedure, she indicated the shelves of heavy, bound volumes in the middle of the hall and explained that the wills were indexed under the surname of the testator and the year in which the document was lodged with Somerset House. It was for Cordelia to trace the catalogue number and bring the volume to the desk. The original will would then be sent for and she could consult it for a fee of 20 pence.

Not knowing when George Bottley had died, Cordelia was in some perplexity where to begin her search. But she deduced that the will must have been made after the birth, or at least the conception, of Mark, since he had been left a fortune by his grandfather. But Mr. Bottley had also left money to his daughter and this part of his fortune had come on her death to her husband. The strong probability was that he had died before her, since otherwise he would surely have made a new will. Cordelia decided to begin her search with the year of Mark's birth, 1951.

Her deductions proved correct. George Albert Bottley of Stonegate Lodge, had died on 26th July 1951, exactly three months and one day after the birth of his grandson and only three weeks after making his will. Cordelia wondered whether his death had been sudden and unexpected or whether this was the will of a dying man. She saw that he had left an estate of nearly three quarters of a million pounds. How had he made this, she wondered? Surely not all from wool. She heaved the heavy book across to the counter, the clerk wrote the details on a white form and pointed out the way to the cashier's office. Within a surprisingly few minutes of paying what seemed to her a modest fee, Cordelia was seated under the light at one of the desks near the window with the will in her hands.

She hadn't liked what she had heard about George Bottley from Nanny Pilbeam and she didn't like him any better after reading his will. She had feared that the document might be long, complicated and difficult to understand; it was surprisingly short, simple and intelligible. Mr. Bottley directed that all his possessions should be sold, "since I wish to prevent the usual unseemly wrangling over bric-à-brac." He left modest sums to servants in his employ at the time of death but there was no mention, Cordelia noticed, of his gardener. He bequeathed half of the residue of his fortune to his daughter, absolutely, "now that she has demonstrated that she has at least one of the normal attributes of a woman." The remaining half he left to his beloved grandson Mark Callender on attaining his twenty-fifth birthday, "by which date, if he hasn't learned the value of money, he will at least be of an age to avoid exploitation." The income from the capital was left to six Bottley relations, some of them, apparently, only distant kinsmen. The will created a residual trust; as each beneficiary died his share would be distributed among the survivors. The testator was confident that this arrangement would promote in the beneficiaries a lively interest in each other's health and survival while encouraging them to achieve the distinction of longevity, no other distinction being within their reach. If Mark died before his twenty-fifth birthday the family trust would continue until all the beneficiaries were dead and the capital would then be distributed among a formidable list of charities chosen, as far as Cordelia could see, because they were well known and successful rather than because they represented any personal concern or sympathy on the part of the testator. It was as if he had asked his lawyers for a list of the more reliable charities, having no real interest in what happened to his fortune if his own issue were not alive to inherit it.

It was a strange will. Mr. Bottley had left nothing to his son-in-law yet had apparently been unworried by the possibility that his daughter, whom he knew not to be strong, might die and leave her fortune to her husband. In some respects it was a gambler's will and Cordelia wondered again how George Bottley had made his fortune. But, despite the cynical unkindness of its comments, the will was neither unfair nor ungenerous. Unlike some very rich men he hadn't attempted to control his great fortune from beyond the grave, obsessively determined that not one penny should ever get into unfavoured hands. His daughter and his grandson had both been left their fortunes absolutely. It was impossible to like Mr. Bottley but difficult not to respect him. And the implications of his will were very clear. No one stood to gain by Mark's death except a long list of highly respectable charities.

Cordelia made a note of the main clauses of the will, more because of Bernie's insistence on meticulous documentation than from any fear of forgetting them; slipped the receipt for 20p into the expenses page of her notebook; added the cost of her cheap day return ticket from Cambridge and her bus fare, and returned the will to the counter. The storm had been as short as it was violent. The hot sun was already drying the windows and the puddles lay bright on the rain-washed courtyard. Cordelia decided that she ought to charge Sir Ronald for half a day only and spend the rest of her time in London at the office. There might be post to collect. There might even be another case awaiting her.

But the decision was a mistake. The office seemed even more sordid than when she had left it and the air smelt sour in contrast to the rain-washed streets outside. There was a thick film of dust over the furniture and the bloodstain on the rug had deepened into a brick-brown which looked even more sinister than the original bright red. There was nothing in the letter-box but a final demand from the electricity board and a bill from the stationer. Bernie had paid dearly—or rather, had not paid—for the despised writing paper.

Cordelia wrote a cheque for the electricity bill, dusted the furniture, made one last and unsuccessful attempt to clean the rug. Then she locked the office and set off to walk to Trafalgar Square. She would seek consolation in the National Gallery.

She caught the eighteen-sixteen train from Liverpool Street and it was nearly eight o'clock before she arrived back at the cottage. She parked the Mini in its usual place in the shelter of the copse and made her way round the side of the cottage. She hesitated for a moment wondering whether to collect the gun from its hiding place, but decided that this could wait until later. She was hungry and the first priority was to get a meal. She had carefully locked the back door and had stuck a thin strip of Scotch tape across the window sill before leaving that morning. If there were any more secret visitors she wanted to be warned. But the tape was still intact. She felt in her shoulder bag for the key and, bending down, fitted it into the lock. She wasn't expecting trouble outside the cottage and the attack took her completely by surprise. There was the half-second of pre-knowledge before the blanket fell but that was too late. There was a cord around her neck pulling the mask of hot stifling wool taut against her mouth and nostrils. She gasped for breath and tasted the dry strong-smelling fibres on her tongue. Then a sharp pain exploded in her chest and she remembered nothing.

The movement of liberation was a miracle and a horror. The blanket was whipped off. She never saw her assailant. There was a second of sweet reviving air, a glimpse, so brief that it was barely comprehended, of blinding sky seen through greenness and then she felt herself falling, falling in helpless astonishment into cold darkness. The fall was a confusion of old nightmares, unbelievable seconds of childhood terrors recalled. Then her body hit the water. Ice-cold hands dragged her into a vortex of horror. Instinctively, she had closed her mouth at the moment of impact and she struggled to the surface through what seemed an eternity of cold encompassing blackness. She shook her head and, through her stinging eyes, she looked up. The black tunnel that stretched above her ended in a moon of blue light. Even as she looked, the well lid was dragged slowly back like the shutter of a camera. The moon became a half moon; then a crescent. At last there was nothing but eight thin slits of light.

Desperately she trod water, reaching tentatively for the bottom. There was no bottom. Frantically moving hands and feet, willing herself not to panic, she felt around the walls of the well for a possible foothold. There was none. The funnel of bricks, smooth, sweating with moisture, stretched around and above her like a circular tomb. As she gazed upwards they writhed, expanded, swayed and reeled like the belly of a monstrous snake.

And then she felt a saving anger. She wouldn't

let herself drown, wouldn't die in this horrible place, alone and terrified. The well was deep but small, the diameter barely three feet. If she kept her head and took time, she could brace her legs and shoulders against the bricks and work her way upwards.

She hadn't bruised or stunned herself against the walls as she fell. Miraculously she was uninjured. The fall had been clean. She was alive and capable of thought. She had always been a survivor. She would survive.

She floated on her back, bracing her shoulders against the cold walls, spreading her arms and digging her elbows into the interstices of the bricks to get a better grip. Shuffling off her shoes, she planted both feet against the opposite wall. Just beneath the surface of the water, she could feel that one of the bricks was slightly unaligned. She curved her toes around it. It gave her a precarious but welcome foothold for the start of the climb. By means of it, she could lift her body out of the water and could relieve for a moment the strain on the muscles of her back and thighs.

Then slowly she began to climb, first shifting her feet, one after the other in tiny sliding steps, then humping up her body inch by painful inch. She kept her eyes fixed on the opposite curve of the wall, willing herself not to look down, nor up, counting progress by the width of each brick. Time passed. She couldn't see Bernie's watch, although its ticking seemed unnaturally loud, a regular obtrusive metronome to the thumping of her heart and the fierce gasping of her breath. The pain in her legs was intense and her shirt was sticking to her back with a warm, almost comforting effusion, which she knew must be blood. She willed herself not to think of the water beneath her or of the thin, but widening cleft of light above. If she were to survive, all her energy must be harnessed for the next painful inch.

Once, her legs slipped and she slithered back several yards before her feet, scrabbling ineffectually against the slimy walls, at last found a purchase. The fall had grazed her injured back and left her whimpering with self-pity and disappointment. She scourged her mind into courage and began climbing again. Once she was gripped by cramp and lay stretched as if on a rack until the agony passed and her fixed muscles could move. From time to time her feet found another small foothold and she was able to stretch her legs and rest. The temptation to stay in comparative safety and ease was almost irresistible and she had to will herself to start again on the slow torturous climb.

It seemed that she had been climbing for hours, moving in a parody of a difficult labour towards some desperate birth. Darkness was falling. The light from the well top was wider now but less strong. She told herself that the climb wasn't really difficult. It was only the darkness and loneliness which made it seem so. If this were a fabricated obstacle race, an exercise in the school gymnasium, surely she could have done it easily enough. She filled her mind with the comforting images of rib stools and vaulting horses, of the fifth form shouting their encouragement. Sister Perpetua was there. But why wasn't she looking at Cordelia? Why had she turned away? Cordelia called her and the figure turned slowly and smiled at her. But it wasn't Sister after all. It was Miss Leaming, the lean pale face sardonic under the white veil.

And now when she knew that, unaided, she could get no further, Cordelia saw salvation. A few feet above her was the bottom rung of a short wooden ladder fixed to the last few feet of the well. At first she thought that it was an illusion, a phantasm born of exhaustion and despair. She shut her eyes for a few minutes; her lips moved. Then she opened her eyes again. The ladder was still there, seen dimly but comfortingly solid in the fading light. She lifted impotent hands towards it knowing, even as she did so, that it was out of reach. It could save her life and she knew that she hadn't the strength to reach it.

It was then, without conscious thought or scheming, that she remembered the belt. Her hand dropped to her waist feeling for the heavy brass buckle. She undid it and drew the long snake of leather from her body. Carefully she threw the buckled end towards the bottom rung of the ladder. The first three times the metal struck the wood with a sharp crack but didn't fall over the rung; the fourth time it did. She pushed the other end of the belt gently upwards and the buckle dropped towards her until she could stretch out her hand and grasp it. She fastened it to the other end to form a strong loop. Then she pulled, at first very gently and then harder until most of her weight was on the strap. The relief was indescribable. She braced herself against the brickwork, gathering strength for the final triumphant effort. Then it happened. The rung, rotted at its joints, broke loose with a harsh tearing sound and spun past her into darkness, just missing her head. It seemed minutes rather than seconds before the distant splash reverberated round the wall.

She unbuckled the belt and tried again. The next rung was a foot higher and the throw more difficult. Even this small effort was exhausting in her present state and she made herself take time. Every unsuccessful throw made the next more difficult. She didn't count the number of attempts, but at last the buckle fell over the rung and dropped towards her. When it snaked within reach she found that she could only just buckle the strap. The next rung would be too high. If this one broke, it would be the end.

But the rung held. She had no clear memory of the last half hour of the climb but at last she reached the ladder and strapped herself firmly to the uprights. For the first time she was physically safe. As long as the ladder held she needn't fear falling. She let herself relax into brief unconsciousness. But then the wheels of the mind which had been spinning blissfully free, took hold again and she began to think. She knew that she had no hope of moving the heavy wooden cover unaided. She stretched out both hands and pushed against it but it didn't shift, and the high concave dome made it impossible for her to brace her shoulders against the wood. She would have to rely on outside help and that wouldn't come till daylight. It might not come even then, but she pushed the thought away. Sooner or later Miss Markland would come to the cottage. Sooner or later someone would come. She could hope to hold on, thus strapped, for several days. Even if she lost consciousness there was a chance that she would be rescued alive. Miss Markland knew that she was at the cottage; her things were still there. Miss Markland would come.

She gave thought to how she could attract attention. There was room to push something between the boards of wood if only she had something sufficiently stiff to push. The edge of the buckle was possible provided she strapped herself more tightly. But that must wait until the morning. There was nothing she could do now. She would relax and sleep and await rescue.

And then the final horror burst upon her. There would be no rescue. Someone would be coming to the well, coming on quiet and stealthy feet under the cover of darkness. But it would be her murderer. He had to return; it was part of his plan. The attack, which at the time had seemed so astonishingly, so brutally stupid, hadn't been

stupid at all. It was intended to look like an accident. He would come back that night and remove
the well cover again. Then, some time next day
or within the next few days, Miss Markland would
blunder through the garden and discover what
had happened. No one would ever be able to
prove that Cordelia's death wasn't an accident.
She recalled the words of Sergeant Maskell: "It
isn't what you suspect; it's what you can prove."
But this time would there even be suspicion?
Here was a young, impulsive, over-curious young
woman living at the cottage without the owner's
authority. She had obviously decided to explore
the well. She had smashed the padlock, drawn
back the lid with the coil of rope which the killer
would leave ready to be found, and tempted by
the ladder, had let herself down those few steps
until the final rung broke beneath her. Her prints
and no one else's would be found on the ladder,
if they took the trouble to look. The cottage was
utterly deserted; the chance that her murderer
would be seen returning was remote. There was
nothing she could do but wait until she heard his
footsteps, his heavy breathing, and the lid was
drawn slowly back to reveal his face.

After the first intensity of terror, Cordelia waited
for death without hope and without further struggle. There was even a kind of peace in resignation. Strapped like a victim to the uprights of the
ladder she drifted mercifully into brief oblivion
and prayed that it might be so when her killer returned, that she might not be conscious at the

moment of the final blow. She had no longer any interest in seeing her murderer's face. She wouldn't humiliate herself by pleading for her life, wouldn't beg for mercy from a man who had strung up Mark. She knew that there would be no mercy.

But she was conscious when the well lid began slowly to move. The light came in above her bowed head. The gap widened. And then she heard a voice, a woman's voice, low, urgent and sharp with terror.

"Cordelia!"

She looked up.

Kneeling at the rim of the well, her pale face immense and seeming to float disembodied in space like the phantasm of a nightmare, was Miss Markland. And the eyes which stared into Cordelia's face were as wild with terror as her own.

Ten minutes later Cordelia was lying slumped in the fireside chair. Her whole body ached and she was powerless to control her violent shivering. Her thin shirt was stuck to her wounded back and every shift of movement was pain. Miss Markland had put a light to the kindling and was now making coffee. Cordelia could hear her moving to and fro in the little kitchen and could smell the stove as it was turned high and, soon, the evocative aroma of coffee. These familiar sights and sounds would normally have been reassuring and comforting, but now she was desperate to be alone. The killer would still return. He had to return, and when he did, she wanted to be there to meet him. Miss Markland brought in the two mugs and pressed one into Cordelia's shivering hands. She stumped upstairs and came down with one of Mark's jumpers which she wound round the girl's neck. Her terror had left her, but she was as agitated as a young girl sharing her first half-shameful adventure. Her eyes were wild, her whole body trembled with excitement. She sat down directly in front of Cordelia and fixed her with her sharp inquisitive eyes.

"How did it happen? You must tell me."

Cordelia had not forgotten how to think.

"I don't know. I can't remember anything that happened before I hit the water. I must have decided to explore the well and lost my balance."

"But the well lid! The lid was in place!"

"I know. Someone must have replaced it."

"But why? Who would have come this way?"

"I don't know. But someone must have seen it. Someone must have dragged it back."

She said more gently:

"You saved my life. How did you notice what had happened?"

"I came to the cottage to see if you were still here. I came earlier today but there was no sign of you. There was a coil of rope—the one that you used, I expect—left in the path and I stumbled over it. Then I noticed that the well lid wasn't quite in place and that the padlock had been smashed."

"You saved my life," said Cordelia again, "but

please go now. Please go. I'm all right, really I am."

"But you aren't fit to be left alone! And that man—the one who replaced the lid—he might return. I don't like to think of strangers snooping around the cottage and you here alone."

"I'm perfectly safe. Besides, I have a gun. I only want to be left in peace to rest. Please don't worry about me!"

Cordelia could detect the note of desperation, almost of hysteria, in her own voice.

But Miss Markland seemed not to hear. Suddenly she was on her knees in front of Cordelia and pouring out a spate of high, excited chatter. Without thought and without compassion, she was confiding to the girl her terrible story, a story of her son, the four-year-old child of herself and her lover, who had broken his way through the cottage hedge and fallen into the well to his death. Cordelia tried to shake herself free from the wild eyes. It was surely all a fantasy. The woman must be mad. And if it were true, it was horrible and unthinkable and she could not bear to hear it. Sometime later she would remember it, remember every word, and think of the child, of his last terror, his desperate cry for his mother, the cold suffocating water dragging him to his death. She would live his agony in nightmares as she would re-live her own. But not now. Through the spate of words, the self-accusations, the terror recalled, Cordelia recognized the note of liberation. What to her had been horror, to Miss Markland had been release. A life for a life. Suddenly Cordelia could bear it no longer. She said violently:

"I'm sorry! I'm sorry! You've saved my life and I'm grateful. But I can't bear to listen. I don't want you here. For God's sake go!"

All her life she would remember the woman's face, her silent withdrawal. Cordelia didn't hear her go, didn't remember the soft closing of the door. All she knew was that she was alone. The shaking was over now although she still felt very cold. She went upstairs and pulled on her slacks then unwound Mark's jumper from her neck and put it on. It would cover the blood stains on her shirt and the warmth was immediately comforting. She was moving very quickly. She felt for the ammunition, took her torch and let herself out of the back door of the cottage. The gun was where she had left it, in the fold of the tree. She loaded it and felt its familiar shape and heaviness in her hand. Then she stood back among the bushes and waited.

It was too dark to see the dial of her wrist watch but Cordelia reckoned that she must have waited there immobile in the shadows for nearly half an hour before her ears caught the sound for which she was waiting. A car was approaching down the lane. Cordelia held her breath. The sound of the engine reached a brief crescendo and then faded away. The car had driven on without stopping. It was unusual for a car to pass down the lane after dark and she wondered who it could be. Again she waited, moving deeper into the shelter of the elder bush so that she could rest her back against the bark. She had been clutching the gun so tightly that her right wrist ached and she moved the pistol to her other hand and rotated the wrist slowly, stretching the cramped fingers.

Again she waited. The slow minutes passed. The silence was broken only by the furtive scuffling of some small night prowler in the grass and the sudden wild hoot of an owl. And then once more she heard the sound of an engine. This time the noise was faint and it came no closer. Someone had stopped a car further up the road.

She took the gun in her right hand, cradling the muzzle with her left. Her heart was pounding so loudly that she felt its wild hammering must betray her. She imagined rather than heard the thin whine of the front gate but the sound of feet moving round the cottage was unmistakable and clear. And now he was in sight, a stocky, broad-shouldered figure, black against the light. He moved towards her and she could see her shoulder bag hanging from his left shoulder. The discovery disconcerted her. She had completely forgotten the bag. But now she had realized why he had seized it. He had wanted to search it for evidence, but it was important that, finally, it should be discovered with her body in the well.

He came forward gently on tip-toe, his long simian arms held stiffly away from his body like a caricature of a film cowboy ready for the draw.

When he got to the rim of the well he waited and the moon struck the white of his eyes as he gazed slowly round. Then he bent down and felt in the grass for the coil of rope. Cordelia had laid it where Miss Markland had found it, but something about it, some slight difference perhaps in the way it was coiled, seemed to strike him. He rose uncertainly and stood for a moment with the rope dangling from his hand. Cordelia tried to control her breathing. It seemed impossible that he should not hear, smell or see her, that he should be so like a predator yet without the beast's instinct for the enemy in the dark. He moved forward. Now he was at the well. He bent and threaded one end of the rope through the iron hoop.

Cordelia moved with one step out of the darkness. She held the gun firmly and straight as Bernie had shown her. This time the target was very close. She knew that she wouldn't fire but, in that moment, she knew too what it was that could make a man kill. She said loudly:

"Good evening, Mr. Lunn."

She never knew whether he saw the gun. But for one unforgettable second, as the clouded moon sailed into the open sky, she saw his face clearly; saw the hate, the despair, the agony and the rictus of terror. He gave one hoarse cry, threw down the shoulder bag and the rope and rushed through the garden in a blind panic. She gave chase, hardly knowing why, or what she hoped to achieve, determined only that he shouldn't get back to Garforth House before her. And still she didn't fire the gun.

But he had an advantage. As she threw herself through the gate she saw that he had parked the van some fifty yards up the road and left the engine running. She chased after him but could see that it was hopeless. Her only hope of catching up with him was to get the Mini. She tore down the lane feeling in her shoulder bag as she ran. The prayer book and her note book were both gone but her fingers found the car keys. She unlocked the Mini, threw herself in and reversed it violently onto the road. The rear lights of the van were about a hundred yards ahead of her. She didn't know what speed it could do, but doubted whether it could out-pace the Mini. She trod on the accelerator and gave pursuit. She turned left out of the lane on to the subsidiary road and now she could see the van still ahead. He was driving fast and was holding the distance. Now the road turned and for a few seconds he was out of sight. He must be getting very close now to the junction with the Cambridge road.

She heard the crash just before she herself reached the junction, an instantaneous explosion of sound which shook the hedges and made the little car tremble. Cordelia's hands tightened momentarily on the wheel and the Mini jerked to a stop. She ran forward round the corner and saw before her the gleaming, headlamp lit surface of the main Cambridge road. It was peopled with running shapes. The transporter, still upright, was an immense oblong mass blocking the sky line, a barricade slewed across the road. The van had crumpled under its front wheels like a child's toy. There was a smell of petrol, a woman's harsh scream, the squeal of braking tyres. Cordelia walked slowly up to the transporter. The driver was still in his seat, gazing rigidly ahead, his face a mask of dedicated concentration. People were shouting at him, stretching out their arms. He didn't move. Someone—a man in a heavy leather coat and goggles—said:

"It's shock. We'd better drag him clear."

Three figures moved between Cordelia and the driver. Shoulders heaved in unison. There was a grunt of effort. The driver was lifted out, rigid as a manikin, his knees bent, his clenched hands held out as if still grasping the immense wheel. The shoulders bent over him in secret conclave.

There were other figures standing round the crushed van. Cordelia joined the ring of anonymous faces. Cigarette ends glowed and faded like signals, casting a momentary glow on the shaking hands, the wide, horrified eyes. She asked:

"Is he dead?" The man in goggles replied laconically:

"What do you think?"

There was a girl's voice, tentative, breathless.

"Has anyone called the ambulance?"

"Yeah. Yeah. That chap in the Cortina's gone off to 'phone."

The group stood irresolute. The girl and the young man to whom she was clinging began to back away. Another car stopped. A tall figure was pushing his way through the crowd. Cordelia heard a high, authoritative voice.

"I'm a doctor. Has anyone called the ambulance?"

"Yes, sir."

The reply was deferential. They stood aside to let the expert through. He turned to Cordelia, perhaps because she was nearest.

"If you didn't witness the accident, young woman, you'd better get on your way. And stand back, the rest of you. There's nothing that you can do. And put out those cigarettes!"

Cordelia walked slowly back to the Mini, placing each foot carefully before the other like a convalescent trying her first painful steps. She drove carefully round the accident, bumping the Mini on the grass verge. There was the wail of approaching sirens. As she turned off the main road, her driving mirror glowed suddenly red and she heard a whoosh of sound followed by a low, concerted groan which was broken by a woman's high, single scream. There was a wall of flame across the road. The doctor's warning had been too late. The van was on fire. There was no hope now for Lunn; but then, there never had been.

Cordelia knew that she was driving erratically. Passing cars hooted at her and flashed their lights and one motorist slowed down and shouted angrily. She saw a gate and drew in off the road and switched off the engine. The silence was absolute. Her hands were moist and shaking. She wiped them on her handkerchief and laid them in her lap feeling that they were separate from the rest of her body. She was hardly aware of a car passing and then slowing to a halt. A face appeared at the window. The voice was slurred and nervous but horribly ingratiating. She could smell the drink on his breath.

"Anything wrong, Miss?"

"Nothing. I've just stopped for a rest."

"No point in resting alone—a pretty girl like you."

His hand was on the door handle. Cordelia felt in her shoulder bag and drew out the gun. She pushed it into his face.

"It's loaded. Go away at once or I'll shoot."

The menace in her voice struck cold even to her own ears. The pale, moist face disintegrated with surprise, the jaw fell. He backed away.

"Sorry, Miss, I'm sure. My mistake. No offence."

Cordelia waited until his car was out of sight. Then she turned on the engine. But she knew that she couldn't go on. She turned off the engine again. Waves of tiredness flowed over her, an irresistible tide, gentle as a blessing, which neither her exhausted mind nor body had the will to resist. Her head fell forward and Cordelia slept.

Chapter Six

CORDELIA SLEPT SOUNDLY but briefly. She didn't
know what woke her, whether the blinding light of
a passing car sweeping across her closed eyes
or her own subconscious knowledge that rest
must be rationed to a brief half hour, the minimum
necessary to enable her to do what had to be
done before she could give herself over to sleep.
She eased her body upright, feeling the stab of
pain in her strained muscles and the half-pleasur-
able itch of dried blood on her back. The night air
was heavy and odorous with the heat and scents
of the day; even the road winding ahead looked
tacky in the glare of her headlights. But Cordelia's chilled and aching body was still grateful for
the warmth of Mark's jersey. For the first time
since she had pulled it over her head she saw

that it was dark green. How odd that she hadn't noticed its colour before!

She drove the rest of the journey like a novice, sitting bolt upright, eyes rigidly ahead, hands and feet tense on the controls. And here at last were the gates of Garforth House. They loomed in her headlights far taller and more ornamental than she remembered them, and they were closed. She ran from the Mini praying that they wouldn't be locked. But the iron latch, although heavy, rose to her desperate hands. The gates swung soundlessly back.

There were no other cars in the drive and she parked the Mini some little way from the house. The windows were dark and the only light, gentle and inviting, shone through the open front door. Cordelia took the pistol in her hand and, without ringing, stepped into the hall. She was more exhausted in body than when she had first come to Garforth House, but tonight she saw it with a new intensity, her nerves sensitive to every detail. The hall was empty, the air expectant. It seemed as if the house had waited for her. The same smell met her of roses and lavender, but tonight she saw that the lavender came from a huge Chinese bowl set on a side table. She recalled the insistent ticking of a clock, but now she noticed for the first time the delicate carving of the clock case, the intricate scrolls and whirls on the face. She stood in the middle of the hall, swaying slightly, the pistol held lightly in her drooping right hand, and looked down. The carpet was a formal geometrical design in rich olive greens, pale blues and crimson, each pattern shaped like the shadow of a kneeling man. It seemed to draw her to her knees. Was it perhaps an eastern prayer mat?

She was aware of Miss Leaming coming quietly down the stairs towards her, her long red dressing-gown sweeping round her ankles. The pistol was taken suddenly but firmly from Cordelia's unresisting hand. She knew that it had gone because her hand felt suddenly lighter. It made no difference. She could never defend herself with it, never kill a man. She had learnt that about herself when Lunn had run from her in terror. Miss Leaming said:

"There is no one here you need defend yourself against, Miss Gray."

Cordelia said:

"I've come to report to Sir Ronald. Where is he?"

"Where he was the last time you came here, in his study."

As before, he was sitting at his desk. He had been dictating and the machine was at his right hand. When he saw Cordelia, he switched it off, then walked to the wall and pulled the plug from the socket. He walked back to the desk and they sat down opposite each other. He folded his hands in the pool of light from the desk lamp and looked up at Cordelia. She almost cried out with shock. His face reminded her of faces seen grotesquely reflected in grubby train windows at night—cavernous, the bones stripped of flesh, eyes set in fathomless sockets—faces resurrected from the dead.

When he spoke his voice was low, reminiscent.

"Half an hour ago I learned that Chris Lunn was dead. He was the best lab assistant I ever had. I took him out of an orphanage fifteen years ago. He never knew his parents. He was an ugly, difficult boy, already on probation. School had done nothing for him. But Lunn was one of the best natural scientists I've ever known. If he'd had the education, he'd have been as good as I am."

"Then why didn't you give him his chance, why didn't you educate him?"

"Because he was more useful to me as a lab assistant. I said that he could have been as good as I am. That isn't quite good enough. I can find plenty of scientists as good. I couldn't have found another lab assistant to equal Lunn. He had a marvellous hand with instruments."

He looked up at Cordelia, but without curiosity, apparently without interest.

"You've come to report, of course. It's very late, Miss Gray, and, as you see, I'm tired. Can't it wait until tomorrow?"

Cordelia thought that this was as close to an appeal as he could ever bring himself. She said:

"No, I'm tired too. But I want to finish the case tonight, now." He picked up an ebony paper-knife from the desk and, without looking at Cordelia, balanced it on his forefinger.

"Then tell me, why did my son kill himself? I take it that you do have news for me? You would hardly have burst in here at this hour without something to report."

"Your son didn't kill himself. He was murdered. He was murdered by someone he knew well, someone he didn't hesitate to let into the cottage, someone who came prepared. He was strangled or suffocated, then slung up on that hook by his own belt. Last of all, his murderer painted his lips, dressed him in a woman's underclothes and spread out pictures of nudes on the table in front of him. It was meant to look like accidental death during sexual experiment; such cases aren't so very uncommon."

There was half a minute of silence. Then he said with perfect calmness:

"And who was responsible, Miss Gray?"

"You were. You killed your son."

"For what reason?" He might have been an examiner, putting his inexorable questions.

"Because he discovered that your wife wasn't his mother, that the money left to her and to him by his grandfather had come by fraud. Because he had no intention of benefiting by it a moment longer, nor of accepting his legacy in four years' time. You were afraid that he might make this knowledge public. And what about the Wolvington Trust? If the truth came out, that would be the end of their promised grant. The future of your laboratory was at stake. You couldn't take the risk."

"And who undressed him again, typed out that suicide note, washed the lipstick from his face?"

"I think I know, but I shan't tell you. That's really what you employed me to discover, isn't it? That's what you couldn't bear not to know. But you killed Mark. You even prepared an alibi just in case it was needed. You got Lunn to ring you at college and announce himself as your son. He was the one person you could rely on absolutely. I don't suppose you told him the truth. He was only your lab assistant. He didn't require explanations, he did what you told him. And even if he did guess the truth, he was safe, wasn't he? You prepared an alibi which you dared not use, because you didn't know when Mark's body was first discovered. If someone had found him and faked that suicide before you had claimed to have spoken to him on the telephone, your alibi would have been broken, and a broken alibi is damning. So you made a chance to talk to Benskin and put matters right. You told him the truth; that it was Lunn who had rung you. You could rely on Lunn to back up your story. But it wouldn't really matter, would it, even if he did talk? No one would believe him."

"No, any more than they will believe you. You've been determined to earn your fee, Miss Gray. Your explanation is ingenious; there is even a certain plausibility about some of the details. But you know, and I know, that no police officer in the world would take it seriously. It's unfortunate for you that you couldn't question Lunn. But Lunn, as I said, is dead. He burnt to death in a road accident."

"I know, I saw. He tried to kill me tonight. Did you know that? And earlier, he tried to scare me into dropping the case. Was that because he had begun to suspect the truth?"

"If he did try to kill you, he exceeded his instructions. I merely asked him to keep an eye on you. I had contracted for your sole and whole-time services, if you remember; I wanted to be sure I was getting value. I am getting value of a kind. But you mustn't indulge your imagination outside this room. Neither the police nor the courts are sympathetic to slander nor to hysterical nonsense. And what proof have you? None. My wife was cremated. There is nothing alive or dead on this earth to prove that Mark was not her son."

Cordelia said:

"You visited Dr. Gladwin to satisfy yourself that he was too senile to give evidence against you. You needn't have worried. He never did suspect, did he? You chose him as your wife's doctor because he was old and incompetent. But I did have one small piece of evidence. Lunn was bringing it to you."

"Then you should have looked after it better. Nothing of Lunn except his bones has survived that crash."

"There are still the female clothes, the black pants and the bra. Someone might remember who bought them, particularly if that person was a man."

"Men do buy underclothes for their women. But if I were planning such a murder, I don't think buying the accessories would worry me. Would any harassed shop girl at the cash desk of a popular multiple store remember a particular purchase, a purchase paid for with cash, one of a number of innocuous items, all presented together at the busiest time of the day? The man might even have worn a simple disguise. I doubt whether she would even notice his face. Would you really expect her to remember, weeks afterwards, to identify one of thousands of customers and identify him with sufficient certainty to satisfy a jury? And if she did, what would it prove unless you have the clothes in question? Be sure of one thing, Miss Gray, if I needed to kill I should do it efficiently. I should not be found out. If the police ever learn how my son was found, as they well may do since, apparently, someone other than yourself knows it, they will only believe with greater certainty that he killed himself. Mark's death was necessary and, unlike most deaths, it served a purpose. Human beings have an irresistible urge towards self-sacrifice. They die for any reason or none at all, for meaningless abstractions like patriotism, justice, peace; for other men's ideas, for other men's power, for a few feet of earth. You, no doubt, would give your life to save a child or if you were convinced that the sacrifice would find a cure for cancer."

"I might. I like to think that I would. But I should want the decision to be mine, not yours."

"Of course. That would provide you with the necessary emotional satisfaction. But it wouldn't alter the fact of your dying nor the result of your death. And don't say that what I'm doing here isn't worth one single human life. Spare me that hypocrisy. You don't know and you're incapable of understanding the value of what I'm doing here. What difference will Mark's death make to you? You'd never heard of him until you came to Garforth House."

Cordelia said:

"It will make a difference to Gary Webber."

"Am I expected to lose everything I've worked for here because Gary Webber wants someone to play squash or discuss history with?"

Suddenly he looked Cordelia full in the face. He said sharply:

"What is the matter? Are you ill?"

"No I'm not ill. I knew that I must be right. I knew that what I had reasoned was true. But I can't believe it. I can't believe that a human being could be so evil."

"If you are capable of imagining it, then I'm capable of doing it. Haven't you yet discovered that about human beings, Miss Gray? It's the key to what you would call the wickedness of man."

Suddenly Cordelia could no longer bear this cynical antiphony. She cried out in passionate protest.

"But what is the use of making the world more beautiful if the people who live in it can't love one another?"

She had stung him at last into anger.

"Love! The most overused word in the language. Has it any meaning except the particular sentimental connotation which you choose to give it? What do you mean by love? That human beings must learn to live together with a decent concern for each other's welfare? The law enforces that. The greatest good of the greatest number. Beside that fundamental declaration of common sense all other philosophies are metaphysical abstractions. Or do you define love in the Christian sense, caritas? Read history, Miss Gray. See to what horrors, to what violence, hatred and repression the religion of love has led mankind. But perhaps you prefer a more feminine, more individual definition; love as a passionate commitment to another's personality. Intense personal commitment always ends in jealousy and enslavement. Love is more destructive than hate. If you must dedicate your life to something, dedicate it to an idea."

"I meant love, as a parent loves a child."

"The worse for them both, perhaps. But if he doesn't love, there is no power on earth which can stimulate or compel him to. And where there is no love, there can be none of the obligations of love."

"You could have let him live! The money wasn't important to him. He would have understood your needs and kept silent."

"Would he? How could he—or I—have explained his rejection of a great fortune in four years' time? People at the mercy of what they call their conscience are never safe. My son was a self-righteous prig. How could I put myself and my work in his hands?"

"You are in mine, Sir Ronald."

"You are mistaken. I am in no one's hands. Unfortunately for you that tape recorder is not working. We have no witnesses. You will repeat nothing that has been said in this room to anyone outside. If you do I shall have to ruin you. I shall make you unemployable, Miss Gray. And first of all I shall bankrupt that pathetic business of yours. From what Miss Leaming told me it shouldn't be difficult. Slander can be a highly expensive indulgence. Remember that if you are ever tempted to talk. Remember this too. You will harm yourself; you will harm Mark's memory; you will not harm me."

Cordelia never knew how long the tall figure in the red dressing-gown had been watching and listening in the shadow of the door. She never knew how much Miss Leaming had heard or at what moment she had stolen quietly away. But now she was aware of the red shadow moving soundlessly over the carpet, eyes on the figure behind the desk, the gun held closely against her breast. Cordelia watched in fascinated horror, not breathing. She knew exactly what was going to happen. It must have taken less than three seconds but they passed as slowly as minutes. Surely there had been time to cry out, time to warn, time to leap forward and wrench the gun from that steady hand? Surely there had been time for him to cry out? But he made no sound. He half rose, incredulous, and gazed at the muzzle in blind disbelief. Then he turned his head towards Cordelia as if in supplication. She would never forget that last look. It was beyond terror, beyond hope. It held nothing but the blank acceptance of defeat.

It was an execution, neat, unhurried, ritually precise. The bullet went in behind the right ear. The body leapt into the air, shoulders humped, softened before Cordelia's eyes as if the bones were melting into wax, and lay discarded at last over the desk. A thing; like Bernie; like her father.

Miss Leaming said:

"He killed my son."

"Your son?"

"Of course Mark was my son. His son and mine. I thought you might have guessed."

She stood with the gun in her hand gazing with expressionless eyes through the open window to the lawn. There was no sound. Nothing moved. Miss Leaming said:

"He was right when he said that no one could touch him. There was no proof."

Cordelia cried out, appalled:

"Then how could you kill him? How could you be so sure?"

Without releasing her hold on the pistol, Miss Leaming put her hand into the pocket of her dressing-gown. The hand moved over the desk top. A small gilt cylinder rolled over the polished wood towards Cordelia, then rocked into stillness. Miss Leaming said:

"The lipstick was mine. I found it a minute ago in the pocket of his dress suit. He hadn't worn that suit since he last dined in Hall on Feast night. He was always a magpie. He put small objects instinctively into his pocket."

Cordelia had never doubted Sir Ronald's guilt but now every nerve was desperate for reassurance.

"But it could have been planted there! Lunn could have put it there to incriminate him."

"Lunn didn't kill Mark. He was in bed with me at the time Mark died. He only left my side for five minutes and that was to make a telephone call shortly after eight o'clock."

"You were in love with Lunn!"

"Don't look at me like that! I only loved one man in my life and he's the one I've just killed. Talk about things you understand. Love had nothing to do with what Lunn and I needed from each other."

There was a moment's silence. Then Cordelia said:

"Is there anyone in the house?"

"No. The servants are in London. No one is working late at the lab tonight."

And Lunn was dead. Miss Leaming said with weary resignation:

"Hadn't you better phone the police?"

"Do you want me to?"

"What does it matter?"

"Prison matters. Losing your freedom matters. And do you really want the truth to come out in open court? Do you want everyone to know how your son died and who killed him? Is that what Mark himself would want?"

"No. Mark never believed in punishment. Tell me what I have to do."

"We've got to work quickly and plan carefully. We have to trust each other and we have to be intelligent."

"We are intelligent. What must we do?"

Cordelia took out her handkerchief and dropped it over the gun, took the weapon from Miss Leaming and placed it on the desk. She grasped the woman's thin wrist and pushed her protesting hand against Sir Ronald's palm, pulling against the instinctive recoil, forcing the stiff but living fingers against the soft unresisting hand of the dead.

"There may be firing residue. I don't really know much about that, but the police may test for it. Now wash your hands and get me a pair of thin gloves. Quickly."

She went without a word. Left alone, Cordelia looked down at the dead scientist. He had fallen with his chin against the desk top and his arms swinging loosely at his sides, an awkward, uncomfortable-looking pose which gave him the appearance of peering malevolently over his desk. Cordelia could not look at his eyes, but she was conscious of feeling nothing, not hatred, or anger, or pity. Between her eyes and the sprawled figure swung an elongated shape, head hideously crooked, toes pathetically pointed. She walked over to the open window and looked out over the garden with the casual curiosity of a guest kept waiting in a strange room. The air was warm and very still. The scent of roses came in waves through the open window, alternately sickening sweet and then as elusive as a half-caught memory.

This curious hiatus of peace and timelessness must have lasted less than half a minute. Then Cordelia began to plan. She thought about the Clandon case. Memory pictured herself and Bernie, sitting astride a fallen log in Epping Forest and eating their picnic lunch. It brought back the yeasty smell of fresh rolls, butter and tangy cheese, the heavy fungoid smell of summer woods. He had rested the pistol on the bark between them and had mumbled at her through the bread and cheese. "How would you shoot yourself behind the right ear? Go on, Cordelia—show."

Cordelia had taken the pistol in her right hand, index finger lightly resting on the trigger, and with some difficulty had strained back her arm to place the muzzle of the gun against the base of the skull. "Like that?" "You wouldn't, you know. Not if you were used to a gun. That's the little mistake Mrs. Clandon made and it nearly hanged her. She shot her husband behind the right ear with his service revolver and then tried to fake a suicide. But she pressed the wrong finger on the trigger. If he'd really shot himself behind the right ear he'd have pressed the trigger with his thumb and held the revolver with his palm round the back of the butt. I remember that case well. It was the first murder I worked on with the Super—Inspector Dalgliesh, as he was then. Mrs. Clandon confessed in the end." "What happened to her, Bernie?" "Life. She'd probably have got away with manslaughter if she hadn't tried to fake a suicide. The jury didn't much like what they heard about Major Clandon's little habits."

But Miss Leaming couldn't get away with manslaughter; not unless she told the whole story of Mark's death.

She was back in the room now. She handed Cordelia a pair of thin cotton gloves. Cordelia said:

"I think you'd better wait outside. What you don't see you won't have the trouble of forgetting. What were you doing when you met me in the hall?"

"I was getting myself a nightcap, a whisky."

"Then you would have met me again coming out of the study as you took it up to your room. Get it now and leave the glass on the side table in the hall. That's the kind of detail the police are trained to notice."

Alone again, Cordelia took up the gun. It was astonishing how repulsive she found this inert weight of metal now. How odd that she should ever have seen it as a harmless toy? She rubbed it thoroughly with her handkerchief erasing Miss Leaming's prints. Then she handled it. It was her gun. They would expect to find some of her prints on the butt together with those of the dead man. She placed it again on the desk top and drew on the gloves. This was the more difficult part. She handled the pistol gingerly and took it over to the inert right hand. She pressed his thumb firmly against the trigger, then wound the cold, unresisting hand round the back of the butt. Then she released his fingers and let the gun fall. It struck the carpet with a dull thud. She peeled off the gloves and went out to Miss Leaming in the hall, closing the study door quietly behind her.

"Here, you'd better put these back where you found them. We mustn't leave them lying around for the police to find."

She was gone only a few seconds. When she returned, Cordelia said:

"Now we must act the rest just as it would have happened. You meet me as I come out of the room. I have been with Sir Ronald about two minutes. You put down your glass of whisky on the hall table and walk with me to the front door. You say—what would you say?"

"Has he paid you?"

"No, I'm to come in the morning for my money. I'm sorry it wasn't a success. I've told Sir Ronald that I don't want to go on with the case."

"That's your concern, Miss Gray. It was a foolish business in the first place."

They were walking out of the front door now. Suddenly Miss Leaming turned to Cordelia and said urgently and in her normal voice:

"There's one thing you had better know. It was I who found Mark first and faked the suicide. He'd rung me earlier in the day and asked me to call. I couldn't get away until after nine because of Lunn. I didn't want him to be suspicious."

"But didn't it occur to you when you found Mark that there might be something odd about the death? The door was unlocked although the curtains were drawn. The lipstick was missing."

"I suspected nothing until tonight when I stood there in the shadows and heard you talking. We're all sexually sophisticated these days. I believed what I saw. It was all horror but I knew what I had to do. I worked quickly, terrified that someone would come. I cleaned his face with my handkerchief dampened with water from the kitchen sink. It seemed that the lipstick would never come off. I undressed him and pulled on his jeans which had been thrown over the back of a chair. I didn't wait to put on his shoes, that didn't seem important. Typing the note was the worst part. I knew that he would have his Blake with him somewhere in the cottage and that the passage I chose might be more convincing than an ordinary suicide note. The clattering of the typewriter keys sounded unnaturally loud in the quietness; I was terrified that someone would hear. He had been keeping a kind of journal. There wasn't time to read it but I burnt the typescript in the sitting-room grate.

Last of all, I bundled up the clothes and the pictures and brought them back here to be burnt in the lab incinerator."

"You dropped one of the pictures in the garden. And you didn't quite succeed in cleaning the lipstick from his face."

"So that's how you guessed?"

Cordelia didn't reply immediately. Whatever happened she must keep Isabelle de Lasterie out of the case.

"I wasn't sure if it was you who had been there first but I thought it must have been. There were four things. You didn't want me to investigate Mark's death; you read English at Cambridge and could have known where to find that Blake quotation; you are an experienced typist and I didn't think that the note had been typed by an amateur despite the late attempt to make it look like Mark's work; when I was first at Garforth House and asked about the suicide note you spoke the whole of the Blake quotation; the typed version was ten words short. I first noticed that when I visited the police station and was shown the note. It pointed directly to you. That was the strongest evidence I had."

They had reached the car now and paused together. Cordelia said:

"We mustn't waste any more time before ringing the police. Someone may have heard the shot."

"It's not likely. We're some distance from the village. Do we hear it now?"

"Yes. We hear it now." There was a second's pause then Cordelia said:

"What was that? It sounded like a shot."

"It couldn't have been. It was probably a car backfiring."

Miss Leaming spoke like a bad actress, the words were stilted, unconvincing. But she spoke them; she would remember them.

"But there isn't a car passing. And it came from the house."

They glanced at each other, then ran back together through the open door into the hall. Miss Leaming paused for a moment and looked Cordelia in the face before she opened the study door. Cordelia came in behind her. Miss Leaming said:

"He's been shot! I'd better phone the police."

Cordelia said:

"You wouldn't say that! Don't ever think like that! You'd go up to the body first and then you'd say:

"'He's shot himself. I'd better phone the police.'"

Miss Leaming looked unemotionally at her lover's body, then glanced round the room. Forgetting her role, she asked:

"What have you done in here? What about finger prints?"

"Never mind. I've looked after that. All you have to remember is that you didn't know I had a gun when I first came to Garforth House; you didn't know Sir Ronald took it from me. You haven't seen that gun until this moment. When I arrived tonight you showed me into the study and met me again when I came out two minutes later. We walked together to the car and spoke as we have just spoken. We heard the shot. We did what we have just done. Forget everything else that has happened. When they question you, don't embroider, don't invent, don't be afraid to say you can't remember. And now—ring the Cambridge police."

Three minutes later they were standing together at the open door waiting for the police to arrive. Miss Leaming said:

"We mustn't talk together once they're here. And, afterwards, we mustn't meet or show any particular interest in each other. They'll know that this can't be murder unless we two are in it together. And why should we conspire together when we've only met once before, when we don't even like each other?"

She was right, thought Cordelia. They didn't even like each other. She didn't really care if Elizabeth Leaming went to prison; she did care if Mark's mother went to prison. She cared, too, that the truth of his death should never be known. The strength of that determination struck her as irrational. It could make no difference to him now and he wasn't a boy who had cared over much what people thought of him. But Ronald Callender had desecrated his body after death; had planned to make him an object, at worst of contempt, at best of pity. She had set her face against Ronald Callender. She hadn't wanted him to die; wouldn't have been capable herself of pressing the trigger. But he was dead and she couldn't feel regret, nor could she be an instrument of retribution for his murderer. It was expedient, no more than that, that Miss Leaming shouldn't be punished. Gazing out into the summer night and waiting for the sound of the police cars, Cordelia accepted once and for all the enormity and the justification of what she had done and was still planning to do. She was never afterwards to feel the least tinge of regret or of remorse.

Miss Leaming said:

"There are things you probably want to ask me, things I suppose you've a right to know. We can meet in King's College Chapel after Evensong on the first Sunday after the inquest. I'll go through the screen into the chancel, you stay in the nave. It will seem natural enough for us to meet by chance there, that is if we are both still free."

Cordelia was interested to see that Miss Leaming was taking charge again. She said:

"We shall be. If we keep our heads this can't go wrong."

There was a moment's silence. Miss Leaming said:

"They're taking their time. Surely they should be here by now?"

"They won't be much longer."

Miss Leaming suddenly laughed and said with revealing bitterness:

"What is there to be frightened of? We shall be dealing only with men."

So they waited quietly together. They heard the approaching cars before the headlamps swept over the drive, illuminating every pebble, picking out the small plants at the edge of the beds, bathing the blue haze of the wisteria with light, dazzling the watchers' eyes. Then the lights were dimmed as the cars rocked gently to a stop in front of the house. Dark shapes emerged and came unhurriedly but resolutely forward. The hall was suddenly filled with large, calm men, some in plain clothes. Cordelia effaced herself against the wall and it was Miss Leaming who stepped forward, spoke to them in a low voice and led them into the study.

Two uniformed men were left in the hall. They stood talking together, taking no notice of Cordelia. Their colleagues were taking their time. They must have used the telephone in the study because more cars and men began to arrive. First the police surgeon, identified by his bag even if he hadn't been greeted with:

"Good evening Doc. In here please."

How often he must have heard that phrase! He glanced with brief curiosity at Cordelia as he trotted through the hall, a fat, dishevelled little man, his face crumpled and petulant as a child when forcibly woken from sleep. Next came a civilian photographer carrying his camera, tripod and box of equipment; a fingerprint expert; two other civilians whom Cordelia, instructed in procedure by Bernie, guessed were scenes-of-crime officers. So they were treating this as a suspicious death. And why not? It was suspicious.

The head of the household lay dead, but the house itself seemed to have come alive. The police talked, not in whispers, but in confident normal voices unsubdued by death. They were professionals doing their job, working easily to the prescribed routine. They had been initiated into the mysteries of violent death; its victims held no awe for them. They had seen too many bodies; bodies scraped off motorways; loaded piecemeal into ambulances; dragged by hook and net from the depths of rivers; dug putrefying from the clogging earth. Like doctors, they were kind and condescendingly gentle to the uninstructed, keeping inviolate their awful knowledge. This body, while it breathed, had been more important than others. It wasn't important now, but it could still make trouble for them. They would be that much more meticulous, that much more tactful. But it was still only a case.

Cordelia sat alone and waited. She was suddenly overcome with tiredness. She longed for nothing but to put down her head on the hall table and sleep. She was hardly aware of Miss Leaming passing through the hall on her way to the drawing room, of the tall officer talking to her as they passed. Neither took any notice of the small figure in its immense woollen jersey, sitting against the wall. Cordelia willed herself to stay awake. She knew what she had to say; it was all clear enough in her mind. If only they would come to question her and let her sleep.

It wasn't until the photographer and the print man had finished their work that one of the senior officers came out to her. She was never afterwards able to recall his face but she remembered his voice, a careful, unemphatic voice from which every tinge of emotion had been excluded. He held out the gun towards her. It was resting on his open palm, protected by a handkerchief from the contamination of his hand.

"Do you recognize this weapon, Miss Gray?"

Cordelia thought it odd that he should use the word weapon. Why not just say gun?

"I think so. I think it must be mine."

"You aren't sure?"

"It must be mine, unless Sir Ronald owned one of the same make. He took it from me when I first came here four days ago. He promised to let me have it back when I called tomorrow morning for my pay."

"So this is only the second time you've been in this house?"

"Yes."

"Have you ever met Sir Ronald Callender or Miss Leaming before?"

"No. Not until Sir Ronald sent for me to undertake this case."

He went away. Cordelia rested her head back against the wall and took short snatches of sleep.

Another officer came. This time he had a uniformed man with him, taking notes. There were more questions. Cordelia told her prepared story. They wrote it down without comment and went away.

She must have dozed. She awoke to find a tall, uniformed officer standing over her. He said:

"Miss Leaming is making tea in the kitchen, Miss. Perhaps you would like to give her a hand. It's something to do, isn't it?"

Cordelia thought; they're going to take away the body. She said:

"I don't know where the kitchen is."

She saw his eyes flicker.

"Oh, don't you, Miss? You're a stranger here, are you? Well, it's this way."

The kitchen was at the back of the house. It smelt of spice, oil and tomato sauce, bringing back memories of meals in Italy with her father. Miss Leaming was taking down cups from a vast dresser. An electric kettle was already hissing steam. The police officer stayed. So they weren't to be left alone. Cornelia said:

"Can I help?" Miss Leaming did not look at her.

"There are some biscuits in that tin. You can put them out on a tray. The milk is in the fridge."

Cordelia moved like an automaton. The milk bottle was an icy column in her hands, the biscuit tin lid resisted her tired fingers and she broke a nail prising it off. She noticed the details of the kitchen—a wall calendar of St. Theresa of Avila, the saint's face unnaturally elongated and pale so that she looked like a hallowed Miss Leaming; a china donkey with two panniers of artificial flowers, its melancholy head crowned with a miniature straw hat; an immense blue bowl of brown eggs.

There were two trays. The police constable took the larger from Miss Leaming and led the way into the hall. Cordelia followed with the second tray, holding it high against her chest like a child, permitted as a privilege to help mother. Police officers gathered round. She took a cup herself and returned to her usual chair.

And now there was the sound of yet another car. A middle-aged woman came in with a uniformed chauffeur at her shoulder. Through the fog of her tiredness, Cordelia heard a high, didactic voice.

"My dear Eliza, this is appalling! You must come back to the Lodge tonight. No, I insist. Is the Chief Constable here?"

"No, Marjorie, but these officers have been very kind."

"Leave them the key. They'll lock up the house when they've finished. You can't possibly stay here alone tonight."

There were introductions, hurried consultations with the detectives in which the newcomer's voice was dominant. Miss Leaming went upstairs with her visitor and reappeared five minutes later with a small case, her coat over her arm. They went off together, escorted to the car by the chauffeur and one of the detectives. None of the little party glanced at Cordelia.

Five minutes later the Inspector came up to Cordelia, key in hand.

"We shall lock up the house tonight, Miss Gray. It's time you were getting home. Are you thinking of staying at the cottage?"

"Just for the next few days, if Major Markland will let me."

"You look very tired. One of my men will drive you in your own car. I should like a written statement from you tomorrow. Can you come to the station as soon as possible after breakfast? You know where it is?"

"Yes, I know."

One of the police panda cars drove off first and the Mini followed. The police driver drove fast, lurching the little car around the corners. Cordelia's head lolled against the back of the seat and, from time to time, was thrown against the driver's arm. He was wearing shirt sleeves and she was vaguely conscious of the comfort of the warm flesh through the cotton. The car window was open and she was aware of hot night air rushing against her face, of the scudding clouds, of the first unbelievable colours of day staining the eastern sky. The route seemed strange to her and time itself disjointed; she wondered why the car had suddenly stopped and it took a minute for her to recognize the tall hedge bending over the lane like a menacing shadow, the ramshackled gate. She was home. The driver said:

"Is this the place, Miss?"

"Yes, this is it. But I usually leave the Mini further down the lane on the right. There's a copse there where you can drive it off the road."

"Right, Miss."

He got out of the car to consult the other driver. They moved on slowly for the last few yards of the journey. And now, at last the police car had driven away and she was alone at the gate. It was an effort to push it open against the weight of the weeds and she lurched round the cottage to the back door like a drunken creature. It took some little time to fit the key into the lock, but that was the last problem. There was no longer a gun to hide; there was no longer need to check the tape sealing the windows. Lunn was dead and she was alive. Every night that she had slept at the cottage Cordelia had come home tired, but never before had she been as tired as this. She made her way upstairs as if sleepwalking and, too exhausted even to zip herself into her sleeping-bag, crept underneath it and knew nothing more.

And at last—it seemed to Cordelia after months, not days, of waiting—there was another inquest. It was as unhurried, as unostentatiously formal, as Bernie's had been, but there was a difference. Here, instead of a handful of pathetic casuals who had sneaked into the warmth of the back benches to hear Bernie's obsequies, were grave-faced colleagues and friends, muted voices, the whispered preliminaries of lawyers and police, an indefinable sense of occasion. Cordelia guessed that the grey-haired man escorting Miss Leaming must be her lawyer. She watched him at work, affable but not deferential to the senior police, quietly solicitous for his client, exuding a confidence that they were all engaged in a necessary if tedious formality, a ritual as unworrying as Sunday Matins.

Miss Leaming looked very pale. She was wearing the grey suit she had worn when Cordelia first met her but with a small black hat, black gloves and a black chiffon scarf knotted at her throat. The two women did not look at each other. Cordelia found a seat at the end of a bench and sat there, unrepresented and alone. One or two of the younger policemen smiled at her with a reassuring but pitying kindness.

Miss Leaming gave her evidence first in a low, composed voice. She affirmed instead of taking the oath, a decision which caused a brief spasm of distress to pass over her lawyer's face. But she gave him no further cause for concern. She testified that Sir Ronald had been depressed at his son's death and, she thought, had blamed himself for not knowing that something was worrying Mark. He had told her that he intended to call in a private detective, and it had been she who had originally interviewed Miss Gray and had brought her back to Garforth House. Miss

Leaming said that she had opposed the suggestion; she had seen no useful purpose in it, and thought that this futile and fruitless enquiry would only remind Sir Ronald of the tragedy. She had not known that Miss Gray possessed a gun nor that Sir Ronald had taken it from her. She had not been present during the whole of their preliminary interview. Sir Ronald had escorted Miss Gray to view his son's room while she, Miss Leaming, had gone in search of a photograph of Mr. Callender for which Miss Gray had asked.

The coroner asked her gently about the night of Sir Ronald's death.

Miss Leaming said that Miss Gray had arrived to give her first report shortly after half past ten. She herself had been passing through the front hall when the girl appeared. Miss Leaming had pointed out that it was late, but Miss Gray had said that she had wanted to abandon the case and get back to town. She had showed Miss Gray into the study where Sir Ronald was working. They had been together, she thought, for less than two minutes. Miss Gray had then come out of the study and she had walked with her to her car; they had only talked briefly. Miss Gray said that Sir Ronald had asked her to call back in the morning for her pay. She had made no mention of a gun.

Sir Ronald had, only half an hour before that, received a telephone call from the police to say that his laboratory assistant, Christopher Lunn, had been killed in a road accident. She had not told Miss Gray the news about Lunn before her interview with Sir Ronald; it hadn't occurred to her to do so. The girl had gone almost immediately into the study to see Sir Ronald. Miss Leaming said that they were standing together at the car talking when they heard the shot. At first she had thought it was a car backfiring but then she had realized that it had come from the house. They had both rushed into the study and found Sir Ronald lying slumped over his desk. The gun had dropped from his hand to the floor.

No, Sir Ronald had never given her any idea that he contemplated suicide. She thought that he was very distressed about the death of Mr. Lunn but it was difficult to tell. Sir Ronald was not a man to show emotion. He had been working very hard recently and had not seemed himself since the death of his son. But Miss Leaming had never for a moment thought that Sir Ronald was a man who would put an end to his life.

She was followed by the police witnesses, deferential, professional, but managing to give an impression that none of this was new to them; they had seen it all before and would see it again.

They were followed by the doctors, including the pathologist, who testified in what the court obviously thought was unnecessary detail to the effect of firing a jacketed hollow-cavity bullet of ninety grains into the human brain. The coroner asked:

"You have heard the police evidence that there

was the print of Sir Ronald Callender's thumb on the trigger of the gun and a palm mark smudged around the butt. What would you deduce from that?"

The pathologist looked slightly surprised at being asked to deduce anything but said that it was apparent that Sir Ronald had held the gun with his thumb on the trigger when pointing it against his head. The pathologist thought that it was probably the most comfortable way in which to hold the weapon, indeed the only comfortable way, having regard to the position of the wound of entry.

Lastly, Cordelia was called to the witness box and took the oath. She had given some thought to the propriety of this and had wondered whether to follow Miss Leaming's example. There were moments, usually on a sunny Easter morning, when she wished that she could with sincerity call herself a Christian; but for the rest of the year she knew herself to be what she was—incurably agnostic but prone to unpredictable relapses into faith. This seemed to her, however, a moment when religious scrupulosity was an indulgence which she couldn't afford. The lies she was about to tell would not be the more heinous because they were ringed with blasphemy.

The coroner let her tell her story without interruptions. She sensed that the court was puzzled by her but not unsympathetic. For once, the carefully modulated middle-class accent, which in her six years at the convent she had unconsciously acquired, and which in other people often irritated her as much as her own voice had irritated her father, was proving an advantage. She wore her suit and had bought a black chiffon scarf to cover her head. She remembered that she must call the coroner "sir".

After she had briefly confirmed Miss Leaming's story of how she had been called to the case, the coroner said:

"And now, Miss Gray, will you explain to the court what happened on the night Sir Ronald Callender died?"

"I had decided, sir, that I didn't want to go on with the case. I hadn't discovered anything useful and I didn't think there was anything to discover. I had been living in the cottage where Mark Callender had spent the last weeks of his life and I had come to think that what I was doing was wrong, that I was taking money for prying into his private life. I decided on impulse to tell Sir Ronald that I wanted to finish the case. I drove to Garforth House. I got there at about ten-thirty. I knew it was late but I was anxious to go back to London the next morning. I saw Miss Leaming as she was crossing the hall and she showed me straight into the study."

"Will you please describe to the court how you found Sir Ronald."

"He seemed to be tired and distracted. I tried to explain why I wanted to give up the case but I'm not sure that he heard me. He said I was to come back next morning for my money and I said that I only proposed to charge expenses, but that I would like to have my gun. He just waved a hand in dismissal and said, 'tomorrow morning, Miss Gray. Tomorrow morning.'"

"And then you left him?"

"Yes, sir. Miss Leaming accompanied me back to the car and I was just about to drive away when we heard the shot."

"You didn't see the gun in Sir Ronald's possession when you were in the study with him?"

"No, sir."

"He didn't talk to you about Mr. Lunn's death or give you any idea that he was contemplating suicide?"

"No, sir."

The coroner doodled on the pad before him. Without looking at Cordelia, he said:

"And now, Miss Gray, will you please explain to the court how Sir Ronald came to have your gun."

This was the difficult part, but Cordelia had rehearsed it. The Cambridge police had been very thorough. They had asked the same questions over and over again. She knew exactly how Sir Ronald had come to have the gun. She remembered a piece of Dalgliesh dogma, reported by Bernie, which had seemed to her at the time more appropriate advice for a criminal than a detective. "Never tell an unnecessary lie; the truth has great authority. The cleverest murderers have been caught, not because they told the one essential lie, but because they continued to lie about unimportant details when the truth could have done them no harm."

She said:

"My partner, Mr. Pryde, owned the gun and was very proud of it. When he killed himself I knew that he meant me to have it. That was why he cut his wrists instead of shooting himself, which would have been quicker and easier."

The coroner looked up sharply.

"And were you there when he killed himself?"

"No, sir. But I found the body."

There was a murmur of sympathy from the court; she could feel their concern.

"Did you know that the gun wasn't licensed?"

"No, sir, but I think I suspected that it might not have been. I brought it with me on this case because I didn't want to leave it in the office and because I found it a comfort. I meant to check up on the licence as soon as I got back. I didn't expect ever to use the gun. I didn't really think of it as a lethal weapon. It's just that this was my first case and Bernie had left it to me and I felt happier having it with me."

"I see," said the coroner.

Cordelia thought that he probably did see and so did the court. They were having no difficulty in believing her because she was telling the somewhat improbable truth. Now that she was about to lie, they would go on believing her.

"And now will you please tell the court how Sir Ronald came to take the gun from you?"

"It was on my first visit to Garforth House

when Sir Ronald was showing me his son's bedroom. He knew that I was the sole owner of the
Agency, and he asked me if it wasn't a difficult
and rather frightening job for a woman. I said
that I wasn't frightened but that I had Bernie's
gun. When he found that I had it with me in my
bag he made me hand it over to him. He said
that he didn't propose to engage someone who
might be a danger to other people or herself. He
said that he wouldn't take the responsibility. He
took the gun and the ammunition."

"And what did he do with the gun?"

Cordelia had thought this one out carefully.
Obviously he hadn't carried it downstairs in his
hand or Miss Leaming would have seen it. She
would have liked to have said that he put it into a
drawer in Mark's room but she couldn't remember whether the bedside table had had any drawers. She said:

"He took it out of the room with him; he didn't
tell me where. He was only away for a moment
and then we went downstairs together."

"And you didn't set eyes on the gun again until
you saw it on the floor close to Sir Ronald's hand
when you and Miss Leaming found his body?"

"No, sir."

Cordelia was the last witness. The verdict was
quickly given, one that the court obviously felt
would have been agreeable to Sir Ronald's scrupulously exact and scientific brain. It was that
the deceased had taken his own life but that
there was no evidence as to the state of mind.

The coroner delivered at length the obligatory warning about the danger of guns. Guns, the court were informed, could kill people. He managed to convey that unlicensed guns were particularly prone to this danger. He pronounced no strictures on Cordelia personally although it was apparent that this restraint cost him an effort. He rose and the court rose with him.

After the coroner had left the bench the court broke up into little whispering groups. Miss Leaming was quickly surrounded. Cordelia saw her shaking hands, receiving condolences, listening with grave assenting face to the first tentative proposals for a memorial service. Cordelia wondered how she could ever have feared that Miss Leaming would be suspected. She herself stood a little apart, delinquent. She knew that the police would charge her with illegal possession of the gun. They could do no less. True, she would be lightly punished, if punished at all. But for the rest of her life she would be the girl whose carelessness and naïveté had lost England one of her foremost scientists.

As Hugo had said, all Cambridge suicides were brilliant. But about this one there could be little doubt. Sir Ronald's death would probably raise him to the status of genius.

Almost unnoticed, she came alone out of the courtroom on to Market Hill. Hugo must have been waiting; now he fell into step with her.

"How did it go? I must say death seems to follow you around, doesn't it?"

"It went all right. I seem to follow death."

"I suppose he did shoot himself?"

"Yes. He shot himself."

"And with your gun?"

"As you well know if you were in court. I didn't see you."

"I wasn't there, I had a tutorial, but the news did get around. I shouldn't let it worry you. Ronald Callender wasn't as important as some people in Cambridge may choose to believe."

"You know nothing about him. He was a human being and he's dead. That fact is always important."

"It isn't, you know, Cordelia. Death is the least important thing about us. Comfort yourself with Joseph Hall. 'Death borders upon our birth and our cradle stands in the grave.' And he did choose his own weapon, his own time. He'd had enough of himself. Plenty of people had had enough of him."

They walked together down St. Edward's Passage towards King's Parade. Cordelia wasn't sure where they were making for. Her need at present was just to walk, but she didn't find her companion disagreeable.

She asked:

"Where's Isabelle?"

"Isabelle is home in Lyons. Papa turned up unexpectedly yesterday and found that mademoiselle wasn't exactly earning her wages. Papa decided that dear Isabelle was getting less—or it may have been more—out of her Cambridge education than he had expected. I don't think you need worry about her. Isabelle is safe enough now. Even if the police decide that it's worthwhile going to France to question her—and why on earth should they?—it won't help them. Papa will surround her with a barrage of lawyers. He's not in a mood to stand any nonsense from Englishmen at present."

"And what about you? If anyone asks you how Mark died, you'll never tell them the truth?"

"What do you think? Sophie, Davie and I are safe enough. I'm reliable when it comes to essentials."

For a moment Cordelia wished that he were reliable in less essential matters. She asked:

"Are you sorry about Isabelle leaving?"

"I am rather. Beauty is intellectually confusing; it sabotages common sense. I could never quite accept that Isabelle was what she is: a generous, indolent, over-affectionate and stupid young woman. I thought that any woman as beautiful as she must have an instinct about life, access to some secret wisdom which is beyond cleverness. Every time she opened that delicious mouth I was expecting her to illumine life. I think I could have spent all my life just looking at her and waiting for the oracle. And all she could talk about was clothes."

"Poor Hugo."

"Never poor Hugo. I'm not unhappy. The secret of contentment is never to allow yourself to want anything which reason tells you you haven't a chance of getting."

Cordelia thought that he was young, well-off, clever even if not clever enough, handsome; there wasn't much that he would have to forgo on that or any other criteria.

She heard him speaking:

"Why not stay in Cambridge for a week or so and let me show you the city? Sophie would let you have her spare room."

"No thank you, Hugo. I have to get back to town."

There was nothing in town for her, but with Hugo there would be nothing in Cambridge for her either. There was only one reason for staying in this city. She would remain at the cottage until Sunday and her meeting with Miss Leaming. After that, as far as she was concerned, the case of Mark Callender would be finished for good.

Sunday afternoon Evensong was over and the congregation, who had listened in respectful silence to the singing of responses, psalms and anthem by one of the finest choirs in the world, rose and joined with joyous abandon in the final hymn. Cordelia rose and sang with them. She had seated herself at the end of the row close to the richly carved screen. From here she could see into the chancel. The robes of the choristers gleamed scarlet and white; the candles flickered in patterned rows and high circles of golden light;

two tall and slender candles stood each side of the softly illuminated Rubens above the high altar, seen dimly as a distant smudge of crimson, blue and gold. The blessing was pronounced, the final amen impeccably sung and the choir began to file decorously out of the chancel. The south door was opened and sunlight flooded into the chapel. The members of the college who had attended divine service strolled out after the Provost and Fellows in casual disarray, their regulation surplices dingy and limp over a cheerful incongruity of corduroy and tweed. The great organ snuffled and groaned like an animal gathering breath, before giving forth its magnificent voice in a Bach fugue. Cordelia sat quietly in her chair, listening and waiting. Now the congregation was moving down the main aisle—small groups in bright summer cottons whispering discreetly, serious young men in sober Sunday black, tourists clutching their illustrated guides and half-embarrassed by their obtrusive cameras, a group of nuns with calm and cheerful faces.

Miss Leaming was one of the last, a tall figure in a grey linen dress and white gloves, her head bare, a white cardigan slung carelessly around her shoulders against the chill of the chapel. She was obviously alone and unwatched and her careful pretence of surprise at recognizing Cordelia was probably an unnecessary precaution. They passed out of the chapel together.

The gravel path outside the doorway was thronged with people. A little party of Japanese, festooned with cameras and accessories, added their high staccato jabber to the muted Sunday afternoon chat. From here the silver stream of the Cam was invisible but the truncated bodies of punters glided against the far bank like puppets in a show, raising their arms above the pole and turning to thrust it backwards as if participating in some ritual dance. The great lawn lay unshadowed in the sun, a quintessence of greenness staining the scented air. A frail and elderly Don in gown and mortarboard was limping across the grass; the sleeves of his gown caught a stray breeze and billowed out so that he looked like a winged and monstrous crow struggling to rise. Miss Leaming said, as if Cordelia had asked for an explanation:

"He's a Fellow. The sacred turf is, therefore, uncontaminated by his feet."

They walked in silence by Gibbs Building. Cordelia wondered when Miss Leaming would speak. When she did, her first question was unexpected.

"Do you think you'll make a success of it?"

Sensing Cordelia's surprise, she added impatiently:

"The Detective Agency. Do you think you'll be able to cope?"

"I shall have to try. It's the only job I know."

She had no intention of justifying to Miss Leaming her affection and loyalty to Bernie; she would have had some difficulty in explaining it to herself.

"Your overheads are too high."

It was a pronouncement made with all the authority of a verdict.

"Do you mean the office and the Mini?" asked Cordelia.

"Yes. In your job I don't see how one person in the field can bring in sufficient income to cover expenses. You can't be sitting in the office taking orders and typing letters and be out solving cases at the same time. On the other hand, I don't suppose you can afford help."

"Not yet. I've been thinking that I might rent a telephone answering service. That will take care of the orders although, of course, clients much prefer to come to the office and discuss their case. If I can only make enough in expenses just to live, then any fees can cover the overheads."

"If there are any fees."

There seemed nothing to say to this and they walked on in silence for a few seconds. Then Miss Leaming said:

"There'll be the expenses from this case anyway. That at least should help towards your fine for illegal possession of the gun. I've put the matter in the hands of my solicitors. You should be getting a cheque fairly soon."

"I don't want to take any money for this case."

"I can understand that. As you pointed out to Ronald, it falls under your fair deal clause. Strictly speaking you aren't entitled to any. All the same, I think it would look less suspicious if you took your expenses. Would thirty pounds strike you as reasonable?"

"Perfectly, thank you."

They had reached the corner of the lawn and had turned to walk towards King's Bridge. Miss Leaming said:

"I shall have to be grateful to you for the rest of my life. That for me is an unaccustomed humility and I'm not sure that I like it."

"Then don't feel it. I was thinking of Mark, not of you."

"I thought you might have acted in the service of justice or some such abstraction."

"I wasn't thinking about any abstraction. I was thinking about a person."

They had reached the bridge now and leaned over it side by side to look down into the bright water. The paths leading up to the bridge were, for a few minutes, empty of people. Miss Leaming said:

"Pregnancy isn't difficult to fake, you know. It only needs a loose corset and judicious stuffing. It's humiliating for the woman, of course, almost indecent if she happens to be barren. But it isn't difficult, particularly if she isn't closely watched. Evelyn wasn't. She had always been a shy, self-contained woman. People expected her to be excessively modest about her pregnancy. Garforth House wasn't filled with friends and relations swapping horror stories about the ante-natal clinic and patting her stomach. We had to get rid of that tedious fool Nanny Pilbeam, of course. Ronald regarded her departure as one of the subsidiary benefits of the pseudo pregnancy. He was tired of being spoken to as if he were still Ronnie Callender, the bright grammar school boy from Harrogate."

Cordelia said:

"Mrs. Goddard told me that Mark had a great look of his mother."

"She would. She was sentimental as well as stupid."

Cordelia did not speak. After a few moments silence Miss Leaming went on:

"I discovered that I was carrying Ronald's child at about the same time as a London specialist confirmed what the three of us already guessed, that Evelyn was most unlikely to conceive. I wanted to have the baby; Ronald desperately wanted a son; Evelyn's father was obsessional about his need for a grandson and was willing to part with half a million to prove it. It was all so easy. I resigned from my teaching job and went off to the safe anonymity of London and Evelyn told her father she was pregnant at last. Neither Ronald nor I had any conscience about defrauding George Bottley. He was an arrogant, brutal, self-satisfied fool who couldn't imagine how the world would continue without his issue to supervise it. He even subsidized his own deceit. The cheques for Evelyn began to arrive, each with a note imploring her to look after her health, to consult the best London doctors, to rest, to take a holiday in the sun. She had always loved Italy, and Italy became part of the plan. The three of us would meet in London every two months and fly together to Pisa. Ronald would rent a small villa outside Florence and, once there, I became Mrs. Callender and Evelyn became me. We had only daily servants and there was no need for them to look at our passports. They got used to our visits and so did the local doctor who was called in to supervise my health. The locals thought it flattering that the English lady should be so fond of Italy that she came back month after month, so close to her confinement."

Cordelia asked:

"But how could she do it, how could she bear to be there with you in the house, watching you with her husband, knowing that you were going to have his child?"

"She did it because she loved Ronald and couldn't bear to lose him. She hadn't been much success as a woman. If she lost her husband, what else was there for her? She couldn't have gone back to her father. Besides, we had a bribe for her. She was to have the child. If she refused, then Ronald would leave her and seek a divorce to marry me."

"I would rather have left him and gone off to scrub doorsteps."

"Not everyone has a talent for scrubbing doorsteps and not everyone has your capacity for moral indignation. Evelyn was religious. She was, therefore, practised in self-deception. She convinced herself that what we were doing was best for the child."

"And her father? Didn't he ever suspect?"

"He despised her for her piety. He always had. Psychologically he could hardly indulge that dislike and at the same time think her capable of deceit. Besides, he desperately needed that grandchild. It wouldn't have entered his mind that the child might not be hers. And he had a doctor's report. After our third visit to Italy we told Doctor Sartori that Mrs. Callender's father was concerned about her care. At our request he wrote a reassuring medical report on the progress of the pregnancy. We went to Florence together a fortnight before the baby was due and stayed there until Mark arrived. Luckily he was a day or two before time. We'd had the foresight to put back the expected date of delivery so that it genuinely looked as if Evelyn had been caught unexpectedly by a premature birth. Dr. Sartori did what was necessary with perfect competence and the three of us came home with the baby and a birth certificate in the right name."

Cordelia said:

"And nine months later Mrs. Callender was dead."

"He didn't kill her, if that's what you're thinking. He wasn't really the monster that you imagine, at least, not then. But in a sense we did both destroy her. She should have had a specialist, certainly a better doctor than that incompetent fool Gladwin. But the three of us were desperately afraid that an efficient doctor would know that she hadn't borne a child. She was as worried as we were. She insisted that no other doctor be consulted. She had grown to love the baby, you see. So she died and was cremated and we thought we were safe for ever."

"She left Mark a note before she died, nothing but a scribbled hieroglyphic in her prayer book. She left him her blood group."

"We knew that the blood groups were a danger. Ronald took blood from the three of us and made the necessary tests. But after she was dead even that worry ended."

There was a long silence. Cordelia could see a little group of tourists moving down the path towards the bridge. Miss Leaming said:

"The irony of it is that Ronald never really loved him. Mark's grandfather adored him; there was no difficulty there. He left half his fortune to Evelyn and it came automatically to her husband. Mark was to get the other half on his twenty-fifth birthday. But Ronald never cared for his son. He found that he couldn't love him, and I wasn't allowed to. I watched him grow up and go to school. But I wasn't allowed to love him. I used to knit him endless jerseys. It was almost an obsession. The patterns got more intricate and the wool thicker as he grew older. Poor Mark, he must have thought that I was mad, this strange, discontented woman whom his father couldn't do without but wouldn't marry."

"There are one or two of the jerseys at the cottage. What would you like me to do with his things?"

"Take them away and give them to anyone who

needs them. Unless you think I ought to unpick the wool and knit it up into something new? Would that be a suitable gesture, do you think, symbolic of wasted effort, pathos, futility?"

"I'll find a use for them. And his books?"

"Get rid of them too. I can't go again to the cottage. Get rid of everything if you will."

The little group of tourists was very close now but they seemed engrossed in their own chatter. Miss Leaming took an envelope out of her pocket and handed it to Cordelia.

"I've written out a brief confession. There's nothing in it about Mark, nothing about how he died or what you discovered. It's just a brief statement that I shot Ronald Callender immediately after you had left Garforth House and coerced you into supporting my story. You'd better put it somewhere safe. One day you may need it."

Cordelia saw that the envelope was addressed to herself. She didn't open it. She said:

"It's too late now. If you regret what we did, you should have spoken earlier. The case is closed now."

"I've no regrets. I'm glad that we acted as we did. But the case may not be over yet."

"But it is over! The inquest has given its verdict."

"Ronald had a number of very powerful friends. They have influence and, periodically, they like to exercise it if only to prove that they still have it."

"But they can't get this case reopened! It practically takes an act of parliament to change a coroner's verdict."

"I don't say that they'll try to do that. But they may ask questions. They may have what they describe as a quiet word in the right ear. And the right ears are usually available. That's how they work. That's the sort of people they are."

Cordelia said suddenly:

"Have you a light?"

Without question or protest Miss Leaming opened her handbag and handed over an elegant silver tube. Cordelia didn't smoke and was unused to lighters. It took three clicks before the wick burst into flame. Then she leaned over the parapet of the bridge and set fire to the corner of the envelope.

The incandescent flame was invisible in the stronger light of the sun. All Cordelia could see was a narrow band of wavering purple light as the flame bit into the paper and the charred edges widened and grew. The pungent smell of burning was wafted away on the breeze. As soon as the flame tinged her fingers, Cordelia dropped the envelope, still burning, and watched it twist and turn as it floated down small and frail as a snowflake to be lost at last in the Cam. She said:

"Your lover shot himself. That is all that either of us need to remember now or ever."

They didn't speak again about Ronald Callender's death, but walked silently along the elm-lined

path towards the Backs. At one point Miss Leaming glanced at Cordelia and said in a tone of angry petulance:

"You look surprisingly well!"

Cordelia supposed that this brief outburst was
the resentment of the middle-aged at the resi-
lence of the young which could so quickly recover from physical disaster. It had only taken
one night of long and deep sleep to return her to
the state which Bernie, with irritating coyness,
used to describe as bright eyed and bushy tailed.
Even without the benison of a hot bath the broken
skin on her shoulders and back had healed
cleanly. Physically, the events of the last fortnight
had left her unscathed. She wasn't so sure about
Miss Leaming. The sleek platinum hair was still
swathed and shaped immaculately to the bones
of the head; she still carried her clothes with cool
distinction as if it were important to appear the
competent and unharassed helpmate of a famous
man. But the pale skin was now tinged with grey;
her eyes were deeply shadowed, and the incipient lines at the side of the mouth and across the
forehead had deepened so that the face, for the
first time, looked old and strained.

They passed through King's Gate and turned
to the right. Cordelia had found a place and had
parked the Mini within a few yards of the gate;
Miss Leaming's Rover was further down Queen's
Road. She shook hands firmly but briefly with
Cordelia and said goodbye as unemotionally as
if they were Cambridge acquaintances, parting

with unusual formality after an unexpected meeting at Evensong. She didn't smile. Cordelia watched the tall, angular figure striding down the path under the trees toward John's Gate. She didn't look back. Cordelia wondered when, if ever, they would see each other again. It was difficult to believe that they had met only on four occasions. They had nothing in common except their sex, although Cordelia had realized during the days following Ronald Callender's murder the strength of that female allegiance. As Miss Leaming herself had said, they didn't even like each other. Yet each held the other's safety in her hands. There were moments when their secret almost horrified Cordelia by its immensity. But these were few and would get fewer. Time would inevitably diminish its importance. Life would go on. Neither of them would ever forget completely while the brain cells still lived, but she could believe that a day might come when they would glimpse each other across a theatre or restaurant or be borne unprotestingly past on an underground escalator and would wonder whether what they both recalled in the shock of recognition had really once happened. Already, only four days after the inquest, Ronald Callender's murder was beginning to take its place in the landscape of the past.

There was no longer anything to keep her at the cottage. She spent an hour obsessionally cleaning and tidying rooms which no one would enter, probably for weeks. She watered the mug of cowslips on the sitting-room table. In another three days they would be dead and no one would notice, but she couldn't bear to throw out the still living flowers. She went out to the shed and contemplated the bottle of sour milk and the beef stew. Her first impulse was to take both and empty them down the lavatory. But they were part of the evidence. She wouldn't need that evidence again, but ought it to be completely destroyed? She recalled Bernie's reiterated admonition: "Never destroy the evidence." The Super had been full of cautionary tales to emphasize the importance of that maxim. In the end she decided to photograph the exhibits, setting them up on the kitchen table and paying great attention to exposure and light. It seemed a fruitless, somewhat ridiculous, exercise and she was glad when the job was done and the unsavoury contents of bottle and pan could be disposed of. Afterwards she carefully washed them both and left them in the kitchen.

Last of all she packed her bag and stowed her gear in the Mini together with Mark's jerseys and books. Folding the thick wool, she thought of Dr. Gladwin sitting in his back garden, his shrunken veins indifferent to the sun. He would find the jerseys useful, but she couldn't take them to him. That kind of gesture might have been accepted from Mark, but not from her.

She locked the door and left the key under a stone. She couldn't face Miss Markland again and had no wish to hand it back to any other member of the family. She would wait until she got to London, then send a brief note to Miss Markland thanking her for her kindness and explaining where the key could be found. She walked for the last time round the garden. She wasn't sure what impulse led her to the well but she came up to it with a shock of surprise. The soil around the rim had been cleared and dug and had been planted with a circle of pansies, daisies and small clumps of alyssum and lobelia, each plant looking well established in its hollow ring of watered earth. It was a bright oasis of colour among the encroaching weeds. The effect was pretty but ridiculous and disquietingly odd. Thus strangely celebrated, the well itself looked obscene, a wooden breast topped by a monstrous nipple. How could she have seen the well cover as a harmless and slightly elegant folly?

Cordelia was torn between pity and revulsion. This must be the work of Miss Markland. The well, which for years had been to her an object of horror, remorse and reluctant fascination, was now to be tended as a shrine. It was ludicrous and pitiable and Cordelia wished that she hadn't seen it. She was suddenly terrified of meeting Miss Markland, of seeing the incipient madness in her eyes. She almost ran out of the garden, pulled the gate shut against the weight of the weeds and drove finally away from the cottage without a backward glance. The case of Mark Callender was finished.

Chapter Seven

NEXT MORNING she went to the Kingly Street office promptly at nine o'clock. The unnaturally hot weather had broken at last and, when she opened the window, a keen breeze shifted the layers of dust on desk and filing cabinet. There was only one letter. This was in a long stiff envelope and was headed with the name and address of Ronald Callender's solicitors. It was very brief.

"Dear Madam, I enclose a cheque for £30.00 being expenses due to you in respect of the investigation which you carried out at the request of the late Sir Ronald Callender into the death of his son Mark Callender. If you agree to this sum, I would be grateful if you would sign and return the attached receipt."

Well, as Miss Leaming had said, it would at

least pay part of her fine. She had sufficient money to keep the Agency going for another month. If there were no further case by that time, there was always Miss Feakins and another temporary job. Cordelia thought of the Feakins Secretarial Agency without enthusiasm. Miss Feakins operated, and that was the appropriate word, from a small office as squalid as Cordelia's own, but which had had a desperate gaiety imposed upon it in the form of multi-coloured walls, paper flowers in a variety of urn-like containers, china ornaments and a poster. The poster had always fascinated Cordelia. A curvaceous blonde, clad in brief hot pants and laughing hysterically, was leap frogging over her typewriter, a feat she managed to perform with a maximum of exposure while clutching a fistful of five pound notes in each hand. The caption read: "Be a Girl Friday and join the fun people. All the best Crusoes are on our books."

Beneath this poster Miss Feakins, emaciated, indefatigably cheerful and tinseled like a Christmas tree, interviewed a dispirited trail of the old, the ugly and the virtually unemployable. Her milch cows seldom escaped into permanent employment. Miss Feakins would warn against the unspecified dangers of accepting a permanent job much as Victorian mothers warned against sex. But Cordelia liked her. Miss Feakins would welcome her back, her defection to Bernie forgiven, and there would be another of those furtive telephone conversations with the fortunate

Crusoe made with one bright eye on Cordelia, a brothel madam recommending her latest recruit to one of her fussier customers. "Most superior girl—well educated—you'll like her—and a worker!" The emphasis of amazing wonder on the last word was justified. A few of Miss Feakins' temporaries, beguiled by advertisements, seriously expected to have to work. There were other and more efficient agencies but only one Miss Feakins. Bound by pity and an eccentric loyalty, Cordelia had little hope of escaping that glittering eye. A series of temporary jobs with Miss Feakins' Crusoes might, indeed, be all that was left to her. Didn't a conviction for illegal possession of a weapon under Section 1 of the Firearms Act of 1968 count as a criminal record, barring one for life from socially responsible and safe jobs in the civil service and local government?

She settled down at the typewriter, with the yellow telephone directory to hand, to finish sending out the circular letter to the last twenty solicitors on the list. The letter itself embarrassed and depressed her. It had been concocted by Bernie after a dozen preliminary drafts and, at the time, it hadn't seemed too unreasonable. But his death and the Callender case had altered everything. The pompous phrases about a comprehensive professional service, immediate attendance in any part of the country, discreet and experienced operators and moderate fees, struck her as ridiculously, even dangerously, pretentious. Wasn't there something about false representation in the

Trades Description Act? But the promise of moderate fees and absolute discretion was valid enough. It was a pity, she thought drily, that she couldn't get a reference from Miss Leaming. Alibis arranged; inquests attended; murders efficiently concealed; perjury at our own special rates.

The raucous burr of the telephone startled her. The office was so quiet and still that she had taken it for granted that no one would call. She stared at the instrument for several seconds, wide-eyed and suddenly afraid, before stretching out her hand.

The voice was calm and assured, polite but in no way deferential. It uttered no threat, yet to Cordelia, every word was explicit with menace.

"Miss Cordelia Gray? This is New Scotland Yard. We wondered whether you would be back at your office yet. Could you please make it convenient to call here sometime later today? Chief Superintendent Dalgliesh would like to see you."

It was ten days later that Cordelia was called for the third time to New Scotland Yard. The bastion of concrete and glass off Victoria Street was, by now, fairly familiar to her although she still entered it with a sense of temporarily discarding part of her identity, like leaving shoes outside a mosque.

Superintendent Dalgliesh had imposed little of his own personality on his room. The books in the regulation bookcase were obviously textbooks on law, copies of regulations and Acts of

Parliaments, dictionaries and books of reference. The only picture was a large water colour of the old Norman Shaw building on the Embankment painted from the river, an agreeable study in greys and soft ochres lit by the bright golden wings of the R.A.F. Memorial. On this visit, as on previous occasions, there was a bowl of roses on his desk, garden roses with sturdy stems and thorns curved like strong beaks, not the etiolated scentless blooms of a West End florist.

Bernie had never described him; had only fathered on him his own obsessive, unheroic, rough-hewn philosophy. Cordelia, bored by his very name, had asked no questions. But the Superintendent she had pictured was very different from the tall, austere figure who had risen to shake her hand when she first came into this room and the dichotomy between her private imaginings and the reality had been disconcerting. Irrationally, she had felt a twinge of irritation against Bernie for so putting her at a disadvantage. He was old of course, over forty at least, but not as old as she had expected. He was dark, very tall and loose-limbed where she had expected him to be fair, thick set and stocky. He was serious and spoke to her as if she were a responsible adult, not avuncular and condescending. His face was sensitive without being weak and she liked his hands and his voice and the way she could see the structure of his bones under the skin. He sounded gentle and kind, which was cunning since she knew that he was

dangerous and cruel, and she had to keep re-
minding herself of how he had treated Bernie. At
some moments during the interrogation she had
actually wondered whether he could be Adam
Dalgliesh the poet.

They had never been alone together. On each
of her visits a policewoman, introduced as Sergeant Mannering, had been present, seated at
the side of the desk with her notebook. Cordelia
felt that she knew Sergeant Mannering well having met her at school in the person of the head
girl, Teresa Campion-Hood. The two girls could
have been sisters. No acne had ever marked their
shiningly clean skins; their fair hair curled at precisely the regulation length above their uniformed
collars; their voices were calmly authoritarian, determinedly cheerful but never strident, they exuded an ineffable confidence in the justice and
logic of the universe and the rightness of their
own place in it. Sergeant Mannering had smiled
briefly at Cordelia as she came in. The look was
open, not overtly friendly since too generous a
smile might prejudice the case, but not censorious either. It was a look which disposed Cordelia
to imprudence; she disliked looking a fool before
that competent gaze.

She had at least had time before her first visit
to decide on tactics. There was little advantage
and much danger in concealing facts which an
intelligent man could easily discover for himself.
She would disclose, if asked, that she had discussed Mark Callender with the Tillings and his

tutor; that she had traced and interviewed Mrs. Goddard; that she had visited Dr. Gladwin. She decided to say nothing about the attempt on her life or about her visit to Somerset House. She knew which facts it would be vital to conceal: Ronald Callender's murder; the clue in the prayer book; the actual way in which Mark had died. She told herself firmly that she mustn't be drawn into discussing the case, mustn't talk about herself, her life, her present job, her ambitions. She remembered what Bernie had told her. "In this country, if people won't talk, there's nothing you can do to make them, more's the pity. Luckily for the police most people just can't keep their mouths shut. The intelligent ones are the worst. They just have to show how clever they are, and once you've got them discussing the case, even discussing it generally, then you've got them." Cordelia reminded herself of the advice she had given to Elizabeth Leaming: "Don't embroider, don't invent, don't be afraid to say you can't remember."

Dalgliesh was speaking:

"Have you thought of consulting a solicitor, Miss Gray?"

"I haven't got a solicitor."

"The Law Society can give you the names of some very reliable and helpful ones. I should think about it seriously if I were you."

"But I should have to pay him, shouldn't I? Why should I need a solicitor when I'm telling the truth?"

"It's when people start telling the truth that they most often feel the need of a solicitor."

"But I've always told the truth. Why should I lie?" The rhetorical question was a mistake. He answered it seriously as if she had really wanted to know.

"Well, it could be to protect yourself—which I don't think likely—or to protect someone else. The motive for that could be love, fear, or a sense of justice. I don't think you've known any of the people in this case long enough to care for them deeply so that rules out love, and I don't think you would be very easy to frighten. So we're left with justice. A very dangerous concept, Miss Gray."

She had been closely questioned before. The Cambridge police had been very thorough. But this was the first time she had been questioned by someone who knew; knew that she was lying; knew that Mark Callender hadn't killed himself; knew, she felt desperately, all there was to know. She had to force herself to an acceptance of reality. He couldn't possibly be sure. He hadn't any legal proof and he never would have. There was no one alive to tell him the truth except Elizabeth Leaming and herself. And she wasn't going to tell. Dalgliesh could beat against her will with his implacable logic, his curious kindness, his courtesy, his patience. But she wouldn't talk, and in England there was no way in which he could make her.

When she didn't reply, he said cheerfully:

"Well, let's see how far we've got. As a result of your enquiries you suspected that Mark Callender might have been murdered. You haven't admitted that to me but you made your suspicions plain when you visited Sergeant Maskell of the Cambridge police. You subsequently traced his mother's old nurse and learned from her something of his early life, of the Callender marriage, of Mrs. Callender's death. Following that visit you went to see Dr. Gladwin, the general practitioner who had looked after Mrs. Callender before she died. By a simple ruse you ascertained the blood group of Ronald Callender. There would only be point in that if you suspected that Mark wasn't the child of his parents' marriage. You then did what I would have done in your place, visited Somerset House to examine Mr. George Bottley's will. That was sensible. If you suspect murder, always consider who stands to gain by it."

So he had found out about Somerset House and the call to Dr. Venables. Well, it was to be expected. He had credited her with his own brand of intelligence. She had behaved as he would have behaved.

She still didn't speak. He said:

"You didn't tell me about your fall down the well. Miss Markland did."

"That was an accident. I don't remember anything about it, but I must have decided to explore the well and overbalanced. I was always rather intrigued by it."

"I don't think it was an accident, Miss Gray. You couldn't have pulled the lid free without a rope. Miss Markland tripped over a rope, but it was coiled neatly and half-hidden in the under-growth. Would you have even troubled to detach it from the hook if you'd only been exploring?"

"I don't know. I can't remember anything that happened before I fell. My last memory is hitting the water. And I don't see what this has to do with Sir Ronald Callender's death."

"It might have a great deal to do with it. If some-one tried to kill you, and I think that they did, that person could have come from Garforth House."

"Why?"

"Because the attempt on your life was proba-bly connected with your investigation into Mark Callender's death. You had become a danger to someone. Killing is a serious business. The professionals don't like it unless it's absolutely essential and even the amateurs are less happy-go-lucky about murder than you might expect. You must have become a very dangerous woman to someone. Someone replaced that well lid, Miss Gray; you didn't fall through solid wood."

Cordelia still said nothing. There was a silence, then he spoke again:

"Miss Markland told me that after your rescue from the well she was reluctant to leave you alone. But you insisted that she should go. You told her that you weren't afraid to be alone in the cottage because you had a gun."

Cordelia was surprised how much this small

betrayal hurt. Yet, how could she blame Miss Markland? The Superintendent would have known just how to handle her, probably persuaded her that frankness was in Cordelia's own interest. Well, she could at least betray in her turn. And this explanation, at least, would have the authority of truth.

"I wanted to get rid of her. She told me some dreadful story about her illegitimate child falling down the well to his death. I'd only just been rescued myself. I didn't want to hear it, I couldn't bear it just then. I told her a lie about the gun just to make her go. I didn't ask her to confide in me, it wasn't fair. It was only a way of asking for help and I hadn't any to give."

"And didn't you want to get rid of her for another reason? Didn't you know that your assailant would have to return that night; that the well cover would have to be dragged clear again if your death were to look like an accident?"

"If I'd really thought that I was in any danger I should have begged her to take me with her to Summertrees House. I wouldn't have waited alone in the cottage without my gun."

"No, Miss Gray, I believe that. You wouldn't have waited there alone in the cottage that night without your gun."

For the first time Cordelia was desperately afraid. This wasn't a game. It never had been, although at Cambridge the police interrogation had held some of the unreality of a formal contest in which the result was both foreseeable and unworrying since one of the opponents didn't even know he was playing. It was real enough now. If she were tricked, persuaded, coerced into telling him the truth, she would go to prison. She was an accessory after the fact. How many years did one get for helping to conceal murder? She had read somewhere that Holloway smelt. They would take away her clothes. She would be shut up in a claustrophobic cell. There was remission for good conduct but how could one be good in prison? Perhaps they would send her to an open prison. Open. It was a contradiction in terms. And how would she live afterwards? How would she get a job? What real personal freedom could there ever be for those whom society labelled delinquent?

She was terrified for Miss Leaming. Where was she now? She had never dared ask Dalgliesh, and Miss Leaming's name had hardly been mentioned. Was she even now in some other room of New Scotland Yard being similarly questioned? How reliable would she be under pressure? Were they planning to confront the two conspirators with each other? Would the door suddenly open and Miss Leaming be brought in, apologetic, remorseful, truculent? Wasn't that the usual ploy, to interview conspirators separately until the weaker broke down? And who would prove the weaker?

She heard the Superintendent's voice. She thought he sounded rather sorry for her.

"We have some confirmation that the pistol

was in your possession that night. A motorist tells us that he saw a parked car on the road about three miles from Garforth House and when he stopped to enquire if he could help he was threatened by a young woman with a gun."

Cordelia remembered that moment the sweetness and silence of the summer night suddenly overlaid by his hot, alcoholic breath.

"He must have been drinking. I suppose the police stopped him for a breath test later that night and now he's decided to come up with this story. I don't know what he expects to gain by it but it isn't true. I wasn't carrying a gun. Sir Ronald took the pistol from me on my first night at Garforth House."

"The Metropolitan Police stopped him just over the force border. I think he may persist in his story. He was very definite. Of course, he hasn't identified you yet but he was able to describe the car. His story is that he thought you were having trouble with it and stopped to help. You misunderstood his motives and threatened him with a gun."

"I understood his motives perfectly. But I didn't threaten him with a gun."

"What did you say, Miss Gray?"

"Leave me alone or I'll kill you."

"Without the gun, surely that was an empty threat?"

"It would always have been an empty threat. But it made him go."

"What exactly did happen?"

"I had a spanner in the front pocket of the car and when he shoved his face in at the window I grasped that and threatened him with it. But no one in his right senses could have mistaken a spanner for a gun!"

But he hadn't been in his right senses. The only person who had seen the gun in her possession that night was a motorist who hadn't been sober. This, she knew, was a small victory. She had resisted the momentary temptation to change her story. Bernie had been right. She recalled his advice; the Superintendent's advice; this time she could almost hear it spoken in his deep, slightly husky voice: "If you're tempted to crime, stick to your original statement. There's nothing that impresses the jury more than consistency. I've seen the most unlikely defence succeed simply because the accused stuck to his story. After all, it's only someone else's word against yours; with a competent counsel that's half-way to a reasonable doubt."

The Superintendent was speaking again. Cordelia wished that she could concentrate more clearly on what he was saying. She hadn't been sleeping very soundly for the past ten days— perhaps that had something to do with this perpetual tiredness.

"I think that Chris Lunn paid you a visit on the night he died. There's no other reason that I could discover why he should have been on that road. One of the witnesses to the accident said that he came out in the little van from that side road as if all the devils in hell were following him. Someone was following him—you, Miss Gray."

"We've had this conversation before. I was on my way to see Sir Ronald."

"At that hour? And in such a hurry?"

"I wanted to see him urgently to tell him that I'd decided to drop the case. I couldn't wait."

"But you did wait, didn't you? You went to sleep in the car on the side of the road. That's why it was nearly an hour after you'd been seen at the accident before you arrived at Garforth House."

"I had to stop. I was tired and I knew it wasn't safe to drive on."

"But you knew, too, that it was safe to sleep. You knew that the person you had most to fear from was dead."

Cordelia didn't reply. A silence fell on the room but it seemed to her a companionable not an accusing silence. She wished that she wasn't so tired. Most of all, she wished that she had someone to talk to about Ronald Callender's murder. Bernie wouldn't have been any help here. To him the moral dilemma at the heart of the crime would have held no interest, no validity, would have seemed a wilful confusion of straightforward facts. She could imagine his coarse and facile comment on Eliza Leaming's relations with Lunn. But the Superintendent might have understood. She could imagine herself talking to him. She recalled Ronald Callender's words that love was as destructive as hate. Would Dalgliesh assent to that bleak philosophy? She wished that she could ask him. This, she recognized, was her real danger—not the temptation to confess but the longing to confide. Did he know how she felt? Was this, too, part of his technique?

There was a knock at the door. A uniformed constable came in and handed a note to Dalgliesh. The room was very quiet while he read it. Cordelia made herself look at his face. It was grave and expressionless and he continued looking at the paper long after he must have assimilated its brief message.

She thought that he was making up his mind to something. After a minute he said:

"This concerns someone you know, Miss Gray. Elizabeth Leaming is dead. She was killed two days ago when the car she was driving went off the coast road south of Amalfi. This note is confirmation of identity."

Cordelia was swept with relief so immense that she felt physically sick. She clenched her fist and felt the sweat start on her brow. She began to shiver with cold. It never occurred to her that he might be lying. She knew him to be ruthless and clever but she had always taken it for granted that he wouldn't lie to her. She said in a whisper:

"May I go home now?"

"Yes. I don't think there's much point in your staying, do you?"

"She didn't kill Sir Ronald. He took the gun from me. He took the gun—"

Something seemed to have happened to her throat. The words wouldn't come out.

"That's what you've been telling me. I don't think you need trouble to say it again."

"When do I have to come back?"

"I don't think you need come back unless you decide that there's something you want to tell me. In that well-known phrase, you were asked to help the police. You have helped the police. Thank you."

She had won. She was free. She was safe, and with Miss Leaming dead, that safety depended only on herself. She needn't come back again to this horrible place. The relief, so unexpected and so unbelievable, was too great to be borne. Cordelia burst into dramatic and uncontrollable crying. She was aware of Sergeant Mannering's low exclamation of concern and of a folded white handkerchief handed to her by the Superintendent. She buried her face in the clean, laundry-smelling linen and blurted out her pent-up misery and anger. Strangely enough—and the oddness of it struck her even in the middle of her anguish—her misery was centred on Bernie. Lifting a face disfigured with tears and no longer caring what he thought of her, she blurted out a final, irrational protest.

"And after you'd sacked him, you never enquired how he got on. You didn't even come to the funeral!"

He had brought a chair over and had seated

himself beside her. He handed her a glass of water. The glass was very cold but comforting and she was surprised to find how thirsty she was. She sipped the cold water and sat there hiccuping gently. The hiccups made her want to laugh hysterically but she controlled herself. After a few minutes he said gently:

"I'm sorry about your friend. I didn't realize that your partner was the Bernie Pryde who once worked with me. It's rather worse than that, actually. I'd forgotten all about him. If it's any consolation to you, this case might have ended rather differently if I hadn't."

"You sacked him. All he ever wanted was to be a detective and you wouldn't give him a chance."

"The Metropolitan Police hiring and firing regulations aren't quite as simple as that. But it's true that he might still have been a policeman if it hadn't been for me. But he wouldn't have been a detective."

"He wasn't that bad."

"Well, he was, you know. But I'm beginning to wonder if I didn't underrate him."

Cordelia turned to hand him back the glass and met his eyes. They smiled at each other. She wished that Bernie could have heard him.

Half an hour later Dalgliesh was seated opposite the Assistant Commissioner in the latter's office. The two men disliked each other but only one of them knew this and he was the one to whom it didn't matter. Dalgliesh made his report, concisely, logically, without referring to his notes. This was his invariable habit. The A.C. had always thought it unorthodox and conceited and he did so now. Dalgliesh ended:

"As you can imagine, sir, I'm not proposing to commit all that to paper. There's no real evidence and as Bernie Pryde used to tell us, hunch is a good servant but a poor master. God, how that man could churn out his horrible platitudes! He wasn't unintelligent, not totally without judgement, but everything, including ideas, came apart in his hands. He had a mind like a police notebook. Do you remember the Clandon case, homicide by shooting? It was in 1954 I think."

"Ought I to?"

"No. But it would have been helpful if I had."

"I don't really know what you're talking about, Adam. But if I understand you aright, you suspect that Ronald Callender killed his son. Ronald Callender is dead. You suspect that Chris Lunn tried to murder Cordelia Gray. Lunn is dead. You suggest that Elizabeth Leaming killed Ronald Callender. Elizabeth Leaming is dead."

"Yes, it's all conveniently tidy."

"I suggest we leave it that way. The Commissioner incidentally has had a telephone call from Dr. Hugh Tilling, the psychiatrist. He's outraged because his son and daughter have been questioned about Mark Callender's death. I'm prepared to explain his civil duties to Dr. Tilling, he's already well aware of his rights, if you really feel it necessary. But will anything be gained by seeing the two Tillings again?"

"I don't think so."

"Or by bothering the Sureté about that French girl who Miss Markland claims visited him at the cottage?"

"I think we can spare ourselves that embarrassment. There's only one person now alive who knows the truth of these crimes and she's proof against any interrogation we can use. I can comfort myself with the reason. With most suspects we have an invaluable ally lurking at the back of their minds to betray them. But whatever lies she's been telling, she's absolutely without guilt."

"Do you think that she's deluded herself that it's all true?"

"I don't think that young woman deludes herself about anything. I took to her, but I'm glad I shan't be encountering her again. I dislike being made to feel during a perfectly ordinary interrogation that I'm corrupting the young."

"So we can tell the Minister that his chum died by his own hand?"

"You can tell him that we are satisfied that no living finger pressed that trigger. But perhaps not. Even he might be capable of reasoning that one out. Tell him that he can safely accept the verdict of the inquest."

"It would have saved a great deal of public time if he'd accepted it in the first place."

The two men were silent for a moment. Then Dalgliesh said:

"Cordelia Gray was right. I ought to have enquired what happened to Bernie Pryde."

"You couldn't be expected to. That wasn't part of your duties."

"Of course not. But then one's more serious neglects seldom are part of one's duty. And I find it ironic and oddly satisfying that Pryde took his revenge. Whatever mischief that child was up to in Cambridge, she was working under his direction."

"You're becoming more philosophical, Adam."

"Only less obsessive, or perhaps merely older. It's good to be able to feel occasionally that there are some cases which are better left unsolved."

The Kingly Street building looked the same, smelt the same. It always would. But there was one difference. Outside the office a man was waiting, a middle-aged man in a tight blue suit, pig eyes sharp as flint among the fleshy folds of the face.

"Miss Gray? I'd nearly given you up. My name's Fielding. I saw your plate and just came up by chance, don't you know."

His eyes were avaricious, prurient.

"Well now, you're not quite what I expected, not the usual kind of Private Eye."

"Is there anything I can do for you, Mr. Fielding?"

He gazed furtively round the landing, seeming to find its sordidness reassuring.

"It's my lady friend. I've reason to suspect that she's getting a bit on the side. Well—a man likes to know where he stands. You get me?"

Cordelia fitted the key into the lock.

"I understand, Mr. Fielding. Won't you come in?"